RAGE

A Dark Romance Anthology for Reproductive Rights

Volume 2

Jo Brenner   Poppy Jacobson   MT Addams   Heleva Risque

Mae K Knight   Rianne Burnett   Adelaide King

Torrence Robb   L.R. Douglas   Inara Gage   K. Rose

Beatrix Hollow   Molly Briar   Lucy Smoke   O'Junea Brown

C.B. Frey   Jenn Bullard   Sherelle Green   Aiden Pierce

Ashley Pines   A.H. Monroe   Amanda Cessor   Marla York

C.J. Willis   Britt Bee   Sarah Daniels   B.L. Brown

Cassia Quinn   C. Hallman   Theia Luna   Maisie Kane

L.B. Martin   Shar Khan   Evie Dawn & Ava Kade

Rebecca Rathe   M.M. Riott   A.B. Daniels-Annachi

Sarah Bale & Everleigh Blake   Maree Rose   ED Crowe

Mira Raven   Skylark Melody   Allie Maddox

Kenya Goree-Bell   Cait Alvarez   Lily Prince   R.K. Pierce

Daniela Romero   Pandora Cress   Cover Designer: Baddies

Illustrated by Sarah Seidel

Illustrated by Snowarox

Illustrated by Luaartiste

Wet Ink Publishing House, LLC.

Contents

Foreword

Organizers' Note

Rage, by itself, is easy. After all, there is so much to rage about—racism, misogyny, queerphobia and transphobia, Islamophobia, anti-semitism, xenophobia, bigotry of all kinds. But how do you confront a cruel and unequal world, and channel that rage to affect change, rather than shake your first at the sky, railing against injustice?

We can't always fight darkness with darkness. We can't always fight darkness with light, either.

But what we can do is help the people already doing the work. No one person, no one *anthology*, can fix this. But there are organizations out there that have been fighting this fight for years, day in, and day out, making sure that folks who need access to reproductive care get it. As anthology organizers, readers, authors, and artists, it's not our job to reinvent the wheel—our job is to put our money where our mouths are, and support those who got that wheel rolling long before us.

The Chicago Abortion Fund provides financial, logistical, and emotional support to those denied access to abortion care in the midwest. They, in their own words, "boldly affirm a person's right to bodily autonomy"—and so, dear reader, do we.

And we hope you do, too.

Within these pages are standalone stories, bonus scenes, and epilogues from previously published novels. They run the gamut of relationship types and perspectives. But what they have in common is twofold: Our deep-rooted rage, and our determination to give you and everyone happily ever afters. (Or happily for nows, in some cases, but the point still stands.)

We are so grateful to you for supporting the Chicago Abortion Fund with your purchase and page reads, and helping us help the CAF get abortion care to those who need it. We invite you to donate on your own, as well.

Thank you so much. Together, we can make sure that the true bad guys don't win so easily. Together, we can fight.

Sometimes, we need to write our own villain origin story.

This is ours.

In solidarity,
    Jo, Poppy, and MT

Volume Two

Rapture & Reckoning

By: Theia Luna

A Dark Sapphic Romance

About Rapture & Reckoning

When men lead to the downfall of society, women must rise to eliminate the worst of them all: the Beasts.

For three years, Lenora has kept her compound of people safe by methodically hunting Beasts, leading hundreds to a peaceful existence. But when her hunting party finds a beautiful and lone doctor in the wild, her carefully laid plans come crashing down like a house of cards. With the compound low on medical personnel, Lenora must put the needs of her people over her growing desire for the sweet doctor.

Davey has survived the end of times by hiding with her brother. Now that he's gone, she has no choice but to follow the petite, pink-haired leader to her compound and try to do her part to help. But when there's only one bed to share and it has been years since Davey felt any passion, can she silently take matters into her own hands?

Soon, they both will realize morality is a sea of grey during the apocalypse. It's us, or it's them.

Content Note:

Mature content. For readers 18 & older. Verbal description of past rape, kidnapping/ captivity, threat of rape and forced pregnancy, graphic descriptions of violence.

Relationship type: FF

Chapter One
LENORA

There are days when the icy touch of metal on my calloused hands brings me peace, when welding and sculpting my art calms my mind and quiets my anxieties. The metal hilt in my hand breeds a different calm, a controlled one that reminds me I'm in charge. No one, not even a Beast, can stop me.

"In ya head again, Lenora?" At sixty-six years old, it's a wonder Antonia is part of the hunting party. Yet, here she is, strong and surprisingly nimble as we trudge through a dusty wasteland.

"You know me—the endless silence makes me daydream," I answer quietly. I should be on alert, but we haven't come across a Beast or any usable supplies in our night of travel. I hate to think this trip could be fruitless.

Her sturdy palm lands on my shoulder with a gentle squeeze, and we share a quick smile. On hunts, we keep talking to a minimum. The last thing we need is an ambush.

In the early days, they would prowl in packs, searching for women, but we've eradicated most Beasts with the help of Antonia's skills as Special Ops in the Marine Corps. Three years have passed already, and we've adapted, mobilized, and overcome the fall of society.

The forest around us is barely that. Most trees in this area are barren, long dead. Sighing, I take a moment to stare at the dark sky above, painted with bright stars. The only safe time to travel for long is after sunset and through the night. Hell hath no fury like Mother Nature scorned. Now, according to the last checks we made before technology failed, Earth is consumed by fires that slowly eat away at civilization. So much can happen in three years, and I wonder if any other groups fared as well as we did.

Jones' luminescent skin practically glows in the moonlight ahead of me. She's only twenty, but she found her place among us as a scout for the hunting party. So, when her steps halt and her hand curls into a fist above her head, my chest squeezes.

The three of us stop in our tracks and listen for what may lie ahead. My grip tightens on the hilt of my knife, and I itch to let out some of my restless energy. Hours with no one in sight. Hours of encampment after encampment yielding nothing of interest. If we've used up all the local resources, we need to relocate our compound, which could leave us well and truly fucked.

Her eyes connect with ours, and her hands come together in an "X." It's not a Beast. A ring around her blonde hair indicates a woman is up ahead.

It has been over a year since we've found anyone in our territory. Most of the women are secure in the compound, and we work tirelessly to ensure our safety. How has a lone woman survived this long? It was hard enough in the beginning, when the civil unrest turned to all-out war. But now, when supplies are scarce, how has she managed to survive?

My palms sweat with anxious nerves. I float all the possibilities of a lone woman surviving this long, in this territory, without us coming upon her prior to tonight. This could be a trap. Thankfully, the three of us are a team. Silently, we stalk forward, and just barely, I can make out the figure of a woman kneeling on the ground. When she finally hears our approach, her wild curls swing towards us, and I'm stunned by the twin pools of her eyes, the brown bright from her tears.

"Who are you?" Her voice is strong, with a slight rasp. When she stands, she towers over all of us. Jones is around five-foot-eight, so she must be close to six feet tall. Like a goddess, her glossy dark hair shines in the moonlight. Fuck, she's beautiful. Still, the protective way she guards the ground around her doesn't do much to ease the tension in my shoulders.

Moving to the front of our hunting party, I look up at her. "We're a hunting party out to find supplies for our compound. Are you alone?" I don't move to shake her hand or take my eyes off her. Beautiful or not, no one can be trusted these days. Trust in a stranger is a luxury only the foolish can afford.

A mask of pain and sadness covers her beautiful features. Her eyes trail to the ground, and her voice is barely a whisper. "I'm alone now. My brother—I just buried him." Her hiccupped cry slices at my heart. We all know loss. For some of us, that is all we know.

It started with the loss of family. Divisions cropped up as The Beasts decided to use all their manipulation and influence to rise to the most powerful positions in the country. Then, faster than anyone expected, came the loss of shelter. Extreme weather all over the world destroyed our homes and entire swaths of land. No one was safe.

The Beasts wanted more power regardless of all the damage they had done. They took our rights, our safety—they took everything. And when we dared to fight back by no longer having children or entertaining their demands, civil unrest led to war. Then, we lost technology. Component failures and lack of supplies led to crumbling infrastructure. It was a fucking hellscape, but we survived.

"I'm sorry for your loss." There's no knowing whether he was a Beast, and that makes this next part even more of a balancing act.

"For our own safety, I have to ask: are you a sympathizer?" I cast a pointed look at the upturned earth behind her. A grave for a man isn't a common thing these days. She must have deeply cared for him.

Her demeanor shifts, eyes turning hard. "What? No! He was only nineteen and still tried to defend me when a pack of Beasts attacked us. We just wanted to go quietly, but they know no peace."

"A pack? Was it around here?" My ears perk up, and my eyes scan the land around us. That can't be. We haven't seen more than a single Beast here and there in months. Antonia and Jones share a look. They don't believe her, but we can't leave a lone woman out here. None of us is safe without a community. There is safety in numbers.

"It was about two hours from here. That was where we lived. But I guess I don't live there anymore." Her eyes mist while her face contorts in dawning horror.

"Look, our compound is a few hours south. We have food and shelter. There are around 200 of us, and we all pull our weight to keep each other safe, fed, and clothed. You should probably come with us." I extend my hand, and for a moment, I think she won't take it.

When her palm touches mine, a spark ignites within me. Even in this wasteland, she is warm and soft. I can't remember the last time my hands felt remotely this soft. She releases my hand with a start.

"Do you have any skills?" Jones pipes up from behind me. She's leery of everyone, Beast or not. When we found Jones, she was seventeen and beaten badly. She was from a family of Beasts and sympathizers. Poor kid.

"Yes! I used to be an OBGYN. I can help your medical team. Do you have one? I owned my own practice, so I can be useful." The hope in her voice is foreign. We don't hear a lot of hope around here. It has been over a year since we've found anyone, so maybe I've forgotten what it's like.

"That's great. We have a mortician and two paramedics, so any medical experience is a plus." Her wide eyes tell me everything I need to know. "Yeah, it's been quite the experience." Huffing a laugh, I lead the way back towards the compound. It's going to be a long night.

Chapter Two
DAVEY

The group decided to rest after a few hours. The blonde one keeps looking back at me. She's pretty squirrelly, so the next time I catch her glancing back at me, I try to be friendly. What other option do I have if I plan to live with them?

"I'm Davey, by the way." She doesn't return my smile, but that's alright. I don't expect a welcoming party in this day and age. Her steps slow as she matches my pace, leaving the tiny leader at the front of the group.

A petite woman with a grown out pink bob leading a senior citizen and a teenager through the nothingness of the world. She is quite the sight.

"That's Lenora. She runs the compound." Maybe she caught me staring. "I'm Jones, and that's Antonia. We're the compound hunting party. I'm—I'm sorry about your brother."

When I look down, she's looking straight ahead, and her shoulders square.

"Thank you. You look like you're around the same age. He's only nineteen, but he's a good one, if you'd believe it. He was a good one." Memories of changing his diapers and teaching him to ride a bike swarm my mind, and it takes everything inside of me to push the grief into a box where I can shut the lid. I have to keep going. I have to survive, or all of this was meaningless.

"I'm twenty. But yeah, I believe there are still good ones. We have around thirty guys back at the compound. They all came in as sons of the women we saved. Some were babies and some were teens. They're the only men I trust in this world." Shadows from the moon dance across her face.

"You saved them all? So you were there in the beginning?" I want to learn as much as possible about these women. It's miraculous that they have survived, and thrived, this long. My curious brain takes over.

"No. Lenora started it all. She is the toughest person I know. She's the one who saved me from my family. Beasts and sympathizers. They tried to kill me, but Lenora found me and took them out one by one. She's my hero." The hint of adoration in her otherwise stoic voice warms me.

But the easy way in which she recounts the murder of her family leaves me with more questions than answers. Lenora killed her family? That tiny pink haired pixie of a woman killed people?

"She killed them all?" I can't mask my surprise.

"Yeah. Three brothers, two cousins, and my dad. They purged my mom early on. I think she got off the luckiest." I can see the hint of a smirk on her face.

Holy shit. The desensitized way she recounts their deaths is the perfect reminder she is a part of a hunting party. Despite that, Lenora looks to be about five foot three and built like a teenager. How did she take out so many people and save Jones? My eyes catch on her pink hair and the hilt of her blade in its holster. It gleams at me like a secret wink.

A shiver climbs up my spine. To kill that many, she must be quick and lethal, probably fast. Warmth fills my belly, and I shift in my jeans at the pooling arousal between my legs. That should not turn me on at a time like this, but I can't help it. Part of me—okay, all of me— wonders what else her talented hands can do besides kill.

No. That is crazy. I'm a doctor. I save people. Maybe my grief is manifesting in some crazy way that makes murderers seem attractive. That has to be it.

"Sorry for all the questions. It's been so long since I've talked to anyone besides my brother. I'm socially awkward." My laugh catches on the wind, and Lenora shoots a quick look my way. Her round blue eyes are like denim in the moonlight, stopping me in my tracks.

"We try to keep quiet so we don't attract anyone," Jones supplies in her low tone.

Right. The Beasts. Good job, Davey. How many more graves can you dig today? *No. Stop.* Keep the lid closed.

We finish the walk in silence. Time passes and the moon drifts in the sky, unaware of the destruction down below. When we stop for a break, Lenora finally talks to me.

"Don't worry. We'll keep you safe." Her wide blue eyes stare into the white of the moon and, for a moment, she breathes in the night's light. "I have to admit, it was surprising to hear about how your brother passed. I've eradicated most of the packs in this area. Sorry, by the way." Her words are direct but still sincere. It doesn't feel like an empty platitude filled with pity for the poor, lonely woman. I may not have been around many lately, but even being with this small group of women feels different. They understand the indignities, the trauma, the hardships, like no other. We all know there's no time for pity and grief when death is hot on our heels every day.

"Thank you. He's a good one. He was a good one." Fuck. I don't think I will ever get used to referring to him in the past tense. The lid on my box of grief threatens to open while I pile brick after brick on top, willing myself to go numb.

"I'll take your word for it." Her eyes catch mine, steady, serious. "But he was lucky to travel with you. We don't ask questions when we find packs or lone Beasts. If they get the advantage, it makes my job that much harder."

Her job. Murdering. She's a murderer.

Even with our height difference, she is intimidating. She exudes a rare powerful aura that's refreshing. But her words give me pause. What a one track mindset, one that can cause so much more harm than necessary.

"Not all men are Beasts. My brother is proof of that." I can't repress my look of disgust. That she would kill before even knowing whether someone was lost or needed help is astonishing. How can someone so beautiful be so callous?

"Thinking like that gets women hurt." Her tone hardens. "It's them or us. If you want to live among us, you'll get used to that now. We don't have the privilege of asking questions first. That time passed three years ago when this bullshit started." Her eyes blaze with passion.

"I'm a doctor. I cared for all kinds of people in my career, and I can't just shut off my empathy. I'm not a sociopath." The words are out of my mouth before I realize what I've implied. "Shit, I didn't mean—"

"No. It's alright." She takes a measured step back, taking her citrus and earthy scent with her. "You keep your empathy. And I'll keep the sociopathy that keeps my community safe. Think whatever you want about me. I've got a job to do." She stalks over to Jones, pink hair swaying, and lowers her voice to barely a whisper.

Well, that could have gone better. For so long, I was the one who wore a brave face and took care of someone. It's going to be tough to change that. The warm breeze coats my lungs, and I bathe in the light of the moon. A long night indeed.

Chapter Three
LENORA

How could someone so stunning be such a pain in my ass? I'm a sociopath? Well, she isn't totally off, but it's what has kept me alive! Maybe one day, she'll appreciate it when it keeps her ass safe. Speaking of her ass, I can't help but picture how lovely it fits in her jeans. Why are the pretty ones always a problem?

Her wild mane of dark curls and soft body makes her look like an Amazonian come to life. Just imagining her with a weapon at my side, fighting for our people, has my mind cloudy with thoughts of more. It has been years since I have felt a genuine passion for anyone. Before I can relive the last time someone touched me, I squash the memory in my mind. I flatten it until it's paper thin and store it in a box of horrors I don't have time for.

"Her name is Davey, and she seems pretty nice. Maybe too nice?" Jones says, breaking me from my reverie about the beautiful doctor who will now be a part of our lives.

Davey.

Jones did her job to suss her out and determine if we were

harboring a sympathizer. No matter how stunning, I can't risk my people. I'd slice her slender throat myself if I needed to.

According to Jones, it was just her and a teenage brother together for a while. How they survived, I'll never know, but now, she's under my watch. So she follows my rules, whether it goes against her precious empathy or not.

"Thanks, Jones." Antonia walks up to us, leaving Davey sitting on the dusty ground, staring into the endless night with a blank expression. I know the look. We all do. It's the mask we all wear when we hide our deepest traumas and swallow our grief to survive this hellhole.

"So? We have about an hour's walk left. We can take her out now if she raises any flags. It's far enough away that if someone finds her body, any Beasts wouldn't track it back to the compound." Is it sociopathic to plan a murder twenty feet from the target? No. This is the greater good. I can't afford to live in a world of whimsy where Beasts may be redeemable or where we have time to question before we kill. I shake out the silly notion she planted into my head. Antonia is right. We have a choice to make as a group, but they will leave me with the decision because they trust me. It's how we function. It's how we survive.

"Jones said she didn't get sympathizer vibes. I don't either, but she was protecting a brother with no other women, so I think she lived in a bubble for the past three years."

"We need medical staff at the compound. I think the pros outweigh the cons. She can integrate over time and be helpful to us all." Jones may be young, but she is tactical and intelligent.

"Agreed," Antonia chimes in.

"Agreed," I say to both of them.

* * *

An hour later, the sun is almost on the horizon and we have precious little time to get back indoors.

"You all live here?" Davey asks, mesmerized by the size of our compound.

"Yeah. It used to be a summer camp, so we luckily had lodges and beds, but we are a little cramped. We've been here for three years, and our growth out-paces our building upgrades, but we're working on it," I answer.

Jones and Antonia head off to get some sleep, and I motion for Davey to follow me.

"You're with me until we can figure something else out." I shoot over my shoulder as I walk up to my cabin. It's a small cabin towards the back of the compound. Originally, we think it functioned as the sleeping quarters for the director of the camp because it's a one bedroom log cabin with a tiny kitchenette and a simple indoor bathroom.

As I catch her eyes over my shoulder, I trace her line of sight to my knife. Either that, or she's staring blatantly at my ass, which is nothing to write home about.

"Eyes up here, doc," I say with a smirk and turn just as her face bursts with red and she averts those big brown eyes of hers. Adorable.

After settling in, we both take quick showers with what little water my tank has. Conservation is key, and she has way more hair and body than I do.

Don't think about that hair and body soaking wet, you pervert.

"Thanks for letting me borrow some clothes. I didn't have much in our cave, anyway. It's surreal to be indoors again. I was almost used to roughing it." She laughs. There is no way she was used to roughing it.

Her skin is glowing, and errant drops of water trail down from her damp hair to caress her shoulders. But that's not what has me gaping like an imbecile at her. My pajamas are usually just shorts and a tank top. On my petite frame, it works perfectly fine to cover everything up, but all the clothes do for her is stress her impossibly long legs and dark nipples, which pebble beneath the fabric.

Oh, I am in fucking trouble. There is no way. How can someone possibly look like this during an apocalypse? Is this a test? Some kind of cosmic retribution for all my kills? That a supple goddess just happens to be in my hunting path and will soon be in my bed? Not mine to touch, but mine to protect?

My eyes roam her body without a care for her comfort. I know I shouldn't be so overt, but the length of the shorts barely grazes the tops of her thighs. I wonder if she's wearing panties. When my eyes finish their perusal and make their way back to her face, she's three shades darker with wide eyes.

"Come. Sit."

On my face.

Don't say that.

I pat the tiny couch cushion next to me. Normally, I prefer to be alone, but the way she takes up my space doesn't put me on edge the way other people do.

I try to shut away the last time my body felt this way. There's no use in living in the past when the present is fleeting. "If you want, I can sleep on this couch and you can take the bed. We can both fit on my bed, but I don't want to make you uncomfortable." Her nose scrunches up as she considers my offer, and it gives her a sweet, youthful appearance.

"If all you have are these tiny clothes, it'll be cold. It's smarter if we share body heat." Ah, so she's taking the scientific approach. I wonder if she also likes women. Most of us lie somewhere on the spectrum of sexuality. Would it be weird for me to mention?

"So, Jones was telling me you started all of this. How did you pull that off?"

I scoff. Everyone underestimates me because of my size, and that's fine with me. I'm not the one six feet under.

"I think you need to work on your bedside manner, Doc." I can't help the smirk that grazes my lips. Again, color washes her cheeks and her eyes brighten in that sweet way.

"I'm sorry. I have only talked to the same person for three years, and I practically raised him. I didn't mean anything by it. It's just that you're fairly petite, not that there's anything wrong with that! You're beautiful! Jones was talking about you taking out grown men, and it was crazy to me. Not that women aren't powerful. Obviously, I *know* that. I'm a *feminist* through and through. You have all survived and-and—" A sharp inhale precedes her next bout of word vomit, so I hold up a single hand. Her mouth snaps shut, and she takes her bottom lip between her teeth.

Is it because she blushes so easily? Is it because she's someone new? It has been ages since I've felt a shred of desire for another person; I just assumed I was asexual now. But sitting close to her warm body makes me wonder what if? What if I had someone to come home to? I rub at the pain blooming in my chest and battle the rush of loneliness that threatens to escape.

"I did what I had to do to survive. It was hard, but I couldn't sit by and watch as they murdered innocent women, or worse."

"Is there something worse than death?" Davey asks, unconsciously edging closer to me the more we speak. From here, I can smell the slight lavender scent of my shampoo wafting off her long curls.

"Yeah, Davey. We're living it." I don't like to think about what's worse. Everyone has this fairy tale that death is some all-encompassing blackness that extinguishes life and leaves your consciousness in a vacuous space, drifting for all eternity. That's a walk in the park compared to living. The grit and nerve we all have, the determination to make it through another scorching sunrise. No, death is simple. What they did to me, I welcomed death every second. But death is cowardly and only sneaks up on you when it's good and ready, a slave to none and a master to all.

I remove my butterfly knife from my pocket and swing it open and closed. The repetitive actions help me find a meditative state where I can have conversations with normal people. Because that is so alluring about Davey: she's normal. She was alone with a sibling since society crumbled, locked into a bubble of safety. She probably lived in that cave insulated from the surrounding devastation.

"Look. I know that life is different now for everyone. But what you've created here? It's powerful. You should be proud." Her smile is warm, and I am having a tough time returning the gesture. When is the last time I've felt the heat of another body, the warmth of a genuine smile? "I haven't even seen everything but, from what Jones mentioned, you're a leader here and I'm happy to help your compound in any way I can. I can be useful again. Honestly, I miss the hustle and bustle of delivering. There are no births at the end of the world." Her eyes look right through me, and a familiar darkness looks back out at me.

A familiar chill runs up my spine, leaving my skin feeling tight. The knife flips faster in my hand as I count my breaths methodically. As the icy blade closes in on itself, a hand closes around my fist, holding it steady. My eyes shoot up to Davey, who is smiling at me with those warm chocolate eyes, defrosting the ice around my heart. For a second, there is no sound, only the rhythmic dance of our breaths as they ease in and out.

"You—you could have hurt yourself!" I say as I stand, and she drops my hand.

"Relax. I have fantastic reflexes, and even if I hurt myself, I'm a doctor, remember? I can patch myself up." She offers her smiles up so easily. Why is she always smiling?

Before I can stop myself, my hand reaches forward and grasps her chin between my fingers. As I tilt her face up to mine, the smile falls from her face.

"Don't take your safety lightly. You're one of my people now. We are a team here, so we all contribute and we all follow the orders that keep us safe. Do you understand?" It's too harsh. It's too much. She has been through so much tonight, but I can't stand the idea of her being so cavalier about this. It's my job to keep everyone safe, and that includes her now.

I expect her to shove me away, maybe a slap to my hand or face while she's at it. What I don't expect is the hazy way her pupils expand and her mouth parts for me. I don't expect her breathing to be heavier while my eyes trail down the long expanse of her neck. When they catch the soft swells of her breasts, her nipples pebble against the thin fabric.

Oh, fuck.

She nods, her chin still captured between my fingers. "I understand," she whispers. It would be so easy to tilt my head down and feel those soft lips with my own. The easy way she understands, the delicious way she stares up at me. It's addicting. I can't afford to mess around with anyone, let alone someone we just brought in, so I release my fingers and take a step back from her, back into the coldness of the cabin. Maybe I *should* sleep on the couch tonight.

Before I mention it, she stands and stretches her long body towards the ceiling with a yawn. I drink in the smooth expanse of her skin, the way her top grazes the swells of her breasts. Those fucking nipples are just staring at me, and I'm trying my hardest not to drool, or reach out and tug.

Shaking my head, I take the hint. "Right. You must be exhausted. The bedroom's over here." A sincere smile lights up her face, and I know for a fact that I will not sleep tonight.

Chapter Four
DAVEY

The bed is soft below me, cradling my body, and even though there's a chill in the air, my body is burning up. Next to me, Lenora, sound asleep, rests her face on her hands, her petite body facing mine. My fists clench as I let out a frustrated sigh. It's all I can do to not turn to the side and stare at the way her perfect tits just squeeze together, almost bursting from the small tank top. I can't stop from glancing over every five minutes and praying that she moves just a little so that, perhaps, one falls right out of its confines. Such easy access. What was I thinking, agreeing to share a bed?

You were thinking you want her to sit on your face.

I groan then shoot a glance her way to make sure I didn't accidentally say that out loud. Then, I throw my arm over my eyes. Fuck it. If she's asleep, I can handle this quickly. With one last glance towards her lax face, my hands trail over my skin—one down to the wet spot in between my legs and the other to squeeze and pluck at my nipples that are begging for attention at the moment. Even the tiny clothes she gave me are turning me on. Is it sick to think that her body was in these clothes at one point? That her pussy was exactly where mine is now? A pleasurable shiver wracks my body at the thought.

Wetness coats my thighs, and I make a mental note to take another shower when I wake up. These underwear are ruined. When and where can I wash my clothes? Shaking my head, I focus on the task ahead. My eyelids slide shut, and I take my bottom lip between my teeth to muffle my moan as I circle my throbbing clit.

Her pink and brown hair is splayed out on the bed underneath me, and the dripping pussy in my hand isn't mine. I conjure that vicious and possessive gleam in her eyes, only for me. My tongue makes a path to her chest so I can taste her skin. Her body bows as I lave her nipples with attention.

But her strength is overwhelming, and she rolls me over to return the favor. Except when her hot mouth suctions on my needy body, she uses her teeth to mark me, bites and bruises that remind everyone I'm hers.

Of course, my delusions give me a sadistic version of her that wants my pain and my pleasure.

Inhaling, I can smell her next to me, and it does nothing but stoke the flames of my imagination. I wonder what she tastes like.

Fuuuuck. Circles around my clit become tighter and tighter until my other hand tightens on my straining nipples. I dip two fingers into my core that's weeping for the deadly hunter in bed next to me, using the heel of my hand to rub my clit. It's times like these I wish I had more hands.

A little more. I'm so close.

"More. More. Bite me. Mark me. I'm Yours," I pant, begging for her attention. *She makes her way to my pussy; I'm glistening and ready for her mouth. Using her thumbs, she holds me open, stripping me bare and leaving me nowhere to hide. A blush covers my chest as I whine and shake with anticipation. Her knowing smirk and the gleam in her eyes disarm me.*

"You'll get everything you need soon. Let me look at what's mine. What a gorgeous pussy; so messy for me. Look how needy your little clit is." As she watches me, spread open, she pinches my clit between her fingers, and I scream out. "That's it, pretty girl. Scream for me."

Right.

There.

My back arches off the bed, and I do everything in my power to hold my moan and keep my movements as small as possible.

So, when a stifled groan sings its way to my ears, my eyes pop back open and find those icy blue eyes glazed over and glued to mine. My hand stays buried in my shorts, trying to wind down. But those eyes.

My hand speeds up again, and a second orgasm rips through me with a shout I can't contain.

Stars burst behind my eyes and, for a moment, all sound evaporates as a vacuum of pleasure sucks me into the abyss. I can't remember the last time I came that hard—or twice, for that matter. As my heart finds its way back into my chest and my breathing evens out, I replay the little vignette I'd created. But then I remember the groan and her eyes boring into me.

Mortified, my head rolls to the side, too spent to turn my whole body, to see Lenora is indeed there. Not only is she awake, she's seen me come right next to her. How did I survive the end of the world only to die of embarrassment three years later?

"I-I" What the fuck do I say to her? My post-orgasm brain is insisting I kiss her, but I can't trust my sex-addled mind right now.

"Do you always come twice like that?" Her voice is huskier from sleep and, my god, I feel like I can come a third time just by listening to her.

"What?" I don't even know how to finish my own thoughts.

She scoots closer to me, which pulls the tank top dangerously tight across her perfectly small tits, and my eyes glide down to her nipples that are now completely visible.

"I'm not a pervert, I swear." That's the only idiotic thing that spews from my mouth. Her laugh is close, and I can feel the heat of her breath across my face.

"Are you sure you're not a pervert?" My heart speeds in my chest. Fuck. I've ruined everything. Where will I go if she kicks me out?

"I-I swear. I'm so sorry," I breathe. The need to cry is strong. At once, all the overwhelming things of the day come crashing down around me, and my breath saws in and out of my mouth.

"Prove it," she whispers, watching me intently. My misty eyes do nothing to erase the look in hers. Is she enjoying this? I pull my hands from my shorts, her shorts, but before I can jump from the bed and throw myself into the burning sun, her hand catches mine. The same hand that was just inside of me, dripping with my arousal.

I didn't even see her move, her obvious skills ramp my desires back up. Wow, maybe I am a pervert.

"You should know," she begins, fingers tightening around my wrist and pulling me closer to her. "We share most things in this compound. We're a community. Do you want to be a part of that?"

Why is she talking about this now? My brain was already hazy, but now, my confusion is making me wonder if I'm hallucinating. "Yes, of course! I'm really sorry!" I plead in a strained whisper.

"Good." That one word is my only warning before my fingers are enveloped in her warm mouth. My breath catches. Her eyes are hungry as they bore into mine, giving me no reprieve. Her moan elicits my own, and I couldn't turn away if I wanted to. She releases my fingers with a pop, and a smile curves her lips.

"I've wanted to know what you taste like since you came out of that shower. My imagination didn't do it justice." She's so cocky and sure of herself, it momentarily takes me off guard. What the fuck is happening? Am I still in my daydreams?

"Tell me what you like." The commanding tone of her voice has me clenching on nothing. Can I be honest with her? I have never said these things out loud.

My whole life, I've been too busy for relationships. The scattered one night stands didn't give me time to open up to anyone about my needs. They were just to blow off steam. It was too embarrassing to tell someone I just met that I wanted to be degraded and praised, *loved*. The perfect student, the perfect daughter, the perfect sister. I took care of everyone and let myself fall to the wayside while life passed me by. What do I have to show for it? A career that means nothing, a dead brother, and only my hand to keep me company. I'm pathetic. And I need someone to tell me exactly that.

"I've never told anyone this," I start.

"Tell me what you need and I'll take care of you." *You*. Not *it*.

My heart pounds a staccato beat out of my chest, and I lift the lid on my heart-shaped box, buried deep and covered in dust.

"Help me shut my brain off. Give me the kind of pain that will replace the one in my chest." I can't quite place why I trust her with this information, but tomorrow is guaranteed to no one. So, if she'll have me, I'll take whatever I can get.

Her icy eyes widen at my admission, and I gasp, hoping I didn't cross a line.

"Do you have a safe word? I won't hurt you in any way you don't want." Her fingers around my wrist rub soft circles into my skin, warming me, easing me into what's coming next.

"I've never had one before, but I guess 'hopscotch' works." She snorts a laugh before training her face back into a mask of desire. Fuck, she looks deadly like this. Wetness leaks between my legs, and I rub my thighs together to try and get some relief.

Lenora's hands push through my curls, holding my head in her hands as she rolls on top of me. I don't know if I'll ever get used to her strength or speed.

Her lips brush against mine as a desperate moan falls from my mouth. She uses the opportunity to explore my mouth with her tongue, leaving me no option but to open up and let her in. As she straddles me, her strong thighs squeeze against my body, holding me in place.

"You're so needy," she whispers against my lips, and I can't help the groan and push of my hips against her. Hands tighten in my hair and pull back, leaving my neck open to her kisses and bites. Every time her teeth hit my skin, a shiver wracks my body, ready for more. After every bust of pain, a soothing tongue follows its path.

She releases my hair and runs her hands around my face,

touching as much skin as she can. "Tell me what you want to be called." I've never had a partner so open to communication. It's almost off-putting, but her hands rove down to my neck, and my breath hitches. As one hand lightly holds my throat in place, I miss the other headed for my breasts. The sharp pinch on my nipple has my eyes rolling to the back of my head.

"I asked you a question." Her fingers squeeze tighter, and I moan at the delicious pain. "Do you want to be my baby, my girl, my little pervert?" My breaths hitch, and a tear escapes my eye at the pressure of her pinch. I pant through my teeth. What was the question?

Her face lowers to mine, and her tongue follows the trail of my tear. "Oh, you want to be my slut, don't you?"

"I'll be anything. Everything," I pant, unable to pick just one. I want it all.

"Greedy girl with a greedy pussy. I like it." She releases my poor nipple and replaces her hands with her mouth, licking and sucking both breasts as I writhe below her. She climbs off me as she looks down at my body.

"Take everything off," she commands, and I obey, hoping to get everything I've ever needed from her. I'm entranced.

Now unoccupied, one hand lowers to my abdomen and then to the apex of my thighs. "You've already come twice and you want more, don't you?" I nod furiously at her question.

"Words," she seethes as her once-soft hand comes crashing down on my clit, making me cry out.

"Yes! Yes, I want more. Please. Give me more. I'll be good," I moan, shifting my head back and forth on my pillow, frizzing up my curls.

"Good? I don't think this pussy can be anything but trouble." Her fingers lightly stroke up and down my center with nowhere near enough pressure.

"You couldn't even wait until you were alone. No. You touched this pretty pussy and tried to keep quiet while I slept right next to you. You are a perverted little slut, aren't you?"

"No!" I whine. Embarrassment coats my words as two fingers spear me. I cry out as her laugh rings out above me.

"Don't lie to my face. You won't like the consequences. Now, tell me what you did while I was sleeping next to you." Lazily, her fingers pump in and out of me, barely brushing my clit innocently. I'm so wound tight, I can barely think.

"I-I can't." I throw my arm over my eyes, overwhelmed with the way she stares down at me, stripping me bare, seeing right through to my debaucherous center. I've never been more turned on in my fucking life.

"Wrong answer, my little pervert." With one hand, she holds my arms down to the bed, leaving me incapable of hiding. Then, her thumb rubs my clit as her fingers push against my front walls. My orgasm barrels towards me. So close. But just as I'm about to crest, she removes her fingers and spanks me, again between my legs.

"FUCK!" I shout, writhing and moaning at my ruined orgasm.

"Let's try again. You said you wanted to be good, but I think I may have to teach you." She sucks my wetness off her fingers and laughs at my frustration. "You did this to yourself. Now, tell me what you were doing while I was asleep."

After my body relaxes into the mattress again, her fingers lazily trace my lower lips and circle my clit. The throb is deep, and my stomach clenches. "I touched myself," I whisper.

"That's a good start," she says as her fingers increase the pressure on my clit, driving me insane. No longer holding my arms down, her free hand finds its home on my throat.

"And what was my little slut thinking of?" she asks casually as she tightens her grip on my neck, just enough to feel me swallow.

"Y-you," I mutter as I climb higher and higher under her lethal hands.

"Mmm. I like that." Two fingers enter me again, and I choke a moan under her hand. "I love feeling your moan beneath my hand. I wish I could parade you around like this. Then everyone would know who you think of when you touch this messy pussy at night. They'll all know what a perverted little slut you are."

I moan through my teeth as the hand around my neck tightens, a necklace I want to wear as a tattoo from now on.

"Oh, you like that. Your pretty pussy just clamped down when I mentioned humiliating you around the compound, showing everyone the little slut you are." Her laugh is taunting, and it drives me insane.

"Do you want to be my pet? Can I walk you around on a leash and force your face between my legs whenever I feel the need to come? Hmm? Oh, baby. You're giving away all your perverted little kinks." Her vicious smile is what brings me to the brink. So close. My legs tingle with anticipation.

"Do you want to come?" she asks as her ministrations speed up.

"Yes, please, please, please, please.," I chant, not caring that I'm begging or that the hand around my throat has tightened.

"Come for me, slut. Show me how good you can be for me."

My toes curl, my breath caught in her hands, and I'm completely and utterly useless to do anything about it. Nothing can stop the pressure from breaking and throwing me into the abyss of my third orgasm.

Lungfuls of air flow into my mouth as Lenora releases me and gently strokes my core, bringing me back down to Earth. Then, as if the last fifteen minutes didn't happen, her hands wrap around me as she rolls us to the side so we're tangled in each other's limbs, my breathing the only sound.

Her hands rub and knead at all the muscles she can reach, and a soothing kiss lands on my brow. She holds me close to her body and her heartbeat steadies me. A hand in my hair massages my scalp as her lips take mine in a less urgent kiss than earlier. This kiss is sweet, gentle, and brings me comfort I've never felt.

This experience will live in my mind rent free for the rest of my life, but part of me will relive the cuddles too, the delicate warmth she brings me when I'm vulnerable.

"Are you okay?" she whispers into my temple, leaving warm

kisses in her wake. My heart warms at the care and concern in her voice. This is what I've always wanted, needed, but could never express. The lid on my heart-shaped box slides off and leaves me open.

"Thank you." My voice is wobbly, and I realize I'm crying. "I'm sorry. I don't know why I'm crying. It was amazing, seriously." I swipe at the tears but still my hands when she gently wipes and kisses the rest away for me.

"Shh. It's okay. Sometimes, a lot of emotions and adrenaline can cause a little drop off afterward. I've got you." As I'm wrapped in her arms, my eyelids get heavy as I drift off to sleep, hoping this wasn't all a dream.

Chapter Five
DAVEY

The days bleed into weeks, and I can't tell if I've died and gone to hell, or if Lenora just hates me. My first night was the last time she touched me. Once the sun wasn't too harsh in the sky, she introduced me to members of the compound and found space for me away from her bed. I still haven't met everyone, but the ones I have are nothing but kind.

My new position as head doctor is something I never expected. I'll be seeing all the women in the compound at least once so I can get a feel for what they will need medically. Most people forget that an OBGYN does more than deliver babies. We are also there to care for all aspects of reproductive health. I can't do testing, and there aren't any labs available, but just talking to people about what's going on in their bodies is helpful in a small community like this one. Flexing this part of my personality again is a little painful, but it feels good, like scratching a muscle that has gone sore with disuse.

But the one woman I want to see has done everything in her power to avoid me. It has been about three weeks since I've arrived, and she has been "busy" since. I know she is the leader here and everyone depends on her, but can't she make time for me? Am I being needy? Maybe it was just a one night thing. That's fine, totally fine. It's not like she was my literal wet dream come true. It's not like she was the first person I've been intimate with in the last three years. I think I'm going to throw up. Or maybe scream? Nope. Brooding. I'm definitely brooding.

"Wow, Doc. You look cute pouting over there," a soft voice calls from the other side of the room. Penelope was once a paramedic. I've gotten to know her over the last few weeks, and not only is her voice very soothing, but so is her presence. I like to think of her as human Prozac.

"Is it that obvious?" I sigh.

"She's right, Doc. What's got your panties in a twist?" Tina chimes in, our resident mortician. She's hysterical and less morbid than I thought a mortician would be.

"Nothing, really. Have you seen Lenora lately? I feel like I haven't seen her since I got here." I'm aiming for nonchalant, but I don't think it's working, because they share a look before meeting my eyes.

"The hunting party has been busy lately," Penelope says.

"Oh, she told me they had pretty much kept everything safe around here in the last year." Why would they be so busy if there were no more Beasts in the area?

"Well, since they found you Doc, they've had to increase patrol. Lenora is vigilant. She won't risk anyone getting hurt or letting any Beasts nearby." Tina's eyes shift left and right, as if we're not the only ones in this small cabin full of medical supplies that were no doubt scavenged during their hunting parties. "You didn't hear it from me, but Lenora had me patch up a nasty gash on her arm the other day after she came in covered in blood. At first, I freaked out, but I realized, as she held her hand out, the majority was not her blood. So she definitely took one out recently."

"That's our girl," Penelope says in her light voice. They talk about killing another human being in this detached way that borders on callous.

My stomach turns as I remember her hands on me, bloodstained hands. I question whether she listened to anyone's story, but it's obvious she's just a cold-blooded killer. A sharp tug behind my breastbone has my hand rubbing the spot idly. How can she be so passionate, so warm, yet so cold and calculating? Should I even seek her out again?

"You look green, Doc. You alright?" Tina's eyes shine with concern.

"Yeah, I'm fine." I wave away her concern. "I'm a doctor. I'm used to helping people and doing what's in their best interests to keep them safe. The idea of just killing any person who comes near is really cruel, isn't it?" I can't stop my mouth from running.

"I mean, obviously, she didn't kill me, and my brother was already gone." I stop to clear my throat. "But would she have just killed him? How do we know they're all Beasts? What if it's one of the good ones who are just on their own, looking for others like us? I can't help but think we could help them."

"Lenora has been keeping us all safe since she found this place. She doesn't need to give them the benefit of the doubt. Why does she owe it to someone to give them the upper hand? She's quick and deadly, and with Jones and Antonia at her side, we're lucky. For every Beast she kills, she keeps us safer for another day," Tina responds, incredulous at my questions.

"Look, I know the Beasts are just that. But how can she not worry if she's making a mistake?" I respond, trying to explain all the thoughts warring in my mind.

"She's made that mistake once, Doc," Penelope says before bringing a hand to her mouth.

"That's not our story to tell. If you have so many questions, you should ask her yourself." I can tell that the conversation is over, and I don't want them to think I'm being unreasonable so we go on, counting inventory and chatting about the compound they all call home.

Chapter Six
LENORA

Sluggish, I bring myself back to the compound after my second shift of perimeter searches, the second one wider than the first. Last week, we found a lone Beast, and it left me anxious. I can't shake the feeling that whoever attacked Davey will find us eventually and try to attack us as well or finish the job. Was it the one I took care of? Will it be a pack? No matter. I'll be ready. That's the only option.

For years, I have kept this compound safe on the principle that I gathered these people here. Therefore, it's my duty to help protect them. But one night with Davey has done something irreparable to my brain. Night in and night out, she's there, in the forefront of my mind. I haven't been avoiding her, per se. Patrols increased, which means I'm just working more. But when my mind can finally wander and linger on a memory of the past, I no longer remember my pain, or my loss. No. Now, I remember her—her warmth, her wild hair and soft body.

How can someone surrender so willingly and still carry on as if nothing happened? Some days, I see her near the medical tent with the others, but I try not to stick around and distract anyone. We all have jobs that need to be completed before sun up. Right now isn't the time. I can't protect her if I'm distracted, and the thought of something harming her causes an odd ache in my chest that I can't identify.

As I enter my cabin and remove my coverings that are caked in mud and debris from outside the compound, a tingle shoots up my spine. Carefully, my non- dominant hand reaches for the small blade holstered to my thigh.

The cold handle centers me as I lunge towards the dark figure standing near my couch, teeth bared and ready to shed some blood. But what meets me isn't a Beast; no, it's terrified brown eyes and wild, curly hair.

"Oh my God!" she screams as I pull back at the last second and stare incredulously at the woman in from of me.

"Are you insane? I could have killed you! You're lucky this is my cabin and not Antonia's or Jones'. They would have filleted you!" My mind races with the possibility of hurting her in this sacred place where we shared the best night of my life.

"I'm so sorry! I just wanted to talk, and I figured you'd be back eventually. I didn't really think." Holding up a hand, I halt her excuses and sheath my dagger.

"Thank you for not killing me indiscriminately," she whispers. Not this again. She will never understand the need for safety when she led a charmed life in the aftermath. Not all of us had a trustworthy travel partner.

"Don't think for a second I wouldn't have slit your throat if we were outside of the compound gates. Never, and I mean never, sneak up on me. I don't like it, and I've practically trained myself to use the fear and adrenaline to push my knife deeper." When I'm sure she understands, we take a seat on the couch, and I'm reminded of the first night we spent together.

"But doesn't this prove there's good reason to stop and think before," she swallows before continuing, "killing? What if you accidentally hit Antonia? Or Jones?"

In an effort to contain my ire, I roll my eyes and sigh. "That's why we train, Davey. That's why we have hunting parties and perimeter searches in shifts. We've spent years planning and honing our skills while setting up this plan, and you think you're qualified to comment and make suggestions, because, what? You're a doctor? Because we slept together? That's not how this works." The lid on my box of fury and grief rattles, threatening to burst open.

"No! No of course not! That's not what..." she sputters. "What you're doing is wrong! Humans weren't made to kill with no remorse. It's why we have empathy. When I took my oath, I promised to treat others with respect, without judgment, and to minimize suffering. I vowed to do no harm!" She raises her voice and stands, looking down on me, and the fragile hold on my lid slips on my hidden box, letting all my deep seated feelings run rampant.

"And after I was brutally assaulted three years ago by a group of beasts, I made a vow to get revenge for the girl they killed that night; to never be unprepared or unwilling to get the job done because of something as silly as morals!" I scream. "They didn't stop, not even when I *begged*. They didn't offer me the mercy of death." Raw energy radiates from my body as I pace the small space.

"But they took from me something I will never get back, something you so desperately cling to. Why do I need to exercise a moral high ground when they *never* will!? Morals have no place in a world beyond saving, a world where it's kill or be killed." I can't even look at her. She doesn't know what it was like. There are nights when I can still feel the hands on my body, smell the stench of my blood and urine, see the twisted smiles as they stripped me of my humanity.

"If *I* don't protect them, what the fuck was the point of creating this compound? This community of people who want to live free and be respected? You live in a fairytale where there's time to question whether someone is going to hurt you instead of knowing the odds are never in your favor as a woman. Not anymore."

I can't catch my breath in the deep and heavy silence that stretches between us.

"Lenora, I..." she starts, and I can see the tears in her eyes, the pity she holds for the young woman who was ripped away from everything and thrown into the fire with no one to save her but herself.

"Don't you *dare* pity me, Davey. Just do your job and follow the rules." I don't stop to see what she does. I can't be in the same room with someone so disconnected from reality that they think there are Beasts worth saving.

The cold shower does little to unravel the knot of my thoughts. After a few minutes, I turn the water warm for a bit. I wonder if she left. Is she still out there, crying into the void? There's that cutting feeling deep in my chest. Fuck. Why do I care about her? A bleeding heart doctor of all people. Why can't I just ignore her and move on? Instead, I want to comfort her and tell her it'll be okay because I'll teach her everything I know about the Beasts.

But will she ever see my point of view without that well of pity bubbling over in her warm eyes? Can she truly grasp the heinous past that so many of us share? Sometimes, I wonder if I'll ever be more than the empty monster she sees when she looks at me. But what's a Beast to a Monster?

Chapter Seven

DAVEY

After Lenora yelled at me about her rape, I've given her space. I was wrong to impose on her sanctuary and try and change it to suit me when I'm only a small cog in the inner workings of the compound. After that day, I promised to be more open-minded and think of myself as one of the group. We all work so hard to keep this place running, and it would be a shame if my hubris were to bring it all crashing down.

Today is finally the day I make it up to Lenora. I want to prove to her that not only can I be useful, but I can also be good company when she's lonely. Let's face it: I'm lonely all the damn time, and I am praying that after tonight, she invites me over. I don't even care if it's just for one night. I'll take what I can get.

When the sun is low enough in the sky, I leave my cabin and jog over to Lenora's in the hopes of finding her before her perimeter check. Bingo. She exits her quaint cabin and stretches her lithe body. When her arms reach for the sky, a sliver of her hips show, and my eyes latch on immediately.

No. Stop it.

This isn't the time for that.

Maybe later, though.

"Hey, Lenora!" I call over, heeding her words about the dangers of sneaking up on her.

"Davey? Hi." She turns to me and cocks her head in a way that has her pink hair tilted to the side. She's so pretty.

"I wanted to ask if I could join you on your walkabout today. You know? To check the perimeter and stuff?" *Smooth.* What is wrong with me?

She eyes me skeptically. I guess I would too, considering.

"I also wanted to apologize and figured a walk would help get out any awkwardness." *Yes, bring attention to it. That is exactly how to get around it.* Mentally, I slap myself. I am a respected OBGYN. I talked to patients for years without sounding like an idiot. What is it about Lenora that reduces my brain to mush?

Her smirk is small but brings hope to my heart. "Sure. But don't think I won't kill something just because you're with me," she says as she walks ahead of me.

"Don't you mean *someone*? You know what, never mind! So! That apology."

We walked in companionable silence for about half of the check. After some needling, she did accept my apology, but only if I focused on my job and had more empathy for the people in our camp than the Beasts.

That one hurt, but from her perspective, that is exactly what I was doing. It's impossible to see a viewpoint opposite to yours when you believe there is no shared bond between you.

The truth is, the tenuous string holding together our paths is weaved in an inexplicable way that is glaring if we look hard enough. We're all survivors of the end times. We all live together, work together, for a common goal. My holier than thou attitude did nothing but distance me from people who can be my tribe, my support. Lenora has taught me so much; I can only hope to repay her kindness one day.

Up ahead, there's a foreign sound that breaks our silence. It has been so long since I've heard a child's voice that it stops me in my tracks. "There's a girl crying over there!" I whisper harshly to Lenora as I point to a figure, huddled low to the ground, sobbing and clutching her gaunt knees to her chest.

Before I can move forward, her arm swings out and catches me across the chest. My oomph is louder than I mean it to be, and she shushes me afterwards.

Sorry, I mouth to her. With a soft whisper, she leans into me.

"This doesn't feel right. There's no way a lone girl survived this long. Let's get back to camp." She turns on a dime and begins treading back the way we came.

What is she talking about? This girl is a child!

"Wait," I breathe, catching back up to her. "It's a child. She looks hurt. We have to check her out at least. You found me alone too, remember?" It wasn't too long ago that I was in the same situation, except I was burying my dead brother. I can only imagine what causes her to wail into the night sky.

"Do not approach until I think of a plan." She pins me with her steely gaze, but it makes no sense.

"What could happen? She's a child, for Christ's sake, Lenora!" I make my way towards the crying girl, and the closer I get, the more I can make out. She's in a tattered dress, maybe a nightgown? And there's blood. She's covered in it. Forgetting to keep my voice down, I call back to Lenora, my doctor hat firmly in place.

"She is bleeding. I won't know why until I can examine her. Help me bring her back to the camp."

"No. Davey, wait!" But her pleas fall on deaf ears. I rush to the young girl's side and start my assessment.

"Hello? Can you hear me?" I ask, hoping she can at least communicate with me. She moans, holding her stomach, where the patch of red on her nightgown grows dark with blood. Fuck. I may be a doctor with medical practice, but I haven't handled non-pregnancy emergency situations since my first residency.

"My name is Davey. I'm a doctor. I'm going to turn you onto your back so I can see what's going on with your stomach. You'll be alright." I try and calm her, but she's shaking like a leaf, and I can't help but wonder if it's from the cold or from blood loss.

When I turn her over, tears streak her eyes, and her hands fall away from her stomach. I palpate the area and don't feel any wound that would result in so much blood loss. Confused, I try and talk to her again.

"What's your name?" I ask, wondering what she could be doing out here all alone. And that's when I realize my series of mistakes. How could she be so close to the compound, alone, when no one has been in this area in over a year? Chills skate down my spine as I scramble to my feet.

"I'm so sorry," she whispers, and her sunken eyes catch mine and hold on for what feels like an eternity. There's pain and sorrow in those eyes, begging for forgiveness.

"Well, well, well. What have we here? Looks like we've caught ourselves a new whore," a deeply masculine voice says to my right.

Lenora was right. It was a trap.

Chapter Eight
DAVEY

"She's bleeding. I won't know why until I can examine her. Help me bring her back to the camp." My heart twists into knots as she trots away from me, throwing off every alarm bell my body can muster.

"No. Davey, wait!" But she doesn't wait. She falls into her role as a doctor, so I have to fall into my role as a killer, as a protector, because something isn't right.

Carefully so that my footfalls are less audible, I slip further away. Everything inside me screams to run toward her, but I have to use my brain. So, I slink away and try to approach the girl from the other side.

There's little cover, but there are boulders scattered in this area that will help. As my feet glide over the barren land, I reach the closest outcropping and catch my breath. I can keep an eye on them from here and see if anyone tries to ambush us. That way, they won't have the upper hand.

Just as I regain my bearings and turn to Davey as she crouches near the girl, all sane thoughts vanish from my mind, leaking from my ears like warm blood, making me delirious.

Beasts.

Two Beasts. One brown haired and the other a sandy blond; tall, slim, haggard.

As they get closer to Davey, all my nightmares come rushing back to the surface.

They'll take her, they'll rape her. They'll break her.

"Well, well, well, what have we here? Looks like we've caught ourselves a new whore."

My feet carry me forward, and dirt kicks up in the wake of my footfalls. Even after three years of hunting, I'm still disturbed by their singular focus on wrecking the world around them. I'll never understand their incessant need to conquer, destroy, and sully everything in their path.

I can't remember grabbing the blade strapped to my thigh, but its cold weight in my hand is a balm to my nerves. Davey stumbles away from the girl but not fast enough. Her beautiful hair is twisted around a bony fist, and her head whips to the side as a fist collides with her jaw.

"No!" I lunge forward to the nearest Beast, the one not holding Davey, and jump onto his back. The element of surprise works in my favor as I bring my blade to the front of his neck and, with practiced precision, slide the steel against the Beast's throat faster than he can shake me off.

Blood runs in a river down his throat, coating my hand, but there's no time to waste. I hop off the collapsing body underneath me and wipe my hand across my clothes in an effort to re-grip my weapon.

"What the fuck!?" the one holding Davey screeches. They had to have known there was two of us. It's not my fault they're incapable of intelligent thought.

His beady eyes dart between the two of us, then to the sky. The sun is lower, and night is approaching fast.

"Let her go, and I won't kill you." It's a lie, but he doesn't need to know that.

For a brief moment, I make eye contact with Davey, on her knees, head wrenched to the side in pain. Yeah, I am going to enjoy seeing the light go out of those black eyes. Her eyes widen in fear, true fear, that she may not make it through the night. I try and convey that I have things under control, but there is only so much silent communication you can have with someone in a situation this dire.

If we had more time, I'd do more than tell her she's safe. I'd tell her she'll always be safe with me as long as she stays by my side.

Weighing his options, the Beast's eyes land on his companion, lying in a pool of his own blood, face permanently stuck in a mask of shock. There's a slight tremor in his hands as he comes to terms with the situation he's caused.

"You'll let me go?" he asks with false bravado. What a fucking coward. Just die like the scumbag you are and move on. I need to talk to my girl, the pent up feelings I have for Davey springing forward, unable to be held back any longer.

"Only if you let her go and let her walk over to me right now. I won't ask twice." I stretch out my hand and lock eyes with Davey. Giving her the briefest of nods, I train my eyes on my next target.

Using the fist in her hair, he throws her forward onto her knees, and I take off to catch him before he can run away. Hurdling over Davey, I wrap my arms around the Beast's waist and bring him to the ground.

"You lying bitch!" he roars.

Dirt and dust coat my bloody clothes and my face. My fist connects with his jaw, a little payback for Davey. As a red haze floats over my vision, I pummel his face and body. I feel a kick or punch to my ribs that forces a scream from my lungs. With a better grip, I roll on top of the Beast and plunge my knife into his chest. I won't stop until he's dead. I won't let him hurt my people. I won't let him take Davey from me.

"Lenora! Lenora!" Distantly, I hear a voice drifting through the fog of my brain. If the Beast is alive, I can't let her near it.

The crunch of bone fills the air, and I can feel the slip of his warm blood around me from head to toe. There's no more resistance to my blade as it punches down into the bloody grave that was once his chest cavity.

Warm arms envelope me, and my downward strikes stop. After a few breaths, the world around me slowly comes into focus, like a lens shifting on reality.

"He's dead. He's dead, Lenora. It's okay." Why is she comforting me when they were going to take her?

Looking down at the Beast brings me to my feet. Gone are his beady eyes and gaunt face. In their place is an empty cavern filled with blood and bone, a macabre soup of the Beast he once was.

My heart aches at the what-ifs of the night, and I throw my arms around the only person who can bring me back from the brink of my bloodlust.

"Are you alright?" Holding her at arm's length, I check her over. A rustle of feet catch my attention, and my head snaps to the small girl who helped these Beasts attack Davey. With my sight focused on her, she freezes, tears tracing down the soft planes of her dirty face.

"Thank you," she whispers before fainting in the dirt.

"What the fuck was that?" Davey asks.

"A trap. They used her as bait," I answer.

"We have to bring her back with us. She's just a kid. If they had her, it couldn't have been of her own free will," Davey pleads. I breathe out through my nose and try to center myself.

"We can't just bring her to the camp and expect everyone to welcome her with open arms. She could be a sympathizer. What if I just killed her father, brother, or worse: her lover?" Bile rises in my throat at the idea of this young girl having a lover in one of the Beasts laying lifeless around us.

"We can quarantine her and have Antonia or Jones keep watch, just until she can tell us what the hell this was all about. Don't you want to know how they got this close?" Fuck. She has a good point. Part of survival is knowing when to collect intelligence. If they have a base somewhere nearby, we may have a problem. If they were the last alive, we could scavenge and find supplies. But by the looks of their frail bodies, it doesn't seem like they had a continuous supply of food.

"Fine, I'll carry her. You just follow me." As I bend to pick up the girl, a sharp pain lances my side, and I scream out. "Oh, fuck!" My knees hit the dirt, and I try to breathe through the pain on all fours.

"Lenora? Lenora! What's wrong?" Davey is at my side, but her face spins in my vision. I push my hand against the pain, and she snatches it, bringing it to her face.

"Blood. Lenora, you're bleeding." Her eyes dart around and land on the Beast behind us. "He had a knife, Lenora! Oh my God, it's a stab wound. We have to get you back." Her voice is growing hazy and distant.

"Give me a minute. I'll get up in a second." It's harder and harder to breathe through the pain. Her face swims in my vision.

"Lenora! Stay with me! I'll get us back."

At least, that's what I think she said before the darkness swallows me whole.

Chapter Nine
DAVEY

I grab the girl, shaking her awake. This is no time to faint. We need to get Lenora back to the compound, fast. As she rouses on the ground, I grab her arm and haul her up, her small frame much too light for her apparent age.

"Please, I'm so sorry. They made me do it! I swear!" Her voice is thin and childlike.

"I don't care. Can you help me? Just follow me back to our compound. I can carry her, but I may need help if something is in the way." I bark the orders at her and reach for Lenora, careful not to aggravate her gaping wound oozing blood through her shirt and onto my hands.

As we make our way back, the night is balmy and, for once, I miss the old days, when winter weather would sweep this side of the country and leave us in snow. Cold would help her body right now. As it stands, I won't be able to do anything until I can get her somewhere safe and peel back her shirt.

That idea used to be so appealing, I would lose myself in daydreams of the very act, but now, all I feel is cold dread. Why the fuck didn't I listen? Am I so fucking dense that I ignored a trained fighter? Someone who has done this hundreds of times and survived while creating a thriving little community of her own? While I was, *what*? Living in a fucking cave with my dying brother, wondering what day or time it was? Useless. That's what I am.

"I'm Celia," the girl says, her dead eyes trained on the ground at her feet as she walks.

"Davey. This is Lenora. She runs a compound very close to here. Once I get her there, I can see if I can," I swallow down the bile rising in my throat, "do something to save her."

"Are there Beasts there?" she whispers. This poor kid. I can't imagine the horrors she faced.

"No. Lenora and her team took them all out. You'll be safe there after you go through some questioning."

For the first time, her wide, blank eyes shoot to me. Then, they shutter and turn back to the ground. "I swear, I had to do it, or they would have forced me to have children. That's what he said. 'Do your job, or we'll keep you knocked up for the rest of your life.'"

Her reedy voice lacks emotion, like she's reciting a news story and not her own life experiences. She must have been a child when they took her, or perhaps she was the child of a sympathizer. Even their own flesh and blood mean nothing; just look at Jones. Celia has the same hard eyes, the ones that hide pain and absorb the shock of life around them by retreating deep into the recesses of the mind. One day, I hope she comes out, but for her sake, I hope that day isn't today.

* * *

Fourteen hours. That's how long I've been hovering over Lenora's prone body on the cot in front of me. The shallow stab wound in her side wasn't as terrible as I initially thought. I stitched her up, but she has been asleep since. Resting. Recuperating.

"She hasn't really slept in days," Antonia says from the door of Lenora's cabin. We moved her three hours ago, when she just seemed to be sleeping and not in any immediate danger.

"Why not?" I ask incredulously.

"She's had a bad feeling since we found you. I'm guessing the two Beasts you found were what tripped her spidey senses." Her head nods, affirming her own statement. "She's been nonstop with patrolling and fortifying everything she comes into contact with. I think she was on the verge of telling everyone to just stay inside." She barks a laugh that brings a smile to my face.

Antonia was in charge of interrogating Celia, though it was really more of a therapy session. That poor girl; I hope she can manage living after everything that has happened to her. Survival really is for the fittest. But, after helping me get Lenora back to camp, she stayed by my side as I detailed everything I was doing to Lenora's wound. Maybe she'll want to help us on the medical side of things once she gets older.

"Lenora's also been a little distracted." Her warm eyes meet mine, and heat climbs to my temples.

"I just want her to wake up so I can apologize. I was so stupid, Antonia. I should have listened to her and never ran ahead to check on Celia. Even if my instincts took over, I should have rubbed my two brain cells together and realized how bizarre the whole situation was. I'm a fucking idiot, and I'll never forgive myself if she just keeps sleeping. Though, she is really pretty like this. The angry little divot between her eyebrows is gone." I manage a small smile and brush her pink hair away from her face.

Antonia leaves me there with a knowing look.

"Tell me again how much of an idiot you are," her voice rasps from the bed, dry from disuse.

"Oh my God! Lenora!" Dropping to my knees, I wrap her in my arms, and she hisses out a breath as I pull away. "Sorry! Sorry. I'm so sorry. I should have listened. I understand if you hate me. I got you stabbed! I'll listen from now on, I promise!" Tears flow freely from my eyes as I grasp her hand in mine.

"Will you?" is the only response I get. No forgiveness, not yet.

"I'm serious. I'll always listen to you. I never want this to happen again." Her slim fingers, the same that were caked in blood and wrapped around a deadly weapon not too long ago, catch one of my tears.

She crooks a finger, beckoning me closer so she can whisper, "Take off your clothes." Her breath tickles my ear, and a shiver races down my spine.

"What? You could get hurt!" I start.

"So you lied? You won't listen to me?" My body wars with the need filling my stomach. I want her so badly. I throw off my top and shorts, left in nothing.

"No underwear? When did you take them off, you little slut?" She bites her lower lip to hide her growing smile, and I'm on fire for her. The way she looks at me and devours me with those icy eyes has my nipples standing at attention.

"I never wore them. I wanted to run into you yesterday to walk the perimeter," I admit, embarrassed at how needy it sounds when said out loud.

"So you wanted me to touch your pretty pussy? Come here." I move closer to the bed, standing directly next to her. Her fingers slide between my folds, already slick with arousal for the killer in bed next to me, the protector.

"Tell me the truth: did you hate seeing me kill in front of you?" Her eyes lose their softness as she waits for my answer, never moving her fingers from my core, just holding them there, waiting for my body to betray me.

"No," I whisper, eyes wide. I remember her covered in blood, the animalistic look in her eyes as she sliced and stabbed through the Beasts with ease, all to save me.

A smile curves her mouth and, gently, she reaches deeper. I stifle a whimper and try my best to remain standing.

"Did it turn you on to see me kill for you?" Her strokes become teasing again, and I moan at the loss of pressure.

"No," I lie right to her face because the truth is embarrassing. How can I admit that?

"That's not what this pretty pussy says. Did you want to bathe in their blood with me, Davey? Let me finger you right there, over their bodies, after they tried to take what was mine?"

"Oh, fuck, Lenora," I moan and double over. The image she paints filters through my mind, and I can't help but play the scene out.

Us. Naked. Writhing over their bodies after she kept me safe by cutting them down.

"Can I touch you?" I moan, trying to keep some composure as she lazily strokes me.

"Since you asked so nicely." She pulls off the blanket covering her body. I never redressed her after tending to her wound. I can't lie and say I didn't look a few times at her beautiful body, so toned and strong.

I scoot next to her in bed and stifle a giggle.

"What?" she asks, raising a single brow.

"This reminds me of the first night we were together," I say with a small smile. I want to stay here, with her. Will she let me?

"Thank you for saving me, Davey." The earnest look in her blue eyes is striking. As her small, capable hand reaches to touch my cheek, I lean into it, and my eyelids slide shut.

"I'm glad I could help."

Gently, she pulls me down, and her soft lips brush against mine, setting my body ablaze. Slow, languid strokes of her tongue against mine have me writhing for any friction. Finally, I trail my fingers down her small breasts. Everything about Lenora seems small, save for her presence. It's big enough to command an entire group of people to safety. I'm awestruck by her resilience and strength in the face of all her experiences.

Careful not to touch her wound, I slide my hand between her legs, and I'm captured by her warmth.

"Let me make you feel good," I whisper, trailing kisses down her slender neck, all the way to her waist. I lick my way down her body; she's a heady aphrodisiac.

"I'm actually fine with that, seeing as I can't move much at the moment." Her lopsided grin is so carefree and soft, my heart almost pounds out of my chest.

With no rush, I make my way between her legs and taste her for the first time. She's a heady mix of salty and sweet. My groan reaches her ears, and her hand fists in my hair as I stroke her softly with my tongue.

Divine.

"You taste so good. Tell me what you like. I want this to be good for you too."

"Davey, there is nothing you could do down there that wouldn't be good. I can't come from penetration, so as long as you touch my clit, I'll be just fine." She huffs and inhales as I use my fingers to massage her outer lips, squeezing and gently releasing, helping the blood flow exactly where I want it.

"Oh, fuck. What was that?" She moans above me, and the praise makes my heart soar.

"Shh. Just relax and enjoy it," I murmur, never taking my eyes off her pink, puffy core. The more I massage, the stiffer her clit gets, and I can tell by the arousal leaking from her pussy that she's turned on.

Pressing the flat of my tongue against the bundle of nerves, I swipe up and down as her body writhes and shakes underneath me. I take a second to admire her as I blow softly on her clit.

"Shit, please, Davey. More," she wheezes. Hearing her beg is not something I ever imagined, but it shoots pleasure directly into my veins.

I latch onto her aching clit and suck gently then flick the tip of my tongue. Her back almost bows, but her wound keeps her attached to the bed. Then, I do the most unhinged thing I have ever done in my life: I trace my name on her clit. I'm exactly where I want to live for the rest of my life—right between her legs.

When her body shakes and a scream explodes from her mouth, I lap at her wetness, drinking down everything she has to give me. As she catches her breath and comes down from the high of her orgasm, I make my way back to the pillows and stare at her.

"That was...insane. Holy shit."

"Thank you for saving me too, Lenora." I can see safety in her eyes, and when she grabs my hand and interlaces our fingers while drifting back to sleep, I know I've found my home.

THE END

If you enjoyed this story and want more filthy spice made to entice, check out my series The Rowdy Reunion where three besties learn what happens when they try and fail to run from their past kinky conquests. Each book is a steamy dark romance full of kink and consent. There are guaranteed HEAs and no cliffhangers.

About the Author

Theia Luna is a bisexual and genderfluid indie author. She loves to write about relationships and people who feel authentic to her experience in the world. When she isn't in her garden reminiscing about her days in roller derby, she can be found walking her dog or spending time with her wonderful family, who support her smut peddling.

Crimson Dress

By: A.H. Monroe

About Crimson Dress

"I'm going to smear you in blood, my little raven."

I thought I could escape *him*. I thought becoming the new queen of the Savage Serpents would free me from the man who once claimed my soul. But on my wedding day, as I stood ready to embrace a new life, one bullet from Adam shattered it all.

My fiancé is dead. My dress is painted crimson. And the one man I swore to escape now holds me tighter than ever.

Adam is dangerous, lethal, and a complete psycho obsessed with me. And the most twisted part? I crave him. Together, we flee the ruins of my wedding, leaving behind a trail of bodies, destruction, and the wrath of my father, the king of the Savage Serpents.

I've spent my life on the edge of a knife. Now, it's my turn to wield it.

This is my story. And by the end, the world will know my name.

Content Note:

This story has a HEA, but it has trigger warnings. Graphic violence, dubcon, possessive MMC, orgasm control, anal play, psychological abuse, toxic relationships, stalking, gun violence, parental betrayal, torture and mutilation, sexual content, and murder. Mature content. For readers 18 & older.

Relationship type: M/F

Chapter One
Adam

T he air in Eretha is cold tonight, just like the revenge I am about to extract. Did Sara believe she could run away from me? I line up my sniper rifle and look through the scope. I see her. She is so fucking beautiful. Sara is devastatingly gorgeous with her long black hair, slightly tanned skin, and bright blue eyes. My raven-haired beauty is wearing her floor-length white wedding dress, and she looks like she is happy. That earns a chuckle from me. I know she is completely devastated, fully aware that we belong together. I'm going to smear you in blood, my little raven.

I'm on the roof of her parents' castle, and I have the perfect view of the wedding in their barn. A wedding is an event meant to be celebrated, and I'm about to celebrate the fuck out of this joyous union. My cock is starting to swell, considering that in a matter of minutes, I will turn her dress into the prettiest shade of crimson. My fingers trail over my Mk-22, my favorite sniper rifle, and I point at the heart of her soon-to-be-dead husband. Sara notices the red dot on his heart and whips her head around. She knows this is my doing.

Yes, little raven, I'm here.

I shoot once I have my target in sight. The bullet flies through the air and hits his heart. Haris slumps to the ground and I am smiling. But. Sara is not. She is furious and shocked. Don't worry, Fury, I'm coming.

* * *

Sara

The atmosphere in the air changes from fake bliss to utter devastation. Once the bullet hit Haris, chaos erupted. The moment his body hits the floor, I look outside. My eyes are looking for *him*, but I can't see him. Yes, ladies and gentlemen, my ex just shot the man I thought I was going to marry. I throw away my bouquet, and I kneel beside Haris. I check his pulse, and, yes, he is very much dead. As I was processing him being shot, I didn't register everybody fucking shouting. And I definitely didn't notice the two strong hands leading me outside the barn. One of my father's bodyguards is dragging me outside. We are almost outside, but my eyes find my father. I can see a flicker of anger in his eyes.

Why the fuck is he angry at *me?*

It's not like I shot my husband. Every attendee is rushing to get outside, but my father's men are keeping them back, likely to interrogate each one and see if anyone knows what really happened. They can question my fucking ass since I am done. I don't need this family.

Once we are outside, the cold air hits me. I am looking everywhere because I need confirmation on whether it was him. My father's bodyguard slams the barn doors closed, and I turn around to look at him. He takes a step forward, and I find myself going to the barn again. My dad's main bodyguard has scared me for years, and I hate how he still has such an effect on me.

"You fucking knew about this, didn't you?" my dad's bodyguard, Eren, quizzes me.

Before I can even react, he points his rifle at me. I take a few steps back and bump into one of the closed barn doors. My breathing slowed down significantly, and I can't utter a single word. I have grown up in this dangerous world of assassins, so I have taught myself proper ways to calm down.

Eren looks at me with an expression capable of killing any regular woman, or man, instantly. But not me. I am the daughter of one of the most feared assassins in the world. The irony isn't lost on me, an assassin princess afraid of a contract killer who is beneath her in rank. I look at him with no expression on my face, well, this just pisses him off. Do I care? Not one bit. He cocks his rifle, which is still pointed at me.

"I know I am going to do your dad a favor by killing you. Goodbye, princess." His finger is going over the trigger, and, shit, I am going to die.

Splat.

I close my eyes, and once the taste of crimson hits my mouth, I lick my lips. It doesn't take a genius to know that this is blood. I wipe Eren's blood off my face, but then I notice that his blood is also all over my wedding dress.

"Could this night get any worse?" I ask nobody.

"Hello, Fury." Before I can whip my head up, a hand closes around my throat. I close my eyes once again, and I relish this sensation. Choking has always been one of my kinks. But there is only one person who knows about this. I open my eyes, and I see *him.*

"Adam."

Chapter Two
Adam

My name on her lips is like an aphrodisiac. The compelling tones of her voice send a straight shot to my dick. I look deeply into her eyes, and I squeeze her throat a little bit tighter. Sara keeps the beast in me alive, and I don't plan on letting him stay in this cage forever. While my right hand is enfolding her throat, my left hand is going to my waist to grab my knife. The shiny object is like a vessel of power in my hands, and I plan on exerting that power over her fucking dress. But not just yet. I release her throat and the audible gasp she releases is unmistakable. She fucking wants this.

"My hand will go around your throat again, Fury," I tell her while my voice is low. Barely above a whisper. The hunger in her eyes is replaced by anger.

"Like I fucking want that." My little spitfire is as edgy as ever. I let out a chuckle and walk over to the dead sack of shit on the ground. I plunge my knife into his heart, and I let his tainted blood coat my knife. I stand up from the ground, not letting the glee fade from my face. My feet take the way, and I stand in front of Sara again. I show her my knife which is soaked in blood.

"I promised you if you ever got married, I would paint your dress crimson." She gasps because she remembers my promise.

"Now, open up those pretty legs, Fury." Sara takes a deep breath, and she does what she is told to.

"You are such a good girl, Fury." My voice is coming out in a heavy but quiet tone. I take my knife, and I lay it flat on her dress-covered chest. I glide the knife across her chest and then down to her waist. Dear Lord, I am not a religious person, but Sara's terrified state could make me believe He might exist.

She is fucking beautiful.

I take a step back to admire my handiwork, and it makes me realize that I can't stop. I will never stop loving her. She puts up her right hand.

"What the fuck do you think you are going to do?" she quizzes me. When her eyes look into mine, she knows she is staring at a dangerous man. I know what I want, and I always get what I want. And she is my prize known as life. I do the only logical thing I can think of so I can show my devotion to her.

I lunge at her.

She screams, hoping that somebody will hear her. I actually don't give a shit if somebody catches us, or watches. Let them, she is mine. I drop to my knees, and when I look at her, she is secretly asking me to never stop.

"I hope you weren't too keen on the bottom half of your dress," I say to her.

"What do you m-" Before she can respond, I cut that part of her dress off.

"How dare you? This dress was incredibly expensive!" Sara yells at me. I furrow my brows. Why is she still so hung up on her dress? It's not like she would ever get married in that thing.

"Since I want to do this" My smile unwavering with the lingering promise I just gave her. I hike her dress up, and I get to work. I rip her panties open and throw them on the ground next to us. My dick is aching from how much it wants to be in her, but I let him rest for just a second. My tongue is taking over his job, for now. I need to fuck her with my tongue like an animal.

"Adam, please, don't," she asks me through cries of pleasure. Did she honestly think I would stop? Fuck. No. My tongue is licking her folds with long strokes, and then I plunge into her cunt. I let my knife hit the damp ground so I can grab both of her thighs. My fingers are digging into her flesh driven by the desire to leave marks on her body. I want her to remember how I own every single part of her body.

"Fucking hell, Adam! Please don't-" Sara can't finish her sentence, and I feel her getting wetter.

"Do you want me to stop? Your dripping pussy is telling me otherwise," I point out to her. Then she reacts the way she always does when she wants to keep this sensation going. Her fingers tug my black wavy hair hard. Fuck, she didn't forget I like that. I dive, again, into her burning core, and I go so deep that my entire tongue is in her cunt.

"Fuck. Me." *Don't mind if I do, Fury.* I stand up while my right hand is cupping her pussy. I insert two fingers into her cunt, and I curl them so the sensation builds up in her body.

"You will come on my hand, Fury. I want your juices all over my fucking hand. Now, fucking come!" I command her in a harsh tone. Her lips part, and she starts panting. Her hands are now on my shoulders, and it feels like her nails are trying to tear the fabric of my black pullover.

"What if I can't do that? It has been a while, Rage." The glimmer in her devious eyes is making me ravenous. I take another blade from my waistband, and I go over her dress to pick up some of the blood. I let the knife go over her lips while the blood is coating her plush pillows.

"Listen to me, Fury. This blood is a sign that I would kill any man, or woman, who stands in my way to get you." My eyes are searching for a flicker of hesitation in her eyes, but it doesn't come.

"You fucking asshole."

Chapter Three
Sara

"You fucking asshole," I tell him while my orgasm rips through me. This burning sensation for Adam didn't happen overnight, I have always had this intense desire for him. For the last three years, he was all I could think about. We broke up as I thought that my rightful place was with someone my dad picked out. I also wanted to leave because Adam is unhinged. For Christ's sake, the man shot my future husband.

"You were saying?" he asks me with a smug grin plastered all over his face. My hands are still latched onto his shoulders. I scratch his shoulders, trying to harm him, but my attempt was pointless. Adam loves pain.

"Tsk, tsk, tsk, Fury. You are going to pay for that." *I am, and I want to.* Maybe this momentary lapse of judgment will give me enough bliss so that when I escape, I can hold onto some memories of pleasure. Adam's left hand goes to his zipper, and he frees his big dick. I don't dare to look down, knowing this is going to hurt. With his dick out, he grabs my jaw and makes me look into his green eyes. He is mad.

"If you ever try to look away from me again, I will fuck your mouth with so much ferocity it's going to hurt." This psychopath is making me breathe even faster. His words are like poison, yet my body is still yearning for them.

"You wouldn't fucking dare," I say to him. I release my hands from his shoulders, and I try to smack him. To my disappointment, he grabs my right wrist and pins it above my head, while his other hand is still around my jaw.

"Fury, I wouldn't even care if you got blisters into your mouth from sucking my cock." The glee in his eyes confirming it. "On second thought. Do that now." He releases my jaw and grabs my hair with a forceful tug. I look into his eyes and silently plead with him not to do anything.

"Adam, please, I don't want to." He smirks. Adam releases my wrist and trails his fingers over my collarbone.

"You might say no, but your body is saying yes. Come on, Fury, get down and suck my dick." He pushes me onto the ground so I can kneel before him. I look up at him while he is still tugging my hair with his left hand. The glee in his eyes is replaced by a need to control me.

Fuck. Me.

Both of my hands trail along his legs up to his dick. I have two things I can do, either I suck his dick, or I can try to escape. The nerves are building up in my entire body, and I can't stop shaking knowing I am afraid. Or something else? With Adam, I never knew. In a split second, I tug on his balls with my left hand while I punch his dick with my right fist. That seems to do the trick because Adam's hand, which was in my hair, is coming up to his mouth. He bites down hard on his knuckles, likely to mask the agony he's in. I quickly stand up and push him to the ground. My sudden choice of actions must have caught him by surprise since he tumbles down onto the ground.

"Atta girl," I hear him say. This is not good, beyond fucked up.

When he says *that* it's time for me to run. It's time for me to face the consequences.

"You have ten seconds before I start running. And, Fury?" he asks me while standing up. I nod at him.

"Run."

Chapter Four
Adam

Did she honestly think that she could run away from me? Or, more importantly, I wouldn't catch her? I stand up and I see her running away into the forest next to her parents' estate. I am contemplating on giving her fifteen seconds instead of ten, but I decide against it. I need to fuck her. Hard.

My feet are taking the lead into the forest, and I don't see my Fury, yet. For a moment, I stand in the middle of the forest, listening for even a snap of a branch. Then, I hear it, her breathing. As a professional sniper, it's my job to look for any details. I can't miss anything, so naturally, all of my senses are heightened. I close my eyes, and while I can hear her breathing, I can also taste her anxiety. It's like the first strawberry of the season on my lips, delectable. She must be close and behind one of these tall maple trees. Very silently, I pick up a rock and throw it to the side. I wait for a reaction, and then I get what I want. The crackle of some leaves has left me fucking elevated. My footsteps are deliberately quiet due to the fact I want to surprise her. I know that my Fury will be excited to see me.

I round up the tree closest to me and see Sara with her back turned. I grab her by the back of her hair and yank her to me. Her back is now plastered to my front, and I put my mouth close to her ear. At the same time, my other hand goes to her throat.

"Now you are going to scream from how hard I'm going to fuck you," I say to her in a deadly whisper. She tries to wiggle out of my loving embrace, but it's pointless.

"Adam, don't do this. I do not want this." Her pleas are falling on deaf ears since I know her. While she is telling me to stop, her hand moves to mine, and she starts stroking it. This is what I live for.

"Fury, your body is my sanctuary. You are going to come on my cock like a good little girl," I say to her. My hands move away from her throat and hair, and I push her onto the ground. She lands on her hands and knees. My dick is getting harder by the second.

"Don't you dare to stand up. Stay in that position, Fury," My voice is unwavering. I lower my pants and boxer briefs, and I am now positioned behind her big fucking ass. My favorite place in the world. I don't give her any time to adjust to her new reality. I start ramming, viciously, into her cunt, and I make her cry.

"Cry for me, Fury, I want your tears," I tell her.

"You are fucking sick!" she screams at me, breathing heavily. Sara's cries for help are silenced by her meeting me thrust for thrust. My fingers find her clit, and I start drawing circles. My touch is sending her into overdrive and her screams are becoming louder. Her sounds are echoing throughout the entire forest. Sara is calling out to God to save her, but I am here. What does she need God for? To prove my point, I push one more finger into her and her reaction is making me ferocious.

"Adam! Adam!" Her voice gives her away, she likes this. My fingers are working in a punishing rhythm, like my dick. Her pussy is getting wetter, and I feel her juices all over my fingers. *Oh hell no.*

"Did I tell you that you could come?" I grab her by the back of her hair, which makes her gasp, audibly.

"I hope you fucking die, Rage!" Would you look at that? She still loves me. Sara only calls me Rage when she truly cares about me. I push my fingers, which are soaked in her cum, into her mouth.

"Suck on them, and taste yourself, Fury." My command is leaving no room for interpretation. Her mouth clamps down onto my fingers, and her hums of appreciation are only fueling my addiction to her. She needs to remember this, I am the only one who can, and will, make her feel this way. Her orgasms are mine. Her screams are mine.

She. Is. Mine.

I am imagining her sucking my dick, and that does it.

"I am going to come inside your pussy," I exclaim while trying to catch my breath. I am going even more crazy over this woman than before. My dick empties himself inside of her, and I am seeing stars. But it's not enough. I flip her over onto her back, and I start fucking my cum back into her. Her arms fly over her head, and a small smile sprawls over her face. Leopards don't change their skin.

When she sees my smirk, she immediately changes her attitude. Sara is a fool for thinking she can deprive me of her smile. I grab the knife from my waistband and I bring it up to her lips. While I am still fucking her, I look deep into her eyes.

"Don't you fucking dare to hide your smile, Fury. If you do, I will carve out a smile," My serious tone is making her shiver just a little bit. Sara might crumble under my touch, but she is not afraid of me. Of anybody, for that matter. Fury is still the daughter of one of the most feared assassins in the world. Her dad is dangerous, but my boss is evil to the core. I empty myself again in her, and I slump down beside her. We are lying side by side, and all is good in the world. I look into her eyes, and I can't believe my luck. I have her again.

"We are going to be so happy, Fury," I promise her.

"How the fuck do you think we are going to be happy? You snatched me away from my wedding." Her tone is starting to irritate me.

"Sara, I love you and you love me, so naturally, we are going to be together forever."

"You are insane. I'm not going anywhere with you, Adam."

"It's funny you think that you have a choice." The resolute tone in my voice is unwavering. I get up and I extend my hand to her. She huffs, but she accepts it.

"So, where are we-" A bullet flying past her hair cut off her sentence. In a split second, I decide to grab her by the shoulders and push her down to the ground. Sara stays silent, knowing any sound could give us away. The bullet didn't fly from a great distance, so it wasn't the work of a sniper. I crouch down right beside her, and I close my eyes to heighten my sense of listening. I need to be totally focused. I hear someone breathing very, very close to us. I put my mouth to her ear.

"You are going to lay down on the ground once I shout." My voice barely above a whisper, she nods at me. I reach for my gun, which has a silencer on it, from the back of my waistband, and I point it in the direction I heard the noise coming from. I look straight ahead of me, and I was right.

"Get down!" I shout at Sara. She gets down onto her stomach, and I fire one bullet through the asshole's skull. A smirk is forming on my face.

"I told you that you would always be safe with me. Now-" I'm cut off by someone taking me down. I am now on the ground with a huge man on top of me. I look at his face and see that it's one of Sara's dad's guards. Fuck, he has my legs pinned down. I try to reach for the knife in my waistband, but it's not there, and my gun is behind the asshole. He puts his gun to my temple, and he is not fucking laughing.

"Her dad sends his regards." His finger goes over the trigger, but my Fury stops him. She jumps onto his back and starts scratching his eyes out. Her nails are digging into his eyes, and I know what she is doing. Sara has always been a fan of removing one of the six senses in a fight. The bodyguard screams out in pain, but he manages to get ahold of her wedding dress. Sara flies to the ground, and she looks completely disheveled. He is about to jump on her, but I am quicker. I get the knife, and I run up to him and put it under his chin. He rises to sit up on his knees, and I can feel my blood boiling. He wanted to hurt what's mine.

"You made a very big mistake. I will cut every vein in your body, but I will leave you with an inch of your life," I say as I cut his cheek. Then I move over to his neck, and I make a superficial cut. My knife travels to his arm, but Sara stops me by standing up. She goes to stand right in front of the bodyguard and stretches out her arm, not looking at me. I give her the knife, and she happily accepts it.

"Give my dad my regards." She takes the knife and stabs his right eye. The second the knife penetrates his eye, blood gushes out. The bodyguard raises his hands, but I stop him by holding his arms in one place. The screams coming from his body are the icing on the cake for this perfect evening.

My Fury is back.

She stabs his other eye, and I couldn't be more proud of her. Sometimes, we have to go through Hell first so we can get our happy ending. She drops the knife, and I drop the bastard like a sack of potatoes. His screams are becoming quieter, probably due to him slowly bleeding out. Once he is dead, I look at her and I see it. She missed this.

Chapter Five

Sara

"Now you are going to let me suck your cock," I tell him while my chest is heaving up and down.

"Right here?" he asks me while coming closer to me. I drop onto my knees, and they hit the pool of blood. My dress is now fully covered in it, and it's a transition as I see it. I don't need this whole empire, because I have Adam. He lets me be myself. I unbuckle his pants, take his briefs off, and he steps out of them. His cock springs out and I grab him. I spit on his dick and I start licking his balls. Adam grabs my hair and starts moaning.

"Fuck, Fury, I forgot how fucking perfect you are." And I believe him. I put my mouth on his cock and I start sucking him. I hollow my mouth so I can take more of him. This obsession I always had with him, isn't something I can bury. All of these months I thought my place was in my dad's empire, but he betrayed me. Adam never did. He was always honest with me, and I need that. Is he insane? Yes. Is he obsessive? Yes. But, is he mine? Fucking yes. He pushes his dick further into my mouth so it's hitting the back of my throat. Tears are starting to form in my eyes.

"Take this dick in your mouth, Fury. Show me how much you

have missed me." So, I do. My right hand is holding onto his dick, while my left-hand goes under my wedding dress. I start rubbing my clit to heighten this exquisite feeling.

"Push two fingers into your throbbing pussy and fuck yourself with them. But don't you dare come onto your fingers, otherwise I will make you drink up this asshole's blood." His commands always make me even more wet. I know I shouldn't want this, him, but I can't seem to walk away. Per his instructions, I push two fingers into myself. In and out is the rhythm I'm holding onto, and all the while I am imagining it's his dick. My hand, which was around his cock, is now scratching his leg. This is my sign to tell him that I'm almost there.

"Oh, I don't fucking think so," he tells me. Adam takes his dick out of my mouth, and when he looks down at me, I only see trouble. His eyes are laughing for him, his maniacal side showing. He is now standing behind me and with his foot, he pushes me into the pool of blood. I make sure to close my eyes and mouth before my face hits the blood-soaked ground. I prop myself up on my elbows to give myself some grace. Adam lowers his body onto my back, and I am immediately enveloped in his warm cocoon. With one swift move, he enters from behind, and I cry out in ecstasy. His dick is hitting all of the good spots, and my orgasm is gushing out of me. The waves of pleasure are running down my thighs. Adam comes inside of me, and when I try to get away, he pushes his cum back into me with his thick fingers.

I stand up, and when I look at him, I see the look of complete satisfaction. I should've expected this look. He is zipping up and picking up his knife and gun. He puts the knife back into his waistband and holsters the gun.

"See how easy it is to listen, Fury?" His question is laced with sarcasm. I cross my arms.

"Don't make me regret this, Adam. You may have remembered our promise, but you did it quite brutally," I tell him, and he just shrugs. Months ago, I broke up with Adam since I didn't want my life to be controlled by him. I felt like he wasn't seeing the real me, but in hindsight, he was the only one that ever did. To make him even more pissed off, or so I thought, I told him that I was getting married. My first thought was that Adam wasn't going to let me go at that time, but he did. When I asked him why, he told me no matter what I did, or with whom, I would always end up with him. I was so stunned by his revelation he promised something to me. He assured me he would get me, no matter the cost. I didn't think he'd follow through, so I one-upped him with my addendum to his promise. I told him if he could break through the security of my wedding, he could do whatever he wanted to get to me. Well, he succeeded.

What also makes me go with him so easily is because of what I overheard between my now-dead fiancé and father. Yesterday, I was looking for my dad, and when I stood outside of his study, my blood ran cold. He wasn't ready to give up his throne to a woman, and that's the sole reason why he wanted Haris to marry me. That piece of shit would have gotten my rightful place as the king of one of the most feared assassin syndicates. I couldn't run away, being under the watchful eye of my dad. I made my peace with the fact I was going to be in an abusive marriage. So imagine my surprise, despair, and happiness when my dress was painted gorgeous red.

I may not get the throne, but people should be afraid of me. My name is Sara, and my dad better watch out.

Chapter Six
Adam

After a mile-long walk, we are finally in my car. Sara and I are in this comfortable silence, and I swear I can't stop smiling. The realization Fury will be mine forever is something I can't comprehend. I look over at Sara and fall in love all over again.

"Why are you looking at me like that?" she asks me while pulling all the pins out of her hair. Her black hair is now falling over her shoulders, down to her hips.

"Because we are together again." My statement makes her smirk.

"And why do you think that?" Her question is something I didn't see coming. Why is she questioning this? I pull over to the dark road.

"Why the fuck did you do this?" she asks me. I unbuckle my seatbelt and then hers. My hands fly to her hair, and I pull her lips to mine. When we break free, I stare into her beautiful eyes.

"You and I are going to be together forever. You should remember that, Fury. I did everything to get you, I held on to your promise. So, now you are mine," I tell her.

"Adam, I am grateful that you saved me, but where is this going?"

"To Brussels."

"Wait, what? Why the fuck would I go to Brussels?"

"Because my boss needs someone to oversee his operations for the Benelux, and he appointed me."

"I do remember that you liked going to Brussels."

"We will talk more about this at the hotel, Fury."

* * *

After twenty minutes, we arrive at the hotel of an acquaintance of mine, Amar. He actually pisses me off, but, he can keep a secret. Lover's Hideout is a hotel on the outskirts of Sarajevo, guests like me frequently use. That's the only reason why the hotel staff didn't give us a second look when they saw Sara in her crimson dress. I got us the best room, my lady deserves all the luxuries in life. We go up to our room and it's beautiful. Since it's nighttime, the soft moonlight is adorning the whole room.

The plush velvet curtains are framing the breathtaking view of the mountains of Sarajevo. In the middle of the room is a king-sized bed, draped in satin sheets set beneath a crystal chandelier, creating an atmosphere whispering of a night full of passion and endless possibilities.

"I can't wait to take my dress off and be in normal clothes," Sara tells me as she goes to the bathroom. Without thinking, I follow her into the bathroom, but not before I take the little syringe out of my bag that was in my car. I hold it behind my back. She won't like this, but I don't care. Sara is shimmying out of her dress, and beneath it is a sinful red lingerie set. Her makeup is taken off in less than five minutes, and when she looks up, my eyes linger on her lips.

"If you keep looking at me like that, I'm going to stab you." And I know she is not kidding. Sara looks at what I'm holding behind my back; she furrows her brows. I am purposefully closing on her very slowly. The anticipation is gradually eating away all of my nerves. Normally, I am very calm when I am about to inject someone, but this is *her*. My cool demeanor comes in handy in my job as a hired assassin. The man I work for has an entire network, just like the Savage Serpents. Those fuckers are spread across Europe and North America, handling devious matters. It's an organization that has trained killers, the best snipers, and tech-savvy people. If you want to take someone out, call them. But, if you want excellence, call me.

"What are you doing?" she asks me, as she is still standing in front of me in her sexy lingerie. Slowly, I run my fingertips from her wrist up to her collarbone. Every second over her smooth and delicate skin feels like a balm to my soul. It's like God is forgiving me for every bad thing I did. Well, I hope he is going to forgive me for this. Sara is noticing the gleam in my eyes, and then she finally realizes what I'm holding.

"Wait, Adam, don't do it," she tells me.

"Oh, Fury, it's for your own good." I take the syringe from my back, and with the speed of lightning, I ram the pointy syringe into her upper arm. I throw the syringe behind my back, and when I look at her, I see anger. Sara is looking over at the spot where I injected her.

"Adam, you have three fucking seconds to tell me what you did. Even though I have a strong suspicion," she exclaims. I don't like this line of questioning, why is she making this so hard? I make a face you can decipher one thing from, I'm thoroughly confused. My hands fly around her thick thighs and I push her onto the counter. I spread her thighs and pin them down with my hands.

"Do you expect me to believe that you don't know what I did?" I ask her. She huffs and puffs.

"You know I don't like brats. So, for your good, you should be honest." My tone does not leave any room for interpretation. She nods her head.

"But, I'll be clear this once. You," I say, and pause to kiss her by the corner of her mouth, "are," another one right on her cheek, "fuck-ing", the last pecker goes on her neck, "mine". I gaze into her eyes again, and now she is confused by my sudden kind intrusion. Well, that will be short-lived. I dig my nails deeper into her thighs until I can almost feel the flesh underneath her delicate skin.

"Fury, I didn't inject you with a poison or a drug," I tell her.

"I thought you injected me with some truth serum." She laughs her concerns off.

"Shit like that doesn't exist. And we both know you are willing to give anything up to me."

"Who made that decision?"

"I did." I roll my eyes. "Anyway, I injected you with a microscopic tracker. You can try to take it out, but I would advise against it."

"Adam, you can go fuck yourself. Why did you put a tracker in me?"

"Because I'm not letting you go, like ever. Why are you so confused?" I ask her, genuinely.

"All my life I tried to walk away from men who try to decide everything for me. I want freedom, and now you are doing this to me. Can't you see how fucked up this is?"

"Fury, I'll show you what your legs are made of. So-" She interrupts me by holding out her right hand.

"Adam, if you see me moving my lips, it means I am talking. This means you need to shut the fuck up." Her ferocity is so fucking hot. Her breathing slows down as she stares into my eyes. I feel like she is trying to uncover my secrets this way, and I might give up all of them. Her brown eyes are an aphrodisiac I can't get enough of. Then something happens, and her face softens. God, I love it when she is like this. Sara crooks her finger at me, and I happily oblige. I lower my face to hers because I am much taller than her. Her lips graze over mine, and every nerve in my lip is on fire.

"Have fun catching me, asshole." Wait, what?
Whack.

I tumble over, and I lose my grip over Sara. When I look down at the floor, with my right hand massaging the right side of my scalp, I see her feet. I am now on my knees, maybe unwillingly at first, but not anymore. She looks down at me with a certain happiness to her, and I don't dare stand up.

"You do something like this ever again, and I will poison you with cyanide." I know she will—Sara can get her hands on that stuff pretty easily. While I am dangerous, I am not stupid. My Fury may be perceived as this prissy princess of a big assassin group, but she is lethal. Her delicate fingers are now threading through my hair, and I revel in the sensation. But then she tugs hard on my hair.

"Let me show you what I will use my legs for. I'm going to get dressed, and you will kneel on this floor like a good whimpering boy. Do you understand me?" I nod at her. The urgency in her voice is making me go feral and fucking horny. I stay on my knees while I am watching her get dressed in the next room. She is going through the duffel bag I packed with some clothes for her. Sara puts on black pants, a dark green long-sleeved shirt, brown combat boots, and a black leather jacket. Her hair is up in a long ponytail, and I am foaming at my mouth.

"I know that you will find me, but let's make this interesting?" A rhetorical question I don't dare to contradict.

"I am giving myself a head start of fifteen seconds. After fifteen seconds, you can start searching for me. Nod if you understand me." So I do. "Have fun hunting, Rage."

With that gleam in her eyes, she is out of the door. And I know that she wants me to find her. How do I know this?

My Fury called me Rage.

Chapter Seven
Sara

Oh, I did it again. This push and pull between Adam and me is what dreams are made of. Healthy relationships? No. Relationships where they always challenge each other? Yes. And that's what I need. I need someone who will contest my words, decisions, and actions. That way I know somebody is *actually* listening to me and paying attention. While I do make it intentionally hard for Adam, I really do love him. That's why I told him to chase me, it's our thing.

"It's your turn, whimpering boy," I say to myself as I race through the lobby of the hotel, and now I'm outside. I make a run for the shed next to the hotel, which is luckily abandoned. Adam is not the only one who visits this hotel once in a while.

"Oh, hell yes, it's all untouched," I say to myself, and the shed. This little space is not your typical shed, it's a space for people like me to gather supplies for their business. You can compare it to a library, but with weapons. Because I am *very* skilled with knives, I gravitate toward them. I make my way to the wall with the shiny objects, and I choose a meat cleaver and a small blade. I sit at the table in the back of the shed, and I wait. While I'm waiting for Adam,

I can't help but think of the time I started learning about the veins in humans.

"I miss you, my dear neurosurgeon friend," I say as I look at the meat cleaver. Maybe I can hit him up when I'm in Brussels?

"There you are, Fury," Adam says, snapping me out of my thoughts.

"I for sure am, Rage," I say.

"Now, what are you doing with that cleaver, baby?" he asks me as he starts walking toward me. Like a lion about to feast on his prey.

"You probably do remember that me and knives have a special relationship, don't you?" I ask him.

"I know, Fury. What are you going to do with them?"

"I am not sure. Do you want me to carve a pretty 'S' into your chest? That way I am branded on you."

"You can do that, but you don't have to. Fury, you have made a permanent imprint on my heart." Fucking asshole. He is now standing before me. When I look at him, I notice that he has his waistband on again. His belt always consists of three things, two blades and a gun with a silencer on it. He is also holding an AK-12. I lay my knives down beside me, and he lays his assault rifle down.

"Did you honestly think you could run away from me?" Adam asks me as he pulls down my pants, along with my panties. I'm now naked before him, except for my shirt. He runs his fingers along my thighs, and, for the first time, I am happy I am completely hairless. I want to be able to feel the callousness of his fingers. Every single cell under his skin needs to be connected with mine. When his fingers come up to my pussy, they tease my entrance.

"You know I love your full bush, but this is a pleasant surprise," he tells me, without averting his gaze from me.

"I know you like my pussy wax-stripped raw," I ask in a hush.

"You know I fucking do, but, I also like it when you have a full bush," he tells me. While he is still on his knees, his fingers are entering my pussy at a punishing pace. I grab the sides of the table and lose my breath. The only thing I'm doing right now is sweating.

My legs open up even further so that Adam can have better access. I throw my head back, the anticipation is killing me. I need to have his wicked tongue on my pussy, and I need him to lap up every single one of my juices. The wetness that is accumulating is something I can't control. All of my inhibitions are laid out in front of this insane man, and I can't seem to get enough. I sit up a little bit straighter so I can look at him. And this psychopath looks right at me, with a vile smirk.

"Do you think you deserve my tongue?" he playfully answers, while his fingers are stroking the inside of my right thigh. The tiny, but powerful move is sending shockwaves through my body. Yes, Haris was good fuck, but nothing compares to Adam. His touch is helping me to get free from the imaginary shackles around my neck.

"I, for sure, do. Come on, just lap up my pussy," I tell him.

"Oh, Fury, I'm going to do much more." The bravado on my face changes from that to being confused. Adam doesn't even give me time to decipher his sentence, he starts tongue-fucking me, and for once, I shut up. Being able to form a coherent thought is out of the question. Adam's tongue is circling my entire entrance, before diving back in.

"Now you can scream." His hot breath on my skin is heightening all of my senses. He plunges his tongue back into my cunt, and I die. Adam is sucking on my folds like his life depends on it. My wet cunt is his last meal, and he intends to feast.

"Fuck, Rage, dear Lord!" I scream. My voice is becoming hoarse from how much I'm screaming.

"When you say my name like that, I never want to stop eating your cunt."

"Then don't!" I yell back at him. I can feel him smiling against my pussy, and I don't have any time for niceties. I need Adam to set me free so I can finally be myself. The imaginary bars around my whole life are almost all gone, and this will make me see the blue skies again. He grabs both of my thighs forcefully.

"Don't worry, Fury, I am not letting you go again." His promise is everything I need in this life. Adam pushes his tongue back into my pussy, and I can feel it against my walls. I don't even care if somebody would walk in right now, that's how much I love having this man on his knees.

"Detonate, Fury, unleash your cum on my face." So I do. Those words are like the fuse that lit the fuel in my entire body. The temperature is rising, and I don't want it to stop it.

"Oh fuck!" I scream out one last time before I come on his face. I release the sides of the table, and I collapse on my back. Adam unhooks his hands from my thighs, and now he is moving over my body. I didn't even realize that he is naked from the waist down, and I don't care. I need his dick inside me.

"There is no escape for you from me." That wasn't a question. It sounded like a lifeline he is hanging onto. Adam is lying on top of me, and I can feel the heat radiating from his body. Our souls are connecting once again.

"Rage, I hope you are ready for a lifetime of me making you mad every step of the way," I say with a smile that I cannot and will not contain. He does the same as he is running his fingers through my hair. This simple gesture is so sweet, and I am becoming addicted.

"Are you going to get up right now?" I ask him as I try to wiggle out of his embrace. He shakes his head in disbelief.

"Trust me, Fury, we are just starting."

Chapter Eight
Adam

I grab her hands and bring them up over her head.

"I am going to fuck you now." She just nods at me. Good girl, I think to myself.

"Let your hands stay like this, and if you don't, you will be punished," I tell her. She cocks her head, and her lips lift to a smirk. Fuck, I forgot that Sara loves to be handled like a problem.

"Put your legs around my neck, Fury." She complies beautifully. In these moments, she only confirms my love for her will never burn out. When her legs are around my neck, I crack my neck by moving it side to side. I tease her entrance by sliding my cock up and down her slit. I use her cum as lubrication. When I hear her moan, I know it's time to push into her. My cock is so deep in her, and her hole is so tight it's creating such a tightness I could get lost in forever. Her cunt is so tight, I almost don't want to move. I don't do that, though.

"You are fucking divine, Fury," I tell her as I pepper her calves with kisses. My own eyes shut so I can feel the intensity even better. This position is giving me the best angle ever, and it causes deep penetration. Sara can adjust her legs, but she's not, since she loves this butterfly position.

"Dear Lord, your dick is even bigger than I remember, Rage."
Her compliments are like music to my ears. They could become my
favorite soundtrack, but her cries will always hold the number one
spot. I am the only one who can demolish her entire being and make
her shatter.

"Did I tell you that you could talk?" I ask her. She slits her eyes at
me and closes her mouth.

"Good girl. Now, shut the fuck up and let me rail you into next
Sunday." She bites her lip, likingmy promise. The sweat is dripping
from my hair down my face and onto her shirt. Sara is making me
ravenous. I am hungry like a wild animal, and this woman is happily
my prey. I started with a slow pace but that's not something I can
hold onto for long. I increase my speed, and to heighten her pleasure,
I start rubbing circles onto her little nub.

"Scream." And my Fury does. Her screams are something that
needs to be studied, it's the sound of angels. This is what heaven
looks and sounds like. Sara cries out in pleasure, and she comes again,
and so do I. My cum is now in her, and it will stay like that. This
woman will carry my children, I promise you.

"It was so fucking hot," my angel exclaims, while she is laying on
the table with her hands above her head. I put her underwear and
jeans back on, then I do mine. I motion to her to sit up straight, and
she does. For a couple of seconds, we don't say anything. We breathe
each other's energy in and let all doubts fade away. Our relationship
is not conventional, and I am not normal. But I can't bring myself to
give two fucks. Sara matches my freak, and I am grateful for her.

"Can I hug you?" I ask her. Her face reveals something, my question has taken her aback. Her mouth opens and closes again.

"Wait, you are asking me to hug me?" she asks me back.

"Why is that so weird?"

"Because you are asking me for permission to touch me. Just
saying."

"Fury, just this one time." My smile widens. She holds her arms
out, and I step into them. Sara nuzzles into my neck, and I can't stop

smelling her hair. My beautiful girlfriend smells like a raging storm. Her scent invades my entire being, she is like the promise of shelter in a storm. Sharp and unyielding. Leather and crushed herbs. I could bask in this all fucking day.

"I love you, Sara." While I love calling her Fury, she is my Sara first and foremost.

"I love you too, Adam," she says sweetly. Life can't get any better.

"So, I thought-" My sentence is cut off with Sara reaching for the blade beside her. When I look at her, she is looking for something, or someone, behind me. She pushes me to the side and throws the blade.

"Get down!" she yells. I don't question her combat intelligence, and I get down. I look at the dead sack of shit on the ground, and I don't recognize him. But Sara does.

"Who is there?" I ask her, and while I stand up to grab my gear, she grabs hers as well. When we are ready, she looks at me, looking incredibly pissed off. She is also holding a bottle of water.

"Why are you carrying a bottle of water?" I ask her. She shrugs, and I let it go.

"My father's men are here. They tracked us down. Somebody at the hotel must have tipped them off. Do you know who?" She asks me, while she is leading us outside of the shed.

Amar.

"I know. It's an acquaintance of mine." We walk back into the hotel, and I start looking for the weasel.

"Isn't he a friend of yours? And where is he?" she asks me while I'm looking for Amar. We go to the basement of the hotel, and we are standing in front of Amar's personal quarters. I turn toward Sara, and I grab both of her hands, and I kiss them.

"He is right through here, and no he is not a friend. He is just someone who I thought could keep his mouth shut," I say truthfully.

"My dad probably promised him a seat at the table. Wait a minute." She looks at the door and then back at me. "This looks like a set-up."

"Your dad is probably on the other side of this door. They knew we would come here. He wants you to go back to your old life."

"That is never going to happen, I want to leave that life behind."

"Sara, you can't. You can only leave our life behind if you give up your throne."

"And I will. But I will also need to kill my dad."

"Why the fuck would you need to do that?"

"When the heir to the throne wants to leave the Savage Serpents, they need to kill the current king or queen. It's a stupid old rule."

"Can you kill your dad?"

"He never meant anything to me. I just thought I needed to tolerate him due to the fact I deserved the throne. But now I don't want it."

"Well, what do you want?" I ask her gleefully. She smirks at me.

"We will talk about that later. Are you ready?" I nod at her, time to bring my murderous lady home.

Chapter Nine
Sara

I open the door to Amar's quarters, and the first thing that hits me is the smell. It smells clean. But I'll change the scent when I smear their blood all over the walls while their intestines are oozing out. Like a watchdog, Adam follows behind me. When I step into the room, I stand still. Amar and my dad, Denis, are sitting on the couches.

"Well, this looks nice, I guess," I tell them. I step closer to them, and my heart is pounding. I am going to murder my father. I take a seat across from them. Adam stands behind the couch, with his assault rifle in his hand. I look around the room and it's bland. The walls are grey, there aren't any carpets, and there is one black desk behind the couch where those two assholes are sitting. The room feels cold and distant, and yet, I feel like these walls could talk. The room is way too clean, the smell of bleach invading my nostrils.

"You knew we were coming here. How?" I don't have time for small talk. My father looks at me with his black eyes, while Amar is nursing a glass of scotch. Denis is a silver fox at fifty-five years old. Appearance is everything apparently, so my dad works out every day. He is keeping up his physique, and the only way you can tell he's older is due to his pepper-colored hair. My dad crosses his legs with a smile is on his face. With a very meticulous smile, I return the favor.

"Well, head Serpent, why did you run away?" my dad asks me.

"You were going to give away my throne to Haris," I answer him.

"Sara, no. Yes, you were going to act as the new queen to the Savage Serpents, but Haris was going to be the real brains behind the operation."

"Haris couldn't tell a knife from a gun even if I held it before him. He was stupid beyond recognition."

"He wasn't the smartest of the bunch, but his family trained him to fight."

"Only with his fists. He was cruel and physically abusive, Denis." My dad laughs as if he can't believe what I'm saying is a problem. He is the embodiment of why women chose the bear over the man.

"Sweet child, marriage isn't based on love. Besides, I could never let you run everything on your own. Even if you are the smartest Serpent." Now we are getting somewhere. I always suspected Denis to be a raging misogynist, but this is absurd. I am the most skilled fighter in our organization, the smartest one, and the most manipulative one. You don't want to close a deal? Watch me change your mind.

"Denis, cut to the fucking chase. You didn't want me to run the Savage Serpents entirely on my own for one reason," I tell him while remaining completely emotionless. While I am portraying myself as calm, I am anything but. The rage is building up inside of me. I position myself a little bit more steadily. I uncross my legs and let my feet hit the floor. My underarms are now leaning on my upper thighs.

"You are a woman, Sara. I could never let a woman do everything; women can't do that. I would rather eat a dick than see a woman at the helm of my organization." There it is ladies and gentlemen. I scoff and I start laughing like a maniac. Once I calmed down, I can see Amar has set his drink down. He is like a child who is watching a fight between his parents. Useless.

"Denis, you were afraid because I could do your job better. And I did, didn't I?" I ask him. He is gritting his teeth. *Get mad, asshole.*

"All of the clients of the Savage Serpents have told you business has been extremely good. More hits, or should I say, better-planned hits that don't result in cleaning up?" If steam could come out of someone's ears, it would have been out of my dad's. While my dad was completely in charge the last couple of years, clients started dropping him. It was all due to the incoordination and sloppy work of the assassins we had back then. Their screw-ups forced us to clean up for free. We lost a lot of money from it. That's when my dad had me come in to take over some tasks, and once I did, business was good again.

"You had help. Your cousin Eldin helped you." He can't bring himself to admit I am just *that* good.

"No, he didn't. Yes, he was helpful, but I was training him," I tell my dad. He furrows his brows at me.

"You see, I think Eldin will be a great Serpent King." And with that, my dad stands up and points his Glock at me. I smile at him.

"Is this what has become of the great current Serpent King? I could vomit of how pathetic you are," I tell him while making a disgusted face. Denis looks at Amar and nods at him. The short guy is now pointing his assault rifle at Adam, and he is just laughing. Did Amar honestly think he could scare Adam?

"Amar, shoot him," my dad commands him, his fingers move over the trigger.

"Amar, stop. Before you shoot Adam, let me tell you something about my dad." My voice is strong, and Amar lowers his rifle.

"My dad promised you a seat at the table, but how could he? All of the seats are filled up. You should have done your research, leech." Amar's eyes open wide, and he is looking mad. He now points his rifle at my dad.

"Do you also know the true meaning of power, Amar?" He shakes his head without even looking at me. The number one rule as a Serpent Savage is, that if a higher-ranking officer talks to you, you must look at them. Like I said, he is completely useless, and a testament to what my father has become. Desperate.

"Me. I am the true meaning of power. And one more thing, you didn't look at me." Amar realizes his mistake and looks at me. I bite my lip since I am in my element and I snap my fingers at Adam.

"Rage." And with that one-letter word, Adam points his rifle at Amar and shoots him through his skull. My dad looks at the dead body that's lying in front of him, and he grips his Glock even tighter. He looks at me and then at Adam.

"I hope you are ready to die, Sara," my dad tells me. Adam doesn't have enough time to stop my dad from shooting me, so I close my eyes.

"No!" I hear Adam shouting. Before Adam can shoot my dad, something happens and everyone frazzles, except me. My dad's gun is empty of bullets. He throws the unusable firearm onto the floor, and remains quiet. You could hear a pin drop in the room.

"Oh, I had a backup plan. You see, a day before the wedding I had a feeling you would do something, so I emptied your favorite Glock." When the words leave my mouth, they cling to the walls. The grey cages are eating every word up.

"What the fuck did you do?" Denis asks me. I stand up and I pull the blade out of the waistband Adam put on me earlier on.

"You have become predictable, an abomination to this society. You forgot the weight of a loaded gun. For special events, you always carry your favorite gold weapon." This is only the beginning.

"The only abomination is your subordinate to your father!" I sigh at his childish outburst.

"Anyways, you haven't used your Glock in a while, so I emptied a night before the wedding." I wiggle my eyebrows at him. This always made him mad but I don't fucking care anymore. I am mad too.

"I will never let you have the throne. Do you hear me!" What's this yelling about?

"I don't want it, Eldin will take over," I tell him.

"Eldin is weak like you. He will run it into the ground."

"No, he won't, because I taught him. Anyway, you have two options now. Either you die with dignity, or you die with me killing you very slowly."

"No, silly little girl, not if I kill you first." My dad grabs a knife from his back pocket, and he starts running toward me. I unscrew the bottle of *water* I found in the shed, and I murmur *come at me,* under my breath. My dad raises his knife to cut me, but I'm faster. I spill the contents of the bottle onto his eyes, and he starts screaming. He collapses onto the floor, and he trashes around.

"Hold his arms down, Rage," I command Adam. He stalks over to my dad, and he holds him down. I drop down to my knees and sit beside my piece of shit dad. I take out my blade and I raise his sweater so that his stomach is exposed. I take my blade and start carving.

"Was that acid, Fury?" Adam asks me while I am carving my dad. I nod. My dad is screaming in pain, and his cries are like a symphony. I am avoiding carving any deeper because that's not the main objective of *this*. I want to convey a message to whoever finds him. But I have to admit one thing, the feel of my blade entering my dad's lower abdomen is amazing. The way the flesh under his skin is turning red is a sight to be seen. It's like I am one with my blade and I can feel every pulse and nerve I am hitting.

"Can you do something for me, Rage?" I motion for him to come to me. He lets go of my dad and I whisper my command in his ear. He nods gleefully at me and goes over to Amar. My dad can't see, but he can still talk.

"You fucking bitch! What the fuck do you think you are doing?" my dad asks as he moans in absolute agony. I smile as I finish my craft. I look up at Adam who returned with the *thing*. He hands it over to me and for a moment I want to puke, but I don't.

"I am leaving this organization, and you are going to choke on Amar's cock," I tell him.

"Don't, Sara, don't!" he screams. I shove Amar's severed dick in his mouth. My dad starts choking on the bloodied dick.

"Didn't you tell me that you would rather choke on a dick than to see a woman at the helm? Now, you will." My tone is dangerously low, and it tells you not to mess with me. I take my cleaver from my waistband, and I slice him from ear to ear. Why? Because it's my sign-off. That way everyone will know I did this, along with the message I carved into his lower abdomen. Blood starts splattering from his cheeks and mouth, and I make sure that it keeps gushing out by doing it slowly. This is, after all, a work of art.

"Fury, this is magnificent," Adam tells me, and I smile at the compliment. For my final move, I slice his throat in one swift move. I stand up and I am honestly so happy. He is finally dead. I stand beside Adam, and he puts an arm around my shoulders.

"I, Sara, hereby decree that I abdicate my throne to my cousin Eldin. He will now be the Serpent King. If any of you try to find me, you will face death even worse than Denis," Adam reads my message out loud.

"At least they will leave me alone. Eldin will be the best Serpent King," I tell Adam. I turn around and I put my arms around his shoulder. I kiss him with passion and our mouths are fusing. I break the kiss, and I can't stop grinning.

"Do you think your boss will have a job for me?" Adam smirks at me.

"I'll talk to M," he promises me.

"Now, are we still going to Brussels?"

"Yes, we are, Fury. Are you ready to start our new lives?" he asks me.

"I for sure am. I am so happy you painted my dress crimson."

"It was the best decision of my life. I love you, Sara."

"I love you too, Adam."

THE END

About the Author

A.H. Monroe is a romance author with a heart as diverse as her heritage. She began writing at the age of 18, and her stories often explore the depths of emotional connection and the beauty of vulnerability. While she loves her golden retriever book boyfriends, dark romance book boyfriends will always hold a special place in her heart. When she's not writing, Monroe enjoys spending time with her wonderful husband and their young son in Belgium, often finding inspiration in the little moments that make life truly special.

https://www.instagram.com/authorahmonroe/

The Traveling

By: Skylark Melody

About The Traveling

Set in the backdrop of the Dust Bowl Era, childhood friends are torn apart when one sacrifices himself for the other so that she can escape the fabled winds as they touch down on the Plains, bringing with them rumors of horrors, destruction, and death. Years later, unable to forget him, she returns to say goodbye but finds herself in the eye of the storm. It will be up to her to decide if this is a chance for redemption, or death.

Content Note:

Gore, Violence, Blood, Kidnapping (passive, implied)

Relationship type: MF

The Traveling

You didn't know him as a man, you knew him as a boy, before he got broken and crushed. You were both children then, his voice not yet taken by the baritone of adolescence, and your form not yet molded into curves. Neither of you had the crossness of maturity, not even in the times that came to be, when your young days of chasing butterflies by the creek and savoring sweet mulberries before they were picked off by the birds became hard and long.

Tired as the two of you were, him working in fields that were more dust than crops, and you caring for more mouths than could be fed, in starlight you'd meet by the creek that was no longer, reminiscing of the butterflies that had moved on. You held hands in youthful hope and gave each other smiles which creased the dirt hard labor had embedded on your faces.

Life was easier when there was a soul who made you forget the misery but never the butterflies.

They arrived one particularly hot and dry day. The winds had so thoroughly cracked the Plains that torrential rains would need to fall for months on end to heal the calloused earth. And rain had been in short supply.

There was never any warning, though there were stories. But the stories had unknown origins, and they were stories not warnings, changed and retold for the benefit of the teller. Perhaps they brought more coin that way, or a bite of sup— both hard to come by in these times.

There had been no crops to pick that day, no fields to tend to, and so he'd taken a small reprieve at the place where the butterflies used to be. He imagined the grass was still as high as your shoulders, and you'd run as fast as your little legs could manage until you'd reach the creek. He always caught you, hauled you up and back into the grass. But one day you decided to be a little more clever. You out ran him and were already at the water's edge when he saw you. You squealed and in an act of childlike boldness, jumped on a rock visible in the shallow clear depths. You didn't know how slippery moss could be, or how much it would hurt to slice your hand on the edge of stone.

He'd waded in with no hesitation, soaking his only pair of britches, been there to wash the pain away and kick the rock for being the cause of your tears.

Your ma had not been happy.

"I ain't got no time for injuries!" She'd screamed, bandaging you up in old rags, telling you to stop daydreaming with the boy next door and warning you not to come home if he gave you a growing belly.

In another life, she could've been a gentle woman, your ma, but in this life, at least the rags were clean.

The sun was hurting his eyes but he was too preoccupied laughing at the memory, wishing the grass grew tall so he could find you again and again, when the earth gave a shudder. They had said there was no warning but years later after piecing together the fragments of his memory, he would know that moment heralded it..

On instinct he jumped to his feet. After all, the Plains didn't give much time to think things over if a storm was coming through. But there was nothing. Nothing but the stories. And the instinct that had been bred into him saw to it that his legs made haste back to the farm.

He'd screamed into the sky, the thick air muffling the sound, keeping it away from its intended targets. He arrived breathless, sweat dripping from under his cap that had somehow survived the sprint.

You came out wiping flour, a commodity as rare as gold, on your apron. You'd planned on sneaking him a slice of sugar pie later on. After months, your ma's voucher had finally been good for it and some eggs and milk. It was just cause to celebrate.

Someone had spared him a drink, and between gulps and pants and a growing audience, his eyes met yours.

"Go," he told them, but he was speaking only to you.

The two of you often talked under the stars about what you'd do if the stories turned out to be true. You'd said it might be an excuse to get out of dodge. He'd said it didn't matter what happened as long as you were beside him. Maybe then was the first time your girlish lips felt his still-boyish ones, you weren't sure, because the world faded away and there were only the stars and him, and maybe even a few butterflies.

Some believed him and scattered immediately to collect their paltry provisions. Most were on foot, letting their toddlers ride in carts dragged by the men while the women shouldered the ones too small to walk. Others lucky enough to have kept a horse or two alive hitched up their wagons to ride West with the rest. There were stories about the West too, but they were more like fairytales written by those two foreign brothers, not mysterious nightmares.

Yet these nightmares came from somewhere. Someone must have dreamt them.

It was hard to breathe with the frenzy of panic kicking up more dust that swirled and carried the dry heat.

Your shaky hands worked frantically. Together with your ma, you secured the cargo and corralled and soothed your frightened siblings. All the while you kept one eye out for him. To your dismay, on your last trip back to the house for supplies, you saw him with your pa, helping him tack Old Rosie, instead of gathering for himself what little he possessed.

He had no family, for years he'd been a wanderer. Always considered tall for his age, he sported a good pair of hands, and a strong back. He slept where he could and took whatever job he could get.

That's what caught your pa's eye. He saw an able body with a sharp mind and an eagerness to earn his keep, but soon enough what caught you was his heart.

Your pa was a good man, but the years had aged him far quicker than was fair. He was bent by the stress of heavy labor and even heavier thoughts.

When the Earth shuddered again, they all felt it. Those who had made good time packing and leaving and were already on their way picked up their pace. But others showed that good people facing a crisis find the desperate evil within.

His hands found the shotgun your pa had packed. An old Remington with exactly three rounds to her name. Your heart beat wildly, thinking of what may come. You were lifted at the waist one handed and just as easily as he'd plucked the shotgun from her place, he tucked you in it.

Pa already held the reins and was having a time of it coaxing Old Rosie to move. Glass breaking jolted you and your siblings to duck down. In the corner of your eye you saw the shattered window of your old homestead and the man tumbling out of its frame while another climbed through, having no care for the shards that tore his hands.

They stopped their sacking long enough to notice the full wagon, the frightened children, and the lack of men.

He was between the men and the wagon in no time at all, the Remington mounted proper and one finger on the trigger. Your pa taught him how to shoot, you knew he wouldn't miss. But you didn't want it to come to bloodshed, you needed him here in the back with you, tucked into the safe nook of his lap, getting out of dodge like you always planned.

A wail tore through the air, one of despair and fear. The quake that it seemed to trigger came from all directions, above and below, left and right. It had no origin, like the stories, yet it was everywhere. A wall of churning, angry belligerent dust began to form, seeking to become a circle. It rose, aiming to block out the sun, and over the roar of dirt and fury you heard your pa begging Old Rosie to fly. Your siblings were beside themselves and your ma pressed and needled your pa to do something more.

Crack went a hard slap made by the heel of the gun, as he beat Old Rosie's right flank. The poor horse, not accustomed to such chaos and abuse, reared once, uttered a neigh and flew, leaving him behind.

The wall was closing in on itself faster than Rosie's gallop. She overtook those on foot, their haste and headstart all for naught. You climbed over your brothers and sisters, and used a sack of flour for leverage. Your hair came free when the wind stole the handkerchief that kept the wild spray of dark curls moderately tamed.

Dark curls he loved so much. They held their softness in these tough times, just as you had. He couldn't hear your screams over the thunder of dust, but he saw your lips moving and your arm extended beyond the wagon, pleading to take his. He ran with all his might, caked in the dirt the old rusted wheels of the wagon kicked in their wake.

Your eyes met for one glorious second when your outstretched fingertips almost met his and you had the nerve to feel hope that they may have found purchase. But Rosie chose that moment to find the courage to dive into that ever-closing gap between dust and damnation.

The wagon gave a great creak of grinding, rusty spokes, and rough hands pulled you back into a huddle of arms and shivers and chattering teeth. They held you down amidst your cries and your ma, somehow finding gentleness in the eye of chaos, smoothed your hair and said a prayer for the boy you never thought you would see again.

Before you succumbed to the pull of sleep brought on by a broken heart, you dared a glance behind, but there was nothing there but the vast Plains of grief. In front lay salvation granted by too big a sacrifice and in your palm which had almost held his you clutched a handful of that damned dust instead.

And off you rode to the West.

* * *

He didn't know what to call the force that pulled him back from you, but he knew he'd managed a smile as it knocked him off his feet. He landed hard, scraping his elbows into the earth dried of any give.

He never took his eyes off you or the wagon disappearing beyond the waves that became his prison and that's why he smiled.

He was not alone. There were others, non-believers who regretted their choices, and those who had had none, who had remained stuck because of unfortunate circumstance. They trudged together to form a circle within the one that confined them, and only then did he notice that he still held the Remington in his hand.

The wind picked up, dirt and dust heaved and bellowed, forcing eyes to close and ears to be covered. There was no sun, it was like a twilight made of smoke and fog had descended upon the land, and then.

It stopped.

The dust...fell.

Not like gentle fluttering of snow or the light patter of rain. No. It just...dropped, dense like lead or the heavy pull of a weighted curtain.

And beyond the curtain of settled dust lay the impossible.

The circus had come to town.

Either here because desperation and sadness had willed it to come. Or the storm had picked its destination blindly, the stories didn't say, but yet here it was. As large and imposing as the dust bowl it had traveled in on.

No one moved.

The sky gleamed clear like the first dawn after cleansing rains, and sunshine made the white of the spired tents too bright for tired eyes.

The faint lull of the mandolin—or was it the banjo?—drifted through stands flowing with more food than could be right. Chocolate sweeties, drumsticks with drippings oozing down their sides, trays piled with fruit, some too exotic for the simple folk bearing these sights. A child's laugh came from somewhere and between the red and white, bobbing along were mountains of balloons, spun cotton sugar, and lollipops, palm-sized in colors which put a rainbow to shame. Stages, though silent, held the promise of music and entertainment.

Yet there wasn't a soul in sight, as if all of this appeared only to taunt and disappear upon the first sign of movement.

The people were spent and wretched and scared. They didn't want to trick their hearts and minds and stomachs into believing what simply could not be true. A mirage in these times would be cruel, and folks didn't have the constitution for such things anymore.

From within the huddle, someone took a step forward, unable to curb curiosity or temptation. While the rest held their collective breath, his stupidity—or bravery— seemed to break the spell.

Merry men on stilts appeared from behind the cover of the tents. The lull of music turned to orchestral tunes played by musicians on stages no longer empty of performers. Booths with happy attendants and their beguiling smiles waved at the children, entreating them to come play their games. Prizes hung proudly in the back. Bears and lions for the boys and sweet, pink dollies for the little girls. The first smile in years broke upon a child's face and parents, saddled with worry for bringing babies into these trying times, didn't allow much begging before they followed their ecstatic sons and daughters into the jubilee.

All the while, he stood there in awe. His heart remained heavy with guilt and concern. He had sent you away. He thought he was so wise, making sure of your escape. He had been so certain it was the right thing to do, to see to it that you weren't part of the stories that were told.

He stared at the abundance that surrounded him and almost cried, in anger, in sadness, that he should be the one standing here while he had driven you from it.

The stories had lied. How could he live with himself, sending you out into the unknown when paradise was in front of him? Upon the liveliness that had sprung up, the grouping had broken, and dragging his feet, he decided to explore.

Attractions popped up at every turn, friendly smiles that never wavered. Everything was to the heart's content. A man with a painted smile appeared before him, and bowed in his oversized shoes and bright dress, presenting a goblet of milky drink. He didn't have to take it to know it was chilled, and suddenly seeing the drink, he realized how parched he had been, and for so long. How refreshing the first gulp would be.

But what he'd done to deprive you made him hesitate. Why would the stories tell such untruths? He had vague memories of his childhood, and in it the same stories had been told to him nearly every night.

Run. Because The Traveling will bring nothing but sorrow. It will bring drought and famine. Rip children from their mother's bosoms.

Here it was and it was nothing like the stories. He saw children in their parent's arms, with bright smiles and full bellies. Some had painted faces much like the man still in front of him, patiently waiting for him to take his offering. It was too much, and so he shook his head at the refreshment, and meant to go on his way.

He stopped as pain from something dull and searing invaded his body. It robbed him of breath, blurred his vision until it left him sightless. In the dark he slowly lost command of his body as well. First it was his arms which fell to his sides, the Remington slipping from his fingers. He struggled to keep control but felt himself falling to his knees and tried to moan, but his voice was stolen as well.

His arms were brought over his head and gripped together and he was dragged for what had to be miles because pain could not last that long otherwise. The ground burned his skin and scraped it off slowly in bits. He wore his teeth into his lip to silence himself even though he had no voice to scream. For a moment, he abetted as he grew airborne..

The air stung his wounds, but the ground hurt more as he was dumped on what felt to be a wooden platform. Without his sight, he could simply guess. The air felt cooler here, and held a touch of damp. Even barely breathing, he could smell the rancidness, like rotten meat and curdled milk, and his stomach heaved.

There was no time to be sick because he heard the steps, not those of one by their lonesome, and not the two by two of dual companions. No this was an odd beat, and in the travails of nausea and fear, he could not for the life of him make it out.

Liquid splashed on his face, restoring his sight. He winced in the light and he wished he'd remained blind.

He'd heard the circus had freaks, but this was not worth a few pennies to throw on the stage and laugh at their misfortune. He'd empty his purse if it meant he could scour out his eyes.

A woman, or some semblance of, as big as three, waggled forth. She wore but her own skin, which hung upon her in layers like tallow from beef. Her face had no shape, neck and shoulders and chin melded together into one form, and on each step, veins barely contained under overstretched skin, threatened to burst and drown the whole world in blood.

He mustered the energy for a cough and a gasp and then a silent cry when what he had thought was this thing's own flesh moved on either side of her chest. It was not one but two heads like the twins he'd heard about from the Orient. Each had their own malformed nose and a mouth of crooked chipped teeth; and onto their chins ran a line of drool he recognized as a familiar milky drink.

At this realization he became most violently ill. These *things* had been *nursing*.

Three sets of sunken eyes peered at him, and perhaps in the worst twist of all, the mouths stretched into simultaneous smiles. Haggard, they were. Creatures that would make monsters resign the designation and live out the rest of their days spreading the gospel instead. They had come for him first, knowing he was the one because he'd declined the offered libation at his worst state of thirst.

His hair was grabbed hard at the roots and his head bent back. Above him he glanced at a painted mouth. The odd beat resumed until the heat from the thing and the odor it produced were closer than before. He gagged as a finger entered his mouth to pry his jaw apart. He bit down on the foreign appendage but it was too late.

Hot milk was poured into his throat, thickly, languidly, ensuring he could taste the vile creamy sweetness coating his tastebuds. The painted man laughed til he cried while the liquid burned and bubbled on its way down.

"This one will grow up to be useful," they said, the Grim Mother and Her Children and let him keep his wits but only as dreams. They were once daughters and in her need for control, The Mother had sewn them into herself and kept them alive with the poison she created. They squeezed her breasts dry and made certain he drank every drop until there was no more. On the final swallow his brain scrambled, memories became distant, but even then his thoughts were of nothing but you.

Many years later...

You stood at the borders of what used to be, a wilderness of skeletons, some tangible, some bones of the past. It wouldn't be recognizable if you hadn't held onto the memories and never let yourself forget.

You knew the empty shell of your homestead the second you saw it. Though the wood was but dry rot and the gabled roof pitched and sagged so low and sad to the ground, it would make anyone else mourn what was once there. Not you, the anger festered, feeding on the years that passed. You weren't bitter, you were starved. You didn't know for what but that deep hunger never left your spirit, never let you rest.

In those memories of hardship swam ones of cold spring waters in the creek and the boy that ran into them to avenge you from the rock that drew your blood.

You hadn't married. Your heart closed the same day your fist had around nothing but dust. Dust you wore around your neck, bottled so you could never forget.

Your ma begged you to let go of him on her deathbed, your pa before her. They saw how you tortured yourself. What they thought was just puppy love was ripping you apart. But you couldn't let go, not without one day coming back and pouring the damned dust onto that accursed land and giving him a proper goodbye.

And so here you were, standing where it began and ended. You weren't scared, not that you'd admit. The stories said it never came to the same place twice, like lightning. But being here again with that hunger rumbling inside you, making your bones shake, how you wished it would strike a second time.

Every step you took around what was your old life cast you into a deeper gloom. Rumors plagued you throughout your new life of a lone family who escaped. They reached your ears but no one suspected. They didn't want to believe it could be true. Loss was easier to handle if there was no other choice.

You walked and walked, seeing more relics of houses, trees and farms that skillful hands had built and planted.. A few cornstalks had been spared. They stood upright, dry and shriveled, no moisture in their veins to allow them to bend. One gentle breeze and they'd be, what else—dust.

The stillness sat heavy, and while your childhood had been hard, there had still been *life*. This was death, captured and preserved in a moment in time.

With the sun setting, you circled back. You might have hesitated, but then you picked yourself up and ascended the old rotted stairs of the porch and into your home. Everything was almost as you'd left it, save a few possessions, remnants of a ransack. You'd planned to explore but stopped short at the kitchen entrance, the old coal oven catching your eye. The iron was still black as obsidian; rust had not found its place there. But the door hung open and slightly askew, and in it you saw the spoiled remains of that sweet sugar pie.

And you screamed.

Screamed and screamed and screamed.

You tore at your hair and tugged at your dress. It wasn't insanity. It was fire, rage, and despair. You screamed yourself hoarse, then cried some more, grabbed at the bottle around your neck, and with all your might smashed it to the ground.

Though no bigger than a thimble, glass sprayed everywhere, the dust spread, and didn't stop. It flowed like clouds on a breezy day, spreading throughout the four corners of your home, and spilling outside. You lay there momentarily stunned, watching the hazy mist move as though alive.

Calling you to it.

When you didn't move, it shook the earth as persuasion. And you knew what was to come. This time though, you wouldn't fly, you wouldn't run. You would stay and see if the stories were true.

There was no great circle of dust keeping you prisoner. It seemed to know you'd stay. A faint note of music caught your ear, a jeering tone of horns and the deep vibrato of tubas, peaking with a calliope that thrummed the walls and forced you to your feet.

Night had fallen upon the homestead. You studied how the pitch black darkness made the fire of torches more garish, their dance sinister. You hadn't taken a breath, forgotten to. How could you think of breathing when your wish had come true–lightning had indeed struck again.

It stretched as far as you could see, to where the night swallowed the torchlight. You took a step then another, shivering from a mix of excitement that blended into fear.

Rows upon rows of decadence enticed you, trays of succulent

meats and fruits, stands with their lines full and spiraling of people waiting to swap coin to play. A whip snapped in the distance, followed by a creature's roar, garnering the loudest applause.

You stepped through the crowds and gasped as you recognized those you thought lost. The neighbor's young daughter, wearing her yellow gingham she loved so much, not having aged a day. Her father right behind her, in overalls and his old leather hat. You raised a hand in greeting and began to approach with a hurried pace, forgetting all formalities as the question you wanted most to ask was about to spill from your lips when both father and daughter passed through you in an icy whiplash of chill.

Stumbling back in shock, numbed by the encounter, you took a closer look around. Shadowy shapes surrounded you. They moved without acknowledging your presence, they themselves there but not there, frozen in time.

Your hand absentmindedly went to the chain broken around your neck and you wondered, had you called this back? Had you done this? And if so, had it come to claim you too?

You tried to retrace your steps, but there was no way out. There was no childhood homestead leading you back to reality, only the circus and its shadows every which way you looked.

You pressed your clammy palms into your skirt, and jumped at another round of applause, louder than the last. But it was the voice that quieted the crowd that stomped your fear and sent you running past and through the blurry shapes that paid you no mind.

It was older, yet spoken with the same cadence that you knew so well, but you wouldn't believe what you couldn't actually see.

He kept speaking, taunting the audience while you ran. The place was a maze and though the beings weren't corporeal, the structures, awnings, flags and the like obstructed your view. It wasn't until you arrived at the great clearing, expecting a throng and seeing nothing and no one there but him standing on the stage with a painted smile.

The trap had been set, and you were the mouse.

His eyes appeared cloudy but blazing.

THUMP THUMP THUMP

The sound ground itself in your ears as tears streamed down your face, for the boy who looked just as you remembered him, but had been made into something you knew not.

Your eyes grew wide at the shotgun he used instead of a circus master's whip, before the torches went out all at once and everything became black. There was no denying your fear now as you heard him draw closer, dragging it behind him. The clang of metal ominous in the darkness.

You trembled in a world gone cold, when a lit match danced before you. The comforting scritch brought a second of relief until you saw the lifeless eyes and artificial smile it illuminated. And before you could scream, the wooden heel of that familiar gun smashed into your mouth.

Blood spurted from your face and you fell back. Laughter, mocking and evil, echoed in the night, bouncing across the shadows. He stood over you, taking you in, then bent a knee to hover near your injured face. He rocked his head back and forth as if to shake something, and for one moment the cloudiness disappeared and he spoke in a tired voice.

"I've dreamt of you before."

The cloudiness returned and with it your rage.

You fought back as he held you down and forced open your mouth. Scratched and clawed as an odor so foul frightened the shadows and advanced. But mostly you fought to awaken the boy that was taken from you and reduced to this. You grabbed at his wrists and ripped at the fabric of his shirt and just then did you realize you were holding on to something real.

Fabric and flesh.

And you doubled your efforts despite the pain in your jaw and the knee that kept your back firmly planted on the ground.

The revolting smell grew and your stomach lurched at the monsters that loomed above your head. Three faces, three mouths, and pounds of flesh, the Grim Mother and her Daughters needed a fresh soul.

Through muffled words you begged him to remember, choking on the taste of milk that hit your tongue.

In a husky breathless voice the Mother commanded silence and he lay down the match and gun to use both hands to keep you still.

Milk dripped across your face and the offending flavor further instigated your fight. Within each drop was a memory, of lives taken, of spirits broken, of souls trapped to serve Mother and Child.

You wheezed as the liquid went down the wrong pipe, flailing as one arm broke free and settled around the very tangible heel of your father's old gun.

In one movement you swung, landing a blow directly to the side of his head, knocking him aside. The Mother screeched at him to get up, but blood streamed out the side of his head and he lay still.

You turned slowly, the world fading in and out. Everything was spinning. Three heads became six, then nine.

But your grip on the gun kept you focused.

THUMP THUMP THUMP

You weighed it in your hand. Three times for good measure. Three times for three shots.

Your pa had taught him how to shoot, and he'd decided to teach you too.

The first landed squarely in the left daughter's head, which twitched slumped forward, another right through the skull, bits of it landing and scratching The Mother's eyes, the last you saved for the crone herself. Not a kill shot, no. She'd sit with her dead for a while before she bled out. So you aimed for the chamber directly above her heart.

You watched blood ooze from the dead and the dying. The first drop hit the fire still burning from the match and ignited.

He groaned and your heart leapt, first in happiness then in fright. Your steps were cautious and you knelt, the old Remington still in hand.

Behind you, The Mother twitched, engulfed in flames, embers of flesh flying into the night. He stared ever so curiously, watching them burn and fly.

"What are you thinking of?" you asked, keeping your distance.

His clear eyes made contact with yours and he smiled and replied,

"Butterflies."

Do you like your fantasy with a side of angst, emotional damage and heartache? Then you should definitely follow Skylark on Threads and IG: @skylark.melody.author and preorder *A Fate Drawn to Flame*, Book One of her genre-blending debut fantasy series here: https://a.co/d/9VTPclc

About the Author

Though most of her writing falls in the fantasy and fantasy romance genres, Skylark used this opportunity to indulge in her not-so-secret obsession with the strange, macabre and morbid (and for this she has Vincent Price and Mary Shelley to thank).

A Boston native, she loves cold weather, the mountains, caffeine, and thick books.

Circus Psychos

By: Aiden Pierce

A Sinner's Sideshow Short Story

About Circus Psychos

Welcome to Sinner's Sideshow, the most obscene, blood-pumping, skin-crawling creep show this side of Hell.

Circus Psychos contains supplement scenes from the Sinner's Sideshow series and features four men who worship and empower their woman in a depraved and shameless circus act not meant for the faint of heart. Reading the main series first is not required, but you may enjoy the following content more if you start with *Circus Creeps*.

Content Notes:

This is a dark paranormal romance and contains certain themes that might be triggering to some such as gore, murder, violence, horror elements, knife play, breath play, degradation, demonic clowns, spitting, sharing, consensual non-consent, exhibitionism, voyeurism, and other graphic sexual content.

Relationship type: MMFMM

Chapter One

"Spooks and specters, creeps and cunts..." The smooth-as-sin voice rumbled through the big top, making the hairs on the back of my neck rise. I peered through the pinned-up tent flap the troupe used to enter the ring, squinting through the murk to see the ringmaster floating over the house near the center pole, keeping the audience on the edge of their seats.

No matter how many shows I witnessed, I still got this little thrill through my veins every time Alistair made his opening spiel.

"Crawling out to you from the Downside's underbelly is the greatest spectacle on Earth, featuring haunts and horrors known to give the vilest of monsters nightmares."

"Look who I've found, Rifton," a familiar voice said behind me. I turned to see my favorite green-haired harlequin sauntering through the backyard, slinking his way between the makeup tables where the other members of our circus primped and preened. "Creeping on the boss. Hanging on to his every word."

Right behind him, like a shadow, faithfully following just a beat behind, was his younger twin—younger by a few minutes.

Riff's exaggerated red mouth flexed into an unsettling grin that had my thighs clenching. "Oh yeah, she just *loves* watching the boss work. Bet if we checked, we'd find those panties soaking."

"Get bent, fuck clowns," I said with a grin of my own.

The brothers cackled, each one coming to stand on either side of me, their arms snaking around my waist to tuck me between their lanky bodies. Riff and Raff were well over six feet, and at my five feet, zero plus inches, they towered over me, making me feel like a toy between them.

I fucking loved that feeling, and just like hearing Alistair in his element, addressing the monsters who traveled far and wide to see our show, I'd never get tired of it.

"You ready for the show, Hell Bat?"

I nodded and caught my reflection in one of the mirrors mounted to the makeup table behind Riff. My short bubblegum pink locks were styled to perfection, laying artfully around the set of black pointed horns protruding over my hairline. I wore a purple bodice with an upside-down heart cutout between my breasts and a ruffled skirt so short it left most of my ass exposed.

Unlike the twins, I was barefaced.

Catching me staring at myself, Raff's hands clamped over my hips, and he pivoted me to face the mirror. His brother stretched out my black, leathery wings, which were small compared to any other succubus since I was only a half-demon.

"You are so fucking beautiful," Riff murmured, pressing a kiss to my temple while Raff did the same to my other side, his tongue licking its way up my horn. Knowing how sensitive they were, his lips curved against the exposed bone as I shivered.

His grin melted when he caught onto the anxiety radiating from my aura.

As sex demons, we had the ability to read and feed on emotions like no other creature. It made sex a religious experience. Other times, when I preferred to keep certain things to myself, it was a pain in the ass.

Raff caught on a moment later. "What's wrong?"

"It's nothing. It's stupid..."

Unlike most nights, I wasn't performing with the twins in tonight's show. We had our own acts. This pang in my chest wasn't pre-show jitters. I never got those. I was just sad I wouldn't be doing the usual fuck show with the twins.

It was probably silly, feeling put out like this. I'd begged Alistair to give me my own act, and now I had one. But God, did I love being out there in the ring, wrapped like a pretzel around every appendage these males had, while the crowd looked on in envy.

"Tell us what's going through that pretty head, Hell Bat."

"We won't be performing together tonight. I still want everyone to know I'm yours."

My hand went to the leather collar around my throat, and I fiddled with the metal spikes. Everyone knew I was mated to Daemon. I wore his collar, and it never came off. Alistair's true form was as big as a building, so when he'd marked me, the scar took up my whole thigh.

The twin's mating marks were more inconspicuous.

Riff stretched out both my wings again, a twinge of lust bleeding into his aura when a small moan slipped from me—my wings were even more sensitive than my horns. "Everyone will know you belong to us, Meg."

The incubus bent to brush his lips over the mark he'd made on my wing months ago, in the tunnel of sin ride at the carnival. Then he moved to kiss his brother's mark on the other wing.

Small shock waves of pleasure worked through my body, and I burrowed closer to both of them. Suddenly, I was ravenous for a meal. Not for food, but for *them*.

I chewed my lip, examining my bare facial features in the mirror. "I wish I'd painted my face so we could match tonight."

Through the reflection of the glass, the twins exchanged one of their telepathic looks over my head, and Riff smirked. "Seems like our girl needs some attention before she goes on. Smooth some of those 'jitters.' Know what I'm saying, Rafferty?"

The green-haired demon gave an enthusiastic nod, his spade-tipped tail lashing the air behind him like that of a feisty cat.

Before I could parse the mischief rolling off them in powerful currents, Riff turned me around, picked me up and set me on the table with my back resting against the mirror.

"Guys, whatever you're planning, we don't have time. I go on in—*Oh.*" My protest died in my throat as Raff pushed my legs apart and shoved his head beneath my skirt.

My hands instinctively dropped to his curved horns, making for the perfect handlebars. The air grew hot and heavy with his need, and I could practically taste it.

His index finger hooked into my panties, pulling down the strap of fabric covering my entrance. He chuckled against me when he found that his brother had been right; I was soaking.

"Fuck." My hips bucked, desperate for more of the heat that barreled from the clown's mouth with every breath he took. He nipped my labia, causing me to cry out in pain, which melted into a grunt of pleasure on the next breath as he sank his tongue past my folds.

We weren't the only ones in the backyard, either. This was the area behind the big top where the troupe got ready for the show. Some of the other clowns sat at the nearby tables, applying their paint and smearing their faces as their attention veered in our direction. My fingers clenched tighter around Raff's horns, and my tail wound around his throat, pulling him deeper into my apex. We didn't care that they watched us. We feasted on the attention.

The low din of applause from the big top sounded, and my eyes drifted shut, pretending for a second they were clapping for us.

I opened my eyes when the table jerked beneath me to find Riff ripping open one of the drawers and sifting through the makeup. His upper lip curled, disappointed by the selection. "Why does everyone around here insist on using the cheap crap? Don't have time to go back to our trailer and get the good shit."

"It doesn't have to be the good stuff." My laugh fractured with a lewd groan as Raff's tongue pressed deeper inside me.

Riff shook his head in disagreement. "Only the best for our girl."

The blue-haired demon closed the drawer with a flick of his tail, then propped a hip against the table, watching the way my face contorted from his brother's ministrations with a thoughtful look in his eyes. Raff pulled his tongue from my pussy to prod my clit while his finger replaced his tongue and curved to hit that secret place that had stars dancing across my vision.

Riff's face lit up. His hand disappeared behind his back to appear on the next pound of my pulse, twirling one of his famed knives. "Do you trust me?"

"You mean, do I trust the psycho sex clown with a thing for watching people bleed?" The way the blade flashed in the light leaking from the big top had my nerves lighting up like a circuit board. I was a perfect match for the twins. For Alistair. For Daemon. For this whole damn circus. Because I was just as depraved as all of them.

A dreamy smile lifted my lips. "Always."

Chapter Two

Raff feasted on me like a starving animal.

The wet noises coming from under my skirt had my cheeks burning and my lust building. My toes curled in my sneakers, my tail applying just enough pressure to leave the demonic clown gasping for air against my pussy.

Riff's finger pressed under my chin, guiding my attention back to him. His manic smile filled my vision. The painted diamonds around his eyes wrinkled with this *look* he wore—an expression that oozed sex and violence.

He tapped the blade of his knife to his nose. "You want to look like us, yeah? You want every one of those monsters who watch you tonight to know you're ours?"

I licked my lips, nodding eagerly.

He gave the blade a twirl, and I watched the weapon dance around his slender fingers. I was constantly amazed by what those digits could do. "Then let me mark you up."

Riff wasn't talking about mating marks. We'd already exchanged those. I met him grin for sadistic grin. "If you cut me, Daemon will have your dick."

Raff laughed against me, the reverberation causing me to jerk against him in a shock of pleasure. "That supposed to deter him?" The green-haired demon caught my gaze and held it, all while sinking a second finger inside me at a pace that had me writhing against him, desperate for more. "Greedy succubus cunt. Can never get enough, hmm? Even with four mates. Insatiable little slut."

My thighs started to tremble, and my breath came out in stunted huffs. My fingers slipped from his horns, nails sinking into his scalp hard enough to make him nip my clit in retaliation. My orgasm mounted, and when pleasure was at its peak, Riff's shadow consumed me as he closed in.

I caught a wicked glint of his knife just before being hit with a brief sting of sharp pain, which only pushed the radiant warmth spreading through my core to new heights.

Every muscle in my body tightened as I came. When I rode out the final waves of the climax, they loosened, and I instantly felt like jelly.

Riff licked my blood from his blade and gestured at me with the point. "Take a look at my handiwork, bro."

My heart leaped in my chest when Raff pushed to his feet, and I saw how his lips were drenched with my arousal. "Fuck. She looks so damn good." He glanced in the direction of their trailer, then back at his brother. "Wonder if the boss would kill us if we decided to ditch and—"

"You know the boss wouldn't dirty his hands with your blood, imps. He'd leave the honor of killing you to me," a new voice cut in, and I perked up as Daemon stomped over to us.

The small throng of troupe members that had gathered around to watch our impromptu backstage performance parted as they made way for the hellhound alpha. They knew better than to get in the way of Alistair's personal guard dog.

Daemon was always intimidating, especially when he wore his stage fit. The Bitch Tamer wore tight black leather pants that left little to the imagination and a harness that accentuated his tattooed pectorals. His shoulder-length black hair was slicked back, with a leather biker-type cap and a whip in hand. It was that leather and ink-wrapped package that had the audience shaking in their seats with equal parts pleasure and fear.

I was a particular fan myself.

I held my arms out to Daemon and gave my hips a little wiggle. "Aren't you going to kiss your mate for good luck?"

Daemon's amber orbs practically glowed in outrage as he scanned my face. His attention snapped to the knife clutched in Riff's hand. "What did you do to her?"

Raff rolled his eyes. "Daddy, chill. She's a supernatural, remember? She'll heal by the end of the night."

I'd been a part of Sinner's Sideshow for six months now, though most days, it felt longer than that. It was a perfect dream I never wanted to wake up from. By now, the hellhound shifter had pretty much gotten over the whole possessive thing that was common among his kind—they weren't used to sharing their mates.

Daemon had really warmed up to the incubi brothers. He even embraced his attraction to them, which I found especially fun on the nights he got to show off how good he'd gotten at the whole sharing thing. But he was still overly protective and probably always would be.

While the "imps"—as Daemon referred to them—had grown on him, he still thought they were reckless with me.

I didn't see the twins as reckless, at least not with me. They knew my limits, and they loved getting nice and cozy with that line. But they'd never cross it.

Alistair knew that. One day, maybe Daemon would too.

I hopped off the makeup table and turned to examine my face in the mirror. Riff had carved four delicate and fairly shallow lines into my face—two over each eye and two below to resemble harlequin makeup. Only, instead of makeup, he'd used my blood.

When I grinned, the lines of displeasure carving Daemon's

features deepened. "I can't believe some of the shit you let them do to you."

"Oh, come on. You do some pretty dirty shit to me, too." I spun around and stretched onto my toes. He had to bend to kiss me. His growl was dark and delicious and snaked into my mouth, the taste of him renewing my lust. Raff was right. I was insatiable.

"If you kissed me, you could taste her other lips," Raff offered with one of his signature grins and a wink. His lips were still wet with my arousal.

He'd been joking. Or, at least months ago, it would have been nothing more than a joke. A way to crawl under Daemon's skin.

That line had long been blurred.

Daemon kept one arm around my waist while his other snapped out to seize the incubus by his throat. Raff wasn't a small man but he looked slight in stature compared to Daemon's body-builder physique. Especially with his thick fingers and the way they easily swallowed Raff's throat.

Before I could fully process what was happening, Daemon's mouth crashed into Raff's. To call it a kiss would be inaccurate. It was more like a battle for supremacy, which Daemon promptly won. The green-haired demon surrendered, allowing the alpha to lick at his lips —lapping up every last drop of me off Raff's skin.

Raff hummed in approval, his palm smoothing over Daemon's chest. I liked sharing my hellhound's embrace with my other mates, it was just usually with Alistair. This was still pretty new territory for us.

"Shit," Riff muttered under his breath as he watched from the sidelines with the rest of the troupe. "Makes me think we should be selling tickets to *this* show."

Growing bold, Raff's hands slipped down the ripple of Daemon's abs. Then, one hand dipped into his pants. Before he could find what he was looking for, Daemon snatched his wrist and twisted his arm at an angle that would have any other man crying in pain.

Raff only grinned, his clown paint making him look truly deranged.

Daemon shoved his sneering face into Raff's, putting on that big cagey caveman show he did better than anyone else. But there was no missing the lust radiating from Daemon's aura. He was eating up every depraved second of this stolen moment before the show.

"You don't touch me unless I give you permission, imp."

At that, Raff started to cackle like a hyena, and his brother joined in. "Yeah... See, I'm not the obedient little sub-type. You want me to behave? You're gonna have to get out the whip and paint me black and blue like one of your French girls, Jack."

With that, he ripped his arm from Daemon's grip and sauntered away with one last look that slid to me. "Break a leg, baby. We'll see you in the ring."

The hellhound stared after the clowns for several seconds before his gaze turned back to me, softening. "Why did he call me Jack?"

"You really have to watch more movies, Daemon. I think you'd understand the twins better."

He shrugged a meaty shoulder. "I've stopped trying to figure them out. I kind of like the mystery anyway. That's half of Alistair's charm, too."

A deafening round of applause punctuated the end of that moment, and several of the troupe members made their exit. The opening act was done, and now it was time for the bigger names to grace the ring.

"Presenting the seductive creature who's wrapped your tiny cocks around her wings, it's the half-blood Hell Bat!"

"That's your cue, Pup," Daemon muttered, a hint of a whine in his words. Like he was sad that he had to let me go. He kissed me again, and this time, his lips tasted of Raff.

Chapter Three

The crowd was an easy one tonight. This was an area Sinner's Sideshow had never been to before—filled mostly with werewolves. They were easy to impress, and their manners were more agreeable than a lot of audiences we'd had in the past.

Our audience was always monsters, sometimes hungry, mean ones who looked at me and saw a meal.

It was a good night if no one was jumping into the ring to act out whatever disturbing, impulsive thoughts played through their head as they watched me with my men.

So far, no one had been slaughtered by my possessive mates, no appendages chopped off, no innards ripped out by Daemon or his hellhound pack. Not yet, anyway, but the night was still young.

I stood on the round platform that gave every seat in the house a perfect view of me, twirling my sword to the rhythm of my signature song, "Boss Bitch" by Doja Cat, before sliding my sword down my throat and swallowing all twenty-five inches of pure steel.

They all clapped and whistled, but the lust rolling off them was lackluster. Barely a meal. I'd fed from the twins' lust pre-show, but it hadn't been enough.

As a circus brat, I grew up in show biz, so being in the ring was as natural as breathing. As a succubus, I loved being the center of attention in a place like this because it kept me sated. It was my feeding ground.

I pulled my sword from my throat and, making a show of it, took the blade's point and sliced my top off. I gave the audience a shake, my nipple piercings glinting under the lights.

The crowd went wild. Lust bled into the air. I breathed it in like a drug, spread my wings and gave another slow turn on the platform, drinking in their adoration, their envy, their hunger for me.

I didn't even have to use my succubus charm powers. All it took was a flash of my tits, and I had them eating out my hand—while they jacked off into theirs.

What happened next unfolded all in a breath.

A man in one of the first few rows, the death seats as we referred to them, lunged out of his seat and over the divider that separated the house from the ring.

In midair, he shifted into a great brown wolf with beady red eyes honed on me.

"*Mine!*" His growl exploded through the big top like dynamite, making everyone jump in their seats.

Before the werewolf could pounce on top of me, a black hound twice the wolf's size appeared seemingly from nowhere. His maw closed around the wolf's throat and snatched him out of the air. Both beasts hit the ground hard, making the lighting overhead sway and shadows shift.

Daemon had transformed back into a man, naked and glistening under the lights. He pressed his foot on the wolf's throat, looking down at him like he was less than dirt.

"I'd ask if you have a death wish, but seeing as you came from a death seat, I know the answer."

The death seats were named because that's exactly what they

were. A monster bought a ticket for a death seat only if they had no intention of walking out of our grisly show alive.

We were the demon circus straight from Hell, and for a price, we'd send you there in style.

"Yeah, I bought a death seat," the wolf wheezed beneath the pressure of Daemon's foot. "So fucking kill me already. I'm ready to meet Discord."

"That's not how this works. We decide how you die, not you."

Alistair melted from the shadows, his umbral form taking shape into flesh. His stature was somewhere between Daemon's and the twins, tall with an athletic form that filled out his maroon ringmaster's uniform to perfection.

The music had faded, and the click of his cane as he walked echoed through the tent, his long, shadowy hair billowing behind him.

He approached where Daemon stood with the wolf pinned beneath his foot, cocking his head. "You've lost your privileges to look at my star."

With that, the shadow demon pressed his cane into the creature's eye socket. Purposefully slow, making a show of it.

The werewolf thrashed and screamed, but before he could wiggle from Daemon's hold, dozens of shadowy tentacle-like tendrils shot from all directions of the room and strapped him to the ground.

The ringmaster's unhinged smile could be seen beneath the shadow of his brim, stretching wider as the wolf's screams grew louder.

With a tug of his wrist, he pulled the cane from one eye socket and moved to the other. A mix of disgust and fascination rolled off the audience. Alistair finally pulled away. This time, the eyeball stayed speared to the cane's tip.

Turning to face the audience, the shadow demon leaned against the ring divider and held the cane out to a random soul in the first row. It was as if he was offering a carnival snack on a stick rather than a werewolf's eyeball.

"Eat it."

The monster—some kind of ghoul—stiffened in his seat. "What?"

"This is Sinner's Sideshow. You came here for the entertainment. No one promised you it was for *your* entertainment. Now go on." Alistair gave the cane a flick, making the eyeball's cornea jiggle. "*Eat* it."

My succubus urge to feed on his terror quickly squashed the human urge to pity the ghoul.

Unable to resist, I drank it in. Just a small taste. Goosebumps pricked my skin. *By Discord's dick*, I was so damn ravenous it took every shred of willpower to keep from gorging myself on the ghoul's terror as he obeyed Alistair's command.

However, I previously got sick from feeding on too much fear. My emotion of choice was lust. Sure, it was a bit of a cliché for a sex demon, but with mates like mine, could I be blamed?

The ghoul swallowed the gooey mass and struggled to keep it down. Ghouls were known to eat flesh, but the humiliation of it all had him gagging.

Satisfied, Alistair turned away from the audience with his emerald glare trained on me while he continued to address the entire house. "You pathetic Upside wretches are lucky I allow you to look at her at all. I should pluck out every last one of your eyes."

A shiver shot through me, and Alistair's smile widened. His mark on my thigh grew infernally hot under his attention.

"But no..." Alistair went on. "Tonight, I'm feeling magnanimous." The shadow demon approached me. He was so tall that the platform I stood on brought us to eye level. One of his shadow tentacles caressed over my face, sweet and gentle at first. Then, it slid to the back of my neck, gripping me possessively. "Perhaps we should demonstrate who you really belong to, Little Demon?"

Chapter Four

At the suggestion, my mouth went dry, and my pussy soaking wet.

All eyes were on me. Waiting for me to respond, to say yes. Alistair knew I was starving. That I needed to feed on my mates' lust and that the best meals were always when we fucked with an audience. Still, he was asking for consent.

I nodded.

The tentacle wound around my throat and pulled me closer to Alistair. Even without the tether, I found myself leaning toward him. It was so easy to get sucked into his aura. "Use your words, Megaera. Tell us what you want."

"I want my mates to own my body right here. Right now. I want everyone to see who I belong to."

The ringmaster's eyes lit up in that devilish way that set my soul on fire.

The wolf's cries had died down and were extinguished completely when Daemon brought his foot down on its skull, crushing it with one swift stomp. The crunch of bone echoed through the big top, and when he turned, my jaw damn near dropped to my feet.

Since he shifted, his muscular body was completely naked, wearing nothing but the complicated mural of tattoos, which was now splattered with a shock of red—the werewolf's blood.

His eyes glowed white hot as they slithered down my body, licking his lips when they landed on my bare breasts.

"My hound is always hungry right after a kill. I think he's found his next meal."

Daemon started for me with purpose in each stride, the look on his face causing pure lust to sweep through my veins like wildfire.

"I can scent your arousal dripping down your thigh. The little clown slut is so eager to be torn apart."

"Fuck you," I snapped, even though everything inside me screamed fuck *me*.

He chuckled at my faux defiance. "Maybe I should put your bratty little mouth to better use." His hand trailed down the ripple of his abdominal muscles, dipping lower until he gripped his monstrous cock. It was erect now that it had my full attention.

I wanted nothing more than to crumple to my knees and lick off the werewolf's blood drop by drop. But we were putting on a show here, and the audience loved it when I put up a fight. Almost as much as my guys and I did.

Alistair's shadows had released their grip on my neck, allowing me to scramble off the platform. Whirling around, I slammed into a hard chest and found myself staring up at Riff, his face paint making him look diabolically sexy. "Where do you think you're going?"

Raff appeared from behind Riff, grinning over his shoulder. "Where do you think you're going?" he echoed his brother, his tone mocking. "Come on, Hell Bat. Let's give your adoring fans a show they'll never forget."

Taking hold of each of my arms, Riff and Raff dragged me to the center of the ring, where Daemon stood with his dick still clutched in his hand. Waiting.

The twins forced me to my knees and leaned over me, crowding together so their painted faces blocked out the audience for a moment. Their eyes glowed a soft green and blue—their hue muted from their white contacts.

"How do you want this to go down, baby?" Raff asked in a lowered voice. "Make it look rough, or do you want a more authentic experience?"

I raised my gaze to theirs and nibbled my lower lip. "Make it hurt."

The incubus flicked his attention to his twin, whose aura buzzed with excitement. "Fuck yeah. God, you're so damn perfect. We love you, baby."

"I love you too." The second the last word left my mouth, I spit into Riff's face. He blinked, the glob of spit slipping down his cheek and smudging the white makeup. He laughed, and as he laughed, he slapped me hard enough that the entire house heard, hard enough to make my eyes water and my cheek sting.

Both twins parted, allowing Daemon to stride between them.

Music started playing again, this time, "Circus Psychos" by Diggy Graves.

Raff tugged on my hair, jerking my head back and Riff wrapped his tail tightly around my throat, both of them holding me in place for the hellhound alpha.

I blinked up at him through my tears, enamored by his chiseled muscles and inked flesh that glistened under a sheen of sweat and blood. This demon was violence. He was sin, and he was looking at me like I was a favorite toy he had every intention of destroying.

"Be a good pup and open that bratty mouth."

I kept my lips firmly sealed, and just as I hoped, one of the twins —Riff by his chipped back fingernails—roughly shoved two fingers inside my mouth and pried my jaw open by force.

Raff bent down and spit in my mouth, getting most of it on my tongue. The rest covered my face, making the fresh cut lines his brother had sliced burn.

The degradation had me eager to sate the blaze of arousal inside me.

"I said, open your fucking mouth." Daemon's command was hard as steel, warning me not to disobey. Being the brat I was, I was certainly tempted. But I was so hungry for him, for all of them, that this time, I obeyed.

He pushed his cock past my lips, and I moaned as his flavor hit my tongue. Warm, masculine, with notes of leather and salt.

The beat of the music filled my ears.

The burn of every eye in the house was hot on my skin.

The tail coiled tight around my throat, just tight enough to leave me gasping around the thick cock driving in and out of my mouth alongside Riff's fingers.

The intoxicating flavor of both men seeped into my taste buds.

It was overwhelming—and I ate up every depraved second.

Daemon gripped both small horns as best as he could with his huge hand and thrust into me at a harsh pace that had his balls slapping against my chin.

The hellhound shifter's grunts of pleasure and growl-laced pants coming from over my head were the sexiest sounds to ever meet my ears.

I strained my eyes, looking up as far as the cock jammed in my mouth would allow. Riff and Raff stared at me with feral expressions that had my pussy aching.

Riff stroked my cheek with the pad of his thumb, his claw raking against my flesh. "Fucking beautiful..."

Daemon rammed his cock deep down my throat, a less-than-subtle way of pulling my attention back on him.

Whatever he found in my eyes had his thrusts stuttering and his cock throbbing. His brow scrunched, and his perfect mouth dropped into an "O."

On the next breath, a torrent of molten cum shot onto my tongue, and seconds later, he pulled out with an obscene moan.

I got ready to spit his load back at him, and it was like he could read my mind. He grabbed my jaw, his grip brimming with power. He could crush my bones with a single twitch, yet he was more careful with me than any of my mates. There was nothing better than being held like a delicate treasure in the hands of a brutal monster who could destroy you with a look.

I licked my lips, a thick bead of his cum slipping down my chin.

Daemon's eyes lit up with something primal. "Don't you fucking dare waste what I give you, Pup. You're going to swallow me. Every last drop."

Again, I obeyed.

"Now let me go," I seethed, even though I wanted anything but.

All three laughed in unison, cold and cruel. They were good actors. We all were.

"They're just getting started, Little Demon," Alistair said from where he leaned against the ringside beside the wolf's corpse. In our shows, dead bodies never hampered the mood. "They're going to unload every last drop of cum they have inside your needy little holes."

The crowd went wild with excitement, hooting, hollering and throwing popcorn into the ring.

We were all so perfectly in our element. To most people, to normal people, this place was Hell. But for me, it was home, my paradise.

I caught Alistair's smile. He'd had this new skin for months now, but now and then, it still gave me chills, thinking where it had come from. What that man had been like. What he'd tried doing to me. My attention dropped to the hand missing a thumb. I found myself smiling at the dark thoughts stirring in my mind.

As a rule, Alistair never joined in on our fuck shows. All five of us went to bed together, sure, but never in the ring. Maybe one day, someday soon, he would.

I was foisted from my thoughts when Raff appeared in front of me holding my sword. He tossed Daemon one of his mischievous looks, a green brow arching. "I think I want to see her swallow this from the other end now."

Chapter Five

My heart skipped several beats. I shook my head no, but my body dripped at the suggestion.

"Don't worry, baby," Riff snickered. "He won't use the pointy end. Not if you're good."

I swallowed thickly, pretending to struggle as he placed a boot on my back between my wings and guided me down so I was on all fours. Peering over my shoulder, I saw Raff kneeling behind me.

The muscles in my stomach tightened, and I forced my breathing to even as I felt the blade brush my skin. He wasn't as skilled with sharp weapons as his twin, but he still had more experience than most, and I trusted him.

I trusted him with my life and then some.

The incubus slipped the blade under the strap of fabric covering my pussy and sliced it open. I sucked in a breath at the rush of air licking against my most intimate place.

"What a pretty little pussy. Desperate for the same treatment your mouth just got."

He flipped the sword, and I swallowed a gasp when he caught it by the blade. I scented the blood in the air for a second before petals of red dribbled down his arm and peppered the dirt ground between us. He didn't give two shits.

Sex demons were fucking crazy.

The cool kiss of the sword's hilt was bliss against my throbbing hot pussy.

Riff's gaze slithered to Daemon's. I knew that look. The way his tail whipped the air behind him, that lopsided grin. The way his thumb hooked in the waistband with the rest of his middle and forefingers drumming the button of his jeans while his free hand raked his blue hair. He was using his charm powers on the alpha.

Daemon was immune to most of that shit. All it did was piss him off. He didn't like giving up control.

I braced for the explosion. It never came.

"Whatever you're thinking, spit it out, fuck clown."

Riff canted his head, his tongue prodding the corner of his ear-to-ear smirk. "You made some pretty sexy sounds when you busted your load inside our girl's mouth, hound. Wonder if you'll whimper like that for me?"

Both of Daemon's brows rose. I looked past his shoulder to Alistair, who for once, seemed just as eager as the audience to see how this played out.

A tense moment stretched through the big top as Daemon seemed to debate his next move. Murmurs rippled over the crowd. Most of these monsters had never seen the show before, but everyone in the supernatural community knew our characters. The Bitch Tamer and the clown twins never interacted.

If Daemon decided to indulge Riff, tonight would be a first.

The moment of silence finally broke when Daemon pointed to his feet and growled, "On your knees, Rifton."

The incubus instantly fell to his knees like a man before an altar, ready to confess his sins and, in Riff's case, ready to commit more.

Daemon gave a dark chuckle and came to stand in front of him. "You're such a desperate little whore."

I peeked over my shoulder to find Raff gaping at what was

unfolding just a few feet away. The corners of Daemon's mouth kicked up into a grin that screamed, *"Watch what I'm about to do to your brother,"* as he gripped Riff's horn and slowly slipped his cock past Riff's lips.

"Jealous, Rafferty—Oh, *fuck*." Before my taunt had left my lips, Raff pushed my sword's hilt inside me. This wasn't the first time one of the twins fucked me with an object that had no business being inside me, mostly the handles of Riff's many knives. However, this was the first time I'd swallowed this part of my sword before. It stretched me more than the hilt of a knife as it was thicker and longer. Raff reached around to press his fingers into my clit, and I gasped at the sensation, my pussy clenching around the metal.

I looked down between my legs to see the sword sticking out of me like some grotesque popsicle stick.

"Keep your eyes ahead of you, baby girl. I want you to watch them..." There was a wicked smile in Raff's voice.

My attention went back to Daemon, fucking Riff's mouth. It was true what they said about sex demon fluids. We made more of everything for moments just like this. Copious amounts of saliva dribbled from Riff's mouth, down his jaw to drizzle onto his chest. Every time Daemon drove back inside him, a wet smacking sound rose over the music.

"Tell them how good it feels," Raff muttered, soft at first, and then his tone grew to a growl loud enough for everyone to hear. "Tell them how good it feels to fuck my brother's throat. After all the shit you've given us, how much your attraction to us pissed you off... Tell them."

The pure pleasure twisting Daemon's features morphed into something darker. "It feels good—*Discord*." A string of curses was followed by another series of growls and moans as Riff gripped Daemon by the balls and squeezed. "His mouth is like everything I'd imagined," the alpha admitted.

"How many times did you imagine it?" Raff pulled the hilt from my pussy with an embarrassing wet sound and shot Daemon a teasing grin as he licked my juices off the metal. "How many times did you imagine this..." His demonic tongue wound around the sword's hilt, long enough to encircle it twice.

Daemon shivered as Riff did exactly what his brother was demonstrating with my sword. "Fuck. So many times." His voice broke. "I lost count—"

Heat lashed through my core like a whip, pure pleasure thrumming through my system. Was there anything better than seeing Daemon like this with Riff? Yes. Getting fucked by Raff while I watched.

I wiggled my hips, and my green-haired incubus took the bait. Tossing the sword aside, Raff took hold of my tail and wrapped it around his hand like a leash. His other hand lifted from my hip, and a beat later, I heard the sound of a zipper.

"Are you going to take my cock like a good little succubus?" Raff's voice came out husky and low. My head bobbed in a resounding "yes" since my ability to form words was gone.

He sheathed his claws for me before pushing a finger inside my pussy, quickly chasing it with a second. "Fuck, you are *so* wet."

I trained my focus back on Daemon, who wrenched Riff off his cock just as the muscles in his shoulders and the veins in his arms started to bulge—a sign that he was moments from coming.

"I'm a sex demon, asshole. We're not done until you come," Riff snarled in frustration. He tried to take the alpha's cock back in his mouth, but Daemon held him firmly in place by his horn.

Daemon leered down at the incubus so close that his luminous eyes cast the film of sweat coating Riff's painted face in an amber glow. "If the cum hungry fuck clown is so desperate for it, maybe he should offer me a tighter hole."

Chapter Six

Riff's gaze turned feral in a flash. He tongued one of his fangs, snapping the string of pre-cum—or incubus spit—webbing from the tip of Daemon's cock to the clown's exaggerated red grin.

The lust rolling off the both of them was thick enough to choke on.

"Fuck me, Daddy." Of all the times Riff had jokingly called Daemon daddy, this was the first time those two syllables were spoken like *that,* dark and laced with desire.

Daemon stood there, jaw flexing. Wrath and hunger poured off him, an energy so powerful and intoxicating that the entire audience was drunk off it.

"Fuck the clown!" the audience started to chant, some of them pumping their fists while others had their hands full. "Fuck the clown!"

Daemon's gaze shifted to Alistair, who gave the tiniest nod of approval.

Raff pulled his fingers from me and spat on my ass. Goosebumps crawled up my spine as I felt a thick gob of saliva slipping down the crack of my ass and oozing between my labia. He cursed as he took in the sight, appreciating the obscenity of it all before pushing his fingers back inside me and spreading them wide. My nails dug into the dirt floor, and he hummed at the lewd sounds crawling up my throat.

"Fuck, I can't wait to hear the filthy little sounds you make when I stretch you with my dick."

He paused, and I knew he'd decided right there that that was exactly what he was going to do. Withdrawing his fingers from me again, his arm banded around my middle, and he plucked me off the ground, pulling me with him as he sat up with his back propped against the platform where I'd opened the act.

I settled down in his lap with my chest to his back, legs spread wide. Gripping his thighs, I pushed myself up, allowing him to line our bodies up. His arm jerked me back down, spearing me onto him. A scream wrenched from me when his cock punched into a much tighter place.

"Wrong hole!" I choked out in a way that had Alistair smirking from across the ring.

Raff's mouth brushed the shell of my ear, and I felt his smile stretching against my skin. "You don't have any wrong holes. Not to me."

Luckily, his sex demon saliva made for the perfect lube, allowing him to slip in easily. My own weight pushed him in so deep I swore I could taste him in the back of my throat.

Movement jerked my gaze up to see Daemon, with his grip still tight around Riff's horn, walking him toward me. With the last few steps, Daemon gave him a push.

Riff was more than a clown, more than an incubus, more than a knife thrower. He was also an accomplished acrobat. He could have caught himself, but we were performing for an audience here so he knew his role in the moment.

The clown pretended to stumble, falling on his hands and knees as he skidded through the dirt, so close to us that when he lifted his head, his breath fanned over the place where his brother and I were connected.

Daemon dropped to his knees, sunk his hand into Riff's hair and wrenched his head up, forcing our eyes to lock. "I want you to feast on this pussy like it's your last meal while I fuck you from behind."

Riff gripped me by my thighs and tossed me a wink before allowing Daemon to shove his head between my apex.

It was a pretty picture, seeing that mop of blue hair framed between my thighs while the ridges of his horns rubbed my flesh raw as he devoured my pussy.

My head dropped back as I stared up at the center pole. The tent's black and white stripes started to blend as Raff savagely fucked my ass while Riff painted lick after sloppy lick to my center, from my clit down to his brother's cock.

Their searing body heat danced over my skin like fire, and the crowd's attention on us only added to the flame.

Pretending to be helpless while the twins used me however they pleased was a fan favorite. In turn, their dark lust fed me, filling my veins with power—making me anything but helpless.

My eyes glowed pink as I drank in the carnality of it all. It was a drug I couldn't get enough of.

Raff slowed his thrusts so he could bury his face into the crook of my neck. Each fang-filled kiss he planted to my skin was like a little zap of electricity, pleasure and pain winding tight.

"Feeling full?"

Was he referring to the meal I took from our audience, or the fact that he was buried balls-deep in my ass with his brother's tongue stuffed into my pussy? Either way, I nodded, since the answer to either question was a *fuck yes*.

My enthusiasm drew a chuckle from Raff, his fingers biting into my hips as his rhythm picked up. "You feel like fucking Heaven."

Riff grunted in agreement which had my toes curling as the vibrations of his voice sunk into my pussy.

"What would two demons know about Heaven?"

"With you as a mate?" Raff's voice in my ear was tight and breathless. "Everything."

Riff opened his mouth, as if to add on to his brother's statement but all that came out was a soft gasp as Daemon reached around to undo Riff's pants, ripping them down his hips. Then he pulled on one horn, lifting his head while he held his palm in front of his face. "You know the drill. Spit."

He did. Daemon released his horn, and Riff returned to torturing my clit with tantric little flicks of his tongue.

I was right on the edge of coming. So close, so worked up. My senses were a buzz, and every eye in the house held in my rapture only pushed my pleasure higher. Riff, Raff and I were all feeding on the attention. Literally. This made us wetter, harder, stronger, our stamina never-ending.

We could screw like this for the whole show if that's what Alistair wanted. With how the shadow demon was watching us with those demonic green eyes, maybe we would. His will was our pleasure.

With his cock properly lubed with Riff's saliva, Daemon pushed himself inside the incubi's ass. Slowly. Teasing out his invasion.

Riff shot a scathing look back at the hellhound shifter that was equal parts frustration and rapture. "While I'm still young, mongrel."

Riff new that Daemon loathed that nickname. To my surprise, the hellhound only smirked, for once not taking the bait. With the way Riff's entire body trembled, it was easy to tell just how overwhelmed he was by the sensuous and tortuously slow pace.

Tonight, it seemed Daemon's obsession for crawling under the twin's skin was evolving.

"Fuck, your ass feels so good," the alpha hissed, his face pinching in unholy reverie. The corners of his mouth curved with a rabid grin. "I think I just found my new favorite hobby."

Riff's tail coiled around Daemon's neck like a collar. The hellhound's brow furrowed at the power move, but he didn't stop him.

With one last nudge of his hips, Daemon filled Riff up, and the incubus subsequently moaned into my pussy, causing my eyes to roll back into my head.

Something snapped. Probably Daemon's control, since at that moment, he started to fuck the incubus with savage thrusts, the friction making Riff's mouth grind violently against my cunt.

It was sloppy, yet somehow coordinated all at the same time.

Pushed to my limits, I came with a scream that filled the entire big top. The audience cheered, and I screamed half-hearted obscenities at them while I rode out the most delicious orgasm I'd ever experience.

Riff lifted his head, and I met his eyes—that hint of blue gleaming from behind the milky haze of his contacts.

His lips silently formed my name, and he reached for me, his dirt-crusted fingers shaking as they brushed my lips. "Beautiful."

A blush burned under Riff's fading face paint when Daemon reached around to fist his cock.

"Goddamn, Daemon." His timbre had a quality to it I'd never heard before, pained with a need that went deeper than lust.

So many years of these three butting heads, resisting that chemistry that was so palpable now I wasn't sure how I'd ever missed it.

Riff's body obstructed most of what Daemon was doing to his cock, but I knew just how much pre-cum was leaking from his tip when a wet rope of hot fluid fell onto my foot. This didn't go unnoticed. Daemon's strokes were frantic, his motions twisting and turning as the fluid Riff leaked made for perfect lubrication. "What a needy little toy you are."

"I'm... I'm gonna come," Riff panted, raw and guttural.

"What do you think, Little Pup?" Daemon turned his attention to me. "Should we let him come?"

Riff was so close to the edge. In this moment he was no longer an entertainer. He was a starving sex demon with an instinctual need to feed and fuck, until that monster inside him was fully sated.

"First, he has to ask nicely."

Riff blinked at me, his glazed eyes trying to focus on my words.

Understanding sparked on the next harsh breath. "Please... Let me come."

Raff muttered a curse in my ear. "I love it when you make my brother beg for it, Hell Bat."

I nodded the okay to Daemon who had Riff hovering right there on the precipice. Each stroke of his hand mimicked the motions of his hips as he fucked into the incubus. Riff came with a ragged growl and the next moment cum spurted from him with enough force to paint my feet, my thighs and my exposed pussy.

Daemon's shoulder muscles bunched, the tendons in his thick neck tightening. He was right behind Riff.

A low whimpering sound wrenched from his throat.

God, that sound. That sweet, swollen sound coming from a ferocious male like Daemon was music to my ears.

I went limp in Raff's grip, feeling like a deflated fuck doll as he thrust inside me once, twice more. Seconds after Daemon's release, Raff followed. He throbbed inside me, a hot torrent of cum filling my ass.

His hold on me loosened, and I dropped back onto his chest.

We all sagged in a sweaty pile of tangled limbs as the deafening roar of applause drowned out the final notes of the last song on the track, "Pussy Liquor" by Rob Zombie.

Then everything became white noise.

We were in a tent with an audience of several hundred monsters, but down here in the ring, it was just us. In our own little fucked up world.

I watched, completely mesmerized, as Daemon tilted Riff's chin to lick the last of my juices from his lips. He then looked to Raff and grinned. "Tomorrow's show, you're next."

I couldn't help smiling to myself. I'd hoped this would happen.

Daemon was opening up to the twins. In turn, they were allowing him to see past the jokes and the makeup. And at what he found there, he was sinking in deep. They had him now. Hook, line and sinker.

If it wasn't the post-orgasm haze scrambling my perception, I could tell by that glazed look in the hellhound's eyes that he was all too aware of how fucked he was for these two unhinged sex clowns and that fighting it was futile.

Alistair strode over, crouching down beside us where we were still connected. With a gloved hand, he pushed a sweaty lock of my pink hair behind my ear. "You put on quite the spectacular show, pet. You all did."

I melted under our ringmaster's praise, the sadistic smile on his face making my heart skip a beat. "Maybe you can join us next time."

He held my chin in a gentle yet possessive grip. "Whatever my star wants. If you ask the world of me, I'll do my best to give it."

My eyelids snapped open, and my chest filled with warmth as I registered the unguarded admiration on his face. I turned my head to look at Riff, Raff and Daemon, then moved back to Alistair with a smile.

"You've already given me the world. All I want now is to share the ring with you. The public deserves to see what those shadow tentacles can do."

The ringmaster chuckled. "Alright, Megaera. My magic can be unpredictable when I'm distracted, so there might be a few more casualties than usual."

"What kind of psycho-sex circus would this be if there wasn't?" I sat up, grinning, the cuts on my face stinging with the movement. "Bring on the tentacles and the murder."

The End!

If you enjoyed these characters and would like to see more, you can find them in the *Sinner's Sideshow Duet* by Aiden Pierce.

About the Author

Aiden Pierce is a writer of dark paranormal romance and erotic horror. Her love stories are on the spooky side and usually end up with the monster or the villain getting the girl. She lives in the Pacific Northwest with her husband and their three fur babies.

FIND AIDEN ELSEWHERE:

Instagram
TikTok
Author Website

Sin & Sacrifice

By: Shar Khan

The First Heir made her a saint
The Second will make her a sinner

About Sin & Sacrifice

Raised in the shadow of a pleasure house, Scarlett Emerson was taught many things, but the one thing she longed for was a fairy tale, one that seemed impossible in the heart of Nameless City. When Jordan Singh, the First Heir to the Black Throne, sweeps her off her feet with love and devotion, an unexpected pregnancy after a failed Alteration feels like just another complication.

But as the promises of the First Heir unravel, Scarlett discovers the heartbreaking truth—he was never anything more than empty words.

Enter Josephine Singh, the formidable Second Heir and infamous Silver Tyrant. Scarlett is irresistibly drawn to the woman's commanding presence, and when Josephine offers her an escape from her Darling chains with a disarming smile and whispers of safety, Scarlett finds herself ensnared in a dangerous game, one she can't resist playing even as the stakes grow ever higher.

Content Note:

Sex trafficking, pedophilia, rape, forced sex work, threat of forced abortion, child abuse. All of these are off page and loosely mentioned.

Relationship type: FF

Chapter One
Silver Tyrant

J oseph Singh, the youngest of the heirs, had one sister—older by two minutes—and two brothers—older by eight and five. He hated them. He hated all of them with every bone in his body. Trust the feeling was mutual, and that's why he'd been strewn across the wooden grounds of his suite, bleeding out from the silver bullet in his neck.

His pants lay twisted around his ankles, and the girl he'd taken from the nearby elementary school was still draped across his bed. He didn't have time to fulfill his vices, for the bullet came from the shadows at his back, and he had a feeling he knew who it was.

She wasn't known as the Reaper or the Maiden. Vigilantism didn't interest her, though it was clear she had the skill for it. As she moved through the bedroom, Joseph heard the sharp click of her combat boots on the wooden floor. The gun she carried was Omar Singh's, but the suppressor that muted the shot? That was hers.

Her dark hair was a long braided tail held together by a band, and as she stopped to cast her gaze over the child on Joseph's bed, he saw the first inkling of utmost disgust creeping over her face."I told Mother we should've killed you when you were a boy." Her voice had either set in from the brisk winter winds outside or the inhalation of her black-gold cigarettes. "You've always been a degenerate, but I suppose I can't blame you. It runs in the family after all."

She stripped the blazer off her arms and draped it over the child's legs. Then, with a sigh, she sat on the corner of the mattress.

That's when Joseph saw it; the kohl that dripped down her cheeks like streams of war paint. The tattoos that swept down the valleys of her arms. The gold jewels that hung from around her neck matching the blown-out pupils that looked down on him; a dark angel come to claim justice.

She was a Singh who walked the hollows of Nameless City. But now, faced with the predicament before her, she had become something else. A silver bullet in an empty chamber, a reluctant savior of children swallowed by darkness. Yet it was that terrible smile she wore that revealed what she truly was. A reminder.

"Mother loved you most. What a fucking insult... And to think she protects you even when you do something like this." She gestured towards the child at her back, the one she refused to look at now. "They're helpless, vulnerable creatures of our society. You? You're a parasite that needs to be eradicated." She leaned forward, elbows digging into her thighs, the gun dangling loosely from her fingers as though it were an afterthought. "I said that too about Jackson. Right before I killed him. Remember?"

Joseph did.

He remembered the sound, a scream, and a snap. He remembered the palace in an uproar. He remembered the look on her face when everyone pointed up the gilded steps and screamed, *"A jinn with red eyes and war paint! Look at her!"*

"The next thing I know, I'm boarding a plane to London, rising into the Guild as one of the finest echelons that could ever exist. I grew to enjoy the taste of wine and women, the sight of a briefcase overflowing with cash, and shrines for the dark gods that answer my call when no one else does." She popped the cartridge open and showed him its intricate little insides. "I can't die. I've won three lives from Baal in a round of blackjack, and I hear he's splitting his tongue open with rage." With an extra bullet in the chamber, she prepped the gun and set it against the side of her head. When she pulled the trigger, it locked. When she pointed it back at him, it burst from its insides, nuzzling an inch from Joseph's hand.

He choked while his sister tilted her head back and laughed, the sound louder than a bullet ever could be.

Staring up at the ceiling, she continued, "Fatima used to call me Jinn. All the men in our family have done worse than I ever will, but I'm Accursed because I learned how to talk to the shadows and bend them to my will, the same ones who helped our great ancestors carve a hollow in the earth and tether us to them—interlopers through and through." She moved off the bed then. Knelt onto the wood, and peered into Joseph's decaying soul. "When you see them, let them know who sent you."

"Jo-Jos-Josephine..." he gurgled.

"In the flesh."

Then, she raised her gun and shot him between the eyes.

One Singh down, two to go.

Chapter Two
Darling Scar

The Doll House could be seen from three counties away, flashing like a beacon in the night. A neon pink sign that hung from the side of its building pulsed in a languid manner. The ever-changing outline of a girl with long, flowy hair parting as she slid down a pole gave the illusion that Upper Encino hosted some of the finest shows for the finest gentlemen, but even the Federation knew the truth.

They were the ones that helped cover up all the little wrongdoings for the right price. Pigs in uniforms, smiles that never reached their hollow eyes, hands that touched even though they weren't supposed to.

Scarlett blinked up at it, numb to her senses. It was so different seeing the Doll House from outside, and while many would say it was liberating to have earned their bodies back from years of servitude, she shook as the brisk winter winds came sweeping in from the sea.

The fur coat that had been delivered to her room hung off her shoulders, letting smooth, white skin grow flush from the cold. She looked like a million dollars with silver hair cascading over one shoulder, and while Pigs came lusting after her blood, the sight of white chains wound tight around her neck made it clear who she really belonged to.

A woman like Scarlett Emerson didn't step into the Red-Light District of her own free will. She was dragged from Lower Salem, torn from her mother's embrace while her father had been counting hundreds by the lamplight.

Then, the First Heir walked through the districts and caught sight of her beauty on the northern terrace. He fell in love, and House Mistresses began telling the younglings about how their work for the prestigious Syndicate would earn them a place alongside the Highborns.

Scarlett would beg to differ, but if she did, she would lose more than just her title.

Her thoughts came to a screeching halt when the headlights of a sleek black Mercedes stopped before her. A man stepped out; handsome with dark brown hair curling against his forehead and harsh, green eyes that flattened against Scarlett's face. The first time Liam Caldwell retrieved her, he'd given her that same stare; something that made her insides churn with nerves. But then he smiled, and the darkness fluttered away, replacing his features with a softness crafted by the gods.

"Most chauffeurs make sure Darlings know their place," she'd once said boldly.

"Good thing you don't," he returned.

And from that day on, they became something of friends.

Liam came around to pop the passenger door open. "You look beautiful, Ms. Emerson." Formal. Stern. Straightforward.

The cars were tapped. Ever since a Driver and a Darling left Nameless City, the First Heir found himself struck with grief. No matter how many Interlopers he sent after them, their heads came back in boxes with pretty bows and their bodies were never found. If Liam had something to say, he'd have to get creative. And shifting his tone to that strong, stoic chauffeur that served the city's darkest family with a scar gnarling his bottom lip would do just that.

Scarlett sank into the plush leather of his car, grateful for the seat warmers soothing heat. The interior was toasty, jazz music played softly in the background, and the tinted windows offered a rare sense of privacy, what little she could ever hope for.

Liam returned to his seat and pulled the car onto the main highway. Then, for five minutes, the two only communicated through idle glances. She, peeking at him with an arch to her left brow, and he, subtly fixing the rearview mirror, the jewels on his pinky, ring, and middle finger clicking against the surface.

Morse code.

"YOUNGEST BROTHER DEAD. MIDDLE SISTER BACK."

Scarlett's hand closed around the clutch of her purse.

It'd been a long time since the Singhs were at war. The last Scarlett had witnessed was two sparring matriarchs. Fatima, wife of the late-king Omar, and Amina, Mother of Heirs. They sat at the war table with a map of Nameless City unfurled before them. Little pawns dyed in white, black, and red were scattered across the three districts. From all of this emerged the matriarch's true calling, one that became clear shortly after Omar's assassination.

Nameless City needed a new heir.

Fatima wanted it for herself.

Amina wanted it for her child.

The halls of the Dark Palace ran red with blood.

Then, the streets followed.

Scarlett was moved to Upper Encino where favored Darlings hid in suites that day. The news that came in was horrendous. Fire catching, gunshots ringing, Federation sirens screaming throughout the night.

Scarlett would never forget what it was like when daylight came creeping through the broken curtains.

Where young Darlings slept huddled together, she'd stayed up, awake, suspicious of the Interloper meant to guard them.

Amina was alive and well. The righteous colors of a new dawn clung to men and women—Servants of Cerberus, so they were called. Any man who had beseeched his loyalty to Fatima Singh, Maharani of the Birzan Dynasty, were dead and so were his greatest legacies.

House Mistresses hung from street lamps. Dolls were raped and killed. Esteemed estates from West Hall to South Gate were set ablaze, no child spared. Gambling dens were pillaged of their worth, the flesh of priestesses torn from their bodies, bullet farms and the slaves that labored within blown sky-high.

It was mayhem.

It was carnage.

It was insidious.

When Scarlett left with the Darlings that were spared their life, she knelt before Amina and couldn't bring herself to meet a gaze made from vengeance and fear. Because any woman that would torture another was no woman at all, just a monster cut from the same cloth as Man.

A *thunk!* brought Scarlett back to the present. She was still in Liam's car, roused by the great sound of his ring clattering against the vent where the pleasant heat had suddenly become suffocating. "Our rajkumar has done well dressing you for the night. I'd think a gown like that would come with a mask."

With a small smile, Scarlett retrieved the mask from behind her clutch. She'd held onto the two like a lifeline while waiting for her chauffeur. Alas, with Liam's eyes beaming at the sight, she couldn't help but say, "Our rajkumar forgot all about it. I can't blame him. He's had a lot on his mind." A swift cover-up. "I went with Margot to the Moon Market and had it custom-made."

His fingers thwacked against the vent again.

"DAINTY AND SWEET TONIGHT. NO EXCESS TALKING. TENSION IN THE AIR."

Scarlett nodded; her lips carefully pressed into a thin line.

Her nail clicked off the clutch of her purse.

"MIDDLE SISTER?"

Liam nodded.

"CODE NAME: SILVER TYRANT."

Silver Tyrant.

It was rare for a woman of such stature to let her name spill into the streets. Whether by accident or design, Scarlett knew the middle sister would become a problem. She tried to remind herself that it wasn't her place to act as the First Heir's hand. Her role was far simpler: to be a docile ornament at his side, paraded like a show dog that only barked when commanded and sat when instructed.

Today, the Silver Tyrant would learn that the First Heir was close to taking the Black Throne. That she would not win this war should it begin, for he had an armada ready to march.

The Pigs were in his pocket, gambling dens flourished, Sharks bloodied the Lowlanding waters, and artillery farms on the outlying counties waited to deliver. The bars on each level of the Doll House were to ensure none of his birds could ever take flight, and the war between Federation and Anarchists kept the people busy while the First Heir stayed his hand closer and closer to what he truly wanted.

The Silver Tyrant won't meet its mark, Scarlett thought, staring out the window. *Not if I can help it.*

Chapter Three
Wicked Grace

A masquerade ball felt dramatic, but those who ruled the Birzan Dynasty had a flair for theatrics.

Scarlett had entered the Dark Palace a thousand times before, but never with this many eyes watching her. Interlopers and Pigs were one thing. She learned how to co-exist among them even if her skin crawled at their lingering stares. But esteemed guests from near and far? It seemed as overwhelming as a set of molten eyes watching from the veranda.

That was all Scarlett could see from the black crow mask that shaped the woman's face. It hugged most of her brown flesh and kept more than enough to the imagination. Dressed in a striking suit with an onyx-bone corset and gilded daggers proudly displayed, she stood with a woman on each arm—both poised in their laughter, skillfully crafting stories to keep her entertained.

Alas, the strange figure seemed interested only in the First Heir's most treasured Darling, the one that hadn't realized she stopped walking until the crow set a hand against the balustrade and tilted her head.

"Scarlett!" She snapped forward, eyes wide as she met the blonde beauty that came sweeping up the aisle, parting a sea of guests with her gusto.

Margot remained a permanent addition to the Dark Palace. Trust, she had her life only because she was the late-king's favorite, and Fatima's most treasured source of gossip. Not many knew Margot White was a Darling. Not until they looked close enough to find the chains around her neck matching whatever gown she was meant to preen in for the day. She'd been one of the first girls to help Scarlett find her footing when she was brought into the Doll House twenty years ago.

They were close in age. In fact, Margot was just two years older, which made Scarlett's time in the Doll House less miserable. Despite the odds, their friendship had sustained itself. They lived what little of their childhood with each other, and by the dark gods' grace, aided in the grand ascent to appease the Singh's.

Margot wrapped Scarlett into her embrace. She smelt of wine and lavender, which wasn't off the mark for a nightingale that enjoyed the sound of her own voice. Even after Fatima's murder, Amina had use for her. *The daughter I never had.*

"You look breathtaking," Margot gasped, holding Scarlett at arm's length.

It took her a moment to remember she'd entered prepped for the ball. Her emerald mask in-laid with black and gold was carefully set against her face. The matching ball gown that once spooled across her bed now clung to her curves. The gorgeous neckline fell down her sternum, and delicate embroidery gave the illusion of spring meadows and forest floors.

It suited the white of her hair that tumbled over her shoulder, the bright blue of her eyes that looked like a burst of spilled ink on a painter's palette. More, it made her look fit for royalty.

"I think that'd be you," Scarlett said, envying the embodiment of a white swan that cast Margot in reams of silk. "All my problems would be solved if I looked like you."

It roused Margot's beautiful laugh and Scarlett's smile, but a compliment like that always held a layer of truth.

Scarlett didn't like looking at herself in the mirror often. She hid behind heavy fabrics and baggy pants. She would write poetry on the days that self-loathing shaped her free will. It would be a scrawl of letters on napkins and papyrus and anything she could get her hands on, really. She would hope, with every fiber of her being, that she would wake the next day and be in someone else's shoes. Someone like Margot, beautiful and social. Someone like a girl in the Lowlands, greasy-haired and forgotten. Someone like anyone that wasn't her.

"Come, you little creature." Margot took her hand, "Jordan won't be able to keep his hands off you."

There came the knot of anxiety again, the one that made Scarlett clutch her purse and set her hand low on her stomach. She tried thinking of all the perfect things the First Heir had said to her during their love making. How he would always protect her, cherish her, celebrate her.

Those couldn't be empty words despite the vast rumors that now followed his near ascension.

Her eyes flickered towards the veranda again. Instead of meeting the brimming eyes of a black crow, she found the two women with frowns, elbows against the stone, missing the charismatic stranger who had long since disappeared.

* * *

Jordan Singh was situated on a dais in the throne room. The seat which his late-father occupied remained, and he wouldn't be sitting in it until he was ready. Instead, he sipped from a silver goblet full of wine while those that attended his masquerade were occupying the expansive floors.

He donned a dress shirt that had been unbuttoned, and his brown flesh seemed to glow under the white-blue lights swiveling around the hall. Though his mask held gray and silver detailing, Scarlett could make out the sheen of intrigue that shaped his violet eyes. Of all the Darlings that approached him and curtsied, she was the only one he stood out of his seat for, the only one whose hand he took, whose fingers he kissed, who smiled against her skin and said, "I've missed you, Darling Scar."

Scarlett forced herself to smile. Whereas his words would warm her soul, tonight it brought nothing but absolute dread. He'd been oblivious to it, of course. The way his large hand caressed her face and brought their lips together meant he cared only to flaunt what he had. She was a Darling, he was an Heir—the First of them all.

"I've waited all night for you, Crown Prince," she whispered, voice small.

But this time when he heard the tremble in her voice, his smile vanished and replacing it was...concern? Genuine concern. "What's wrong, my love?" He took her hand and led her around to the chair beside him.

He had it reserved for you, she thought. *It'll be okay. Tell him.*

She tried. Her lips parted and the words were there at the tip of her tongue when Jordan sighed and said, "Look at this atrocity," before nodding towards a flurry of guests, forgetting all about her and her grief. "What do you see?"

Scarlett took in the sight of them. They were some of the most beautiful men and women she'd ever seen, what little she could see of them with their identical masks on. Yet each had been distinguishable by a silver band around their arm and matching corsets. Some of them held pocket watches they often peeked down at when they were bored of their conversations, others carried daggers with familiar pommels.

"Have they—" She stopped, remembering Liam's words too late.

Dainty and sweet...

She cleared her throat. "You know best, love."

Jordan leaned back in his seat, one leg crossing the other. The obsidian rings on his finger obscured his tattoos, though Scarlett had traced them enough to know them by heart. A dagger, an arrow, a sword, a cross—significant kills to keep the throne reserved for him and him alone.

"I see the legacy my dear sister wrought. I wanted to send word of it to you, but with Interlopers changing allegiances, I feared putting you in danger. Joseph is dead, and the predicament he was found in..." Jordan sighed, closed his eyes, and squeezed his temples. "My brother has done a lot wrong in his life, but the whole of the Syndicate is brimming with madness. Now, my sister sits as a dashing hero to the common folk, saving an unsuspecting girl kidnapped from the gates of Saltview, her purity intact because of a silver bullet that took from me my right-hand. And Mother? She's lost her mind. Sits and wallows in the Northern Ward willing her dead son back to life while the Federation have a field day at the morgue. One Singh down, two to go."

Scarlett's hand tightened around his bicep.

Jordan paused, looking down at her long fingers with another sigh. "When Amina was pregnant with us, they said she was to have triplets—all boys. Healthy, strong thoroughbreds growing in her womb. The day Mother's water broke, the one that parted Joseph, Jackson and I was a girl no one expected. The one whose eyes shone bright gold, the one who laughed instead of cried. It was a curse from the beginning. Fatima saw it. It was the only good thing the bitch had ever said in her life, and out of sheer spite and hatred for her mother, Amina refused to betray her girl. Now, the supposed *Silver Tyrant* is back, pulling the rug out from under me."

Scarlett chewed on her bottom lip. "What will you do now?"

"I cannot take the throne if there is another competitor. The Second Heir has done just that, invoking the Nameless Council that sits fat and pretty."

"Would they be so quick to give her what you've worked so hard for?"

Jordan brought his thumb to his mouth, teeth snagging the torn flesh around his nail. "Her qualifications are excellent, Darling. That too without flaunting all her assets." He dropped his head against his knuckles. "I'm thankful Josephine doesn't have a cock. With all the Highborn women lining up, she'd be bound to produce an Heir and steal the hearts of the Council before a session can so much as come together."

"There's your leverage," she whispered.

Jordan turned his head in her direction. "What do you mean?"

Scarlett dropped her gaze. "I'm pregnant."

"Impossible," he said without a moment's hesitation. "You were Altered. Sure, it's rare to heal from it but...you've always taken extra care of yourself. The House Mistresses gave you tea, ensured you took your medication, that you were pure."

She looked at him, her mouth ajar. "I am pure. I'm *yours*."

Jordan growled, squeezing his temples again. "For fucks sake, Scar! Look around you!" His hand cast out in front of him, guiding him from left to right. "These are esteemed guests. They are men and women who have a name, a title. Words like *Doll* and *Darling* don't get you a seat at the War Table; don't allow your voice to be heard, your opinions warranted! What the Council would think if they heard that I impregnated a whore..."

Jordan wasn't attuned to her. All his pleasantries, all his niceties, those were false. They were just bits and pieces of the bigger picture she had failed to see. Even as he said, "I'll arrange for you to get rid of it," she thought of the idea that kept her alive at night. The one where she was spun in red silk, married to the man whose smile she felt pressed against her lips. Where she birthed all his heirs and watched them grow in a dark place now grown bright.

But a whore could dream, couldn't she?

And when she rose from the seat beside him and left, he didn't follow.

Chapter Four
Black Crow

The world around Scarlett seemed to be closing in. The wide corridor she stormed through felt narrow, forcing her to bump into Highborns that were chatting and drinking with one another. Up the stairs she went, her heels thudding off the carpeted floors. She tore the mask off her face, threw it away from her as if it was made from acid. Her chest heaved for breath, the gown and its cinched corset a tad bit too tight.

She gripped the chains around her neck, pulling them with a clench of her teeth. It wasn't the first time they had been the target of her rage, but unlike the fabric torn from her body or the bruises marking her flesh, this was the one thing that remained unbroken.

Jordan painted such kind words of his ownership of her when he placed it around her neck. When he kissed along her shoulder from behind and said, *"It's because you're my favorite."*

Was this how a favorite was treated? Made to give up everything, anytime he asked? Made to submit, coerced into it to be exact. And now, a choice that should've been hers made without consent.

While many Dolls were told not to daydream by their House Mistress, Scarlett couldn't help herself. She spent days easing red pillowcases over her hair, pretending it was a veil of vermillion silk. How often she practiced her vows to the First Heir, the one that told her under the cover of night how much she meant to him. She bore her soul to him, her heart, her body. And in one menial sentence, he cast it all aside, making her feel small, used, and worthless.

Scarlett's face twisted with grief, the sob now falling from her lips unable to be contained. Even slapping a hand over her mouth did nothing, just made her body crumple against the banister on the fifth-floor landing,

Her mascara ran down her cheeks. Whatever cheap kohl had smudged by her tear-duct burned her gaze, blinding her to the world. Sconces flickered in lapping bits of orange and yellows, highlighting the blood-red walls and the silverite mandala patterns. And when the banister rattled only slightly, drawing Scarlett's attention, she couldn't make out anything but a familiar crow mask just out of reach.

"Why so sad, Little Dove?" While her sultry voice seemed to withhold a mocking edge to it, there was nothing but genuine concern.

Scarlett wiped her eyes, smearing her makeup. "What the fuck do you care?"

The Crow set her arms against the banister. Situated on the opposite side of Scarlett, those cold, calculating eyes had since turned away. There were ten floors to go before reaching the rooftop—Scarlett's original plan. She thought throwing herself from the top would at least teach Jordan what it was like to dim the little light she had in her life. At least then she'd have an inkling of control as opposed to crying her heart out in front of an Interloper.

Scarlett wasn't stupid. A woman like that—the Crow—earned her place. She started at the bottom like all the others, took things with a smile like a babe who refused to share. And much like all other High-born women, she didn't know when to stop talking. Because she looked at Scarlett then and said, "Lover's quarrel?"

Heat touched Scarlett's cheeks as she rounded on the woman.

Her sight had since cleared, giving way to the Crow's vivacious smile; all white teeth, sharp fangs, and a long tongue carefully lapping at the bottom of her lip. Poised, confident, beautiful. "Don't you have some poor Darling girl to harass?"

"You're here, aren't you?" Their eyes met, madness and mischief fighting for dominance.

Scarlett clenched her teeth. "Not for the likes of you."

"But for the likes of the First Heir?" The Crow clicked her tongue. "Bad move."

"Jordan Singh saved my life."

"Jordan Singh is a parasite and Scarlett Emerson lives in her own head."

How does she know my name?

"I know everyone's name," the Crow answered. "I know everything about everyone. It's common for a solicitor of the Assassin's Guild. The one who created it, I mean."

Scarlett wished she could remember what that meant. She knew about the EU Underground, the one that had burned under the Federation's eye and was rebuilt by a terrifying order known as the Assassin's Guild. Alas, the moment of clarity and knowing passed, for the Crow eased off the banister and moved towards her like a cat slinking through the halls.

She crossed one foot in front of the other, looking Scarlett up and down. Whereas the men who came easing through the mahogany doors of the Doll House did so as if she were a slab of meat, the Crow accessed her as if she were a canvas. Something to be placed within The Louvre, something to be marveled at—hand to the heart, small little quivering gasps, a tear to be shed from such unnerving beauty.

"You don't care much about the Singhs or the Syndicate. You don't care about Nameless City and all its terrible little secrets. You," the sound of a theatrical melody came sweeping through the Dark Palace, harps and violins melting into a breathtaking chorus, "want to dance."

Scarlett blinked stupidly. "What?"

The Crow put out her hand. Black leather hugged her fingers like second skin, and when Scarlett took too long to move, the woman beckoned her forth with a finger. "All doves enjoy the sound of music."

"I'm not some fragile little creature," Scarlett seethed, entranced still by those molten eyes.

The Crow took hold of Scarlett's hand, startling the girl. She had no idea when the distance between them closed nor when she'd given herself up to the stranger behind the mask. And even when the Crow set a hand on her waist and guided Scarlett's to her shoulder, the Darling didn't object.

She was swept across the plush red floors, weightless and floating. The Crow's grip tensed only when she took the brunt of Scarlett's weight, lifting and twirling her with ease. The world seemed to have quieted since their meeting, for now the sound of the masquerade ball came spiraling up the steps, blessing Scarlett with the sharp trill of violins, the elegant rise of a quartet, the harmonious melody of vocalists she could only imagine in her mind's eye.

"What's the point of dancing if you take all the credit?" she meant it as a serious question, but it fell from her tongue in a bout of curiosity.

"You've already taken a lot of the spotlight today. All eyes were on you when you arrived, Little Dove."

"Yours included."

Dangerous, said the voice in her head.

"Very dangerous," the Crow agreed.

Scarlett's grip tightened. "How are you doing that?"

"I'm just reading you is all." She twirled her out, their long, slender arms pulled taunt against each other. Then, the Crow pulled her back. The music rose through the never-ending high-rise, and through it all, Scarlett could see the hint of a smile filling the Crow's eyes. "It's how I got your name and that beautiful little secret you have nestled in your womb."

Scarlett froze as she looked at the woman before her and saw little else. "I know who you are."

"Oh?" Their fingers laced together; white dove and black crow locked in the faraway ramparts that loomed above. "Who am I?"

The Crow twirled her again, spinning Scarlett around her frame. As she did so, the Darling's hand shot out, taking the mask and wrenching it from her face. The world spun and snapped. At arm's length, Scarlett saw the truth.

The black-gold mask that matched the cigarette case peeking through the Crow's pocket fell from Scarlett's hand, draped in elegant shadows.

Of course, the woman who had created the Assassin's Guild from the bottom up was not an Interloper. She was the Second Heir, and she was standing there with fingers easing over her jawline; the place Scarlett marked with her sharpened claws.

"Josephine."

"In the flesh." Now, when the woman smiled, her sharp fangs glinted off the light. "Heard of me?"

The Silver Tyrant who killed Joseph.

The Black Crow that Jordan feared.

With a jolt, Scarlett was pulled back into Josephine's embrace, chest pressed against hers, head tilted, eyes blown wide with shock, fear, and intrigue. "Aw, what happened, Little Dove? Don't want to play with me anymore?"

"I'm not your plaything," came her snarl.

At that, Josephine lifted her brows. Astonishment painted her features. It was almost surprising she hadn't seen those words coming. One full of self-loathing and hatred. Alas, the tremble in Scarlett's voice was subdued and only a quiver of her lips remained. One that drew Josephine's gaze.

"Do you want power, Ms. Emerson?"

Scarlett pulled away, a scorned laugh breaking the barrier between them. "What?"

"The First Heir seeks the throne with a proper wife at his side.

He doesn't see you as an opportunity. He sees you as a possession, as something to be had and used. That's what he said, didn't he? That's how he cast you away? Will you be in the good graces of my brother only after you get rid of the very thing you want?" A hand caressed Scarlett's face, and the woman wondered how she continued closing the distance between them so easily. "Poor Little Dove. Jordan's trapped you in a cage and told you pretty lies so you'd never leave. You think looking up into the sky means you'll fall into it?"

Her fingers took Scarlett's chin, tilting her head up only an inch before she looked up.

High above, past the hanging chandeliers, was stained glass that led to the heavens. Light cascaded through the storm clouds above Nameless City. Another dying day in a dying city where the Lowborns starved and the Highborns ate to their heart's content.

"Oh." A purr. "You look like you want to fly."

"I don't think I know how," came her restless whisper.

"Marry me and I'll teach you."

Scarlett's eyes dropped unto hers, molten gold churning red. Scarlett's jaw clenched as she remembered what Jordan said, of a sister who had parted three brothers at the womb, a plague ripe for the taking, empty promises and a call for pawns...

"Fuck you, Jinn. I won't be part of your game."

Josephine dropped her hand, though there was no insult or dejection in her eyes. Only intrigue. Constant intrigue. "But you already are. Whether you like it or not, you'll dance with me again. Only next time, you'll enjoy it."

Chapter Five
Lamb To Slaughter

L iam's gorgeous eyes filled with shock at the latest red light. Normally, he would hold Scarlett's gaze in the rearview mirror and affix her with the strongest emotions he could conjure. Today, when she'd signed the words to him, he thought it was a mistake.

"PREGNANT?" he returned with a twist of his hand.

A teary-eyed nod was his response. **"JORDAN WANTS ME TO GET RID OF IT."**

The snort that left his mouth carried down the street. It was rush-hour, the worst time to be driving in Mid-Town for any and all reasons. But then, there wasn't an hour in the day when the streets weren't overrun by sleek black cars and Lowborns running between them, hoping for a coin or two.

"HE'S A FOOL. THE POWER HE COULD HAVE…" Liam's hand hovered in the air, mind moving a mile a minute. **"NOT MANY KNOW HOW DEEP AMINA'S TALONS HAVE SUNK. IF HE WAS SERIOUS IN TAKING THE THRONE, COMING FORTH WITH NEWS OF A CHILD**

WOULD MAKE HIM THE DEADLIEST HEIR THE BIRZAN DYNASTY WOULD EVER SEE."

For a chauffeur to have known so much meant only one thing: Liam had a deeper connection with members of the Singh family.

"Interlopers changing alliances."

Jordan's words came to her just as Liam took a detour. He went left through an alley, the GPS on his car blinking rapidly.

RETURN TO YOUR ROUTE flashed across his screen before his steering wheel locked. Liam didn't seem to panic, not the way Scarlett did, tensing in her seat, struggling against the seatbelt that felt more like a noose around her neck.

Whatever intercepted Liam's car warped his screen. A static hum and a bar ran through the middle as if cracked. Only when the words started typing in real time did Scarlett realize they'd been hijacked.

"First the Tyrant and now you? Something big is happening. Make sure you stick to your allegiances, Interloper. Would hate scraping your guts off the sidewalk. - Lamb."

But what startled Scarlett the most was Liam's throaty laugh. One she had no idea he could make. "Ease up back there, Ms. Emerson."

"Don't tell me you—"

"—were so enthralled by Josephine's return that I turned my back on the First Heir? No. I'm not that cliche, but I do know the run-down."

"Such as you would, Interloper." Her eyes caught his in the rearview mirror again, this time through narrowed slits. "So, what, selling me to the highest bidder?"

His tone softened. "Jesus Christ. Of course, not. You're my Darling and I'm your Driver. I just think you need to see what Jordan really had in store for you."

Scarlett quieted then, thoughts running a mile a minute, gaze leaving his and easing over the screen. She allowed Liam to drive. He wasn't the type to fill silence with menial ramblings, and they'd known each other—at least to an extent—for quite some time. Enough that he knew she would rather simmer in her thoughts and do the only thing she had a choice over: cry.

It was like that for the next thirty minutes.

From Mid-Town to Outcoast, if Scarlett had felt that Liam was delivering her to the ends of the earth, she didn't have the energy to care anymore. At least not until she realized Outcoast was where Jordan kept his hidden trade routes. Usually, international cargo that docked on Port Nine was hauled there where a subdivision of the Birzan medicine men would conduct their screenings.

Arriving at the Slaughterhouse gave way to all her anxieties. Because this is where the Singhs would send their broken toys.

Scarlett met Liam's gaze in the mirror. "No. Jordan wouldn't do this. He said he wanted me to get rid of the child. I agreed—"

"Agree or don't agree, you've posed a threat. You either disobeyed the House Mistress and refused your tea, or you—Scarlett Emerson—were the only Darling with a penthouse suite that healed when she wasn't supposed to."

Nonetheless, it happened. One where the imposed Alteration of a woman still bore consequence. But that was the way the world worked. A man only ever held sin in their bones, and the women bore their sacrifice.

Liam pulled up alongside one of the outlying farmhouses. Under twenty miles, the motor turned quiet. The hum of the engine came to a stop, and the headlights that illuminated the grassy path layered them in darkness.

He sat back in his seat, gesturing to the cargo haul full of pregnant Dolls. Scarlett couldn't look too long. Not when she realized some of them were only children, bare-foot and bright-eyed despite the terrible hand they'd been given.

According to Liam and the sight of the farmhouses, it was clear her time was up. Or, at least that's what Jordan wanted.

"The First Heir lied to you." Liam's voice was a pin drop. It was almost lost to the howling winds that buffeted against the open windows in the back.

Scarlett set her elbow against the armrest, balancing her chin against the top of her knuckles with tears glistening in her eyes. "I loved him," the words were merely a whisper.

"No, you didn't." That low, terrible voice didn't sound so terrible today—the Jinn of Many Names. Josephine's hands were in her pocket, her right shoulder leaned up against the back door. "Love doesn't exist for women like you."

Scarlett felt like she'd been slapped. With tears streaming down her cheeks, she pushed the door open with force. Josephine easily side-stepped the hit as Scarlett fumbled onto her feet, flinging her finger into the Second Heir's face. "What do you know about love, Jinn? You, who built an empire from the bones of her enemies—"

Josephine snorted. *"Bones of her enemies'?* What, you take enough of my brother's dick to start talking like him? Does that make you feel powerful?"

The slap came quick, shooting Josephine's head to one side. Scarlett's hand burned, yet she relished the way strands of black hair fell over the Second Heir's face.

That *makes me feel powerful.*

Josephine's low chuckle hadn't prepared Scarlett for the way those horrible, yellow eyes flashed when they swiveled back to meet her. "It should. Not many can land a hit on an Heir and still have their life." Scarlett gasped when Josephine struck. Like a snake entrapping a field mouse, her hand wrapped like a vice around her neck. She squeezed so hard, Scarlett could see black spots dotting her vision. Even the small little ember in Josephine's eyes burned bright, red churning in its depths. "You owe me your life now that I've let you have it."

"Bullshit," she seethed.

"No?" A tilt of the head, a mocking laugh. "Your chauffeur put his life on the line turning his back on the First Heir. If not for the quick involvement of the Guild's most enthused hackers, a bullet would've killed you faster than the Pigs." Josephine tipped her head towards the farms, the line of laughing women and young girls finding solace in each other. Lambs led to slaughter.

"You give me my life and you forsake theirs. You're not as kind as you think you are," Scarlett wheezed.

"Who said anything about kindness, Little Dove?" Josephine wrenched the woman into her embrace. With Scarlett's back to her front, she turned, forcing them to watch men in lab coats and poised smiles coming to collect their victims. "You're all pretty pawns pushed to their limit by shadows that care little for them. You gave your love to Jordan Singh, a man who has done you no favors."

Scarlett shook her head. "He loves me too."

"Is that what he said when he raped you?"

Her eyes watered. "He's not some Pig."

"All men are pigs if you stab them just right." Her gloved hand carefully moved from her neck, easing Scarlett's hair over one shoulder. The cool touch of leather grazed the woman's skin, leaving a trail of goosebumps in its wake. "They squeal loud enough to make you wonder where they get their power. The same power used to break your wings, to make you think the cage they put you in is locked while the door remains wide open."

Scarlett wrenched out of Josephine's grasp and whirled on her. "So that's it? Show me the truth and make me submit before you? Oh, how grateful I am! How merciful you are! Should I worship you like I would my Creator?"

"You are your own Creator. You worship only yourself." Josephine said it so casually, it pulled a scoff right from Scarlett's mouth.

Worship? She only knew how to worship the men who bargained with her body. She only knew how to worship the First Heir who had given to her gifts that he could easily take away...

The Silver Tyrant's mischievous eyes had since grown full. They were soft—willfully so—but not pitiful. "I brought you here so you could see how easily disposable you are in my brother's eyes. I brought you here because you know why Broken Dolls are sent to the Slaughterhouse. When they heal from their Alteration, when they bear the consequence of men and are regaled as filth for merely being able to carry the essence of life..." She shook her head, turned away, flashed a simple color of emotion that made her so terribly human it all but tore Scarlett's heart in half.

"So, you brought me here to see all that and more. You also hope that I'll change my mind; that I'll take your hand as you asked."

"You're smart, Little Dove." Josephine smiled as she said it, head still turned away. "You play pretend and live in your head. It's kept you alive all these years, but aren't you tired of hiding? Don't you want to see your true potential?"

"A businesswoman through and through," Scarlett laughed. "You may have won all of Europe, but you won't win me so easily."

"I offer you an easy way out. All you have to do is marry me. If you wish to keep your child, you will be protected. If you wish to get rid of it, I will have the best of the best at your service come morning. No matter how it ends, you would live in my estate."

"As your prisoner."

"As my wife."

"And if I accept all that and choose to disregard your hand?"

"Then it'd be your choice."

Scarlett shook her head. "You lie."

"I'm not the curator of a Doll House. I'm not a Mistress that makes you balance books atop your head, tightens the strings to your corset, makes you dance for men as old as your grandfather. I'm a businesswoman," she parroted, lifting her head coolly. "You are a wonderful creature, Little Dove. Men look at you and see a shell. I look at you and see what lies within."

"What do you see, Jinn?" Scarlett asked, her brows knotted with grief, her top teeth sinking into her bottom lip to still her pain.

"I see a queen. Someone who can turn those chains into jewels. Who can fill the streets with scarlet blood."

Scarlett said nothing. Her hand merely rose, settling on her collar and its dainty little charms. She watched Josephine's gilded eyes drop to her bosom and turn away, the reality of their dance as depressing as the truth.

Little Dove and Silver Tyrant.

Slave and Liberator.

"Fine," Scarlett said, startling herself as much as Josephine.

The silence between them grew so loud, they could hear the faraway echo of those that came and would not return. The laughter of girls and the ancient sound of serpents treading over dirt.

Eventually, Josephine straightened her posture. She stood shorter than Jordan by a few inches. Six-foot-three, maybe taller with the set of heels she had on now. She carefully fixed her suit, the padding on her shoulders making her look bulkier than Scarlett knew she was, what with those lean muscles carved from hours of training, and a body that she had only known from their dance just a mere night ago.

Finally, Josephine rapped her knuckles against the driver's side window. Liam rolled it down without thought. "Take Ms. Emerson back to the Willow Estate."

"Your brother will call for Inter-War when he finds out she didn't make it here, Heiress." It was the first time Scarlett had seen Liam look worried.

Josephine, however, glanced at the woman from the corner of her eye. "Good. I've been waiting for a fight."

Chapter Six
Red Willow

The Willow Estate was a lavish home, but it lacked the grandeur of the Dark Palace. In fact, it had been left in disrepair for quite some time.

Scarlett quickly learned that this was the place where Amina lived while pregnant with her quadruplets. She'd been forbidden from setting foot in the palace, all because of her mother-in-law—the very same woman Amina had strung up by her entrails when power surged through her veins.

The Willow Estate earned its name after the death of Jasmine Singh, the youngest of the Heirs, a would-be Fifth if she survived. But then the terrible rumors of the Jinn With Many Faces returned, tales of how Josephine set a bassinet on fire just to see if the babe would scream.

Liam touched the small of Scarlett's back, making her jump. "I can't go further."

"You've already done so much. What's walking a girl to her front door?" she joked.

Liam merely said: "I only compromised my own safety because the First Heir sought to dispose of you. When Josephine came with her proposition, I knew I had to take it. I don't trust her. I don't trust any of them...but I love you. You're my friend, Darling Scar. And whatever happens, I want you to be safe." He gestured towards the door and added, "Knock three times when you're ready."

Scarlett shed enough tears to last a lifetime, and while she couldn't surmise anymore, she hugged Liam, breathing her love into him. She felt secure when his arms wrapped around her waist, when his hand flattened against her back and left an everlasting impression when he left.

He'd settled in his car when she did as she was told, rapping her knuckles against a panel made from onyx and steel three times in all. The door then opened of its own accord and let in a stream of light from outside. It also closed when Scarlett stepped over the threshold, losing herself in the delicate furnishings that made the place feel like home.

While the outside stood in ruins, it was clear Josephine had returned to Nameless City quite some time ago. She merely sat in the pockets of land that held no promise, lived in would-be squalor as she plotted her family's demise.

Elegant sconces flickered with warm light, the same as the night of the ball. They were evenly placed along the corridors and every time Scarlett passed one, it would darken. At first, she thought the electricity was bugged, that the estate hadn't been powered in a long time and therefore faulty. But when a sconce lit up on the second floor just by the rounding staircase, she knew it was a sign.

As she held the ends of her skirt and ascended, she took in the delicate tapestries and elegant wallpaper. While she did not believe in enchantments much, she believed in Josephine. When she danced with her, when she read the little thoughts in her mind, answered them, and smiled as if it were a party trick...

She was the first Singh to surprise her. But then, women who ruled over the Birzan Dynasty were full of those. They were enchantresses that withheld magic unable to be burnt from their system. Who did business better than any man ever could. Who smiled and laughed while slitting their wrists, weaponizing the splatter of their own blood.

Such was the nature of Singh women, or so it was told. For only they could war against the world and win. For only they could smile as their husbands took the throne, died for it a thousand times if not more, and struck only when they felt necessary.

Amina and Fatima would hold no significance now that the War of Heirs began.

The sconces disrupted Scarlett's idle thoughts. They flashed and reddened when she aimlessly wandered, drawing her back with a set of entranced eyes. They flickered and often bathed her in darkness, nothing that so much scared her.

Eventually, she found herself in a suite that put the penthouse to shame.

While the doors to the terrace closed, she could see through the stainless glass and into the gray stone outside. It overlooked the whole of the courtyard and out into the dazzling city. Heavy, dark curtains were pulled back to allow her sight, and the plush carpet underfoot prompted Scarlett to remove her shoes. She set them against the door, her gaze averted for only a moment before the curtains fell from their hold and shielded her from the twinkling lights outside.

Scarlett looked up in time to find the candles come alive. Their wicks burst with golden flames, keeping the darkness at bay. And just when she eased towards the four-poster bed big enough to hold a family of five, she turned towards the tall stick of wax with the biggest flame and said, "How're you doing this, Jinn?"

A *tap, tap, tap* eased over the wall of her bed frame.

"MAGIC."

Scarlett couldn't help the smile on her face. Not when she asked, "Are you next door then?"

"PRAYING TO THE DARK GODS. YES."

"Won't you bid me goodnight? Or do the dark gods look down on common courtesy."

Silence encumbered the suite for only a moment before Scarlett felt it, that presence one would miss if they weren't searching for it.

Josephine stood by the open door, her arms crossed over her chest and her eyes all knowing. Scarlett faced her with a strange surge of confidence. "You didn't answer my question."

"I did." Josephine lifted a hand, two fingers—index and middle—held before her. A small wave, and the sheer veil came tumbling over the bed, encasing the silken sheets with a curtain of privacy. "Magic."

"There's no such thing as magic, Jinn."

"Of course there is. You just need to know where to look."

"Then it's safe to say you can read all my thoughts? Play with small little knick-knacks with your mind?"

"I can only read a person who is close to me. I can only alter what's mine. And you, Little Dove, compel me. You have since our dance."

"I suppose I should be flattered. I've insulted an Heir, slapped her, and now I'll sleep in her bed."

Josephine's eyes gleamed with mischief. "And you'll dream of her too."

"So sure of that?" Scarlett asked.

The Silver Tyrant tilted her head back against the handsome frame and smiled. The gesture caught Scarlett off guard. What bit of bravado she had fluttered like butterfly wings in her stomach. The sight was breathtaking. It lit up Josephine. Made her cheeks bunch up at the highest points of her face and the corner of her eyes crinkle.

The laugh that accompanied it was breathtaking. It put the cathedral bells to shame. And where Scarlett had hoped, had prayed the Second Heir would take a step forward and say to her a plethora of things full of admiration, she instead said, "Goodnight, Ms. Emerson. I'll see you in the morning."

Chapter Seven
Winged Dove

The night had grown cold and no matter how heavy the sheets were, Scarlett found herself curled up for warmth. When she awoke, she thought it was morning before realizing the candlelight that bathed her chambers in a sheen of orange too dim to be the sun. And when she moved, the cold mattress made her wince and pull back.

It was ritualistic, it seemed. Every hour, the wax melted a little more and the frigid breeze eased through her suite. But it was only when she finally found a bit of peace that it had been disrupted again. It came like a shadow falling over the partition of her four-poster bed with long, beautiful fingers carefully threading them to one side.

Scarlett sat upright with a gasp, the sheets falling off her like rivulets of water.

Years of paranoia painted her grief with panic. Now, she was staring at the partition, at the way it moved of its own volition. There was no wind, for the doors and the windows were closed. And there was no one else in her room. At least that she could see.

She looked from one painted corner to the other, shadows moving and melding to their own accord.

It was only when she pulled her knees into her chest that it struck.

A set of hands wrenched her by the ankles. Just the shock of it had stilled Scarlett's scream, that is until she was on her back with Josephine hovering over her.

"Not even a sound?" the Second Heir asked with a tilt of the head. "You really are full of surprises, Little Dove."

"As if I would've given you all that power." In place of her ire, Scarlett found herself trembling under the woman's form, her voice muted by desire.

Josephine smiled, tongue trailing over the tips of her sharp teeth. "But you'll give me something, won't you?"

With every ounce of strength, Scarlett pushed herself up. It wasn't enough to overpower Josephine, but she had yielded, allowing the Darling to ease her back against the plush mattress, the cold sheets warming with each passing second. Straddling her hips, Scarlett carefully set a hand against Josephine's neck. Unsure at first and then, squeezing just there at the base. "I'm sick of men coming to take what they're due."

The black of Josephine's hair haloed out behind her. "You think me as terrible as them?"

"No," Scarlett whispered, her fingers easing down the trail of Josephine's unbuttoned dress shirt, feeling the soft of her brown flesh down to the naval. "If you were, you would've already taken more than just my dignity."

The muscles in Josephine's core tightened as she sat up. With ease, she slung her arm around Scarlett's waist and turned, pressing her into the sheets around them. It was almost terrifying when the Second Heir took Scarlett's hand and brought it to her lips, kissing along her fingers with adoration. "I will take only what you ask me to."

Heat blossomed across Scarlett's cheeks. "My lips then?"

Josephine peered into those blue eyes for only a moment before leaning forward, close enough that their noses brushed, and kissed her. It was soft with a touch of yearning, deepened only when Scarlett wrapped her arms around Josephine's neck, felt the tension there in her shoulders when hands went guiding along the valleys of her back.

Lust flared to life in the cover of darkness. Scarlett had done this a thousand times with men who bathed her in gold jewels and promised her riches. But this? This was passion.

It was passion in the way Josephine had taken Scarlett's face in her hands. Those long, jeweled fingers eased down the soft canvas of the Darling's flesh. But it was also passion in the way Scarlett wrapped her legs around Josephine's waist, drunk off the touch of whiskey on her tongue. It was the only reason she gripped her shirt and tore it off her shoulders.

"I'm not surprised by much, Little Dove," Josephine said, "but I'm yet to figure you out."

Scarlett sat up, arms slung low around her form. "Oh, but I'm not yours to figure out."

"You're not?" Josephine asked, feeling the woman's tongue trail between her breasts. "You have the Silver Tyrant in your bed."

"She came here of her own volition," Scarlett whispered, peppering kisses along the Heir's collarbone.

Josephine grasped Scarlett by the back of her hair. She wound those long, thick tresses around her hand, using it as a leash to hold her at bay. The Darling let out a breathy sigh, melting at the center. "Perhaps I did, seeing what I could claim should you let me."

Scarlett took Josephine's free hand and set it against her chest. The full of her breasts swelled under that soft nightgown, and while she spread her thighs only slightly, Josephine looked at her—curiously intrigued. "You can claim whatever else I give you. But this is my bed," the Darling murmured, "and you're my guest."

Twice now, Josephine smiled. And how beautifully she obeyed.

With the fluidity and grace Scarlett could only dream of,

Josephine's lips trailed along Scarlett's hand, down her wrist, tightening only when she pinned her to the sheets. A breathy exhalation lingered, a brief moment of doubt—something no Singh would ever allow to be seen. No one but her.

That molded into something else as she trailed her lips down Scarlett's long neck. Josephine's hand took hold of that pesky nightgown and pulled the fabric down over her chest.

Scarlett squirmed impatiently, for the Second Heir had taken her time pressing kisses to her chest, her thumb stroking over the hardened bud of her nipples. Just the softest lap of her tongue, the way her sharp teeth brushed her flesh, had Scarlett arching her back with a moan.

Just like that... she thought.

Josephine pulled her hand between Scarlett's legs. "Like what? Like this?" She slipped her fingers under Scarlett's panties with seamless ease. Practiced, confident—like she'd done it a thousand times.

Scarlett tried closing her thighs. "Careful."

"Oh, I'm always careful, Little Dove." Josephine ripped the lace with a mere shift of her fingers. Scarlett gasped at the feel of cold air against her wet pussy. And then when Josephine dragged open mouthed kisses down her body, lapping at the softness between her legs.

Scarlett let out a startled moan, clamping a hand over her mouth to stifle her pleasure. "Don't hide," Josephine carefully guided Scarlett's hand from her mouth and situated it between her legs. Two fingers pressed against her clit, and it took the Darling some time—through a spark of lust that made her vision hazy—to understand that they were her own. "I have a feeling you haven't been taken care of before," Josephine whispered, her hand over Scarlett's. "Let's change that."

Scarlett propped herself up on her elbow, her legs parting inches wider, a wordless invitation. No matter how much she wanted to quip back, Josephine's beauty and confidence left her stunned into silence. She seemed to be embraced by the shadows and the flickering orange light from the nearby sconces, the same ones that bent to her will.

At least like this, she could watch the way Josephine's soft lips pressed along the inside of her thighs. Made her wait until her tongue found its way back to the heat emanating between her legs. No matter how much Scarlett wanted to anticipate the touch, she couldn't. Not when she was touching herself, fingers moving in a slow, calculating manner.

Josephine parted only slightly, her warm breath still hot on Scarlett's center. Two long fingers sheathed her, drawing a strangled cry from Scarlett's mouth. A third had her top teeth burrowing into her bottom lip, struggling to keep composure. But every little nerve in her body screamed on alert. From the way she stroked herself to Josephine's rhythmic pulse–a slow, agonizing pump of the fingers–to her tongue lapping the warmth seeping from her cunt.

Scarlett drove her hips down against Josephine's mouth and her fingers. It earned a soft bout of laughter that made their sinful dance nothing short of innocent. The Heir pulled back, licking her lips as she did. She pressed her hand into the plush sheets beside Scarlett, trapping her with that brilliant, hovering presence.

Scarlett couldn't look away even if she wanted. She was entranced by the Second Heir's mysterious aura, that too with the feeling of Josephine's pace quickening. "How are you where I needed you most?" Scarlett whispered, her lashes fluttering.

Josephine's brow quirked. "Do you mean figuratively or literally?" She spread her fingers, prompting Scarlett to tilt her head back until the touch of the sheets caressed her.

She turned away, a wave of blush touching the hollows of her cheeks, dropping across her chest, spreading through her core. "You know what I mean."

"Perhaps. I'm just shocked you've strained against that little collar my brother donned on you. What did he say? That they were jewels bathed in the ancient waters of our people?"

"Blessed by monks," Scarlett sighed in bliss. "For seven—"

"—days and seven nights, guarded in a temple on the top of a mountain path where the desert met snow and the spirits came to bless an offering meant for the bosom of a good, dutiful girl." While there was no humor in Josephine's words, it had blossomed against her features in mockery and a tinge of anger. "A girl that forsook her freedom for love, not knowing she could have both."

"You made that up," Scarlett accused, her eyes flashing. With daring boldness a Darling could never have, she moved her hand to clutch Josephine by the hair, yanking her up from between her so their frames were close. "You lie through your teeth."

"That would be my brother, Little Dove," Josephine said, hands roving down the sides of Scarlett's nearly naked body, her gown immodest. With fingers stopping at her hips, she added, "But if you want to make me your villain for a night, I don't mind." Scarlett's grip tightened around her hair, cutting off Josephine's words with a strangled grunt. She rolled them until she was straddling her again. "So long as you finish—"

Scarlett rolled her hips, and that small, simple gesture had thrown Josephine's head against the mattress, a growl of pleasure rumbling in her throat.

Her right hand moved from Scarlett's hip and eased under her gown for only a moment before the Darling pushed it away. "You said you wanted me taken care of."

"I did," Josephine leveled.

"Then let me use you the way I intended."

Scarlett's assertiveness drew a breathy chuckle from the Second Heir's mouth. It was a riveting feeling, being on top, pinning Josephine against her bed knowing she could've easily taken the upper hand as all men had.

But Josephine Singh wasn't a man. With her hips steadily rolling out her pleasure, fucking her without doing so, Scarlett didn't even think she was a woman. Maybe a dead god, what with that inquisitive way she looked at her through half-lidded eyes, the flare of her lashes, the muffled moans on her tongue.

Scarlett's hand left Josephine's neck, quickly burrowing under her gown and rubbing hard against her clit. She tilted her head back, nearly losing herself if not for Josephine's hands on her hips, rooting them together with an unbroken vice.

The Second Heir met her thrust for thrust, their clothes askew, their hair disheveled, until the very moment Scarlett cried out her orgasm with a knotted brow.

Her body shook against Josephine's, carefully riding out the tension before the candlelight flickered and she remembered where she was. In the Willow Estate with flares of magic dancing along the fingertips of her lover. Atop the Second Heir who looked at her as if she'd never seen another woman. Leaning down to catch Josephine's mouth with hers, soft as if to give thanks.

"You're a beautiful thing, Little Dove," she whispered. "I wonder what you'll be like when you wake up."

It was almost immediate. That earth-shattering revelation that pulled Scarlett up with a gasp, hand pressed to her chest, feeling the flutter of her heart. She was still situated in the Willow Estate. Her suite hadn't changed, for there were still sconces burning along the wall. The side tables were shrouded by her transparent veil, but Scarlett could make out the book she'd pulled from the shelf before bed, *Pride and Prejudice*, hanging off the edge.

The sheets were warm, and so was she. That is until she pulled them back and realized she was practically soaked by her own desires, one roused by terrible dreams of Josephine Singh.

One where she wanted her more than she wanted anything else.

Chapter Eight
Red Or Blue

While the Willow Estate wasn't too well-furnished, its emptiness didn't bother Scarlett. She enjoyed it more than she cared to admit, given that she never knew what it was like to be solitary.

The sun sat high in the sky by the time she got out of her bed. Her body ached as if she'd spent the night rolling around with the Silver Tyrant; a strange, mysterious enigma that gnawed at her wandering thoughts.

While hunger clawed at her bones, Scarlett's curiosity kept her from the kitchens and her feet trailing through each of the rooms. There was an office that held a desk, a laptop that was open with a document full of Birzhagi—a language made by the curators who claimed the Black Throne. While there were no bookshelves, many texts had been stacked haphazardly across the floors, taking water damage from the leaky spots in the ceiling.

Scarlett shifted through them, smiling at the oddities of classic fiction and historical romances. If these belonged to Josephine, then she had a type.

Only when she went trapezing through a half-open door with the words **DO NOT ENTER** written across it did she find a spare change of clothes. They were simple: a band tee, a pair of ripped jeans, and a note atop them that read: *"You're a troublemaker, Little Dove. One day, it'll get you killed. Breakfast is downstairs. Liam will come in an hour (1:30PM) to pick you up."*

Scarlett had questions. Mostly how Josephine knew of her sleep schedule, perfectly timing Liam's arrival, and the creation of breakfast in a home that held nothing. The latter part of those questions had been answered with a bowl of cereal.

When Liam arrived at 1:30PM on the dot, he retrieved her with a small smile. And when she asked him where they were going, he raised his brows and said, "To the clinic."

* * *

Scarlett hated the drive. She hated Jordan for putting her in this predicament, making her regret every little thought of admiration she had towards a man that proved he was just that and nothing more. She hated Amina, Mother of Heirs, for producing them. And she hated Josephine for giving her answers she didn't want.

There was a reason why Dolls and Darlings didn't ask questions. It was better to kill a bird when they felt loved. When they brushed their beaks against the open palm of their master, not knowing when their neck would break.

Josephine took that to the grave. She'd turned Liam's obedience, used his care for the girl he'd chauffeur, and took her to the Slaughterhouse where she got to see the truth. As theatrical as the Second Heir had been since their paths crossed, Scarlett was thankful for one thing: when it came to the well-being of those around her, Josephine wasn't as terrifying as her brothers.

The clinic was a facility that stood alongside the medical district; a long strip of land, maybe ten miles in length, that anyone could get lost in. It was the only place where Singhs and their rampant number of enemies couldn't brawl. And here, Medics sat with their pockets full and their hearts fuller. They cared for all people despite their sins.

For Scarlett, sitting in a room with four white walls and navy blue seats that made her feel at home was strange. So was the woman that had come to aid her with a smile. Tell her that she and the expansive crew of Medics would be prepared to help her in any way possible.

Then came the facts.

Scarlett was almost a month and a half pregnant. It was too early for her to be showing any signs other than the occasional dizzy spell, terrible headaches that ripped through her frontal lobe, and an excessive touch of fatigue. Thankfully there was no morning sickness. "Not yet at least," said one of the women with a smile.

Past the pap smear, the blood test, and the ultrasound screening, she was in good shape.

"Stress and anxiety is a cause for concern, Ms. Emerson. But before we go into a plan for helping you reduce that, I have strict orders from the Second Heir."

Scarlett's heart was in her throat. What was it? A terrible motive, a choice to be made without her permission, a revelation of secret plans she'd naively walked into–

"How would you like to proceed? Would you like to terminate this pregnancy or carry to full term?"

The question hung in the air for some time. Scarlett blinked back her shock with raised brows and long lashes. "What does Josephine want?"

"It's not about what the Second Heir wants. It's about what *you* want, Ms. Emerson."

Scarlett nodded, her heart in her throat. She never had a choice in the matter. Not when she was told what she could and couldn't eat, beaten if she stepped out of line, pushed into holding her tongue.

The only thing she could do was stand from the little gurney she'd been settled upon, hands clutching each other like a vice. "Can I come back later and give you my answer then?"

She was expecting a raised brow of annoyance, but the Medic

merely smiled warmly and said, "Of course. I'll call you after your test results are in. Take care, Ms. Emerson."

Scarlett shook the whole way out. But when she popped the passenger door open to Liam's car, she looked at him with all the conviction she had and said, "Take me to Josephine."

Chapter Nine
Scarlet Blood

Hightown was crafted with Grecian architecture fit for royalty that matched the interior of the Dark Palace. It was a place where nobles ran rampant, layered in fashionable drapes of silk and chiffon, eating to their heart's content, and spoiling themselves with material items while the rest of Nameless City suffered.

Scarlett already felt rotten, blinded by Jordan's dance and her eventual fall at the hands of an Heir.

She wanted to be like the women with shopping bags lining their long, slender arms. She wanted to be as beautiful as them, shining in the sunlight. She wanted the diamond jewels that touched their fingers, that made them a goddess among heathens. She wanted all that and more.

Liam couldn't go further. She'd gleaned that from the way the lens of his glasses darkened along with the car windows. If anyone found out he'd turned on the First Heir even slightly the consequences would be dire.

Instead, he kissed her cheek and offered her a pristine smile, one she hadn't seen before, and said, "You'll be okay."

Scarlett didn't shed a tear until she left the expanse of his car and watched him pull away. Then, she turned towards a building known as Phantasm and carefully stepped over the threshold.

Scarlett knew Doll Houses.

She'd known them intimately, dressed in the finery of a grown woman when she was anything but, bore the consequence of her beauty at the hands of Pigs and more.

For moments Scarlett wandered the halls of Phantasm with a hand to the chest, heart in her throat, worried Josephine Singh was just like her brother—maybe worse.

Her anxieties were quelled when she met with a breathtaking woman in a dainty dress, goosebumps on her flesh from the chill that swept around the lobby where several women (a bit like Scarlett—out of place) sat about, twiddling their thumbs.

"I'm sorry, I was dropped here by my chauffeur. I'm looking for Josephine." Her eyes strayed upon the love marks that purpled the woman's collarbones.

"Oh, of course! You must be Ms. Emerson. You're the one Joey put up at the Willow Estate. She talked up a storm about you. She's been entertaining a few guests this morning, but I'm sure she can make some time. Come."

Scarlett could do nothing but shoot a glance in the direction of the lobby, of the girls who refused to meet her gaze. She had questions, too many questions, yet followed after the nameless woman in a nameless city.

She wondered what kind of company Josephine could possibly be keeping. Something to help bloodlet the poison that seeped into the Dark Palace, to overthrow the First Heir and whoever else stood in her way.

But then, when the woman stopped by a single golden door and threw it open, Scarlett wasn't thinking of anything at all. She was merely startled at the sight of an inner chamber from 15th century relics and forsaken architecture. The slanted goth ceiling that led to a hidden nook accessible by a ladder tucked away, reachable only by a particular device, sported a strange glow to it.

The two posters that held up the nook were draped with satin black curtains and while the remainder of the chamber was layered in rosewood, Scarlett couldn't help the blush seeping into her cheeks when realizing she'd walked into a sex party.

It shouldn't have embarrassed her, what with every piece of furniture occupied with writhing, naked bodies. Cast in red and orange lowlights that flickered from the nearby sconces, it reminded her much of last night; a mere figment of her imagination, a dream she wished was reality.

Women in all shapes and sizes were enamored by each other's presence, caring little for where they were so long as who they were around. They were intertwined limbs kissing and touching to their hearts desire. They dug their nails into the wide hips of their lovers, knotted them in thick strands of hair, rousing moans that rolled through the chamber like prayers at dawn.

There were no plastic baggies full of X or lines of coke prepared for consumption. Only euphoria fueled Phantasm's inner circle, pulling carnal pleasure from the depths of their soul.

And through it all, Scarlett's gaze stopped on Josephine Singh who sat on a throne, for lack of better word, checking her nail beds as if she were bored.

Scarlett was bold when their eyes met and a look of knowing surpassed the Second Heir's face. It was as if they'd shared a secret. When she bid the girl goodnight and came to her in her dreams, when the shadows danced at her back, when the sconces flickered... It couldn't have been a coincidence.

Scarlett pushed forward.

Her heels clicked off the tile, lost from the sounds of ecstasy and soft music pulsing through the lounge. Lost to everyone but Josephine whose hooded eyes locked onto her, whose boredom turned into excitement, made her sit up, made her alert and intrigued.

When Scarlett finally stood before her at the bottom of a three-step dais, a man and a woman—suited for business—looked her over with raised brows full of shock.

"You won over the obedience of a Darling and you haven't even been home a week," said the woman, her flashing red eyes painted with mischief. "Impressive."

"Don't mind my partner," said the man, his broad shoulders squared and handsome face lit up with a smile. "It's a compliment."

Josephine gestured between the two. "Ms. Emerson, I'd like to formally introduce you to Zahira Mostafa and Frank Castelo." War Maiden and Frankenstein. Nameless City's most feared Anarchists. "*But* it looks like we'll have to cut our meeting short. It's not proper to neglect a lady."

Zahira and Frank shared a knowing glance before drawing their fists to their chests. They dipped their heads in unison and left without sound. Only the courtesans flanking Josephine's throne remained, their envy of Scarlett making them tight-lipped and sour.

"I'm glad you found your way to me," the Heir admitted.

"I take direction well, *Joey*."

The woman smiled, her eyes uncannily large and her teeth sharper than Scarlett remembered. "Oh, Cassidy let that one slip, did she? Only those of my closest circle are allowed to address me as such."

"Then it seems I'm long overdue. Lest you've forgotten where you let me rest my head. I'll cut to the chase. I want to accept your offer. The one you gave me the night of our dance."

Josephine's laughter was low and husky. Amusing, breathtaking—and with the way she looked down the bridge of her archaic nose—victorious. "Who's to say that offer is still valid? I mean..." she made a pout of her lips, eyes scanning the inner sanctum, "it's not every day I ask a woman to be my wife."

A blonde haired woman set a hand on Josephine's shoulder, nails like talons. "You proposed to marry a whore?"

"What the Highborns would say if they knew," tsk'ed another, her black hair in long, luscious curls down barren shoulders.

"Will you take all of your brother's playthings?" That last one felt like a slap to the face, the red-head who'd spoken it flashing only the wickedest of smiles.

Josephine sighed. "Apologies, Ms. Emerson. They tend to envy what they don't have."

Scarlett swallowed a lump in her throat yet remained as strong as she could. "You dismiss your business partners, but you lend your ear to courtesans who don't know how to respect your guests. Seems you're just like your brother."

Her words were static tension that made the shadows dance along Josephine's throne. What humor the Second Heir had vanished, and now her jaw clenched, her eyes dulled. Gone was Josephine's wit and charm. Replacing it was a look of unadulterated rage that sent a shiver down Scarlett's spine.

She lifted her hand, gesturing for the lot to leave. "Clear out. All of you."

It brought Scarlett far too much pleasure seeing the gorgeous trio slinking after the others. It took no time at all for the place to hold only two beating hearts, that is if Josephine still had one left.

"Marrying me thinking it would save your dignity would do the opposite," Josephine began. "You're not my brother's first victim and you won't be his last. The Singhs don't care about the trouble they cause, not when they're the forerunners of weapons manufacturing and trade."

"Trade as in sex trafficking," Scarlett snapped.

"Little Dove—"

"Stop it. Stop trying to use pretty words thinking it'll change how I feel or what's been done. You don't know about this family the way I do. You don't know what I've been through. You were sent to Europe, got into Ivy Leagues at the bat of a lash, learned how to work the Underground. You know what I got?" She got close enough to see Josephine's emotionless face, the way her eyes danced along hers. "I got pulled from my mother's arms at eight. I was raped by Pigs and what did my father get in return? Ten thousand dollars per mark, per bruise, per desecration of my soul. It continued for twenty fucking years and now, you want your turn, don't you? Come back after two decades and think you know what's best. Just know this. I can marry you, but I'll never be owned by you. You and your filthy bloodline can go to hell."

Her chest heaved, her hands shook, and she could barely look at Josephine with tears obscuring her sight. But there was no ire in the Heir's voice when she asked, "You don't remember me, do you?"

Scarlet recoiled at the sudden change in conversation. "What?"

"We were in the same class. Grade 2. You don't remember."

Scarlett agreed, "I don't remember a lot about my youth."

"I liked you," Josephine said with a smile. "When I saw you for the first time, I told Nan how a girl with snow in her hair made my heart hurt. You had so many friends. Enough to fill your yearbook with tiny little signatures, even me."

"You?" Scarlett asked, brows furrowed.

Josephine let out a groan as she stood, as if her body ached and bore the brunt of a thousand invisible cuts. "I was quiet. Did my work and went home. You were nice to me. You were so nice that when Zeke stained your dress, I held his puppy over the ravine near Crestwood and made him promise to never bother you again." Scarlett stepped back as Josephine stepped closer. "And when Jackson said he wanted you for himself, I pushed him down the stairs hard enough to break his neck. Cockroaches, my brothers. All of them." Another step and she was towering over Scarlett. "I suppose I should clear the air. I didn't ask for your hand because I want to control you, Little Dove. I asked for your hand because every time I dream of a wife, I see you."

Scarlett was taken aback by the pleading tone in Josephine's voice. Her brows furrowed together in despair, and she stood there, hands tucked behind her back, waiting for a response.

"What're you saying? Are you saying you love me? Some schoolyard crush turned you into a fucking psycho?"

"There are worse things in Nameless City than a psychopath."

"Like what?"

"Like men."

She had a point.

Josephine was a weapons specialist and socialist, the face of the Birzan Dynasty if she succeeded at eradicating those who stood in her way. She was a businesswoman who wasn't opposed to shaking hands with the enemy, because the enemy of her enemy was her friend. And more than that, she had magic in her veins. Scarlett didn't know to what extent, but it was there, dancing at the lapse of her consciousness.

That made her dangerous, but not dangerous enough to keep Scarlett at bay.

"I'm keeping her," Scarlett said. And when Josephine's brow twisted in confusion, she set a hand against her stomach and said, "My baby. I'm keeping my baby. I want out of the Dark Palace unless it's reborn under your hand, I want the Doll Houses eradicated, and I want my father's head on a platter. But more than that, I want to see your brother burn."

Josephine nodded. "As you wish."

"That's it?" Scarlett asked, flabbergasted. "I'm using you," she emphasized with a sneer.

"To the world you'd be my wife. You'd be the face everyone sees, one they respect. You feed me information; you tell me about your sufferings. You command me to change the wrongdoings of this city, and you're carrying *my* child to term. Am I not using you as well?"

Scarlett said nothing else. She merely swallowed the growing lump in her throat, set a hand against her chest at the fluttering of wings trapped inside. "You're not as bad as they say, Jinn."

Josephine pulled a signet off her hand. Made from brambles and thorns wrapped around gold, the jewel was a blaze of scarlet red. Then, she took the Darling's hand and slipped it onto her ring finger, a perfect fit.

"Not to you, wife. *Never* to you."

About the Author

Shar Khan is a multi-genre author, daydreamer, and professional introvert. Unsure of which path to take, they graduated with a BA in Creative Writing, English, and Sociology. Indecisive much? You can keep up with them on Instagram and Threads, though one is a bit spicier than the other. (@shariva.writes)

The Untaming of Ivy Allaway

By: Allie Maddox

About The Untaming of Ivy Allaway

After years of living in a veritable hell on earth—first with my mother, then the Forresters—I'm finally getting out. Finally breaking free. But what will freedom cost me?

And can I survive this new pack long enough to see what my future looks like?

Content Note:

This story has a HEA, however Ivy goes through quite a bit to get there. This story is set in the Shifters of Northpeak world but is separate from any current stories.

Content includes graphic violence, past trauma including abandonment, neglect, and abuse, current abusive environment for MCs, matricide, loss of a parent, suicidal thoughts, mental health struggles, previous cannibalism, attempts at forced breeding, and other dark themes. Mature content. For readers 18 & older.

Relationship type: This story involves an MMF relationship, however the MM relationship does not have sexual content on page.

Chapter One
Ivy

My phone buzzes on the table, and I flick my gaze over as it lights up. Pain shoots through my spine when he shifts in his seat—he hears it too. Garrett's heels dig into my back, and I bite down on my lip, stifling the cry I want to let out. He's right on the fresh wounds from yesterday, and the bastard is well aware of it.

"Who the fuck is calling you? It's a godsdamned Sunday, Ivy!"

I know the rules and that my phone is supposed to be put away when the guys are home. Even when they're gone, I'm limited in what I'm allowed to do, but considering Garrett dragged me out of my bed last night and left me on the floor of the living room when he and Acton were done with me, he can't be too surprised that I got bored and retrieved it. Candy Crush was calling my name. Though the rage flashing in his eyes right now tells me that he's none too pleased with me.

Good.

Maybe this time he'll fucking kill me. Put me out of my misery.

I let my head drop, knowing he won't let me pick it up.

Booted footsteps on the hardwood make my stomach drop, and I suck in a breath, holding it as one of the others approaches.

"Don't fucking bother," Garrett growls, but a moment later I hear another deep voice.

"Hello?" Hurst answers, going quiet for a moment.

I don't dare pick up my head, nausea creeping up as I recall what I did last week in a moment of rebellion. A moment where I finally broke down and decided to fight back.

It can't be.

Not that quick.

"No, she's not available right now," he replies succinctly. "May I take a message?"

Fuck. Fuck! Fuck! Fuck!

Tears prick in the corner of my eyes as Hurst says, "I understand, ma'am. Will do," and disconnects, my phone clunking back down on the table.

"Well?" Garrett asks, irritation in his voice.

"Get your fucking feet off of her," Hurst rumbles.

Garrett scoffs but does as his older brother says. A moment later Hurst is crouching down in front of me, his black eyes stern as he grasps me under the armpits and lifts me to my feet. He deposits me in a chair, and my knees scream with the motion, aching from being crushed against the floor for the last three hours.

I swallow hard as Hurst stares down at me, and I don't dare rub the pain out of my knees. I just sit there, shivering against the cold leather and wait.

"Do you want to tell him who that was, or do you want me to?" Hurst questions, cocking his head to the side with a small smirk.

He's not a good guy, none of them are. But Hurst is the reason I'm still alive. Which makes me hate him more than the others. Even if he's never harmed me, he's still a fucking monster.

They all treat me like shit, but Hurst is always the voice of reason. *Give her a break. Let her take a bath. Make sure you feed her. Don't fuck her until she's in heat.* All the reminders he gives them to keep me in somewhat-working condition. Because without that, I'll never go into heat. Even if he finds the stupid drugs he's been looking for this entire time.

"I—I don't know what you're talking about," I croak out, my voice scratchy from lack of use.

That smirk grows, and Hurst picks up my phone, tossing it to me. I catch it and stare at him until he nods. Swiping it open, I click on the little green icon, and there it is. Accepted call at 7:56pm on a Sunday.

Fear and excitement roll through me, colliding in my chest like some sort of super-storm that crashes against my rib cage and makes my heart beat out of control.

"What's it say, Ivy?" Hurst demands.

I glance up, and Garrett is glaring at me just as Acton waltzes into the room.

His nostrils flare as he senses my fear, and there's a flash of fang before the last brother in the pack appears to finally read the room.

Taking a deep breath, I close my phone and let my gaze land on each of the brothers, settling last on Hurst. "The Calldrene Shifter Blood Bank."

Chapter Two
Ivy

To say the men of the Forrester pack took my news in stride would be the understatement of the century. And unfortunately, to my great displeasure, Garrett did not put me out of my misery. Although, my grocery shopping detour to the Calldrene Shifter Blood Bank last week may have put the final nail in my coffin.

"Fuck this! Why do we have to let her go? She's close to a heat, I can smell it on her," Garrett screams, lifting his beer and flinging it across the room.

It smashes against the wall, and I flinch, trying my hardest to keep from curling up in a ball in front of them. I've shown these men enough weakness and now, when I want to cower in fear, I'm realizing I have no reason to.

They aren't going to hurt me anymore.

"She's not our mate," Hurst says in a matter-of-fact tone. "And we don't have the drugs to make her that, so we have to let her go."

"We don't have to," Acton pipes in, leaning against the wall as he watches me.

He's always fucking watching me. Learning all the things that bother me, that scare me, that hurt me. Fucking psychopath.

"They might not want her once they find out she's a mutt."

Fuck.

Acton is right, and my stomach sinks. His lip curls up as he tilts his head to the side, examining my body language.

"Mutt or not, we clearly weren't expecting this, and CSBB says she needs to call back to schedule a time to go in," Hurst explains.

"So we don't let her call," Garrett replies with a shrug. "Simple as that. She's allowed to change her mind about it."

Hurst shakes his head. "You understand they would have called her mates tonight as well, right? They wouldn't have called her if she didn't have a match. So some wolf out there, or maybe even another pack, just found out their fated mate is alive and kicking. You think they won't come looking for her?" Hurst turns his attention back to me. "Tell me, Ivy, did you give that organization all your information?"

A lump forms in my throat, making it feel like I might just choke on my own spit. I nod.

"Where you live?" he questions. I nod again. "Right," he answers, disappointment apparent on his face.

Garrett lets out a deep growl and lunges for me. My instincts kick in, and I tug my knees up, throwing my elbows and forearms in front of my face to protect myself as much as I can. Pain lances through my back with the sharp movement. I brace for impact, but it never comes.

"You can't touch her!" Hurst yells, and I blink my eyes open, peering through the barricade of limbs in front of me.

Hurst is holding Garrett by the back of his neck, a blade pressed to his jugular.

"How much did you hurt her yesterday?" he asks his brothers.

Garrett shoves at him, scowling at me as he walks away. "I barely touched her," he grumbles.

He's not wrong. Garrett was too drunk to do much last night, preferring to fuck the girl he brought home in front of me, making sure I knew that he thought I was disgusting as he put his cigarette out on my shoulder while he pounded into the girl. She was clearly in pain and not interested in the way he tried to force his knot as far as he could into her, but she was a human and in no position to fight back.

"What about you?" Hursts asks, turning his attention to Acton.

He shrugs, blond hair falling in his eyes. "I just played with her, normal weekend routine."

"Fuck," Hurst seethes, running a hand through his hair. "Fuck!"

The normal weekend routine consists of Acton picking a new activity to try and torture me. He thinks that if he scares me or hurts me enough, maybe I'll shift into a wolf and not stay the pathetic human they all view me as. And each week, when it doesn't work, he reopens the wounds on my back, carving MUTT into the space between my hips with his favorite blade.

The same one I used to turn myself into a monster, just like them.

Acton dissolves into a fit of laughter at my clear disgust, and my entire body shudders. He really is a psychopath.

Hurst sets me with a vengeful glare and fishes his phone out of his pocket.

"I'm calling a friend to come clean her up," he states, punching numbers into the screen. "Call the bank back. Now. I will not have a bunch of feral wolves showing up at my house."

I pick my phone up from where I dropped it on the couch when Garrett lunged at me and swipe it open. Hesitation grips me as my thumb hovers over the number, and I flick my gaze back to Hurst.

"Do it," he orders, and my thumb immediately presses down, months of obedience gripping me in an instant. "And, Ivy," he says as I lift the phone to my ear. "Not a single scar on your body is from us. Your parents disowned you for being a mutt, and we saved you. Never forget that. Not if you want your secret safe and want to live."

Chapter Three
Ivy

My hands are sweating profusely as I follow the nurse through the doors and into a private room. Hurst dropped me off, along with my bag and a reminder that he will kill me if I tell my new mates about my time with the Forrester pack. His words still ring in my ears.

I tamed you, Ivy Allaway. Not this man. Don't you ever forget it.

If I hadn't witnessed them kill five women and two men in the last six months while I lived in that house, maybe I wouldn't believe him, but unfortunately, I do. I can't even take solace in having mates that will protect me, because I don't want to do anything to upset the monstrous men I'm leaving.

I'm getting out by the skin of my teeth.

And keeping my own demons hidden in the process.

I may be filled with scars, burns, brands, wounds, and bruises, but I'm alive. And otherwise intact. That's one thing Hurst seemed relieved about when he was driving me here. That he kept his brothers from doing anything sexual while I was with them, continuously reminding me that if they needed a doctor to check me when I went into heat, I couldn't have any signs of trauma or they would immediately take action and call the police. Meaning my back, shoulders, and arms are covered. Anywhere a doctor wouldn't need to look to assess my ability to carry a child for them.

And thankfully, now I never have to.

Though, to be honest, I'm not sure I could have.

I wipe my hands on my pants as I wait. The nurse speaks to me, letting me know that it's my choice if I want to leave with the man coming in to see me—the mate I've always dreamed of. Oliver, she said his name was. If not, I'm welcome to go my own way—with my one bag of clothes and the twenty dollar bill Hurst gave me before peeling out of the parking lot.

I'd be lying if I said I wasn't terrified. Those men stripped me of everything. My belongings, my livelihood, my inheritance. My dignity.

Everything.

The door creaks open, and I shoot to my feet, the skin-healing tape on my back stretching and causing a stinging sensation. The scars will always be there, but forcing me to push off this meeting for an entire week means the prescriptions they put me on and the medicated tape have had time to clear up most of my issues. Hell, Hurst even brought me to get my hair done the other day. Said he couldn't let Oliver meet me and have me look like the mutt I am.

So sweet, that one.

Oliver strides into the room, and my first reaction is that he's strikingly handsome. His six-something frame towers over my measly five-foot-two stature, but he doesn't have the looming presence the Forrester pack did. Instead, Oliver looks a bit shy and dorky with his swept-over onyx hair and thick black-framed glasses. He's dressed a bit preppy in a sleek, navy-blue button down tucked neatly into khakis.

"Ms. Allaway," the nurse says, interrupting my ogling of Oliver with his warm brown eyes and inviting smile. "This is Oliver Bergman. Mr. Bergman, this is Ivy Allaway. I'll give you two a few minutes."

I barely notice as she leaves, too engrossed in the man in front of me. He's not what I expected. Not that I've had a ton of experience with wolves outside my hometown, and they're a close knit group. Of assholes, that is.

"Ms. Allaway," he croons, stretching out his hand toward me in greeting.

"C—call me Ivy," I state, taking his hand and noticing the way his smile grows even wider.

Gods. He is beautiful.

"Ivy it is," he replies. "You can call me Oliver, or Olly. That's what Ewan calls me anyway."

"Ewan?" I question, confused by his response.

Oliver drops his hand and rubs the back of his neck. "Oh, yes. Sorry, I wanted to wait to tell you. Ewan pulled his information from the bank, but he's my other mate, and that means he's likely yours as well. We didn't want to overwhelm you by both showing up."

Holy shit.

"I have *two* mates?" I ask, trying to keep the hope I'm feeling from becoming too apparent. I'm not supposed to let him know how shitty my life has been thus far.

Oliver nods. "I believe so. I guess we'll know once you meet him. That is... if you want to."

My head bobs fervently despite my attempts to keep myself in control. He has a life. A real life. And another mate. This is my way out. Out of the disgusting town I've been trapped in my whole life. Out of the despair of being a mutt. Out of the guilt and shame.

This is my new beginning.

They don't know who I am or what I am. And they don't need to. I'll figure it out eventually—how to hide it from them. But for now, I just want to get the fuck out and find some peace for once.

"Of course I do!" I blurt.

Oliver chuckles. "Do you want to sit down? Get to know each other a bit before we move forward?"

As much as I don't want to do that, I figure it makes more sense, so I nod my head, moving toward one of the comfortable chairs arranged in the room. Oliver follows behind me, giving me a respectful amount of space and opting for the chair across from me.

It's odd, but I feel a lot more at ease with him having just met him than I ever did in that fucking house.

"I'm a software developer in the city, so I do work long hours, but I take a lot of time off too," he tells me, settling himself back in the chair when the nurse comes to check on us and leaves us with some tea. Oliver thanks her before pouring me a cup and taking a tentative sip of his own. "Ewan is partial to staying home, so we haven't traveled much, but I'm hoping maybe we can change that."

"And what does he do?" I ask, holding the warm mug in my still-sweating hands.

Oliver smiles, but it's slightly different, something seeming off about it as he answers. "Currently he's been painting. Ewan is creative and though he worked as an art professor for years, he decided to retire early and now paints from home. You should know, he suffers from fairly significant panic attacks and agoraphobia, so he won't be getting a job outside of the house again."

"Oh," I reply, unsure what to say. "That's awful to hear. But he's happy?"

"Of course he is," Oliver responds—maybe too quickly? He's obviously protective of his other mate. "He has a friend that spends a lot of time with him. Ewan really is a wonderful soul, I'm sure you'll love him."

I nod, a little nervous when he asks me what I do. "Umm," I begin. "Well, I'm in between jobs right now. Currently looking for a new one, but I don't have a degree or many skills."

Swallowing, I watch for his reaction, but Oliver just appears to relax a bit more. "No? You didn't go to school?"

"No. I lived at home until I was twenty-one and then went to live with some friends this past year when my mother passed away. I—I come from a fairly closed-off community so I wasn't allowed to work or go to school."

It's not entirely a lie. More a mix of a lie with some omission.

"Ahhh," he replies. "Say no more. I'm aware of those little pockets that still exist. Old-world wolves, right?"

I bob my head repeatedly. "Yes."

"No worries at all," Oliver states. "I want you to rest assured, Ivy, I make enough money to take care of both you and Ewan without any concern. I know the bank only allows us this one meeting, but I wanted to extend the invitation for you to come stay with us as we get to know one another. We have a guest room, and there would be no expectations whatsoever."

As crazy as I feel saying yes to him, I find my mouth forming the words. I can't go back to the Forresters. I would rather die.

And those fuckers just won't let me.

Chapter Four
Ivy

"So—umm—you paint?"

I want to slap my hand to my face when I ask the question, feeling like a fool. But it's the only tidbit of information about Ewan I have, and I'm unbearably uncomfortable right now.

Oliver is watching us intently, sitting at the head of the table, with Ewan and I placed directly across from one another. His eyes are more black than brown now, and the weight of his stare is heavy, making me shift in my seat.

Ewan clears his throat, pushing his fork around in his bowl before twirling a noodle onto it. He glances up at me with warm hazel eyes before flitting his gaze back to his meal.

"I do," he replies succinctly, taking a bite.

I wait a moment, but he doesn't continue. "I would love to see some of them—if you wouldn't mind." Ewan lifts his eyes back to mine, and something flashes in them. "My—my dad painted. From what I was told. I don't remember any of it, but I loved the few paintings my mother kept."

His hazel gaze softens, and a small smile forms on Ewan's lips before his stoic mask falls back into place. I'm not sure what I've done to make him uncomfortable, but he feels aloof for someone who is meant to be my mate.

And my body isn't responding that way. Not at all.

In fact, I feel like all of my senses are heightened right now just being in his presence.

Meeting Oliver felt relieving, but not the same as meeting Ewan. Something in him calls to me, and the longer this dinner goes on, the more worried I am that the Forresters were right. That the human half of me will mess up any chance I have at being a real mate.

I take a sip of my water while Ewan watches me.

"Your paperwork mentioned your parents. I'm sorry, Ivy."

I shake my head, waving him off. "It's fine. I was young with my father."

That part isn't a lie. I was young when it happened. But that doesn't mean I wasn't aware of what they did to my dad. Murdering him in order to force my mother to have more children for the wolves of our community. Little did they know she wouldn't be able to carry any of them. And little did they know it would force her into a deep, horrid depression where she was willing to let her only child be physically abused by those very wolves for years. Only to sell her off to the highest bidder once she proved to be too much of a mutt for any sort of use.

"Still," he whispers. "Losing anyone you love leaves a mark."

Ewan's eyes are glassy, and I give him a tight-lipped smile. "Yes."

"Well," Oliver interrupts. "I'm sure you're exhausted after today. I know I am." He pushes back from his seat and picks up his dishes. "I'm hoping we can have more time to get to know one another after I come back from work tomorrow, but Ewan will be here."

Ewan nods to me and continues to eat his dinner quietly. I glance down at my bowl of stir-fry and dig around for a pea pod, popping it into my mouth as Oliver returns from the kitchen and places a chaste kiss to the top of my head. "Get some rest, sweet girl."

His whisper sends a shiver down my spine, but it's not entirely pleasurable. I'm guessing the last six months have made it impossible for any touch from a man to feel pleasant.

Ewan is silent as Oliver takes his leave and treks up the stairs. But the moment the door at the end of the hall clicks shut, he looks back up at me.

"You don't eat meat?"

I swallow my nausea at the memory before shaking my head. "No. Bad experience."

He tilts his head, sitting back in his seat and looking far more relaxed than he did throughout the entire dinner. "Why didn't you tell Oliver?"

After showing me around the house, Oliver had offered to make dinner for us while Ewan was locked up in his studio finishing a painting. He asked if I liked stir-fry, and I immediately answered yes. I haven't been asked what I wanted to eat or what I like since my dad passed away. Even if living with my mother wasn't as bad as the Forresters, it was still bad.

And when I snapped... well, she had it coming.

I take a deep breath and blow it out, determined not to fuck this up.

"I just didn't feel like upsetting him," I say, keeping it truthful but also avoiding giving this stranger too much information, even though my heart is telling me it's safe to talk to him.

I still don't know him. Ewan may be my mate, but the blood work isn't there to prove it, so the feeling in my gut could be nothing more than nerves and discomfort at being in this new place.

He narrows his eyes and runs his tongue over his teeth. My eyes track the movement without even trying, and I feel a pulse vibrate through my entire body.

Well.

What the actual fuck is that?

Ewan's nostrils flare, and he shakes his head. "Oliver was right, you should get some rest."

He grabs my bowl and cleans up both of our plates. I don't follow him into the kitchen, but wait just outside until he comes out. Ewan brushes by me on the way toward the stairs, and I hesitate, every hair on my body standing at attention from the brief physical touch.

He pauses as he gets to the first stair and lets out an audible sigh. "Come on," he says, reaching a hand out behind him.

I'm not entirely sure what comes over me, but the pull I feel to him seems to drag me in, and I take his hand, trekking up the hardwood stairs as quietly as possible behind him. It's odd and sort of surreal to be in this massive home—one that is far bigger than anywhere I've lived before—and to know that this could be my new home. Or rather, it *is* my new home.

I can't help the smile that takes over my face at that thought.

A real home.

Chapter Five
Ivy

A real home plagued with the same horrid nightmares of my previous residence.

Tossing off the covers, I climb out of the queen-sized bed and tug at my T-shirt. It's soaked in sweat, and I sigh as I peel it off and replace it with one of the only sports bras I have in my measly bag.

Oliver didn't say much about my belongings other than asking if I had more back home, and when I responded that I didn't, he said he would give me some money this week. I feel like a low-life letting him pay for me, but I also don't have much of a choice unless I want to continue wearing the same few pairs of black leggings and handful of shirts until I manage to find somewhere to hire me. My sleep shorts don't seem to be as sweaty, which is relieving since I only have the one pair.

I glance over at the bed, which was so nicely made up when I got here, and notice the disarray of sheets and blankets—all twisted up with the fitted sheet ripped entirely off the side I was sleeping on. It's only three in the morning, but I resign myself to the likelihood that I won't be getting any more rest tonight and decide to go get some water.

Anywhere between one to three was usually when Garrett would come get me. Whenever he rolled in for the evening with his fuck of the week so he could make me watch and sit in for his ash tray. The nightmares started long before I moved in with the Forresters, and most nights I would be woken from them by one of the brothers. But if not, I would be up for the day once it happened.

I assume it will take some time for those to go away.

The door is quiet as I slip from my room and pad down the hallway and stairs to the kitchen. I'm grateful Oliver and Ewan live in a newer home. Less creaking that way.

I pour myself a glass of water and catch a glimpse of my reflection in the kitchen window as I walk past. I look pretty terrible right now. My blonde hair hangs in stringy pieces around my face, tangled from all the sweat, and all the light is gone from my icy blue eyes. Leaving behind circles akin to pits of despair. My cheeks were a lot rounder a year ago, but stress has done a number on me, and I'm positive I look closer to thirty-five than twenty-two.

Letting out a long sigh, I take a sip of my water and walk out to the living room, quietly examining the space as I go. It's a weird feeling, but instead of coming off like a well put together home where the owners are neat and tidy, it just feels carefully curated. Like someone was going for that look and wanted the home to be as perfect as possible. Not a picture is out of place on the wall by even an inch, the candles all look brand new, like they've never been lit, and each knickknack and book on the shelves has a very light coating of dust as if no one has ever touched them aside from an occasional cleaning.

I run my finger across the top of one, picking up a fine layer of gray as I do before sifting it between my fingers.

"Have you read that?"

The voice startles me, and I jump, letting go of my glass and instantly dropping into a ball on the ground.

Ewan is on me in a second, snatching the glass out of the air before it hits the wood and wrapping me up in his embrace. He's warm and smells like leather and paint, a drastic difference from the scent I was expecting—tobacco, stale liquor, and burning flesh.

"Shit, Ivy," he whispers, holding onto me tight as he sets my glass on the ground. Ewan drops his entire body down to the floor, enveloping me and holding me tight.

Something in my body still wants to run, to hide, but another part —one that seems to be growing stronger by the moment—wants to stay. To let him hold me and keep me safe. The whimper that falls from my lips when he holds me close is muffled against his bare chest, and I breathe him in, feeling my heart rate instantly start to settle with his scent.

"Breathe with me," he says quietly, and I do, feeling the rising and falling of his chest and recognizing that Garrett isn't here. Acton isn't here.

It takes a while of breathing before I notice that my entire body has relaxed in his lap and that Ewan is rocking me slightly, side to side. I sit up, not fully removing myself from his embrace, and glance up at the man I've just met.

"I—I'm sorry," I state, but Ewan shakes his head.

"Ivy, do not apologize for anything. I may not know exactly what happened to you, but I know where you came from, and I know that how you just reacted means you've been through something horrible. Not to mention, I can see the scars on your back."

My fingers make their way to my lower back, realizing that in my sports bra, the letters would be on full display. And despite the embarrassment and shame that come bubbling up to the surface, I nod my head, listening to Ewan.

"It was the men I lived with before."

He gives me a somber smile. "I figured. You said your parents were dead." He brings his hand over mine against the scars on my back and traces a finger lightly over them. "Is this why?"

I nod again. "Old-world packs don't approve of non-shifter matings. And they especially don't approve of any child who isn't purebred. My dad was killed because of it."

"I understand," he replies softly. "Sometimes the people who love us leave us, and the ones that are left behind are monsters."

"If you only knew," I whisper.

He sighs. "You're not there anymore, and you're not going back there."

I stare at him while he speaks, feeling an overwhelming sense of calm wash over me, even though something about his words makes me question what he's been through and if he would feel the same way if he knew the things I've done.

"Thank you," I respond, tilting my head to place my lips against his in a gentle kiss.

A jolt of excitement fires through me when our lips meet, and I instantly rip my head back, noting the smirk on Ewan's face.

"What was that?" I ask, bringing a finger to my bottom lip and rubbing away the staticky feeling of electricity.

"That, my love, was a mating bond."

Chapter Six
Ivy

"You will if you want her to live. This is time sensitive."

I pause, forcing myself to keep breathing in and out through my nose and willing my eyes to stay clamped shut. The voice doesn't belong to Hurst or the others, and it takes a moment for me to register that there's a body next to me. I focus on the smell and remember I came up to Ewan's room with him after the scare earlier this morning. I never thought I would fall back asleep, but my body calmed in his presence, and here I am, still curled up next to him in his bed.

Ewan tenses beside me, and his palm finds its way to my hip, rubbing gentle circles against my skin as he speaks, but I still don't dare move. The words out of Oliver's mouth are not what I was expecting from my mate. A cold sweat starts to break out across my forehead, but I stay still, not wanting to brush it away. Ewan's hand continues to move, seeming to sense the discomfort in my body.

"You have no idea when she'll go into a heat."

Oliver's voice is low and quiet when he responds. "You can smell her as much as I can, and you know it's coming soon. You push her until she's in one. Use *him* if you have to. You have a week or I'm getting rid of her and starting fresh."

Ewan's voice is calm when he speaks again. "How do you plan to do that? You already killed one of my mates and *he* is rotting away in your basement—this is the only way you continue your line. She can't take your knot if she's not in a heat, and *you* certainly can't put her into one."

"Fuck you!" Oliver seethes, my body tensing with his tone. "I'm going to work. Get your head on straight and don't fuck this up."

He must have noticed my body moving because after Oliver storms out of the room, I hear the heavy sigh that comes out of Ewan. "You can stop pretending. He's gone."

I scramble away from Ewan, sitting upright against the headboard and heaving breath into my lungs. "What the fuck was that? Is he sending me back? What did I do?"

I know my voice sounds incredibly frantic, but that's exactly how I feel.

Ewan's brows furrow, and he scoots his body so he's sitting against the headboard next to me. He stretches out a hand and hesitates. "Can I touch you?"

I nod, and he slips his arm around my shoulders, tucking me in close.

"He's not sending you back, and based on your reaction, I'm not sure I want to know what happened to you there. Who were you living with?"

"The Forrester pack," I reply, glancing up at him.

Ewan's jaw tenses, and he shakes his head. "Alright, we can deal with them later. First, we need to manage Oliver."

"What was that?" I ask, my body still shivering from the terror that ripped through me when he started talking about killing me.

It's funny—I wanted to die every day for the last few months, but now the thought of it scares the shit out of me. Or maybe it's less about dying and more the fear of not dying. Of being stuck in that house for the rest of my life, going through a heat and being tied to them for all eternity.

Ewan swallows. "It's a lot, but I need you to trust me, Ivy. I know we only just met, but you feel it, don't you?"

I chew on my bottom lip but give him a small nod of my head. "Yes, I feel it. With you, but not with Oliver."

He smiles and instantly apologizes. "I'm sorry. I know I shouldn't be happy right now, but I'm so damn glad he found you—even if the circumstances are complete and utter shit."

Ewan leans in and brushes his lips across mine, giving me a soft and quick kiss.

"That man isn't your mate. That's why you didn't feel anything toward him and never will. He's not actually Oliver."

"Wh—what?" I ask, my brows pinching together, my face certainly betraying my clear shock at this revelation.

Ewan rubs a hand over his face, scratching the stubble he has growing on his chin and cheeks. I'm not sure if he always has it or not, but he's beautiful with it. "Can we go downstairs and make some coffee? You thrashed around a lot last night, and it took a bit for me to fall asleep once you settled down."

"Oh—ummm—I'm so sorry. I did—"

"Stop," Ewan states, holding up a hand. "I'm not upset about it. I just have a lot to tell you, and it would be easier with coffee."

* * *

Once we get downstairs and we each have a delightful vanilla latte in front of us, Ewan starts to unpack the reality of my future. And it's bleak as fuck.

"Drake Bergman. That's who you met at the bank, and that's who is pretending to be Oliver. They were twins, and when the two of them sent their blood in, Drake was informed his only mate had passed in a car accident the year prior. Instead of moving on from the tragedy, he got angry. And even angrier when his brother was told he had at least two mates. Florian and myself. That rage he felt grew more and more as the next few years passed and the three of us became closer, purchasing this house and moving in together, discussing how we could start a family. We had no idea there was another mate, that you even existed."

"What happened?" I question.

Ewan swallows roughly. "I'm not entirely sure, but some altercation, and Drake killed Oliver before taking up as him."

"He killed his own brother?" I ask, pausing with the coffee mug resting against my lower lip.

Ewan nods, and tears twinkle in the corner of his eyes.

"When? And what about Florian?"

"It was a year ago now. A little over that. It took some time before he was willing to let me be around other people, but Florian has a much shorter temper than me, and Drake has never trusted him."

"Florian is alive?" I state, not positive how my body can handle more shock or information at this point.

He nods again.

"This... this is all so much. What does he want with me?"

Ewan's face turns somber. "He wants children, and for some reason he won't settle for another route. Drake knows that if I can get you to go into heat, you'll be able to take a knot from any of us, and he fully plans for it to be him. It's the only reason he's kept Florian and me alive. He's aware he may need both your mates for it to happen."

Fucking hell.

My breathing becomes a bit more rapid, and Ewan immediately places his mug down, coming around the kitchen island to wrap his arms around me. No matter how much the Forresters fucked me up, Ewan's touch feels immediately different. My heart rate regulates instantly, and when his breath tickles across my neck, my nipples peak and I feel a pulsing between my legs.

"Shit," I breathe as Ewan drags his nose along my neck.

"Fuck," he groans, pressing himself against my back. "This isn't a good time for you to start."

"Start what?" I ask, feeling his cock hardening against my ass.

"A heat. Have you had one yet? Usually wolves will go through them with their mates, but someone your age has typically had a few already."

I shake my head. "I'm not a full wolf. I'm a mutt. I can't shift, and I don't have heats."

Ewan's hand travels to my waistband, but he pauses, waiting for confirmation. Aside from the one young wolf back in my old town who was willing to slum it with a mutt, I haven't found anyone else willing. And despite still trying to process all the mind-bending information he just dropped on me, I lean my body into him, allowing Ewan to slip his fingers past my waistband.

They trail over my hip and dip lower, cupping over my pussy before he slips them between my legs. I suck in a breath, and Ewan groans again.

"Fuck, Ivy. You're drenched in slick. You're going through a heat soon, whether you like it or not."

As much as I want him to continue, Ewan removes his hands and grabs both my coffee and his before heading back toward the stairs.

"Are you sure? I've never gone through one, even with the Forrester pack."

"They weren't your pack. They weren't your mates. Your body knows you're with us now, and we're going to need to adapt."

I follow behind him at a clipped pace, trying my best to ignore how painful the pulsing between my legs is getting.

"Where are we going?"

Ewan casts me a glance over his shoulder, and the corner of his mouth turns up in a smirk. "I need you to trust me, Ivy. I know this is all happening fast and you don't know me, but you're going to need me. And soon."

I chew my bottom lip again, feeling exactly what he's saying. My body needs him, even if my brain is warring with that fact. "Alright. Where are we going?"

"To meet Florian."

Chapter Seven
Ivy

There's a shuffling noise as we descend the stairs, and once at the bottom, Ewan hits a light switch, throwing the dark basement into a low amber light.

"Flor?" he calls out into the space, and there's a groaning sound from the corner of the room. "Florian, get the fuck up!"

The basement is set up as a nice little apartment with a bed on one side and a small living room and bathroom on the other side. The blankets on the bed shift, but no one comes out from under them. Instead a grumbled, gruff voice calls out, "Go away!"

Ewan looks at me and shakes his head. "Flor is stronger than either myself or Drake. He keeps us from shifting, but Florian has still gone after him more than once. The last time, Drake told him that if he does it again, he'll kill me, and that finally got his attention. Since then, he's been refusing to speak to either of us, trying to shut me out, and the other day he stopped eating. I'm genuinely hoping you can help."

I swallow, trying to take it all in. I thought being with the Forresters was bad, but little did I know the home I would come to would be a veritable hell on earth for my mates.

Ewan walks toward the bed, setting his coffee down on the bedside table before taking mine and doing the same. "May I?" he asks, before settling himself behind me like he did upstairs.

He's a good deal taller than me, and I notice the same as before—my body regulates, my heart rate becoming slow and steady, my breathing less rapid.

"Florian, Drake found our other mate," Ewan calls out from behind me as he sets his chin on my shoulder, and when he drags his nose up my neck, my body reacts just like upstairs.

My nipples tighten as he whispers in my ear, "Do you want this?"

I nod, leaning back against him again. "Yes," I reply, suddenly overwhelmed with his scent and the pulsing throughout my entire body.

The bed shifts again as Ewan finds the waistband of my shorts. I'm hyper aware that I'm still in the sports bra and sleep shorts, in a room with a man I just met and one I've never met. But none of it seems to matter to me in this moment. I just want Ewan to give me what I need.

His fingers slip inside my shorts and travel straight to my pussy, but this time, when he slides them between my legs, I automatically open for him, shifting my stance and leaning more of my body weight against him.

"That's it," he croons, kissing my neck. "I know what you need. Let me help you."

Never in my life did I think I would let a man touch me like this again. Especially not after my treatment with the Forresters, but something is just different with Ewan. Something feels right.

My body is alive like it never has been before, sparks shooting through my system as he finds my clit and rubs soft circles around it. A soft moan escapes my lips, and I reach one of my hands up, snaking it around his neck and pulling him in closer.

Ewan nips at my ear and rubs faster. "Just a little something to take the edge off," he tells me. "You'll be able to focus after. I promise."

My brain has been a jumbled mess this entire morning, and I hope he's right. I don't feel like myself. I feel like I can't concentrate on anything, that all these important details about my current circumstances are being dropped on me, but they slip away in an instant. And I know I should be taking them in, putting together the pieces of a puzzle, and planning my way out, but all I can think about is Ewan and his hands on my body.

He reaches his other hand up, cupping my left breast through the fabric, and brushes his palm over my nipple. It aches, but he keeps going, lightly twisting and playing with it, all the while, his cock growing harder against me. I grind back, and Ewan nips my ear again.

"Not yet, Ivy," he tells me, making me whine in response. "Florian, can you hear her?"

The grunt from under the blankets seems to be a bit less muffled, and I wonder if he's listening. But before I can pay too much attention to it, Ewan rubs me harder, playing with my nipple and swirling his fingers faster against my clit.

Pleasure ripples through my body, causing my legs to spasm and my pussy to clench as my orgasm hits me. I cry out, arching my back, my thighs trembling as Ewan continues, not letting up against my over-sensitized clit.

"Fuck!" I scream as a massive man sits up in the bed in front of me, throwing off the blankets.

His nostrils flare as Ewan pulls his hand from my shorts, covered in my release, and stretches it out toward the man.

Florian rises from the bed, broad chest on full display, a pair of old flannel sweatpants hanging low on his hips.

"What the fuck?" he asks, his voice croaking when he speaks. "Ewan, what are you doing? Who is this?"

Ewan continues to hold me, keeping his hand outstretched and using the other to shimmy my shorts down. "Why don't you tell me?" he asks, as Florian's nostrils flare even more when he leans into Ewan's hand. "Do you still feel needy, Ivy?"

I nod my head, my gaze dropping to Florian's waist as his erection starts to press through.

Between that sight and Ewan behind me, I can't think of anything other than getting fucked by these two men. I step out of my shorts, and Ewan lets go of me, coming around front and blocking my view of Florian. He makes direct eye contact with me and grasps the band around the base of my bra. I lift my arms as he slides it off before dropping his own pants.

His knot is already swelling, and I find myself licking my lips just at the sight.

"You're in charge, Ivy. You're my mate, and I'm here to serve you however you need."

That surprises me, despite my current state, and I tilt my head. "What do you mean?"

Ewan takes a few steps back before lying on the bed behind him, all while Florian watches us intently. His cock is standing nearly straight up, and my body starts to ache even more.

"I mean, you've been around wolves before—men who would hurt you. That's not us, and it never will be. Find your voice and find your wolf, Ivy. And take what you need."

Something deep inside of me seems to come to life with those words, and I stalk toward him, not missing how Florian reaches out his fingers to trail them against my arm as I pass. His touch sends a fresh jolt of desire through me, and I moan at the feeling, unable to help myself as I scramble up on the bed and on top of Ewan.

He stares up at me, those hazel eyes deepening to a dark golden green. And I'm not sure what the fuck comes over me, but I angle myself over him, widening my hips and lowering myself down onto his throbbing cock.

Ewan's mouth opens wide, and I cry out as I take all of him, all the way down to the top of his knot.

"Fucking hell," he breathes, pausing with his hands on my hips for a moment before I start to move.

Everything in me is vibrating, chasing some high that only he can give me. I place my hands on his chest and bounce up and down, reveling in the feel of his cock sliding deeper and deeper inside of me. The sensation of his knot rubbing up against me and pressing on my walls, trying to get all the way into me.

"Gods," Florian whispers from behind me. "She's going into heat."

"She is," Ewan replies, smiling up at me. "And we're going to get her through it."

"What about Drake?" he asks, and my brain seems to catch up, recognizing that I'm in a murderer's house but fucking someone in the basement instead of doing something about it.

"Not now, Florian," Ewan demands before pressing my hips down farther. "Ivy, just focus on me. You'll feel better after."

Listening, I grind down on him, and he groans. "Fuck, that's it. Just like that."

Florian hisses behind me, but I try my best to ignore him, even though I want desperately to reach out to him. His scent permeates my nostrils, a sweeter smell than Ewan. More like musk and vanilla mixed with fresh grass. It's intoxicating, and I close my eyes, riding Ewan and reveling in it.

"Are you ready, Ivy?" Ewan asks, and when I open my eyes again, his face is tense, his orgasm building.

"Yes," I answer, more sure of myself and my current circumstance than I have been in a long time.

Ewan holds my hips tight and juts up into me, making my climax come shattering down around me. I scream out, and he does the same, his knot lodging inside of me and rubbing up against my G-spot, causing a second orgasm to rocket through me right on the heels of the first. Something warm shoots all over my back when I collapse on top of Ewan, and Florian's hands begin rubbing his cum into my skin.

"Shhhh," Ewan whispers, calming me while he kisses my cheek. "You'll feel so much better soon," he promises, petting my hair as I drift off on top of him, the feel of Florian massaging my back relaxing me into oblivion.

Chapter Eight
Ivy

My head is fuzzy and filled with pressure when I wake up, and although the ache between my legs is relieved, it's been replaced by one hell of a throbbing. It's not necessarily painful, but I feel like I've been stretched to my limit, and I suppose I have.

I stretch, and my fingers prick with an odd sensation. I suck in a breath when I open my eyes and glance down.

Claws.

The moment I glimpse them, they shoot right back into my fingers, and I shake my head, convinced I'm seeing things. I've never shifted. I can't shift.

I'm not a real wolf.

"She's waking up," Florian states, and the mattress beside me sinks with the weight of the two men.

"Ivy," Ewan breathes, placing his hands to cup my cheeks. "Are you alright?"

I nod, noticing Florian staring at me. His eyes are this deep brownish gold, and his hair is the same shade, falling down in soft waves around his shoulders.

He's beautiful. They both are.

"I'm fine," I promise, giving him a small smile. "A little sore, but I'll be okay. How long was I out? Is Oli—I mean, Drake home yet?"

Florian winces when I start to say Oliver, and my stomach tightens in a knot, hating that I caused him any pain.

"He's not here yet, but Flor and I have been discussing a plan of action for when he returns."

"A plan?" I question, sitting all the way up in the bed. "What kind of plan? Can't we just leave?"

"You mean run away?" Florian asks, his brows furrowing in clear frustration. "This is our fucking home. This is Olly's home. We aren't going anywhere."

Ewan gives me a somber glance. "He's right. We made a promise to one another that we would stay here. That we would get rid of him eventually, even if it killed us."

Ewan reaches out and grasps Florian's hand, and the man leans in, giving him a kiss. It's tender and makes my heart swell. It's clear there's a lot of love between the two of them, and I know I should feel awkward being here in the middle of it, but I don't. Instead, I feel at home.

"Alright. I can understand that," I respond. "Then how do we get rid of him?"

"He's going to smell that you're going into heat the moment he walks through those doors," Florian replies with a shake of his head. "And he's going to want to fuck you." The last part comes out more like a growl, and Ewan squeezes his hand.

"But we won't let that happen. Drake should bring Florian up to make sure it happens, and that's when we'll kill him."

"K—kill him?" I sputter. "You can't kill him. *We* can't kill him."

"Yes, we fucking can," Florian states. "He murdered Olly, and he deserves to die. He's only keeping the two of us alive in order to find you and breed you. Gods, Ivy! Don't you get it?"

His voice is raised, and I instantly cower back from the hulking man, despite my warmer feelings toward him before.

"Shit, Flor!" Ewan curses, hurling himself onto the bed and scooping me up into his arms. "She's been through a lot. More than we have."

"Fuck! I'm sorry," Florian pleads, kneeling in front of the bed. "I'm so sorry, Ivy. I didn't know." He runs his hands through his hair, dragging them down his face while tears form in the corner of his eyes. "I just don't know how to keep on going if he's not dead. I just... I just need this."

I know what he means... more than he realizes.

Before I know it, I'm crawling out of Ewan's arms and grabbing Florian's head before cradling it in my lap. I run my hand through his hair, reveling in the soft feel as he relaxes beneath me.

"We don't know anything about one another," I whisper, before taking a shuddering breath. "But I know. I understand."

"I hate to break this up," Ewan interrupts, glancing at the watch on his hand. "But Drake should be home in an hour. Florian, you should probably stay down here since he hasn't let you up. I'll call and check in about it."

Florian nods and places a soft kiss on my thigh before standing up. "Fill the room," he instructs, and Ewan gives him a dip of his head in acknowledgment. "And let me know when it's safe."

I follow Ewan as he leads me out of the room and back up the stairs, not able to help myself from looking back at Florian repeatedly. He remains kneeling next to the bed, his golden-brown gaze trailing me as I go.

My heart aches for him as we make it upstairs and Ewan starts speaking to me about what to expect.

"I know this is a lot to process, but we need to move quickly. You'll have to act like you're fully in heat, even though you're not. What happened downstairs? That needs to happen again, except with both Florian and me. Are you alright with that?"

"You mean I need to have sex with both of you?" My voice is higher pitched than I anticipate, and my embarrassment at the thought is obvious.

Ewan's upper lip tilts in an adorable smile at my reaction while we walk toward his bedroom. "We have to make this believable for him, Ivy. It's the only way Drake is going to get close enough to us that we can take him down."

When we walk into Ewan's room, he begins rustling around the edges of his mattress, pulling and tugging at straps and loops, adjusting and moving to the next corner.

"Why can't you shift and kill him? Is he that much stronger than you?"

Ewan glances up at me, and rage fills his eyes. "He's not stronger than me at all. And he's absolutely not stronger than Florian. Flor was clearly the alpha of our trio before Olly was killed."

"Then why haven't you killed him already?" I question, anxiety getting the better of me as I begin to pace his room, watching as he lays out a restraint system on the bed.

I don't want to do this again. I don't even know if I can.

Ewan moves to the closet, removing a floor board before pulling out a variety of different blades. He places one under the pillow, another under the mattress at each corner, and one squeezed between two books on the shelf behind his bed, then keeps moving.

"In the beginning, I was too out of it. Drake had me committed when I broke down at work after finding Olly. I told them all Drake did it, but no one believed me. And when he showed up at my job to collect me—dressed like my mate, acting like my mate—they all believed him and not me. I was committed for a few weeks, fed a slew of medications to get me to calm down, and Drake visited me. Let me know I needed to get it together and get on board or he would keep me there."

"Gods, Ewan," I reply quietly. "I'm so sorry."

He waves it off. "I'm past it now, but it's been a long journey to get here. Florian wasn't so easy to subdue, but I just knew if I waited it out, if I played the long game, it would pay off eventually. And it has."

I understand his not wanting to discuss it too much right now, it's not as if we have a ton of time to get into our histories. And I'm hiding enough with mine.

"The restraints?" I question, chewing on my bottom lip, hating the idea of being held down in any way.

Ewan cringes and shakes his head. "There's no way around it. He's going to want you under control in case you shift."

"I—I can't shift," I reply.

Ewan shrugs. "That makes two of us."

"What do you mean?" I ask, incredulous. "Are you a mutt? You're not a full wolf either?"

His face falls a little. "No, I'm a full wolf. I've shifted plenty in the past, but Florian and I have implants to keep us from shifting. Mine was set when I was in the hospital, and I'm not sure how or when he got to Flor, but we both have them. If we even try to shift, Drake can hit us with a shock that will knock us out." I go to open my mouth, but Ewan shakes his head. "Whatever you're going to say, I guarantee we've tried it. He always seems to know what we are doing or planning. Each time we've attempted any sort of coup against him, he's knocked us out for hours."

My stomach sinks.

"Ewan?" I ask as he finishes hiding all of his blades.

He pauses and looks up at me before letting out a massive sigh. "I know. It's a lot."

"Can we really do this? You can't shift, and neither can I. And you're strapping me down. How are we supposed to make this work?" The more I speak, the more flustered I become, and Ewan stands from his place on the floor, coming to wrap his arms around me.

"Are you afraid of hurting someone?" he asks, and I nod, terrified to tell him the truth. "You grew up with old-world wolves, you haven't been in a pack fight or anything before?"

I chew on my lip.

"I know you've just met me, and I know you have no reason to trust me, but close your eyes for me for a moment, Ivy. Just breathe with me."

I do as he says, letting him hold me close and laying my head on his chest.

"I had never loved someone as much as I loved Olly, but then I met Florian, and things got so much better. I never thought I could love again after Olly died, but then I met you. I can't explain it, but I know, deep down, that this is how things are meant to be. The three of us are mates, and we are destined to go on and live our lives beyond this mess Drake has made."

I breathe in and out, tears welling in my eyes.

"I know it's a lot to ask of you, but please, Ivy. Please do this for us. Please do this for Olly. You never got a chance to meet him, but he would have loved you so damn much, just like I already do. You're a piece of me, part of my soul, and we need you now just as much as you need us."

Pulling back from his chest, I wipe a tear away and nod, staring at my mate. "Alright, Ewan. I'll do it."

Chapter Nine
Ivy

I tug at the restraints against my wrists, trying to keep my wits about me as the force of my impending heat takes over.

Ewan assured me he would start things before Drake came home to keep me sane, to ensure I was already fucking him when the murderer walked in. I may not know a ton about heats yet, but I am fully aware of what I felt earlier, and being in that state of mind is not good for me right now. Not when I have people counting on me. So if it means I need to have an orgasm in front of the man who killed my other mate in cold blood? So be it.

I arch my back as Ewan drags his tongue over my nipple, making it pebble in response.

"Don't get yourself too worked up," Florian reminds him, sitting in the chair in the corner of the room.

"Speak for yourself," Ewan remarks with a grin, glancing back at Florian who is already rock hard just watching us.

After speaking to Drake on the phone and informing him of the reaction I'd been having to the men, he allowed Florian to leave the basement and tend to me in Ewan's room. But Drake was very clear—

neither of them were allowed to fuck me or let themselves get carried away before he got here. Instead, they were to get me ready and primed for him, make it so that I am aching and needy, begging him to give me his knot.

Those were his exact words.

Fucking prick.

I'm finding anger is coming a lot quicker the more time I spend with these wolves. Anger that I haven't felt in a while. Anger at the people who raised me to be this meek girl, fury at the men who hurt me and shamed me into staying that way, and rage at the man who killed someone I was meant to love before I ever had the chance.

"Ivy?" Florian asks as Ewan trails his tongue down my abdomen and inches closer to my pussy.

It pulses in time with my fast-beating heart, and I stare over into his eyes.

"He's going to be here any minute. Are you ready?"

"More than ready," I pant when Ewan's tongue flicks across my clit, sending an electric sensation through my entire body. "More," I breathe as he continues licking and sucking.

The feeling is so intense, like I'm turning into a live wire. But it's not enough. My body is craving more. So much more.

I cry out when he sucks hard on me, and Florian gets up from his seat, coming to stand next to where I'm restrained on the bed. "We can give you more. What do you want, love?"

Ewan shakes his head. "You're playing with fire," he tells Florian who just grins in response.

"Might as well go out with a bang," Florian declares as he unbuttons his pants, dropping them and letting his massive cock spring free.

"Oh shit," I breathe, aware that I feel like someone else has possessed my body as I lick my lips, waiting for him to come closer.

Florian's grin widens. "Open up, love."

As he slides his cock between my lips, Ewan sucks on me, lathing his tongue over my clit and slipping two fingers inside of me. He curls them, making me arch my back. Florian pushes himself farther down my throat, and I hear the gurgle that comes out of me. He reaches out and flicks his fingers over my nipples while Ewan speeds up, thrusting his fingers in and out with force while he sucks harder. I hollow my cheeks around Florian, and he curses just as waves of pleasure crash over me.

I try to cry out, but Florian grabs my head, keeping me in place as he continues to thrust his hips forward. My orgasm just keeps coming, flooding my system and making every single fiber of my being ache for more. Gagging on Florian, I swallow as best I can around him, and my eyes roll back as Ewan breeches my entrance, pushing his engorged cock inside of me.

"Shit, Ewan," Florian gasps. "You said you weren't going to fuck her yet."

Glancing over, I see Ewan grinning down at me. "I couldn't help myself. You're fucking gorgeous like this, Ivy. Stuffed full of both of us."

Something in his words sets me off even more, and I suck harder on Florian while Ewan fucks me slowly. His knot rubs up against me, causing a second orgasm to flow through me, slower and not as intense as the last one, but no less fantastic.

"Oh, gods!" Florian cries out as warmth spreads through my mouth, and I swallow as quickly as I can, gulping down his sweet release. "That's it, baby," he coos, even as cum drips from the corners of my mouth.

"What the fuck do you think you're doing?"

The voice that echoes through the room sends a chill through my entire body, and everyone around me stills. Ewan stops thrusting inside of me, but doesn't pull out, and Florian's cock slides from my mouth as I turn my head to face him.

My head is still foggy, filled with the scent of my mates around me, and my brain is warring with me to keep going, my hips lifting slightly despite the danger present in the room. Ewan glances back at me when I lift my hips and winks quickly before flicking his gaze back to Drake. I take the cue, my brain buzzing with pleasure, but still with it enough to remember what Ewan told me.

I moan, letting the sound fall from my lips and not bothering to hide the fact that my cheeks are streaked in Florian's cum. Bucking my hips up to Ewan, he slowly thrusts again, not breaking eye contact with Drake. I close my eyes and hum in pleasure, trying to keep my wits about me.

"Stop!" Drake yells, but Ewan continues.

"I can't," Ewan tells him. "She's so needy, can't you smell it on her?"

"Of course I can!" he snaps back. "Florian, back away from Ivy."

The mattress dips beneath me, and I'm aware of the blades stuck between the mattress and box spring. Ewan presses a finger to my clit, and my eyes snap back open.

"Fuck," I breathe, focusing on his eyes as they lock on me.

He presses harder circles and slams into me, pushing his knot right against me before rotating his hips. His cock is deep inside of me, but I'm trying to focus on Drake stalking across the room behind Ewan and going straight for Florian. I know Ewan is attempting to make me come as much as possible so I can maintain concentration and not be overwhelmed by the impending heat, but it's hard as shit to get my body to play along. It's all part of the plan, and I'm the distraction for Drake. So far, it seems to be working because he can't seem to keep his eyes off of me as he pauses a few feet from Florian.

"You didn't want to fuck her?" he asks, throwing me off a bit, and I let my gaze flick between their interaction and Ewan. "You're her mate too, aren't you? You didn't want to go against my orders?"

"I—I was trying not to," Florian admits.

"Mmmm," Drake replies, stuffing his hands into his pockets.

Ewan panics as he seems to notice the discomfort in Florian and the confusion playing out across his expression.

"Fuck!" I scream, ecstasy washing over me once more as Ewan pinches my clit. "Fuck me!"

Florian angles his body toward Drake as surges of pleasure continue to race through my body and bloodstream. Just as quickly as he darts forward, Florian's body goes crashing to the floor, jerking as shockwaves ripple through him. The knife in his hand clatters to the hardwood floor, and Ewan jumps back, sliding out of me with another blade held in his hand.

His claws are peeking through, and I recognize that he was likely readying himself to shift when Drake came into the room. Drake doesn't have time to get the other shock button and kneels quickly, trying to evade Ewan when he lunges for him and grabs the knife Florian dropped.

Halfway into his lunge at Drake, Ewan grunts and slumps to the ground in front of him, Florian's body lying still and lifeless on the ground behind them.

"No!" I scream, fear coursing through my veins and swiftly replacing the pleasure I was feeling just moments before. "No, no, no," I repeat, my screams fading to pleading as Drake tilts his head to examine me.

He stands, not bothering to pull out the blade he'd embedded in Ewan, and stalks toward me.

I try my hardest to pull away, but the restraints have me stuck tightly in place. "Please," I beg, while Drake grabs my ankles, streaking them in Ewan's blood.

"Ah, little pup," he croons. "You picked the wrong side. The time for begging was before you aligned yourself with those two."

"Wh—what do you mean?" I ask, feigning ignorance. "You're my mates."

Ewan moves on the ground behind Drake, slowly pulling himself toward the wall. He's silent as he moves, and Drake appears to be unaware, so I keep my gaze trained on him.

He stares down at me, his eyes narrowing behind his glasses and turning a dark shade that's utterly terrifying. Drake makes a tutting noise and unbuckles his belt. "No sense in keeping up pretenses when one of your mates is down for the count and one is bleeding out on the floor. I heard your entire plan." Drake presses his lips together, giving me a condescending look. "I thought you would have known better... mutt."

Chapter Ten
Ivy

Something in me ignites when he says that, and there's a burning that radiates through my entire body, lighting every vein aflame.

"What did you call me?"

Drake's face breaks into a sinister smile as he pulls his belt off, dropping it to the floor and moving to unbutton his jeans. Ewan grunts as he pulls the knife from his abdomen and throws himself at Drake, but the man is quick on his feet. He kicks back, catching Ewan under the chin with his boot and sending my mate reeling backward onto the wood.

It's clear, with a quick glance, that neither Ewan nor Florian are coming to my rescue. That the man in front of me is no different than the Forresters. That no one has ever saved me, and that it isn't going to happen right now.

My fate has been set in stone since day one.

Mutt.

Worthless.

Garbage.

Shame starts to trickle in, shoving at that rage blazing through my system, and part of me wants to let it. To just lay here and let Drake do whatever he wants. This has always been my destiny. If it wasn't him, it would have been Hurst.

"Oh, you didn't hear me?" Drake asks, pulling his pants down and dragging his cock out of his briefs. "I called you a mutt. Dirty half-breed that you are."

I take a deep breath, my vision starting to blur and turn a nasty reddish hue.

"What? Don't like that word? It's just the truth, Ivy. You're not worth much aside from your womb. You can't shift, you can't run a hunt, you can't rule over a pack. So your best bet is to hope your mediocre genetics can produce a full-wolf offspring."

"Then why the fuck do you want me?" I ask, my teeth gritted together to hold my rage at bay.

Drake kneels on the bed in front of me, unable to keep the grin off his face. He reaches forward and swipes his fingers across my opening, gathering my glistening release on the tips and showing it to me. "You're more than ready for my knot. And to answer your question, I want you because you're domesticated."

My fingers ache, and I'm aware those claws that sprouted before are coming back. It may not be much, but I lean into that burning feeling radiating through every pore, every fiber of my being. Even if it's just claws, maybe it can help me right now.

"Domesticated?" I spit, barely able to let up on the pressure of my teeth pressing together.

Drake rolls his eyes. "Docile. Disciplined. Broken. What fucking word do you want to use, Ivy? That's what the Forrester pack told me, and it's clear as day on your face and the scars across your body. You're no feral wolf."

You're broken, Ivy. There's nothing more I can do.

My mother's words swirl in my brain. Her last words.

The look Drake gives me is one of pure and utter disgust and disdain.

My brain spins, my body vacillating between numb and excruciating pain.

"You're tame," Drake seethes.

My vision goes fully red at that statement. Memories of Hurst, Acton, and Garrett collide in some sickening nightmare with my mother. One that makes my stomach churn with nausea.

I tamed you, Ivy Allaway.

Broken.

Tame.

The muscles throughout my body ripple, causing an aching pain that won't let up. Sweat beads along my forehead, running along my temples in rivulets much faster than they should be. The anger and irritation that radiate from Drake shifts like a sudden drop in temperature, and all I smell is confusion.

"What's wrong with you?"

That pain ratchets up about a thousand notches, my spine feeling as though it's being stretched beyond what it can bear, my face cracking as if all the bones are breaking and reforming. But it's not until I glance over and see that the claws I'm sprouting are not just claws, but full-blown paws, that it registers with me.

I'm shifting.

Drake stumbles back from the bed. "Y—you can't shift! You're a mutt!"

The howl that erupts from my muzzle begs to differ, and I yank at the restraints, snapping them with ease.

I can see that Drake is about to shift, his claws pricking at his skin, his nose stretching out, and I lunge. I lunge with all the force I have in me. With all the anger I feel in this moment.

The rage.

My paws slam into Drake's chest, and we both go crashing to the ground. He's not stopping though, and I know I only have moments to get him before his shift takes over. So, I don't think. Just like that day back home.

I bend down, using my canines to tear through his jugular.

Ripping through skin as my maw sinks into his flesh, and as I yank my head back, I hear muscles tear and tendons snap while his warm blood floods my mouth, dripping from my jowls and coating my golden fur in a deep shade of burgundy.

Drake's body stills beneath me, and an overwhelming sense of exhaustion overtakes my entire being. I slump to the ground and immediately black out, hoping beyond hope that Ewan and Florian are still alive.

Chapter Eleven
Ivy

"Ivy?"

Ewan's voice travels through the fog that seems to be clouding my vision and my thoughts, and I sit up, quickly looking around. I'm still covered in Drake's blood, and his body is on the ground, lifeless.

I'm surprised to notice that I'm back on Ewan's bed and both him and Florian are awake and staring at me.

"You did it," Florian states, his face filled with relief. "You killed him."

I swallow hard, but it doesn't help. My gaze darts back to Drake, and bile rises in my throat before I bend over the side of the bed and heave. There isn't a ton in my stomach, and it doesn't take long before I'm sitting back up, my body shaking from the earlier events.

"Ivy," Ewan says softly. "I understand you must be in shock—"

"I'm not in shock," I tell him, cutting him off.

I lock eyes with Ewan, noticing the beautiful golden glow both of my mates have with their distinctly different colors of brown and green. I'm aware that what just happened has me emboldened, and I might regret this, but it's now or never.

"Drake isn't the first person I've killed."

Both men look taken aback, and Ewan shakes his head. "You've never shifted. You told me that."

I shrug. "You're right, I hadn't ever shifted until today." A smile creeps across my face at the memory of that shift, and how glorious it felt. "But that doesn't mean I haven't taken a life."

Taking a deep breath, I resign myself to the fact that I'm a monster and these men may hate me forever.

"After my father was killed, my mother was supposed to bear more pups for the pack but couldn't. She was depressed, more so than a normal depression, and she couldn't get herself out of it. She let the men she slept with abuse me, couldn't get herself out of bed to help me even if I was being dragged out of my own bed by my hair or when I was force fed meat that turned out to be my murdered father. And when I turned twenty-one? She said she was shipping me off to the Forresters, that they were coming to get me. She had sold me off because I was worthless."

Both Florian and Ewan are still staring, their mouths open wide as they listen to me. I glance down at the blood all over my body and remember the day vividly.

"I wasn't going to be sold. I snapped. And I killed her. Drove a blade right into her heart, but I was too late. The Forresters were already there, and they scooped me up anyway. It just gave them more ammunition against me. Not only was I a useless, broken mutt, I was also a murderer. A wolf who killed her own. There's no coming back from that."

"They would have told your old community?" Florian asks, his voice quiet.

I shake my head. "They already told everyone. I had nowhere to go aside from the Forresters. I was a villain back home—a true and veritable monster."

My voice cracks at the end, remembering what Garret and Acton told me. How no one back home would ever trust me or take me back in. And when I glance up at the two men beside me, my mates, I half-expect them to have left, but they're both still there—watching me.

"They isolated you," Florian states.

Ewan scoffs. "They did more than isolate her."

I cringe a little at that but try to shake it off. "I understand if this changes things—"

Ewan holds up a hand to me, effectively pausing me mid-sentence. "It doesn't change a thing, Ivy. Both Florian and I would have killed Drake if we had the chance, and we will forever be grateful that you did it."

"And neither of us are saints," Florian adds with a shrug. "When Olly died and Ewan was in the hospital, I killed anyone that looked at me the wrong way. Racked up quite the body count before Drake tranquilized me and got the chip implanted."

That shocks me a little, but Ewan nods. "We also took out Oliver's father when he stormed in here demanding that Olly leave. Said he needed to find a real mate, a woman, not just a bunch of guys to fuck around with. He came after Olly, and both Flor and I got in between. It didn't go well."

"Gods," I breathe, unable to help the giggle that comes out afterward. "We're all a little fucked up, aren't we?"

Florian grabs my hand and presses a kiss to the back. "We are, love."

"He's gone," Ewan assures me. "And that's enough for Flor and me to rest easy, but I feel like it's not for you, is it, Ivy?"

I glance up into his gorgeous hazel eyes that have a familiar and knowing look in them and shake my head. "No. No, it's not."

Chapter Twelve

Ivy

"Does it bother you to know that I have mates? Real mates that you don't have?" I ask while Ewan slides his hands down my sides and settles his thumbs in my waistband.

"Doesn't change what you are, Ivy," Hurst growls from his space on the couch across from us.

Turns out, it's handy to have been kept prisoner by an abusive man who wanted to make sure you never shifted. Florian was well aware of all the little things Drake had in the house, including drugs to sedate them, extra chips to shock them if they shifted, manacles, and much more. And my mates were more than willing to break into the Forresters' house tonight and use all of those items on them.

So now, Hurst, Acton, and Garrett are chained up in front of me, their sedation wearing off. Each one has tried to shift and been met with the reality that Ewan embedded a chip in the back of their necks.

And, to no one's surprise, none of the men are very happy right now.

"Oh?" I ask, feeling the temperature in my body rise, and not from anger.

Fucking impending heat is killing me right now.

Garrett's nostrils flare, and Ewan nuzzles into my neck. Florian takes a step in front of me, effectively blocking my view of the men, and takes a deep breath.

"You need us," he tells me, and I nod. "Here?"

"Yes," I assure him, realizing I mean it.

"What the fuck are you doing, Ivy?" Garrett spits, pulling at his restraints and making a loud clinking noise echo throughout the room.

Florian sinks to his knees in front of me and unbuttons my pants, staring up at me with his golden-brown eyes the entire time. "Just focus on me, love."

I do just that after stepping out of my pants, and he dips his head to my pussy and starts to lick and suck like his life depends on it. He lifts one of my legs up over his shoulder as Ewan tugs my shirt up over my head. I'm not concerned about any of the men seeing me naked, not anymore.

Florian sucks on me hard, just as Ewan twists my nipples, and I cry out.

Garrett starts to laugh. A noise that goes right through me and snaps me out of my hazy, heated stupor. He's laughed at me too many times. When I was hurt, when I was aching.

"Fuck you, Garrett," I seethe, dropping my leg from Florian's shoulder and stepping away from my two mates.

Neither of the men try to stop me, they just stand back, giving me the freedom to deal with my abusers however I see fit while I walk toward Garrett on the couch.

"I just hoped that maybe you would sound better. Like a real mutt whore when you got all worked up and into a heat. Not like some meek little cunt."

My hand snaps out and grasps his jaw. Garrett smiles like the prick he is, until my claws flick out and stab into his skin. He hisses, and I press harder, forcing his mouth open wider. When his tongue is fully visible, I reach my other hand in, grabbing it tightly before releasing his jaw and using my claws to slice through it.

Garrett lets out a garbled cry and thrashes wildly at the restraints as I saw away, cutting through the muscle bit by bit. When it finally comes free, he's screaming. The sound is grotesque as blood pours from his mouth and he chokes on it. Sighing, I use my claws to tear through his pants, right at the edge of his hips.

"Too bad you never knew how to keep your mouth shut, Garrett."

When his thigh is free, I kneel down, biting into the flesh and severing his femoral artery. His blood rushes into my mouth and something comes over me, causing my temperature to rise even more.

I pull my head back and cry out, holding on to Garrett's hips as slick gushes from me. I need Florian and Ewan, but I still have work to do.

Acton doesn't even need to move before I lunge toward him, ripping his eyes from their sockets with my fingers. They make a sickening popping noise, and I shove them down his throat before dragging my claws across his neck.

And as his two brothers bleed out, I grab Hurst by the neck and slam him onto the floor, allowing my hands to shift fully to paws.

"Y—you're a wolf?" he asks, incredulous.

"I am," I tell him, before picking up the lamp from the side table and bringing it down on his temple.

"So much for taming me," I state as his skull indents, and I hit him again, over and over until it's fully crushed and pouring onto the floor.

My body continues to spring to life, my hands switching from paws to fingers and back again as my bones ache, and my veins feel filled with fire.

"Shit, Ivy," Ewan curses, coming up behind me. "Let us help you."

He moves in front of me, settling himself on the ground beside Hurst's lifeless body. "Come here," he tells me, lifting me from the ground and pulling me onto his lap.

My pussy pulses, and I lick my lips, tasting the coppery tang of Hurst's blood on my skin.

I lower myself down onto Ewan, feeling painfully full as his cock fills me up. But it's still not enough.

"More," I breathe, leaning forward and placing my hands on Ewan's chest.

When I start to bob up and down, Florian is there, gathering the slick running down my legs and scooping it up to rub along my ass. I suck in a deep breath as he drags his cock along that tight hole before pressing himself inside me.

I scream at the sensation, and my entire body feels alive, like it's finally freed of all the tethers of my life. I can't move, I can barely even recognize what's happening around me, but my men move for me. Ewan thrusts in and out of me, keeping time with Florian as he fucks me from behind, and I'm overcome with pure and utter bliss.

When my orgasm overtakes me, I'm panting and gasping as Ewan's knot locks in tight and Florian spills himself inside me. The warmth that fills me is overwhelming, and I collapse on top of Ewan, Florian falling into a heap along with us.

"Thank you," I whisper, trying to catch my breath while Ewan is still pulsing inside of me.

"Anytime, love," Florian says with a chuckle. "You're fucking beautiful when you rage."

I glance at Ewan, and he tucks a lock of hair behind my ear. "Beautiful and deadly. There's no taming you, Ivy Allaway. And I wouldn't have it any other way."

About the Author

Allie Maddox is a dark romantasy and dark paranormal romance author with two current series, the Daughters of the Keeper trilogy and the Shifters of Northpeak series. Follow her on tiktok and instagram @authoralliemaddox or check out her website and sign up for her newsletter to follow along with new releases www.authoralliemaddox.com

Cover For Me

By: Ashley Pines

About Cover For Me

Olivia needs an alibi and finds it in an alluring stranger in a nightclub bathroom.

Content Note:

On page mentions of drugs (cocaine, fentanyl, xylazine), mentions of orchestrated overdose, murder of a spouse, infidelity, discussions of infertility and issues with conception, alcohol use/abuse, poisoning, sex in public, mentions of physical and emotional violence by a romantic partner.

Relationship type: NBi x F, Queer Pairing, AFAB x AFAB

Cover For Me
Olivia

Praying mantises didn't get enough credit. They truly were the most intelligent women on the planet, ripping their mate's head off and devouring it before they got a chance to get brave and raise a hand to them?

Pure. *Genius.*

Unfortunately for me, unlike in the bug world—a blissful, cop-free utopia—I was facing twenty-five to life if I murdered my husband in cold blood.

If they could prove I did it, that is.

This meant instead of taking a chainsaw to the lying, cheating, money-stealing cunt I called my *'life partner'*, I was going to have to take a page out of another famously murderous insect's book, the black widow.

Well, technically spiders aren't *insects*. But given I was on my third round of Cuervo of the evening I figured I could cut myself a *little* slack for a more fluid metaphor.

The club was heavy with the pound of the base. It'd been ages since I'd been out to a club like this. It just wasn't proper, wasn't good-old-family, or *advertiser*, values for the wife of an NFL footballer in a red state to be seen slurping down scotch and sodas and dancing on tables.

Player though? Their bad behaviour, for the most part, could be swept under the rug. Sometimes it felt like Charlie got away with murder while I was on parole for a crime I didn't even commit.

Until he didn't, of course.

These things always had a way of coming back around.

I was lucky, he'd only managed to steal my early twenties from me—still plenty of fun, going-out years left now that I was twenty-six. Even if it was a horrible time to become a widow. I could almost read my dating profile now.

Oliva Hastings, formerly Beaumont, twenty-six.

Yes, I was married to *that* Beaumont.

And I killed him too, not that I'd include that on Bumble.

Do you think they'd give me a little knife emoji if I put murder under my hobbies and interests?

The air was sticky and sweaty despite the blasting AC, a product of Miami in the dead of August. A viscous, tangible thing you could wade through, slowing my hand as it brought my spicy mango margarita to my lips.

God, I'd missed drinking. Missed clubs too. I loved dancing, even the noise that came with it. Even if after I left I could feel my ears ringing, that tingle of adrenaline in my veins always pulled me right back.

Tonight, the adrenaline wasn't just a tingle. It was a raging ocean of shot nerves and wicked excitement.

Karma was *finally* going to get me what I deserved and all I needed to do was give her a little shove in the right direction.

I'd given up my youth in favour of a white picket fence and attempt after attempt at the two-point-five children Charlie demanded of me. But no matter what I did, it never stuck.

Daily injections. Doctor's appointment after doctor's appointment.

It just never worked.

At first, I'd reasoned this whole thing was my fault.

That Charlie needed an outlet for his disappointment. That there were worse things he could be doing than having a couple of beers and playing cards.

But Charlie didn't need an outlet.

He needed a fucking scapegoat.

I excused a lot of shit that knuckle-dragging cunt did at first—the late nights, the missed dates and dinners, the yelling. Even the first time he shoved me I let go. It was a one-off, I'd said. He'd never hurt a fly.

But then came the lying, the cheating, the drugs.

Oh god, the *drugs*.

I'd spent an hour holed up in my vanity carefully applying layers of colour corrector so it would look just right to avoid suffering the embarrassment of a black eye during game day press, only for Charlie to show up absolutely wired to the field. One moment of indiscretion and he'd outed himself as a cokehead in front of every news publication in the state, along with anyone with a fucking camera phone.

I could handle whatever the Herald had to say, but watching my husband ruining my life in meme format every time I opened TikTok? Honestly, I deserved a medal for not killing him sooner.

It wasn't a surprise when the call came. It didn't do for a star athlete to be a known drug user. What kind of message did it send the kids?

Goodbye NFL.

Goodbye to the American Dream.

Goodbye, the comfort I'd become accustomed to thanks to that big fat footballer paycheck.

Not that Charlie didn't have family money, loads of those pretty boy NFL jerkoffs did, but that wasn't *really* the point.

The point was, I'd married Charlie Beaumont, the NFL star, the running back, the all-American guy. And what I got was an ungrateful loser who couldn't stand by his wife during her infertility issues.

A man who wasted my early twenties on ski trips and a fuckload of mid-range prostitutes.

I wasn't mad at the girls, a John was a John. And for a high-profile, good-looking man like Charlie? It was easy to want to take on the business.

Shame about his performance though. That guy couldn't find the clitoris if it lit up like Rudolph's bright red, shiny nose.

His mistress on the other hand?

Yeah, that was something else altogether.

That's what landed me here.

Well, other than the fact that I needed an airtight alibi about exactly where I'd been tonight, and with whom.

Down the bar, my unknowing accomplice and best friend, Selene, was chatting with a couple of guys in crisp button-down shirts. She always had a *type,* it just looked a little different when we were slamming wine coolers out of the back of her dad's Grand Camino.

Rich. Successful. And major fucking douchebags.

Unfortunately, It was a taste we shared.

The plan tonight was simple enough... I sat here at the bar, perfectly visible to every camera phone that wanted to take a picture, on my third margarita and carefully considering what lucky dickhead was going to spend the rest of the night with me.

No NDA required. How *scandalous.*

Bonus points if they were good-looking. But hey, a girl couldn't be too picky when it came to a quick and dirty alibi solidifying one-night stand.

Down the bar, the first contestant on '*will I be sleeping with you so that the cops don't think I murdered my husband*', a man in what I guessed was his early forties with grey threading the sides of his just on this side of too long, curly hair, was making yet *another* attempt to catch my eye.

Ideally, I'd never fuck another man as long as I lived—much less one with ten years plus on me—but this was Florida, and there wasn't exactly a plethora of options when it came to queer people willing to come up to you in the middle of a bar.

Fucking *appearances.*

I couldn't exactly be seen going into a gay club. It would pose too many questions. Would seem too unusual.

No, instead I came out with Selene tonight, her dark hair falling over her shoulder in a silken, black sheet. She was the type of woman that men liked. Successful, but not so much so that she was intimidating. Funny, but not so talkative they couldn't get a word in edgewise. Fit, with all the right wrappings—nails constantly done, eyelashes artfully glued into place, and just enough filler that her lips were even, not so much that it was terribly obvious she'd had work done.

Then, there were the tattoos. An ample amount of black and grey coated most of her visible skin. Dangerous, but in a way that was palatable. Especially since she didn't want a commitment.

I'd always been too quick with the commitment. Married at twenty-three! What the hell was I thinking?

But Selene, forever the master of the one-night stand, was perfectly happy using men as playthings to boost her ego and nothing more.

She was sort of my hero right now. It was fucking badass that she knew herself so well, and knew how to get what she wanted even better.

Never dating, never chasing.

Always with the same type.

Clean cut. Rich. Athletic.

Never anyone interesting enough that she'd want to get attached —just enough looks or money to make her engine rev and nothing more.

Was I about to become just like her?

A widow at twenty-six, independently wealthy, ready to start life over anywhere that wasn't here. Somewhere, preferably, where no one knew me or my name.

One nostalgic club hit blended into the next as I glanced at my watch.

With any luck, Charlie was already leaving to meet up with Sonya, or Charlotte or whatever trashy JC Penny version of me he'd decided to spend time with tonight.

It was crucial that this didn't go down in my house. I didn't want a fucking corpse rotting on my carpet all night, you know?

Did it look good for me to be out at a nightclub going home with some stranger? Hell no.

But I thought it'd really spice up the headlines.

Besides, it was all about what they'd *believe*. How quickly the investigation was wrapped up and my name cleared of any doubt. I really, *really* didn't want the hassle of a wrongful death trial. It was going to be hard enough as it was to pretend to be distraught when they called me in a few hours.

Looking at it pragmatically, maybe I should've been a *little* upset that my husband was going to die tonight. But really, he could've saved himself at any time. All he had to do was stop drinking, stop partying like he'd promised. Then, my carefully crafted biological warfare would've been made moot.

Hard to kill a rat if it won't eat the poison, you know? Even better, Charlie was about to bring that poison right back to the nest.

When ingested, windshield wiper fluid was fatal, and nearly impossible to get to pull up on a toxicology report.

Unless you know to look for it, that is.

Which is why I couldn't let my beloved husband go into unexplained kidney failure. No, that would bring up too many questions, like why he was pulling money out of the college fund for our future children to spend on Bitcoin and blow.

Funnily enough, I had the same questions.

Though our vows clearly hadn't meant anything to Charlie, they'd meant something to *me*. Especially until death do us part.

As far as I was concerned there was only one way out of this marriage: one of us was going to have to die.

And now that my wrist had healed, I was tired of waiting for Charlie to find the afterlife on his own.

But I'd never touched a gun before, and Charlie was staunchly anti-open carry. And he had a hundred points on me, not to mention over a foot and a half. It wasn't like I could take him one on one.

A fact he'd taken immense pleasure in reminding me, over and over.

Instead, I went for a more simple solution. Adding just a bit of windshield fluid to his alcohol bottles for weeks. Apparently, it tasted like hell, but my gamble that the burn of liquor would mask it proved to be effective enough.

Now that I'd weakened Charlie's liver all that was left was to set the trap.

I knew where he kept the drugs, it was almost too easy to swap his with my own supply, a special blend of fentanyl, cocaine and xylazine—a horse tranquillizer that suppresses the nervous system, my safety precaution in case one of his buddies tried to administer NARCAN.

This might've been my first murder, but I'd watched enough crime drama to know that setting the scene and having an alibi was just about the only way to get away with it.

So, I needed an *accident*. One that no one would question.

Case opened and closed in the same night, a bad batch and a partying playboy. A sad story heard a hundred times over.

That abusive shithead was going to seal his own coffin tonight. He'd probably be all over the news for a couple of weeks while they tried—and *failed*—to find his dealer and then it'd be a sad anecdote once a year from there. If that.

Damn, turns out that celebrity really wasn't for forever.

The worst part was going to the next few months pretending to be a gutted widow—but not *too* gutted. I'd already been feeding blind items to the press about his infidelity, letting the world call me an idiot for staying, for letting it happen, for trying to continue on with my life like nothing was wrong.

And you couldn't miss the cast I'd been walking around with for the last six weeks. That was the night I'd finally snapped, when I'd stopped hoping things would get better and started taking steps towards getting even.

I thought that cunt was going to kill me. The only reason he didn't was his own hubris letting him believe I wouldn't do the same.

Charlie always did have a bad habit of underestimating me.

Which brought me here, *tonight*. Looking for the oldest alibi in the book. A night of drinks and dancing with a girlfriend—trying to cheer me up about the shambles of my decaying marriage, *obviously*—along with a few too many drinks until I made a horrible mistake.

Except, there would be no mistakes.

I was a little buzzed, sure, my first sips of anything harder than white wine in damn near a year hitting me like strawberry wine before my sophomore winter formal. Even so, I was playing it up for the bit. Making sure that everyone in that bar heard me when I ordered another round. And *another*.

Selene returned to my side, rolling her eyes and flashing her hand as she pointed to her ring finger. "Married," she mouthed, not bothering to shout over the music.

I offered her a frown and a thumbs down, along with the rest of my drink.

Back when I was twenty-two and still enjoyed life, clubs like this were fun—*exciting*—the perfect way to blow off steam. But they really lost the draw when every time I went out it was an argument. Or worse, when it turned into bottle service, white lines cut with black Amexes, and media headlines the next day.

There were a lot of things that Charlie ruined for me: giving head, going to restaurants that didn't offer chicken nuggets on the menu, and red wine. But the worst, by far, was dancing.

I used to *love* to dance.

So when Selene hooked her thumb towards the floor, her eyebrows raised in a silent question, I was already eagerly sliding off my stool, wobbling a little in my heels as she grabbed my hand to tug me towards the light-up dance floor.

Selene's dark purple-painted grin was slow, cat-like as we found a space in the middle of the crowd, her hand moving to find my hip as we swayed to the beat.

"I missed this," she shouted over the music into my ear. "I missed you, really."

"I've been around," I called back, wrapping my arms around the taller woman's neck.

She shook her head, lightly upturned nose wrinkling. "Not really, not *you* at least."

I didn't have to ask what she meant, but it did hurt to hear.

Someone bumped into my back, a bit of sticky drink sloshing onto my shoulder, forcing Selene's eyes off me—likely to tell them off. But whatever she saw made her release me quickly, pulling away with a little nudge in the direction of the clumsy asshole that'd bumped me.

I turned, intending to tell the guy off, my lips popping open in surprise as I met a pair of dark hazel eyes.

A soft, apologetic smile tugged the corner of their mouth up into a charming, lopsided sort of expression. "Ah, fuck, gorgeous. I'm sorry about that," they said, using their hand to wipe away the alcohol with a grimace. "Not my smoothest moment."

"I–um—"

The air was too hot, too full as I tried to breathe through the sensation that the world had stopped turning. The pulse of music and the heavy press of bodies making my head spin as the air completely vacated my lungs.

"Let me make it up to you?" they offered, the tilt of their head showing off the finely shaved sides of their hair, the long, shaggy top slightly curled in the humidity as it was painted pink and blue in the lights. "A dance? A drink after?"

Their hand found my hip, the question in their eyes before they made contact washed away by the jerky bobble of my head, so fast it likely could've fallen right off.

My arms slid around their neck as they pulled me close, the warmth of their body only adding to the stifling heat of the club as we moved to the music. Every graze of their fingers against my bare skin felt like the beginnings of a wildfire, like my body was a tinderbox waiting to go up in smoke after years of unanswered desire—met instead with carefully scheduled attempts after temperature checks and rounds of vitamins.

Sweat slipped down my back, making my hair stick to my face and neck as I leaned in close, throwing all decorum out the window as my lips made contact with their strong jaw.

"I'm Olivia," I said, loud enough that they'd hear me over the music.

Not that it mattered, not really. But I needed them to be able to confirm that they knew me if they were asked.

"Kenley," they replied with a low groan as I ground against them, a hand finding my lower back to force me harder against their muscular body. "What's a pretty thing like you doing all alone?" they asked, head bending to graze their lips against my cheekbone.

A girlish giggle escaped me that sounded *way* too much like I'd totally lost sight of my mission. My heart was beating so fast... It'd been years since I'd danced with a stranger at a club. Though Charlie would never dance with me, his ever-present glare worked better than a forcefield to keep people out of my bubble.

There was a time when I'd found his possessiveness romantic, I thought that it meant that he loved me and wanted to protect me. Now I knew better, he just didn't want anyone to touch something that he perceived as his.

Dickhead.

I tilted my face up to look at them through my lashes, falling right into my usual M.O. for flirting like I hadn't been on a five-year hiatus. "Looking for you, of course."

Kenley laughed in surprise, making little crow's feet appear at the corners of their eyes. "Well, gorgeous, you found me."

"Thank goodness," I purred softly, rounding my blue eyes innocently in that way that always seemed to work with guys. "I was getting lonely."

Kenley was visibly queer in a way that usually would've made me nervous. Their stylishly tailored pants tucked over a pair of leather boots. A leather belt with silvery chains hanging over their thigh along with a few charms that caught the light. Their mesh shirt was just see-through enough that I could see their silvery mastectomy scars, the material sticking to their toned chest with the sheen of sweat.

I'd worked hard—at the insistence of my husband—to wipe any hint of my bisexuality away from my appearance. Long gone were the rubberized bracelet I'd worn in college touting my LGBTQ+ status, the bisexual pride pin removed from my gym bag, and perhaps the saddest loss, the pink steak I'd had in my hair through my undergrad.

It didn't matter how I'd felt, it was all about how people saw us, saw *him*.

The irony that me being a girl kisser hadn't done so much as dent the patina of our image, whereas his partying had shoved a wrecking ball through it, wasn't lost on me.

Their eyes followed mine, lopsided smirk returning. "Why don't we find you that drink?"

There it was again, the question in Kenley's eyes, like they were asking permission before they bent, mouth grazing the corner of my lips in a barely there kiss.

"I'm not really that thirsty," I admitted, catching their jaw to hold them in place for a slow, deliberate press of mouths. "Why don't we find somewhere quiet instead?"

Kenley's little raspy groan made my knees wobble, their hand finding my hair to drag me to their lips for another heated kiss. They tasted like whiskey and lime, their soft lips passing over mine unhurriedly but not lazily. Purposeful. Like we had all the time in the world.

And maybe they were right.

Maybe I'd been looking at this thing all wrong. Too worried about the finer details of my plan that I'd forgotten the most important thing.

Tonight was the first night of the rest of my life.

Of *freedom.*

My hands slid to their belt, using it to keep them close as we kissed in steady passes of mouths and gentle nibbles of each other's lips.

I couldn't remember the last time I'd had a one-night stand—did we really ever? One day it was the norm, and then the next it was an anecdote of the crazy shit you'd get up to in college, usually followed by a wistful sigh, dreaming about a simpler time.

But of all the one-night stands I'd secured, of which there'd been plenty—I didn't remember them feeling like this. Kenley's free hand found my ass, squeezing and making me release what was undeniably a moan.

They broke the kiss, lips slightly swollen and glossy with our shared saliva. "S-Somewhere quiet?" they gasped out, a rosy pink blush dusting the bridge of their nose and tips of their ears.

I nodded, their hand finding mine to tug me off the dancefloor. On the way by, I caught Selene's eye, nearly laughing at her bright grin and flashed a thumbs up.

That sealed it. How Kenley made me feel aside, bestie approval was the most sacred covenant out there.

Kenley led me into the ladies' bathroom, pushing me up against the door to kiss down my neck the moment I was inside. "Usually I'd go for the men's," they admitted. "But the girls are usually cleaner."

"Thoughtful," I praised with a definite air of teasing to my tone. Using a hand at the back of their neck, I pulled them back to my lips. "God, I could kiss you forever."

They loosed a little laugh. "Me? Have you seen yourself tonight?"

"Sweaty with my mascara running?"

"As if," they rolled their eyes, manoeuvring me as easily as if I was a doll to press me against the sink, facing the mirror. "So you can see what I do," Kenley murmured, their ringed hand coming to squeeze my breast through the thin fabric of my dress.

I shivered, grinding back into them as their lips met my bare shoulder, tongue slipping between their pink lips to slide along my skin and up my bare neck. My hissed curse was interrupted by a whine as I put my hand over Kenley's to squeeze my breast again, my pebbled nipple pressed against their warm palm.

They nipped and sucked at the side of my neck, free hand wandering to trace along my bare upper thigh where my dress had ridden up against them and the vanity.

"Kenley," I whispered, meeting their eyes in the mirror desperately. "Please."

I hadn't needed to be touched like this in ages. Every scrap of their attention was better than ecstasy as they pushed the hem of my dress north, revealing the tiny scrap of fabric that dared to call itself a thong.

They sucked in a breath through their teeth at the wet spot in the red material. "Do you want to watch how prettily you come for me, Olivia?"

I whimpered as they pinched my nipple, toying with the tight peak with the slip of silken fabric adding to the sensation, nodding my head. "Yes."

Their other hand joined its companion, the myriad of rings decorating Kenley's long fingers catching the dim lights of the bathroom as they slid the straps of my dress down, baring my chest to anyone who walked in.

"Look at yourself," they ordered, voice soft and coaxing, but leaving no room for argument.

Half reluctantly, I met my eyes in the mirror, hardly recognising the needy animal staring back at me. My lipstick was smudged, the traces of it that I'd shared with Kenley left behind on my jaw, throat and shoulders.

"You listen so well," they murmured, rewarding me with a tweak of their fingers against my bare nipples that made me cry out, thighs quivering with the need to be *touched*. "Is that what you came out looking for tonight? Someone to make you come?"

"Yes," I whispered, before I could even think to come up with a lie. My flushed cheeks and chest stared back at me from the mirror as I watched my mouth form the words like they were coming from someone else. "I need to be fucked."

"Is there anything you don't like?" they asked, their breath tickling my ear before they gave it a sharp nip that arched my spine into their hands desperately.

"No choking," I said quickly, a flicker of the last time Charlie'd wrapped his fingers around my throat making me nervous. I licked my lips, my second request leaving me feeling exposed in the low light. Quietly, I added, "And... don't be mean, please."

"Mean?" they asked, sucking at the soft spot between my neck and ear, one of their hands travelling to cup my nearly bare pussy. "Who could say anything cruel to a pretty little princess like you?"

I didn't answer, turning my head to catch their lips in a needy, moan-filled kiss. "Slut is okay."

"Slut is okay," they repeated, diving in for another kiss as their fingers pressed against my clothed clit. I whimpered, pushing against their hand. They chuckled into my lips, the noise full of excitement. "Makes sense, you're such a sweet, needy little slut, aren't you gorgeous?"

I nodded fervently, welcoming Kenley's tongue as it pressed into my mouth, tangling with mine as they circled my nipple with their thumb.

"Yes, sir," I whispered, barely audible over the sound of my blood rushing in my ears. "Fuck me, please."

Kenley moaned at the honorific, rewarding me with rough side-to-side swipes of my clit with their fingers. "Am I going to find my slutty little princess wet for me, Olivia?"

I bit my lip, trying to swallow the horrifically embarrassing whimpers bouncing off the mirror back at us.

"Well?" they asked, a smirk in their tone as their mouth found my shoulder again, strokes becoming more insistent.

"Yes!" I gasped as their hand left my breast to find my hair, forcing me into a rough kiss.

Kenley turned me enough to be able to kiss down my chest, sucking the tip of my breast into their mouth. They hummed, rolling my nipple between their teeth, grazing the tender nerves as they did.

"That feels so fucking good, don't stop," I breathed out, pawing at their shirt with the intention to take it off.

"Are you going to say please?" Kenley asked, voice laced with humour. They looped a finger into the side of my underwear, lifting it away from my skin with the kiss of cool air against my overheated centre.

"I want—" I gasped out, watching as Kenley travelled to my other breast to toy at the peak with their tongue. "Your mouth!"

The idea of undressing them disappeared as I shuddered, the edge finding me quickly with the combination of their fingers and teeth.

"Is that so?" they asked, straightening to brush their lips against mine. "Just a kiss then, gorgeous?"

"What?" I asked, horrified. "No I—I want—"

"Oh," Kenely purred, tucking a lock of my sweaty blonde hair behind my ear. "You want me to taste that sweet little pussy, Olivia?"

I ground my hips against theirs, desperately trying to will their fingers into my aching cunt. "Stop teasing me, please—I can't take it!"

"Don't tell me I'm disappointing you, princess," Kenley murmured with their dark hazel eyes narrowed, the tips of their fingers just barely slotting into my opening.

Another fucking tease, but one that sent me wild as they turned me back to the mirror, half bent over the vanity as they inched their fingers in incrementally deeper.

"No! Of course not—! I—God, *fuck!*" I rocked my hips back against their hand, relishing the relief even this tiny bit of subtle stretch provided.

I wanted them to use me.

To make the sloppy, messy person staring back at me through my eyes shatter into a million pieces onto the sticky bathroom floor.

They didn't make me wait long, easing my knee up onto the vanity so my cunt was as bared to the room as my chest. The view of my skirt bunched lewdly at my waist along with the wet sheen of my thighs made me moan, my forehead making contact with the cool glass as I bent forward.

I should've been mortified, but I'd always had a bit of an exhibitionist streak. And to be caught with someone as beautifully handsome as Kenley? What an ego boost.

Kenley's hands found my hips, angling me the way they wished, digits pressing deeper into my drooling sex. The sound of my slick desire dripping to the countertop was drowned by the music beyond the door, but I could see the small pool beginning to form the longer they fucked me, achingly slowly, with their fingers.

I panted their name, a pathetic, needy noise that made my pussy throb as the glass fogged with my stuttering breaths.

"Look in the mirror," Kenley ordered, their lips making contact with the swell of my ass. "I want you to watch yourself as your slutty little cunt swallows my hand."

I shuddered, using my hand to steady myself against the glass to comply with their request. My reflection obscured slightly in places by my own lewd lip prints.

They met my eyes in the mirror, peering around my body from their place on the floor. "I'm going to make you come so hard you forget your name," Kenley promised, fucking me viciously with their fingers. Their face lit as they slotted a third into me, arching their hand upwards to find my sweet spot. "Is that what you need gorgeous? Someone to fuck you right?"

I nodded, unsteady as loud moans mingled with the wet clap of Kenley's motions. It was all I could do, really. They could offer to take me home right now and I'd happily say yes, but I worried if we stopped in this moment there would be nothing to stop me from fucking them in the cab home.

Kenley used a hand on my hip to pull my sex towards them, trading their finger's from fucking me to rubbing my clit as their tongue teased my slit. They let out a groan of approval, sucking and slurping at my pussy like they were caught between wanting to please me and chasing my taste. They tongued my entrance and I moaned loudly, my free hand flying backwards to push their face further into my centre, hips canting to grind against them as my release threatened with every swipe of fingers and tongue.

"Yes, yes! Just like that!"

Kenley speared me with their tongue, lapping at my arousal like it was their favourite meal and I broke. My moans and pants skyrocketed in desperation, every breath more erratic until I was shaking with the release of it, stars dancing at the corners of my vision as pleasure sparked from every nerve ending.

My mouth was open in a near comical 'O' as I shuttered and whimpered, continuing to grind on Kenley's face in a futile attempt to chase another climax so quickly after the first.

Not that it mattered, Kenley seemed happy to continue on, wrapping their mouth around my clit for a firm suck that made me keen pathetically.

"Have you ever been fucked with a strap before?" they asked, pressing two fingers back into my cunt and scissoring them, making the tightened muscles contract around them.

I shook my head, half sobbing with the pleasure of their relentless attention. "No, never."

"My hotel isn't far..." Kenley said slowly, pressing a sweet kiss against my side totally at odds with the vicious addition of a third and fourth finger, picking up their pace once more. "I'd like for you to come back with me, if you want." Their hand stilled as they leaned around to catch my eye. "I'm not ready for this to be over if you aren't."

I shook my head, cheeks flushed as I met their eyes in the glass.

The door swung open with a wave of heat, music, and the familiar sound of a drunk girl crying. Kenley was up in a flash, setting me onto the floor and covering my body with theirs as they righted my dress. The only evidence of what we'd been doing was the small puddle left on the vanity as a group of girls walked in, talking loudly about one of their ex-boyfriends—or maybe current boyfriends?

Honestly, I wasn't listening hard enough to tell, too focused on the taste of myself on Kenley's lips as they kissed me.

"What do you say, gorgeous? Come back with me?"

"I hope it's not far."

"It isn't, promise."

I told myself it didn't mean anything as I grabbed a paper towel from the dispenser, wiped up my mess and tossed it in the trash before grabbing Kenley's hand to lead them to the door.

But a little voice, one that still had too much hope for the life I'd lived, whispered to me sweetly as we waited for the coat check girl to bring me my purse, that if I'd asked, Kenley would've happily covered for me.

The End... For now.

About the Author

Ashley is a cat-mom of two, wife and spicy romance enthusiast living in Edmonton, AB. You can usually find her curled up on the sofa surrounded by a hundred pillows and reading on her kindle (or, y'know, writing.) Becoming her best friend is easy! You just need an undying love of all things sweet and be cool with watching the same five movies on repeat.

https://bexdeveaulinks.carrd.co/

Night Sister

By: B.L. Brown

About Night Sister

Men are weak. Rhona knows this, even as she is captured and caged by the vampire hunter Declan Margrave. They are weak and it is only a matter of time before she is able to exploit that weakness to secure her escape. And then, will she take her revenge.

Content Note:

Torture, blood play, dubcon, gore, light pet play, Domme/sub, poisonings, awful people, dark vibes, and a very handy stake.

Relationship type: cishet Male, bi Female

Chapter One

The first failing of weak men is knowledge.

They know they are weak. They know they cannot manifest change in the world, and that knowledge makes them cruel.

I suppose knowledge is my failing as well, for as much as I know I should not give Declan Margrave the satisfaction, I do. I know that by screaming and letting him see how much this hurts, how much it enrages me, I'm only urging him on.

Because Declan Margrave is a weak man.

He hides this weakness behind silver chains and cattle prods. Behind the slow drip of holy water and angled mirrors to reflect the dying light. Every whimper and cry that slips from my lips encourages the monster that is Declan. Every bruise I earn thrashing against those silver bars, and the blistering welts the holy water raises on my skin feeds the weak man within the beast.

He paces around my cage like a northern wolf, and my eyes catch on the stake dangling from the belt cinched tight around his trim waist. Hewn from a crucifix, the holywood stake is a favorite toy of Declan's. Leather worn smooth by use wraps around the base, right up to the flared hand guard. Ribbons of mahogany and redwood wind around the shaft, capped by a gleaming silver tip pounded and sharpened to a wicked point.

Torchlight winks off the wretched metal, and my skin prickles in anticipation of the stake's weight. The memory of cold silver against my flesh explodes in my mind. Despite how well I know not to do so, I flinch away, curling into a tight, tiny ball as far from Declan as I can get.

This is not the first time he has captured and tortured me. I wish I could say it would be the last, but I am no longer sure.

Ours is a dance, our fates tidally locked. Wherever I go, no matter how deep I run into the woods, he finds me, and I end up locked in this cage while he tortures me for a crowd.

But there's always someone, some sympathetic Northerlands fool, who finds Declan's work distasteful. I only need to pick them out of the crowd.

Declan pauses at the corner of my cage, obscured by the thick silver-coated frame. Men and women fill the hall, huddling at a safe distance. They leer at my bruises and wounds, their faces twisted in disgust as thick, clotted blood pumps from the cuts on my arms.

"You see?" Declan whips around the cage, driving a blade into my side.

I scream from the shock of it, the pain, furious that I dropped my guard enough to allow him that strike. I press my hand against the cut, deep crimson blood surging between my fingers as I glare at him. The pain recedes to an ache, and the flow slows as my skin stitches back together—a normal blade, then, not silver or doused in holy water.

"They bleed," Declan states, "and anything that bleeds can be killed."

"But they come back!" a villager shouts, too deep in the crowd for me to pick him out.

"Not if you do the job properly." Declan gestures to the rear of the hall, where his men flank the walls on either side of large oak doors. I do not recognize a single one of them, which does not come as a surprise. Declan does not keep them for long. He is weak and cruel. Such men do not breed loyalty.

Still, every time I find myself in this cage, I search for a face I know, only to be met with strangers.

Two of his men peel away from the walls to haul the doors open. Screams fill the hall. Wild, feral screams that make my blood sing in recognition.

Vampire. Sister.

The blood of the First One chills in her veins as it does in mine, like calling to like, binding us together in our undeath.

"We found this one lurking in a village beyond your walls." Declan's voice rings over the enraged cries of my night sister. He paces the length of my cage and back again, pausing to spit. A thick gob splatters against my shoulder. I whip my head around to hiss at him, but he has already moved away, ignoring the beast in her cage.

My night sister wails and spits, fighting against Declan's men as they drag her across the floor. Muscles in her legs twitch and flex, but her feet drag at odd angles. She puts her weight on one, fighting to the last, but her ankle folds, and she drops. Only the men's grip on her arms keeps her from crashing to the cold stone floor.

"The bitch killed three of my men before we subdued her." At this, he lowers his head and presses a hand to his chest, letting his words sit heavy in the hall. "We believe her to be the creature that killed Lord and Lady Beenleigh."

A murmur grows in the crowd. Rumors of the horror in Beenleigh have spread far. The Lord and Lady drained of their blood, and their entrails spread to decorate Marley Hall. There were less than half a dozen survivors of the vampiric massacre, a feat I am still quite proud of.

Feet shuffle, and the mass parts. Finally, I am given a clear view of the manor lord and his wife seated on a low dais at the far end of the room. The lady's cheeks are pale, her pinched features sucked to the center of her face, while the lord sits with his legs set wide. Rolls spill over the high collar of his shirt, and the buttons on his vest threaten to pop off from the strain of covering a rotund belly.

"Drained a flock of sheep before we got there." Declan shakes his head.

"What concern of mine is that?" Lord Stilton scoffs and spit dribbles down his chins.

"The farmers will starve this winter, Lord Stilton. Many of them will die. Who will tend your fields in the spring, hm? Who will plant the seeds that grow the food to fill your tables?"

The crowd murmurs at his words, sharing glances. Lady Stilton darts a look at her husband, and my eyes catch the mottled purpling dotting her neck and disappearing beneath her collar.

Rage simmers in my poisoned blood. If my heart could beat, it would be thundering. Instead, a stillness settles deeper in my chest. I must remain calm because Declan Margrave is weak and cruel and far from done.

"Put her there," he directs his men. My night sister's body slams against the cage. Her screams rise in pitch as silver burns her back and arms. She twitches and jerks against them, and I spot the wounds on her arms, the backs of her calves, and across her ankles.

Yellowed tendons curl against pink muscle. Blood crusts the edges of the wounds like chapped lips, but none falls. At the sight, my night sister's inability to walk makes a gruesome sort of sense— Declan's men took a blade to her Achilles. The stink of rotting meat and burnt garlic reeks from the wounds, explaining the lack of healing and blood. I gag, and Declan's blade slashes down my back.

My scream brings a smile to his face. His eyes flutter closed as he straightens and tips his head back, inhaling deeply and stretching his arms high. His vest stretches tight across his chest, leather creaking as the toggles strain against the swell of muscle.

Above me, my night sister pants against the bars, her screams reduced to rasping wheezes. Silver eats into her flesh like acid, filling my cage with more of the putrid stench of a rotting carcass. Even if she could walk, I doubt she could move now. Chunks of skin and meat drip from her back and arms, splattering against the floor and pushing me further into the corner. Closer to those wretched bars.

"As I was saying, anything that bleeds can die." Declan strides around the cage, running a hand through russet brown hair to sweep the long strands away from his face. "You just have to do it right."

He pulls the leather tassels at the end of his stake, removing it from his belt and spinning the holywood in his fingers, torchlight glaring off the tip as he holds it high for all to see.

"Silvered weapons will wound them if you're lucky, but it only slows their healing." He grips her jaw, fingers digging into her cheeks to force her mouth open. The assembled crowd gasps at what I know is a stub of meat capped in silver. A precaution he adopted to prevent us from using our allure against him and his parade of men. "Now, if you douse your weapons in holy water and rub garlic into the wounds"—he stands before my night sister and presses the tip of his stake just off the center of her chest—"you might stand a chance of surviving long enough to do this."

He raises his arm high. Her shoulders twitch, her wheezes rising in pitch as panic overwhelms what remains of her ability to think. I want to reach for her hand and grasp her fingers in this final moment. I want my night sister to know that her death serves a greater purpose. That she will be avenged; I will reign down a fury on these men so terrible it will become a moment of legend.

Instead, I cast my gaze out among the crowd, searching. There's always one. Someone hurt or hurting, someone who sees these cruel men for what they are: weak.

"I'll give you this one for free, Lord Stilton." Declan grins and drives the stake through her heart.

Her chest shatters like an eggshell. Declan is weak, but his body is muscled and strong—an armor he wears to disguise his failings. The silvered tip pierces through my night sister's back and ash crawls out from the wound. With a final rasp, she dissolves. Gore and viscera pour through the silver bars, and the ash that was her settles like a grim snow on my skin and hair.

A deadly silence blankets the hall, pierced by a high-pitched, drunken giggle. It takes me a moment to realize the sound comes from Lord Stilton.

"Good show," he says between giggles. He grips both arms of his chair, kicking his feet out to gain enough leverage to rise. Lady Stilton grabs his arm, attempting to help her husband stand, and he rips it out of her grasp, backhanding his wife in front of the hall.

I freeze in my cage, eyes fixed on the blooming of red on her cheek. Whether she senses my keen attention or simply needs a place to look that is not one of the people who allow her to suffer her husband's hand day in and day out, I do not know.

All I know is that she looks at me, her chin lifted and eyes sharp.

It takes every bit of my restraint not to smile.

There is always one.

Chapter Two

"Fifty pieces of gold for every vampire we gather in a week's time." Declan jabs the table with a finger. Only the two of them remain, the hall long emptied by Stilton's demand. After hours of their back and forth, I understand why. The man is an abysmal negotiator and has spent more time pushing ale into Declan's hands and peppering him with questions about his weapons, tactics, and training than discussing terms. It is clear he wants to use Declan for his knowledge, no doubt planning to form his own hunting party and attempt to handle the matter of my night siblings himself.

It is also clear that Lord Stilton is not only cruel but a fool as well. Weak men and all.

"And what happens after a week?" Stilton counters. "You continue to rob me blind, dragging your feet as you 'handle the matter'?"

Declan's face remains calm, and a sharp, knowing grin curls his lips, a suggestion of the capabilities he possesses. It reminds me of the many reasons I keep finding myself in this cage.

"If we haven't cleared your lands of the vermin by then," he says, "we can negotiate a lower rate for the remaining pests."

"What guarantee do I have that you won't draw this out?"

"I'll sign a contract if you are so inclined, and if you find me in breach, I'll accompany you to whatever passes in these lands as a court."

His bravado only angers Stilton. He casts a toad's gaze around the hall, watery pale eyes landing on my cage. The man is repulsive, his cheeks mottled red and fleshy lips permanently pursed. Even if I had not noticed his treatment of Lady Stilton, my loathing for this lordling would remain. The wooden beams transversing the hall's ceiling are rotted and darkened by mold, and his servants skitter along the edges of the room, heads ducked and shoulders stooped, all of them winter lean in the flush of summer.

He is a poor lord forsaking the care of his people and the weed-ridden, wild lands I viewed around his manor.

My fangs itch, and as offensive as I find Stilton, my hunger rises.

I need blood if I am to escape. Trapped in silver with unhealing wounds, I am weak, like the men arguing at the table. Any warm body would do, but my sights are set on the putrid lump festering at the table.

Him first, and then I will seek out Declan.

"And what about her?" Lord Stilton's voice booms across the emptied hall. He stands at the bench, a fist against the table and a meaty arm stretched in my direction. "You cannot expect me to house that vile bitch in my hall."

"Put her in the stables for all I care." Declan shrugs. "We need her for bait."

Bait.

What a waste of my abilities. He's right, however. We undying, my night siblings and I, we can scent each other on a windless night. Curiosity draws us like moths to flame. It is dangerous knowledge for a hunter like Declan to hold.

"And have her scare the horses?" Stilton spits three times and glares at Declan. "If she's bait, string her from the yew tree like we do with the pigs."

Calm settles over Declan's features. The smile he wears now is cold and distant, absent all emotion or cunning. A thrill trickles down my spine as he sheds the mask of a jovial hunter, showing Lord Stilton the terrible man who so often puts me in this cage.

He rises to match Stilton's height, places his hands on the table, and leans forward, lowering his voice to a threatening level. "Fifty gold pieces for every vampire my men capture in a week's time. After that, my men and I will leave you to your troubles." He pounds his fist against the table and points at my cage. "And she remains indoors."

Stilton blanches, eyes darting from Declan to me, and his mass deflates. He needs Declan. Vampires have ravaged his lands for weeks, and his tenants and the villagers are scared and growing angry. Many of them witnessed Declan's little performance earlier and gawked at me in my cage, still covered in the remains of my night sister. They know help has come, and if Stilton does not accept Declan's terms, he will leave this wastling lord to the pyre that will no doubt be built for him.

"A week, then," Stilton attempts to keep his voice steady, but I catch the tremble in his words.

Weak.

* * *

Five cages line the far wall at dawn, just beyond the light's reach, and by midnight, seven of my night siblings sit within their bars. They wait, calm as I am, knowing this will only get worse. We are not resigned to our fates as much as we are aware of what happens next.

"What is the meaning of this?" Lord Stilton bursts into the hall. A red velvet dressing gown flutters as he charges toward Declan, cleaning his nails with a knife blade on the edge of the dais.

"We raided a nest," Declan says without looking up. Mud stains his trousers, and blood cakes his arms and vest, streaking down his cheek. I inhale, picking him out of the other scents in the room.

Not his blood.

"Lost a good portion of my men in the doing," he continues. "I'll need to take some of your guard when I go out next."

"To do what? Parade the empty wood?" Stilton stops before Declan, his fist pressed against his side. "You were supposed to slaughter the vermin. Instead, you've brought me a nest; what the hell are they doing in my hall?"

"Marinating." Declan shoots to his feet. He twirls his knife by the hilt and slides it into a sheath at his hip. "You let this go on too long, Stilton. Where there's one nest, you will find half a dozen more. These things breed like rabbits; it is a wonder your entire county isn't overrun."

A blotchy red crawls over Lord Stilton's cheeks. He huffs and jabs Declan's chest with a meaty finger. "Answer my question, boy."

It takes all I have in me not to roll my eyes.

"Was I not clear?" Declan crosses his arms, the leather sleeves of his riding coat creaking. "You let this go too long. Every person in this hall last night witnessed your failure to protect them."

"You have no proof—"

"Don't I?" Declan tilts his head to the side, a jester's grin stretching his face while his eyes remain hard and cold. "Half the villages came out to see us raid that nest. Your tenant women gifted us their garlic, and your men offered their pitchforks. You have a mutiny on your hands, Stilton." He sweeps an arm at the cages against the wall. "They require proof that their lord is not weak. That he is a man who defends his people."

With an easy sweep of his leg, Declan steps over the bench and strides the length of the hall, his eyes fixed on my cage. The flask he pulls from his coat pocket sloshes menacingly. I shrink away, but there is nowhere to run from the holy water. I am trapped, and the monster is walking directly toward me.

"I have seen this dozens of times," he continues. "Weakling lords who wait until a tiny problem becomes a catastrophe. Lucky for you,

I have developed a ... performance, shall we say, sure to rid you of their mutinous behavior." He thumbs open the silver flask and dangles it over my cage. A quick twist of his wrist pours a stream of holy water through the bars. It splashes on the ground, and droplets land on my foot and ankle. The searing pain is immediate, sizzling my skin and burning to the bone. Tears burst in my eyes, and I barely strangle the scream in my throat.

Declan huffs and stares down at me, his stony gaze assessing how I cower, trying to make myself small. The smile he sends me then is no performance. He knows he has enraged me, as he has done time and time again.

"Invite them to your hall at the end of the week." He spins, facing Lord Stilton. "Host a feast, open your cellars, and let them see with their own eyes how terrible the vampire threat was to their lives. Let them see how you care for them. Men are weak, Lord Stilton; remind them of this with a show of your strength."

Lord Stilton's puffy lips flatten, his watery eyes darting from Declan to me and back. His chins wobble as he nods his agreement, and I bury my face in my knees to hide the expression that crawls over my face.

* * *

Declan and his borrowed men fill the cages. They build more from scrap wood and silver stripped from Stilton's walls or melted from his goblets and cutlery. The week passes, and I watch their progress from my cage, which is now in the center of the hall. I am covered by a tapestry during the daylight hours, safely hidden from the sun while my body takes its needed rest, and each sunset, I am rewarded with the sight of my night brothers and sisters sitting quietly in wait.

We are unliving; we are undying. We are patient.

I see it written on their faces and in the steadiness of their stares. They wait, watching me, following my lead. Rumors of Declan have spread across the Northerlands, and with them come the stories of me. Captured, escaped, a terror in the night chased across the moors and highlands by a man with a silver-tipped stake. We are creatures of legend, crafting a warning tale for mortals and immortals alike.

It is a dance, mine and Declan's. We are bound together on the wheel of fate, tipping in his favor as easily as the cards deal my success. I am caged now, but I will not be caged forever. No silver bars can hold me, not when the weakness of men serves my purposes so well.

Not when there is always *one*.

Lady Stilton haunts the hall in the small hours, her wide-set, dark eyes large on her pinched face. New bruises darken arms she no longer hides from my night siblings and me. A limp hitches her step, but with every night that passes, she draws on her courage to come closer.

On the sixth night, I wake to the tapestry torn away and Lady Stilton's face pressed against the bars.

"He will kill you," she hisses, her voice barely above a whisper. "He has had the priests blessing barrels of rainwater all day. Tomorrow, after the feast, the guards will drag your cages into the courtyard at dawn and drown you." Lady Stilton's pulse flutters in her neck, her heartbeats loud enough to deafen. Her eyes skitter over my face, my filthy dress, and the dried, crusted blood on my arms and legs. "He wants to watch you burn before you burn."

In the sun, I assume. What a terrible fate.

"A grand plan for a worm like your husband," I rasp. Each word saws up my throat, and hunger claws in my belly. Six days is a long time to go without a meal, and I was hungry when Declan threw me into this cage.

Lady Stilton's mouth twists in a sneer. "My husband can barely think beyond his next meal. This was the hunter's idea."

Of course it was.

"Please." I press a hand to my mouth, making my eyes widen in fear. "Please help me."

A silence descends over the hall, quieting the mice in the corners and the swallows nested in the rotting beams. As one, my night siblings fall still and face my cage, ears pricked as they listen intently to our exchange. Their silent focus is as loud as the rush of blood in Lady Stilton's veins.

"How?" she asks. Pale, twig-like fingers curl around the bars of my cage. Several are crooked, bones broken and healed, and she is missing the thumbnail on her left hand.

I shuffle across the cage on my knees, hands clasped in plea. "I heard them speaking. Lord Stilton is going to open the cellars. Tell the servants to pour heavy. Get them drunk and—"

"He'll water down the wine."

"They will not notice?" I stop, lowering back onto my heels.

"They never do." Lady Stilton grips the bars, eyes darting as she thinks. "But perhaps ... perhaps if I drug the wine with bergamot and elderflower?" I blink, surprised at how easily she offers to do this. Bergamot and elderflower are a druid's tools, and that knowledge has me eyeing her pale, pinched features and dark, haunted eyes anew. "The taste of the wine would be strong; they will think it fortified and consider him generous. They'll drink more heavily and—"

"And when they succumb, you steal the keys from the hunter." Greasy hair falls in my face as I nod. "Let me out, Lady Stilton, and I will ensure you never have to suffer another night at the hands of your husband."

Her skin blanches the color of the moon, a white so pale she could be one of my night siblings. Blue veins pulse in her throat and along her jaw, and she steps away from my cage, fingers pressed to her tiny mouth. For a moment, murderous druidic tendencies aside, I fear I have overstepped and made one too many assumptions about the caliber of woman before me.

Then she nods. A tiny, tight dip of her chin that bobs and grows into a strong affirmation.

She will do it. She sees the wisdom. Free me and be freed. Her husband drained and discarded—all of his lands, all of his wealth, hers for the taking. I do not care whether she will be a good shepherd of her lands. I only care about escaping my cage and tipping the scales in my favor.

Chapter Three

By the night of the feast, two dozen vampires fill the cages. They huddle together to keep as far from the silver bars as possible, but there is no respite. Declan's men and Stilton's guards have taken to dousing our cages with holy water and cheering loudly when they scream. At the far end of the hall, a quartet of men play a game, guessing the number of blisters that will rise when the water touches a night sister's arm.

She is brave, my sister, and does not scream, but blood wells in her eyes, drawing crimson tracks down her cheeks.

Lord and Lady Stilton sit on their dais with Declan lounging near their feet. Propped on an elbow, he absently twirls the silver-tipped stake in his hands. His dark hair falls loose and soft, curling against the collar of his vest, and stubble darkens a strong jaw. A goblet sits untouched beside him, and he stares down the center of the hall at me. Hunger darkens eyes that gleam a burnished gold in the firelight, and I can't help but notice the bulge pressing against the tight leather of his trousers.

An unwilling shiver trembles through my body, and I tear my gaze away, studying the guests.

I recognize many faces from that first night, though most are new. Tourists come to witness the vampires in their cages and see the slaughter with their own eyes. I would laugh if I were not so hungry.

They feast and drink. The revels grow in volume. Lord Stilton's face reddens red as he drinks and eats. Grease shines on his chins as he raises a goblet to Declan.

"To our hunter!" Wine spills over the rim, splattering like blood against the dais. Red drops bleed into Declan's linen sleeve and collar. He raises a hand to his neck to wipe the ruby-red splatter away. All the while, his eyes never leave mine.

I cannot deny what the sight of that red wine on his throat does to me. How hunger claws as he lifts his chin, showing me the long tendons and flutter of his pulse. It has been more than a week since I last ate. More than a week since I stretched my limbs and fought.

More than a week since I pressed Declan Margrave to the ground, drove my knees into his sides, and turned that silver-tipped stake against him.

My fangs itch, and a deep, cloying need thrums my belly, demanding to be sated.

Soon.

"The hunter!" Men and women cry, raising their goblets to the dais. Lady Stilton subtly lifts a finger from her armrest, and servants flurry into motion. New casks roll into the hall and are quickly tapped. Red wine so deep it is almost purple flows freely, filling the goblets of every man and woman as a sharp, floral scent teases my nose.

She's done it. I do not dare meet her eye, though I can feel her gaze on me as well as I feel Declan's.

My night siblings stir in their cages, no doubt catching the same scent I do. They know, and they will be ready.

The tallow candles in the chandelier burn lower, the moon passes into view through the window at the rear of the hall, and Declan is the first to leave. He lingers by my cage, his hand gripping the hilt of his stake as he stares down at me. Those eyes burn with contempt and something else—something molten and hot, trailing my filthy skin and greasy hair.

"I'll see you in the morning," he says before striding away. I cannot help but watch him, drawn to the easy saunter and sway of his broad shoulders and narrow hips.

And then he is gone, and it is only a matter of time.

The women drop first, cradling their heads in their arms and falling asleep at the table. Then, one by one, the men fall—some beside their women, others to the floor. Lord Stilton holds on longer than I expect, drinking and eating from abandoned plates as he wanders the cages with an ewer of holy water. He pours it over my night siblings, guffawing as their skin bubbles and sloughs off, leaving them raw and bloodied.

"Watch you burn," he slurs in a sing-song voice. "And then we'll watch you buuurn." He fills his goblet a seventh time, downing the contents and throwing his vessel to the floor. Gold clangs against the stone, dented from the strike, and Lord Stilton sways before my cage. He sets the ewer down and grips the frame, leaning close enough for spittle to strike my leg as he hisses, "I will save you for the last."

I say nothing. He is drunk and more of a fool than I had reckoned if he thinks he can goad me to speech. I know better than to give weak men what they desire.

"Declan's *pet*." Stilton fumbles with his waistcoat and trousers. "The bait he never takes for the hunt. Useless bitch." He pulls a stubby worm of a cock free, stroking as his watery eyes trawl my body. At this pathetic display, I remember the second failing of weak men: their predictability. "I will use you if he will not."

He lurches for my cage on drunken legs, tripping and falling heavily. The bars rattle, and the ewer tips onto its side. Holy water rains down, and there is nowhere for me to run. My legs burn. The flesh on my feet bubbles and melts away to reveal bone and charred tendons. This time, I scream, letting the pain and rage shred my throat. Stilton fumbles for his keys, his eyes unfocused and movements slow and clumsy.

But he shoves the key into the lock and manages a half-turn. I shrink back, ignoring the hunger that grows in my belly as his rapid pulse pounds in my ears. The pain is unfathomable, drowning out all thoughts beyond *blood, drink, drain.*

If he gets in, if he gets closer, there is a chance I can override the pain and sink my teeth into his pale, fleshy neck—a chance I can strike a vein.

A loud thunk tears me from my hunger. Lord Stilton gurgles a wet, pained sound, and his mass collapses in front of my cage, revealing Lady Stilton with the ewer in hand. The base is dented, and her face twisted in rage.

"Him first." The ewer flies from her hand, clanking against and rolling across the floor. She twists the key in the lock, hesitating before she opens my cage. "Drain him until his body is as dry as winter wheat."

I nod, lips curled in a grimace—blood thrums in her veins, close enough that I can smell the tang of unpoisoned iron. My fangs descend, and her eyes widen as she sees me for the monster I am. For a moment, I fear she will prove as weak as the man lying on the ground, but then resolve settles on her thin, pinched face.

"Him first," Lady Stilton repeats, jerking the door to my cage open. "And then you and your siblings will kill them all."

"All of them?" I let my surprise show on my face, casting a glance at the unconscious bodies around the hall. "What have they done?"

"Does it matter?" she hisses. "They locked you and your siblings in cages. They reveled in your capture and would witness your death. Take your revenge. Kill them all, and I will shelter you from the sun."

Disappointment overtakes my shock as I see Lady Stilton for who she truly is. Not weak, like Lord Stilton and Declan, no. She is something worse. She is what happens when weakness prevails.

She is cruel.

"Promise me," Lady Stilton presses, blocking the door of my cage.

My only way out is to treat with her, and my body craves what she offers—a chance to feast, to fill my belly with life-giving blood, and heal.

"I promise," I rasp. "I will drain those who sought advantage in my capture. I will take my revenge."

A slash of a smile creases Lady Stilton's cheeks. She rises, leaving a clear path between myself and Lord Stilton, and without a moment to spare, I launch from the cage.

Her shoulders are thin and bony in my grasp, her body creaking as we collide. She claws and scratches, kicking her legs, but I am faster and far stronger than this pitiful, cruel human will ever be.

I tackle her to the ground, and her skin tears like crepe at the gentlest press of my fangs. Lady Stilton shrieks, but anyone who could help her has been drugged by her hand.

Blood bursts from her veins, splashing against my tongue. I groan as the hunger overwhelms me. I have no memory of the taste of wine or meat. No ability to recall the sweetest sugars. There is only the decadence of metal and blood. Filling my mouth, coating my throat, warming my belly, and filling my veins.

This is the tricky part. It is easy to get lost in the bloodlust and become the monsters they think we are. Her body slows, the fight in her limbs overwhelmed by the pleasure of my bite. Soon, her screams become moans, her scratching nails softening until they caress my arms and hair. Ours is a soft death. A lovely death, granted by the venom in our bite, but death all the same.

When her hands fall away from my body, and her pleasured moans turn to sighs, I tear my fangs from her throat. Any pain in my body is a distant memory. My blistered flesh regrown as I feasted; my body returned to its full strength by the gift of her blood. Slowly, I rise, wiping blood from my chin and licking it from my fingers.

Lady Stilton gazes up at me, her small body fragile as porcelain. She lies next to her husband, his putrid mass burbling for every wheeze that escapes her.

"Why?" Her voice is less than a whisper, but no sound is too small for my ears. Not after I have feasted.

"Because you are cruel," I answer. Sweeping the keys from where they fell, I unlock my sibling's cages, greeting them each with clasped hands and soft words. Many nights have passed since I saw them last, and again, they have trusted me to lead them to this moment.

Bait, Declan called me. The lords and their wives never question his choice of words. They let me sit in their hall night after night, blind to the threat I pose.

I am no more bait than I am the trap set to ensnare greedy lords who place themselves above the people and the land. And in every hall we visit, in every manor where I sit in my cage, there is always one who takes the bait.

"Strip the tapestries from the walls and cover the windows," I announce, striding across the hall to stand over Lady Stilton. "The poison should wear off by dawn, and then you may feed. Until then, the silver is in the forge. Melt it down and cast coins using the molds in Lord Stilton's treasury." A handful of my brothers and sisters nod and depart. I do not doubt they will follow my orders. They have for years.

I am a harsh mistress, but I am fair, not cruel. They know a feast awaits them. They know I would never let them languish the way Lord Stilton has allowed his people to flail.

I bend low and tear Lady Stilton's skirt, using a length of cloth to gather the ewer and pass it to a night sister. "Stoke the fire and fetch me a blade."

She nods and departs, knowing what happens next. One of my brothers appears with a leather satchel from Declan's horse. I waste no time stripping off the filthy shift I have worn for the last week and stepping into my leathers and a soft, linen blouse. My knife belt is a comforting weight around my hips, and my fingers deftly lace the corset.

Another sister braids my hair, weaving it into a crown on my head. Once Stilton and his wife are dealt with, there will be time to bathe. For now, there is work to be done.

Lady Stilton whimpers at my feet. I crouch beside her, running my fingers through her thin hair.

"Do you want to know what happens next?" I ask. "Or have you figured it out?"

"Kill me," she wheezes, eyes drifting closed.

"No, no, none of that." I pat her cheek, jostling Lady Stilton to wakefulness. "Stay with me, Lady Stilton. Just a moment longer. There is much to be done."

"The fire's ready," my night sister calls from across the hall. A blaze fills the hearth, burning brighter than all the torches.

"Use the cauldron to melt the ewer," I order, reaching for my knife. "Now, this is the tricky part, Lady Stilton." I show her the blade, wickedly sharp and finely oiled. "I won't lie to you, not when you've been such a gracious host." Leaning close, I grab her jaw, digging my fingers into her thin cheeks to force her mouth open. "This is going to hurt."

Her arms twitch against the floor, eyes rounding like marbles. Fear makes her body tremble, but I am stronger, fueled by her blood and my undying rage. My blade slices cleanly. A garbled scream tears from her throat, and the fat end of her tongue falls away. My mouth waters as blood wells, teasing me with its rich scent. I toss the thick muscle aside, and two of my brothers grab Lady Stilton's arms, holding her down as a sister approaches with the cauldron from the hearth.

"It took us a few tries to perfect the process." I rise to give my siblings room to work. "Lady Beenleigh was our best work to date. She was hardly recognizable by the time we finished. Your own neighbor, and neither you nor your husband batted an eye when we dragged her out. The trick, you see, is to make the alterations *before* we change you. It is the only way to ensure they stick."

I grab a handful of her hair, shearing it away with my knife. Tears stream down Lady Stilton's cheeks, but all fight has left her. She sobs as I work, cutting her hair and nails, carving a wild creature from the lady of the hall. When my sister approaches with the cauldron, I rise and step away, allowing my siblings to do their part.

Silver caps her tongue, the molten liquid burning her lips and vocal cords. Just as Lady Beenleigh before her, I have rendered Lady Stilton mute and left her hovering on the edge of death. She will not be able to speak her story or warn the next hall of the trap they welcomed with open arms. The wretch I have made of her is the vampire she will become.

She will live until her purpose has been served, and her final death will not be in vain.

When the silver cools, I tear my wrist with my fangs, dripping blood into Lady Stilton's mouth. For a moment, she lies still, her chest barely rising and falling, and I fear I have gone too far. When her eyes fly open, they are wild and ravaged by the pain I have inflicted. Her throat works, swallowing my offering, and I see the instant her body awakens to the need. Her limbs tighten, back bowing as hunger hauls her upright. Thin lips latch onto my wrist, and the blunt stump of her tongue prods the wound as if she could tear it wider and drink faster.

My head grows light, but I push her away only when my vision dims around the edges. Lady Stilton reaches for my arm, and a brother moves me out of reach, helping me to my feet while two sisters bundle her in a heavy wool blanket.

"Put her in the cage," I command, thanking my brother with a nod.

When he is certain I can stand, he lets go, attention drifting over the humans in the hall. Some groan in their drugged sleep, while others snore. "And the rest?"

I survey the hall and spy the faint orange glow along the edge of a tapestry covering a window. "The sun rises. Feed, allow no more than fifteen to flee with their lives, and interview the servants. Pull aside those that may be a good fit for our family."

Frowning, he drops his gaze to Lord Stilton's mass. "What about him?"

"The boar drank enough poison to fell a herd." I sneer at Lord Stilton's mass. "Spare him until nightfall. He can be the feast for our newly turned siblings." He smiles at that, fangs glistening in the torchlight. I clasp his shoulder. "We leave before midnight, brother; use the time well."

A smirk pulls his mouth. "You as well."

"I intend to."

Chapter Four

Screams fill the manor like a symphony, punctuated by sobs and scattered begging. I prowl down long hallways and narrow passageways, luxuriating in the sound of terror as I hunt for Declan. More than once, I have found him in the Lord of the hall's bed-chamber, spread across fine linens in a deep sleep. The screams do not bother him, nor does the blood being spilled in part by his hand.

Bait, he called me, as though he were not a part of the trap.

I catch his scent in a richly decorated hall. The carpets are woven in deep maroons and gold, shot through with indigo. Gilt frames line the walls, displaying vibrant oil paintings of Stilton and his ancestors, and crimson silk drapes the length of the ceiling.

All the wealth on the display turns my stomach.

On the road to this hall, we passed through blight-starved villages and fallow fields bordered by plague pits. Stilton was a pox on this land and his people. They will be better off under the leadership of whichever brother or sister I leave as the deputy of this hall. My siblings will work the fields at night while the villages recover. They will divert the streams, build mills, and ingest new life into

Stilton's holding while the wastling lord is neither mourned nor remembered.

But that is work for nightfall. Now, there is a hunter to be dealt with.

"Declan." I sing his name as I turn a corner, trailing my knife along the walls. Sparks fly behind the scrape of my blade, shushing when I cut through a tapestry and across a painting. His scent fills my nose. Salt and sweat, the heat of his muscled body mixing with the earthy smell of horse he can never quite scrub out. At the end of the hall, I close my eyes and inhale, filling my head with Declan Margrave.

Left.

My body moves on instinct, easing into a silent prowl: one door, two, three. I halt at the fourth, smiling when I see Declan has taken no pains to protect himself from me. The lock has been mangled, the knob dangling from bent screws. He forced his way in, stealing this chamber for himself with all the arrogance I expect from him.

I slip into the room, silent as midnight, and the scent of Declan envelops me. My steps falter, hunger itching my fangs. Though I fed from Lady Stilton, turning her drained me. I need to feed again, and the longer I deny myself, the harder it will be to maintain control.

Not that control has ever been a concern where Declan Margrave is concerned. He is weak, and I am not. He may play at being the hunter. He may delight in putting me in my cage and torturing me for the entertainment of wastling lords, but when it is just us, either alone in a room or tangled in the wood, Declan keenly understands which of us is in control.

He lies sprawled across the bed, muscled chest rising and falling in a deep sleep. The candles on the bedside table are nearly burned down, and their meager flames send gold dancing in the strands of his dark brown hair. The sheet is twisted low around his waist, tight against his groin, and heat blooms in my belly as I rake my eyes over him. Hunger and need warring within me.

And then I see it—the holywood stake.

Declan's favorite toy rests on the pillow beside his head, placed within easy reach as an invitation. Golden firelight licks along the silvered tip, liquid and smooth as if freshly oiled. I trail my eyes over the bedside table, noting the bottles and neatly folded squares of linen. Desire puddles warm and hot between my thighs.

I smile, flexing my hand as I decide how to play this. He has been wicked, my Declan, and he must be punished.

My fangs descend as I kneel on the edge of the bed. He does not move when my weight dips the mattress. If anything, his breaths deepen as I lower my face to his hip, jaw relaxing as hunger drives me. This close, his scent is intoxicating. My mind reels, and I allow myself one lapse of control, flicking my tongue out to taste him before I feed.

I lick across a vein, and his pulse throbs in response, tempting me to scrape my fangs across his taut skin. Goosebumps rise as I trace the divot of muscle and bone, and Declan hums in his sleep. The deep, rich sound stokes the fire building inside of me—the need to feed and to punish. To take my pleasure from Declan's body as easily as he doled out pain to mine.

Ours is a dance, a twisting of limbs and minds. When I am caged, I have no choice but to follow him through the steps, but when the bait has been taken ...

Then I take the lead, and my pet is all too willing to dance to my tune.

"You've been bad, Declan," I murmur, my fangs lengthening. Sweet venom pools on my tongue, coating my lips. I swallow it down before pressing my mouth to his hips, sucking to draw a vein to the surface.

He writhes in his sleep, hips rising and falling. A hand comes down on my head, and I smile despite myself. It is better when he wakes for this. Better he when is reminded of what I am so that he and I both know he enters this willingly.

I am a terror. His monster and his master. I would see the hunger and fright in his eyes before I sink my fangs into his hip and slake my thirst.

"Rhona." He groans my name, swallowing the vowels in the low, rumbly way I cannot resist. Fingers burrow into my hair, upsetting the crown my sister braided. "Please, Rhona."

"You are awake."

"Hard to sleep knowing you're in that cage." He rolls his hips, and the swell of his erection butts against my temple. His fingers knot in my hair, and he tugs as if he could guide my mouth to his groin.

"I doubt that stopped you throughout the week." I scrape my fangs across his lower abdomen, relishing each goosebumps and the thickening scent of his arousal. At the second roll of his hips, I know what game he wants to play. "Did you forget, pet, that I own you?"

I score his skin with a fang, banding an arm across his abdomen to keep Declan where he lies. I need to feed, but I am not the weak vampire I was in that cage. Declan hisses, muscles dancing at the pain I have dealt him. His fingers twitch, but his hold remains, so I do it again and again. Cutting and puncturing his skin until the dusting of hair between his navel and groin is dotted and streaked with fat, wine-red pearls of blood.

His scent overwhelms me, driving into my mind and muddling my thoughts. The heat in my belly simmers, hunger clawing at my stomach. More venom drips from my fangs, pooling sickly sweet on my tongue.

"Never," Declan pants. A sheen of sweat makes his skin glow in the candlelight. Each dip, swell, and jut of his body, from the taut muscles in his stomach to the roll of his pectorals, begs for my teeth and tongue. "I'm yours, Rhona. Use me."

I glance up at him, drinking in the strain on his face. His eyes are shut tight, his jaw clenched. Though his fingers pinch my scalp, he lies ready for me, cock jutting like a mast beneath the sheets, his body my willing plaything.

"Tell me what you want, Declan." I lower my voice, speaking with an authority that makes his cock bob. A flick of my tongue catches three ruby beads, and his rich taste floods my senses. I snarl, biting my tongue to keep from sinking my fangs into his copper-rich skin.

"Whatever you'll give me." Damp spreads along the tight stretch of linen over his head, and Declan shivers. "Whatever you ask."

"Good," I purr and give in, lathing his abdomen with the flat of my tongue. He sighs, cock straining against the street. I draw closer and closer, only to skirt away, relishing his frustrated whimper. I know what he wants, but to bite him and draw from his cock would pleasure Declan too greatly. He must suffer first for how he treated me in that cage. He must be reminded that I am the master, despite how he lays stretched across the bed and weak beneath me.

"On your stomach," I rasp as I pull away, sliding my hand over the wounds I have gifted him. The hunger in my belly rails against me, my need to be filled and to feast, fighting against my inborn desire to hear him cry for mercy. Blood smears across his belly, and I pop a finger into my mouth, resting on my knees as I lick and suck. Declan's eyes fly open, dark with desire and trained on the sweep of my tongue and hollowing of my cheeks. His chest rises and falls, and he hesitates long enough that I raise an eyebrow.

It is the only threat he needs. A subtle reminder of who his master is.

Grabbing a pillow, he rolls onto his front and stuffs it under his lower abdomen to give his aching cock room. Not that it will do him any good. I have plans for that cock. It is not the sad, soft nub Lord Stilton threatened me with. No, like the rest of Declan, his cock is a thing of beauty. Thick and red with gathered blood. The vein throbbing along its length is juicy as a worm in spring, and my fangs itch with desire at the thought of hot, rich blood pumping from his cock as Declan pumps into my mouth.

Later.

When he has earned it.

For now, I stretch over his body, reaching for the stake. The warmth of his back radiates against my breasts and belly. I bury my face in the crook of his neck, inhaling deeply before pressing my fangs to the artery. His pulse pounds against my teeth, ramped all the higher by terror and desire. Of me, for me, as it should be.

He does not glance back as I take hold of the stake, instead reaching up to grasp the rails in the headboard.

"Good boy," I murmur into his throat. Declan thrusts his hips back, pressing his rear into my belly. "But you'll not escape your punishment that easily."

"No, Rhona."

I trail the silver tip of the stake down the length of his arm, circling the crook of his elbow. Muscles in Declan's arms strain as he fights against the tickling sensation. He buries his face in the mattress, taking long breaths as I draw light circles along his biceps, armpit, and down the long stretch of his side.

"You stabbed me," I whisper in his ear and jab the tip into his side. Declan grunts, knuckles blanching as his grip tightens. When I remove the stake, red blemishes his tanned skin, the beginnings of a bruise. The blood rushing to the surface of his skin makes my nose itch, like a sneeze I cannot release. "You made me look weak in front of Lord Stilton and his hall."

I jab him again, harder this time. His body seizes beneath me, and the pained whimpers that push from his throat are music to my ears. The tip of the stake is crimson when I pull it away. Blood rushes from the wound, pulsing with every one of Declan's sweet pants, and I can no longer deny myself.

I latch onto his side, digging my nails into the curve of his rear as I suck and tongue the wound. My head spins, my pulse pounding as his blood fills me and strengthens me. The heat of it stokes the fire in my belly, setting off a low, delicious throb in my core. Need overwhelms me, and that is all the warning I need. I snag my lip with my fangs, letting my blood mingle with his. Trace amounts of venom enter his bloodstream, and Declan's body eases, his pained pants softening to light wheezes as pleasure rises.

It is not enough to bring him to ecstasy. Only enough to ease the pain and slow the bleeding so that I may keep working.

"I am not weak, Declan." My voice is raw and guttural, the monster in me closer to the surface than before. I rest on my thighs and take in the meal stretched before me. Blood stains the linens at Declan's side, his sweatslick skin glistening in the candlelight. Muscles twitch and flex as he breathes through pain edged in pleasure, his mind already dropping into the space where I know he is mine and mine alone. "You are weak. A toy. A pet."

I trace my nails over his rear and hip, curving around to his front to hitch him onto his knees, just enough for me to lightly grasp his cock. He jerks against me as I do, a strangled sound bit off by a clenching of his teeth.

"My pet." I stroke to the tip, licking my lips as precum dampens my fingers. "Good, needy pet."

I twist my wrist, and he groans. "Rhona."

"Did I say speak?"

His hands adjust against the bedframe, and Declan rubs his face into the mattress, shaking his head. I am about to lean forward and give him the pleasure of my bite when he thrusts into my hand, seeking the pressure and friction I have denied him.

Anger sparks. I tear my hand away, using all of my vampiric strength to crash it against his backside. Declan growls, more in shock than pain, and glares over his shoulder at me.

"You speak when I say you may speak." I smack him again, my strike drawing blood to the surface. "You are my pet to do with as I please."

"Yes, Rhona."

He closes his eyes when I strike again, brows hitching and lips parting.

"You owe everything to me, pet." And again. This time, he bites his lower lip, nostrils flaring as he takes the punishment I deal. "Everything you are, the life you lead. You breathe because I allow it, understand?"

Declan does not reply. A shudder racks his shoulders, and he presses his face against the mattress. I hesitate, watching each tremor and counting every breath.

"Dawn?" I ask.

The rails creak as he tightens his grip.

"Declan." I press a hand between his shoulder blades. "Dawn?"

"Moonrise," he blurts, voice muffled. "Gods, Rhona, moonrise. Please, don't stop."

A smile overtakes my face. I stroke my hand down his spine, and Declan rolls into my touch, every inch of his glorious body responsive and mine. I bend over his back, scraping his ear with my teeth. Venom sweetens my breath, and I bite the space beneath his ear. Declan's cry of pleasure is music to my ears. A whine tempered with desire that has my cunt clenching.

"Tell me," I ask before puncturing his throat a second time. More of my venom enters his bloodstream, and Declan relaxes beneath me. "Tell me, pet, why do I own you?"

"Because you killed them." His tongue is thick and drunken, words slurring from my bite and the pleasure riddling his body. "You killed them all."

"Why?" I lap at his neck, mind reeling from the richness of his blood. I will never tire of this. All that muscle, all that strength on display for the lords and ladies we hunt, and he is weak for me. Pliant and subservient, taking the punishment I dole and begging for more. "Speak, Declan."

"They beat us and starved us," he says. "They sold the girls for a night of entertainment and pitted the boys against each other in the ring." I kiss my way down his body, rewarding him with every true word he speaks. For grounding me in what we do, hall and after hall. For reminding me why I let him live.

I have forgotten the taste of wine and berries and cakes. If I am not careful, I will forget this.

"They beat us when we lost." He shudders as I drag my fangs across his lower back. "Beat us and tossed us into the cold."

"And then?" I pinch his cheek with a fang, cupping his rear.

"You found me."

"I did." Spreading his cheeks, I breathe against his hole. "Good pet."

Declan wriggles, knowing better than to speak when he has earned a reward. I draw venom and saliva onto my tongue before dragging my fangs down sensitive flesh. His cheeks tense at the pain, no more than a splinter, and then I sweep the meager wounds with my tongue. Declan's moan vibrates through his body, as deep and guttural as his voice the day he asked me to kill them all.

"Every lord," he had rasped. "Every lady. Every wretched piece of filth that treats us like vermin."

And I did. I was new, then. More monster than mistress, and my hunger knew no bounds. I glutted myself on his keepers, drinking until my stomach threatened to burst, and the rest I drained while Declan opened the cells and recruited my brothers and sisters. Hall to hall we went, setting traps and cutting out the rot of humanity. One by one, the children I rescued grew into men and women. One by one, they asked to become my night siblings. To help me cleanse these lands of the festering blemish of humanity.

All but Declan.

"You like me weak," he had said with a cocky grin, and I could not argue. Knowledge may be the first major failing of weak men, but this is not always a curse.

I love him like this, drunk off my venom and liquid beneath my hands. Whimpering and panting. My plaything and lover when the rest have become my kin.

The thought lengthens my fangs, and they pierce the tender flesh beside his hole. Declan curses, legs shooting straight as I leave them inserted and suck. My name leaves his lips like a prayer, the heat of his body rising as I draw blood to his nethers. I swear, it is richer when I drink from him like this. Sweeter and more intoxicating when drawn from a place that gives him as much pleasure as it does me.

Moisture pools in my leggings, the leather teasing my clit as I rock my hips, seeking more friction, the same as Declan. He presses against my mouth, and his scent drowns out my thoughts. There is a hint of lavender and rose. A hint of the lye from a wealthy woman's soap, but the rest is all him. Musk and sweat, the earthiness of his leathers. It has me grasping his cheeks and spreading them wide, pooling venom and saliva on my tongue before I thrust into his hole.

He gasps above me, a restrained cry of pleasure that ribbons into my ears. But soon, his body is lax, and the muscles are all but drawing my tongue deeper. I thrust and roll, massaging his cheeks before I pull away and replace my tongue with a finger. Declan's groan as I insert a digit is pure, mind-bending bliss. I turn my wrist and crook my finger, earning another sweet cry.

"Dawn?" I ask.

He takes a moment to answer, so I crook my finger again.

"Moonrise!" he shouts, back arching so he can look at me. "Moonrise, fuck the Gods, Rhona, please."

"Good pet." I crook again, savoring his moan. "You speak when I say speak." He nods, and I accept his answer, reaching again for the holywood stake. "You come when I say come."

The handle fits my palm perfectly, and the leather is worn to the curve of my fingers. Declan's eyes widen in anticipation, and I remove my finger from his hole to twist the blood-coated silver tip. It pops off with ease, revealing the ridged, blunt end.

He exhales, eyes dark and liquid, and presses his rear toward me. Without a word between us, he releases the headboard and grabs a bottle from the bedside table, easily flicking the cork free with his thumb and handing it to me.

"Good pet," I murmur and coat the stake in oil. Some spills onto my hand, and I use it to stroke and pet my plaything, circling his hole and inserting my finger.

Adjusting my stance, I grasp his cheek and spread him wide, pressing the blunted edge against his hole. Declan grunts, hand flying for the headboard as I insert the ridged head.

"Speak."

"Moonrise." He presses back, telling me with his body and his words how badly he wants this, how he wants me to dominate him. To remind him he is weak. That I am his mistress. I who spared him and cared for him, who heals him with my blood and pleasures him with my tongue, venom, and cunt.

I am his monster, and he is weak for me.

I fuck him slowly with the stake, watching every twitch and tremor in his face. The roll and flex of muscle in his back and arms. Low light from the dying candles gilds his skin. Tight, pleasured whines escape his plush lips, and a flush rides high on his cheeks. His eyes are feverish as he watches me with one cheek pressed against the mattress.

He is beautiful like this.

All too soon, it overwhelms me. His beauty in this moment and the power I wield over him. What we have achieved in this hall and the halls before it. What is yet to come. Declan and I will cleanse this land, creating a new world under the rule of my night siblings.

All too soon, I crave his touch and the stretch of his cock. With a twist of my wrist, the handle of the stake clicks free. I cast it aside, using all my strength to flip Declan onto his back. The move rams the stake deeper within him. He cries out as I draw him upright, pressing his mouth to my throat as I tear the laces of my corset and shred the front of my shirt.

He knows what I want, how I want it. His mouth latches onto my breast, tongue flicking my tightened nipple, and I remove my leathers to straddle him. His cock presses between us, the thick base teasing my clit. I roll my hips, tensing my thighs in search of the friction I crave.

Declan again needs no instruction. Ours is a dance, and while I lead, he is well-trained in the steps. He knows how to please me and ensure I come to him morning after morning for the pleasure none of my night siblings can offer.

A warm body and stroking hands. Fleshy lips and thrumming blood and a cock that can make me see the Gods.

He grasps my hips, lifting me with ease and settling me on his cock. Pleasure shoots through my body at the press of his thick head, stretching me in such a delicious way I cannot help but throw my head back and moan. Easing me down, Declan returns to my breast, sucking each nipple as his fingers grasp my hips hard enough I would bruise if I could. Only when I am seated does Declan ease his grip. He slides a hand between us, thumb brushing my clit. Sparks fly up my spine, throwing my body into a rigor mortis only more of his touch can relax.

"Use me," he growls against my breastbone. His demand ignites something within me—a rage brought on by his insubordination and disobedience.

I snarl and grasp his biceps, nails cutting into his skin. Blood wells, and the scent of it drives me forward. My fangs slide into his throat like a hot knife through butter, and I slam down against him. Molten heat floods my belly and Declan curses. His hand finds its way into my hair, grabbing hold as I rise and slam down again, taking pleasure from his body. Hot blood in my mouth, a thick cock in my cunt. I ride him cruelly, sparks bursting in my eyes every time I crash against him.

The movement jostles the stake in his rear, driving it harder against a place that makes him grunt and groan. His arms tremble, his firm legs quaking beneath me. His thumb circles my clit, and the movement drowns me in bliss. Tension builds as I ride him, drawn together by the sweep of his thumb and the pulse of his blood, filling my mouth and my belly as my venom sends him careening to the ceiling.

I pull my fangs out of him to moan his name, the only warning Declan gets before my cunt clenches around his cock, and euphoria strikes like lightning in my veins.

My back shoots straight, head falling back as I release a ragged cry he interprets as permission.

"Rhona." The groan of my name rumbles against my chest, and his cock seems to thicken and twitch before he spills inside of me. His

seed mingles with blood from the wounds I have inflicted, filling the
room with more of Declan's scent. I am feral, half-mad in the throes
of orgasm, clawing at his back and rocking my hips in search of more
even as he is spent.

Declan falls back, rolling onto his side and slipping out of me.
Before I can fight or move or fully process his absence, he pushes me
onto my back and hauls my cunt to his face. His tongue thrusts inside
of me, writhing and flicking, licking me clean as I wind tighter and
tighter, only to fall apart a second time.

Wave after wave of pleasure overtakes me, and when I come back
to myself, I am panting against the sheets. Distantly, I hear the clunk
of the stake being tossed aside, and then Declan is there, wrapping his
arms around my body and gathering me close.

How long we lie there, lost in the shared bliss of release, I do not
know. When I turn my head, the candles are puddles of wax, and the
room is lit only by the dim glow of day behind the drapes.

Declan's breathing is deep, his eyes closed and face soft in a way
that reminds me of the youth I spared from the cold. As if he hears
my thoughts, his arms tighten around me, and he nuzzles the crook of
my neck.

"What next?"

"Lord Stilton still lives," I answer, pressing back against him.
Declan makes a sound I interpret as surprise. "His blood was too
poisoned to risk. He will be the feast for any new siblings we turn."

"Good." He twists, drawing a blanket from the floor to cover us
both. "And the lady?"

"She has been prepared for the next hall."

"How long do we wait this time?"

"Two weeks." A yawn overtakes me, and I relax into Declan's
arms. Sleep comes on quickly, thickening my tongue as my body falls
into death. "Perhaps three, you'll need time to—"

"Recruit men and let the fear and rumors spread." Declan kisses
my temple as he bands an arm across my chest, pressing me tight
against him. "I know."

He knows.

Of course he does.

"Sleep, Rhona, my love."

A soft smile plays on my lips, and in my last conscious thoughts before sleep takes me, I dwell on the failings of weak men.

THE END
(for now)

If you enjoyed this story, check out my enemies-to-lovers witchy urban fantasy romance series *Witch of the Demesne*, about a formerly wicked witch defending her hometown from multi-level marketing huns, and the hot Scottish witch sent to investigate her.

About the Author

B.L. Brown writes paranormal and urban fantasy romance about disaster witches making increasingly poor decisions. Her books are queer, sex-positive, and full of magic and mayhem. For her social media and direct links to books, visit: https://linktr.ee/brittabrau

Sins Of The Father

By: Rebecca Rathe

A Dark MM Short Story

About Sins of the Father

Levi Asher is determined to expose Senator Mathias Havre as the corrupt politician he believes him to be. To get closer to his target, Levi sets his sights on the senator's perfect son, but Adam isn't what he expects—he's sweet, kind, and innocent in a way that makes Levi ache.

Adam Havre has devoted his life to his family and his faith, but he's tempted beyond his control by the handsome stranger he meets at church. Despite his fear about the forbidden attraction, he sees a light in Levi that pulls him in and convinces him that pleasure this right can't be wrong.

When Adam learns the truth of Levi's intentions, he questions everything he thought he knew about himself and his beliefs. And when Levi uncovers the evidence he needs to expose the senator, he finds himself torn between his feelings for Adam and vengeance.

Can he punish the son for the sins of the father?

Content Note:

This story contains mature content that is intended for readers 18 & older. This is a dark and toxic story that may trigger sensitive readers. Sensitive content includes but is not limited to: religious trauma, manipulation, lies and betrayal, discussion and imagery of a forced medical abortion and injury thereafter, and of course graphic language and sex acts.

Relationship type: MM

Chapter One
Levi

"Heavenly Father, we come before you today, humbled and grateful for your love and grace. Thank you for your gift of salvation through..."

"Jesus, you're serious? What are you—*Oh, God...*"

"...We acknowledge, Oh Lord, that without your strength, we are weak..."

"*Uunnngh—*"

"...your help to live in purity and righteousness. Lord, we pray that you will guard our hearts and minds. Help us to honor you with our thoughts, our actions, and our..."

"Levi? I can't—*Ungh—ahh—*I'm—"

"When temptation comes our way, give us the wisdom to recognize it and the courage to resist. Strengthen our resolve, Oh Lord, and surround us with your peace. We ask you to fill us with the power of your Holy Spirit..."

"Oh. My. *Gahhh—* Levi, I'm gonna—"

"...In Jesus' name, we pray."

"Ohhh *Gooooood!*"

A-fucking-men.

I groan, capturing the jets of Adam's hot load as he spills into my mouth. The bittersweet flavor of his cum coats my tongue and the sounds of his delicious blasphemy fill my ears. Fuck, he's almost loud enough for the congregation to hear him.

The head of his fat cock pushes his cum further into the back of my throat, and the effort to not swallow too much causes me to choke. He stills and pulls back, cock still twitching as it slips from between my lips.

Cool air hits my heated body as Adam pulls his robes up to look down at me. I greet his worried expression with a knowing smirk. He's about to start freaking out. Now that I've sucked the cum from him like a thick milkshake through a thin straw, the post nut clarity is hitting him. He's worrying about the state of his soul when he leaves this earth and stands before the pearly gates. Or what his father would think.

"Are you okay?" He asks, eyes wide. Ever the gentleman, he's making sure he didn't hurt me before worrying about himself. I give it a moment, waiting for it to sink in.

Three... Two... One...

A small, choked gasp leaves him as he steps back, letting his robes fall. His pants are still undone, spent cock hanging out of his underwear and dripping onto the front of his khaki trousers.

The small table behind him jostles when he bumps into it. "Communion," he whispers, remembering what he was supposed to be doing back here. He spins around, frantically touching everything, making sure it's all in place. It is. I've been waiting here like a predator, knowing he'd have to step back here to collect the communion tray for Pastor Reynard.

Adam takes a deep breath, his thickly muscled chest caving inward as his shoulders droop. I stand, adjusting my erection so it's pulled up against my stomach, hopefully hidden well enough behind the waistband of my black dress pants. I smooth out my grey dress shirt while I give Adam a moment to collect himself.

The poor guy has been on edge all morning, trying to avoid

looking at me as I burned holes into the back of his head from the last pew while he sat at the front with his family, hanging on to every word Pastor Reynard said and jumping up to perform his duties as assistant to the pastor. The altar boys, or whatever they call them, are busy getting the recreation hall ready for the potluck. I took a risk and assumed Adam would have to retrieve the communion tray, and it definitely paid off. Honestly, I didn't expect him to cave the way he did. He's been putty in my hands since the first time I made him come by doing nothing more than cupping his crotch and whispering in his ear that I knew his secret.

Sweet, soft, simple Adam, the prodigal son of Senator Mathis Havre. He's the textbook definition of a himbo. Tall, dark, and handsome, built like a renaissance statue, and dumber than a box of rocks. Always ready to show his love of Jesus through the efforts of helping hands and hard work. And since ignorance is bliss, he's always happy. Well, he was. And then I set my sights on him. There was no going back once I noticed the way his hazel eyes burned into me with an interest that I'm pretty sure he still doesn't understand.

I should feel bad for the way I affect him, but the truth is I revel in it. I feed on it like a bloodsucking leech.

Adam wants to believe the best of me. He wants to believe I'm a good little Christian boy just like him, no matter how much I show him otherwise. He's too good—too sweet—to see that I've planted myself next to him to get something I need. To find my way in. A wolf in sheep's clothing that will eventually tear his carcass apart to get what I want.

I'm here for a reason. And I won't be satisfied until I expose every evil bone in his father's body. Until the whole world knows what kind of man Senator Havre truly is and what he's capable of. What he's done to cover his own tracks and keep his shiny public persona squeaky clean.

His son will suffer for his sins.

Adam turns around, face flaming red and sweaty, like he's already being roasted over the pit of hell. A smile, although not exactly a kind one, spreads across my lips.

I step forward, crowding into his space. He freezes, like he always does when I get this close, and sucks in a breath through his teeth when I lift the front of the stupid robe he wears to signify his position in the church. He's a glorified altar boy, all too happy to let the church take advantage of his time and talents for the good of the congregation and ministry.

Keeping my eyes locked on his, I slip my hands under the robe and tuck his cock back into his pants, then zip and button his fly. His lips part when I give his crotch a little pat, like it's been a good boy. Then I surge forward to kiss him. He gasps as I take his mouth with mine, whimpering when I force my tongue inside and feed him the mouthful of his own cum I've been holding just for him.

"You taste so sweet," I murmur against his lips, rubbing my erection against his thigh, letting him feel how hard he makes me. "Do you feel what you do to me?" He whimpers again, and my cock throbs. I fucking love the desperate, terrified little noises he makes. "I'm not done with you, sweet boy. Come find me after the service."

"We have th-the potluck. And the youth group is—"

"—going to go sing worship songs at the old folk's home. Yeah, I know." I pull back, rubbing my thumb across his wet, swollen bottom lip. "But I want these pretty lips around my cock, and I can't wait too long. Find me, or I'll find you."

Adam's pupils grow darker, then he flinches and looks away when he hears the bell announcing communion. He straightens and smooths down his robe, trying not to look directly at me as he picks up the tray and makes his way towards the stage and pulpit where Pastor Reynard waits for him. Before he disappears from sight, he turns his head and nods curtly. The look of uncertainty and his flushed cheeks make my cock jerk.

On my way out, I stop in the lobby to check my reflection. What I see reminds me why I'm here, and my eyes dim. The way hers have. Because of what that monster did to her.

Maybe it's unfair to use someone as soft and sweet as Adam to get my revenge. If I were a better person, I'd feel bad. But whatever good I had inside me has been swallowed by pain and anger. From the moment I saw Adam watching me, I knew I had my target. My way in.

Senator Havre has to suffer for what he did. And I'm going to use his sweet, stupid son to expose his sins to the world.

Chapter Two
Adam

Potluck Sundays are my favorite. After church, everyone comes together in the recreation hall, arms laden with dishes to share. It's usually casseroles. I love casseroles. They're like comfort on a plate, happiness and love in a baking dish, warmed to share with others. And no one, and I mean no one, makes better casseroles than southern church ladies. It's common knowledge.

I don't even care how hard I'm going to have to hit the gym tomorrow, I make sure to get a little bit of each and every dish that the women of our congregation have set out buffet style. It's probably a little gluttonous, but I don't skip even one dish. What if sweet Mrs. Kelse asks me how I liked her cheesy potato bake, and I didn't have any of it? It's not like I could lie to her, and I couldn't bear to hurt her feelings. Surely my gluttony is justified if I'm trying to make others happy.

With a heavily laden plate of delicious comfort food, I make my way across the room to find somewhere to sit. I avoid my father's judgmental stare from the front of the room, where he is sitting with Pastor Reynard and the other church officials, like he normally does. As an upcoming member of the clergy, I should probably go sit with them. They probably expect me to. But the youth group is close to my heart. And Levi is here somewhere...

My mouth dries up when I see him sitting at a long table towards the back of the room. He's talking to Leah, a girl in our youth group who is a few years younger. She's petite and gorgeous, with tanned skin and long, dark hair that reaches her waist. Thick, dark eyelashes frame her amber eyes. It's a sharp contrast to Levi's wavy blond locks and bright blue eyes. Sometimes I think everything about him is made of light. God's light.

Seeing him always makes me feel strange. You'd think I'd be used to him by now, but my skin tingles whenever he's near me. I don't see anyone but him until I notice his hand on Leah's back. They're leaning their heads together, whispering like they have a secret. She seems upset. Levi is down on a knee next to her chair, rubbing her back.

"Leah? Are you okay?"

She sniffs and looks up at me, then shares a look with Levi. Like they know something I don't.

Levi clears his throat and resumes rubbing her back. I barely hear what he's saying through the blood rushing in my ears as my eyes zero in on the casual way he touches her. I have to shake my head out of it, remembering that he's trying to comfort the younger woman.

"Leah's mother is being deported. It's the same issue Mr. Alba had," he says solemnly.

Leah's father had to move back to Guatemala a couple of years ago because of an issue with his work visa.

I look at Leah. "How is that possible? You were born here. Doesn't that mean your parents can stay?"

Leah shakes her head. "That's not how it works."

"That seems wrong."

Leah scoffs and stands up, wiping her face. Her back straightens. "Why don't you ask your father about it?"

What does that mean? I glance over to my father's table, noticing the way he watches Leah flee the room. I can't quite read the expression on his face from here, but my stomach clenches all the same. He has never been as welcoming to the Alba family as he should, never giving them the same kindness and respect as the other members of our congregation.

One of the few times I've ever talked back to my father was around the time that Mr. Alba was deported. I was still in high school, and my father had made an offhanded comment about having "illegals" in the congregation. Considering we have very few church members of color, it wasn't hard to guess what family he was referring to. I'd mentioned that they were good people, hard workers, and active members of the church. He told me I was too young to understand how this country works and gave me a lecture about how illegal immigration was harmful to the economy and dangerous for crime rates.

The Albas were here legally, paid taxes, and were upstanding members of our community. When I pointed that out, he brushed me off as disrespectful and sent me to my room to pray for forgiveness and understanding that he was protecting our way of life. After all, shouldn't I defer to him, as both the head of our household and an elected representative of the government, to make the right choices for us?

I prayed on it, but I never came to the conclusion he wanted me to. Instead, my prayers led me to find quiet ways to help the Alba family where I could. Including writing a letter of recommendation to the university that I recently graduated from. With Leah's excellent grades and extra-curricular work that she does with our youth ministry, she was offered a full scholarship. What happens to that scholarship if her mother's immigration status is challenged, or if her mother has to leave the country before she graduates high school this year? Will she have to leave too? She doesn't have any other family in the states that I'm aware of, and she's only seventeen.

My father's disapproving gaze locks on mine, and I force some pleasantry into my steely expression. I nod in his direction, and he smiles. A little hope unfurls in my chest.

"Maybe I can talk to my dad, see if there's anything he can do." Maybe now that he won the senate race, he could help Leah's family. Surely after all this time he knows they're good people and wouldn't want their family to be separated. All it would take is a letter from him to the immigration offices, I'm sure of it.

Levi lets out a small scoff, prompting me to turn my attention to look at him. "What?" I ask softly. I don't think I said anything funny.

With a small shake of his head, he takes a seat at the table. I pull out the chair directly across from him and sit, trying not to stare too obviously at his face. He's just so beautiful. I know I shouldn't think that way, but he is. So much so that I completely lose control of myself whenever he's too close. I keep letting him—

"You're thinking about it," he says softly, eyes glittering.

A shiver runs through me. It's uncanny how he always seems to know what I'm thinking. If I hadn't seen the evidence of his goodness myself, I'd worry that he's an agent of the Devil, sent to trick me into wickedness. Sometimes I still worry, but the warm feeling I get in my chest when I see him can't be a trick. And this wickedness inside me has always been there. It's something I've never been able to rid myself of, no matter how much I pray. When I begged God for a light when I was feeling trapped in the darkness of my own thoughts, *he* showed up.

I'll never absolve myself of the sins I've committed since meeting Levi. And today, in our house of God, of all places...

"It was wrong."

"Was it?"

"We were in church. Pastor Reynard was leading prayer less than twenty feet away!" I hiss, angrier at myself than I am at him.

Not only is it wrong, but we could have been caught. Anyone could have walked around the corner and seen us like that. With Levi on his knees and me... in his mouth.

"You were praying plenty," Levi purrs. I choke on my own spit, reaching for my glass of lemonade and gulping it down as the seats fill up around us.

Levi's eyes lock with mine, a smirk pulling his lips up on one side.

The kids from the youth group close in around us, talking excitedly about today's performance. I try to clear my nerves so I can engage with them, but I'm too flustered to make any sense.

Jesus.

A shiver races down my spine. The starched fabric of my pants becomes uncomfortably tight.

Tearing my eyes away from Levi's mouth is painful, but I manage to pull myself together enough to look away before my situation gets much, much worse.

"I want these pretty lips around my cock..."

Levi Asher has touched me, more than once, and in more than one way. He's done things to my body that I'm ashamed to admit has me considering that I've been wrong about what it means to commune with God. His hands and mouth have made me forget who I am and the values I grew up with. For goodness' sake, I forgot I was in church this morning when he dropped to his knees and looked up at me with those clear blue eyes.

He's touched me, but I've yet to reciprocate. I've been afraid to. More than that, I've been ashamed of how much I want to. Even now, as much as it scares me to admit to even myself, my mouth fills with saliva at the thought of putting him in my mouth. Kissing him felt like the most salacious act only weeks ago, when Levi showed up seemingly out of nowhere. I was immediately intrigued by him. I couldn't tear my eyes away from how absolutely beautiful he is.

Levi clears his throat and smiles, like he knows the direction my thoughts have fallen. I swallow deeply, clenching my hands where I've rested them in my lap.

"Dessert?" Levi asks, and I nod.

He excuses himself from the table, wishing the youth group luck with their performance this afternoon. They fawn over him, begging him to come with us, but he smiles and makes excuses about visiting his sister.

I've never met his sister. I think she might live outside of town, but not too far, because Levi visits her often. He's staying with his mom while he takes a break from school, before starting a graduate program in the fall.

After giving him a few minutes, I get up from the table, too. We have almost two hours before we have to get on the bus, but we need time to get far away from here.

I nearly collide with my father on the way out. "Where's the fire?" *Did he see Levi leave? Does he suspect that I'm following him?*

Surely not. I'd be shipped off to *Deliverance Summit* in a heartbeat. *Reparative therapy for wayward boys experiencing identity confusion and unnatural predilections*. I flat out heard my father said they torture the patients, to break them and reprogram them. Something my father believes is warranted and necessary.

I idolized my father growing up, always believed he was a good man. He's an official in the church, and was a respected lawyer before serving on the local city council for over a decade. There is a lot we don't see eye-to-eye on, though. He's very old-fashioned. But I still thought he was a good person.

That is until I started listening and noticing more.

Despite being the son of a politician, I never much paid attention to politics. I've dedicated my life to church, family, and sports, in that order. I graduated with my bachelor's degree in Christian Studies a few months ago, and I'm headed to Seminary this summer. There's never been much room in my head for all the squabbling and taking sides worse than sports rivalries. But the events of the past few years, from the George Floyd protests to the Capitol riot in Washington, DC, have opened my eyes to the world around me. I began to notice things, like how the people closest to me treated people who look, love, think, or worship differently than we do. I began to notice that the so-called "traditional values" I grew up with weren't the right path for everyone. I started to see the imbalance in our own home and started paying attention to what kind of world my father was advocating for.

I didn't vote for my father. And I didn't vote for the man he thinks of as a messiah for bringing America back to Christian values. Never mind that he's a convicted felon who, by his actions, seems to be the antithesis of Christian values.

As I stood in the gymnasium of our town community center, I watched my father hover behind my mother while she made her choices. I looked around and saw several couples standing in similar positions. I don't think I would have noticed it before, but just weeks before, there had been a social media advertisement that my father had just about lost his mind over. It was about wives being able to vote however they like, and that their husbands would never know otherwise. Pastor Reynard stood on the pulpit that next Sunday and preached that men are the heads of the household and that the responsibility of decision making should lie on their shoulders as God intended. Wives, he said, should vote as their husbands direct them to, that they are bound by their union to be as one in all things. It's the first time I ever wanted to stand up and walk out, to disagree with the man that I considered my mentor, and who will eventually become my boss once I'm through with Seminary and come to work at the church officially.

On voting day, I strongly considered causing a scene. I wanted to demand that the tall tables with partitions didn't provide enough privacy, that there should be more space between them, that people shouldn't be able to congregate together, even as families, to vote. Because I know if I had been standing next to my parents rather than across from them, my father would have looked at and tried to influence my ballot the way I know he was doing to my mother.

I'm sure he trusted that I was voting the way he'd coached me. Admittedly, it's how I made my decisions the first few elections I voted in. Before I started to pay attention. Back when I trusted that my father had good intentions and cared about his constituents.

"Son?"

I jolt out of my thoughts, remembering that I was trying to come up with an excuse for my hasty retreat.

"Sorry, sir. I'm just a little embarrassed. I got some of Mrs. Mill's chicken pot pie dropped right in my lap, and we're heading to the retirement home soon. I thought I'd just pop home real quick to change. I'll be gone before you and mom get home, but I'll be home for dinner later," I add on, rambling like an idiot.

"We have plans this evening and likely won't be home until late," he reminds me, staring at me a little too intently. Like he knows I'm lying. I've been holding my jacket in front of my pants to hide the stain from my earlier indiscretions, and I take the opportunity to show him now, hoping the spot that I scrubbed at with flimsy paper towels and hand soap will pass as a food slip and not bodily fluids leftover from being drained within an inch of my life. My face flames, and I think it's enough to convince my father. He shakes his head and dismisses me with a remark about being a twenty-three-year-old man child that needs a bib.

Chapter Three
Levi

"Fucking finally," I say, leaning against the bed of Adam's big, shiny, black truck.

"Get in," he hisses, looking over his shoulder to check if anyone is watching. He parks all the way around the back of the lot because his massive vehicle doesn't fit into a normal parking spot, so I don't think he has too much to worry about. But there are only so many things I can pick on him for in one afternoon.

"Why exactly does anyone need a truck this big?" I ask as I buckle myself in, lifting an eyebrow at the pristine condition of the cab. It still smells like new leather and money.

"I probably don't, and it gets terrible gas mileage," Adam replies as he pulls out of the lot and onto the road. I don't ask where we're going, because I don't actually care. He can take me behind a dumpster at an inland seafood restaurant if it means I get to see golden boy Adam Havre on his knees with my cock in his mouth. "It's convenient sometimes, though. Like if someone needs help to move, or if we need to transport fifty cases of water and a ton of other stuff across the state line for hurricane relief."

I nod, trying to focus on his words and not on the way his mouth moves.

He wears his happiness and pride over his usefulness all over his face. His lips are pulled into a broad grin, and I've decided that I've either done something very, very right or I'm being punished in some deviously clever way, because this man has dimples. *Fucking dimples!*

"It is a big truck bed..." His smile drops, eyes wide and serious as he focuses on the road more intently than he was before, squirming in his seat. Just as we're pulling into a long driveway, I unbuckle my seat and lean across the center console to lick his earlobe. "I can think of some things I could do to you in this truck. There's plenty of space—"

"We're here!" he shouts, his voice almost cracking with nerves. Did he forget that we left explicitly to get some privacy? And where is *here*? Was he not driving us somewhere secluded so we can suck each other dry?

Apparently not. Because when I pull my attention from him, I notice we're sitting in a large U-shaped driveway in front of the biggest house I've ever seen up close. A bona fide mansion.

"Is this where you live?" I can't decide if I'm impressed or disgusted, or an anxious mix of both.

"It's my parent's house. I stay here between semesters, though, yeah."

I whistle as I follow him around the side of the house.

"My church clothes not fancy enough to take me through the front door?"

"W-what? No. I— This is—"

"I'm kidding, Adam. Chill."

He makes a face, pausing once he unlocks the door. "I don't know what I'm doing here."

"You needed to change your clothes," I remind him gently. He relaxes slightly. "And suck my cock," I add, leaning in next to him to push the door open. He stumbles inside, and I follow, chuckling. He's too easy.

We enter what looks to be a basement that has been turned into a large living space. It's decorated like something out of a magazine, masculine but also too fashionable to really fit Adam's personality. He strikes me as the collectibles, sports paraphernalia, and framed posters kind of guy. Maybe some fancy model cars.

"You like video games?" I ask, gesturing towards the entertainment center that holds what looks like every gaming console available.

"Not really," he says. "It's all, um, Christmas and birthday presents, I guess." He shrugs awkwardly. "Poor little rich boy," he says sarcastically.

"Not so little," I say, raking my eyes down his muscular body. "Might want to get started changing out of those pants if you're going to make it to the old folk's home on time."

"Retirement home," he corrects. "And I thought... I thought you'd be the one taking your pants off this time?"

His voice is almost sheepish, and he can barely look me in the eye. And just like that, I'm hard. To be fair, I've been halfway here since this morning, but one look at his sweet, shy expression and I'm moments from blowing my load.

"How about we both get naked and see how we're feeling?" I'm desperate to see him in all his glory. So far, all our play has been stolen moments in dark corners.

Like I have all the time and patience in the world, I kick off my shoes. Unbuttoning my shirt as I walk towards him, I lay it neatly over the edge of the couch. I do the same with my pants, letting Adam make a meal out of watching me strip down for him. And then I'm standing there in nothing but a pair of black low-rise briefs that are doing very little to hold back my straining erection. I cup myself and cock my head to the side.

"I want to see you," I tell him, my voice gravelly and low.

As if he'd forgotten what he was supposed to be doing, Adam makes quick work of stripping down to his white boxers. The head of his cock is peeking through the slit in the front.

"All of it."

Like the good boy he is, Adam drops his boxers and lets me see him. All that perfect golden skin and sculpted muscle. And then there's his cock. Of course he has a big, thick, gorgeous cock. Not that mine is anything to scoff at. I'm pretty proud of it. But Adam's cock is something to behold. He's thick and long, much bigger than mine. The head of his cock is bulbous and pink, the circumcised skin taut and flushed with blood flow. He's got neatly groomed pubic hair that manages to look soft and luxurious, and large, heavy balls pulled up close to his body.

I can tell just from the way he's holding himself still, the tremble in his limbs, and the way his breathing comes in small, harsh pants that it won't take much to make him come. He's been pretty quick to the trigger the few times I've messed around with him so far. It makes him so much fun to play with.

"You're dripping for me," I say, eyes glued on the pearls of liquid that drip from his tip.

Slowly, like I'm stalking prey, I move into his space. Brushing a finger over the dark pink head of his cock, I bring it to my lips before changing my mind, reaching out to smear it across his lips instead. Adam's eyes dilate and fix to my mouth. He's near vibrating with tension, or excitement, I'm not sure which is the more prevalent feeling at the moment. Cupping the back of his neck, I pull him closer. I lick at his lips, tasting his cum and his nervousness, before gripping the back of his head with both hands to steady him while I thrust my tongue deep inside his mouth. I kiss him like a starving man, licking into him until he's breathless and needy. His cock glides along mine and presses into my stomach. I don't even think he's aware his body is trying to rut against mine.

I pull my lips from his, still holding his head in place while I look into his eyes. I like him like this. He looks wrecked. Out of his mind with lust, in a headspace that his internalized homophobia and self-consciousness can't reach. All mine to do with as I please.

Without a word, I dig my fingers into the back of his hair. "Get on your knees for me, Adam. Worship my cock."

His eyes shutter. I'm not sure if it's because of arousal or if I've offended his delicate sensibilities, but either way, he drops slowly to his knees in front of me. He doesn't touch me or look away from my eyes. A jolt of arousal shoots through me like electricity when I realize he's waiting for me to tell him what to do. I could give him permission to explore and take it slow, let him ease into it. But we don't have that kind of time and I don't have that kind of patience.

Gripping the base of my cock, I give myself a few slow strokes before guiding the head to Adam's lips. I paint his lips with my precum, making them glossy. His tongue darts out to taste me on his lips, first tentatively, then rolling his lips in to clean them.

"You like that, sweet boy?" The nod he gives me, his eyes dark with need and apprehension, makes my cock pulse in my hand. Is he doing this because he really wants to, or because he wants to please me in return for all the things I've made him feel? Have I made him feel obligated?

Maybe.

"Lick it."

Adam darts his tongue out to give my cockhead a quick, tentative lick, rolling my taste around his mouth before doing it again. This time it's a longer, firmer swipe over the whole head. Then he runs the flat of his tongue up the underside of my cock, from where my hand is holding the base, all the way to the tip. He licks me like a melting popsicle on a hot day, and that's exactly how I'm starting to feel. I watch him for a few minutes, intrigued by his growing confidence and interest in his task. It's taking all the self-control I have not to explode all over his face before he's even sucked me properly.

"That's good. Now open that pretty mouth for me, Adam. Nice and wide."

Adam takes a shaky breath and does as I command. The sight of this Adonis on his knees, mouth open and waiting, has me tightening my grip around my base and pulling my balls roughly to stave off orgasm. Not too slowly, but with more restraint than I thought I had, I feed my cock between his lips and push inside. I rub the head of my cock on his tongue in small thrusts before pushing farther back, all the way until I reach his gag reflex. I don't pull back, holding still. With one hand gripping the base of my cock, I use the other to push a lock of loose hair off his forehead and caress his cheek. My fingers stroke his jaw and slide down his neck, soothing him.

"Breathe through your nose and relax. That's better. Good. So good," I praise as I begin to thrust again.

I can hear his short breaths coming through his nostrils, and his neck all but lolls back, letting me have control of this throat, which I take advantage of. I test the limits of what both of us can take, fucking into him in harder, deeper thrusts.

"God damn. You take me so good."

He gags on a deep thrust, and it does something to me that I should probably be ashamed of. With one hand on the back of his head, and the other on his throat, I indulge in the vibrations of his moans and gags. His hands come up to rest on my thighs, but he doesn't push me away or stop me. He lets me face fuck his virgin throat until the vibrations of his moans and gagging drives me to an edge I can't come back with. Adam falls back on his heels and gasps in ragged breaths when I pull out of his hot, wet mouth.

"*Fuuuuuck,*" I groan, as thick white streams of cum jet from my cock and splash across Adam's sweet, unsuspecting face. He cries out, and I feel something warm and wet hit my inner calf and across one of my feet.

Jesus, did he just come?

"Oh, you sweet, dirty boy. You liked choking on my cock so much you made a mess. Or is it the mess you liked?" I ask, wiping the cum from his eyes. He groans when I force my fingers into his mouth, feeding him my orgasm. "Who knew you'd be such a dirty little cum slut?" His face flames, and he tries to close his eyes, but I'm not having it. "My sweet cum slut," I say, bending down to hover my mouth over his. I lick my own release from his cheek before shoving my tongue into his mouth. He sucks at it greedily.

Adam only balks a little when I straighten and tell him to clean up the mess he made. I tsk and shake my head when he reaches for his discarded t-shirt on the ground. Now that his lust has passed, and he has some mental clarity, he's second guessing himself and what he clearly knows I want him to do. I keep my face impassive but expectant, my lips curving into a cruel smile when Adam bends to complete his task. By the time Adam has licked up half his own mess from my leg and foot, he's nearly hard again.

"Where's your shower?" I ask, checking my phone screen for the time. "We're good if we're quick." There's just enough time for me to make my next move.

Trusting that I have a handle on the time, Adam nods and stands on trembling legs. I follow him to a room that obviously belongs to him. Unlike the main living space, it feels like Adam actually lives here. There's a king-sized bed with a dark blue comforter; the bed is made and the edges are tucked in perfectly. A large mirrored cross hangs on the wall above the bed, but the rest of the dark grey walls are decorated with framed sports memorabilia posters. Several bookshelves surround a large bay window with a window seat. Random nicknacks are scattered through the room, including a few model cars and trophies. It smells so strongly of Adam that I find myself taking deep inhales, as if I could infuse the scent of his subtle cologne into my brain.

Adam leads me to a wooden door that slides open, exposing a lavish ensuite bathroom that would rival an extravagant hotel. I'm tempted to talk Adam into soaking in the massive jacuzzi tub instead of going anywhere, but we both have work to do.

A towel is pressed into my hands, and I look away from the bathtub to meet Adam's smiling eyes.

"I want to live in that," I say, pointing to the jacuzzi I've been ogling.

"I've actually never used it," he says, gritting his teeth in a guilty smile.

"That's blasphemous, Adam."

He chuckles. "I'd say you're welcome to take a swim in it, but—"

"We don't have time. Rain check, maybe."

"Yeah. Maybe."

We stare at each other until enough steam has built up in the room to break our momentary trance.

"Oh, um. The shower's ready for you. I'll be down the hall, but everything you need should be—" I cut him off with a kiss.

"This shower is plenty big enough for both of us," I tell him. "Besides, we don't have much more time. Might as well make the most out of it. Who knows when we'll have privacy like this again?"

Adam doesn't argue or resist when I take him by the hand and pull him into the shower. The moment the door is closed, I attack, pressing him against the frosted glass and kissing him hungrily. His needy cock presses insistently against my stomach. I break our kiss to look down at it, my eyebrow raised. I'm honestly impressed with his recovery rate. Then again, despite coming my brains out less than twenty minutes ago, I'm halfway there myself.

I don't know if it's the heat of the shower or embarrassment turning Adam's cheeks so red. "I love how needy you are for it. How ready you always are."

"I can't help it," he says shyly. "I've spent my whole life holding back, and now it's like I can't stop. I even—" he cuts himself off, but I have to know what he's so embarrassed about.

"Even what, Adam? Tell me."

Mouth pursed into a thin line, he shakes his head. "It's nothing," he says, turning away from me to duck under the spray of the rainfall shower.

"Nothing, my ass," I mutter, moving in behind him and snatching the loofah from his hands. I hold it out for him to pour on body wash, then get to work washing his back, arms, ass and thighs. Instead of turning him around to do the front, I plaster myself to his back and reach around, washing his chest while my now fully hard cock rests against the bottom of his ass. I hum appreciatively when he pushes back against me. When he's turned on enough, he doesn't seem to be aware of what he's doing and lets his instincts take over. I fucking love it. Not just because I am readily available to take full advantage of his needs and curiosity, but because watching him experience even a fleeting moment of freedom when he comes undone is like nothing else I've seen or felt before. It's a fucking beautiful sight, and it makes me regret playing games with him even more.

I didn't expect to have this much of a reaction to him. I've all but forgotten my purpose for getting close to him in the first place and have fully focused all my attention on wanting Adam. My goal of turning Adam Havre into my desperate little cock slut is still firmly at the top of my priorities, but I keep forgetting the why of it all. Exploiting him to get back at his father is an afterthought. Fucking him because I want to, because I want to make him feel good, has overshadowed the anger and hatred that made me decide to pursue Adam in the first place. All I can think about is how badly I want my dick inside that big, beautiful, muscular ass. I want to fuck him so badly, to make him beg for it—

Adam tenses in my arms, and I realize that I'm thrusting against him, just enough that my cock is sliding through his cheeks. I didn't even notice I was doing it, lost in my thoughts of how badly I want him. Jesus, I don't know how it's possible to want someone this much.

Maybe after I fuck him, at least once in every position I can think of, I'll be able to walk away.

"Sorry," I mutter softly, kissing his shoulder. "You're just so fucking sexy."

"It—It's okay. You can t-touch me... *there*."

A pained groan rumbles through me, and I bury my face between his shoulder blades.

"Oh, you sweet, sweet boy." He shivers at the contact of my lips and tongue on his skin. "Put your hands on the wall."

There's a moment of hesitation before Adam complies, and I can tell he isn't completely sure about what's happening. I want to ask him if he trusts me, but hearing him say it will make me feel even more like the piece of shit I am.

I'll just have to make up for it by blowing his mind with pleasure.

With that in mind, I make my way down his body, trailing kisses and lapping at the drops of water rolling down the small of his back. When I'm on my knees behind him, I trail my fingers lightly over his ankles, up his calves, and across the backs of his thighs, where I tap him to widen his stance before I gently grip his juicy ass cheeks and spread him wide for me. His pretty pink hole stares back at me, winking as he clenches his body with nerves. At the first swipe of my tongue, he whimpers so prettily, I could cry.

Chapter Four
Adam

Oh, my dear Lord, help me. I know this is wrong. I know it is.

But it feels so... *unreal*. That's the only word for it, and the only thought keeping me from running away. With my hands on the tile wall, and the steam billowing around me so thick that I can't see the opposite end of the shower, I can pretend this is a dream.

Maybe it is a dream. Because what he's doing to me right now cannot be a real thing. People don't do *this*. Do they?

His tongue swipes over me in slow, soft licks before he presses the tip against me. He swirls it around my rim, teasing it into my opening, flicks it back and forth and then prods again. It tickles and soothes and sends little shivers of electricity into my balls. The head of my penis is dripping again. I don't know if that's normal. Maybe I should see a doctor. Maybe I should see multiple doctors to discuss the insatiable need that's been unlocked inside me, to touch and be touched. I'd talk to a preacher, but I'm not comfortable talking to Pastor Reynard. I'm too afraid he'll tell my father, and that I'll be disowned. I'm an adult. It's not like they can send me to Deliverance Summit against my will, but they can hold Seminary over me, my home, my livelihood. I have nothing without the financial support of my family and my place in the church.

I need to stop this. I've given into temptation and fallen too far.

Tears stream down my face. Confused tears that come unbidden. I don't want to admit that this might be the most amazing thing I've ever felt in my life. It's so intimate and weirdly soothing. I receive his tongue like an offering and take it. Willingly. Enthusiastically.

My hips rock involuntarily as I press back against him, unsure of what I'm chasing. Then his tongue slips inside me, and a bolt of awareness shoots straight through me, more potent than the icy waters of the baptism tub. It's a revelation. A baptism of a different kind. And I'm drowning in it.

What he's doing to me is turning me inside out.

Levi Asher is temptation. But he's also my friend. I've never felt so comfortable around another person, safe to be my true self. Since the moment I met him, I've basked in his presence. He's light personified—he'd never lead me astray on purpose.

Will he forgive me for tempting him in the same way? Will God forgive us if we atone for our sins?

Unable to stop the tears and contradictory thoughts, I resort to the only thing I've ever known for comfort.

Levi's mouth leaves me for a brief moment, and I want to cry harder. "Are you praying?"

"No. Don't... Please don't stop."

"It's okay. Pray for us, baby. Let me hear the words, and I'll show you God."

The words of the prayer leave me on a choked whisper, but they get stronger when Levi's finger replaces his tongue. He stands behind me, whispering the words along with me. We repeat it several times, while Levi's soap-slicked finger sinks inside me and his other hand wraps around my erection. The shock of the foreign stretch and the warm rush of his breath against the back of my neck distract me from the words I've known by heart since I was three years old. Staggered breaths blot out words until they're coming out in breathless pants and a broken, staccato rhythm.

"Our Father..." *breath* "...your name..." *whimper* "...kingdom come..." *moan* "...your will... be... done... heaven..." *breath* "give us... forgive us..." *cry* "lead us... temptation..." *deep moan*.

Before I can even attempt the end of the prayer, I'm delivered straight into the fire. The heat of it rips through my veins and explodes deep inside me. Blinding white light flashes behind my clenched eyelids and I convulse. My cries echo off the glass walls of the shower.

"That's right, let it all go. I've got you, baby. You're milking my fingers so good."

He keeps massaging inside me, some magic spot that I didn't know existed, murmuring soft words and encouragement. He did exactly what he said he would.

I swear I really did see God just now.

The physical and mental release takes me out, and I lose control of my limbs. My legs turn to jelly. Levi pulls his fingers out of me and guides me to the floor of the shower, where I collapse against him. Part of me wants to ask him to leave, not wanting him to witness what is sure to be a pathetic display of weakness. But I can't find the words, and there's a large part of me that wants him to stay.

Levi doesn't hesitate to wrap his arms around me, kissing my wet forehead and holding me while sobs wrack through me. He whispers that I'm okay, I'll be okay, he's here. *He's here.*

Eventually, I come back to myself and realize I have no idea how long we've been in the shower.

"What time is it?" I croak, pulling away and standing up so fast my vision gets fuzzy.

I barely acknowledge Levi as I scramble out of the shower, grabbing a towel on my way to check the time on my alarm clock. *Damnit!* I'm definitely going to be late.

Stumbling around, I do a poor job of drying myself off before tugging on a new pair of dress pants and a button-down shirt. I throw a tie around my shoulders and nearly forget my jacket, which I run back into the closet to get. I nearly collide with Levi, who is wearing nothing but a towel.

I curse under my breath. *Levi.* I won't have time to drop him back at the church to get his car, and his house isn't on the way either.

"Would you mind coming with me? I'm so sorry I lost track of time. I didn't mean to ruin your afternoon. I know you were going to go see your sister, but if I'm any later than I'm already going to be, then I'll have to explain—"

"Slow down. Take a breath," he says. He steps up to me and arranges my tie before tying it for me, talking to me in a low murmur that lulls me into a sense of calm. "I can visit my sister tomorrow. It's fine. But if I go with you, it might look suspicious. I'll call a car to pick me up." He gives me a sweet smile and tugs on my tie, pulling me in to place a gentle kiss to my lips that stuns me more than all the dirty things we've done so far.

Who is this man? He's just so *good.* He's made me feel things I never thought were possible, gave me more pleasure than I've ever felt in my life, and held me while I cried like a baby. Now here he is picking up all the pieces so I can go about my merry way. I don't want to leave him, don't want our time together to be over yet. I need to find a way to thank him without scaring him off because I've gotten so clingy.

"Stay," I blurt. At the incredulous look on his face, I shake off my awkwardness and try again. "You can stay here, if you want. The housekeeper is off today. My parents will probably come home to change, but they're going out so they won't be around long. Their rooms are on the far side of the house, and they never come down here. We can lock the door to the stairs just in case and maybe keep the main lights off. But you could hang out. Watch TV, read a book, play video games, take a nap. Anything you want—" *Ugh, I'm rambling.* "I'd really like it if you were here when I get home. I'd like to make you dinner or something to thank you for..." My words trail off, and a deep red blush heats my face. "I didn't mean—"

Levi laughs. A bright, happy sound that fills me up on the inside. "You want me to hang around so you can thank me for the best orgasm of your life? Sounds promising." He pumps his eyebrows, and I snort out an embarrassed laugh.

I sigh. "I just meant that I'd like to spend some more time with you, and since my parents aren't going to be back until fairly late, it's a good night to do it. Outside of the... sex stuff," I say awkwardly. "You've been a good friend, and I want to be a better friend to you, too. I feel like things have been unfairly one sided." I glance down at the half hard appendage that's tenting the towel and drag my gaze up his amazing body. He has a slighter frame than I do, cut more like a swimmer than a weightlifter. His usually light blond hair is darker when it's wet, the difference made even more obvious with the contrast to his pale skin. His body is mostly hairless, aside from a light smattering on his arms and legs, and a thin trail of dark blond hair that trails down the bottom of his flat stomach. *He's perfect.*

"Did you forget the way you let me fuck your throat?" he says bluntly, making me choke on my own spit for the second time today. He laughs and pulls me in for another kiss, this one deeper and slower. "You better get out of here. I'll stick around, maybe take a dip in that insane tub of yours."

The grin that splits my face almost hurts.

Chapter Five
Levi

Well, mission accomplished. I weaseled my way into the Havre mansion. Adam played right into my plan.

I expected we'd "accidentally" lose track of time fooling around in the shower. What I didn't expect was the raw, emotional moments we shared. He'd cried—*sobbed*—when the release his body was experiencing triggered something more. Something deep and painful. I felt it in my gut, his pain radiating through my bones as if it were my own.

There was a good chance any sort of ass play was going to set off his deep-seated internalized issues about his sexuality. I was expecting that on some level. But this felt different from the melt-down he had after the first time we kissed, or the way he'd freaked after I jerked him off the first time. The hair pulling, muttering to himself, falling to his knees to pray for forgiveness—I understand where it's all coming from. Fortunately, the more that happens between us, the more he seems to come to terms with it. Not that I see him coming out anytime soon. Or ever.

Hell, I'm not out to my family. My mother has always been highly religious. I'm sure my father would be rolling in his grave if he knew his only son likes cock. I'm out at school, at least. And my sister knew. *Before.*

Thinking of my sister gets my thoughts back on track. Worrying over the gut-wrenching acceptance I felt like a hit to the chest won't help the situation. Adam may never forgive or trust me or speak to me again after I'm done with his father, and I need to be okay with that. He's collateral damage, an unwilling sacrifice on my path to avenge the one person I love above everyone else.

He'll be fine. Maybe he'll even be more willing to find a way to live his truth now that he's had some positive experience. I could still be helping him.

That's what I tell myself, like a mantra, as I tiptoe up the stairs. Adam said no one is home, and I should have a little while before they come home to change. On Sundays, his father stays well after the services for official church business meetings, and those get pushed later on potluck Sundays. It's just after 2:30PM. He expects them to be home around 4:30PM, take an hour to get ready, and then be gone until close to midnight. Sunday nights are their weekly country club get togethers, where they rub elbows with the important people and talk about how to take over the world and what they're going to do about the brown people, queers, and dirty poor folks trying to bring them down. At least, that's how I imagine it. I'm probably not very far off.

Adam expects to be home by six, so I can't just wait until after they leave. I'm not exactly prepared, but I'm still going to take this chance to explore. I didn't think I'd get in here so easily. If I can get here once, especially as easily as I did, then I can do it again. And if Adam isn't willing to bring me back after today, I know the Havre's are away from their home most of day and night on Sundays. This is a good start and more than I expected to have after only six weeks of flirting with Adam while trying to avoid his father's attention.

I nearly trip over the too-long sweatpants that Adam loaned me, stopping to roll the bottoms up to my calves and cinch the waist as tight as I can. I don't need to be distracted by my pants falling off until later, when I'm hoping Adam will be the removing them himself.

The house is deathly quiet, and cleaner than an art museum. It feels empty while still being over the top and lavish. Everything is crystal and ornate gold. Massive gilded frames decorate the walls, and the furniture looks like it's never been sat on. The plush carpets are stark white and there are perfect diagonal vacuum marks across each room. I skip all the main rooms, not wanting to tread through in even my socked feet in case I leave behind prints. I stick to the marble tile floors in the hallways, kitchen, utility room, and foyer. The stairs are marble as well, so it's not until I get upstairs that I have to worry about my feet sinking into the plush fibers. Thankfully, it's obviously been walked on this morning, but out of an abundance of caution, I try to only step where someone else has stepped.

Senator Havre's footprints are easy to pick out, since they're much larger than Mrs. Havre's and it seems like she wears heels in the house. Which isn't surprising, she seems like a Stepford Wife if I've ever seen one. A sad, broken Stepford Wife. I wonder if she'll get some freedom when I ruin her husband, if she'll be happier even if they lose this house and all the pretty things they own.

Mrs. Havre almost never speaks, keeps her head down, and does what she's told. I've never seen Senator Havre show her any kindness or affection. I wonder if Adam even notices, or if he's conditioned for the women around him to act that way. As kind as he is to all the ladies at church, I can't imagine that he's okay with how his father treats his mother. That wouldn't be the Adam I've come to know.

Interestingly, but also not surprisingly, the footsteps seem to deviate to different rooms. I follow the larger footprints to what must be Senator Havre's room, which is enormous with ornate crown molding and floor to ceiling windows. The bathroom is the size of my mother's living room and has an actual sauna. Everything is marble and chrome, and I'm careful not to touch anything in case I leave smudges. Back in the bedroom, I use the bottom of my borrowed t-shirt to cover my hands to open the closet, which is unsurprisingly the size of a normal person's bedroom. Everything is so meticulously organized and clean, there's no real hiding places for anything interesting, but I'm able to steal a pair of soft leather driving gloves.

The bedroom is much the same. Even his underwear is folded into neat, starched squares. *Who starches their underwear!?* Honestly, that should be enough proof that the guy is a criminal.

The bedside table might as well be in a hotel. There's almost nothing personal in there at all, aside from some sleeping pills, a loaded handgun, and a journal. My heartbeat picks up when I see the journal, but there's not much of interest in there aside from a couple of nearly illegible notes. Most of what I can make out are numbers. There's a phone number, some scribbling that might be an address, and what looks like possibly a date and time. Then there are some random numbers jotted down that have no explanation:

200 of #1
800 of #2 24-48 hours

I take a photo of the writing before fanning through the pages to make sure I didn't miss anything else. A small bronze key falls out, clattering against the bottom of the drawer, the sound causing me to jump. It breaks me out of my concentration, and I hear a car engine outside.

Quickly, I put everything back as I found it, aside from the key, which I pocket for the time being. The way it was hidden makes me think it might be important, and I need to examine it more to figure out where it came from.

Careful not to touch anything or muss the carpet, I fly down the stairs just as I hear car doors shut. Voices get louder as they move nearer to the front door. Or rather, one voice. Senator Havre is pissed off about something.

Shit shit shit shit shit!

Just as the doorknob turns, I scoot into a dark hallway and hide in the first room I see. I don't have time to worry about where I am, nearly falling on my ass as I slide into the room, slipping on the polished floors in my socks. I scramble up and silently close the door. Thank fuck the Havre's seem to go straight up the stairs, by the sounds of Senator Havre's voice echoing through the house. I don't dare breathe until I'm sure his loud voice is far enough away to be muffled.

Breathing through my nose to calm my nerves, my eyes adjust to the dimly lit room. I'd assumed, incorrectly, that this little hallway would lead to a butler's pantry or something else unimportant. But as the faint smell of cigars hits my awareness, I realize I'm in an office or study.

The room is large and ornate like the rest of the house, but the abundance of large, heavy mahogany furniture and leather sofas fill the space and make it more cozy and lived in than the other rooms. And unlike his bedroom, there are a lot more personal effects in this room. There are framed photos of the senator meeting all kinds of important people, from politicians to foreign dignitaries to the one and only Jeffery Epstein. *Gross.* And in a place of pride, next to an award that I can't quite read the text on, there's a picture of Senator Havre shaking hands with everyone's favorite convict president-elect. I roll my eyes so hard, it's a wonder I can't see my brain matter.

Keeping an ear on the voices and movement from above, I search through the room. There are several locked shelves and file drawers, but none of them match the key I found. Nor does it match any of the desk drawers. Well, fuck. Maybe it's because it's the only interesting or out-of-place item I've found so far, but this key has to go to something important.

In the top drawer, I find some paperclips and an eyeglass repair kit that includes a tiny screwdriver. The desk is pretty old, likely an antique. The locking mechanisms might not be too hard to pick. Chewing on my lip for a moment, I decide it's now or never. I'm here now, and who knows when I'll get the chance again? I feel in my gut that there's something here.

A few minutes later, I manage to get the first drawer unlocked, and nearly deflate when I see it's filled with nothing but bills and mundane files. It seems Senator Havre has yet to embrace technology when it comes to his records.

But there's something off about the drawer. After pulling it open and closed a few times, it feels like the weight isn't right, and the size of the drawer versus the storage capacity doesn't match. On a hunch, I empty the drawer completely and inspect the edges, which are uneven and slightly discolored from the rest of the drawer. *There's a false bottom.*

I have to use a letter opener to pry it open, but once I get the false bottom loose, I know I've hit pay-dirt. Several file folders, a thick stack of hundred-dollar bills, and a small metal lockbox are hidden beneath the panel. When I put the key into the lockbox, it fits. A rush of excitement makes the blood roar in my ears, almost muffling the sound of footsteps stomping down the stairs. *Fuck.*

After replacing the now broken false bottom as best I can, I put all the files and bills back the way I found them, or hopefully close enough that the differences won't be immediately noticeable. Then I close and relock the drawer just as the door opens and a light turns on.

Oh, shit.

There are no less than four loaded weapons in this room alone, not including whatever is in the big fancy gun cabinet against the wall near the door. If Havre sees me, I have no doubt I'll be bleeding out on the plush burgundy rug I'm currently belly down on. If he can't see me yet, he'll surely hear how loudly my heart is beating. It's thundering against my eardrums, thumping so hard I can feel the movement of my chest against the floor. I can't hear anything above it, but I can see Senator Havre's feet in the half-inch gap between the floor and the desk. He walks over to the sidebar, and then backtracks, yelling out the door for Mrs. Havre.

"Rachel! Where's my fucking ice?!" He shouts angrily.

Mrs. Havre's small voice sounds from farther down the hall. The senator stomps out of the room, and I take the opportunity to find a better hiding spot. With the contents of the hidden compartment clutched tightly to my chest, I make a run for the closet. I pull the door shut just as Senator Havre comes back into the room, muttering something about being married to a "good for nothing, barren whore".

I hear the tinkle of ice, followed by a satisfied sigh.

"Let's get the hell out of here. I need to talk to Murphy about a certain VISA appeal letter. That idiot is soft. If I don't get him under my thumb, he'll let these illegals run all over us..." His voice trails off as the Havre's make their way out of the house. I wonder fleetingly if Mrs. Havre actually listens to any of the senator's racist drivel.

I don't dare move from my hiding spot until it's abundantly clear that they're gone and not coming back. A quick glance at my phone shows I still have about an hour before Adam is due back. His parents were much earlier than he thought they'd be.

With my prize in hand, I head directly to the opposite side of the house, through the kitchen, and back down the stairs to Adam's living space. Only when I've turned on the kitchen light and spread my findings across the kitchen island, do I take a proper breath. A breath that promptly gets knocked from my chest the moment I open the lockbox.

Chapter Six
Adam

"Levi?" I whisper-yell, even though there's no one around.

The only cameras that pick up sound are the front and back doors, and my Luddite father never checks the security feeds. Unlike him, I have the security company's app on my phone with full access, so I can go in and delete footage from the day prior. Not that I've ever used that feature before today. Nor have I ever staked out the cameras to watch my parents coming and going, or to make sure a certain blond-haired siren hasn't left yet. I haven't been able to get him off my mind all afternoon.

The youth group did an amazing job, and I normally encourage them to spend some extra time with the residents, but today of all days I couldn't get them to leave. I texted Levi to let him know I was running behind, but the message never showed as read, and he didn't answer when I called from the car when I was finally headed home. I hope he likes Chinese food, because it's too late to cook now.

Just now, as I was walking up to my door, I thought I heard it creak, but the light that normally comes on automatically apparently doesn't work when the camera has been shut off. *Whoopsie.*

The door creaks again, and a faint glow illuminates the dark outline of Levi's body. He doesn't say anything to greet me or kiss me. Not that I was expecting a hello kiss, but considering the goodbye kiss that he sent me off with... Yeah, I was hoping.

I made a decision today while I drove away from Levi, praying that no one discovers him hiding out in my rooms. I decided not to fight this thing anymore, whatever it is. Not that I've been fighting all that hard since the first time Levi kissed me. The feelings he inspires inside me—not just sexual feelings—are too intense to not be something special. If it were just physical, I'd worry more that I've fallen into dark temptation. I am worried, but I know there's more here, something beautiful and pure.

After letting the other youth directors know I'd be meeting them at the nursing home, I called my favorite professor from one of my world theology courses, one who has no personal ties to my father or Pastor Reynard and happens to be married to another woman. She was patient with me while I asked leading questions without any details as to why I was asking them. Thankfully, she couldn't see how intensely I was blushing when I wanted to ask why pleasure was considered a bad thing, when it's the closest to God I've ever felt.

"God loves all of his children, Adam. There are a lot of people who interpret the Bible in many ways, but they are just that—interpretations. Listen to your heart and the instincts that HE gave you. I think you worry too much about temptation and being chased by the devil, but the only devil chasing you is your penchant for punishing yourself. God made the parts of you that feel good so that you can feel good. God made the parts of you that can open up and love another person, whoever they are. God made a beautiful world full of beautiful things for you to enjoy, Adam."

Without realizing it, she backed up the conclusion that I'd already been mulling over. That God brought Levi into my life for a reason, and that he wouldn't put me on this path to punish me with these feelings. Because the things I feel are too good and too pure to be evil. *How could love ever be wrong?*

Levi grasps my wrist and pulls me inside, leading me to the

kitchen island, where there's a mess of papers, pictures, cash, and prescription bottles. My eyes skim over it all, but hone in on the haunted look in Levi's blue eyes.

"Are you okay?" I ask, but it's a stupid question. He doesn't look okay. "What is all this?"

He swallows and fixes me with a pained stare.

"I need to tell you something, but I need you to promise that you'll hear me out. You're going to want to run, you're going to want to hate me, but—"

"I could never hate you," I interject softly.

"Don't say that until you hear what I need to tell you. What I have to say might hurt you, but I need you to stick with me until I've said it all. You need the whole story before you decide."

"Decide what?"

"What you want to do next. Whether you want to be with me."

Be with him? "W-what does that mean, be with you?"

Does that mean *he* wants to be with *me*? How would that even work? Does that mean I'd have to come out, or does he just mean continuing on as we are? There are too many questions swirling around in my head.

"That's something that we'll need to decide, but I think you need to hear this before you can think too hard on it."

"Okay..." I say, sitting in the chair that Levi pulls out for me.

He paces a moment, leans over the counter, fiddles with the piles of papers and other items. I haven't known Levi all that long. It's been less than two months since he came into my life, and only a few weeks since he turned my life upside down. But in all that time, I have never seen Levi look anything less than confident and self-assured. The way he's fidgeting and avoiding eye contact is disconcerting. My brain cannot conjure what he could possibly have to tell me that would make him this nervous.

Finally, he takes the seat next to me, turning to face me. My legs are too long, so he ends up with his knees between mine. A warm tingle follows wherever he touches me—my knees, my thigh, my hand when he takes it in his. He stares down at our intertwined fingers for a moment before raising his eyes to mine. The sky blue of his eyes looks darker than usual, the red rims and puffiness making them seem stormy and unstable, like the sun may never come out again. It scares me.

He takes a deep breath and starts. His voice is low and hoarse, like his throat might be sore or it's hard to get the words out.

"First, I need to tell you that I'm sorry. Even before I started to fall for you, I knew that this was wrong—"

Wrong? Does he mean because we're both men? Wait... he said fall for you. He's falling for me, too?

"I'm falling for you, too. Have fallen, really," I blurt before he can say anything else. "Sorry, I know I'm supposed to be listening. But I feel like you need to know that. And I don't care that you're a man. I mean, I care. I'm terrified. But I don't think that something that feels this right could be wrong. I don't believe that God doesn't want us to experience happiness like this."

A smile slowly stretches Levi's lips, but his eyes are just as sad. I can't tell if he's looking at me with pity, or what. He looks like a kicked puppy.

"Thank you."

That's a weird response.

"What's going on, Levi?" I ask softly, gesturing for him to continue. I'll shut up now so he can tell me what he so desperately needs to.

"I'll, uh, start at the beginning..." He looks down again, mouth twisting.

"Hey," I say, reaching to tip his chin up to look at me. *My, how the tables have turned.* "It's okay. It'll be okay."

How can it not be? I'm in love with him. He just said he's falling in love with me. The rest we can work around. Long distance? Hiding our love from the outside world? Trying to separate my life from my father's? None of it seems insurmountable now that he's said those words.

Leaning forward, I press my lips to his. He sighs into the kiss, opening for me. It's soft and sweet, and yet still makes my pants feel tight. Will that excitement ever dull? I hope not, but even without it, I want to bask in his light for the rest of my life.

Salt mingles with the taste of Levi's lips, and I pull back to see a tear track down his face. I kiss him once more. Twice. When I take his hands in mind, I notice that he's wearing gloves. *Why is he wearing gloves?*

"A few months ago, I was staying with my sister. We were supposed to be going on a cruise to celebrate that she'd graduated from her pre-law program early because she's an overachiever. She'd been working as an assistant at this big fancy law firm, was ready to start law school in the fall. Anyway, we had to cancel the cruise because she was sick. Well, not sick exactly—she was pregnant." He takes a shaky breath. "Everly was terrified about telling our mom, and she'd gotten into an argument with her boyfriend about keeping the pregnancy, but she was still so happy. She was so excited to be a mother, despite the circumstances. She said it was God's will, and she could *feel* the rightness of it. Her boyfriend would come around, and she'd have to put off law school for a year or so, she thought. But she was steadfast in her optimism about it all. Honestly, I believe she could have pulled it off. Even if our mother disowned her, even if the boyfriend didn't come around and she had to do it on her own. My sister would have been the best mother and found a way to put herself through school to become the best lawyer. It's just the kind of person she is—*was*."

Was. He pauses for another shaky breath and my hand tightens around his.

"Later that week, Everly went out on a date with her boyfriend. They'd met for coffee two days before and had been talking on the phone. Just like she said he would, he'd changed his tune. He took her to some overpriced boutique store to make a registry and even put a hold on some fancy nursery furniture. They were sending house listings back and forth, and she was positive he was going to propose. I was worried, of course I was. All I knew about the guy was that his name was Matt, she'd met him at the law firm she worked at, and that he spoiled her." Levi scoffs, and a tear escapes his eye.

"Aside from the morning sickness and living off nothing but protein smoothies, she was okay. Better than okay. She was literally glowing... Until she started cramping and feeling really sick. The bleeding started before she could even get an appointment with her doctor, and I took her to the emergency room."

"Everything happened so fast. Ultimately, she miscarried and hemorrhaged. Lost too much blood and had a stroke."

Dear God. I bring his hand to my chest, cradling it there like I can soothe both our pain. My heart aches for him. "I'm so sorry."

"I called him. The boyfriend. She'd tried to get in touch with him while she was still conscious, but he'd been out of town for work and didn't answer. When I finally got through to him, he didn't say much. All he asked was if she'd live, and if the baby survived. He never showed up. A couple of days later, when I called to update him, the number was no longer in service. Something felt off. I scoured her phone, reading through all her text messages and social media, but she wasn't very active online. I found a few selfies she'd kept on her phone and got some hints from the text message thread."

The way he looks at me feels foreboding. There's a tension in the air that clogs my throat. I know what he's going to say next, even though I don't want it to be true. Why else would he feel the need to tell me all of this?

Levi holds up a phone that was sitting on the counter with all the other stuff that suddenly feels very ominous. The screen is already unlocked, the photos app pulled up. On the screen are multiple pictures of my father with a very pretty young girl. Some of them could be considered innocent enough, but as Levi swipes through the photos, there are a few that I wish I hadn't seen that make it very clear what the nature of their relationship was.

My father was having an affair with Levi's sister.

"The more I dug into things, the more I got the feeling that something was very off." He pauses and swallows again before leveling me with a very serious glare. "I found out that Mathias Havre had closed the baby registry two days before Everly got sick."

"Wh-what?"

Levi nods, like he's waiting for me to catch up, for something to click in my brain. But the opposite is happening. It doesn't make any sense.

"Everly's boyfriend didn't want her to have the baby, but then came around suddenly and was making all these plans. All of his text messages were planning their future together, discussing baby names and what the nursery would look like and whether their future child would have her freckles. But he canceled the registry even while he was telling my sister he hopes the baby is a little girl so he can spoil her. And then, when he was notified that something was wrong, he didn't come to her side. He blocked all communication. Never reached out or checked on her. The last part almost made sense once I found out he was married and a public figure, but the registry thing kept bothering me...."

A wave of nausea rolls through me. The smell of the takeout I set on the table is no longer appetizing, and I consider opening the door to let some fresh air into the room.

Levi clears his throat, and his eyes fall shut. His posture is tense, and I know he isn't done. There's something more. He said he'd done something bad, but all he's talked about is my father and his sister.

"I started following your dad. That's how I ended up at your church. I knew he did something to my sister. I *knew* it. But there he was, smiling and going on with his perfect public image and perfect family. I wanted to ruin him like he ruined my sister. She's alive, but she might never regain her full brain function. She's rotting in a hospital bed, while he's winning elections on a platform of family values. I hate him, Adam."

I suck in a sharp breath. I don't know how to feel. Honestly, I can't really blame him. Especially because I know some things about my father that he doesn't. Things my gut wants me to share with him, but the expression in his watery eyes tells me there's more.

"Why are you telling me this?"

"Do you remember the volunteer project we did with the youth group, the one where we fixed up that old lady's house?"

Uh, yeah, I remember.

I'd noticed Levi the first day he stepped into the church, surreptitiously watched him sit in the back pew week after week. But that project was the first time I really *looked* at Levi. At the end of the day, we were covered in sweat and sawdust. Levi switched his shirt for a clean one before getting in his car to leave. I think I nearly swallowed my tongue when I looked over at the car next to mine and saw him without a shirt. The way he'd grinned when he noticed me looking at him terrified me, but it also exhilarated me. It was after that day that Levi started coming around more, volunteering more, and we started getting to know each other. It was only a week later that he kissed me for the first time, and I'd embarrassed myself with just a light brush of his hand over the crotch of my jeans.

"The moment I saw you look at me like that, I knew I could seduce you. Use you. I started talking to you, flirting with you... doing things to you I knew you were uncomfortable with, but wouldn't stop because I knew you wanted it. I took advantage of you and got close to you with the intent to get back at your father for what he did to Everly. I didn't have a plan. My best-case scenario was that I'd get access to the senator and find something to incriminate him... And I did."

The room is spinning, a burning sensation crawling up my esophagus. It takes a conscious effort to breathe.

Everything I let him do to me, that I did to him... Everything I've been feeling. None of it was real.

My voice is barely audible. "It was all... a lie?"

"It started that way, yes." He gives me a moment to process, but when I don't move, he says more. "It started that way, but something happened along the way I wasn't expecting. I got to know you, and you're so much more than what I saw when I first laid eyes on you."

"And what was that?" I spit out.

"I thought you were surface-level like your dad. Perfect on the outside, but hiding something sinister and ugly on the inside."

He's wrong though. I do have something sinister and ugly on the inside. I always have. A secret I never dared to speak out loud. A secret I tried to deny, even to myself. All the prayers, and self-loathing, and fear of hellfire couldn't burn it out of me, but at least I'd never acted on it. At least I could pretend. Until I met him, and he made me believe that the worst part of me was something beautiful.

"No, Adam," Levi says sharply. "No. Nothing like that. Don't ever think that, please. Even if you hate me, even if you never want to see or speak to me again, I need you to know this—"

This time it's him who makes me look up, cradling the sides of my face in both hands and looking deep into my eyes. His eyes are filled with tears, and the look he's giving me is full of sincerity and longing. It's painful to look at him. He's so beautiful. So full of life. How is it possible that he could be faking something that I felt in my soul?

"You are perfect, Adam. In every way, inside and out. It took one conversation to realize you were nothing like your father. But I'm broken inside, Adam. I still kept pushing you, kept digging, kept trying to get closer and closer to you. And a big part of that, even after I learned you are a good person, was because I wanted to take advantage of that goodness. I could have stopped, could have left you alone and found another way, but I didn't. Because I didn't want to stop."

He sucks in a jagged breath and continues, the pained tone in his voice making it sound like the words hurt as much to say as they do to hear.

"The closer I got to you, the more I wanted you. The more I tasted, the more I hungered for you. I didn't even realize the depths of my feelings for you until I knew it was too late, until the moment I had all the evidence I need laid out in front of me, and I realized that if I did this, if I used the information I found today to take him down and expose him... that I would be losing you."

Pulling away from him, I stand. He moves to follow me, but I hold up a hand. My brain is tired. I don't know what to think or what to feel.

"Why tell me, then? Why not keep stringing me along until you got tired of me? Or is that it—are you done playing with me already? Think it'll be less fun now that you aren't using me to get something you want?"

I'm angry and talking out of my ass, probably not making any sense. Nothing makes sense anymore.

He used me.

"I would love you for the rest of my life if it was a choice."

My stupid, selfish heart restarts itself with a painful lurch. "Then why tell me?"

"Because I can't lie to you anymore. You deserve the truth. And because I don't think I'm capable of letting your father get away with what he's done."

He pushes the items on the counter closer to me, and I focus on them for the first time. A copy of the medical records for Everly Asher, some printed emails from a Dr. Finley at the care facility where she's being treated, asking for progress updates in return for payment. There are records of wire transfers.

Levi's gloved hand rests on a printed list of instructions next to two pill bottles. The labels aren't from a pharmacy, only plain white labels with the name of what I'm assuming the medications are: misoprostol and mifepristone.

"Those are the medications that doctors prescribe to induce abortion, and the instructions on how to use them. Whoever gave them to him specified how much to give and when to give them. There's a note at the bottom that states how much was in each bottle, which was far more than the dosage needed. The note specifically mentions not to give more than the original dose."

Levi picks up the bottles and shakes them.

"They're empty."

He nods. His expression is closed, but I can read the agony in his posture. The anger. The absolute hopelessness.

The pill bottles drop from his hand onto the counter, like they're too heavy for him to hold any longer. His shoulders slump, and I feel his pain so viscerally that it makes my stomach lurch. Stumbling to the kitchen sink, I barely make it in time before I lose the contents of my stomach.

Chapter Seven
Levi

I'm not sure if he wants me near him right now, but I rub Adam's back as he vomits, then hand him a napkin and some water. The bottle of bleach I used to clean up after myself earlier is still next to the sink. After leading him to sit down, pulling the trashcan out next to him in case he might not be finished, I clean and sanitize the kitchen sink and counter. I take longer than I need to, trying to give Adam time to process, and myself time to figure out my next move.

There's more to show him, of course there is. A man who is capable of what his father has done has a lot more skeletons in his closet than even what I've uncovered.

Adam speaks, drawing my attention. "He got the Albas deported."

It isn't a question. He must have already suspected some involvement, but the file in his hands is hard proof, not only that he targeted the Alba family, but that he's been paying off judges. There are more records like that one, where he's paid judges or other officials for various favors.

He sits with this knowledge for a little while, looking through each paper, giving them new attention and focus now that he understands what he's looking at. It's quiet, and I'm wondering if I should leave. He hasn't so much as looked at me since I showed him the worst of it. And he's been understandably withdrawn since I told him the truth of my involvement with him.

Part of me wishes I'd never met him, or that we met under different circumstances. But, honestly, none of those scenarios would have led to a happy ending for us, either. It's a gut-wrenching fact that I have to acknowledge. I don't deserve a man like Adam. And he certainly doesn't deserve me. He's too sweet and soft, everything good in the world, and I'm filled with too much anger and hate. And lust.

All I've done is taint him. Punished him for the sins his father committed. Dragged him to hell with me.

"I have something to show you," Adam says. He sounds like he's still in shock.

He keeps his eyes averted and walks out of the kitchen, to a door near the pool table. Through the door is a small hallway. We pass an impressive home gym on the left, and towards the end of the hallway is a door.

The room is dark. It takes Adam a second to find the light switch, and when he turns it on, I see that we're in a large storage space. There are bins marked with various holidays, most of them Christmas decorations. Along the far wall, there's a row of file cabinets. Adam bends down and runs his fingers along the bottom of the cabinets until he locates a small black box, which he pulls a key out of. He uses the key to unlock the file cabinets and opens a drawer towards the bottom left.

"I lost trust in my father a long time ago. A few years back, during the worst of the pandemic, I started getting suspicious about things. The rest of the world was suffering, people were losing their lives, their jobs, their homes, but we seemed to be thriving. My father was making more money than ever before, despite no longer working at the firm. I felt like something was off."

He moves all the files to the front to reach the back of the drawer, where he pulls out a stack of files. "Turns out he invested in a lot of pharmaceutical companies shortly before official news of the virus started to spread. One might say it was a smart move, and sadly not illegal, but I kept looking. Some of the money transfers and investments seemed off."

Adam hands me the stack of files. "I'm sure there's more, and not all of that is exactly concrete, but I think it's enough to warrant an investigation. Offshore accounts, shell companies, and I'm pretty sure insider trading. I highlighted a bunch of transactions that I wasn't sure about at the time, but now that I've seen what you've found, it could be evidence of more bribes."

Speechless and unsure what I'm supposed to do, I look down at the heavy stack of files in my arms before blinking up at Adam. He still doesn't meet my eye.

"I knew my father was dishonest. Corrupt, even. It seems like all rich politicians are. I prayed for him and had this juvenile plan to donate every cent of my inheritance when he dies. But I had no idea it was this bad. I promise you, I didn't know. I didn't know he was ruining people's lives, hurting them. What he did to your sister..." he gags but holds up a hand when I try to step forward.

"My father is member and donor to The Heritage Foundation. '*Saving babies*' and '*traditional values*' are the top platforms that he's run and won on. He's fought for anti-abortion reform and legislation that even I felt went too far, and then he goes and forces a young woman that he was committing adultery with to have an abortion against her will? This cannot stand, Levi. He can't get away with this."

Adam sniffs and wipes at his nose with his wrist before straightening his spine. "I don't know how to feel about us, and what you did to get close to me. I feel... used. And I don't know if I can ever forget how much this hurts. I thought... God, I'm so stupid." Another sniff, and a deep breath. My eyes are closed, listening to his words but unable to watch the way he can't even look at me. "But I also understand why you did it. And I think that maybe the outcome, getting justice for your sister and all the other people my father has wronged, justifies the means."

"Adam, I—"

"I'm not ready to forgive you. As much as I understand, I'm not strong enough to let this go yet. But I want to help. What else can I do to help?"

It takes several moments to process what he's just said, and even longer to sputter out the words spinning around in my brain. "I—I don't know. This is a lot, though. A good start. Like you said, it should be enough to warrant at least an investigation. I know someone, from my computer forums, that works in Washington. He's an intern at the U.S. Attorney's Office. I already messaged him, and he says he can meet me. It's safer to do in person, so I—"

"I want to go with you."

My eyebrows shoot to my hairline.

"It's a six-hour drive, and we'll have to stay overnight." Or longer, depending on whether it would be safe to return.

As much as I'm dying to keep him close, to find a way to make things right between us, I don't want him to risk anything or be uncomfortable.

"That's okay. I don't really have anywhere else to be right now. I can't stay here."

I nod, understanding what he means. "Okay. Um, pack a bag and then we'll need to stop by my place real quick so I can do the same."

He jogs out of the storage room, and I follow behind slowly, walking like I'm in a trance. This doesn't feel real.

* * *

"You want me to leave the pot?"

I jerk my head up to look at the older woman in a blue apron, my blurry eyes focusing on her nametag. Sal.

"Um, yes, please. Thanks, Sal."

"Long night?" she asks as she tops off my coffee cup.

"You have no idea."

Chuckling, she sets an insulated pot down on the table and says she'll be back around to check on our table when my guest arrives.

Adam is waiting in the car, sipping on his own to-go coffee and waiting for me to do the exchange. We left his truck parked at the church, where we used the office to make copies of everything we have, and took my car since it gets better gas mileage. It will also be harder to track us down if Senator Havre gets suspicious about Adam's absence, but Adam doesn't expect they'll notice him gone until Wednesday night church services. And by then, the deed will be done. Hopefully, an investigation will be underway. It's probably too much to hope for an arrest by then.

A tall, thin black guy with wire-framed glasses and a mess of curly black hair emerges next to the booth.

"Levi?"

"In the flesh," I say, grinning.

Standing, I ignore his offered hand to shake and pull him in for a hug. I've known Freddie for the better part of ten years, but only online. We met playing an online role-playing game when we were middle schoolers and became fast friends even though we've never talked face to face. We've texted, chatted, and thrown conspiracy theories back and forth in our favorite forums nearly every day, and know more about each other's lives than any of our in real life friends do. It's an unusual friendship, for sure. But I trust him, and he has the right connections.

"Wow. So, you are a real person."

I laugh out loud. "I'm going to need to get a selfie so I can show my mom proof that you aren't some old pervert living in his mother's basement."

"I keep telling you I'm not old!"

We banter back and forth until Sal comes to take our orders. I order two club sandwiches and three pieces of pie to go. Freddie just orders a coffee to go since he has to get to the office early enough to talk to his boss. Once Sal walks away, I give Freddie a meaningful look.

"Thank you for meeting me and helping. I have a lot of stuff, but I'm not sure how much of it means anything. I think there's at least enough here to open an investigation, even outside of the evidence regarding my sister."

Freddie knows what happened to my sister, so I told him what I found. After I assured him I didn't touch anything with my bare hands, he told me to put everything back where I found it and take several photos. Once he shows his boss and gets advice from someone higher up, they're going to contact someone that isn't likely to be in Senator Havre's pocket to report the crime to.

Freddie pulls the box over next to him and peeks inside. He whistles. "You're right, there's a lot."

"Those are all copies, but I have the originals, or at least what was in his files. And pictures of everything else, like the pill bottles and the phone. I'll turn it all over to whatever official or police investigator as soon as it's safe."

"You did good, Levi. I'm not gonna lie. I thought you were nuts when you talked about getting close to him to expose him. But you did the damn thing."

"I had some help."

He frowns at me. "I thought you'd be happier."

"Yeah, me too."

Through the diner window, I can see Adam dozing in the passenger seat of my car. My heart twinges. I can't believe he's here with me. The drive was tense and silent. We barely talked to each other outside of bringing up stops for bathroom breaks or caffeine, or to switch off driving duties. Not that either of us slept. I'm glad to see he's resting a little now. The last nine hours have been physically and emotionally exhausting.

Sal brings our orders out, and Freddie pays for everything, despite my protests.

"Go check into your hotel, get some rest. I'll check in with you later today, but it might be tomorrow before John gets through all of this, depending on his court schedule today. Just rest and take it easy, maybe do some touristy shit to get your mind off things."

"Yeah, I will. Thanks, Freddie."

He pulls me in for another hug and thumps me on the back. "I'm happy to help, man. It's really good to see you in person. Maybe if you stick around for a while, we can have dinner or go out? This town has some decent nightlife."

"Sounds good."

We walk out together. Freddie is parked just a few spaces away from my car, and he sees the handsome sleeping man in my passenger seat. He raises his eyebrows and nods like he's impressed.

I wish I could smile back at him and be like, "Yeah man, I know, right? He's just as gorgeous inside as he is out, too." I want to be proud to have him. But he's not mine, and he never will be because I fucked this up so monumentally. Not only did I lose him, but I made him second guess himself. Just when he was coming to terms with having feelings for another man. Just when he'd let go and let himself feel and enjoy.

"Alright, man. I'll check in with you later."

With one last thank you and a wave, I get in the car and place the bag of food in the back seat. Adam sleeps the whole way to the hotel Freddie recommended, and I leave him to check in. When I come back with the key, he's awake but a little disoriented.

"Let's get inside and eat, shower, and sleep—in whatever order works best for you," I say, grabbing my duffle and the bag of food. Adam follows me quietly. Maybe I should have booked him his own room, but I'm worried about him being alone. I might not be his favorite person or the best company right now, but I don't want him spiraling or anything like that.

But then I unlock the door and realize just how much I screwed up.

Chapter Eight
Adam

There's only one bed.

One. Freaking. Bed.

By the look of surprise, then embarrassment, on Levi's angelic face, this wasn't intentional.

"Hold on, I'll fix this," Levi says hurriedly, dropping his bag on the floor and running to the phone. I stand awkwardly in the doorway, staring at the bed, while he argues with whoever is at the front desk.

"You have to be kidding me," he whispers to himself while he waits on hold. His hand rakes through his hair and pulls at the ponytail at the back of his head, shooting nervous glances my way. I shouldn't want to rake my fingers through the loose strands, to soothe him and tell him it's okay.

It's not okay. Or it shouldn't be. The truth is, I don't really want to be alone. But can I handle lying that close to him, when all I want is for him to kiss and hold me and tell me everything is going to be alright.

"You're sure?" He sighs heavily. "Okay, what about a cot or something? No, that's fine. Thanks for trying. I'll call back and let you know what we decide."

Levi hangs up the phone and deflates. "I'm so sorry. I booked the reservation online while we were driving here, and I must have not been paying close enough attention. I expected two queen beds, not one. The front desk says the only other rooms they have available right now are the same size, and they don't have cots."

He seems really incensed by the cots. A giggle bursts out of me before I can stop it, making me snort. Levi gives me a funny look, the side of his mouth quirking up in an involuntary smile.

"Sorry, I'm basically delirious at this point," I say, stepping fully into the room and letting the door shut behind me. I drop my bag next to Levi's and take a seat at the tiny round table in the corner of the room. Levi walks over and sets down the bag of food from the diner. Staring at it, I try to decide if I'm too tired to eat, but then my stomach growls audibly.

"Eat. I'll see about finding us somewhere else to stay," Levi says. His voice is gentle and caring, but I can tell how tired he is, too.

"It's okay. We're both beyond exhausted and need sleep. I'm not sure I could make it anywhere else, honestly. It's just a bed, and we're just going to sleep. It'll be fine."

* * *

It's not fine.

After eating less than half of my sandwich, I couldn't handle staying awake for even another minute and stumbled over to the bed. Levi stood awkwardly for a few minutes before I tiredly patted the spot next to me. "Just sleep," I said, halfway to dreamland already, then rolled over to give Levi some space. I was startled awake when he grabbed my foot and jerked. I hadn't even bothered to take my shoes off. I think I managed to mumble a thank you, or maybe an apology for having my shoes on the bed, but I can't really remember. I felt the bed dip next to me, and then I was out.

I don't know how long I've been asleep. I'm reluctant to open my eyes, but I have to pee.

There are blackout curtains blocking the windows, so it's dark, but there's a faint light coming in around the edges. It's just enough to make out a little detail in the room. I don't need light to see how much trouble I'm in, though. No, I can do that from feel alone.

Levi and I didn't merely roll into each other in our sleep. One of us didn't spoon the other or throw an errant hand over the other's body. No, we somehow completely entangled ourselves while we slept. We're facing each other, arms and legs entwined. My face is pressed into his chest and I'm holding him around his waist like he might try to escape. I'm practically straddling one of his thighs, and his other leg is thrown up over my hips. Thank goodness we both fell asleep fully dressed. Otherwise, the situation stirring behind the fly of my jeans might be a lot more uncomfortable than it is, which is saying something.

I should move away, extricate myself from the complicated knot of our limbs, and get some space, but I don't want to wake him. And, if I'm being honest with myself, I don't want to move away. He's so comfortable, and he smells good—like apples and something musky. I can smell my soap on him, too, which reminds me of our shower yesterday. The way my body lit up like a Christmas tree when he put his fingers inside me. I've never felt anything like it, and I—

Nope. No sir, Adam. Stop it right now. Stop thinking of Levi Asher that way. He tricked you, like the snake he is.

Groan.

He's not a snake. I can't even pretend to hate him, or to distrust him like I obviously should—he admitted to lying to me. Using me.

He admitted to it. Knows he did wrong.

But he did it anyway.

He didn't want to.

But he did. He pretended to be interested in me, touched me, made me want him.

He didn't know it would be like this.

He should have been honest with me from the start.

He was protecting his sister.

He hurt me.

He said he was falling in love.

The two sides of my consciousness war with each other over what I should feel and want and what I actually feel and want.

Tilting my head, I look up at his face in the dim light. Even in sleep, he looks troubled, no sign of the easy-going guy I've come to know. His brow is furrowed, messy hair flopped over his face. I want to brush the errant strands from his face and kiss him awake. I want to tell him I love him, and that it doesn't matter how he came into my life, I'm still glad he's here.

I want to tell him I'm afraid of losing him, that even the thought of never again feeling the way I do when I'm with him hurts more than his betrayal. However uncertain the future is, whatever happens with my dad, the one thing that soothes my anxiety is imagining having Levi by my side. He makes me feel confident and happy.

It's too soon to feel this way, and it's probably unhealthy. But I'm not ready to give him up. The more I think about walking away from him, the more I realize I need him. I need him, and he needs me. He needs someone to lean on and support him under all the weight of his worry and fear and sadness for his sister.

Can we move past the lies, knowing he did the wrong thing for the wrong reasons, but did so from a place of hurt and fear?

If he wasn't sincere, he wouldn't have admitted to the truth. He would have taken his evidence and walked away. Instead, he stayed and confessed, not just to manipulating me, but to falling for me along the way. And he let me come with him when I didn't have anywhere else to go.

He wouldn't go through all of this for nothing.

I want him.

I want him.

Eventually, I can't wait any longer to get up. I need the bathroom and at least six inches of space to think clearly.

Despite my efforts to move slowly and carefully, I'm not able to extricate my arm from beneath his back without stirring him awake.

When he blinks his eyes open, I'm hovering awkwardly above his chest.

"Sorry," I whisper. "I didn't mean to treat you like my own personal stuffed animal."

Levi laughs, his voice deep and husky from sleep. "I don't mind. I can't remember the last time I slept that good, actually."

"It's been a pretty exhausting couple of days. I might have stayed asleep if my bladder didn't wake me."

He hums in agreement, pushing up on his elbows. "What time is it?"

Now that I'm sitting up, I can see the red glowing digits of the alarm clock. "It's just after five in the evening," I answer, surprised at how late it is. We really slept the whole day away.

Levi sits up and reaches for his phone. I excuse myself to the restroom, grabbing my toiletries bag out of my duffle on the way so I can brush my teeth and splash water on my face.

"I need a shower, but I'm going to have a snack first," I say as I walk out of the bathroom. "Do you think the pie is still—"

"Holy shit," Levi says, pushing his hair back. He jumps up from the bed and paces while his fingers fly across the screen. My heart starts beating erratically. "Holy shit," he repeats.

Before I can ask what's wrong, the phone vibrates in his hand, and he immediately pulls it up to his ear. "Freddie, what's happening?"

If it's Freddie calling, it must be news about the evidence we handed over about my father. My stomach, no longer feeling the hunger that it was a minute ago, feels like I swallowed a boulder.

What if the evidence we gave them isn't enough? What if it was?

I know we're doing the right thing, especially where it concerns Levi's sister, but he's still my father and I was raised to honor and obey the will of my parents. Until I was old enough for him to sniff out that I might be different, he was the perfect dad, if not a little absent because he worked a lot. He taught me how to throw a ball and came to every game. He taught me what it was to be a provider and supported me when I chose to join the church, even though he'd hoped I would follow in his footsteps to become a lawyer. But the life he lives behind the scenes is one of corruption and evil, and exposing him is the only way to make it right.

"You're serious? Fucking hell, Freddie, this is insane. I know, I'm sorry, I didn't expect to sleep so hard. No, no. This is good. This is..." Levi looks up at me, a wild look in his bright blue eyes. His expression changes, eyebrows furrowing in what looks like concern. "Yeah, I'm good," he says into the phone. "Tomorrow morning is good. Yeah. Text me the address and I'll be there. And thank you, Freddie."

"What's going on?" I ask, barely able to force my voice out.

"Are you having any second thoughts?" Levi asks tentatively.

I shake my head fervently. "No," I say firmly. "It hurts, I'll admit to that. But this is the right thing."

He lets out a breath. "Good, because your father's house is being raided as we speak."

My mouth drops open. "Ri-right now?"

Levi nods, taking a step forward to steady my elbow when I reel. "Here, sit," he says, guiding me to sit on the edge of the bed. "Are you alright? I know it's a shock. I had no idea things would happen this quickly. Freddie says his boss took one look at the files we gave him and made some calls immediately. They wanted to get in and out before your father suspected anything."

My head nods slowly as I try to process the information. "Th-that's good," I say. "He won't see it coming."

After a few more slow breaths, I look up at Levi, who is still watching me like I might have a breakdown at any point. "What about your sister and the evidence we left behind?"

He squeezes my hand. I didn't realize that I'd reached over and threaded my fingers through his. "They'll find it. Freddie says his boss didn't want to know any details, in case it thwarts the investigation, but that the search will be very thorough."

I'm looking down at our hands entwined in his lap. He loosens his grip, but I tighten mine, not ready to let him go. There are things I need to say, but I don't know if this is the right time, if there's anything we need to be doing to prepare for whatever comes next.

"Do we need to do anything?"

"I'm going to meet with the Attorney General tomorrow morning to give them the original files. If you still think you might want to testify—"

"I do," I say firmly.

Levi nods, a small, sad smile showing on his angelic face. "Then you can come with me. I'm sorry that you have to do any of this."

"It's the right thing," I repeat.

"Thank you," he says. "For understanding. For doing the right thing, even though it's going to hurt your family. For helping me. What I did—"

"You did what you had to do," I say, holding up a hand before he can say anything else. "I'm not saying that manipulating me was okay. It definitely isn't. But you could have left without a word. You chose to stay behind and tell me the truth, even though it obviously hurt you to do it, even though it could have ruined your plans. I could have tipped off my father or destroyed the evidence. I could have easily thwarted everything you worked so hard for, but you took a chance on telling me, anyway."

"It never even occurred to me that you'd do any of that, Adam. Because I know you. You're a good man. A better man than I've ever met before, and I—" I cut his words off with my lips. He grunts in surprise, but kisses me back without hesitation.

Levi lets me take the lead, taking whatever I give him, and in return, I feed him everything I have. I pour it all into this kiss—all my fear and sadness, my heartache, my hope and exhilaration. My budding love.

The kiss deepens, and we end up horizontal on the bed, tangling our limbs together and holding each other as close as possible. But it's not close enough. I need more. I need all of him.

My hands drag down his body, landing on his butt and pulling him against me hard enough that there's no doubt of what I'm feeling right now.

"I don't deserve you," Levi rasps, pulling away from me to suck in a ragged breath. He rolls us so that he's hovering over me and looks down into my eyes. Whatever he sees there darkens his expression, his eyes growing misty.

"I promise you, Adam, I'll never hurt you again. And I'll spend the rest of my life working to be the kind of man that could even come close to deserving someone as good as you. And for as long as you'll have me, I'd do everything in my power to show you what you mean to me."

My chest tightens as the organ inside swells and palpitates. Barely able to speak at all, I hold Levi tightly against my body and choke out two words.

"Show me."

With a groan, Levi descends on me, fitting his body to mine and grinding his hardness against mine. All our clothes are too much, and I'm desperate to feel his skin against mine. Pushing my hands under his shirt, I move my hands up his back until he reaches for the fabric and pulls it over his head. I sit up with him in my lap so he can pull mine off as well, and then we're chest to chest, skin to skin.

"More," I wheeze against his lips, and we scramble to strip every piece of clothing from our bodies, one by one, until we're blessedly bare.

The heat of his flesh against mine is scorching, sweat slicking our bodies as we tangle and writhe together. Hands, lips, and tongues explore every inch of skin we can reach until we're both moaning and desperate. I'm so needy for him I could cry.

Levi's hand wraps around us both, and I moan into his mouth. He strokes us until I'm trembling, so close to orgasm but holding back because I want so much more. I want things I don't understand, things that I'm honestly afraid of, but I want them all the same. I want to be joined together, for there to be nothing between us.

"Levi—" I pant into his mouth, my body tensing against my oncoming release.

He notices my hesitation and pulls away. "Too much?" he asks, breathing heavily. "I'm sorry, I got carried away."

"Not too much. I want more... I want all of you."

I'm not sure how to interpret the look of pain that crosses his face, or the way he kisses me so hard it takes my breath away.

"I want that too," he whispers. "But you're not ready."

"I am ready," I protest, pushing my erection into his. "I want to feel you inside me."

Levi swallows deeply, but shakes his head and pulls back more. I hold him against me, not ready to lose the contact of our bodies. The pained groan makes me second guess myself, and I lift my hands and release him.

"*Oh*. Unless you don't want to. That's okay, of course—" I'd never want him to do anything he isn't comfortable with. What we've been doing is more than fine.

"It's not that, I promise," Levi says, rocking against me as if to prove himself.

"Then what is it?" I ask, sitting up so I can hold him close and kiss the sexy dips of his collarbone.

"You need more time to be ready to take me," he says, which makes me blush so furiously, I hide my face in his neck so he can't see it. "And I need more time to prove myself."

"What do you mean?" I say, forgetting my embarrassment and pulling back to look at him.

"You might forgive me, but I don't know if I'll ever be able to forgive myself. I don't deserve to take anything else from you, Adam."

My hands come up to cup his face, and I look into his eyes so he can see how serious I am. "I want you, Levi Asher. Every part of you."

Whatever he's thinking, he seems to be searching for something in my eyes as well. Then he blinks, hard.

"Then take me."

Chapter Nine
Levi

Adam's forehead scrunches while he tries to figure out what I'm telling him. It takes him a few moments, but his eyes pop wide open when he catches on.

"You... want me... to..."

I nod and try to hold back from smiling too widely. I don't want him to think I'm making fun of his innocence, but his shock is adorable.

"But I thought, or I assumed..." he trails off, not able to verbalize whatever he's thinking.

"I like it both ways," I assure him. "I've never bottomed for anyone as big as you, though, so it'll be kind of like a first time for both of us," I say, somewhat jokingly.

He looks unsure, but his cock is leaking pre-cum at an alarming rate. If he's as excited as I am, this won't last long. I take his mouth again, in a long, deep kiss that makes me nearly forget what I'm supposed to be doing. That is, until my heartbeat takes up residence in my cock, and it's pulsing against Adam's stomach.

"Let me just..." I strain to reach my jeans to get to my wallet, not wanting to leave his lap for even a second. With a chuckle, Adam holds my waist and practically lifts me to hover over the side of the bed before putting me back on his lap. I blink down at him. I knew he was strong, but *damn*. He winks. *Fucking winks.*

"I don't know where this cockiness is coming from," I tell him. "But I'm into it." I huff. "Shit, I'm into everything about you. At this point, you could ask to foot fuck my ear and I'd probably come."

The face he makes is priceless. "Is that a thing?"

"Probably. There's some weird shit out there. Some of which I absolutely plan to explore with you. But for now..." Producing a single condom and packet of lube from my wallet, I rip open the lube and spread some over the tips of my index and middle fingers before reaching behind me. Adam freezes, eyes wide, as he watches me.

I sink one, and then two fingers inside me, not giving myself much time to acclimate because I'm on a mission. I stretch myself, fucking my fingers in Adam's lap, with one arm linked around his neck to steady myself.

"What are you doing?" Adam asks shakily.

"Stretching myself for you," I say, moaning a little when his fingers dig into my sides.

"Can I see?"

"You want to watch me stretch my ass to fit your big cock?"

Adam nods wordlessly, and I lick his lips before turning in his lap. I get to my knees right in front of him and bend forward, steadying myself with one arm on the bed and the other reaching behind to probe my ass with two fingers.

A whoosh of breath leaves his chest and brushes across my exposed ass. As open and confident as I normally am, this position is a little vulnerable even for me, but having Adam watch me finger my ass is making my balls feel heavier. I avoid my prostate in case I set myself off, not wanting to come until he's inside me. I want him to feel what it's like to have my ass clench around him and massage the orgasm from his cock.

I feel his hands touch the back of my thighs and roam up to cup my ass. His thumb swipes over my fingers, then pulls away quickly.

"It's okay," I pant. "You can touch me however you like."

"Can I, uh... can I help?"

Oh, fuck, yes.

Removing my hand, I curve my back and push my ass out like a cat. "You want to stretch me open for you?" Jesus, even my voice sounds desperate for him to do exactly that.

"Yes please," he whispers huskily.

"So polite."

Before I can finish teasing him, his fingers are brushing over my hole. My breath catches. They're wet, so he must have gotten some of the lube from the open packet. He toys with me, although I'm not sure if it's intentional or his uncertainty that keeps him circling my rim. He presses against it, the tip of his finger barely sinking in until I push back against him. He gasps when his finger slips inside to the first knuckle, then moans. His breathing gets heavier as he presses in and out of me, feeling around, sinking the finger in all the way. Unintentionally, he brushes over my prostate.

"There," I pant. "Right there."

His finger moves around again, stopping when I moan. He prods and rubs the spot inside me, feeling the tender fleshy button that has me bucking and pushing back against him. I'm already so close.

"Is that..."

"My prostate, yeah," I say breathlessly. "Give me another finger, stretch me open so I can feel your cock there instead."

A small choking sound leaves him, but he does as I say. His two fingers are definitely larger than mine. The burn of it helps stave off my orgasm, and I'm able to refocus on walking him through prepping me. I barely make it to three fingers before I can't take it anymore. I pull away from him, holding back a chuckle when he pouts like I've taken away his favorite toy. Once I tear open the condom, he snaps back to attention, gripping his cock tightly around the base. His eyes follow my every movement as I remove the rubber from the packet and reach to put it on him. His cock jumps when I touch him, and I can't resist giving him a few soft strokes before rolling the condom down over his thick length. It's a snug fit, but I'm able to roll it down and have enough room at the tip.

"We'll get you a bigger size for next time," I tell him. "And a lot more lube." I chuckle, but he doesn't say anything or move. He just sits there, frozen, holding the base of his cock while I suit it up. He hasn't said a word in a few minutes.

"Are you okay?" I ask. "We can stop. You don't have to do anything you're not ready for." He swallows and averts his eyes, cheeks growing red. I know Adam well enough to know what that means.

"Adam," I say, tipping his chin to make him look at me. "Whatever it is, you can say it. You can tell me anything, and I won't judge you."

"No, it's okay," he says, shaking his head. "I'm just, uh—nothing. We're good. I'm good. I'm ready."

"Adam."

"It's stupid."

"I don't care."

"I—it's just—do we need this?" He looks down at his sheathed cock.

The sausage is straining in the casing, to say the least. I know it would feel so much better without it, but I didn't want to assume anything. Hell, the only reason I have a condom and one packet of lube is because I happen to always keep one in my wallet. Better safe than sorry.

"It's not like I can get you pregnant," he says, blushing furiously now. I can't help but laugh a little.

"No, you can't knock me up. But there are other things to protect against." I give him a thoughtful look. "I've been tested recently, all negative. I've never had sex without a condom."

"I'd never ask you to do something you don't want—"

Without another thought, I run my hand up his length, rolling the condom back up his shaft and then throwing it over my shoulder. It hits the door with a slight splat. Adam's lips twitch, and the tension bleeds from his shoulders.

"You're sure?" he asks, laughter in his voice.

"Are you fucking kidding me? Sweet, sweet boy," I say, crawling into his lap and palming his cock. I spread the rest of the lube over him with a firm stroke before lining him up.

Resting my forehead on his, our mouths a breath apart, I whisper the God's honest truth. "There's nothing more in this world I want to feel than you inside me, hot and bare. I want to feel every single millimeter of your skin," I say, losing my breath as I push myself down just enough to feel the blunt head of his cock start to breach me.

Adam sucks in a breath as I expel mine, a low moan escaping from my chest as I take him into my body. The farther down I sink, the wider I'm stretched, the more I feel like I'm being filled with more than just Adam's cock. By the time I've sunk all the way down, the cheeks of my ass meeting his pelvis, I'm pretty sure I'm having a legitimate religious experience. Adam's mouth has dropped open, head tipped back, eyes clenched shut. A drop of sweat, or maybe a tear, rolls from the corner of his eye. Leaning forward, I trail kisses up his neck and jaw. He meets my lips and kisses me deeply, meaningfully, and I taste salt.

I pull back to look into his eyes, smiling softly. With my eyes locked on his, I lift myself up and sink down again. And again. Slowly. Again. Soft sounds of pleasure and heavy breaths build with the tempo of our lovemaking. Because that's what we're doing, I realize with a tightening in my chest that steals my breath on a cry of pleasure. This isn't any kind of sex I've ever had before. This isn't at all what I thought the outcome of ruining Adam Havre would be. He's ruined me instead. Ruined me by loving me.

Adam says my name like a prayer, his arms tightening around my waist. Warmth explodes deep inside me. I grind down on Adam's cock as he jerks up, burying his hot cum inside me. The friction of his cock pegging my prostate and my cock rubbing between us sets me off, and I spurt all over us both. I keep rocking in his lap, keep kissing him between whispers at how good he was, how good he makes me feel, how much I love feeling him inside me. Until finally I collapse against him, my face tucked into his neck and his arms tightly around me. Eventually, I know I'm going to have to pull off of him. My ass is already aching, but I don't want to lose the contact, and I think he doesn't either. He's holding me around my middle, much like he did when we were sleeping, clutching me to his chest.

I pull back enough to look at him, noticing the wet tracks on his cheeks. Running my thumbs under his eyes, I give him a questioning look.

"I didn't know it would be like that."

"Like what?"

Did he feel that the way I did? Like he was meeting God?

"I didn't know it would be beautiful."

I nod, dropping my lips to his and wrapping my legs around him tightly, hugging him with my whole body. We kiss until I'm squirming involuntarily. Adam rolls us so he's laying over me, the move so sexy my cock gives a valiant twitch despite the ache. I groan softly as Adam slowly pulls out of me, looking down at where we're joined as his cock slips from my ass. A trickle of wetness follows, and Adam's pupils dilate so much I can barely see the color in his irises.

"Please tell me we can do that again," he whispers huskily, and I gasp as his fingers swipe against the mess. I moan when he massages my hole with his fingers, gently pushing his cum back inside me.

"As many times as you want, for the rest of our lives," I promise him. The declaration slips out of me without permission, but I'm not sorry. Not when Adam lays behind me and pulls me into his big, warm body. Not when he makes me believe that everything, whatever may come, will be okay.

No matter how this started, despite my many sins, I found my way to heaven. And his name is Adam. Sweet, beautiful, strong, amazing Adam.

About the Author

Rebecca Rathe is a neurotic, neurodivergent hot mess... but she's got this deliciously dirty mind to make up for it. If you're looking for plot forward books with queer representation, grit, emotion, and a metric ton of spice, check out RebeccaRathe.com

Malevolence

By: Sarah Daniels

A Twisted Metamorphosis Prequel

About Malevolence

I've always been different, void of any emotion.

I never understood why movies made people laugh, why funerals made people cry, why a man cheating on his wife makes her angry. My brain can't comprehend these emotions, and it's led to being poked, prodded, and studied by every shrink in this damn state.

Life wasn't worth living anymore until I met her, Alaina.

Despite not being capable of love, she embraced me, loved me. She's an addict and understands my need to satisfy urges. But she kick-started new urges in me I never knew I could have outside of the need for blood on my hands.

But when I killed to protect her honor, things changed. I need her, and I will kill whoever I have to, to keep her in my life forever.

Content Note:

Mature content. For readers 18 & older.

Mentions of animal dissection (no on page unaliving of the animal), foster care system, homelessness, illegal drug use, injections (mentions of, no on page detail), knife violence, murder, arson

Mental Health: Psychopathy and Antisocial Personality Disorder, Conduct Disorder (as a child), Split Personality Disorder (including mental conversations between two personalities), drug addiction, lack of empathy, unethical treatment from a psychiatrist (purposefully triggering psychopathy with images, videos, medication)

D/s dynamics, dub-con, bondage, lack of aftercare, transactional relationship, exhibitionism, praise with degradation

Relationship type: FF with MF Scenes

Prologue
Tara

(10 Years Ago - 11 Years Old)

I*ntestines...liver...kidneys... I think?*

The cool, spring Nebraska breeze gave me a slight chill as the sun reflected off of the knife in my hand.

"Tara! Oh my god, what are you doing?!" my foster mother shrieked, forcing me to stop trying to figure out which organs these were in the dead bird I had laying on the ground in front of me. The tip of the paring knife I was holding hovered over what I assumed was this bird's stomach.

"It's just a pigeon, Megan," I replied indifferently, refocusing on the bird with its belly sliced open in front of my crossed legs in the grass of our front yard.

"Wh-what...? With my kitchen knife?!" She pointed a shaky finger towards the expensive paring knife in my hand.

"I'm learning about organs in school, and I just wanted to see some real ones," I said, monotone. "Besides, I needed this knife since you took my scissors away."

Scooping up the dead pigeon in my bloody hands, I held it out towards my foster mother. "See? I think I found its stomach, right here..."

I pressed the tip of the paring knife deeper into the bird's stomach, forcing a small trail of blood to fall down the bird's side, pooling in my hand.

Megan doubled over, throwing up into the grass, and I just stared at her with my head tilted slightly, confused by her reaction.

Did I do something wrong?

Was I supposed to be upset?

Why don't I understand why Megan is being so dramatic?

"Get...get inside. Now. G-Go shower and get cleaned up," she stuttered, pulling her knitted cardigan tightly around her chest, and hugging herself.

"But, I'm not done, I–"

"I said, go. Now."

Still confused, I placed the pigeon down on the grass, stood, and tucked the paring knife away into the pocket of my jeans before turning towards the front door.

I'm eleven years old. How can she not believe that I know how to use a knife? I don't understand what she's so freaked out about... Was I holding it wrong?

Quickly dismissing it in my mind, I wiped my bloody hands on my jeans before turning the doorknob to the front door. I stepped inside and looked over my shoulder towards Megan, who had her back turned and her cell phone to her ear.

"Yes, Doctor Halloway? It's about Tara. Again." Megan's voice in the distance was barely audible, but I closed my eyes to focus on listening before closing the door behind me.

"It happened again; a bird this time... Yes... No, this has been too much... Yes... Alright, I'll get her to your office by then... Thank you, Doctor..."

Megan is my third foster mother in six months.

I'm "too much to handle" according to Gemma, the social worker at the group home that I'm now expecting to return to.

I should be upset; why don't I feel a thing?

"Adam, you need to come home. It happened again..."

I had no desire to hear her cry to her husband, so I closed the door behind me and hummed Beethoven's Für Elise while strolling into the restroom. As I turned the sink on to wash my hands, I heard Megan close the front door and sigh exasperatedly.

"Tara?" she called out from the other room. "Can you come here, hun? We need to talk."

* * *

"Tara? Dr. Halloway is ready for you, my dear."

A petite, brunette medical assistant stood in front of me with my file tucked in her arm. Megan and Adam were quick to stand while I remained sitting, observing.

The medical assistant tucked a strand of her shoulder-length black hair behind her ear, giving Adam a strange look as Megan dug through her purse for her vibrating cell phone. Adam looked her up and down like he was starving and she was his next meal, but shifting back to a stoic expression once Megan looked back up. Turning her back, the assistant began walking, and Megan motioned for me to come.

I don't understand why people act like this...

We walked down the sterile hallway towards Dr. Halloway's office, and I shoved my hands in my pockets, not wanting to be here. My fingertips brushed the handle of the small paring knife I still had in my pocket, and I felt something... Comfort? It was a foreign feeling, since most of the time I feel nothing.

The assistant swished her hips back and forth, probably to keep Adam's attention, and opened the door to the doctor's office.

"Please, sit. Dr. Halloway will be in shortly," she said in a professional tone, but gave Adam a subtle wink.

"She must really like attention," I said monotone, as Megan and

Adam sat on the beige couch in the center of the room. I opted for a matching armchair so I could sit alone.

"I'm sure she's just being friendly, hun," Megan said, forcing a smile.

"It's her job to be friendly and professional, Tara," Adam said, leaning back into the couch.

"Uh huh..." I yawned. "So, it's *friendly* to shake her ass when she walks and wink at Adam?"

"Tara! Language!" Megan scolded. All I could do was stare at her, still baffled by why she seemed so... different.

"I'm so sorry for my delay. Good afternoon," Dr. Halloway said, entering the room and sitting in an armchair across from me.

"Good afternoon, Doctor," Adam said with a nod.

"Hello, Doctor," Megan replied with a sigh.

"Hello, Tara. How are you feeling today?" Dr. Halloway asked, shifting attention to me.

"I'm fine. Just a normal day."

"Normal day? I hear you've been busy today," he said, clicking his pen, and opening his portfolio notepad.

"I already told Megan. We're learning about organs in school. I just wanted to see real ones and not fake model ones."

Why is this such a big deal to everyone? It's just a bird... It's not like it was a dead person or anything...

"Why a bird, Tara?" Dr. Halloway asked, looking up from his notes.

"Because it was there? I don't understand why everyone is upset. It's just a bird." I crossed my arm, a tightness in my chest building. Before Dr. Holloway could speak, a gentle knock interrupted him.

"Excuse me for interrupting, but Miss Gemma is here to speak with Adam and Megan," the same assistant from earlier said, standing halfway inside the room.

"Thank you Lila," Dr. Halloway replied, and she closed the door gently behind her. "If you are okay with it, I can continue speaking with Tara. But, I understand if you wish to be present. We can pause while you speak with Gemma."

"N-No, please..." Megan shot up from her seat in a rush. "Please continue; Adam and I will return shortly."

Megan and Adam left the room, and Dr. Halloway pulled out a packet of papers, flipping to the first page. I could see "PCL-R" printed on the cover page.

"Alright, Tara. I'm going to ask you some questions, and just answer honestly." He flipped the page again, and his elbow knocked his portfolio binder to the floor, and photographs scattered across the floor.

"Shoot, I'm sorry. Let me get those..."

My eyes found one photo in particular; a man laying in a pool of blood with his throat cut from ear to ear. Someone tied him to a four-post bed, and he was naked.

I couldn't take my eyes off of it.

What kind of knife cut so clean like that?

How deep is the cut?

My knee began subtly bouncing unconsciously as I studied the photograph. I hummed Für Elise silently in my mind, trying to keep this tightness in my chest at bay.

"How does it make you feel, Tara?" Dr. Halloway said, the tone of his voice darker, deeper. "Tell me, do you like what you see?"

Chapter One
Tara

4 Years Ago (17 Years Old)

"Do you like what you see, Tara?"

Dr. Halloway's deep, ominous voice echoed in my mind as I sat in the same armchair I've been sitting in since I was eleven years old. I was staring at a spot on the carpet of his office, lost in thought.

"Tara?" Dr. Halloway asked, drawing my attention back to him. Shifting in my seat, I crossed my arms over my chest, reciprocating eye contact.

"What now? Everything is fine, just swell. Like always." My voice was sharp, harsh.

"We need to discuss your transition, my dear. Since tomorrow is your eighteenth birthday, you will no longer be with the Haven House."

A tightness built in my chest again; the familiar feeling of my urges surfacing... My urge to feel the warm, silky smooth sensation of blood on my hands. The urge to see the life leave someone's eyes as I steal their last breath...

"I'm fine, *Timothy*," I spat, staring daggers at him.

The image of him spread out on a four-post bed like the image he's shown me every time I've been in his office... I wanted that to be Timothy Halloway tied to that bed with his neck sliced wide open by my knife...

"We've discussed this callousness in your attitude, Miss Hollis."

"We've discussed how I don't give a shit about your little psychopath test, Timothy."

Dr. Halloway stood from his chair, tossing his portfolio to the seat, and walked towards his desk. I watched him pull open a drawer and slam it closed, walking towards me.

"Don't forget who holds the power here, Tara. Your pathetic attempts at manipulation and dominance are useless here."

Dr. Halloway grabbed my wrist, and forced me to grip the handle of my paring knife I stole from Megan, my previous foster mother. At age eleven, having killed a bird with it, he took the knife from me when I was forced to see him.

Feeling the smooth, wood handle in my hands sent a wave of calm over me. My vision became more clear, my breathing more even, my urges jumped to the forefront of my mind. All I could do was stare at the blade, tilting my head slightly, imagining the memories I have made using this knife to kill.

The power he had over me was frustrating.

The social worker forces me to have sessions with him twice a week, and each session he pokes and prods, studying me. "Studying your perfect mind." He calls it.

I'm not stupid. I know what he's doing.

Once I turned sixteen, he began showing me more intense crime scene images and videos. People murdered in various ways, people having sex in unconventional ways, purposefully triggering my urges so I'd kill who he wanted without the blame being on him.

I couldn't fight it and he knew it.

I've always been different, void of any emotion. I never understood why movies made people laugh, why funerals made people cry, why a man cheating on his wife makes her angry. My brain can't comprehend these emotions, and it's led to being stuck in the foster care system. No families could handle me; apparently my birth parents couldn't handle me either.

At least that's what Dr. Halloway and Gemma, the social worker, say.

"What do you feel, Tara?"

"Nothing," I lied.

"I said, what do you *feel*, Tara?" he pressed.

Gripping the knife handle tighter in my hand, I closed my eyes, taking a deep, grounding breath.

"I feel...ready, Doctor."

"Good girl, Tara." He gripped my cheeks harshly with one hand, forcing my mouth open, and placed a small, white tablet on my tongue. "Swallow for me. You'll be even more ready soon."

* * *

Sitting on my bed at the Haven House, I picked at my cuticles, looking at the digital clock on the nightstand next to my bed. It was six in the evening, and I was one sleep away from being forced out of the group home.

My session with Dr. Halloway had me on edge. He's pressed and pressed, trying to get my urges to manifest, and I was struggling to keep them at bay. I was still feeling strange from that pill he forced down my throat.

At least I got my knife back... I thought, stroking the handle with my thumb absentmindedly, proud of myself for swiping it off his desk as I left.

Funny thing about the foster care system; once you turn eighteen, you're no longer the state's problem. They show you the door and wish you good luck in life that they don't do shit to help you prepare for. But I wasn't letting that bitch of a social worker kick me out; I'm leaving on my own terms.

I could hear all the children playing outside on the playground, so it was the perfect time to leave. Standing off the bed with purpose, I reached underneath the bed frame and grabbed my duffel bag. I've never had much here, but I neatly folded my four outfits I owned, and placed my toiletries in a plastic bag on top of my clothes. I tucked my knife away safely in between two pairs of jeans and patted the stack of clothes, making mental notes of where it would be.

I was expecting to be on the streets for a while, so I took my duffel bag to the kitchen. Shuffling through the pantry, I grabbed as many lightweight non-perishables as I could find and shoved them into my bag.

This will have to do for now. I have plans tonight...

Before leaving, I snuck into Gemma's office and picked the lock of her drawer. She keeps her emergency cash in here, and it was mine now.

Once satisfied with the contents of my bag, I pulled up my long, black hair into a ponytail and began humming Für Elise as I slipped silently out the front door.

It was only about a ten-minute walk to Dr. Halloway's house, and he should be home from the office in about twenty minutes. As I turned the corner out of the neighborhood, I reminisced about a previous session with Dr. Halloway last week.

"So, tell me, Tara, how does this make you feel when you see it?" Dr. Halloway asked, showing me an image of a woman sobbing over a flag covered coffin of a loved one.

"I guess she's upset? Some dude must have died in war, I don't know."

"Okay, well, let me ask you this, then. How did you feel when you took Megan's car without asking to go on that joy ride?"

"If she didn't want me using her car, she shouldn't have left her keys out," I yawned.

"Did you have a plan to take the car? Or was it just an urge? Impulse?"

"She left the keys. I took the keys. I drove the car. It's not that hard

to understand," I spat, crossing my arms. Dr. Halloway scribbled away in his notes and I felt the tightening in my chest start again.

"I see..."

Forcing the memory out of my mind, I turned down the corner of his block into a pleasant neighborhood. It wasn't upper class, but a comfortable middle. The homes had neat, manicured lawns, and children out playing in the front yards.

Dr. Halloway's home was about halfway down the block. His BMW SUV sat in the driveway, and lights shone inside. Without hesitation, I hummed my Für Elise tune in my mind and knocked on the door.

"Tara? What's going on?" Dr. Halloway asked as he opened the door, his tie untied, and hanging from his neck.

"Can I crash on your couch until tomorrow morning? I'll be taking the train out of town, and they won't let me buy a ticket until I'm eighteen, which happens tomorrow," I asked, gauging his mood and energy.

"You should be at the Haven House and..."

"Well, I'm obviously not. Please, just for one night. I'll be gone before you wake up." I watched his eyes subtly scan my chest, and I sighed deeply, allowing my breasts to rise and fall, watching him suck in a sharp breath.

"This is completely unethical. You're my patient and..."

"It's fine. I'll find somewhere else to go, Timothy," I interrupted, turning to walk away.

"Tara, wait. Fine, just come inside." Dr. Halloway stepped aside, allowing me entry into the living room.

It wasn't what I was expecting. It was neat, homey. There was a dark, blue-grey suede couch and matching loveseat surrounding a mahogany coffee table, with tall silver lamps and a flat screen television on the wall above his fireplace. A simple dark brown rug was on the floor underneath the coffee table, and there was a single glass of what I assumed was whiskey on the tabletop.

Picture frames of his achievements and diplomas were on the

opposite wall, along with photographs of his family and artwork from his younger patients. A bookshelf full of medical books and vinyl records was on the wall next to the fireplace, and a vintage record player sat neatly tucked away on a rolling cart next to it.

"Please make yourself comfortable. I'll grab some blankets out of the closet for you. Either of these couches are free for you to use. The remote for the television is on the mantle," he said, finally peeling his eyes off of my chest, and turned to walk down the hall.

I dropped my duffel bag on the floor next to the loveseat and plopped myself down onto the cushions. My eyes found his vacant glass on the coffee table, so when I heard his footsteps returning, I sat up and downed it as he returned to the room.

"Tara!" he said, surprised, swiping the now empty glass out of my hand.

"What? It was there," I said with a shrug.

Trying to remember how that assistant in his office acted with Adam, I mimicked what she did when she was giving him looks. I looked Dr. Halloway up and down, forcing a smirk to pull up the corner of my lips. He swallowed hard, visibly affected, and collected himself before speaking.

"Help yourself to anything in the refrigerator. I'll be in my bedroom for the evening; the last door at the end of the hall. Knock if you need anything." He pivoted around without hesitation and walked down the hall, closing his bedroom door behind him.

Standing up from the loveseat, I reached behind me to unsnap and remove my bra to get comfortable, and get ready for what was to come with dear Dr. Halloway. I lifted my duffle bag, placing it on the loveseat, and shuffled through it, looking for my sleep shirt. It was nothing fancy, just an oversized man's undershirt that fit me like a dress, but perfect for my plans. I peeled off my skinny jeans, laying them out neatly on the cushions. Reaching up, I release my hair from my ponytail, letting my black waves fall haphazardly around my face. Shaking out my hair, I smirked as my eyes found my knife in my bag.

Finally...

Gripping the handle, I held it up to eye level, studying the blade on it. I closed my eyes, overwhelmed by the mental image of the sharp metal slicing through the skin of his neck. My "pre-kill calm" I liked to call it, washed over me, and I wandered towards Dr. Halloway's bedroom door. Taking care to keep my knife hidden behind my back, I didn't bother knocking, and just walked right in, wearing just my shirt and black lace thong.

"Tara? Are you alright?" Dr. Halloway placed a newly filled whiskey glass down on his nightstand and looked over the book he was reading in his queen size bed. He was shirtless, wearing only pajama pants, relaxing on top of the comforter, and leaning against the headboard.

"Just looking for the bathroom. Wrong room," I replied, looking around the room.

"It's two doors down on the right and–" He stopped mid sentence as I sauntered up to the foot of his four post bed.

"How does it make you feel, Tara?"

Images of the crime scene photo he always shows me flashed in my mind; the man tied to the bed, the slice in his neck...

"What are you doing? Tara?"

Ignoring him, I climbed onto the foot of his bed, subtly tucking my knife away underneath a blanket draped across the foot of the bed. On all fours, I crawled my way up towards him, in between his legs.

His legs stiffened as I reached his waist, and his confused eyes met mine. Reaching up, I took the book from his hands and tossed it to the floor.

"You're the doctor, Timothy; you tell me."

Crawling towards him made my shirt ride up, revealing my ass in my lace thong. His hands twitched, and I knew he was desperate to touch.

"Tara, this is just–"

"Shh..." I cooed, adjusting my knees to rest outside his hips to straddle him. Reaching above his head, I tossed all the pillows to the floor, so he was laying flat on his back. I hovered over his lap, not lowering myself yet, watching his eyes darken with lust, my hands resting on his bare shoulders.

"How does it feel, Doctor?" I taunted, lowering myself to sit on his lap, rocking my hips, feeling his cock stiffen underneath me. Gently digging my nails into his skin, I dragged them towards me, earning the softest groan from him.

"Tara..."

"Mmm, there it is," I smirked, feeling his now hard cock under me.

"Fuck, Tara... We can't... We can't do this..." He groaned as I started to grind on his cock, his length sliding perfectly along my pussy over my thong.

"I've imagined this every day, Doctor, just like the photo you showed me," I whimpered as his hands slid up my bare thighs, to my ass.

He gripped the flesh of my ass in both hands, guiding my movements.

Finally, I felt something. Arousal.

Before he could continue, I climbed off of him, walking to the sliding door of his closet. Pushing it open, I shuffled around his dress clothes.

"Tara? What are you doing?" he asked, confused.

Perfect.

Reaching for a tie hanger, I pulled out a handful of his neckties, turning back to the bed. His eyes darkened when he saw the bundle of ties in my hand.

"I knew you loved that photo, Tara," he groaned. I forced what I thought was a sultry smile and began tying one of his wrists to a post of his bed.

"Oh, I loved it alright."

Making my way around his bed, I tied him to each of the posts of his bed. Climbing back on top of him, I pulled my shirt over my head, revealing my pierced nipples. He focused his eyes on them and bit his lower lip.

"See something you like, Doctor?" I asked, resuming my grinding on his cock. "Too bad you can't touch," I teased, gripping my breasts, tossing my head back.

"Fuck, Tara..."

Lifting off of him again, I slid my way between his legs, pulling down the waistband of his pajama pants just enough to allow his dick to spring free. He was already leaking pre-cum, and I gripped his cock tight in my hand. Leaning forward, I dragged my tongue up the underside slowly, sucking his tip hard into my mouth. The salty taste of his pre-cum hit my tongue, and I forced myself not to gag in disgust. But I needed to get off, and I'd make sure I did.

Shifting my knees to straddle him again, I pulled my thong to the side, and rocked my hips on his cock again, allowing him to slide along my slit, coating him in my arousal.

"Mmm, Doctor..." I groaned, lifting my hips and positioning his tip at my entrance.

"Fuck, yes, Tara. Take my cock, use me..." he groaned as I lowered myself onto him. Propping my hands up on his chest, I bounced my ass on his lap, chasing my pleasure.

"How does it make you feel, Doctor?" I moaned, sitting up tall, grinding my clit on his pubic bone.

"So fucking good, baby. So fucking good."

"Feel how tight this pussy is for you, Doctor? How wet it is? All for you..." I whimpered, my climax quickly approaching.

Arching my back, I propped myself up on his knees, and continued bouncing on him, his cock getting so deep, hitting the perfect spot.

"Look at your cock inside me, Doctor. I want this to be the last thing you see." Reaching my hand back underneath the blanket, I gripped the handle of my knife.

"What....? Oh fuck, don't stop baby. Don't fucking stop. I'm going to cum so hard in this tight little pussy..." He groaned, closing his eyes.

Sitting up tall, I slammed my hips into his, my orgasm nearing its peak. I leaned myself forward over his body, dragging the tip of my paring knife gently down his cheek. His pathetic shivering and whimpering in fear made me smirk, and the once playful, aroused look in his eyes shifted to fear.

"Oh, come now, Doctor. You're not scared of me, are you?" I taunted.

Grinding my hips into his, he closed his eyes once again in pleasure. I rode him hard and fast, and the moment his eyes opened again to meet mine, I sliced his neck open with my knife.

"You better make me cum before you bleed out," I purred, grinding harder on him as he gargled and choked on his own blood.

His eyes rolled back as he exhaled for the last time, sending me over the edge, my orgasm ravaging my body, giving me the few seconds of emotion I'd been craving for so long.

I cried out in ecstasy as I kept riding him, drawing out my orgasm, until my legs buckled and shook.

"Mmm, thank you, Doctor," I sighed. "Oh, and what was that from your little psychopath test? 'A core trait being impulsivity and risk-taking with no regard or consideration for consequences of my actions?' Trust me, Doctor. I know the consequences of my actions..."

Climbing off of him, I cleaned myself up, humming Für Elise as I got dressed and untied him from the bed.

Sated and satisfied, I lit a fire in his bathroom and bedroom, letting the trail of flames follow me to the living room. Draping my duffel bag across my chest, I casually walked out the door, closing it gently behind me, walking into the night.

Chapter Two
Tara

Present Day (21 Years Old)

"*Do you like what you see, Tara?*"

My dead psychiatrist's voice still echoed in my mind four years after I killed him.

I hid in the darkness next to a dumpster in an alley and watched my next victim, a grungy, homeless looking man, make a drug deal with a known dealer. Reaching into my crossbody bag, I gripped the handle of my paring knife firmly in my hand. I welcomed the familiar feeling of calm to wash over me, as the need to satisfy my urge to kill threatened to overwhelm me.

He bought heroin, and I needed it for Alaina.

Alaina is my girlfriend, if I had to label whatever our relationship was. We met the night I killed Dr. Halloway; the same night I became homeless.

Unsure of where to go after I burned his house down, I wandered, just let my feet take me wherever they wanted to go. The hint of feeling I had after getting off and watching him die was short-lived, and I was back to feeling numb. I ended up here, in a shady part of Omaha, with a pretty heavy homeless population. It was the type of area that you would lock your car doors driving through; the type of area that people avoid. It was the perfect place to satisfy my urges.

People that no one would look for, or notice they were missing... People like me.

Meeting Alaina, though, was... different.

Someone like me doesn't have relationships; they're impossible to keep. People want connection, closeness, intimacy; all of which I'm incapable of. Alaina is the perfect partner for me; bends to my will for the slightest bit of affection I can fake, and for her next drug fix. I must admit, though, using her body to get off and have that temporary moment of feeling anything is addicting.

Refocusing on my task at hand, I studied the drug transaction. I recognized this drug dealer. He was a complete asshole, constantly changing his prices and keeping the overage for himself. It was entertaining to watch the customers panic and struggle to find the rest of the money in their pockets or bags.

I really should kill him tonight also, but I have plans for him.

The dealer goes by "Ro-Ro" and regularly works this block. His boss is based out of the strip club about a half mile to the east, and collectively they are part of a cartel based out of South Dakota.

Holding my knife handle in between my teeth, I reached up and adjusted my ponytail, watching the homeless man walk deeper into the alley with his purchase. He stopped underneath a flickering light on the side of an abandoned building, and I held my knife again, inching out of my hiding spot, approaching him from behind.

He was distracted and his hands shook as he tried to open the little plastic bag when I made my move.

Without a sound, I swung my knife at him, stabbing him through the neck, and releasing the handle. He let out a surprised gasp, falling to his knees, dropping his drugs as he slumped over to the side. I began my ritual of humming Für Elise out loud while observing the growing pool of blood under him. Bending over, I gripped the handle of my knife that was standing straight up in the air, still lodged into his neck, and pressed my foot into his face. I used the leverage to rip my knife free from his neck. As I tore my knife from his lifeless body, a thin trail of blood spattered along the dirty brick wall of the abandoned building.

Holding my familiar paring knife up to my eye level, I studied the blood dripping from the tip of the blade. As if time was moving in slow motion, I fixated on a drop of blood, leaving a crimson trail down the cool metal and pooling on my hand. My temporary feeling of euphoria engulfed my body, but it was gone almost as soon as it came, leaving me feeling empty, shallow.

Kneeling next to his body, I swiped up the small bag of heroin for Alaina before his blood could reach it, tucking it away in my bra.

A wave of memories from when I was a child consumed me.

"How does it make you feel, Tara...?"

"I'm confused."

"What are you confused about, Tara? You're eleven years old. Clearly you know that something is wrong in this photograph?" Dr. Halloway pressed, gripping my chin, forcing me to look at a photograph of a naked woman on top of a man, with another behind her.

"How does it make you feel?" He asked again.

"I don't know. I don't feel anything."

"Look at it."

My eyes scanned the photo again. The woman was making an expression I tried to decipher. She had tears streaming down her cheeks, and her eyes squeezed shut.

"I don't understand. She's crying, but why?" I asked, confused.

"They are using her, Tara. Using her body to feel good."

"I don't know what you mean."

"You will soon enough."

I chuckled to myself; He was right. I found out exactly what he meant. I used him to feel good, even if it was very short-lived.

With a bored sigh, I flipped the homeless man's body, so he was lying on his back, and lifted his shirt, revealing his stomach and chest.

Just like I did with the bird when I was eleven, I pressed the tip of my knife into his skin at his sternum, dragging it down towards his hips, cutting him open.

Intestines...liver...kidneys...

Absentmindedly, I continued to hum Für Elise while sitting cross-legged. Propping up my chin in one hand, I poked at this dead homeless guy's organs in his sliced open stomach with the tip of my knife. The voices from the past continued to echo in my mind.

"I'm learning about organs in school, and I just wanted to see some real ones..."

"Tara! Oh my god, what are you doing?!"

"I knew you loved that photo, Tara..."

"Tell me... Do you like what you see?"

"Fuck, yes, Tara. Take my cock, use me..."

The voices in my mind dissipated, and I grew bored. Wiping my knife clean on his dirty shirt, I tucked it away in my small crossbody bag I carried. Still humming, I rifled through his pockets for anything else of value. Satisfied, I ended up with three dollars and a half-empty pack of cigarettes with an almost spent disposable lighter inside.

"Nice," I said out loud, standing to my feet and brushing the dust off of my jeans.

I continued to walk deeper into the alley, turning the corner around the back of this abandoned building. The main road was about half a block to my north and I needed to get to the highway across the main road, where Alaina and I camped out.

The thought of Alaina letting me use her body in exchange for the fix of heroin in my pocket triggered that hint of feeling I've been craving; killing wasn't enough for me tonight. I needed more.

Jogging across the street, I made my way through a hole in the chain-link fence separating the street from the highway. I carefully maneuvered down the steep decline in the landscaping towards an overpass. Following my usual trail I've created, I approached our tent, discreetly hidden behind tall brush so it wasn't visible to passing traffic.

I could hear Alaina's whimpering from the inside of the tent as I unzipped the door and ducked inside. She was curled up in a ball, shivering and pale. She had kicked off her blankets and was in just a tank top and panties despite the cool night time weather. Kneeling by her side, I brushed her sweaty blonde hair away from her eyes.

"Alaina," I said in a monotone voice.

"T-Tara..."

"Sit up, I got it."

Weakly, Alaina sat up, and leaned against a rolled up sleeping bag. She licked her dry lips and looked into my eyes. She raised her eyebrows as if in pain. I took a moment to assess her and try to sympathize... But I couldn't.

Chapter Three
Alaina

Where is Tara? She's been gone too long...
W   The tremors in my body forced me to curl up into a ball as I tried to keep my withdrawal symptoms at bay. I could not calm my body. I knew what was happening, but my brain could not comprehend it; the anxiety is overwhelming.

Every inhale felt like my lungs were being ripped out of my chest, and every exhale felt like I would vomit the contents of my stomach. All I wanted was Tara, and she's been gone for over two hours.

Tara has been the only light in the darkness of my shitty life.

Things weren't always like this for me. I had the picture perfect life; wealthy parents, white picket fence home, full ride scholarship to Alabama State University, the whole "growing up with the silver spoon" thing. My parents divorced when I was a freshman in high school, and my picture perfect family fell apart.

My dad ended up moving out of state, to "find himself again" and my mom remarried quickly, and moved my stepfather into my family home.

Losing my dad was detrimental to my mental health. He cut off all contact with my mom and I, refusing to be present in my life in any capacity. I was his only child, his only daughter, and he abandoned me.

On my high school graduation day, I walked to receive my diploma as valedictorian five minutes after being notified that my stepfather shot and killed my mother, then killed himself.

I was lost, alone, and turned to alcohol to cope. I didn't want to feel anything anymore; no pain, no heartbreak, no loneliness. My mother left me two hundred thousand dollars in her will, but I quickly blew through it all in less than a year, desperate to find comfort in material things. By the time I turned nineteen, I was out of money, and lost my mother's house, becoming homeless here in Omaha.

My addiction to heroin began when I found friendship with a group of homeless people in their early twenties that were also addicts. It's been five years since it has completely consumed my life.

Now here I am, having withdrawals, relying on my girlfriend to get me a fix.

I still remember the day I met Tara. I was walking down the main street when I saw her. She stopped me in my tracks with how absolutely stunning she was; slim, but fit, with long, jet black hair, and sun kissed skin. Standing in front of the window of an electronics store, she was watching a news report about a burning house with a blank stare.

She had an energy about her... It's so hard to explain, but I felt drawn to her, and I had to know her name. I approached her, nervous, making sure the sleeves of my hoodie covered my embarrassing track marks on my arms. As I approached her, she turned away. Then a homeless man we call "Dom" pulled her into an alley.

Right as I turned the corner to go down the alley, Tara had a knife shoved underneath his chin, and he slumped forward on his knees. She ripped it out and kicked him over before wiping the blade on his jeans.

I was stunned, scared, but still felt that pull towards her. We ended up talking and sharing a sandwich I had gotten from the soup kitchen.

She differs from anyone I'd ever met. Her lack of emotion and empathy was foreign to me as someone who thrives on connection and intimacy, but we needed each other. She was new to being home-less, and I needed companionship. I knew about her traumatic upbringing in the foster care system, and how psychiatrists and doctors kept studying her, using her as a guinea pig for medication and therapy; that had to be the reason for her...coldness.

I had convinced myself that I could help her feel again, help her embrace her emotional side. Our physical relationship took off, and it was amazing at first... But now... It's very one sided. Most of the time she just takes what she needs, then avoids me. The fact that she's a killer should have been a sign that I needed to stay away, but I couldn't. I needed her, and was determined to help her feel love.

Yes, I know. Very much the "but I can fix them" thing.

Every moment Tara was gone, my anxiety grew.

My tears fell as I desperately tried to ride out the tremors and anxiety. My whole body was screaming in pain, and I couldn't take much more.

It was a cool night, but I was burning up. I kicked off my blankets and curled up again in just a tank top and panties. It helped some, but it was temporary.

Just when I thought she'd never return, she did. She brushed my hair aside and her icy, bitter voice rang in my ears.

"Alaina," Tara said coldly.

"T-Tara..."

"Sit up, I got it."

I was so weak, but forced myself to sit up and prop myself up against a rolled up sleeping bag. My eyes met hers, and I tried to keep myself from falling back to the ground. I was in so much pain, and just needed her, needed my fix.

"Is this what you need, baby girl?" Tara asked, holding up a small baggie in my line of sight.

"Y-Yes..." I whimpered, reaching out a shaky hand towards the baggie.

"Show me how bad you want it, Alaina," Tara ordered, removing her cross body bag, kicking off her slip on Vans, and peeling off her black skinny jeans.

Tara prepared a syringe from the little baggie of dope. My whole body was aching, screaming in pain, but I needed it so badly, and I'd do whatever she wanted me to for my high.

She placed the capped syringe down on the ground next to her jeans and sat next to me. I leaned in to kiss her deeply and she pulled my face into hers. I kissed her with every ounce of love and affection I could muster, praying for reciprocation.

Her kiss felt forced, as if she was kissing me from muscle memory.

Lifting my shaking hands, I cupped her cheeks, deepening our kiss, and she grabbed my arm, pulling me on top of her so I was straddling her waist.

"Tara..." I whimpered as she broke our kiss, her hands sliding under my shirt until she was cupping my breasts. Rocking my hips on her lap, desperate for friction, I tugged at her shirt.

Removing her hands from under my shirt, she quickly tore her shirt off over her head, followed by mine, and buried her face in my breasts. She licked and sucked my nipples, and I arched my back as arousal flooded my shaking body. I needed her; I needed her to see how much I love her, how much I want her...

"You want your fix, Alaina?" She groaned after releasing my nipple with a pop.

"God, yes."

"You will not get one drop until you ride me. I want to feel your pussy dripping for me. Do you understand?" She snaked a hand around to the back of my head, fisting my hair at my scalp, and harshly pulled my head to the side so she could lick and nip her way up my neck.

"You see that syringe, Alaina? It's yours if you make me cum like my good fucking girl, you hear me?" she said with hooded eyes, pointing towards the capped syringe on the ground.

"Yes, Tara. Anything... anything..."

"Good girl, baby. Now, take my thong off," she ordered.

I obeyed, climbing up to my knees, hooking my shaking fingers into the waistband, and slowly lowering it to the ground for her to step out of. Her glistening pussy made my mouth water, and I needed to taste her.

Wrapping my hands around the back of her thighs, I pulled her towards me,

"Not yet, Alaina," Tara commanded, stopping me in my tracks. "Take your panties off. Now."

I was dizzy, my vision blurring, but I obeyed, sliding them off as Tara laid down on my blankets.

"Get my pussy over here and ride me, Alaina. You don't get shit until you make me cum."

Desperately trying to ignore the pain in my joints, I straddled her so one of her legs was in between mine, lowering my pussy onto hers. I draped her other leg over my shoulder and held her thigh close to my chest. I rocked my hips on hers, grinding my pussy on her clit in just the right spot.

"Oh my god, Tara..." I moaned, grinding harder and faster.

Tara groaned, panting as she cupped her breasts, tugging on the piercings in her nipples.

"Yes, baby girl, just like that... So wet for me already," Tara praised. I clasped her leg to my chest as she matched my movements. Feeling her clit rubbing against mine was euphoric; the harder I rocked my hips into her, the louder she got, fueling my body to continue.

"Such a perfect pussy, baby girl. Give it to me..." Tara gripped my thighs, digging her fingertips into my skin, and I could feel the muscles in her legs get tense.

"Please, Tara, please... Please... I want you to cum so bad..." I whimpered, grinding my pussy on hers faster. Her climax was building, and I had to make sure she felt every ounce of pleasure I could provide.

Tossing my head back, I mustered up all the strength I had left and kissed up the leg I was holding to my chest.

"Fuck, don't stop, Alaina..." Tara cried out, her orgasm tearing through her body as her hips moved more erratically and her back arched off the ground. I kept going, knowing her clit was sensitive, desperate for her to feel good. She cried out in pleasure,

When Tara's body relaxed, I held her thigh closer to my chest, hugging it with both my arms.

"I love you, Tara." I confessed with watery eyes.

Tara sat up, sliding out from underneath me, reached for the syringe and tossed it onto the ground in front of me.

"Enjoy, baby girl." Pulling the blanket up, Tara rolled over and fell asleep, leaving me alone, still horny, and feeling... used.

Chapter Four
Tara

"Breaking news out of Omaha this evening," a news anchor said on a television in the window of an electronics store I was walking by. It's been three hours since I left Dr. Halloway's home, and I was curious about what was being reported.

"Police and fire responded to the home of Dr. Timothy Halloway at about six-thirty this evening in what appears to be an accidental fire caused by an electrical short in the en suite bathroom..."

The reporter's voice trailed off in my ears, and for the first time in my life, I smiled.

A genuine smile.

For years, he and his colleagues used, studied, and triggered me. They thought they could control me, change me, fix me. But they'll see the monster they created. They'll feel every ounce of pain they cause; every tear I cried as a child will be a drop of their blood that will spill. They wanted to break me, but I'll show them what true rage looks like...

Killing Timothy Halloway was just the beginning.

He triggered my urges, forced me to act on them, coached me, *watched me kill... Now, I'm addicted to the sight of my knife piercing skin, drawing blood. I needed more, and his colleagues would be next.*

Gripping the straps of my backpack, I turned to continue walking, when someone suddenly pulled me into the alley next to the electronics store.

"Well, what do we have here, hmm?" A homeless man said, licking his lips. He reeked of body odor and filth. He looked down at me with hooded eyes, scanning my body. After leaving Dr. Halloway's home, I decided not to wear my bra, so my nipples were stiff peaks from the cold under my thin shirt.

He had a firm grip on a strap of my cross body bag and reached his free, dirty hand to grip my breast, groaning like a starved animal.

"Get off me," I spat, trying to pull free of his grip. He held tighter, smiling.

Reaching his hand into his pants, he gripped his cock, groaning as he pulled it free and—

"Tara!"

I shot up from my dream, panting, drenched in sweat.

My body shook, not in fear, but in rage. Another man thinking he could use me like Dr. Halloway did...

"Tara, are you okay?" Alaina's muffled voice reached my ears, and I couldn't comprehend that she was speaking.

The moment I felt her hand on my shoulder, I spun around, gripping her harshly by the throat, slamming her to the ground on her back. Straddling her, I shifted to grip with both hands, squeezing tightly. She kicked her legs, trying to buck me off of her.

"Tara... It's me..." she gasped.

My eyes found hers through my haze, and I scanned her, searching. I can't explain what I was looking for, why I was even trying, but my mind finally comprehended it was Alaina, and I released her, backing off.

The familiar tightening in my chest returned. My urges were surfacing. Sitting on my heels, I stared at a snag in Alaina's blanket, trying to force my urges into the lockbox of my mind, trying to find control again.

My body trembled as I fought to keep my rage at bay. Needing to do something with my hands, I gripped the hem of my shirt, squeezing as hard as I could. I could feel my nails cutting into my palms as I squeezed, continuing to focus on that spot on the blanket.

"Tara, it's okay, I'm here," Alaina said softly, sitting up in front of me.

Save me...

"I'm going to touch you, okay?" Alaina asked, but I could not respond as I continued my hyper-focus on the blanket.

Her soft, warm hands covered mine, her thumbs tracing soft, comforting circles.

"You're okay, Tara. It's okay."

Something shifted in my mind, something I can't explain. I closed my eyes, focusing on the feel of her hands on mine, absorbing this emotion I was feeling for the first time.

What is this...?

Involuntary tears fell down my cheeks, and Alaina wrapped her arms around my neck, holding me tightly.

"I'm here, Tara. I'm never leaving you. Please let me in, please... I love you so much." Alaina pleaded. Her body trembled as she sniffled, crying with me. "Let me help you, please..."

As soon as the feeling came, it was gone.

I finally felt something aside from my rage... I needed more.

Without a word, I pushed Alaina to lie on her back. She gasped in surprise as I stood to remove my panties.

"You want to help, baby girl?" I purred, looking down at her. Her hooded eyes met mine, and she bit her lower lip when they found my pussy bare for her.

"Yes, ma'am." Her hands reached to hold behind my ankles, and I lowered myself to straddle her.

Leaning in, I kissed her, propping my hands up on either side of her head. Her hands slid up my thighs as she moaned into my mouth.

"Such a good fucking girl for me, Alaina," I said, breaking our kiss, sitting up tall. "Here's what you're going to do for me. Pay attention."

"Yes, ma'am."

"You are going to eat my pussy while I ride your face, you hear me? And you won't stop until you make me cum."

Alaina surprised me, pulling my legs towards her face without a word. Repositioning my knees on either side of her head, I lowered myself onto her greedy mouth. Alaina hummed, wrapping her hands around my thighs to hold me down, dragging the tip of her tongue up my slit towards my clit.

"Fuck, baby girl, that tongue..."

She circled my clit with the tip of her tongue, and my hips moved, rocking and grinding on her tongue. Reaching under my shirt, I squeezed my breasts, digging my nails into my flesh. I could hear Alaina's heavy breathing through her nose as she pressed her tongue deep into my pussy. A wave of arousal shot through my body, and she reached a hand around my thigh to circle my clit with her thumb as she curled her tongue inside me.

The feeling returned.

What is this...? Love?

Forcing it out of my mind, I refocused on Alaina, devouring my pussy like I was her favorite meal.

Removing her thumb from my clit, she gripped my thighs tightly with both hands, curling and dragging her tongue through my slit again. My climax was quickly approaching, and she threw me over the edge the moment she sucked hard on my clit, and biting it gently.

"Oh, fuck, Alaina. Make me cum, baby girl. Do it. Now," I ordered.

Alaina groaned and obeyed me. Her relentless sucking and teasing of my clit threw me over the edge. I felt my pussy soaking her face as my orgasm hit harder than it ever had before. My thighs stiffened and shook as I unconsciously tried to lift off of her face. She held me down tight, continuing her movements, drawing out two orgasms.

I love you, Alaina... I said in my mind, unable to physically speak the words.

Lifting myself off of her, I sat to her side, sated and relieved.

Propping herself up on her elbows, her pleading eyes met mine. I tossed my head back, looking at the ceiling of our tent, taking a deep breath. Looking back at her, she opened her mouth to speak, but I did before she could get any words out.

"I have a surprise for you, baby. Get dressed, we're getting you all the dope you little heart desires."

Her face twisted in what I assumed to be disappointment, and she nodded, silently handing me my panties.

Chapter Five
Alaina

Handing Tara her panties, completely deflated, I turned away, trying to force my tears at bay. She used me. Again.

What do I have to do to get her to love me? I do everything she asks, give her everything she needs, fuck her how she likes... Why doesn't she love me?

"Wear all black, Alaina. Bring the knife I got you last week," Tara said, pulling on her skinny jeans and slipping her feet into her Vans.

"Okay," I said, trying to keep my voice firm and hide my pain.

I was feeling almost normal after the fix Tara gave me last night, but it wouldn't last me long. Standing to get dressed, I watched her shuffle through her cross body bag. The smile on her lips when she saw her favorite knife hit me with a sting of jealousy.

She loves that knife more than me.

"Okay, Alaina, here's the deal," Tara said, scooping up her long, black hair into a messy bun. "I've been watching Ro-Ro and his boss for a few weeks now. I found where they cook all their shit they sell. We're going to get you stocked up so you don't have to worry about the withdrawals anymore."

"Oh, okay."

I know that this was a caring gesture for her, even though it's a very unhealthy one. But after how bad my withdrawals were last night, I think I'm finally ready to give recovery another try.

"Ready? This is the best time to go since we are awake in the middle of the night," Tara said, draping her bag over her chest.

"Y-yes... I suppose."

"Here," Tara said as I approached her. She tucked away my folding knife in the front pocket of my jeans. "Just in case, baby."

Following Tara out of our tent into the cool night air, I trembled, my nerves building up in my chest. We walked in silence down the path we made towards the main street, ducking through the hole in the fence we made.

I didn't like silence, didn't like Tara's silence. The further we walked, the more my anxiety grew, so I reached for her hand, interlacing our fingers. She's capable of so much violence, and just knowing we were going somewhere dangerous where the possibility of her getting hurt or worse had me on edge.

My hand trembled as I gripped hers tightly. Looking at her, trying to gauge her mood, my heart sank when I saw two hollow green eyes. Her hand was lax in mine. She didn't hold mine back, but I ignored the feelings of rejection I constantly felt, following her into the night.

"Here we are, baby," Tara said coldly, turning us down an alley in between two dilapidated looking buildings.

We stopped walking near a dumpster that had fallen on its side in the darkest part of the alley. Before I could comprehend what was happening, Tara shoved me against the wall, pinning me in with her hands on either side of my head. I gasped, startled. I opened my mouth to speak, but she didn't let me.

She kissed me hard. It differed from what it usually was.

Inching closer to me, she pressed her body onto mine as her tongue explored my mouth in the most passionate kiss I'd ever had. Tears streamed down my cheeks as I absorbed every second, every moment.

Reaching my hands up, I wrapped my arms around her neck, pulling her closer. Pulling away, we were both panting and out of breath,

"Alaina..." Tara whispered, resting her forehead against mine.

"I love you, Tara. So fucking much." I tried confessing again, desperate for her to say those words back.

She quickly pecked my forehead, stepping away. My heart sank, shattered all over again.

"Wait here, baby. Stay in the darkness until I come back. Don't move, you understand?"

"Yes," I said harshly, surprising myself with how cold I sounded.

Tara cocked an eyebrow at me, gripping my chin roughly, and pushed me into the wall again. She glared at me, scanning my eyes, trying to understand my shift in mood.

"Yes, what?" she purred.

Lowering my eyebrows, I glared right back at her, heartbroken and angry.

"Don't make me force it out of you, Alaina."

Holding my ground, I held eye contact with her, but couldn't help the shiver of desire dancing across my skin.

"Fine."

Tara unbuttoned the front of my jeans and unzipped them, shoving her hand down the front, underneath my panties. Her chilly hands found my wet pussy ready for her. Pressing my palms into the wall behind me, I panted heavy breaths as she pressed two fingers inside me.

"Is this what you need, then?" She pumped her fingers inside me, deep and rough. When I didn't reply, she reached up with her free hand, gripping my hair at my scalp, yanking my head to the side.

"I asked you a fucking question, Alaina."

Pressing her fingers as deep as she could, she curled them, hitting just the right spot, forcing my hips to move to grind on her hand. Closing my eyes, I leaned my head against the wall, entranced by the sounds of my wet pussy taking her hand. I just wanted to cum so desperately. My focus is always on her and her pleasure. When she was done, we were done, and I couldn't take it anymore.

"Just...Fuck. Make me cum for once, Tara. Please..." I whined, her movements halting.

Opening my eyes to meet hers, I could see her mind trying to comprehend what I said.

"Fine." Her movements continued, and she released my hair to cover my mouth. "But if you make a sound and draw attention to us, you will never cum again, understood?"

I vigorously nodded, desperate for a release.

Her hand shifted to cup my cheek as she added her thumb to circle my clit. She watched me intently, tracing my bottom lip with her tongue. Fighting to suppress my moans, I sucked her thumb into my mouth, humming and dragging my teeth along its length.

"Cum for me, baby girl, I need it now," Tara ordered. I was so close, the swell of my orgasm rising in my core, building and growing. "I said cum for me, Alaina. Cum. For. Me."

Each pause was a harsh, deep thrust of her fingers.

"You like this, don't you, baby? Being in public, riding my hand?"

"Y-yes, ma'am. Fuck..." I whispered.

"I wish someone would walk by and see how perfect my pussy looks taking my fingers," Tara groaned, kissing me deeply. "But I told you to cum for me, and I need it now, or we're done. Fucking cum for me, Alaina. Be a good fucking girl and give it to me," Tara purred, sending me over the edge.

Her thumb pressed on my clit hard as she buried her fingers deep inside me, stroking that perfect spot. My knees buckled as my orgasm consumed me. Tara covered my mouth again as my whole body shook. I wanted to scream out, cry out her name, but I stayed as silent as I could. Once my walls stopped contracting on her fingers, she dragged them out of me, teasing my sensitive clit.

"Good girl, baby," Tara said, sucking her fingers clean, closing her eyes in pleasure.

She helped me lift my jeans back into place and button them

closed. Reaching into my pocket, she opened my knife and handed it to me.

"Wait here. Don't move until I call for you, understood?" Her eyes looked different... Concerned.

"Yes, ma'am." I replied, out of breath and sweating, still riding the high of my orgasm.

"Sit, baby. I'll be back soon."

She kissed me quickly and turned to walk towards the abandoned factory at the end of the alley. Sinking to the ground, I placed my knife down with a shaking hand. I needed a hit again; the familiar anxiety and urges began.

Perfect. I'm alone and craving. Please hurry, Tara...

Chapter Six
Tara

What the fuck is wrong with me? What is this... feeling?
Unable to resist, I sucked on the tip of my pointer finger while slipping into the darkness of this abandoned building. Tasting her pussy on my fingers was intoxicating.

Watching her come completely undone for me in the alley created a shift in my mind... My urges... For the first time in my life, I didn't have the urge to kill. I had the urge to make her cum for me again.

Shaking it off, I hummed Für Elise in my mind, focusing on the task at hand.

I've been following Ro-Ro for months, and memorized his patterns, his interests, his filthy habits. He likes to bring call girls here for an easy lay, and he had a type; me. Slim, athletic, long, dark hair, pierced tits.

Turning into an empty room, I took off my cross body bag, and began adjusting my outfit to better fit his preferences. I had already left my bra at our tent, so I reached into my bag and pulled out my knife. Holding the fabric taut, I sliced a slight cut in the front of my shirt at the bottom seam. With both hands, I ripped it up almost to my breasts, and tied it together, forming a crop top to show off my toned stomach.

My nipple piercings formed small bumps over the fabric of my shirt; subtle but noticeable, which will also work in my favor. Draping my bag back over my chest, I reached up to let my hair down.

Perfect.

Exiting the room, I continued down a dark hallway towards the sounds of at least three male voices. Ro-Ro had a guard shift outside the door of their lab, so I knew he would be alone. Still humming my tune in my mind, I reached into my bag to grip the handle of my knife. I needed the feeling of calm focus it provided.

I'm ready.

Zipping up my bag, I turned the corner, adjusting my stride to swish my hips back and forth, exaggerating the shaking of my hips. We made eye contact, and I flipped my hair over my shoulder, giving him a smirk. He eyed me up and down, adjusting in his seat.

"This is private property, miss. I suggest you leave," Ro-Ro said, lighting a cigarette.

"I'm sorry for the confusion. Mr. Rowe sent me here a day ahead of schedule than your regular girl. I hope it's okay with you?" I asked innocently, twirling my hair around my pointer finger and biting my lip shyly.

He took a long drag of his cigarette, exhaling the smoke above his head.

"Mr. Rowe, huh? How generous."

Lifting my crossbody bag off, I gently let it fall from my fingers on the floor as I approached him slowly. He stared at my breasts as I climbed on top of him, straddling him.

"I'm well aware you're picky with your girls. But I can guarantee you I'm..." I slid and rocked my hips forward on his lap. "... very good at what I do."

He inhaled on his cigarette again, his free hand sliding up my thigh. Looking to the side, he placed his cigarette in an ashtray, exhaling the smoke as he turned to face me again. I could feel his cock stiffening in his pants as I continued to circle my hips, grinding into him.

"Let me see those tits, baby," he groaned, and I started faking my arousal; panting and subtle moaning.

Lifting my top over my head slowly, my breasts bounced as I freed them from the fabric. Immediately, his hands were on me, flicking my piercings with his thumbs.

Images of Alaina getting off in the alley flooded my mind while this asshole played with my nipple piercings.

The way she stayed quiet for me, how insanely wet and juicy her pussy is, how deliciously sweet she is, feeling her walls contract on my fingers...

I moaned louder than I expected to, desperate for a release. Ro's hands found my hips as he guided my movements, sliding me up and down his length.

"Fuck, baby. Let's go to my room. I'm not sharing you with these assholes here."

With a fake, playful giggle, I slid off his lap, pulling my top back on while Ro spoke on his cell phone.

"Hey, Mac. I need you to cover the door for fifteen minutes. Thanks, man." He pocketed his phone, picking up the remainder of his burning cigarette and inhaled it almost to the filter before snuffing it out.

Mac appeared from around a nearby corner and chuckled when he looked at me.

"I'm not covering you for two hours like last time," he laughed as I picked up my bag.

"Better make it twenty minutes just to be safe," Ro said, smacking my ass.

"Whatever, bro. Just get the fuck out of here with her or else you'll have to share."

Grabbing my wrist, Ro led me down the hall and I stopped in my tracks, earning a confused look from him.

"So, what if I told you I had a friend waiting outside? In case, you know... You wanted an extra good time?" I gave him a wink, and a sinister smirk formed on his lips.

"You really know what I like, don't you, baby?"

"Oh, you have no idea," I purred, shoving him into the wall. He grunted in surprise as I lowered myself to my knees, taking what I wanted. Well, what he thinks I wanted.

Tearing his belt open, I forced his jeans down, yanking his boxer briefs down with them. His dick sprung free, already leaking pre-cum.

"You want me to fuck that pretty little mouth right here where everyone can see? Such a perfect slut for me already," he growled, pumping himself in long, languid strokes.

Looking up at him innocently, I moaned and nodded my head.

"Open that filthy mouth for daddy."

Daddy? Really? I chuckled in my mind.

"Yes, daddy," I forced out, trying not to laugh.

Replacing his hand with mine, I took him deep into my throat, sucking and licking as he reached into my hair, holding me in place.

"Fuck yes, baby, take all this cock. Swallow."

Swallowing around his tip, he groaned and pulled my head into him. I gagged and coughed, but held my ground, breathing out of my nose.

"Goddamn, baby. Such a perfect little fuck toy for daddy."

I chuckled in my mind again.

Coughing accidentally because I was holding back a laugh, I played it off and continued to suck him deep down my throat.

Finally releasing my head, he pulled out of my mouth completely, and I sucked in greedy breaths of oxygen. Not waiting for him, I went in for seconds, sucking him hard and deep as I followed the movements of my mouth with my hand. Twisting and pumping him as I sucked made his thighs twitch. Taking him deep in my throat one more time, choking myself, I sucked him hard and slowly released him with a pop.

"Come meet my friend, daddy. Save your cum for her. She needs it so bad," I whined.

"Let's go. Now," he ordered, pulling up his pants. I held his hand, leading him to the exit towards where Alaina was hiding in the alley.

Perfect. My plan is working better than I'd expected.

Chapter Seven
Alaina

*W*hat is taking her so fucking long?
It's been over an hour... I think?
What should I do?
Do I need to call the cops?
Should I go find her?

My anxiety was rising as I experienced my typical withdrawal symptoms again. Tara was gone a lot longer than I was expecting, and I was feeling paranoid and anxious. My hands shook, and I tried to focus on the knife Tara gave me.

It had a smooth, black handle with an "A" painted in a gold calligraphy font. The blade was about four inches long, with a slight curve at the tip. It was extremely sharp and cut through fabric like butter.

But it wasn't me.

I don't like violence and confrontation; I don't like Tara's darkness and what it does to her. While I appreciate her trying to make sure I'm protected; at least that's what I tell myself it is; it's just not who I want to be.

The panic swelling in my chest was becoming overwhelming. My heart was racing, and I was back to the familiar feeling that I'd puke if I exhaled.

Pulling my knees close to my chest, I rocked back and forth, trying to fight the urge to vomit.

Tara's fake giggle pulled me out of my mind, and I peeked out from behind the dumpster. She was holding a man's hand. Fingers interlaced like I wanted her to hold mine...

A surge of jealousy washed over me.

She can hold a random drug dealer's hand, but not mine? After all I've done for her...

Not waiting for her to call me out of the shadows, I swiped up my knife, folded it and returned it to my pocket. Stumbling to my feet, I stormed in their direction. Tara's dark, empty eyes met mine, and I knew he'd die. For the first time, I was fine with it. She held his hand...

"Here she is, as promised," Tara purred, her hand outstretched in my direction.

"Oh, what have we here? An innocent looking one, hmm? My favorite," the man said, a sinister smirk on his lips.

"Ro, this is Alaina. If you like her, you can have us both," Tara said coldly. My gaze immediately shot to hers as she pulled her knife out of her cross body bag. "She happens to enjoy getting fucked in public, especially dark, scary looking places like this alley."

"Oh, is that so? Come here, darling. Let me give you what you want." Ro stepped forward, grabbing my wrist and pulling me towards him. He reeked of cigarettes and whiskey, and it took every ounce of mental strength not to vomit in his face.

Turning around, he led me deeper into the alley, with Tara following behind me. There was an old, dirty couch someone had discarded here, and he sat, pulling me on top of him.

"Daddy needs that pussy, baby," Ro groaned, pressing his hips into me.

He reached up, yanking my top down, revealing my bra, and I gasped in surprise. Before he could do anything else, Tara came up behind him and threw a haymaker punch to his temple, knocking him out cold.

Stumbling backwards off of his lap, I fell to my ass on the ground. Tara rushed over, kneeling in front of me.

"Are you okay, Alaina?" She asked, scanning me for injuries. "I'm sorry, baby, I wasn't expecting him to do that. No one touches what's mine without her permission." Tara's eyes flashed with anger as she helped adjust my shirt.

"You held his hand," I said, shrugging her off of me, and pushing myself to my feet.

"Yes, and...?"

"You wouldn't hold mine on our way over here. What the fuck is so wrong with me that prevents you from holding my hand, knowing full well that I fucking love you, Tara? But you can hold his?!" I was so tired of feeling rejected by her, my pent up anger spewing out of me.

Tara stared at me, confused.

"I brought him for you, Alaina," Tara said coldly, turning her back to me, walking back up towards him passed out on the discarded couch.

She went through his pockets, stuffing at least eight bags of dope in one pocket and a wad of cash in the other. Once finished, she grabbed his legs, pulling him off the couch so he was flat on the ground. His head bounced off the cement harshly, and Tara scoffed, using all her energy to drag him away from the couch.

"Wh-What the fuck..." Ro regained consciousness, bringing a hand to the side of his head and looking around.

"I'm so sorry, daddy. I don't know what happened. Some man wearing all black and a leather jacket came up behind you and hit you. I couldn't stop him..." Tara plastered on a fake, innocent look.

"Black leather jacket? That mother fucker..." Ro sat up, but Tara pushed him down with her foot, pressing onto his throat. "What the fuck do you think you're doing?" He hissed.

"I'm so sorry, *daddy*," Tara said sarcastically. "It's simple, really.

See my girl here? She needs to cum, and you're going to make her cum if you want to walk away from here with your boss' dope and his money.

Tara reached into her pocket and pulled out the bags and cash, waving it in front of his face.

"You fucking bitch..."

His voice trailed off in my ears as my eyes hyper-focused on the baggies in Tara's hand. The adrenaline was wearing off, and my tremors returned. I needed it. I needed it so badly. Tara moved her hand around and my eyes followed them. I heard her giggle. She knew...

"Trust me, you can't resist that sweet pussy of hers. So tight, so sweet. Perfection," Tara praised. I felt my arousal soaking my panties from her words, but I needed those baggies.

"Get over here, Alaina," Tara ordered. My body reacted to her commands, and I joined her by her side. "Take off your jeans and your panties, baby girl."

Without hesitation, I obeyed, dropping them to my ankles, and stepping out of them.

"What the fuck do you think you're doing?" Ro growled, trying to sit up. He almost succeeded until Tara swung her knife into his shoulder, forcing him back to the ground.

"I didn't say you could move, did I?" she purred.

"You need your fix, baby girl?" Tara asked, looking at me with hooded eyes, waving the bundle of baggies in my line of sight.

"Y-yes... please..." I whimpered, my shaking hands reaching for it.

"You'll get what you want after you show me how you make yourself cum. Use him."

Tara tipped her chin towards the whimpering piece of shit dealer laying on his back. "Show me how you like it, baby girl."

She leaned on the brick wall and watched me as I picked up my knife, kneeling next to Ro, and slicing his pants open.

"That's it, baby girl. Take what you need," Tara encouraged as I tore his pants away from him, his half hard cock laying to the side

Ro groaned in pain from his shoulder, but I tuned it out, gripping his cock in my hand, pumping him roughly.

"Fucking hell... Let me up, please... Fuck, let me enjoy getting off at least..." Ro groaned, as I took his cock into my mouth, greedily sucking and stroking as hard as I could.

"You like that, Ro? Pretty fucking perfect mouth, isn't it?" Tara said, crossing her arms casually over her chest.

"God, yes," he groaned.

"Stop stalling, Alaina. I told you to make yourself cum."

Releasing him from my mouth with a pop, I threw my leg over him, straddling him, and reached down to guide his tip into position. Before lowering myself, I slid his tip back and forth through my slit, teasing my clit.

I was so wet for Tara, so needy.

"Fuck, take my cock baby, please," Ro groaned, and I slowly lowered myself onto him.

I cried out in ecstasy, as I bounced my ass into his hips, his cock stretching me in all the right places. Propping my hands up on his chest, I slid my hips back and forth, his length rubbing my clit as I chased my climax.

It's been so long since I've had sex with a man. I miss these sensations, this feeling...

"How does it feel, baby girl?" Tara asked, reaching down to stroke my cheek.

"So...So good. So fucking good," I moaned, grinding on him harder and faster. Ro's hands found my thighs as I continued chasing my climax.

"Good girl, Alana. Cum for me, baby. Let me see how perfect you look when you take what you need."

Tara's words sent me over the edge and I forced his cock inside me as deep as I could while my orgasm crashed into me.

"Fuck yes, that's it. Give me all that cum, baby," Ro groaned, pulling me out of the moment.

Tara noticed my shift, so she ripped her knife out of his shoulder and sliced his throat open.

"You fucking piece of trash. She was fine until you opened your filthy fucking mouth, ruining her moment," Tara hissed.

Climbing off of his dying body, I quickly pulled my pants back on. I could hear police sirens in the distance, and fear set in.

"Alaina, look at me," Tara ordered. I was so scared, I couldn't comprehend what she was saying.

"Alaina!" Tara shook my arms, and I looked into her dark eyes. "Take this, baby girl. Take my bag and go back to the tent as fast as you can. Don't wait for me, do you understand?" She shoved the baggies and cash into her crossbody bag and pushed it into my arms.

"Tara... The cops... We need to go..." I stuttered.

Tara pulled my lips to hers in a devastating kiss. Tears streamed down my face as she pulled away. She cupped my cheeks, gently wiping them away.

"Please trust me, baby. I can't have you tied to this if the cops come before I can take care of it, please." Tara pleaded. Her eyes looked... scared. "Go, Alaina, run. I'll come back for you, I promise. Please go!"

I couldn't help but obey her as she turned back towards a now dead Ro. I ran down the opposite end of the alley into the night towards our tent, away from the love of my life.

Chapter Eight
Dr. Helena Lawson

(Two Years Later)

"Good morning, Marcus," I said into my cell phone, as I placed my suitcase on the bed of my hotel.

"Good morning, Doctor. How was your flight to Omaha?" Marcus Jacobs asked, my contact with the Behavioral Analysis Unit at the FBI.

"It was pleasant, no complaints here. I spent a good amount of time looking at our Miss Tara Wilde's file. Poor girl has had a rough life," I said, stepping out of my pumps and pulling my confidential file on my newest patient out of my briefcase.

"Yes, it's truly a shame. I have scheduled an interview for you with Miss Wilde at eleven in the morning at the Nebraska State ICI. Please let me know if you need anything."

"Thank you, Marcus. I will have an update for you after I meet with her." We disconnected our call, and I picked up Tara's file, opening it across my lap.

"Alright Miss Wilde, let's see."

Tara was diagnosed with Conduct Disorder at six years old;

which is an odd diagnosis. Typically, a diagnosis of this type is given a little later in life at age eight.

She has had... eight psychiatrists in her past.

My god, the poor girl.

Flipping to the next page in her file, a report done by a Dr. Timothy Halloway, he was suspecting her to have a psychopathy disorder.

Miss Wilde shows signs of psychopathy and Antisocial Personality Disorder. While the two always go hand in hand, hers is quite the special case. She shows the following traits as noted from previous in person sessions, and reports from foster family and social workers.

- *Lack of empathy and remorse*
- *Manipulativeness*
- *Impulsivity*
- *Extreme risk taking*
- *Lack of concern for hers and others' safety*

The following behaviors and social patterns have been noted as well

- *Animal mutilation*
- *Pathological lying*
- *Antisocial behaviors*
- *Shallow and short-lived emotional experiences*
- *Inability to feel deep emotions*
  - *Love, grief, fear*
- *Inability to maintain long-term relationships*
  - *Friendships, relationships with foster family members*
- *Extremely callous disregard for others' feelings and rights*
- *Interpersonal relationships are driven by dominance, exploitation, and a lack of reciprocity.*

We have begun Cognitive-Behavioral Therapy to address her

violent urges and lack of impulse control. We have seen no success with this treatment.

Closing the file with a snap, I tossed it to the side. This poor girl was used as a study subject, rather than trying to actually treat the underlying causes or environmental factors that contributed to this "psychosis."

If this Dr. Timothy Halloway had not died in his house fire, he'd make a fine meal for me...

* * *

With my portfolio notebook in hand, I walked into the Nebraska State Institution for the Criminally Insane. It was a cool winter morning, and I unbuttoned my peacoat as I entered the building.

A kind young receptionist greeted me at the front desk.

"Good morning, Doctor Lawson, we've been excited to have you with us today!" She greeted eagerly, and a grin tugged at my lips.

"Good morning to you, my dear. I have an eleven o'clock appointment with Miss Tara Wilde," I said professionally.

The things we could do to her...

My darkness whispered in my mind, but I shut her out, trying to maintain my composure.

"Yes, the warden will see you now to take you to meet her, right this way, please!" She stood from her desk, her strawberry blonde curls bounced as she took light steps. Her hips swayed side to side in her modest pencil skirt; intoxicating.

Following her down the hall to the warden's office, she knocked gently on his door.

"Mr. Daly? Doctor Lawson is here to see Miss Wilde," she said with a wink, before turning back to her desk.

"Thank you, Elaine," Miles Daly replied as she walked away.

Elaine... I like that name.

"I hope you had a pleasant flight from the FBI headquarters, Doctor." Miles stood from his desk motioning me to follow.

"I did, thank you. So, what can you tell me about Miss Wilde?" I asked, preparing my notes as we walked.

"She refuses to speak. Miss Wilde has been here two years and has said a handful of words, refusing to cooperate with any therapists or doctors," Miles said, sounding exasperated.

"Oh? What words has she said? That could help in my profile."

"All she has said to staff is the name Alaina, and the words bag, knife, and hurry. Quite odd."

I noted these words down in my notebook for future reference.

"I'm familiar with Alaina, her girlfriend. She went missing when Tara was arrested after the murder of Ronald Adler, or 'Ro', as he was called. I found her with the help of the FBI, and she will be arriving to join me shortly," I said with dominance.

"Yes, Doctor. We will bring her to you as soon as she arrives. Here we are. Tara is the last cell on the left. Please avoid touching the glass and handing anything through the holes. We left out a chair for you, and have the cameras rolling. If you need anything at all, just say so out loud and we will respond in seconds."

"Thank you, Miles."

Turning to walk down the hallway towards Tara's cell, the clicking of my high heels echoed off the walls. My darkness hummed in my mind, ready to assess our Miss Wilde.

If she is what I feel she is, we must help her. She will be instrumental in my plan with the FBI. I said to my darkness in my mind.

Your plan with young Camden Sullivan, I assume? She replied.

Yes, Camden. That young prodigy and I have plans. He just doesn't know it yet.

Reaching Tara's cell, I stood next to the folding chair the warden had left out for me.

"Good morning, Miss Wilde. My name is Doctor Helena Lawson, and I'm here to speak with you," I said calmly, sitting down in the chair. She was in her state issued white jumpsuit, with her back to me.

Her long, beautiful black hair was a tangled mess, and she had scratches up and down both arms. With her back still to me, she turned her head to speak.

"I've heard it all before, Doctor. What do you want me to say? Daddy touched me in the wrong places? Mommy didn't love me enough? I killed that fucker because I could, and that's all there is to it, so spare me all the shrink bullshit and leave me alone."

Mmm, she's perfect.

My attention was drawn to the end of the hall, where the warden had a timid-looking Alaina standing in front of him. I nodded, motioning for her to come.

"Tell me, Tara. What do I need to do to earn your trust? I'm an open book," I purred, gauging her reaction.

"Something you can never give me, Doctor," Tara spat.

"And what might that be, Tara? Because I'm confident that you'll like what you see."

Alaina joined me at my side, covering her mouth timidly with tears streaming down her cheeks. She was skinny, pale, exhausted, and one year sober.

"T-Tara..." Alaina whispered.

Tara whipped her body around so fast, running up to the glass, pressing her palms to it, trying to reach for her.

"Alaina... Alaina... Oh my god. Alaina..." Tara fell to her knees sobbing, and Alana followed her to the floor, reaching for her.

"I'm so sorry, my dear. We cannot touch the glass," I cradled Alania as she sobbed in my arms.

"Please, Doctor, please. You have to help her, please..." She sobbed relentlessly into my shoulder as Tara watched, her own eyes became glassy with tears.

"Alaina, I love you," Tara confessed. "I don't feel a damn thing except the love I have for you. It's always been there since we met, I just...I didn't know what it was. I love you, baby girl. Please know that," Tara sniffled, burying her face in her hands.

"Tara, I love you too. So much. I got sober for you. My life is for you."

Pressing a button on my phone that I had rigged this morning to disable the audio on the surveillance cameras, I released Alaina from my arms.

"Tara, you listen to me, my dear. They cannot hear us, but it will only last thirty seconds. I know you have an eidetic memory, so listen closely. Tomorrow at noon, you are being brought to a physician's office for a physical. Once you are there, you are to locate the hand-cuff key I will leave in the doctor's drawer in their office; top right. You will be handcuffed to a wheelchair, so you will need to figure that out."

Tara stared at me, studying my every word, imprinting it to her memory.

"Once you exit the rear of the building, there will be a white Ford Focus with an Alabama license plate; the keys will be in the ignition and ready. There is an address written on a card that will be in the center console with an envelope of cash. You will go to this location, tell no one, and meet me there. Do you understand?"

"Yes, Doctor." Tara said with purpose.

"Is everything okay here, Doctor? We lost the signal on the cameras for a moment." The warden came running in just as we finished our conversation. Alaina was in a stunned silence, and I placed a gentle hand on her shoulder.

"Everything is fine, warden. Tara here does not feel the need to cooperate with me today, so I will take my leave. I will not press her if she is not ready. Good day, Tara."

Guiding Alaina out of the hall with me, the heavy metal door locked behind us, leaving Tara in her cell alone.

"I apologize, Doctor, it's been the same with us regarding Miss Wilde," the warden shrugged, opening the front door of his facility for Alaina and I.

"It's quite alright, it takes time to build trust. I will return soon, very soon."

About the Author

Hi babes! I'm Sarah Daniels, a dark romance author, specializing in BDSM, horror, psychological thriller, and all the smut your dark little heart could ask for. Lets keep in contact!

https://linktr.ee/authorsarahdaniels

How The Shadows Fell

By: Britt Bee

Prequel to *In the Dark*

About How The Shadows Fell

Let's go back in time to the era where Katherine and Rhett reigned supreme, to the dandelion picking, to the sweet high school love they shared.

Until it was stolen from them.

Find out what made Katherine break from the mold of her own making, what made her tick, what drove her to measures she never expected. Find out the reasons behind current-day Katherine's antics and thoughts in this prequel to IN THE DARK. Dive in and see HOW THE SHADOWS FELL.

Content Note:

Mature content. For readers 18 & older. This story is the prequel to *In the Dark*.

This book contains sensitive material relating to: Blood/Gore, Explicit Language, Murder of a Loved One, Murder, Violence, Foster Families/Adoption, Abusive Foster Parents

Relationship type: MF

Chapter One
Katherine

12 Years Old

Why didn't anyone want me?

Being in foster care sucks balls. The last few families I had been placed with were nice at first. But I always managed to somehow do something that they didn't like. The last family told my case worker that I spoke poorly, and that they weren't keen for me to be speaking how I did with them and their posh children.

They lived in a big, white, colonial house with grounds people, cleaners, and every type of service available. Their children, three of them, wore uniforms for school and had their own driver.

Why they wanted a foster kid was beyond me. But they accepted me with semi-open arms. Though, in the end, I was only there for a total of three weeks.

The final straw? The foster mother had asked me how school had gone and my response had been, "It sucked balls today."

That was that. And now I'm back at the public school I had been at less than a month ago. But my once friends aren't speaking to me now. They act like I don't exist at all, actually. I only had a few select friends, but I feel the blow of their abandonment, nonetheless.

Going about seventh grade with no friends is a slow type of torture. Walking to and from classes in the clustered halls is no joke. I hear the whispers and the snickers, and I can see when they stare. Their eyes burn into my back and the side of my head like drills. But I do my best to ignore them.

I'm in a group home now. There are several girls here, but none are my age. They're all younger and still in elementary school, so I don't have friends here either, even though one of the first graders follows me around like a lost puppy. Her eyes still shine with hope and determination. I know mine did for the longest time, but no more.

It's been almost a month since I came back from my last placement, a whole month of being lost at school and at the group home, when I nearly run into another kid in the hall. I round the corner after math class and all but collide into a scrawny chest.

Large hands grab my upper arms, steadying me. "Whoa there, my bad." His voice hasn't completely dropped yet, so there's still a bit of a higher pitch to it.

I stutter a response, "I-it's okay." I don't know what comes over me, but I stare at the boy in front of me. My brows crease as I take in his mousy brown hair, but it's the white streak in the front that catches my attention.

He notices my stare. "You can ask about it, ya know?"

Blood rushes to my face as embarrassment covers me like a shroud. I tuck my wayward hair behind my ears as I continue to stare at him. "Did you do that yourself?" I ask him, my voice somehow not trembling.

He chuckles. Chuckles! Once he catches his breath, he answers, "It's actually a birthmark." Combing it back and forth with his deft fingers, he continues, "It just grows in like that. I've had it since I was a baby."

"No way!" I gasp. "That's so cool!"

His smile is full and cheesy. "What's your next class?"

"English," I tell him.

"Cool, that's my next class, too. Wanna walk there together?" He stands next to me, nearly shoulder to shoulder. He's taller than me, so much so that I have to crane my neck to see the white streak in his hair.

I nod, gripping my books tighter against my chest.

"My name's Rhett, by the way. What's yours?"

"Katherine."

"So formal," he says with a smirk and a twinkle of humor in his eye. "And pretty," he adds more genuinely.

"Thanks." I blush.

"So, Kath, tell me more about you."

Chapter Two
Katherine

16 Years Old

Moving in with a new foster family always sucked, especially if they already had the kids they actually wanted. Nine times out of ten, foster kids were just a means to get a government check. I hauled my garbage bag up the small staircase into the living space of the bungalow. The outside looked well kept and had a swing set in the backyard. They obviously had kids already, so chances are, these people just want another form of shitty income. Too bad it's at my expense.

The foster mom, I don't even know her name yet, guides me through the living room. She shows me the gallery wall, full of wedding photos and baby photos of at least two other children. She goes on and one while I stand awkwardly, clutching my plastic bag until my knuckles turn white. My shoes are scuffed ten ways to Sunday and my pants could definitely use a good wash. When was the last time I washed them? I can't even remember.

She's droning on about how the kids are smart and favor their father's looks. One has his nose, and the other, his chin and eyes. "I wish they looked a little bit like me. Seems so unfair since I carried them for almost ten months," she remarks.

Her tone is sassy, like she hopes her husband hears her or something. But there's that unmistakable tick in her voice that tells me she's dead serious. If I didn't know any better, I would dare to assume that she feels a hint of resentment towards the children and her husband for this slight against her. As if any of them actively chose not to look like her.

This is going to be splendid.

We round the corner and step from the living area to the kitchen. It's homey, I'll give it that. The table has clutter on it. School books are stacked on the corner with some kind of poster board project filling the middle. Markers and pens in every color are also scattered across the tablecloth. The chairs are wooden, and some are pushed into their spots while one is halfway across the room. The sink has a few dishes in it, but not so many to where I think I'm going to be forced to clean them day in and day out. A shiny, silver dishwasher hides beneath the counter, and I praise whatever God there might be because handwashing annoys the hell out of me.

Before we get any further into the impromptu tour of the over-sized house, the foster mother turns toward me, complete with a look of shock etched on her shiny face. "I nearly forgot, how rude of me!" she exclaims. "Please, call me Debbie. And my husband is Daniel."

The fridge is one of those fancy ones that has two doors for the fridge section alone, with a pull-out drawer on the bottom for the freezer. The curtains are blowing softly in front of a half-cracked window, and the smell of fresh cookies lingers in the air. I don't spot the cookies, however, even as I scan the counters and subtly look toward the floor.

Debbie gives me a tour of the kitchen. "Here's the table, sink, fridge. Help yourself to anything in the fridge at any time," she frets, before turning toward a sealed door. "Here's the pantry. The bottom shelf is where the kiddos' snacks live. You're more than welcome to help yourself any time, day or night." She claps her hands together as she spins back to me. Her blonde hair is shoulder length and pin straight. Her cheeks are rosy, and her smiles widens uncannily. I eye her warily. There's something...off about this woman, even though she's hit every benchmark thus far. I'm not sure what lurks beneath her glassy, perfect skin, but I'm determined to figure it out before I'm thrown under the bus, again.

The rest of the house tour goes the same. "Here's the bathroom, bedrooms. Here's where we do laundry. Just throw your clothes in one of the hampers in the bathrooms and I'll get it done and folded for you to put away. I try to do a load at least every other day, so you should never be without." Her smile cracks open her face, the generosity making me pause. I choose not to dwell on it for now.

Finally, after what seems like years, we make it down the end of the hall to a lone door. She eases it open with practiced grace and beckons me inside. "This will be your space while you're here. There's sticky-tac in the desk drawer, so please feel free to put any photos or posters you want on the walls. We can even order some prints online and get them set up for you." She's spinning around the room as she talks, forcing her skirt to billow out around her willowy legs. She's a tall woman, I note.

"Okay, well, I'll leave you to get settled in for a bit. Dinner is nearly complete. It's a casserole with noodles and lots of cheese, so I'll come grab you when it's ready. The kiddos are with their dad on an outing, so you won't have to meet everyone right away." She pats my shoulder as she walks by. "I'm so glad you're here, Katherine," she tells me. I wouldn't believe her if it weren't for the wet look in her brown eyes. She seems genuinely excited that I'm here and, for now, I can accept that.

* * *

The rest of the evening goes by smoothly. There are no hiccups at dinner and the casserole is pretty tasty. I devour more than my fair share of the dish, but Debbie allows it. She offers even more as I push my bowl away, but I shake my head as I finish chewing my last bite. "That's all I can handle for tonight," I whisper.

She nods her head quickly, her blonde hair bouncing against her shoulders. "That's fine dear. Don't forget about the snacks in the pantry if you get peckish tonight."

She begins clearing the table, even grabbing my bowl and spoon before I can. She pauses with the bowls in her hands, looking down at me. "Don't worry about it, dear. I'm just going to throw these dishes in the dishwasher, and I'll probably head up to bed soon. You can use the adjoined bathroom in your bedroom to shower and get ready for bed when you're ready. But feel free to roam about." She balances the bowls in the crook of one arm as she opens the dishwasher with the other. She glances back over her shoulder to me, the smile still present on her face. "Just knock on my door if you need anything. Daniel and the kiddos will probably be back home soon, but don't feel pressured to interact with them tonight. He's going to send them straight to bed before he does the same."

I nod, the only response I'm capable of giving her.

* * *

Waking up in an unfamiliar bed has become so normal to me at this point that I end up sleeping like the dead. I don't have a phone or an alarm clock, so I wake as the sun is beaming into the room. It burns my retinas as I crack open my eyelids, but I quickly shudder awake.

My pajamas are rumpled from being in my garbage bag, but they do the job and are the warmest thing I own. I stumble down the stairs into the kitchen and am greeted by five sets of eyes watching me.

Debbie is busy at the table with the kids, who don't look surprised to see me. They smile their crusty grins before shoveling more fork-fuls of pancakes into their awaiting mouths. Daniel stands tall over the range, flipping even more pancakes onto an already tall stack. He looks over his shoulder, catching my gaze before wiping his hands on his apron and facing me. "Good morning, Katherine. I'm just whipping up some pancakes. Take a seat and I'll bring you some," Daniel tells me enthusiastically.

This family is too bright and cheerful in the morning. I don't even know what time it is, but my soul knows it's too damn early. I scrub my tired eyes awake and take a seat at the large kitchen table.

As Daniel sets a plate of pancakes in front of me, a door closes down the hall. Is someone else here? I look at Debbie and her face registers a split second of "oh fuck" before she faces me.

"Katherine, dear, this was very last minute, but we had another placement early this morning."

I audibly gulp. Are they sending me away already? I *just* got here and someone new is moving in and forcing me out. I steel myself, looking down at the fluffy pancakes that I will probably never eat again after this morning.

"Don't worry, Katherine. You aren't going anywhere. We have another spare bedroom for him."

Him. A *boy* is staying here? How old is he? Who is he?

"Good morning," a voice smooth as butter greets us as someone enters the kitchen.

My ears must be playing tricks on me. Surely it isn't who I think it is. It's been several years since I've seen him. He was sent away to live with a foster family a few towns over and we lost contact.

But I've never forgotten. I could *never* forget.

I glance up. And it's him.

"Good morning, Kath." Rhett flashes me a smile as grand as the famous canyon.

Chapter Three
Katherine

17 Years Old

A milestone has been reached. I've been in the same foster home for nearly a year. I've eaten so many pancakes in that time that I'm pretty sure I'm at least seventy-five percent pancake at this point.

And the best part? Rhett is still here, too.

We have most of the same classes together at school and we're constantly together. Seeing him again after several years apart was something that shocked my system. After the initial shock, however, I was so ecstatic that I nearly pissed my pants./ Debbie and Daniel weren't alarmed that we knew one another. We were both orphans after all and all orphans know each other apparently.

Seeing Rhett, and even living with him has been a dream come true. We were friends, good friends, before, but now we don't talk to other people or have other friends. We have each other, and that's all we need.

He gives me this feeling deep in my gut and in my heart that makes me settled, content. I'm happy here. Even the foster family's kids are nice to me. They're sweet little kids who are in elementary school and just want to be included with us "big kids". It's endearing, if not a little annoying. Debbie even gave the both of us permission to tell her real kids "no". Talk about an improvement over other foster placements I've been in.

But Rhett. Just thinking about him makes my heart giddy. It pounds in my chest, vibrant and alive for the first time in what feels like forever. Walking back from school now, we're on our regular route. "How was your day, Kath? Break any hearts?" He asks me this question every single day. It's a running joke between us at this point.

I shake my head, glancing at him from the corner of my eye as we continue down the cracked sidewalk. "Nope, sure didn't. What about you?"

He turns his megawatt smile on me, it's whiteness blinding. How he gets his teeth so perfect is a wonder to me. Mine aren't necessarily yellow, but they definitely don't look like *that*.

"Sure didn't, had one girl on my mind too often to give a shit about anyone else."

"Oh, just one girl, huh?" I tease, already knowing how the conversation will play out.

"Just a singular girl, Kath." He winks.

"And who is this girl you're speaking of? Do I know her?"

We pass a large field, the building that was once there long since gone. Thousands of dandelions litter the field. Rhett scoops down low and plucks several stems from the lush grass. He turns to me, spinning on his heel, offering the displaced dandelions to me in a flourish. "For you, my singular lady," he sings.

I feign astonishment, bringing my hand to my forehead. "Oh my God, Rhett, you shouldn't have," I cry.

"Only the best florals for my lovely woman." He stands quickly, rushing me. His lips graze mine as I sink into him. The dandelions are crushed against our chests, but I'll still cherish their crinkled petals. They'll be placed in the box under my bed where all of our dandelions go. Every single day, at least during the right season, I have two or three, maybe even four to add to the ever-growing box of stems and petals.

We've been talking about our future lately. The dandelions are a promise of that, of our shared future where we can fully be together. It's difficult having to hide this part of ourselves when we're at home with the foster family. But it's something we've agreed we've agreed to do. And it'll be worth it in the end.

Chapter Four
Katherine

1 Week Before 18th Birthday

It's the time of day when the sun sinks into the horizon slowly. It dips lower with each breath we take. The sun casts an orange glow around the street, the taller buildings silhouetted against the sky. The air is crisp, but enjoyable with the sweater I threw on. I grip it tighter as a gust of wind blows through my hair.

"You're in your own land again, Kath."

I smile, a shyness washing over me as his words coat my skin. "I'm admiring the sunlight, appreciating the wind." My eyes float to him, looking up until I meet his gaze. His eyes are a wondrous shade of green, bright and warm. His hand catches mine and we continue down the block. "What do you think of the sunset?"

Rhett wraps his arms around my shoulders, pulling me tightly against him and dipping his head against my crown. "I think the sunset is beckoning us to walk into it, to feel its warmth. I think the sun is going home after being high in the sky all day." We pause on the sidewalk, his hand cupping my cheek. "I think the sun's brilliance highlights the darkness of your hair." He runs his fingers through my long mane, his fingertips pulling on the ends with a gentle tug. "As dark as the closet we were in that one time."

A giggle falls from my lips. "Of course, you'd remember that closet!" I playfully shove his shoulder and strong arms twine around my torso, bringing me impossibly closer. I fold my arms around him and lay my hands across the base of his spine.

"Now, how could I possibly forget our very first kiss?" He pecks my nose quickly then returns to press his lips against mine.

I roll my eyes. We unwrap our bodies, and our hands find their places together. Forever entwined.

"It's almost time for me to head back to the foster fam." I shrug as his arms tighten.

"And I have to get back to the dorm to get some homework finished," he pouts.

"My eighteenth is close. Then we can finally have those sleepovers we've been dreaming about," I tease.

I bark out a laugh. "Well, Debbie did see us kissing in the laundry room, Rhett." I sigh, "You know that created a huge shit storm."

Rhett pecks my forehead. "Debbie was fucked up. She viewed us as full siblings, like, what the fuck?"

I shake my head, stuck between wanting to forget the whole ordeal and laughing my ass off at the ridiculousness of it.

Debbie and Daniel aren't too bad, if you forget the whole overreaction of the kissing incident. I don't think they'll be adopting me, but with my eighteenth on the horizon, I don't really need it. Thankfully only a few weeks after the kissing incident, Rhett turned eighteen. He packed up, moved out, and graduated within a few weeks, moving on to college.

I peek up at him as we walk. His hair is longer than he normally styles it, but the stark white streak in the front section is prevalent as ever. When I first asked him about his hair, he told me it was a birthmark, just in his hair. I didn't believe him at first, but when it never changed or moved, I started to. I want to run my fingertips across his scalp, pull him closer until we merge as one.

"How many classes do you have tomorrow?"

"Only a few. I'll be done by four, I think." Rhett tugs me closer to one side of the pavement so a mother and stroller can squeeze by.

"That's great. Do you want to work on homework together at that one cafe?"

Rhett halts on the sidewalk. "I believe I can accommodate you, my sweet lady." He grins as he tugs our clasped hands to his chest, spinning me.

Tires grinding on the road pull my attention from Rhett.

A small car peels down the road, tires almost hitting the curb. Rhett jerks my arm, *hard*. I try to peer around his arm as he forces me behind him.

The car barrels towards us.

A man, probably in his late twenties or early thirties, hangs halfway out of the back window. His elbow leans on the car door, supporting a long-barreled rifle.

My eyes widen.

Rhett retreats a step, slighting turning his jaw. "Do not say a word, Kath. I mean it."

The man leans further out his window. "Boy, you've really fucked up this time, you know?" His voice doesn't match his body. It's higher pitched than I anticipated and doesn't match his burly exterior.

When neither of us respond, the man continues, "You should have known better than to fuck with the Sandman!"

Rhett turns, his face full of determination. I attempt to grab his arms, but he shoves me in the chest. I lose my balance and fall to the sidewalk, the rough concrete cutting my palms and knees.

A spattering of *pops* erupts.

Rhett's body pulses once.

Twice

Three times.

He staggers as the tires grind the pavement. The car peels away, leaving the smell of burnt rubber heavy in the air.

Rhett collapses as I reach for him.

He's barely on the ground before a large pool of blood seeps from his torso. It coats the sidewalks, following every crack perfectly. I loom over him, shoving my hands anywhere I can reach on his chest. I push down hard enough to make him sputter.

"K-kath," he chokes.

Hot tears burn down my cheeks as I cry, "No, Rhett, baby, don't say anything. You're going to be alright." Snot is pouring from my nose as my hands are bathed in my love's lifeblood. "Just hang on, baby," I plead with him.

Rhett's eyes are glassy and unfocused as he tries to look at me. "K-kath," he cries again, more blood spilling over his rounded bottom lip.

I push harder against his torso, the blood hot and sticky between my fingers. It coats my hands and wrists. "R-rhett," I stutter. I run a bloodstained palm through his hair, coating that magnificent white streak and turning it pink.

"I I-love y-you," he whimpers.

"No! No, don't you close your eyes!" I scream. Rhett's eyes flutter several times. "Rhett, baby, please," I beg, but to no avail.

Rhett's eyes dim as they close for the final time.

And all I can think of is that I didn't say it back.

Chapter Five
Katherine

19 Years Old

The one year anniversary of Rhett's death was last week and yesterday was my nineteenth birthday.

The last year of my life has been crushing, a guide map on duality. I grieved harder than I ever have, even more than when I lost both my parents. The grief hasn't left me, contrary to popular belief, you don't get over it. I haven't gotten over it, at all in fact. I transformed my grief into a powerful beacon of anger. Some days my anger is frigid and decrepit, turning my skin to ice and my mood to stone so sharp a single word can shrivel someone's mood. On the opposite hand, however, my anger is an inferno, an internal fire that burns so hot, just waiting to escape, or be freed.

The wait is nearly over.

I moved out of my foster family's house only two weeks after Rhett's tragic end. I glossed over my birthday, not wanting to celebrate without the single most important person in my life. Debbie tried to get me involved with a birthday cake made up with fancy candles that looked like fireworks and creamy blue buttercream.

But it didn't work.

I barely touched my cliche, telling the kids to eat as much as they physically could and, damn, did they deliver.

Now, here I am, standing on the sidewalk, cloaked with the shadows that stretch out around me. I trot over a few paces. I bend at the knees and place a hand, palm down, on the pavement. The concrete is cold; I'm not sure why I expected it to be warm or lively. But the last time I touched this piece of concrete, Rhett's lifeblood was flowing freely through my fingers.

I was so meek.

So powerless.

So *frightened*.

Not anymore.

The past year has been filled with kickboxing classes. I've bulked up just enough to show hints of muscles beneath my skin. I'm not ripped by any means. In fact, I'm still roughly the same size I was pre-Rhett. My stomach is rounded and plush, but I love the security is provides me. And my arms aren't thin and willowy, but they *are* strong.

I need "strong" right now.

I cannot afford anything less.

Besides moving out and picking up kickboxing, I've been searching for Rhett's killer since my eighteenth birthday. Searching and researching, visiting various locations around town hoping that I'll run across the Sandman or one of his lackeys.

They love evading but they can't hide forever.

My patience is wide and growing every day, but even still, I feel the ends fraying. My blood pulses with new vigor. I can't, *won't*, stop until the thirst inside me has been quenched.

Blood demands blood.

The score needs to be balanced, settled.

No one cared that Rhett died. No one except for me. He didn't have family– I was his family. No one mourned him alongside me. No "friends" from college, no former foster siblings. No. One.

No *one* but fucking *me*.

Rhett was my reason for living. Like a cloud in a nice, clear blue sky. He was there and I was there. We were there...*together*. And that's all that mattered to us. Tears freely fall down my sodden cheeks. I wipe my face with the sleeve of my hoodie. The cuffs are slightly tattered, complete with stringy bits and holes created by those freaky closet moths.

I don't linger around the cold concrete for long. My plan begins today. I can't fuck it all up on the first day, with the first stage.

The walk is long, and I thank whoever the fuck is upstairs for allowing me to get back into shape this year. I'll need the stamina for what's coming.

Chapter Six
Katherine

Things would be so much simpler if I was above legal drinking age. At least then I could walk into the bar that looms ahead. But, no, I'm stuck at nineteen. I spend several nights a week walking past this bar, just wishing I could waltz in and down a few amaretto sours to drown out the constant static that lives in my head. Between the static and the reverbating pusles that I've categorized as some level of trauma from watching Rhett be shot over and over.

I don't have a deep desire to drink, but god damn, do I wish I could drown out those sounds. The vivid memories of his blood coating my skin. The visceral reaction his torso had to my hands pressing so firmly against it as it fought to keep his breath steady.

Sometimes I feel like I'll never move on, never love someone the same way as I did Rhett. I have to continuously remind myself that I deserve some type of love. I've accepted that I'll probably never encounter a love like Rhett's, something that started as a brisk friendship that evolved over years of close encounters and just plain old interaction.

It's fine with me.

I've had the great love of my life.

I was so lucky it held me in its warm embrace so young. But it does make it that much more difficult because now I have to spend the rest of my shitty existence remembering it and feeling the emotions from the catastrophic fallout.

A fallout that should have never fucking happened in the first place.

Hearing the gunman shout at Rhett, spewing hatred from the Sandman, has fueled my anger just as much as Rhett's physical death. Who was the man hanging halfway out that window? The man who pulled the trigger and riddled Rhett's beautiful body with bullet holes.

Whoever *that* man was, he's going to fucking pay if I have anything to do with it.

* * *

Leaving the sidewalk where I last saw Rhett alive and breathing is laborious, but I manage to scrape myself off the concrete and stand to my full height. I'm on the shorter side, so it isn't much. Nonetheless, I stand tall and begin walking downtown.

I know he's right where I want him.

Alone.

In the basement of the building. The garage section where fancy ass mafia dudes roam freely with guns strapped to their waistbands inconspicuously.

I'm doing the same.

The small handgun I saved up for has been burning a hole in the back of my pants ever since I left my shitty apartment this morning. I bought it under the table and have practiced shooting and following targets. I've taken it completely apart, cleaned it, and loaded it. I've rebuilt it several times over.I'm more comfortable handling it than making a fresh dinner at home. I could take it apart with my eyes closed at this point, but I won't since there's the possibility I could shoot myself in the foot. Metaphorically and physically. I'm not going to take that chance today.

The shadows along the edges of the buildings surrounding me grow longer and richer the further I walk. Before long, the streetlights flare and I know it's getting down to the wire. I need to find that son of a bitch.

I keep walking.

After an hour of walking and looping through and around buildings, I sigh a breath of relief when I see the establishment around the corner. Taking a deep breath and double-checking my positioning, I pick up my pace and quickly arrive at the entry door to the run-down, hole-in-the-wall, pizzeria.

A mafia-owned pizzeria.

I swallow glass as I enter, noting the way a dozen or more heads flit in my direction on instinct alone. They can't hear me over their own raucous laughter.

I ignore them all as their beady eyes follow me to the front counter. An older woman, probably in her sixties, glances up from her sudoku game book and does a double take on my face. "Good evening, miss. How can I help you?" Her voice is motherly, holding the same rasp as every grandmother before her, like some kind of ancestral chant.

Noting the lack of menus, I tell her the only thing that comes to mind. "Just a medium pepperoni pizza, please." *Don't be rude to the grandmother of the fucking mafia*, I remind myself. Mafia women aren't to be fucked with. She's probably killed more people than all the jackasses in here combined.

She doesn't write down my order. She stays still as a rock, staring me down to my socks. I feel the seam running across the tops of my toes and scrunch them subconsciously, trying to realign the seam so it doesn't piss me off.

"Will that be for dine-in or to-go?" Her sweet voice is riddled with hoarseness. She definitely smokes. The rasp of her voice is like a gentle caress to my ears. She's lived.

"Dine-in, please."

The grandmother only nods, still never letting her eyes leave me. She doesn't glance around or fidget. She smooths her hands down her blouse and over her thinning apron. "That will be up in about fifteen minutes. Sit wherever you feel comfortable." She doesn't offer any other pleasantries. She just pivots and darts through the doorless archway to what I assume is the kitchen.

Am I actually going to be getting a pizza? I wasn't necessarily planning on that. But pizza sounds damn good right now, too. I definitely won't be passing it up.

I turn from the counter, looking back at the dining room. Red leather booths line the walls with various sized circle tables filling the middle. Their red and white checkerboard tablecloths look to be vinyl, the shininess of them gleaming in the harsh, yet dim light. I conduct a mental survey, trying to calculate what the best option for seating will be.

The booths aren't all occupied, however, there's not much room between filled tables. In the far-right corner sits a corner booth, about half the size of the others. It's missing the harsh glare of the lighting and shadows cast over it mysteriously. It has good vantage points of both the entry and the counter that the grandmother abandoned.

A perfect option for me, then.

I slink my way over to the booth, refusing to look anyone in the eye. I don't need to start drama where there isn't any. I'm here for one reason, and one reason only.

One *man* only.

Sitting in the booth is a visceral experience. The red leather is *real* leather and sticks to any exposed skin. Luckily, I'm wearing jeans, or my thighs would be sticking and peeling off it. Small miracles and all. The tablecloth isn't sticky, and I don't see any visible residue from previous patrons.

Have there ever been other patrons? Or is this only an establishment for members of the mafia? I shrug to myself, not really giving a shit either way. Regardless of if there's been other patrons outside of the mafia rings, I'm here now, and I'm outside of those rings.

But apparently Rhett wasn't.

That's the thing I haven't been able to decipher in the last year. What was he doing? Who was he working for? Was what the gunman said even true? He called Rhett out by name, so there must have been some kernel of validity to his statements. Resting my chin on my fist, I lean on the table. The window to my right is covered with thick blinds and sheer red curtains. Not much light peeks through, but what does manage to seep in is bathed in red. The haunting glow of the light makes my stomach churn.

Not in apprehension, anxiety, or grief.

But in excitement.

My plan has been brewing for so long, it's time for the action to come into play. It's time for me to get what's mine: revenge.

While I'm lost in thought of murder and rage, the grandmother slides from the kitchen carrying a large circle tray propped on one arm. She chatters lightly to the men seated organically in the dining room, smiling and carrying on like there's no tomorrow.

Once she reaches me, she gently places the tray onto my table. The pizza is perfectly cooked, with a light brown crust that's covered in butter, and cheese so melted it could cause a heart attack from looks alone. I waft in the delectable smells of the gooey cheese and crisp pepperoni, smelling the thyme, parsley, and oregano that must fill out the robust scent of the sauce, which I assume is homemade by the grandmother still standing over my table.

I halt my wafting and stare up at her. Her face isn't pursed like I thought it would be, but instead her lips are clipped with only the corners being lifted ever so slightly. "I'll bring your check out in a moment," she tells me matter-of-factly.

"Thank you," I reply earnestly. *Don't piss off the grandmother of the mafia.* My mantra does little to settle my soul. The grandmother gives me one more long look, her eyebrows pulling tight in their centers. She gives me one more look before returning to the other individuals in the room. She continues her talking and walking until she makes it safely back into the kitchen.

I dive into the pizza, savoring the flavors as they explode across my tongue. I devour several slices in an inhuman amount of time all while keeping my eyes locked on the entry door. Waiting, watching.

I'm blotting my lips of grease when the tiny bell on the door chimes, welcoming a medium-built man with no hair and bad posture. My eyes lock on him, following his every movement as he saunters up to the grandmother's counter. She's nowhere to be found. He waits for several moments, tapping his sneakered foot against the tiled floor.

I shovel another slice of the best pizza I've ever eaten into my mouth as I nondescriptly stare at the man. He's the *man*, the one I've been looking for. He's the man who gunned down the love of my fucking life.

Chapter Seven
Katherine

I finish my pizza with glorious speed. I know I'm going to regret it later when the heartburn fueled by a thousand suns hits my gut and chest. I can't find it within me to really give a shit, though. Good pizza sometimes results in heartburn, and if that's my cross to bear, so be it. The pizza was so fucking delicious that it's worth every bit of pain I'm guaranteed to have later.

As I wipe my hands, I keep my eyes locked on the man at the counter who continues to stand at the front longer than I'd expected him to. As I watch him, he hops from foot to foot, displacing his weight effortlessly. His subpar build doesn't intimidate me and I'm grateful that he isn't one of the six-foot-tall men that reside in one of the booths here. He doesn't exude brutality like the others. But I know the truth.

He's more brutal than most.

Gunning down teenagers.

Murdering a teenager.

I still don't know how I managed not to get hit with one of the stray bullets.

It makes sense, though. He was shooting a rifle, not an automatic weapon. He wasn't blasting off dozens of rounds toward us, he was aiming. Those bullets lodged in Rhett's chest and never left.

I refocus on the man. His name is Whitman. Once I discovered his identity nearly six months ago, my plan truly began to come to life. I had the help of a hacker, thankfully, or I never would have found him.

About eight months ago, I was sitting on the living room floor, browsing sites I had no business browsing. I started chatting with a hacker, whose name I still don't know, and one thing led to another. Eventually, I had the name: Whitman. The hacker didn't want any payout or any credit for their work. It always seemed suspicious to me, but I took a random, albeit stupid, leap of faith and prayed it wouldn't kick me in the ass later on.

It was probably, no, *definitely*, a bad idea, talking to an unnamed hacker who seemed to know more about the situation than I did, but at the time, I didn't give a fuck. I still don't, not really. I have one thing on my mind: revenge. I will harness that revenge if it's the last thing I do.

Whitman leans against the front counter, his elbows against the wooden top with his head hanging between his shoulders. I wipe my mouth, pushing away the tray that once held the best pizza of my life, and cradle my chin in my hands as I lean against the table. He has to be leaving soon.

Finally, Whitman pushes against the front counter, letting himself rock back on his heels. He lets out a low whistle, probably pissed that the grandmother of the mafia didn't fly out to take his order. He turns to leave. I smooth my jacket down my chest and subtly check the gun in my waistband. After making sure it's still secure, I begin to scootch across the red leather seat, toward the aisle.

Before I stand fully, I quickly pull a crumpled twenty from my pocket, followed by two fives. I placed them under the rim of the large tray so the grandmother of the mafia can easily locate them. I don't know the exact protocol for tipping someone of her nature, but surely a few extra bills won't offend her.

Whitman exits. He's outside, most likely rounding the building. I've scoped it out enough so that I can predict his patterns. He will turn left and head for the alley off the side of the street. While I haven't interacted with Whitman at all since the fatal day of the shooting, I've been watching him.

With the help of my friendly hacker, I've been given access to cameras that are placed around the streets near the pizzeria. I can sit in the comfort of my own shitty apartment, headphones on, and laptop in my lap and just observe. Many times, the hacker friend will join me in a voice call and we chat. They use a voice app or something to synthesize their voice. I assume they're a man, but I could be completely wrong. We've never video chatted or seen one another.

They've been a rock this entire time. Without them, I would have never found Whitman and I definitely wouldn't have been able to garner access to the cameras.

Whitman most likely doesn't even remember me, honestly.

He'll know my name after tonight, though.

Chapter Eight
Katherine

The evening air is crisp and heavy with possibilities. I walk briskly, but not quick enough to garner any unwanted attention. There are men posted on every other corner. I assume they're the Sandman's men. This is their part of town, and they keep their presence seen. I avoid catching anyone's attention as I come up to the mouth of the alley that I know Whitman just sauntered into.

The alley is...well, an alley. There are a few garbage dumpsters scattered around and more trodden cardboard than I could have imagined. A small family of racoons skitters about near one of the dumpsters, their tiny freaky hands carrying old food. I watch where I step, careful to avoid any plastic or debris that could give away my location.

Whiteman is roughly fifty feet ahead of me. He walks with an atypical gait, indicative that his previously broken leg is bothering him. Good. I can work with that.

I quickly shorten the distance between us. At twenty feet, I let my hand roam along my waistband.

At ten feet, I grip the handle and halt abruptly. I'm still silent as a mouse, my steps light and quick. I keep my hand on my weapon as I draw it from my waistband and pull it to my side. I keep the nose of it pointed down, my pointer finger twitching toward the trigger.

"Whitman," I nearly yell out his name.

He stops, stock still and suddenly taller. I maintain my composure. I've worked too fucking hard to fuck this up now. I swallow any lingering fear, letting my stomach acid bobble around before dissolving it.

Whitman faces me. His face is covered with shadows, like a masked man. But I know better. I know his pock-marked face, his shitty excuse for a beard, and his wayward eyebrows that are in desperate need of a trim.

"Who the fuck are you?" His voice is higher pitched, an ounce of vulnerability seeping into his words.

"You don't need to know my name," I respond callously.

He scoffs, "Whatever, bitch." He turns to walk away, wanting to ignore me.

I'm not willing to be ignored.

The cold metal of the gun bites into my skin.

"Turn around or I'll put a bullet in your ugly fucking head,?" I scold.

Whitman turns around, not hiding his laugh as he cups his mouth. "You on something, girl? What's your poison?" He begins stepping toward me.

I stand my ground, refusing to give him any hold over me. I have a plan. I came here with one intention only.

"The only poison around here is *you*."

He laughs more. The audacity of this fucker. I hate him. I hate him. *I hate him.*

I step closer. "You killed him." A fat, lone tear slides from my eye.

"I've killed a lot of people, honey, you're gonna have to be more specific than that."

I hate him.

"Rhett."

"You're talking about that pretty boy from last year?"

I nod, not trusting my voice for once today.

Whitman lets out a long sigh, rubbing his forehead with the back of his hand. "Of fucking course you're talking about that bitch kid." He looks directly at me, and from this distance, I can see his face now. He doesn't look well, and that gives me a bit of hope as well as some sick satisfaction.

"You riddled his body with fucking bullets."

"Yeah, that's usually what happens when you gun someone down, sweetheart." His voice is a knife in my heart. *I hate him.*

"Why'd you do it?"

"Why did I kill the kid? Well, that's an easy answer. Sandman wanted it to happen, and when boss says jump, you ask how high."

"Why?"

"I don't ask boss questions. It ain't my place to question. The kid had to die."

The kid had to die.
The kid had to die.
The kid had to die.

Tears blur my vision. I can barely see Whitman, who has somehow closed the distance between us. He's barely an arm's length away now. I swallow thickly.

"It's best you keep going, girl. Don't make me doi something you don't want me doing."

"Oh, yeah? Like what? Murdering the love of my life?"

He laughs. Again. "What are you? Like eighteen? He wasn't the love of your life. Fucking dramatic ass teenagers. Move on."

I raise my arm and the gun touches his chest. My finger doesn't twitch, my muscles steady in their decision.

Whitman doesn't pale. He doesn't move or say anything new. His eyes just bore into mine as his lips turn up. Does he want me to kill him? Is this what he wants? Why isn't he grabbing my arm and snapping it in half?

"I see you've got yourself some questions."

I only nod.

"Well, you ain't gonna be getting any answers from me," he steps impossibly closer, burying the gun into his chest even more. "So. Do. It."

I pull the trigger.

A loud *bang* shocks through the alley as vibrations race from my hand to my wrist to my arm and shoulder. Whitman's eyes widen before quickly looking down at his chest. His hands grasp the barrel of my weapon, forcing it down. He doesn't use much force, however. He can't.

I shot him square in the chest.

He's a dead man walking.

Just like Rhett was.

As Whitman crumples to the nasty ground, I turn, walking down the alley as my breaths come in waves. The gun isn't linked to me directly, the serial number having been wiped by the seller, so I toss it in one of the dumpsters I pass.

I'll never forget tonight. It will haunt my dreams until I fucking die.

But I can rest, even just for a bit, knowing that the man who killed Rhett, my sweet, beautiful Rhett is eliminated from his own fucking pitiful existence.

Walking down the alley, my phone rings. My hands burn from clenching them into fists for the last several blocks. I slowly withdraw my phone from my pocket, and see an unknown number flashing against the dim screen. I answer, knowing the voice will be synthesized and comforting.

"Hello?" I answer the call.

The hacker barely calls me, but I knew they would tonight. They need to start, if they haven't already, wiping the cameras in the streets of my presence. It's all a part of the plan. The delicious plan we baked up together.

But their voice isn't the same electronic one I've been hearing for the past several month. I halt as I listen.

"Kath, did you get the job done?"

Kath.

Before I can respond to the ghost, a heavy *thunk* meets the back of my head and I crumple like a doll to the cold concrete of the place where Rhett was last seen.

About the Author

Britt Bee is a newer author who writes romance that features some darkness with sweetness curled up next to it. If you want to read what happens after this prequel, then look for *In the Dark* and check out her instagram @britt.bee.books

Taming His Lady

By: Sarah Bale and Everleigh Blake

A Dark, Contemporary Reimagining of
Lady and the Tramp

About Taming His Lady

The Lady

She presents herself as a lady, someone people should aim to be. But I know the truth. I've seen her true nature. How far will she go to become my pet?

The Tramp

He's known as a womanizer, someone who is irresistible. But I know the truth. He's a mobster who takes what he wants. And now his gaze is set on me, and I fear I won't be able to survive his rage.

Be prepared to devour this dark and angsty age gap, forced marriage, dark romance about a violent man who does whatever it takes to protect those he loves, and a sheltered woman caught in a web of darkness, whose innocence might save them all.

Content Note:

Mature content. For readers 18 & older. This book contains themes such as: Kidnapping, Stalking, Graphic Sex, Age gap, Revenge, and Forced Marriage.

Read at your discretion.

Relationship Type: MF

Chapter One
Wren

UNKNOWN NUMBER

Unknown: Why do you stay, little bird? Letting them shit all over you...

Me: WHO IS THIS???

When the mystery texter doesn't reply, I look around, willing him to reveal himself. Based on the video I got the other night, I know it's a 'he.' My cheeks heat—the one where he was stroking himself with a pair of my panties. I should have been horrified. And I was. How did he get my panties? Was he in my house? Is he watching me there as well as here? All things I should worry about, but my arousal quickly took over until all I felt was heat.

My swallow is audible and has me reaching for the drink on my desk.

The thing is, he's not wrong. Why do I stay here? Because they *do* shit on me. Take now, for example. My boss just embarrassed me in front of a new client and several of my coworkers to make himself look better. Like it helped much. In fact, the only reason the CEO of Rossi Enterprises is here is because of *me*. Not that any of these fools would admit it.

Mr. Rossi's gaze lands on me, as if I've summoned his attention. I hold his icy blue stare for two seconds before looking away. I grab my phone for good measure and act like I'm reading something.

Gideon Rossi, the self-made millionaire of Rossi Enterprises, has a reputation that precedes him. Womanizer. Vicious. Ruthless. Some have even echoed the word 'Mobster' when describing him. All seems accurate to me. Especially the last bit. I mean, the man screams danger. Upon first glance, he appears to be civilized. Tom Ford suit that's altered to fit his muscular body like a glove. Custom cologne that lulls you into a false sense of security. Black hair that's styled to perfection with flecks of silver at his temples. All in all, a *very* good-looking man.

When you take a closer look, that's where things reveal themselves. Not even his tailored suit can hide the tattoos that mark his chest and arms. Even now, I can see some of the colorful inked lines snaking from under his shirt onto the top of his hand. If the rumors are true, the tattoos all have to do with the Rossi Mafia. His well-maintained appearance can't hide the scars on his face and hands. Scars that are rumored to be from knife fights. Can you imagine? *Knife fights.*

I have to admit that his danger is what made him so appealing to me. The company I work for invests money for high-end clients like Gideon Rossi, taking their millions and turning them into billions. No one in the city wants to touch Gideon or his money, as rumors run rampant that he killed the last person involved with his finances. To me, I see a challenge. High risk equals high rewards for all involved. And god knows I need all the financial rewards I can get.

The thought has me frowning just as my boss asks me a question. He sees the look on my face as he looks up and says, "If you can't be professional, Ms. Copeland, then perhaps you should leave this meeting."

Before I can reply, Mr. Rossi swoops in. "I believe Ms. Copeland stubbed her toe right before you asked her the question, Bart." He gives my boss a charming smile. "Show a bit of compassion."

My boss nods. "Of course. Apologies, Ms. Copeland."

My smile is tight. "No worries at all. I will excuse myself, though, so I can get the paperwork for Mr. Rossi and send it to his office."

I duck out of the conference room without waiting for anyone to reply. As I walk, I curse my boss under my breath. Each step brings a new curse word or insult. Prick. Asshole. Douche. Dick. Bastard. Jackass. Dookie-head. Okay, that last one is me reaching deep into the insult section of my brain.

I'm almost to my office when a strong hand touches my arm, making me let out a sound somewhere between a scream and a yelp.

"Pardon me, Ms. Copeland. I thought you heard me call out your name." Gideon Rossi looks down at me, his lips lifting upward. "Though I suppose it might be hard to hear me over all the names you were calling Bart. What was the last one? Dookie-head?"

"I'm so sorry, Mr. Rossi. I didn't know you were behind me."

"Would that have stopped you from calling Bart all those names?"

"Of course."

He looks disappointed. "Pity. I admire a woman who isn't afraid to speak her mind."

I laugh before I can stop myself.

"Something funny, Ms. Copeland?"

"Yes. It's funny that you think women have the luxury of going around speaking their minds. Do you know what happens when a woman speaks her mind, Mr. Rossi?" I wait a beat. "They're called emotional and unstable as if I haven't seen Bart throw a phone across the room in a fit of rage. But does anyone call him emotional and unstable? No."

"I see."

"No, I don't think you do. Did you know that I was the one who reached out to your company proposing the meeting? I'm also the one who did all the research and found out where we could help you." I let out another small laugh. "When Bart found out what I had done, he immediately went to his bosses and claimed credit, which is why your meeting was with him and not me."

"I did notice he knew little about my company."

"That's putting it mildly, I'm sure, since the only thing Bart cares about is getting high."

My lips snap shut as soon as the words leave my mouth. Shit! Shit! Shit! I shouldn't have said that, not to a client and not when the paperwork hasn't been signed.

"I'm sorry, Mr. Rossi. That was uncalled for."

"You have a bad habit, Ms. Copeland. One that pisses me off to no end." He takes a step closer. "One that I'll spank your ass for later."

Heat shoots through my body, and at the same time, my brain screams 'danger.'

"Wh-what do you mean?"

"You'll see soon enough." He puts a respectable amount of distance between us. "Have a good day, Ms. Copeland."

He walks away without another word. When he's gone, I sink into my chair, exhaling.

What in the hell was that?

Chapter Two
Gideon

My finger taps on the top of my desk as my right-hand man, Raul, tells me all the reasons this is a bad idea.

When he realizes that I'm not listening, he sighs.

"I'm not going to talk you out of this, am I?"

"No."

"Why her?"

"Why not?"

"You know what I mean. Why go through all this to get the woman who you believe betrayed Boris?"

"Why not?"

"Dammit, Gideon, this isn't funny."

"Am I laughing?" I wait a beat. "I know what I'm doing."

Raul is silent, which isn't always a good thing. He lets me act on my impulses and then is there to remind me he was right when the shit hits the fan. This isn't one of those cases because I *know* I'm right.

Wren Copeland killed my best friend, and now she must pay.

Raul stands. "I can see I'm not going to get through to you."

"No, you're not."

"Let me leave with this parting word. Wren isn't the one who killed Boris."

I jump to my feet, pulling my gun on my second in command. To his credit, he doesn't even flinch. Not even with my finger hovering over the trigger.

"Tread carefully."

"She didn't kill him, Gideon. Her father did. Just remember that before you punish her."

I let out a laugh before I can stop myself. "We both know that's not true. She was the one he was trying to save. She was the one who begged him for help. If he hadn't listened to her pleas, he would be alive."

Raul's gaze searches mine as if he thinks he'll find an answer to something he's looking for.

Finally, he says, "You're the boss, Gideon. I will follow your orders."

I know he will. I don't keep disloyal men around. If he doesn't do this, he will be dead before sunrise.

"Good. I want her brought to me tonight."

Raul dips his head before leaving. When he's gone, I set my gun on the desk and sit in my chair, leaning back. I've studied Wren Copeland to the point of becoming obsessed. I know everything about her. And I'm going to use it all against her. By the time I'm finished with her, she will wish she had never met me.

Chapter Three
Wren

I've just kicked off my shoes when there's a knock on my front door. Today has been hellish, and getting up is a struggle. My knee aches as I walk, a harsh reminder of what happened a year ago today.

The thought has me pausing. How is this the first time I've thought about that day? For months, it was all that consumed my mind. The kidnapping. The torture. The man with the kind eyes who saved me. My breath hitches. I can still hear his cries as he died in my arms. Moments later, I was rescued by my father's men. If they had been there a minute sooner, Boris wouldn't have died. I did my best to find out about the man who tried to save me but didn't come up with much. Heck, the coroner's office wasn't even sure Boris was his real name.

Another knock brings me out of the troubled thoughts of my past, and I hurry to the door. I open it without looking through the peep-hole, thinking it's the Chinese food I ordered. A large body pushes through my doorway before I have time to process what's happening.

"Sorry about this, ma'am." He says as he grabs my arm, spinning me so my back is to his chest.

Something sharp pierces the skin on the side of my neck right before everything goes dark.

* * *

I come to with a pounding head.

"Shit," I grumble as I sit.

It takes me all of three seconds to remember what happened. I reach for my neck as if I'll still find the needle and syringe there. All I find is tender skin, which is likely bruised since I bruise so easily. The pain morphs into panic as I look around. I'm locked in an actual cage. It reminds me of the kennel my mother used to keep her cocker spaniel in. Four walls with iron bars keep me inside. The top and bottom are solid and there's not enough room to stand. No, I'd have to be on my hands and knees to get out...

"I see you're awake."

I turn toward the voice to find Gideon Rossi sitting in a chair that faces me. It's right next to a massive bed. Am I in his bedroom?

"Why am I in a cage?"

His lips lift. "Strange that the cage is your first worry."

"Oh, there's plenty more on my list, but the cage is preventing me from slapping the shit out of you."

He laughs, and I bite back a silent curse because that's a sound I could get used to.

"Thank you for being honest, little bird."

"Little bird?" My pulse thrums in my neck. "You're the one who's been sending me the texts."

I don't mention the video, even though it's what I think of first. Heat creeps up my neck, and I pray he can't see it.

He says, "You are correct. I'm the one who's been texting you." He leans forward. "I'm also the one who's been watching you. I know everything about you, Wren, and now that you're here, we can move to stage two of my plan."

"Plan? What does that mean?"

"You're about to find out."

He stands, going to the door. When he opens it, a man in a suit steps in. My lips part.

"Father O'Malley?"

"Good evening, Wren, and congratulations."

"Congratulations? What are you talking about? Help me!"

He can see I'm in a cage. Why isn't he helping me?

Father O'Malley ignores me and turns to Gideon. "Mr. Rossi, it's a pleasure to serve you tonight. I'm sure somewhere, both of your parents are smiling down at you."

Gideon snorts. "Doubtful, but thank you for the words, Father."

"Where shall I stand?"

"Wherever you'd like," Gideon says as he comes to a stop next to the cage.

Two more men enter the room, closing the door behind them. I recognize one as the man who shoved the syringe in my neck. I glare at the man, and he lifts a shoulder in a shrug. What a jerk!

Father O'Malley turns, so he's facing us. "We are gathered here today to witness the marriage between Gideon Rossi and Wren Copeland."

A loud buzzing fills my ears, and everything around me spins. I hold on to the bars, trying to steady myself.

"This is where you say, 'I do,'" Gideon says, though it sounds like he's far away.

"No."

"I wasn't asking." His voice is closer. "If you don't do this, your father dies."

"Please don't make me do this."

"Say it, Wren. Say you're willing to be my wife."

Blinking, everything comes into focus. "I do."

"Such a good little bird."

Father O'Malley says, "By the power vested in me, I now pronounce you man and wife. You may kiss your bride, Mr. Rossi."

Gideon smirks. "I think we'll skip that step, Father. Did you bring the paperwork?"

"I did."

He reaches into his pocket, pulling out a document. Gideon takes it, signing his name. He hands it to the two men, and they sign, too.

When he turns to me, I shake my head. "You can't make me."

"Father, have a look out that window over there."

Father O'Malley does as he's told without questioning Gideon.

Gideon turns to me. "You're going to learn that my word is law. I understand that this is new, but when I tell you to do something, I'm not asking, and the longer you stall, the worse your punishments will be."

"Punishments?"

"Yes, my little bird, all pets must be trained. Tamed, even." He reaches into the cage, tucking a piece of brown hair behind my ear. "It's up to you how painful that training will be."

"Why are you doing this, Gideon?"

"Sign the paper, Wren. Make things easier on yourself."

My gaze searches his icy blue one. "Will you tell me why you're doing this if I sign?"

"Yes."

I hold out my hand. He hands me the paper and a pen. I skim the document, even though I already know what it is. A wedding certificate and marriage license. I add my name next to his and hand it back to him.

"Will you tell me now?"

He moves away from the cage. "Gentlemen. Father. I thank you all for being here for my wedding. Mrs. Rossi and I would like some time alone if you know what I mean."

Father O'Malley is the only one who laughs at the poor joke. The man who stabbed me with the syringe hands Father O'Malley a thick envelope and leads everyone from the room, leaving just me and Gideon.

Gideon turns to me. "Now, let's get you some answers."

Chapter Four
Wren

My heart pounds as he reaches into his suit jacket, pulling out a gold key.

"You're going to let me go?"

His lips lift in a smile. "No. Your training is beginning, little bird. I'd suggest being quiet. I still haven't forgotten that stunt at the office."

"Stunt? What stunt?"

"You're going to make this oh-so-fun for me, aren't you?"

I close my mouth, even though I'm dying to ask a million questions.

"Good girl," he praises.

I've seen that term a million times in the romance novels I like to read and never saw the appeal. But hearing Gideon say it in his deep, growly voice... well, let's just say that now I get it. And I hate the heat that is now swirling deep in my stomach.

He unlocks the door, letting it swing open.

"Crawl to me."

It's on the tip of my tongue to question him. Or maybe even tell him to go to hell. One look at the gleam in his eyes tells me that's exactly what he's hoping I'll do. Silently, I lower to my knees and place my hands on the floor of the cage. And then I crawl to Gideon Rossi.

"Very good, pet," he says as he moves toward the bed, sitting at the foot of it. "Come over here so I can punish you, and then we can get on with our wedding night."

It's killing me not being able to ask him anything, but I'm not going to test him. Not when I've heard of the terrible things he's done. I come to a stop at his feet.

"Up."

He pats his lap, so there's no questioning what he means. My swallow is audible as I climb into his lap, laying across his muscular thighs. I regret wearing a skirt to work today because cold air licks my skin. Gideon must be thinking about my skirt, too, because his hand settles on the back of my leg, creeping under the material.

"No panties. Another thing to be punished for, wife."

There's a low humming in my ears as reality hits me. Oh, my god. I'm his wife.

"Why am I getting punished for that? I wasn't your wife until moments ago," I murmur, unable to keep silent.

"There she is," he says.

I get the feeling that if I were to look at him, I'd find him smiling. So I don't look.

"No reply. Smart little bird. Very smart." He pauses. "Ten for the stunt at your job. Ten for back-talking me. And ten for not wearing panties."

Nothing happens, and then my skirt is yanked up over my hips. A moment later, his hand makes contact with my butt cheek in rapid-fire succession. My god. I've never been spanked before, not even as a kid. My dad thought it was uncivilized.

Tears stream down my cheeks, but I don't make a sound. I won't give Gideon the pleasure.

But after number fifteen, I can't stop the moan that leaves my lips. Because somehow the pain has mixed with pleasure. Gideon's hand comes down lower, making me bite back another moan. The contact presses my clit against the material of his slacks. It's enough friction that jolts of pleasure shoot deep into my stomach.

How in the fuck am I getting turned on by this?

Gideon delivers the rest of the spankings, bringing me to the edge of an orgasm. When he's finished, I try to scurry off his lap, but he stops me.

"Oh, no, little bird. What kind of man would I be if I didn't make sure you received aftercare?"

There are so many things wrong with what he just said, but all thoughts go out of my mind when he kneads the tender flesh he abused moments ago. His hand moves between my legs, and he runs his fingers through my drenched slit.

"Such a good little wife," he praises. "You took your punishments so well, Wren. Do you know that?"

My reply is stuck in my throat as he reaches my clit, rubbing it in slow circles that send me closer and closer to climaxing.

But then he stops, and I hate myself because I want to beg him to finish.

"Up," he orders.

I do as he says and stand on wobbly legs. He stands, too.

"I'm going to give you two choices, wife. Think carefully before answering." At my nod, he continues, "One, I will give you all the answers you seek, but I won't touch you again. You will stay locked away in that cage until the entire world forgets about you. But you'll die with the truth. Two, I will give you what you so clearly want—what I want, too—and you will become my pet. You will obey me no matter what. You will be happy, Wren, but you won't get the answers you seek."

My mind races. Can I live with this man, not knowing what drove him to do all of this?

"May I ask one question?"

"You may."

"Will my father be safe?"

Something dark flashes in his eyes. "He'll be safe for as long as you're my pet."

"Then I choose option two."

Because I value my father's life more than needing to know what has driven Gideon to go to extremes to marry me.

Shock is etched in his expression.

I take a step back from him, pulling my top over my head.

"You said earlier today that you wished I would speak my mind. Is that still true?"

"It is."

"Will I be punished for it?"

"Such a quick learner, little bird. No, you will never be punished for telling me the truth."

I nod once. "My truth at this moment is that I want you to fuck me. *Husband.*"

Chapter Five
Gideon

Something snaps inside of me as soon as she calls me *husband*. This entire plan has been based around revenge, but the moment she willingly crawled from the cage into my lap, things changed. For the first time in a year, I could see a future for myself. One that didn't revolve around revenge. Does that make me weak? Well, that's yet to be determined. I'm sure Raul is going to give me shit when he hears that my plan has changed, but I'll deal with that later.

"Get naked," I tell her.

She does as I say, and I watch in awe. She's all curves, and it fucking turns me on. Her body is perfect, and so I tell her.

Her cheeks are pink. "No, it's not. I'm too fat..."

"Who in the fuck told you that? Never mind. I don't want to kill someone on my wedding night."

I move closer, brushing my lips against hers, but she stills.

"No kissing on the mouth. It's too personal..."

"No kissing on the mouth," I agree. But only for tonight. After I'm done with her, every inch of her body will be mine.

I push her down to her knees, so she's eye-level with my cock. She takes the hint and licks the tip before wrapping her lips around my dick. Her head bobs back and forth and she makes a sexy sound of pleasure. But it's not enough. I wrap my fingers through her hair and shove myself further into her mouth. She gags, and tears leak from her eyes, but she doesn't try to stop me. Instead, her throat contracts as she takes me deeper. She's so damn good at this that there are bursts of white spots behind my eyes.

"Fuck yes. Goddamn, Wren. Suck me."

Air rushes from my lungs, and my head tilts back. Her mouth feels so goddamn amazing wrapped around my dick. When I come, she swallows every drop.

"Mmm." She moans. "I knew you'd taste sweet."

I pull her to her feet and push her onto the bed. I shove her legs apart and return the favor. She's wet and tastes so fucking good. I lap her pussy until she comes. And then I keep doing it until she comes again.

She tugs on my hair, and I move up her body, kissing her soft stomach. When I get to her breasts, I latch onto a nipple and suck. Hard. She cries out but pulls me closer.

"We ought to get these pierced," I tell her as I move to the next one.

"If I'm going through something like that, then so will you," she answers as she reaches down, gripping my cock through my pants.

I grin. "Message received, wife."

Her body is covered in sweat, and the scent mixes with her arousal. It's hot as hell. I lick the skin between her breasts and then blow.

"Gideon, fuck me. Now."

I stand, undressing. I love how her eyes roam my body.

"I'm not going to wear a condom," I warn her as I move over her. "I know you're clean, and so am I."

"Wha— how do you know I'm clean?"

"I know everything about you, Wren, which is how I also know you want a family. So, wife, I'm going to go bare in you. You're going to feel every inch as I pound into you. And when I come, I'm going to put a baby in you."

She fucking whimpers but doesn't tell me no. She can't. We both know this is what she wants. And I did promise to give her everything she wanted if she picked option two.

She wraps her legs around my waist, and I enter her in a single thrust. We both moan. It's been a long time since I've fucked someone without a condom, and it feels fucking amazing, especially knowing she's my wife. *Mine...*

I move slowly at first. I don't want to hurt her. I flick her nipple, and her pussy clenches. The next thrust is easier as she gets wetter. Soon, she's so wet that I'm sliding all the way into her tight pussy. Her tits shake with each thrust, and it's so fucking sexy. She is so sexy that I rock into her as my fingers dig into her thick hips.

Tears fall from her eyes when she comes. I'm right behind her. My stomach tightens, and my balls feel heavy. I come, thrusting so hard that she cries out. When I'm done, I pull out of her, falling next to her on the bed.

She turns to me and says, "That was..."

"Agreed."

"I have to ask... Why did you take my panties when you broke into my apartment?"

This woman and her questions. There are a million other things she could ask me, but that's what she wants to know?

"Seemed like a good idea."

She snorts, and it's fucking adorable.

"Oh."

"That's it? That's all you want to ask me?"

She shakes her head. "We both know there are a million things I want to ask you, but I won't. Instead, I have a request."

"And that would be?"

"Next time, I want you to fuck me in the ass."

My greedy cock twitches, liking that thought so much that it hardens.

"I can do that."

We lie there, both catching our breath.

"Why haven't you left that shithole company?"

She turns to me. "I don't know, to be honest. They gave me a job as a favor to my father when I graduated, and I guess I got comfortable. Too comfortable."

"Has Bart ever tried anything with you?"

"A few times, but I can handle him."

Rage coils deep in my chest, and I rub the spot as if it will help.

"I don't want to talk about Bart," she says as her hand moves lower, wrapping around my dick. She pumps me slowly, applying pressure at different spots.

"I think you should come to work for me," I say.

"Doing what, Mr. Rossi?"

I groan when she cups my balls.

"Whatever you want."

She releases my dick and begins touching herself. It's fucking hot being this close to Wren while she masturbates.

"Is my wife being naughty?"

She lets out a throaty moan. "Touching you made me horny."

"Funny. I was just thinking the same thing."

I join her, and we work her pussy together. When I slip a finger inside her, she rocks her hips.

"Turn over," I tell her, pulling out.

She does as she's told, so her back is against my chest. I wrap my arm around her and resume toying with her clit. She comes, bucking against my hand. I spread her juices around, coating her anus.

"Ever been fucked here before?" I ask, flicking my finger over the puckered opening.

"Only by myself."

I nip her ear and reach into the nightstand next to the bed, grabbing lube. I squirt some on my finger, spreading it around her anus. She groans as I slip my finger inside the tight opening.

"I can take more than that," she breathes.

Who am I to disagree?

I press my dick against her opening, sliding slowly in. Her body grips me, and it feels so fucking good. She bucks against me and flicks her clit, sighing. I take the hint and begin toying with her from both ends. Soon, we're fucking in earnest. She's so tight that I know I'm going to come first.

"You're a filthy slut, letting me fuck you like this," I growl in her ear. "My fucking slut."

She pants something incoherent.

I spank her butt cheek. "This ass is mine. Say it, wife. Say you're mine."

"I'm yours, Gideon!"

She screams my name as she comes, and I'm right behind her. My orgasm is almost violent because her anus clenches me so hard.

Gently, I pull out, and she moans.

Fucking hell. That was...

Wren yawns, snuggling against me.

"Thank you."

"For what?"

"For showing me how it could be."

Chapter Six
Wren

Gideon and I settle into an easy routine over the next month. I quit my job and went to work for him. It's everything I dreamed it would be. When we're not in the office, we spend as much time together as we can, to the point that I fear I might be falling in love with him. But I can't fall in love with him. Not when I'm nothing more than his little bird—his pet that he likes to play with.

I'm deep in thought when he enters our room.

"What's the frown for, wife?"

"Nothing."

His gaze darkens. "Is that a lie, little bird?"

I look at him and answer, "Yes."

He sighs as if I've disappointed him. "Why did you lie to me, Wren? I thought we were doing so well."

"How can we be doing well when I don't know why I'm here?" Hot tears fill my eyes. "You say you want to give me everything. Everything but the truth."

"You want the truth, little bird?"

"Yes."

"Even if it means things will change between us?"

"Why will they change?"

"Because once I bring up the past, I won't be able to look at you the same!" He says the words with so much raw passion that I flinch.

But I'm not going to back down.

"I love you, Gideon Rossi, but this marriage won't work unless we're both truthful."

He's silent for a moment, and I fear he's going to shut me out. But then he crosses the room and sits next to me on the bed.

"A year ago, I was approached by your father. He wanted to make a deal with me but didn't have the money to tempt me into considering it. So he offered his biggest asset." His gaze lands on me. "He offered you. I turned him away. I may be a lot of things, but I don't trade in human flesh."

I let out a dry laugh. "It doesn't surprise me he offered me. He's always acted like women must serve men."

"And yet you begged for his life. Agreed to stay with me, even."

We're both turning a new leaf today. One that revolves around the truth. That means it's time to tell him my father's secret.

"My father's mistress just had twin girls. My little sisters. I begged for his life because they deserve a chance to know their father."

"And what happens when he decides they, too, can be used as pawns?" He shakes his head. "A few weeks after I turned him down, I heard that you were kidnapped. My gut said he had something to do with it, so I sent my best man to get you back." His voice is thick as he continues, "Boris sent me one last text before he died. Said he knew where you were and that he was going to get you back."

His words shock me to my core. "Boris was your man?"

"Yes."

I let out a watery laugh. "I've tried to find out everything I could about him since he died. It was like he was a ghost." I turn to Gideon. "Did he have a family?"

"Only me."

My hand finds his. "I'm so sorry for your loss, Gideon. He was a wonderful man. He did everything he could to get me out of there..."

"Your father is the one who had you kidnapped Wren. Who killed Boris. I found out after he died."

I let his words settle over me. "There was a part of me that always knew it was him, you know?"

"I'm sorry."

I brush at the tears streaming down my face. "There's nothing to apologize for, Gideon. You aren't the one who hurt me. He was."

"But I blamed you for Boris' death."

"Do you still blame me?"

"No."

"Then we're good. I promise."

But that's not the truth either.

"Actually, we're not good."

His eyebrows lift. "Little bird, I will get on my hands and knees and beg for your forgiveness if that's what it takes to make this right."

"No. There's only one thing that will make this right. Killing my father."

His eyes are full of dark promises. "I'll make it happen on one condition."

"And that is?"

"That you rule at my side, as my lady. My queen. My equal."

I lean over, brushing my lips against his. "Silly man. I'm already your lady. Now, let's go get my father."

THE END

About the Author

Sarah Bale's family always knew she was destined to write romances when they saw the elaborate stories she created for her Barbie dolls. When Sarah isn't writing, she enjoys spending time with her family and friends and also planning what she'd do in a zombie apocalypse. She is a USA Today Bestselling Author residing in Oklahoma and doesn't plan on leaving any time soon.

Stay in touch by joining her newsletter: https://bit.ly/Sarah BaleVIP

Everleigh Blake is the not-so-secret pen name of Sarah Bale. If you enjoyed this story, be sure to follow Sarah to stay up to date on what's happening with Everleigh Blake books!

Paper Ring

By: C. Hallman

About Paper Ring

He gave me a diamond ring, but it might as well have been made out of paper.

Emmett Carter runs the city.
He's gorgeous, powerful, and cunning.
There isn't a soul who doesn't know him, and nearly everyone fears him. Then there's me.
I'm his wife, but no one even knows I exist... until now.

Content Note:

This is a dark romance, including some content that might be triggering for some, such as violence, forced proximity and dub-con.

Relationship type: Male/Female

Chapter One
Gwen

Just when I thought this night couldn't get any worse, red and blue lights flash in my rearview mirror. *Fuck!*

I glance down at the speedometer. 79mph. *Fuck, again.* I'm pretty sure the speed limit is 65 here.

Unreasonable fear creeps up my spine. Yes, I'm speeding, but that's it. It's not a big deal. People speed all the time. I'm gonna get a ticket and go on with my night. Nothing to worry about. At least, that's what I keep telling myself as I pull onto the side of the highway.

We're just outside of town, and it's a cloudy night. The area is completely dark without any illumination from the sky or the city, making the cruiser's headlights behind me seem even brighter.

I put my car in park and squint my eyes, watching the black silhouette of the police officer get out of his car and walk toward me.

My heart is racing, and my fingers tremble as I reach for the button to let my window down.

Why am I so nervous?

"Good evening, ma'am," the cop greets as soon as he is close enough to peer down at my face. With one hand on his gun holster, he grips a flashlight in the other, searching the inside of my car like I'm hiding a drug dealer in here.

"I'm sorry I was speeding," I blurt out after cursing Gia in my head for making me do this again. "My roommate called and asked me to pick her up from this guy's house, and I was just trying to get there as fast as I could. I know that's not an excuse. I should definitely drive the speed limit, especially at night. I know that, but—"

"Is that why you're in your pajamas?" The cop interrupts my rambling, shining his flashlight directly on my chest.

I lower my head and stare at my bare legs, covered only by a pair of thin plaid shorts. The white tank top I'm wearing is not much better, considering there is no bra beneath it. My cheeks turn hot, and I'm sure they redden to match my embarrassment.

I let my long, uncombed hair fall into my face, hiding my shame with an auburn curtain. "Um, yes. I was asleep when she called. I didn't really think clearly."

"That happens." The cop smiles. "Sounds like you were just being a good friend." He lowers the flashlight, letting me get a better look at him for the first time. He appears to be in his early forties, judging by the gray in his hair and the frown lines on his forehead.

"I'm sorry again."

"No worries. I'm just gonna have to check your license and registration, and you'll be on your way to pick up your friend."

"Of course!" I turn to reach for my purse, which I usually have on the passenger's seat. Today, there is only my phone. "Shit. I must have forgotten my purse while I was rushing out, but I have my registration here somewhere... I think."

Flipping on my interior lights, I start rummaging through the glove box. There are fast food receipts, unopened mail, random flyers, and take-out menus, but nothing that looks like a registration.

"Let's start with your name and birthday, okay?"

"Gwendoline Anne Baker. I actually turned 18 yesterday." Not sure why I mentioned that part. It's not like he cares.

"Well, happy belated birthday," he says flatly while scribbling something down on a notepad.

"Um, thanks. What exactly does a registration look like?" I ask like a complete dumbass. The officer raises one eyebrow at me, as if he's wondering if I'm joking.

"Who is this car registered to?"

"Me, I think? Or maybe my... husband," I murmur that last part. Even after two years of being married, I'm still not used to saying it. Mostly because I haven't seen my so-called husband our entire marriage. I don't even know why he gave me this car, and right now, I don't know why I've been driving it for two years without once questioning who it's registered to.

He was right... I am a naïve child.

My nerves are already on edge, but the cop manages to kick them up a notch when he starts walking around the car and saying something I can't make out into his radio.

I give up my search for this stupid registration and keep my eyes on the police officer, who is coming back to the driver's side now. I'm about to apologize for a third time when he suddenly reaches for the handle of my door and pulls it open.

"Get the fuck out of the car, with your hands where I can see them!" His voice blasts into my ear like I'm in the front row of a concert.

I flinch away from him, shocked and freaking out by what is happening. The cop's gun is pointing straight at me. My hands come up automatically to protect my face, as if my fingers could stop a bullet.

"Get out!" he orders again, less patience in his tone.

"Okay!" I yell back, making sure he can hear me over the loud, erratic beating of my own heart.

My whole body is shaking, and it has nothing to do with the temperature and everything to do with the man holding a gun against my head while screaming at me. "Turn around!"

I spin around so quickly I slide out of one of my flip-flops and almost fall to the ground.

"Hands behind your back," he orders, and again, I do what he says without thought. A moment later, he grabs my wrists roughly, pulling my arms back uncomfortably while he secures handcuffs on me.

Tears well in my eyes as the cool metal presses against my skin. The cop twists me around towards his cruiser, never even letting me put my other flip-flop back on. He sets me in the back seat of his cruiser, letting my legs dangle out the side.

"Do you have any idea what kind of shit you're in? Stealing a car?" He shakes his head. "You look like such a nice girl. Why do stuff like this? Do you even know who you stole from?"

"I didn't steal this car. It's mine."

"So, it's your car, but it's registered to someone else?"

"I told you, it might be in my husband's name."

"You can cut the shit, okay. Husband my ass. You are not even wearing a wedding band." He shakes his head. "There is no way out of this. Just sit tight until backup gets here. I'll have a female officer come and take you in." He gives me one last disapproving look before walking to the back of the car to lean against the corner.

I guess all I can do now is wait.

Chapter Two
Gwen

I spend the next ten minutes trying not to cry. I don't even know why the tears keep rolling down my cheeks. I'm not scared anymore. I'm more angry than anything. Angry with Gia for making me pick her up in the middle of the night. Angry with Emmett for giving me this car and definitely angry with myself for being so naïve and stupid.

The headlights of an approaching vehicle have me looking up into the road. This must be the female police officer. The vehicle slows down and pulls up behind us. I watch as the door opens and a large figure heads toward us.

It doesn't take me but a moment to realize that this person is not another cop. It's the one individual I wouldn't have expected to see tonight... or ever again, for that matter.

Emmett Carter. My husband.

He walks past the cop without glancing at him, his eyes trained on me the entire time until the moment he stops in front of my feet. His gaze moves up and down my body as if to scan every inch of me. I don't want to imagine what he sees right now; how pitiful I must look to him.

"Mr. Carter." The officer clears his throat and stands a little straighter beside us. "I called—" That's all he gets out before Emmett twist his body and slams his fist against the cop's jaw, making his head snap to the side. His eyes roll back, and his body goes down.

My gasp is masked by the thump of him hitting the ground at full force. His head bounces off the pavement like a basketball, making me cringe and yelp out in pain for him.

"Why did you tell him your name was Baker?" That's the first thing out of the mouth of the man who married me two years ago, just to dump me the same day.

"What else was I supposed to tell him?" I'm surprised by how even my voice is at this point.

"Your real last name."

"I wasn't sure if you wanted anyone to know. I figured you might be ashamed." I actually have no idea if he would be. I have no idea what he wants since he's never shared a fucking thing with me. Even on our wedding day we barley exchanged any words.

He ignores my comment completely and counters with another question instead. "What the fuck are you wearing? Your top is basically see-through. I can see your tits, and looking at the length of your shorts, I bet I can see your ass if you stand up."

My mouth pops open, and I suck in a sharp breath, feeling like I just got slapped. How dare he criticize my outfit. As if he has any right?

"What do you care?" He's never cared about me before. "You don't get to tell me what to do! If I want to walk around naked, I fucking will!" Two years ago, I would have never spoken to him like this. My parents taught me better. From a young age, they trained me to be a perfect wife to a man like Emmett. Taught me everything there was to know about pleasing and obeying a powerful man. Talking back was definitely not on that list.

I'm not that girl anymore. Two years of hating him, of being angry and hurt, are all coming to fruition at this very moment.

The cop groans again, but I can't make myself glance over. It's like Emmett is holding me under some kind of spell. I can't look away from his scowling face. His strong, clean-shaven jaw is twitching like he is trying not to grind his teeth too hard. And his brows are pinched together just as tightly as his lips are pressed shut. But what really draws me in are the stormy blue eyes now holding me hostage.

I should probably apologize, for both making him come out here tonight and the way I just spoke to him. Yet, I force my own lips shut and swallow back the apology sitting on my tongue. I don't owe him anything.

He moves so quickly that I don't have the time to even try to get away before his hands grab my upper arms, and he pulls me from the car. With only one flip-flop and my hands still cuffed behind my back, I'm so unsteady on my legs that I have no choice but to fall against his firm chest.

Turning my head away, I try to twist my body away from him, which only makes him dig his fingers deeper into my arms. I wince in pain, jerking from his touch. He suddenly lets go, and for a second, I think I'm going to fall back against the car. Emmett grabs me once more. This time, around my hip. Then he lifts me up and throws me over his shoulder so roughly it knocks the wind out of me.

"Wait!" I croak after I catch my breath. "My friend. I need to pick her up."

"I already sent someone to get Gia," Emmett says casually while carrying me back to his car.

"What? How do you know my friend's name... or where she is?"

"Forget about her; you have yourself to worry about now." His voice is low and gravelly, promising pain and whatever else he has planned for tonight.

His threat hangs heavy in the air as he lowers me to my feet, just to shove me into the back of another car. I almost hit my forehead on the door, but Emmett pulls me back just in time, sitting me up before sliding in next to me.

Someone else is sitting in the driver's seat. Like Emmett, he is wearing a dark suit, his hair is cut neat, and his shoulders are broad and muscular.

"Sir?" he asks.

"Home," Emmett growls out the order.

The driver pulls onto the highway, and I awkwardly try to sit sideways with my hands still tied together behind my back. I turn away from Emmett, looking out the window into the black night.

"Lean back," Emmett orders, grabbing my shoulder. If it wasn't for his hand pulling me toward him, I wouldn't think I even heard him right.

"What are you...?" The words get lodged in my throat when the side of my head meets his warm thigh. Suddenly, my mouth goes dry. What the hell is he doing? His fingers wrap firmly around my throat, not tight enough to restrict my breathing but tight enough to have me worried.

I'm facing him now, trying to look anywhere besides his crotch, which is only a few inches away. Squeezing my eyes shut, I concentrate on calming my breathing and not passing out. Closing them helps only a little because I can still feel his hands on me. Still smell his spicy cologne and hear his heavy breathing.

Fuck, he must be angry. Who knows what I interrupted him doing tonight? My thoughts are running rampant with scenarios of how his night started and how mine is going to end.

My mind comes up with many outcomes... and none of them are good.

Chapter Three
Gwen

I startle awake, disoriented and panicked because I don't know where I am.

"Relax." Emmett's gravelly voice vibrates through me, and I'm catapulted back into reality.

I'm still lying across the back seat of his car, cuffed, half-naked, and with my head propped up on his legs. His hand is still on my neck, but it's cradling the side now, his thumb softly stroking my jawline.

For a moment, I wonder if I actually fell asleep or if he choked me out without me realizing it. I wouldn't put it past him.

"We're almost there."

"Where are you taking me?"

"Home." I know right away he's lying. If he were taking me back to my apartment, we would have been there already.

"This is not the way to my place."

"Your new home," he explains calmly.

"Why are you moving me? I like my apartment, and I love my roommate." His fingers tighten slightly around my neck at the word love. It happened so quickly I'm not sure that it happened at all.

"You are my wife; you should live with me. I'll have your things moved in the morning."

The fact that I'm in a vulnerable position at the moment, one where he could easily snap my neck, apparently doesn't help me control my anger, and I lash out. "Now! Now, you want me? After two years of ignoring me, you suddenly changed your mind and find me worthy of living with you?"

The bastard has the audacity to smile. He fucking smiles like this is all a joke. Like my entire life is nothing but a joke to him.

The car comes to a stop, and the driver steps out as soon as the vehicle is in park. The interior light flickers on, blinding me for a second. I force my eyes open, wanting to at least see coming whatever he has planned.

The front door closes, and the back door opens a moment later. Instead of getting out, Emmett stays seated. "I don't want anyone to see her. Make sure all the men are gone."

"Of course. I'll take care of it," the driver confirms before stepping away.

"How am I supposed to live here if no one is allowed to see me? You can't keep me a secret forever, you know."

"Everyone who works for me knows about you."

"Sure they do." I don't believe a word he says. "Then why can't they see me?"

"Because if one of my men sees you in this outfit, I will use my favorite carving knife to cut his eyeballs out and feed them to the sharks."

Sharks? I don't know why that's my first thought after that monster of a sentence. Probably my sleep-deprived brain's fault. I try not to read too much into what he just said, mostly because the last time I let myself believe he actually liked me, he dumped me.

The driver didn't close the door, making it easy to hear his approach. "All clear."

Emmett wastes no time. Grabbing me under my arms, he pulls

Run...

me out of the car with him. My feet barely touch the graveled driveway when I'm lifted up in the air again and thrown over his shoulder.

Too tired to fight him, I just let my head hang low as he walks me into his house and up the stairs. With each step he takes, my body bounces against his shoulder.

"If you don't put me down, I'm gonna throw up," I warn, not joking one bit.

My stomach churns as he throws me down onto a soft bed. I fly off the mattress slightly, landing on my front with my face shoved into the blanket... a blanket that smells like him. Oh, god. I'm in his bed.

Turning my head to the side, I blink my eyes open and scan the room. "Take the cuffs off, please. My arms hurt."

"I should leave them on tonight as your punishment."

"My punishment?"

"For leaving the house like that."

My mouth opens to counter with a witty remark, but whatever I was thinking evaporates into air when Emmett's hand lands on the back of my calf. Slowly, he runs the rough pad of his thumb along the inside of my leg, and up my thigh until he's almost touching my shorts.

I don't move. I don't even breathe. Too stunned to do anything. Emmett has never touched me like this. Actually, no one has ever touched me like this.

His fingers run over my skin, leaving a tingling hot path behind that feels so intense I worry it will leave a permanent mark. Even worse, I want it to. I want him to mark me, so I can hold on to the moment forever, so I never forget what this feels like.

His hand inches up painfully slow. His thumb is now brushing against my shorts, sending a shiver down my spine.

Suddenly, he pulls away, leaving my skin cold and wanting more. I don't even realize I'm making a disapproving sound until Emmett chuckles. *Asshole.*

Turning my face, I bury it into the soft comforter, thankful that I don't have any makeup on. He might have seen my puffy eyes from my angry tears, but at least I don't have black streaks running down my cheeks.

With my face hidden, I listen to Emmett move around the room. He opens then closes a door, maybe the walk-in closet. Then he gets something from a drawer near the bed. The sound of clothes being taken off has my stomach in knots.

Does he think I'm going to sleep with him?

The bed dips with Emmett's weight as he climbs onto it. "Wait! What are you doing?" I wiggle away from him, but he quickly places his hand between my shoulder blades and holds me down.

"Relax," he says. As if that was so easy. His hand moves to my wrists, where he does something to the handcuffs. The metal bites into my skin, causing me to hiss out in pain. Then, suddenly, the right cuff pops open, and my wrist is free.

Emmett rubs the part where the metal was pinching my skin before placing my arm by my side. My shoulder is stiff, making the movement feel both painful and relieving. A moment later, my other wrist is free, and Emmett gives it the same treatment.

"You've had a long night, so I'm going to let you go to sleep now, but tomorrow, I'm going to strip you bare and fuck you senseless."

"The hell you will!" I sit up, all exhaustion forgotten in a heartbeat. "You can't just say shit like that after not talking to me for two years!" I spin around to face him, realizing he is not wearing anything besides a pair of boxers.

"You are my wife. Why shouldn't I fuck you?"

"Because I don't want you."

"Are you sure about that? I remember you throwing yourself at me at—"

I don't let him finish. "I wanted you two years ago! I was ready then."

"No, you were not. You were a child, molded into the image of a perfect wife by your parents. You were groomed for so long you didn't even know how to be normal. I didn't want a brainwashed wife. Not then, and not now."

"Then what do you want?"

"A queen."

Chapter Four
Gwen

queen? What the hell is that supposed to mean? That's the big question running through my mind as I sit on Emmett's king-sized bed while he waits for me to respond.

Problem is, I don't know what to say. His bare torso is not helping to keep my thoughts organized at all. For being in his late thirties, his body is remarkably toned. My eyes are drawn to the intricate tattoos painted across his taut skin. The artist must have drawn on him directly; the artwork is moving so perfectly with the shape of his physique.

There is a large skull on the center of his chest with a snake swirling around it and coming out of one of the eye sockets. Around it are wilted roses that are so detailed and realistic-looking that I want to run my fingers over them just to see what it feels like.

Emmett clears his throat and folds his arms over his chest.

Shit, what was the question again?

"I'm tired," I rasp out, flustered. "I want to go to sleep now." I get up from the bed to stand on my wobbly legs. "Where is the guest room?"

"You are sleeping here... with me... in *our* bed." I open my mouth to protest, but he is faster. "Trust me, it's not worth fighting about. You are not going to win. So save your energy and get comfortable."

"Fine!" I yell, throwing my hands up. "But I'm not sharing a blanket with you." I climb back into the bed and lie down on the edge farthest away from him.

This is probably the most childish thing I have done, but I couldn't care less. The truth is, it's not worth the fight. He is right about that. I know I'm not going to get past him, but I don't have to make it easy on him either. Just because he's decided he wants me now doesn't mean I still do.

Emmett sprawls out on his side of the bed, pulls the comforter up to his chest, and flips off the light. "Suit yourself, but this is the only one I have, I'm afraid."

Sure it is. I roll my eyes in the dark. He lives in a fucking mansion with only one blanket.

Turning onto my side, I curl up, pulling my legs to my chest in an effort to stay warm. It's not particularly cold in here, but lying still, on top of being exhausted, makes it difficult to get comfortable.

At least I won't have to worry about falling asleep, which I'm not planning on doing. I need to stay up, so I can leave before he wakes up.

For a long time, I remain in this position, forcing myself to breathe evenly to make it sound like I'm asleep. As time passes, it gets harder and harder to stay still and not shiver.

Did he turn up the air conditioner on purpose?

With a deep sigh, Emmett moves around beside me. He is not touching me anywhere, but I know he must be closer now from the way the mattress has dipped slightly. My own body wants to get closer, seeking out the warmth he would provide.

Just thinking about it has me shivering a little more. Exhaustion has made me weak, and I turn my body toward him out of instinct.

He is closer than I thought because I only move a few inches, and I'm close enough to feel his body heat.

I shouldn't, but I can't help myself. Moving the last couple of inches, I find myself pressed against his side. The heat of his body resonates through me, and I bite back a sigh.

Now that I'm warming up a little, my courage starts to build, and the exhaustion fades a bit. No matter what, I can't fall asleep here. I have to escape, find a way out.

The minutes tick by at a snail's pace, but Emmett's breathing finally evens out enough that I'm certain he is asleep. I have no idea where I'll go once I'm out of this room, but I'll figure that out later.

I shift against the silk sheets, like I'm rolling over in my sleep. My heart hammers against my ribs, the fear mounting deep in my gut.

What if he wakes up? What if I can't escape the room? The questions compile, and before I let myself wallow in the fear of what-ifs, I scoot closer to the edge of the bed.

I'm teetering, a breath of an inch away, when I finally do it. I roll out of bed and onto my feet, the mattress dipping ever so slightly as my weight shifts off it.

Once on my feet, I pause for a moment, my breath escaping me like I've run a mile. Emmett remains sleeping, his eyes closed; his gorgeous features appear almost serene.

Like a mouse trying to escape a mousetrap, I back away slowly, my steps small and quiet. Every few seconds, I look over my shoulder to check if he is still sleeping. By the time I make it to the door, the bed seems like it's a million miles away.

Air escapes my lungs as I take the brass knob into my hand and twist it. It's so quiet you could hear a pin drop. Peering over my shoulder one last time, I see Emmett sitting up in the bed, and the invisible rope around my neck tightens.

"Did you really think escaping me would be that easy?"

His voice sends a shiver down my spine, and instead of doing the sensible thing, I do the only thing that makes sense in my mind: I run.

I've barely made it over the threshold when I hear his heavy footfalls behind me. Each step forces me to move faster, my muscles burning as my fight or flight instincts kick in.

One step, two steps... I can do this. I panic at the last moment, trying to decide which way to turn in the dark hallway, giving me a poor sense of direction. It's that indecision that gets me caught.

The air swooshes out of my lungs as a thick, muscled arm wraps around my middle. A scream rips from my throat, and I'm hauled backward against what could be considered a wall of steel.

His hard muscles press against my backside as he lifts me up and carries me back to where I ran from. "There is no escaping me, Gwen. No fighting this. You're my wife, and it's time I made good on that transaction."

Every word rumbles out of his chest and into me as I struggle against his grasp, my legs flailing and my fists forced to my sides.

The bedroom gets closer, and the window to escape disappears. Once we step back into the room, he releases me and slams the door; the sound echoes through the space, rattling my insides.

Chest rising, he growls, "Strip."

I lift my chin, wanting to defy him, all while knowing I'll end up doing it anyway.

"And what if I don't want to..." I'm not sure how I get the words past my lips without sounding weak, but somehow, I manage.

Emmett lurches forward, his fingers grasping the front of my shirt, and he pulls the fabric tightly. The cotton rips at my shoulder from the force, and cool air kisses my skin.

This man might be my husband, but he's not the same man who showed disinterest in me two years ago.

"Take off your clothes, or I'll take them off for you, and believe me,"–his hot breath fans against my cheeks–"you don't want me to be the one to do it. I'm not in the mood for pleasantries. I want you naked, my willing wife, and your pussy ready for me to use."

Chapter Five
Gwen

A tremble works its way down my spine. Does he have to be so vulgar? I swallow my fear, refusing to show him how terrified he truly makes me.

"Let me do it," I say, trying my best to keep my voice sound strong. He merely nods and steps back. I can tell the effort it takes for him to allow me to do this myself. He says he's not patient, but he's clearly trying for me. I slowly pull the shirt off and over my head.

My nipples harden the moment the cold air kisses my skin, but I pretend that I'm not affected by the temperature or him. I look up and toss the shirt onto the floor at his feet. Emmett licks his lips. His gaze darkens, burning a path across my skin as he follows the movement of my fingers when I shove them into the waistband of my shorts.

"Has my wife let another man touch her before?" His tone is icy cold, and I sink my teeth into my bottom lip as I push down my pajama shorts.

I could lie and tell him *yes*, or I could tell him the truth. "Yes, more than once." The lie rolls off my tongue fluidly. "I've been on many dates."

Emmett tips his head back and barks out a laugh that's dark and sinister. "I'm going to give you the opportunity to change your answer since I already know you're lying." My mouth goes dry, but I somehow hold myself together.

"I'm not a virgin. If that's what you are asking," I quip.

Taking a step forward, he reaches out, and his knuckles gently caress the underside of my breast.

"You're a shit liar, and I know it because I've watched you every fucking day. I made certain that no one else touched what was mine."

Whatever my response might have been gets lodged in my throat when his knuckle brushes against my nipple. A gasp parts my lips at the onslaught of sensations that ripple through me from that one simple touch. I don't want to react, but how can I not?

His hand brushes against my chin, and he gently lifts it, forcing my eyes to meet his.

"I'm going to fuck you, my wife, and when your virgin pussy comes around my cock, the blood of your purity coating the skin, we'll both know that you were lying."

"And you'll discover I wasn't." I fire back, using the last of my strength. Like a man starved of air and life, he pounces on me, his lips find mine like a beacon of light, and he devours me from the inside out.

I can't protest or speak. All I can do is drown inside him. He makes quick work of his clothing, tossing the articles onto the floor as he guides us back toward the bed.

I should at least attempt to get away again, but the truth is, I don't want to run. I've wanted Emmett since before I became his wife.

Dipping his head, he kisses me with a tenderness I don't expect. His tongue presses against the seam of my lips, begging for entrance, and I open for him, letting him massage my tongue with his own. I've never French kissed anyone before, but the sparks of pleasure kissing brings makes me feel as though I've been missing out.

Emmett's hands are everywhere, in my hair, trailing along my body, and clawing at my panties. His body blankets mine once we're on the bed, and this sense of protection and security washes over me.

He breaks the kiss and sinks his fingers into the waistband of my panties. He's completely naked now, his straining cock between us.

"You make me so fucking hard, so fucking crazy. Two years I've waited for you. Every day that I've had to stay away has been torture, but you're here now, and I'm going to make you mine. Officially. Forever."

"What do you mean you've waited two years? As in... you didn't sleep with anyone else?"

"Would you be jealous if I had?" The bastard smirks.

"No," I lie again, my mother's lessons coming through. She always told me I should look the other way at my husband's cheating. Men of power can have any woman they want; all you have to do is satisfy him enough to stay married.

"We really need to work on your honesty, but that's going to have to wait," he chides and rips my panties down my legs. Without the protection of my underwear, I'm vulnerable.

Emmett eases my thighs apart and stares at my pussy.

"Nothing but a thin strip of hair..." he says, but I get the feeling he's talking more to himself. My mother always told me I needed to be ready for a man, whenever, and that no man wanted a woman who wasn't groomed.

His fingers dip between my legs, and I draw in a ragged breath when he spreads my pussy lips and moves his head between my thighs.

"What are you doing?" I croak. I know what he's doing, but I can't seem to imagine he would want to do it with me.

"I'm tasting my wife's virgin cunt," he growls against my folds without even looking up. Then he's on me; his mouth suctions against my clit while his tongue flicks the tiny bundle of nerves.

It takes everything inside me not to scream. The pleasure is unlike anything I've ever felt before.

With each lap of his tongue, I grow wetter, my arousal mounting while the impending orgasm claws at my insides.

"Oh... god..." I squeak, my muscles tightening.

"Come on my fucking tongue." His voice rumbles against my folds, and his fingers sink into my skin, holding me in place, with no possibility of escape. The pleasure builds and builds like a storm, and I'm blinded by it.

But right at the height, seconds before I'm about to catapult over the cliff's edge, he pulls away.

"Don't stop!" I beg, looking up at him through my lashes.

He smirks, the bastard actually smirks, and then he does something I never expected. He slaps my pussy. At first, I'm shocked. The slight sting of pain is jarring, but then he does it again, and I find myself gasping, the air getting caught in my lungs.

"You like me slapping your pussy, don't you?" All I can do is nod as he delivers another slap, this one right over my clit.

"Do it again," I beg, wanting the release that I know is coming.

Emmett leans forward, his nose brushes mine, and I can taste the desire he has for me in the air.

"You come when I say you come. Your pleasure is mine, Gwen. Your pain is mine. You're mine, and nothing, not even time, will fucking change that."

I feel his fingers at my entrance. I'm sopping wet now, ready to come at any second. He enters me slowly, and I know he can feel what I feel. A smile graces his lips.

"So tight and ready for my cock. Like you could make me believe that another man had you? Not when I sink a finger inside you and can feel how tight you are."

"I've been with others," I continue the charade.

"We'll see..." He grins and starts to pump his thick finger inside me while keeping pressure against my clit. "Come for me, liar... gush on my fingers."

The stimulation is enough to push me over the edge, my muscles quake, and I clench around his finger, abiding by his demand as I ride the wave of euphoria.

I'm trembling when I come back down. He's added a second finger, and a slight sting of pain fills my center as he stretches me.

He fucks me with his hand for a few more moments before pulling his hand away, bringing fingers to his mouth, and licking them clean of my arousal. The image is so erotic I find it hard to divert my eyes, but when he moves up the bed, his body covering mine, and I feel the brush of his cock on the inside of my thigh, I manage to direct my attention elsewhere.

He is huge, the head thick while his length's veiny and long. Fear tingles low in my belly. Perhaps I made a mistake by lying to him.

"Ready to eat your words, wife," he says a moment before his lips press against mine. He swallows my response with his kiss, and I fall deeper into the pleasure.

I'm vaguely aware of his cock pressing against my entrance, but I'm so caught up in his kiss, in the way he's touching me, hiking my thigh up over his hip, and holding me in place, that I don't register it's happening until he's slid all the way inside of me.

I gasp against his mouth. The pain clashes with the pleasure I felt previously, and it's like I'm being pulled apart. The burning in my core intensifies, and I want to tell him to stop, but I grit my teeth and stare deep into his eyes, feeling the tears welling there.

"You're a liar, wife, but that's okay. You're my little liar," he snarls and then sets a grueling pace, slamming into me at a punishing pace. The pain is searing, and I gasp every time he thrusts forward, but there is pleasure beneath the pain, and as his grunts and the slapping of flesh fill the air, another orgasm builds.

Beads of sweat slide down the side of Emmett's face. "Fuck, your pussy is so tight I don't know how much longer I'm going to last. I'm going to blow right inside your cunt, but first, you're going to come. You're going to strangle my cock with this virgin pussy."

"I don't know if I can," I whimper.

"You can, and you will," Emmett growls.

He slows his pace and snakes a hand between our bodies. He finds my clit and starts rubbing circles against it, igniting a fire deep in my abdomen that I've never felt before. Suddenly, I realize he was right. The pleasure builds and builds, and he starts to move a little faster.

My muscles tremble, and I bite my lip to stifle the scream that's threatening to escape.

"Come, come now!" Emmett orders, and like an obedient wife, I do. I explode, my entire core tightens, and my eyes drift closed as I pulsate around his cock.

"Oh, shit, fuuuuck..." he snarls, and then he's fucking me, his hands holding me in place with a bruising force. I'm so lost in him I have no idea what is up or down. I simply hold on to him, letting him drown in me like I drowned in him moments ago.

Then I feel it; he explodes. His warm cum fills me in spurts, coating my insides while he slows, his eyes squeezed shut and the muscles in his neck tight. He continues to come, so much so that I can feel the sticky liquid dripping out of me.

Sagging against me, he buries his face in the crook of my neck. We're both panting and sweating, and I know that he knows I was lying now. Still, I wait for him to rub it in my face.

Instead, he lifts his head, his gaze collides with mine, and he whispers, "You're mine now, forever and always, wife."

* * *

Thank You so much for reading Paper Ring!
For more J.L. Beck & C. Hallman books check out our website
www.bleedingheartromance.com

Witch's Revenge

By: R.K. Pierce

About Witch's Revenge

This is Merik, where the High Majesty's will is law, and women are little more than property.

We don't ask questions and we do as we're told, ever the obedient servants they want us to be.

My entire life, I've kept my head down and stayed in line. I've done what was asked of me, not eager to incur the wrath of the High Majesty.

Until now...

Now, I'm out for *revenge*.

Content note:

Reader discretion is advised. This story includes subjects such as violence, gore, mentions of sexual assault, mentions of abuse, murder, and graphic sexual content.

Relationship type: FF

Chapter One

August 23, 2050

The sound of a gunshot explodes through the commotion. My ears ring, and a body in the crowd crumples to the ground—*dead*.

No one dares move a muscle.

The Peace Officers pointing guns at us won't hesitate to shoot again.

Sickly yellow light from the setting sun casts long shadows over the officers' faces, contorting their features until they resemble what they really are: demons. It's no secret that 'peace' has nothing to do with their station. They're all cold-hearted, evil bastards who'll do anything to please the High Majesty.

The collar of my work dress clings to the back of my neck with sweat, and a bead of perspiration rolls down my temple. My stomach is growling after five hours of gardening and harvesting the limited herbs and vegetables left for the season. Every inch of me aches. All I want is to go back to our sleep quarters, shower, and rest, but we aren't going anywhere until everyone lines up and is silent.

This is the way, as it must be.

I lean forward slightly, my gaze falling between the cluster of gatherers to see the unmoving form on the ground. All I can make out is the black veil covering her face and the puddle of crimson slowly pooling around her abdomen. I don't yet know which of our house sisters won't be returning with us, but I'll find out soon enough.

I wish I felt anything more than a slight depression in my chest. Rage, hatred, contempt, sadness, *anything*. But for the most part, I'm numb.

From birth, I've been desensitized to the cruel, harsh conditions of our society. I've seen so much pain, torture, and death in my nineteen years that it doesn't faze me anymore. I'm hardened to the difficulties of my reality, as much as I wish they were different. All I can do is keep my head down, follow orders, and try to survive.

This is Merik. This is the will of the High Majesty.

This is the way, as it must be.

Thankfully, no one else moves. The leading Peace Officer swings his gun left and right, the barrel directed at each of us for a fraction of a second. He wears the same red coat all Peace Officers wear, a pointed, red hood covering most of his dark hair. The pale skin of his face is creased with wrinkles, but it doesn't matter what he looks like.

All the officers are the same. Nameless loyalists with a dangerous hive mind, only interested in one thing: pleasing their ruler.

My stomach pitches when the barrel of the gun points at me. As much as I try to reassure myself that I haven't done anything wrong, that doesn't ensure my safety.

Nothing ensures my safety.

"I told you bitches to shut the fuck up and get in line," he growls, his black eyes gleaming with malice. "I'll kill every fucking one of you and tell the High Majesty it was a pack of wild dogs. Now, *move*."

A sensation hooks behind my navel, and my feet move of their own accord, obeying the command. We line up, just as we do every morning, noon, and night. At nineteen, I'm the oldest harvester in our group—one year from aging into the breeder faction—so I lead our group to and from our daily activities. The rest follow me, oldest to youngest, with the thirteen-year-olds bringing up the rear.

A glance over my shoulder gives me the answer I've been dreading. There's an empty space between me and the next girl in line where another person should be. It dawns on me that the second eldest of our faction, Rebeka, is the one lying in a crumpled heap on the ground a few feet away.

She turned eighteen just last month, and now she will forever be eighteen.

"Stop wasting my time," one of the Peace Officers snarls. "Move."

Swallowing down any hint of emotion, I follow orders, keeping my head low so the dark fabric draped over my head masks my face. I march us back toward the tiny village we call home, a mile away on the other side of the crop fields. The crunch of our footsteps on the dirt is the only sound in the oppressive silence that strangles us.

The village consists of five large ranch-style houses, positioned perfectly around a circular clearing. They represent and house the female factions of our state: younglings, gatherers, breeders, homemakers, and elderly. In the middle of the clearing there is a platform with a single noose hanging from it, a constant reminder of what awaits any who disobey.

This is the way, as it must be.

After depositing our harvest into several wooden bins outside of the homemakers' house, we file into our own without a word. Peace Officers stand on either side of the door until we close it behind us, and all but one of them heads back to the men's mansion for the night.

One officer always stands guard, making sure no one leaves their house until morning when they come to collect us for breakfast.

We may be trapped in the house with no way out, but at least we're safe for the night.

We survived another day.

Chapter Two

O nce the officers are gone, I breathe a little sigh of relief and hurry to my room on the second floor. It's small, barely big enough for the two sets of wooden bunk beds that sit in opposing corners. A wardrobe for clothes is positioned at the end of each, and a threadbare rug covers most of the hardwood floor. There are a few decorations, mostly hand-made ones plastered on the walls, but it's not much.

I share the room with three other girls. Two are gatherers—they load into the back of a truck every morning and are driven miles away to collect things like firewood and drinking water—and the fourth is a thirteen-year-old harvester from my group. We may not be blood-related, but the three of them are the closest thing I have to sisters.

Only when I'm back in my room can I remove the black veil and strip out of the uncomfortable work dress I'm forced to wear. A wave of cool air washes over my hot skin, and I immediately crave a shower. I need to wash off the sweat and the memories of the day before I crawl into bed. Besides, the hot water will do my sore muscles good.

Gathering my pajamas, the standard issue gray pants and cotton shirt that all girls get when they age into our faction, I grab my towel and head down the hall to the nearest bathroom. There are four on this floor, eight total in the house, which is hardly enough to accommodate forty-eight—forty-*seven* now—girls, but we manage.

I hurry inside and close the door, exhaling a deep, tired sigh. Moments of solitude are few and far between in this world, and I cherish each and every one. For a moment, however brief, I am alone.

I am not the collective.

I am not a worker or property.

I'm just *Torri*.

"About time," a voice says behind me. Goosebumps prickle over my skin in a wave, and I stiffen.

Turning around slowly, I take in the person standing before me. She too is nineteen, but she ages out of the gatherer house in a couple of months. She's wrapped in nothing but a worn, frayed towel, her dry blonde curls spilling over her shoulders. Her gray eyes gleam when I look at her, dancing with secrets only she and I know.

"Keep your voice down, Lita," I whisper sharply, flipping the lock on the door. I test the handle anxiously to make sure it's locked before looking back at her.

She rolls her eyes. "I've told you I don't care who knows."

"And I've told you I won't let them hurt you."

I glare, my gaze boring into hers.

We go through this at least once a week or so, but I mean it when I say I won't let them hurt her. If that means calling things off and pretending like none of this ever happened to keep her safe, I'll do it, no matter how much it pains me.

"I know you won't." Her voice is low as she steps closer, and my heart rate kicks up speed, the way it does anytime she's near.

Lita is everything I never knew I wanted and everything I can't have. She is both my lifeline and my death sentence. She is a reminder of the dark world we're trapped in and my only ray of sunlight in the gloom.

She stops in front of me, and I exhale a shaky breath.

"Well, come on," she whispers, dropping her towel. "We don't have much time."

I immediately drink in her tanned skin and perfect curves, tracing her scars in my mind, mapping out every inch of her that I've memorized. My last shred of restraint snaps, and the next second my lips are on hers. My towel and pajamas drop to the floor as my hands eagerly roam over her skin.

She smells so fucking good, a mix of earth and flowers from the woods she works in all day. I've never seen them because I'm restricted to the vegetation fields, but she tells me how beautiful they are all the time. *Beautiful like her.*

"You stink," she whispers into my neck as I reach for the knobs in the shower and turn the water on.

"I guess you should wash me." I chuckle, dragging her under the spray of water with me and pinning her against the wall.

I kiss her like it's the last time, the same way I kiss her every time, because all of this could easily blow up in our faces. The only faction allowed to have sex are the breeders, and even they aren't allowed to sleep with other women.

What we have is dangerous, a flame that could combust and incinerate us at any second.

It's also addicting, and my favorite way to dance with fate.

I slide my hands over her hips, dragging her against me, and I swallow the little gasp that leaves her lips. Heat swells in my stomach, making the spray of water against my back feel cold, and I slip my fingers between her thighs.

"I want you, Torri," she whispers as I move my digits through her folds, teasing her clit before sinking two fingers inside her. My need to have her, feel her, *taste* her, blots out the rest of my thoughts, drowning my anxiety and fear. "I-I don't care. Let them know. What are they going to do to me?"

I press my mouth against hers to cut off her questions and pump my fingers into her. She's so tight and warm around my digits, her channel pulsing with every thrust, but it's not enough. I want to feel more of her, drink her in, drown in her.

"They'll kill you, and you know it," I say before dropping to my knees in front of her. I nudge her legs further apart and paint a lick over her seam.

My heart is racing, beating in my throat as the taste of her arousal blooms over my tongue. If anyone finds us like this, they'll kill us both. They'll make a spectacle out of us in the square and leave us dangling there for days as a reminder to never disobey the High Majesty.

But I can't stop.

Lita is the only thing in this entire world that makes me feel something. The numbness fades, replaced by a flutter in my chest and a warmth in my veins whenever she's near. When I touch her, jolts of electricity dance through my limbs.

The way I feel doesn't have a name. It doesn't exist in Merik, but I know it's real.

She comes with a whimper, clamping a hand over her mouth to keep quiet, and I kiss my way back up her body. When she reaches for the apex between my thighs, I brush her hand away.

"When are you going to let me touch you?" She pokes out her bottom lip, pouting, and reaches for her wash towel.

"One day," I say, even though I don't know the answer. I press my lips against hers in a quick kiss to reassure her.

Dark memories begin to bubble up, but I mentally skirt over them, stuffing them down deep where they belong. Just because a Peace Officer isn't *supposed* to do something, doesn't mean they always follow the rules.

And if they break the rules, they're never punished.

The violent memories of hands on me, touching me—violating me—is enough for me to tell Lita no. Even if she doesn't understand why, and probably never will because I won't tell her, she respects my decision and washes me instead, taking her time to scrub the day's work off my skin.

She kisses me one final time before slipping out of the bathroom alone and making her way to the opposite end of the hall. I wait, counting out a full minute before I follow after and hurry to my room.

When I lie down for the night and close my eyes, wishing with all my strength that things could be different, a sense of hopelessness settles over me as reality sets in.

This is the way, as it must be.

Chapter Three

September 2, 2050

My eyes are focused so intently on the bathroom door that I'm surprised my gaze hasn't bore a hole through the wood. I've been waiting for nearly half an hour, expecting Lita to slip in at any moment, but she hasn't shown. It's odd because her group got back hours before ours today.

She should have been here by now.

Did she fall asleep? *Is she avoiding me?*

I run through the same questions I've been asking myself over and over as I pace the tiny room, trying to figure out what's going on. Is this her way of telling me things are over between us?

My stomach sinks.

With her birthday quickly approaching—and inevitably the day she ages into the breeder faction—we've spent every chance we could together. Stolen moments in hallways, shared glances, sweet whispers.

When we're apart she consumes my thoughts, and when we're

together I drink in every second, begging the universe for more time with her.

But now... something feels off. *What's taking her so long?*

The reasonable part of me knows I should just shower and head to my room for the night. After all, we aren't supposed to be together, and investigating may raise a red flag to the other girls. It's best if I turn in and ask her tomorrow in the light of day why she didn't show.

However, the unreasonable part of me demands attention, curiosity burning through me like white-hot fire.

I chew the inside of my cheek, indecision mounting as I reach for the shower knobs. I wash myself quickly, the numbness spreading through my veins like a disease, and quickly dry off. I drag on my pajamas and wrap a worn towel around my long, dark hair, indecision tugging at my gut.

I should head back to my room and turn in for the night.

I definitely should *not* barrel down the hall to Lita's room and demand answers.

Swallowing hard, I slip out of the bathroom and stare down the long corridor, battling with my conflicting emotions. Every logical thought is overshadowed by a burning need radiating from my bones. A need for answers, something we're rarely given here in Merik.

If anyone finds out about us they'll kill us both...

And maybe that's a fate I'm willing to face because a life without Lita hardly seems like a life at all.

Mind made up, I hurry down the hall, passing my room without a backward glance and making my way to the other half of the house. It isn't against the rules to venture to each other's rooms, but I've consciously avoided Lita's room since we started... *whatever this is...* months ago.

Going there now feels wrong, and guilt prickles over my skin like a swarm of spiders.

I shouldn't be here, my intuition screams at me, but I press on until I'm planted outside the wooden door that's identical to my own; white and old with peeling paint and a few dings here and there. I lean closer, listening for voices, but the room beyond is silent.

My stomach turns as I lift my fist, my heart slamming in my chest. Trembling, I knock, the sound impossibly loud in the silent hallway.

A shaky breath escapes my lungs as I wait, the seconds dragging on for what feel like hours, until movement behind the door makes me freeze. Slowly, the doorknob turns, and the door cracks open. Just enough light from the hall spills in through the opening to make out the worried face of sixteen-year-old Sara.

"Yes?" she whispers, her eyes bouncing from me to the empty hall behind me. "What is it?"

I shift in place, put off by her unexpected behavior. Why the hell does she look so afraid?

"Is Lita in there?" I ask, keeping my voice low.

Immediately, the girl's brown eyes widen, and her throat bobs with a swallow. "No, she's not."

"What?" My chest seizes. If she's not in her room, where else could she be? It's nearing curfew; she'll be in trouble if she's not in her room soon.

This doesn't make sense.

Before I can ask anything else, the door starts to close, and I put a hand up to stop it. Sara's eyes widen.

"Where is she?" I fight to keep the desperation out of my voice. Every inch of me is on fire, boiling alive, and the only thing that will alleviate my suffering is knowing where Lita is. I need to know she's okay, that she's safe, that she didn't decide to break up with me without so much as a warning.

I need to see her more than I need my next breath.

"We don't ask questions," Sara reminds me in a nearly inaudible whisper. She tries to shove the door closed, but it doesn't budge against my hold.

"I know but..." Emotion clogs my throat. I can hardly believe I'm behaving this way. All my life I've fallen in line, obeyed orders, kept my head down to stay alive. And now... now I'm willing to risk it all for answers. "I just need to talk to her. *Please.*" My voice finally cracks.

After a painful moment of silence, the door swings open slowly.

"Hurry," Sara whispers harshly, urging me inside. The door snaps closed quickly behind me, and I step to the middle of the room. It's nearly identical to mine.

Two curious pairs of eyes glare at me from the bunk beds, but the room is only illuminated by a candle in the corner so I can't make out their faces.

My eyes fall to the two empty bunks. One is untidy, like Sara had just crawled out of it to come answer the door. The other is perfectly made and undisturbed.

Lita...

"Where is she?" I repeat, fighting past the lump in my throat.

It isn't time for her to age out of our faction. We've been carefully counting down the days together until she transfers to the breeder house. We still have time.

We still have time.

"We don't know," Sara answers softly, her eyes bouncing to the other girls in the room. "The High Majesty requested to see her after we finished gathering for the day. Her and another girl from downstairs."

"For what?" I gasp, fighting to keep my voice level. I know she doesn't have answers. We aren't allowed to ask questions, and the information we *are* given is often limited. We know what the Peace Officers deem necessary, which isn't much. "Did they say anything?"

Sara shakes her head, and I notice for the first time that she's trembling. "Nothing."

I run a hand over my face as the corners of my eyes prickle, my fingers lingering on my lips as I try to wrap my mind around Lita's absence.

Is she coming back? Is she aging out early? *Is she safe?*

"I don't understand," I say, my voice barely a whisper.

Sara shakes her head. "We don't either, but we're... *afraid.* What if they've changed the rules without telling us? What if they plan to take more of us?"

Knots twist my stomach as I meet her troubled gaze. Her fear radiates through the room until I feel it too, sinking through me, sitting heavy in my stomach, but I'm not afraid of aging out early. I've been mentally preparing my whole life for whatever they plan to do to us—to *me*—but that all pales in comparison to my fear of losing Lita.

"Torri," Sara says, snapping me out of my thoughts. I bite the inside of my cheek to keep myself from crying as she watches me, but my emotions are mounting, making it harder and harder to fight back the tears. "I'm sorry. Truly."

The apology hits like a blow to my chest, and I take a step back. Why else would Sara apologize so sincerely unless she knew what was going on between Lita and I? Unless she understood the depth of my distress?

I can't bring myself to ask. I've already risked too much by coming here and asking questions. The only thing I want to do right now is disappear, to fade into the darkness and never come out. I want to run, to scream, to cry. I want to burst into the breeder house and find her, if only to see her one last time.

All I can manage is a feeble "thanks" before I turn and head for the door, tears blinding me as I go back to my room.

Chapter Four

September 9, 2050

Seven. Days.

It's been seven days since Lita was summoned by the High Majesty, and nothing has been right since.

As each day passes, any hope I had of her returning slowly dies, smothered by more intense emotions and crushing disappointment. A throbbing pain in my chest beats in time with my heart, bleeding through my thoughts, hitting me in random waves that I can't escape.

I've asked girls around the house, trying not to raise suspicions, hoping one of them may have information about what happened to Lita and the other girl. No one wants to talk about it, not that I can blame them.

We're discouraged from asking questions. If it's important, the Peace Officers will notify us, and obviously the absence of two house members isn't enough for them to bat an eye at.

This is the way, as it must be.

Still, knowing things are as they must be, I can't help but question. Curiosity has sunk into my bones, throwing my imagination into overdrive. I wonder. I worry. I *think*, and I keep my thoughts to myself.

Death would be the kindest punishment if Peace Officers found out what I was debating, the thoughts and desires occupying my mind as I gathered herbs and spices in the field. They're dangerous, infectious ideas that slowly consume me, burning through my veins like a disease, and once they take hold, I can't shake them no matter how hard I try.

I spend hours contemplating how difficult it would be to sneak past the Peace Officers...

How easily Lita and I could run into the forest...

How quickly we could escape...

Yet, for all my daydreaming, I can't summon the courage to act on it. Even if I manage to get past the guards and sneak into the breeder house, I have no way of knowing if Lita's there. I'm guessing at this point, clinging to a sliver of hope that she's even still alive.

Until I know for sure, I can't defy orders. I must stay and obey, just like I've always done, until I know she's safe.

This is the way, as it must be.

After another long day in the field, I stare up at the dark ceiling of my room, my thoughts refusing to be tamed. My mind wanders, images of Lita tangling together with my desire to escape this place until I'm a mess of confliction once again.

I sigh deeply, my jaw clenching.

How much unrest can one person tolerate before they lose their ability to comply? Before they *snap*? I fear I'm well on my way to finding out.

Forcing my eyes closed, I take a few deep breaths, trying to slow my racing pulse. Minutes drag by, but eventually I settle down, slowly slipping into unconsciousness.

Then a frantic knock at the door has my eyes flying open again.

I shoot up in bed, heart leaping straight into my throat, and I look frantically across the room. Elaine—my youngest roommate—is sitting up too, staring at me nervously.

What is happening?

Another frantic knock at the door has fear shooting through me.

"Torri," a voice calls through the door. My muscles tense at the sound of my name.

I scramble off the top bunk, tripping across the room to the door despite the protests from the girls behind me. I pop the door open a couple of inches, my eyes falling to the girl standing in the hall, and my insides freeze when our eyes meet.

It's Sara.

"What is it?" The words fly out of my mouth before I can stop them. "What's wrong?"

"It's Lita," she whispers, her bottom lip wobbling. "She's back but..."

I don't hear the rest of her words as my muscles move automatically, stepping into the hall and following her toward their room. A few doors are cracked open as we pass, curious eyes watching as we hurry by, but I'm not paying them any attention. My entire focus is on seeing Lita, my fingers tingling with anticipation.

"Is she okay?" I ask, my gaze sliding over to Sara. For a moment, she says nothing, and my steps slow. "Sara?"

She stops abruptly, and I follow suit, standing in the middle of the hall. Worry contorts her features, her brows furrowed and lips pressed firmly together.

"I-I didn't ask questions," she starts, sounding uncertain. "She just asked me to come get you, but Torri... She's not well."

Nausea turns my stomach, and I swallow down the bile burning the back of my throat. "What do you mean? Is she hurt?"

The way Sara's features contort even more gives me my answer, and I'm sprinting before I can stop myself, my eyes set directly on Lita's room. My legs won't move fast enough, but I still beat Sara by several seconds. I grab the handle and shove open the door.

My eyes immediately go to Lita's bottom bunk, and my knees almost give out when I see her sitting there. Only, she doesn't look like she did the last way I saw her.

Her normally perfect hair is a tangled mess, and dirt smears cover her skin. There are dark bags under her eyes, making her look exhausted and much older than her nineteen years. She's wearing a thin, lacy gown much different from the clothes the harvesters wear.

"What happened?" I mutter, stepping closer to her. She flinches at the movement, but her expression immediately softens as I kneel before her, carefully inspecting every inch of her exposed skin.

A sickening realization nearly makes my dinner reappear, and I fight back the urge to vomit all over myself. They aren't dirt streaks on her skin.

They're bruises.

Chapter Five

Cold numbness sweeps through me as I drag my eyes up to meet Lita's gaze. There are tears in her eyes, and it's all I can do to keep from crying myself.

"What happened to you?" I ask, my voice barely audible over the blood pounding in my ears.

Disbelief swirls with relief to create a vicious tangle of emotions. I want to throw my arms around her and hold her close, to never let her go. But at the same time, I don't want to touch her. I don't want to hurt her. The way she flinched when I got close was like a sucker punch to the gut, and the last thing I want is to make her feel unsafe.

Lita opens her mouth to respond, but a sob racks her chest. She claps a hand over her lips to cut off the sound, and I shoot a daring look over my shoulder. It's past curfew. We should all be in bed by now, but I want a few moments alone with her. If only for answers; I need everyone to leave.

Maybe then she'll be able to tell me what happened.

Maybe...

"Sara," I say, and my voice cracks. I can't even get the words out.

The silent plea in my eyes must be enough though because Sara motions for the other girls to follow her, and they file out into the hall. The door closes behind them with a soft click, and a flutter of whispers erupts in the hall.

I don't know if we have a few seconds or a few minutes alone, but I plan to make them count.

Looking back at Lita, I dare to cup her chin in my hand, the touch of her skin against mine setting my flesh on fire. It feels so fucking good to be near her again, but I never imagined it like this.

"You have to tell me what happened," I demand, keeping my voice low. I brush my thumb over her cheek, hating the way a muscle in her jaw ticks at the motion. "What did they do to you?"

She opens her mouth, and her lip wobbles. She's trying hard to keep it together, and it doesn't help when I bring my other hand to her face, gently holding her head between my palms.

"Lita," I say, keeping my voice as gentle as possible despite the anger bubbling beneath my skin. "You can tell me."

Finally, slowly, she speaks. Her words are hardly more than a whisper.

"The High Majesty..." She takes a deep, steadying breath. "He's looking for a new wife and asked the Peace Officers to bring him girls who haven't been bred. He... he used us, *forced* us..." Her voice trails off as panic flashes behind her eyes.

I can't imagine the things she's seen, *felt*.

I don't want to think about the things that vile creature did to her before sending her back looking like... this.

My heart sinks like an anchor, and I fight to keep my expression emotionless. Losing my temper isn't going to help anything right now, and I need answers.

And Lita needs me...

"You're safe now," I say, leaning forward to press my forehead against hers. "You're safe."

I hardly believe the lie as it leaves my lips.

Truthfully, none of us are safe. We never have been, and we never will be.

The High Majesty may have sent Lita back in one piece, but in just over a month, she'll be sent to the breeder house. There they'll do whatever they want to her, however they want, until she conceives a child...

No, we are not safe from the cruel men who rule this world. They will never see us as anything other than inferior. They will never see us as people, as *equals*, only property that they can order around, rape, and kill.

Our only chance at safety is freedom.

The thought resonates so clearly in my mind that it sends a chill vibrating down my back. It's what I've been thinking for the past week, the poisonous thought that'll get me killed or worse. What I want more than anything is to escape from Merik with Lita and to run far, far away.

We could go anywhere, do anything... but no one has ever escaped the High Majesty's rule.

Some have tried, and they've been killed in the square to show everyone what awaits them should they transgress.

Obedience or suffering. Those have always been our options.

But now, as the truth of our reality truly sinks in, I find myself longing more than ever to leave. Consequences be damned; this is no way for anyone to live.

I have to get Lita out of this place. I have to try.

Even if I die trying.

"Torri." Lita's voice drags me out of my daydream, and I blink at her. A fresh tear slips down her cheek and falls onto the silk gown clinging to her skin, sparking a bone-deep well of rage I've been harboring for a while, possibly forever.

"They're going to pay," I say through clenched teeth, even though I'm not really sure what I'm saying.

I'm just a gatherer; I'm no match for a single Peace Officer, much less an army of them, but that doesn't matter. What matters is that I cling to the rage brewing in my blood, harnessing it and channeling it to exact my revenge. Its power gives me confidence I otherwise wouldn't have, and my limbs move automatically as though they've made the decision for me.

I stand, not missing the way Lita's eyes widen in horror.

"Every one of them will pay." My voice vibrates with unholy anger, and I clench my fists. "Every. Last. One."

This is the way, as it must be.

Chapter Six

"Get your things."

I know the words are insane even as they pass my lips, but I can't find it in me to care. Or rather, I do care, entirely too much for us to spend another second in this house.

My eyes roam over the bruises on Lita's skin again, twisted thoughts of what she had to endure blooming to life in my mind. I taste bile, but the urge to succumb to nausea is overshadowed by an all-consuming feeling threatening to burn me from the inside out.

Rage.

"W-what do you mean?" Her voice shakes, and she doesn't move. She just stares at me like I've just asked her to do something crazy... like walk out in front of a firing squad. Maybe I have.

But the intuition urging me on, coupled with the white-hot fury pounding through my veins, doesn't give me an option. Something is screaming for me to go, to run. I can't describe it other than an invisible power forcing my movements, directing me even as my brain threatens to shut down.

If we stall, we may miss our chance.

We have to go.

Our best chance to escape is *now*, in the dead of night. A single guard stands watch outside each house; normally, there are many more guards and watchful eyes looking after us. If we can sneak past them, we can make a run for the woods. I'm too angry to work out an actual plan, moving on instinct rather than logic.

I'll fight if I have to. I'll do whatever it takes.

Even if I get killed in the process, it'll be the chance Lita needs to escape. I won't let her endure any more pain.

I've never considered myself a martyr—I've always followed orders and done my best to slip under the radar—but seeing Lita battered and bruised at the hands of the High Majesty... it's the final straw that breaks my resolve to bend to their orders.

I won't be complacent in our mistreatment any longer.

"Grab what you can carry," I urge, not bothering to keep my voice down.

The girls in the hall will find out what we're up to sooner or later. If they decide to follow us, that's their choice. There's a very real chance that leaving the gatherer house is a death sentence, but it pales in comparison to what awaits us if we stay.

Still, knowing our chances of escape are slim to none, the power dancing through my limbs forbids me to stay put. I've never had such a compulsion to trust my gut, but this feels too powerful to ignore. Like my body knows something I don't, and it's trying to warn me, guide me.

I reach for Lita's hand and drag her off the bed and into my arms. "We're leaving."

"You're insane," she says, shaking her head. Clearly, she doesn't understand how serious I am. "You know we can't leave."

"But we *can*," I say, brushing a stray lock of blonde hair away from her face. What I wouldn't give to drag her into the bathroom and bathe her, to wash away the awful memories clinging to her skin, but there isn't time. "Just trust me."

She blinks up at me, her jaw slack as she tries to form an argument. I know everything she's thinking because I've thought it all before. The danger, the guards, the punishments... I've considered all of them, but right now none of that matters.

The ache in my bones grows, transforming into a throbbing pain that beats through my system in time with my heartbeat. If I don't get out of this tiny room soon, I'll combust. I don't know how I know, but I do.

"You know I trust you, Torri, but you've lost your mind." Lita's eyes glimmer with tears as she fists her hands in the front of my pajama shirt. "They'll kill us."

Something inside me snaps—probably my last shred of sanity—and a well of hot fire churns through my stomach. It hurts, aching all the way down to my bones, and I can feel it seeping into my muscles. Deep, ancient strength that I can hardly wrap my mind around.

Words can't describe it, but I know this feeling, this deep-seated fury, is going to be our ticket out of here.

"They will never lay another finger on you," I assure her. I'm sure it sounds like an empty promise, but I don't know what I can do to prove it to her right now. We're wasting precious seconds standing here while the rest of her roommates eavesdrop from the hallway, and we need to go. "I will protect you. We will escape, do you understand?"

She swallows hard, and her eyes twinkle as she stares up into mine.

I will save you. The words don't come, but she must sense them from the look in my eyes because she finally nods.

"Okay," is all she says before she slips out of my hold and jumps into action. She rips off the silk dress and fumbles for her pajamas, pulling them on just as the door to the room cracks open again.

Sara's curious gaze turns inquisitive as Lita grabs her work dress and stuffs it into the burlap satchel she uses to gather every morning. She tosses the strap over her head and ties her tangled hair into a knot at the nape of her neck.

"You aren't serious, are you?" Sara's voice is soft but critical as she slips into the room, followed closely by Lita's other two roommates.

I know she thinks we don't have a shot in hell at escaping. Walking out of the house is a death sentence, and everyone in the room knows it.

Everyone except me... and now Lita.

"If we escape we'll come back for the rest of you," I assure her.

An awkward beat of silence passes, and we all exchange glances.

"And if you can't?" Sara's eyes bounce between Lita and me. "If you die trying?"

I open my mouth to speak, but Lita answers instead. "If dying is our only chance to truly live, so be it."

Chapter Seven

My eyes snap to Lita, and I admire the fire that's returned to her. She's still afraid—she'd be crazy not to be—but dressed in her pajamas, she looks like herself. The strength and vibrance I love about her flickers like a dull flame, waiting to ignite, but it's there.

I'm glad she's on board with my psychotic plan, and I don't have to drag her out of the house kicking and screaming.

Sara's expression turns somber, but she knows better than to try and stop us. If we're caught, everyone will be questioned; it's best if she stays out of our way and pretends not to know what we're doing.

"Godspeed." She nods her head slightly before stepping out of our way.

We hurry down the hall to my room, and I grab the few things that I own: a small knife for cutting roots, a few feet of twine I swiped from some dead vegetable stalks, and my shoes. It isn't much, but it's all I have.

Then, we head downstairs.

Everyone must have gone back to sleep because all the bedroom doors are closed. There aren't any curious eyes trailing us as we creep down the stairs and tiptoe across the kitchen, which only heightens my anxiety. We're completely on our own, just the two of us against a handful of Peace Officers.

For the first time, my confidence wanes, but Lita squeezes my hand for reassurance. I meet her gaze, and the fire roaring through my veins burns hot enough to make me sweat.

I'm doing this for her...

Originally, my plan was to burst out the front door and run past the Peace Officer. Maybe if we caught him off guard and ran fast enough, he wouldn't catch up. However, I quickly decided that was a terrible plan and shifted my focus to the only other way out of the gatherer house: the windows.

There's a small window above the kitchen sink with a view of the youngling house that opens to let in a fresh breeze every now and again, and a slightly wider one in the common room with a clear shot of the distant woods. That one, on the other hand, is nailed shut.

Before I was born, someone tried to escape through the kitchen window, but they were caught and hanged in the square. No one's tried since. Fear keeps them obedient, so why would the Peace Officers do anything more than hammer a few nails into some wood to keep the gatherers trapped inside? They'd never expect anyone to try and pry the window open, knowing what consequences awaited.

I tiptoe across the floor and pause by the common room window, peering through the narrow slit between the curtains. A wide stretch of grass runs from the back of the gatherer house to the tall trees in the distance, bathed in the white glow of moonlight. It's beautiful, peaceful, with no signs of Peace Officers. Yet, nothing has ever made me more nervous.

"What's the plan?" Lita whispers in my ear. I wish I had an answer for her, but I don't.

Get to the trees. That's my plan.

Run for our lives, because that's exactly what we'll be doing. If anyone sees us, if we're followed, I'll stop to give her time to escape.

"Run," I finally tell her, straining my eyes for anything out of the ordinary. "No matter what, you run."

We exchange glances, and I can see the fear flickering in her eyes. I want to reassure her, to tell her everything is going to be okay, but I don't want to lie to her face. Besides, we don't have any more time to waste.

It's now or never.

Chase freedom or stay here, never truly living.

"Torri..." she says, but I'm already crouching in front of the window. I dig my knife out of my burlap sack and set to work, slowly wrenching the metal nails out of the wood. It's painstaking, and I nearly give up a time or two, but finally the last one pops free and clinks on the hardwood floor.

I carefully shove the window up, grimacing at the groan it makes. Cool air blooms in through the opening, licking against my skin. I'm pouring sweat, and adrenaline beats through my veins like a war drum.

"What if we don't make it?" Lita whispers.

I ignore her, not willing to entertain the thought. I'm staring at the trees in the distance, my heart slamming against my ribs as I try and fail to calculate how far of a run it is. It'll take us several minutes to get there, but it's doable.

We'll make it.

She'll make it.

"Torri..."

I finally look at Lita, and she's shaking.

Against my better judgement, which is screaming at me to hurry up and run, I pause and cup her face between my hands again, gently brushing my thumb over her cheek. I'm doing all of this for her, and she deserves my reassurance. She deserves to feel the power flooding my veins, the rage that spurs me on.

She deserves *everything*, and that's what I'm trying to give her by making sure she escapes.

"I won't let them hurt you ever again," I say, meaning every word down to my marrow. "You have my word. We're going to make it, but you have to promise me that you won't stop running. Do not slow down and do not look back."

She opens her mouth to argue, but I cut her off. "Do. Not. Look. Back. Do you understand?"

I can tell she wants to argue. Of course she does. But instead, she nods, and I dip to press my lips against hers. She gasps against my mouth before sinking into my kiss, our tongues tangling together eagerly like it's the very last time we'll have this chance.

For all I know, it could be.

I pull away gasping and stare into her eyes a final time, losing myself in their depth for a moment, before turning to the window. I crawl out carefully, my feet hitting the ground with a muffled thud, and I freeze. Caution prickles up my back as nerves hit me in full force, and I search the area again.

There's no movement. No sign of any Peace Officers.

I turn to look back at the window, staring up at Lita through the pane of glass. She could slam the window shut and go back to bed, forgetting about my insane plan. She could call for the guards and have me captured. She could walk away.

A million crazy thoughts spiral through my brain as I wait with bated breath for her to follow. It's agonizing, even though it only lasts a couple of seconds, wondering what will happen next. Finally, she crawls out the window and lands beside me.

I take a deep breath, letting the cool night air fill my lungs. Only several yards separate us from the woods. From there, we can flee into the mountains in the distance. After that? We'll figure it out. It's an insane plan but no more insane than staying here to be treated like property. To be owned, enslaved, trapped...

"On three," I whisper, excitement rattling through me as the seconds tick by.

Lita meets my gaze and mouths, "One."

The weight of what we're about to do lands on my shoulders, sparking doubt. We should have planned longer, worked out the exact details of what we're going to do when we're free. Because it's not just about escaping oppression but figuring out how to live in the wild. We have nowhere to go.

"Two," I whisper.

Who knows what awaits us in the forest, or even if we'll make it that far. This whole thing seems more and more irrational as the seconds tick by, and I'm beginning to wonder if I just put Lita in more danger than she would face in the breeder faction.

It's not too late to turn back...

"Three," I say before I can change my mind.

We take off running toward the trees, our footfalls uncomfortably loud in the silent night. For a moment, I think this is way too easy. No one has seen us or set off any alarms. We've made it out of the house without being spotted, and now we're home free.

Free...

The thought is fleeting, shattered by a booming voice yelling after us.

It's soon followed by the explosion of a gunshot.

Chapter Eight

S*hit.*

Terror slices through me as another shot is fired, the bullet whizzing past us and landing in the dirt.

"Run, Lita!" I demand between breaths. I half-expect her to slow or look back, but she follows my orders and keeps sprinting toward the trees. Her blonde hair falls out of its bun and flies along behind her as she goes.

Logic tells me to keep running after her, to head for the trees where it'll be easier to hide, but the unbeatable intuition forcing my movements urges me to slow, to stop. My heart is racing so fast; I'm worried it'll beat straight out of my chest, but I turn on the spot to face the approaching Peace Officer anyway.

If I must die, at least Lita will be safe...

"On the ground," the Peace Officer demands, aiming his rifle at my chest. He marches forward, eliminating the space between us. "Get on the ground or I'll shoot." His voice is loud, echoing over the clearing, and I know it won't be long before the other Officers come running.

"No." The voice that escapes my lips doesn't sound like my own.

I hardly feel in control of my body as the Peace Officer gets closer, like I'm watching through someone else's eyes as everything unfolds. I can no longer fight against the urges trying to control my movements, so I give up. I relinquish control and let the powerful force take hold.

The Peace Officer pauses and aims his gun directly at me before pulling the trigger. I suck in a sharp breath and close my eyes, bracing for the searing pain of impact, but it never comes. Another shot erupts, but no pain follows.

Confused, I pry an eye open. The Officer is staring at me with just as much bewilderment as I feel, and my gaze drops to the ground in front of me. There, nestled in the grass at my feet, are two bullets.

What the...

The thought evaporates when the Officer runs straight for me, snarling as he swings the butt of his gun at my face. Unlike the bullets, this blow lands, white-hot pain lancing through my head as I crumple to the ground. He's on top of me a second later with his hands around my throat.

"You should have listened, you stupid bitch," he growls, saliva spraying from his crooked lips and landing on my face. I fight the urge to gag. "Now, you're gonna pay."

Panic lights my body up as I claw at his skin, digging my nails into his hands and wrists. I draw blood, the crimson liquid dribbling over his skin before soaking into my shirt, and he squeezes my throat tighter.

"I'm going to fucking kill you and then have my way with your dead, rotting corpse," he spits.

The edges of my vision fade to black as I slowly lose consciousness, kicking and bucking against the large man with the little strength I have left. My breaths slow, along with my heartbeat as his fingers wind even tighter around my throat.

The only thing I can think of is Lita and how she'll finally be safe. We might not be together the way I imagined, but I did what I set out to do...

A loud *thud* is followed by a string of garbled curses, and the hands around my neck release their hold. I gasp for breath, choking down air as the weight on top of me disappears, and I blink hard to focus my hazy vision.

A few feet away stands Lita, a rifle clutched in her trembling hands. The Peace Officer is cradling the bleeding side of his head with a hand as he lurches for her.

"No!" I choke, scrambling to my feet.

Lita fumbles with the gun, trying to aim at the Peace Officer, but it doesn't go off when she pulls the trigger. She tries again, frantically backing away as he lumbers closer, and it's all I can do to stand without stumbling.

He manages to grab the gun, wrenching it from her hands before raising a giant boot and kicking her to the ground. She cries out as she hits the earth, and my stomach drops.

No, no, no. Why didn't she run like I told her to? Why did she come back?

The sound of scrambling footsteps follows, and I know the rest of the Peace Officers from the village are on their way.

Shit.

"Two for the price of one," the Peace Officer chuckles, directing the barrel of the gun between Lita's eyes as she whimpers on the ground. "Too easy."

The safety on the gun clicks off, and the Peace Officer's finger finds the trigger. Once again my vision goes red, the invisible force from before surging through my limbs and tearing a scream from my lips. Unable to fight it again, I relinquish control of my body to the power guiding me. It consumes me.

My hands raise and come together, my fingers forming a diamond shape. Unfamiliar words fall from my lips, an ancient incantation that I've never heard before, but clearly I know them deep in my soul.

Bright white light explodes from my fingertips, flickering and sparking before shooting toward the Peace Officer like an arrow. It slams into him with such force that he stumbles and falls to the ground, his robes sparking with a flame where the light hit. He screams and rolls on the ground in an attempt to smother the fire, but it only seems to grow bigger until it consumes him completely.

A gunshot goes off behind me, the bullet landing nearby in the grass. I tear my gaze away from the burning Peace Officer, whose screams become more garbled and indistinct by the second, to find four more officers standing shoulder to shoulder a few feet away. The barrels of their guns are all aimed at me.

"You're a w-witch," one of them stammers, visibly clutching his gun tighter like it will save him.

I smirk, raising a hand as more white light sparks to life from my fingertips.

"Correct," I say, my voice once again not sounding like my own. "But I won't be the one to burn."

Chapter Nine

All at once, the Peace Officers fire, shooting round after round until they run out of ammo. Every bullet stops just short of me and falls to the ground, creating a modest pile of spent ammunition at my feet.

I wait, patiently biding my time, watching as their faces contort in horror. Finally, when the clearing falls silent again, I chuckle.

"My turn."

Once again trusting my intuition, I raise my hand and point to one of the Peace Officers. A jet of white light bursts from the end of my finger, racing toward him and wrapping around his throat like a whip. A pitiful whimper escapes his lips as the magical glowing lasso tightens around his neck.

Rage hooks in my gut, fueling my power, and the light grows brighter. He grabs onto it, screaming when the light blisters his bare skin, and tries hopelessly to pull free. His attempts are in vain, and the light begins to splinter, tendrils stuffing into his mouth, down his throat. They light him up from the inside, making his skin glow an unsettling shade of red.

The others stare in horror, backpedaling as fast as they can, giving the entrapped Peace Officer a wide berth.

They're afraid, as they should be.

I smirk and kick up the power even more, the white-hot whip burning so bright it makes my eyes ache to look at it. Everyone else shields their eyes as the Peace Officer's skin begins to bubble and boil as he's cooked from the inside. A minute later, I recall the magic, and he falls to the ground, a smoking hunk of charred flesh.

For a moment, no one dares to move. The three other Peace Officers watch in horror, trying to decide what their best option is. Should they run? Fight?

I can't help but revel in their fear, letting it stoke the rage burning within me into an uncontrollable inferno.

Every one of them will pay.

Every. Single. One.

The Peace Officer on the right turns and runs, but he isn't fast enough. My magic whips across the clearing, seizing him by the ankle and dragging him slowly while he struggles to get free. The light burns his flesh, searing through the muscle, down to the bone. After a sickening crackle, the foot is severed from his limb, and it falls limply to the ground.

The Peace Officer shrieks in horror, and the other two run in the opposite direction.

"Going somewhere?" I ask, my voice somehow carrying despite not being very loud.

More magical whips lash out, grabbing the officers by their throats. They slam backward onto the ground with the wind knocked out of them, and I stride over casually. My previous haste is gone, replaced by a deep desire to draw out their pain.

I want them to suffer.

I want them to regret every second of their miserable lives.

I want them to know the fear the women in Merik feel every single day, the pain they've endured at the hands of Peace Officers like them.

They're crying, begging for their lives, but their pleas fall on deaf ears. Nothing they can say will save them.

"P-please," one mumbles as my white light branches out and snakes over his body, burning blistering trails wherever it touches. His robes catch fire, the blaze catching quickly as he's unable to roll around to put them out.

"Please what? Have mercy?" I laugh, the maniacal sound twisted and distorted. My eyes shift to the other officer who's fighting to free himself, desperately trying to undo the magical rope around his throat despite it burning the flesh off his fingers. "The way you've shown us such mercy, is that right?"

"P-Please, let us—" The magic squeezes their throats, slicing through their flesh. It cuts through the muscle and bone, decapitating them both. Their heads loll to the side, their unseeing eyes staring blankly up at the star-flecked sky.

Much better.

My eyes bounce back to the last breathing Peace Officer who's frantically crawling around the corner of the gatherer house, almost out of sight.

For a moment, I think about letting him go. After all, Lita and I are perfectly free to escape. We can run into the forest and be long gone by the time he raises the alarm and notifies any other officers.

But he'll still be able to alert them.

I'll buy us much more time if all the loose ends are properly tied up and disposed of.

Mind settled, I march after him, grinning when his babbled pleas hit my ears.

"Please, please don't kill me," he says.

I shove him over with my foot, and he lands flat on his back, bringing his hands together in a mock-prayer motion.

"Please, I'll do anything. *Anything*," he sputters, tears leaking down his face.

"Anything?" I ask, crouching beside him and staring into his dark beady eyes. "Like defy your precious High Majesty? Stand up for what's right and not just what benefits your self-centered ass?"

He nods frantically. "Yes, yes. I'll do whatever you say."

My brows furrow together, my anger ticking up another notch. "You should have done that a long time ago."

I hold out a hand above him and he wails, begging me not to hurt him. The ground around him rumbles as deep roots stir to life, breaking through the top layer of soil and wrapping viciously around the Peace Officer. He thrashes against their hold, but the roots only grow stronger, wrapping around him until he's suffocating beneath their strength.

"May no one ever find you or care to search for you." I chuckle as the roots begin to drag him under the dirt.

This is the way, as it must be.

Seconds later, his screams are silenced by the dirt folding in on top of him. He's gone, with nothing left of him but a severed foot somewhere behind us.

Satisfied, I stand, and the power surging through me finally dissipates. Once again, I'm in control of my extremities, unbothered by intense impulses. I'm no longer the vengeance-bent witch from moments ago. I'm just *me*.

Lita must think I'm a monster.

My chest clenches at the thought of her, and I look up expecting her to be long gone. After all, I just murdered five Peace Officers in a couple of minutes. I'm obviously dangerous. Why would she hang around?

To my surprise, however, she's there. Her eyes are wide with uncertainty, and I slowly make my way over, not wanting to scare her further.

"Lita," I say gently, stopping short when she takes a half-step back. "Lita, it's okay. I'm not going to hurt you."

"How did you—" Her eyes move past me to the corpses lying on the ground. "What the hell was that, Torri? When were you going to tell me you were some kind of psycho witch with powers?"

"No, I... Lita, I don't even know what just happened," I attempt to explain the chaotic thoughts racing in my mind. "But they hurt you... I couldn't let them get away with it. As for the light, I have no idea. I'm just as surprised as you are."

She glares at me in disbelief.

"I'm *serious.*" I don't know how I can possibly make her understand. Besides, we shouldn't be standing here arguing; we should be running. Just because a couple of Peace Officers are dead doesn't mean we're any safer. "We can't stay here Lita. We have to go."

Another moment of hesitation. Her conflicting emotions are evident on her face, and I think she may change her mind. Would she really want to go on the run with a monster like me?

Chapter Ten

It feels like we waste countless minutes staring at one another in the silence, even though I'm sure it's only seconds. I can feel the weight of curious gazes on me from the darkened windows nearby, but I don't care.

Let them see the destruction I've caused.

Let them know what they're capable of.

They may not have crazy witch powers—or maybe they do—but we are not helpless animals like the Peace Officers would have us believe. We are so much more, and we're capable of great things. All we need is to trust ourselves.

Trust in our power.

"Torri, I..." Lita's voice trails off, and my gut twists with unease. Is she going to change her mind? Will she want anything to do with me after what I just did? "You're right."

"I am?" I gasp with relief, before clearing my throat. "I mean, of course I am."

"We need to go. *Now.*" She glances over my shoulder at the gatherer house, probably looking for wandering eyes. Walking past me, she crouches to grab two of the officers' rifles and tosses one to me. "They're out of ammo, but these may come in handy."

They definitely will, especially if we're coming back for the rest of the girls like I promised. Not tonight—we're not prepared enough to take all forty-five of the harvesters with us—but soon.

"Come on." I jerk my head toward the forest and we run, sprinting like our lives depend on it.

We don't stop at the treeline, instead we weave between giant tree trunks and maneuver through the underbrush for nearly an hour before we stop. We're exhausted and pouring sweat, but the relief of freedom outweighs everything else.

We're free.

Of course, there's a chance they'll send Peace Officers after us. They'll want retribution. They'll want to make a spectacle out of us, because if everyone believes they can be free, who will be left to keep their state running?

Who will feed them? Nurture them? Breed for them?

We retreat into a small cave hidden perfectly at the base of the mountains, elated to find shelter for the night. It's small and cozy, just wide enough for Lita and I to curl up together, but it's perfect otherwise.

I use her satchel as a pillow, and she settles into the crook of my arm with her head on my chest.

For what feels like the first time in my entire life, I relax.

I close my eyes and breathe in the sweet smell of our new life, letting it fill me to the brim. We're not entirely out of the woods yet, and we have a lot of work ahead of us, but in this moment—this slice of perfection we've managed to find ourselves in—I finally have a name for the feeling I get when I'm with Lita.

It doesn't exist in Merik, but out here in the wilderness, away from Peace Officers and the High Majesty's rule, it makes sense.

I'm *home.*

About the Author

R.K. Pierce is an author by day, feral chaos gremlin by night who routinely curses the blood of her enemies. While not a big coffee drinker, she does enjoy margaritas, and usually prefers socks with toes over the mitten kind. For fun, she reads or jousts. During downtime with her family, she tends to keep things low key by impersonating Elvis for funeral events or watching trashy TV shows.

R.K. Pierce's Links:
linktr.ee/authorrkpierce

Her Spark

By: C.J. Willis

About Her Spark

Anna is a strong woman who has faced more in her short life than most while climbing out of the gutter. She and her best friend Lucy attend a hospital fundraiser for a night of fun where she crosses paths with a man who takes her breath away. When their conversation is cut short by a phone call revealing new information, it shakes the foundation of their budding relationship.

Aldo is a man at the top of his organization. At a hospital benefit, he meets a woman who knocks him off of his feet. When their conversation is cut short, he is left with a longing not only to explain the situation but to be a part of her life. He uses all of his resources to keep her safe and only asks for one thing, a chance to be honest and answer her questions before she cuts him out.

With secrets in the air and outside forces applying pressure to both of them, will their new relationship survive or crumble?

CONTENT NOTE:

Your mental health matters. Please take notice that the things listed here are parts of the story. If you have questions or if you feel that something needs to be added to this list, please email me at cjwillisauthor@gmail.com : Sexually Explicit Scenes, Trauma, Mentions of Sexual Assault (Off-page), Mentions of Human Trafficking, Violence and Murder, Arson, Kidnapping, Stalking, and Cheating (not between the main characters)

Relationship Type: Male, Female

AUTOR NOTE:

This book takes place in the same world as His Revenge and is canonically set in the year 2000. Due to the timeframe in which this story takes place, you will not find cool modern technology that is in other pieces. I hope that you love it.

DEDICATION

To the villain we all could have become and the person who held us in the darkest moments.

Chapter One
"Pain is relative but feeling anything is a gift."

Aldo

I bring my bourbon to my lips again to keep from scowling at the snobby suits in the room. Today isn't about my pension for destroying empires of perverts but about helping to fund the local medical college and sponsor more doctors to put on our payroll. The more medical hands we have on deck, the fewer of my friends I have to bury.

"Mr. Angelini, it's my understanding that your family is matching the donations made here tonight," she says to me through half-lidded eyes, looking at me as dollar signs and the power that I hold instead of a person. I wish this was the first time that I was openly flirted with at these events, but it's no secret that the only thing between my wife and I is a written agreement.

"Yes, we strongly support the medical needs in our region. It's for the betterment of the community that will outlast us all," I answer, faking the pride that I know is expected to be in my voice. She reaches out to put her hand on my arm and I take a step to the side avoiding the contact. Just as my mask is about to slip, Enzo steps between us.

"My Apologies, Mr. Angelini has an important call that needs to be taken. We hope that you enjoy the evening and look forward to matching your donation." As the last word leaves his mouth, we turn and walk to the back staircase and the executive offices. The other guards flank us, stopping and standing at the base of the staircase, ensuring our privacy.

"Anything I need to know, Enzo?" I inquire, part of me hoping it was an escape from the power trip of the wealthy and part of me hoping it's a bloody matter where I get to set my beast free. Taking my seat on the couch overlooking the party, I can see the opulence pouring off of each of the wealthy guests and the gruff violence thinly veiled for all of the mafia families present.

"Fabbri sent us a message pinned to a corpse at one of our warehouses. Nothing was taken; it looks like he was making a point."

"Fuck. What's the message?" I ask, grinding my teeth and slamming back the rest of the bourbon in my glass.

"You sit on a throne of lies, written in blood on his body." Enzo cringed as the last word left his lips. He must have known the man who died in us getting this message and I note to check in on him again when we are safe in the compound. I pace the room, contemplating the most effective way to handle his retaliation. Fabbri has been fighting for his seat with the most dangerous families in our region, but most of these seats are generational and we are very divided over the decision.

"He thinks that he can kill one of our men in our territory and get away with it. Instead of going in hot-headed, as he expects, I'll call a council meeting locally and provide this to them and any further proof of his blatant disregard for our rules and order," I say as I come to a full stop in the room, a rueful smile caressing my lips. Enzo nods, pulling out his burner cell phone and making the call.

"Less, I know you are still at the location. Gather as much information as you can and bring it home. We'll meet you there later."

An angry vibration settles in my bones with the plan agreed upon and I know that I need to make my way back to the party downstairs. I take one final deep breath as I walk through the dark hall, past the guards, and over to our table. Everyone seems to be having a fun-filled evening of dancing and I recognize most of the faces in the room from other charity events. I pan across the crowd and suddenly the world stops around me.

The only thing that I see is her.

Her laughter floats with the music like a siren song pulling me in and I stand, intending to make my way to her. I quickly remove my plain wedding band and drop it in my pocket with little thought towards my loveless marriage before waltzing to her. She continues to laugh and banter with the woman next to her as they sway to the music. Neither of them are in designer dresses but even if she were dipped in diamonds, her smile would outsparkle even the most rare jewels. Before I can think it through, I make my way to her side, the smell of lilac filling my senses as I take her in entirely.

"Hello, beautiful," I say softly, enamored by the way she moves freely in this space filled with vultures.

"Hello, tall, dark, and handsome," she responds, a glimmer of mischief in her eyes. She matches the movement of her friend without missing a beat until the dark-haired woman looks at her, nods her head in my direction, and walks toward the bar at the opposite end of the room. I extend my hand, hoping that she'll take it. While I may take blood and truths by force, I will never take a woman by force. She pauses for a moment to contemplate her decision before meeting my eyes and placing her hand in mine.

The moment our skin makes contact my heart soars and the rest of the room fades away. Nothing else matters. All I want is to make her smile and I will beg, borrow, and plead to make it happen. As the music changes we adjust to the beat, swaying, dancing, and laughing together as we find our rhythm. With each turn, the colored lights overhead reflect on her purple sequin dress, accentuating her beautiful curves and soft pale skin.

Song after song plays and I have no interest in moving from this spot but I see the sheen of sweat on her skin and a primal need to take care of her steps in. I stop dancing, get her attention, and nod toward the bar. She nods in agreement as we wander over to get a drink and the design of the room lessens the acoustics so you can be heard. As we step up to the bar, the bartender hands me my signature bourbon and I indicate for her to get anything she wants.

"Can I get a Shirley Temple?" She asks, the red of embarrassment tinting her cheeks. The bartender nods, putting the drink in front of her. We step outside to the plaza and find seats under one of the cherry trees. Comfortable silence falls around us, and for the first time in my life, I feel content. Our eyes meet in the moonlight and I finally understand what all of the love stories through history were about. There isn't a thing in this world that I wouldn't fight to be with her and keep her safe.

"I want to kiss you but I need to know you want the kiss first," I tell her, gently placing my hand just below her cheek, waiting for her permission to touch her again. Just because she gave me permission to touch her on the dance floor doesn't mean that invitation extends to our more intimate setting. A soft smile lights up her face before she places her cheek in my hand and nods in agreement. Not wanting to miss the moment, I lean forward, one hand moving her drink out of the way and the other finding its way to the back of her head, tangled in her hair as our lips meet. The kiss is like an atomic bomb in my life, any idea of her importance to me has multiplied and the entire axis of my world has changed. We pull closer together as the kiss deepens, both of us losing ourselves in the magic before footsteps sound in our direction.

"Mr. Angelini, I apologize for interrupting but we need you urgently for this call with your father-in-law."

And then the magic was broken and I watched it disappear from her eyes.

Chapter Two

"When reality hits you hard, don't let it ruffle your feathers."

Anna

At that moment the beauty of the night shatters and any potential future that we had flushes down the toilet. I look into his eyes and I see the hope and want there, but I won't do it. There are some things that I will not allow myself to become and a side woman hiding in the shadows helping some lying bastard cheat on his unsuspecting wife isn't one of them. Then it hits me. Angelini. That's one of the big mob boss families and I was just kissing his lips like we had a future. I stand and turn to walk away when there is a delicate clasp of my hand.

"Can I at least know your name?" He practically begs, and the man who interrupted us raises an eyebrow. While he deserves nothing from me, it's bad form to piss off a mob boss, even a lying and cheating one.

"Anna," I whisper as I step away from him and make my way outside with tears blurring my vision. All the colors and people blur together but I cannot crack right here. Not where anyone can see me break down. I reach into my purse, flip open my phone, and call Lucy as I push through the front doors. Taking steps toward the car, I slide my key into the door and unlock it as my phone rings.

"Anna, is everything okay?" she asks without missing a beat. I can hear her over the music, but barely as she navigates to a quieter part of the room. The tears are freely falling at this point and I can't hold them back.

"Meatloaf," is all I have it in me to say through the sobs that wrack my chest.

"Fuck, I am on my way outside right now to the car. Are you already there?" she asks me, knowing that if I use our safe word I need her right now.

"Yes."

"Okay, get in the passenger seat, baby girl. I am coming and I will drive us to your place," she instructs me before the line goes dead. Using the back of my hands, I wipe away the tears that have fallen before switching sides in the car. Sitting there, I wait for the shimmer of Lucy's red dress to come through the front door of the event. Reaching into the backseat, I find the soft blanket that I keep because Lucy always runs the air conditioning and this was our compromise to keep me from freezing to death.

I see the shimmer of her dress exit the door, followed by the guy who interrupted the best kiss of my life. She turns around straightening her spine, and the world freezes. She puts her finger on his chest and while she is too far away for me to hear, I can tell by the heaving of her shoulders she is yelling at him. Without a fear in the world, she finishes yelling at him, doesn't wait for his response, and storms over to the car.

"Sorry, Babe. Bozo number one stopped me to make sure that I wasn't under the influence before I was allowed to drive you home," she says as she slams the door shut and starts the car.

"Lucy, they are mobsters. It would probably be in your best interest not to piss them off," I say, fear leaching into my voice for my fearless friend. She'll do anything to defend those she loves and sometimes puts herself in danger doing it.

"Actually, they are mafia men, and they don't like to make scenes in public with people who are not involved with the families. Although, that is the first time I have seen so many dangerous men in tuxes in one room," she corrects me as we pull away, headed in the direction of my apartment. The tears fall down my cheeks as the city blurs in the darkness.

By the time we get into the parking garage and park in my spot, the tears have dried up. Stupid men. Stupid lying, dirtbag men. Stupid heart that doesn't understand that he's married. Before I know it, Lucy's at my door, thrusting it open and pulling me into her arms. Sobs still wracking my chest, I hold onto her. The one bright part of my life. Through foster care, running away, and all of my struggles to get where I am today, Lucy has persisted as my person. She never judges me but always tells me the truth even when I am making bad decisions.

"Let's go upstairs. I want to know everything from the moment I left," she tells me while petting my back to comfort me. We walk in solemn silence from the garage into the elevator and up to my floor. I feel numb like my whole life just got ripped away from me, but it was only a kiss. We reach my door before I know it and get inside so that I can fall apart in the safety of my home. After my front door shuts, I can feel Lucy at my back unzipping my dress, freeing me from its confines. She steps away for a moment, going to my bedroom and grabbing something from my drawer. When she comes back she has two large t-shirts in hand and I feel my bottom lip tremble again. My best friend knows me so well that I don't even have to tell her what I need, she just does it for me because I can't. She drops her dress to the floor with utter disregard and throws on the other shirt. We curl up on the couch and turn on the radio before I tell her everything. The farther into the story I get, the more my heart feels like it has been ripped out of my chest.

"So you're telling me that he is one of the only men you have been genuinely interested in as an adult and he's married. He didn't tell you that before he asked if he could kiss you? Hold on," she says with fire and determination in her eyes. Lucy walks over to her discarded bag and pulls out her cell phone. Before I can think of words to stop her she presses the dial button and holds up her finger for me to wait.

"I was hoping you would call me after our broom closet adventure. Miss me already?" he asks her with a cocky tone in his voice that causes my eyebrow to rise.

"No, this is a message I need to get to your boss. You do work for Mr. Angelini, correct?"

"You know my affiliation, Rose Petal." The warning tone in his voice makes my blood boil and I see the challenge in her eyes.

"Tell your boss that if he is going to kiss a woman and make her complicit in his adulterous behavior he could at least let her make that decision." Then without waiting for a reply, she hangs up on him and I am stunned into silence.

"I'm sure he will get the message. Did you want to watch TV or curl up and get some sleep? You've had a long night," She asks, always knowing what I need before I even do.

"Will you stay with me tonight? I'm scared to be alone" I admit, the defeat evident in my voice.

"Of course."

Chapter Three

"Miscommunication is a bitch and so is knowing when you have fucked up."

Aldo

A knock on the door pulls my attention from the paperwork in front of me, not that I was able to keep my focus centered on these agreements anyway. All I can think about is the way she looked destroyed when she left the event. My heart hurts for the first time in my life. I never wanted anything before her. I knew my path from a young age, where people wanted to be doctors and astronauts. I knew I would take over the family business and I was never allowed dreams outside of that.

"Come in," I answer the knocking bleakly, hoping for a small distraction from the pain in my chest. When the door opens I see Gio on the other side of it with trepidation in each of his steps.

"Boss," he greets me in a formal manner, easing his tension a bit. He won't meet my eyes and I know that whatever he has to say won't be easy, but needs to happen. I grab the bourbon on my desk, swig it, and clear my throat to encourage him to speak.

"I got a call late last night from the friend of that girl you were with...." he starts and all of my focus finds him. She better be okay, I had him follow them to her apartment to ensure that she made it home safely. I stand and walk over to him grabbing him by the throat and pushing him against the door he came in before I grab the gun at my waist and put it to his temple.

"Finish what you were saying before I lose the last shred of my sanity," I utter in a deadly tone trying to get my point across.

"She told me to let you know that if you were going to kiss a woman and make her complicit in your adulterous behavior you could at least let her make that decision. There is one upside, I not only have her address but I also have a number to call to connect us to your girl."

"You are so lucky that you are well connected and know exactly what I need. Pack a bag quickly and wait outside my office to be released. Your punishment is that you are to leave and sit outside of her apartment and watch her. She was seen on my arm last night and even if she isn't speaking to me at the moment I need her alive to forgive me," I say, releasing his neck and going back to my chair. It is a little easier to focus on the contract that I need to sign now that I know what I am going to do. Grabbing the notebook from the top drawer on the right side of my desk I start to pen a note.

Dear Lilac,

My shining star in the dark of night. I know how bad this looks but I beg for the chance to explain. Please, if you felt anything that I did last night you will have coffee with me and offer me the chance to explain myself.

Signed,

Do

I stand up and walk to the door of my office before pulling it open. Gio is standing there at attention waiting for further instructions.

"Slide this under her door," I instruct him before turning around and letting a smile find my life for the first time since my lips were on hers last night. With a pep in my step and determination in my soul again I find my way to my desk and the stack of contracts is much easier. Hours pass while I meticulously read each one and note any questions I have that need to be run by our attorney. Once I have finished everything that I can behind a desk, I pull out my phone and call Enzo.

"Hey, we need to meet and discuss your endeavors for the company," before hanging up the phone, getting myself another drink, and getting cozy for a minute while I wait for my friend to arrive. Enzo and I grew up together, he was younger than me, and being part of the family business already, we were both safe to be friends as children. He has never experienced love but I know he has had his eye on a female serial killer that I have been asking him to keep an eye on to see if she is problematic for us. So far he seems to be helping keep her under wraps but in the decades that we have known each other, the man has never asked for a favor so I let this be without question. I know that if she were a danger to us she would no longer exist. My thoughts are disrupted by my phone ringing, so I shake my head to clear them away and answer the phone.

"Boss, your message has been delivered," Gio's voice rings through the line and my heart shudders in my chest.

"Hold on, her friend is calling," he says momentarily before I hear the hold music. I can barely breathe, I am so nervous. Every nerve ending feels like it's on fire and the seconds are moving at a molasses pace. Each beat of my heart reverberates in my ears as the anticipation grows.

"She is in. She will meet you for coffee at Sly Fox Coffee at 7:00 am," Gio says triumphantly. While I am extraordinarily happy to be seeing her tomorrow, Gio has a long night ahead of him.

"Good, you can watch her tonight and follow her to the shop in the morning where you will be relieved."

"Understood Boss," is all he was able to get out before I hang up the line and hear a knock on my door.

"Come in," I give the go-ahead to Enzo who has arrived just in time this evening. He opens the door, walks to the liquor cabinet, and pours himself some peanut butter whiskey before sitting down across from me. We both take sips of our drinks before diving into the business. We discuss the real estate that we manage for all of our people to ensure that everyone is able to have a safe space to sleep at night and raise their kids. Then we transition into the strip clubs and bars that we own all across the state to help clean the dirty money that comes in from the weapons trades that we deal in. I had asked him for the specs on a specific building and how difficult it might be to acquire the apartment building that my lilac lives in.

The information is easy, it's a faceless corporation and I can get it for market value and then increase the safety and security. Even if she doesn't want me after I explain myself, she was seen with me and I will not let anything happen to her because of me. She deserves so much more than I can provide her but I so desperately want to be enough for her. The next thing that I had Enzo do was put a GPS tracker in her car and a video feed of the hallway outside of her apartment. The last file Enzo hands me is the background check. There are still a few requests outstanding since information isn't at the tips of our fingers, but I have her driving record from the DMV and her police record from our detective at the local precinct.

I open the file and read up on how she was only questioned once in a bar fight because someone touched her and she laid them out cold. It brings a smile to my face that my lilac can defend herself when she needs to. She has been pulled over for speeding before, but always seems to talk her way out of a ticket. It says here that her fingerprints were sent to the local hospital for their records since she is an employee there. If she fixes people, maybe she can fix the broken parts of my soul. I lose hours digging into the file and Enzo sits there answering any of my questions and making a list of necessary security updates to her building. By the time I look up, I realize how late it is and that I need to get to my room and get some sleep if I plan to win over my lady tomorrow morning.

Chapter Four
"When in doubt, drink more coffee. What can go wrong?"

Anna

I am way too early, but I couldn't sit still and watch the clock anymore and if I just went to the coffee shop I could get in at least one cup before he gets there. The warm caress of the coffee will calm my nerves. My mind wanders as I walk through the streets to see the shop around the corner. I don't see anything out of the ordinary or any dangerous men as I complete the walk from my apartment. The last steps into the coffee shop bring peace to my soul. The only other place that has ever brought me hope is the library where I could find heat, escape, and adventure no matter how little funds I had. Smelling the warm beans and fresh pastries wafting around the space, I feel some of my anxiety dissipate.

My head turns as the door jingles while other patrons enter the shop, but I am looking to see the man who brought me to life. The barista takes my coffee order and is kind enough not to comment on my obvious reaction at the door. Once I finish ordering a white chocolate mocha with caramel and whole milk, I pay with cash before waiting on the other end of the coffee bar for my drink. I can see the door from where I stand and my body vibrates with the violent combination of hope and anger.

"Anna," the barista calls out from behind the counter before setting down my drink and turning back toward the coffee station. I pick up the warm cup and find my way to a table in the corner where I have a clear view of the door. After I sit down I reach into my bag, pull out the vampire book that I have been reading, and pretend not to be bothered while I wait for him. The jangle of the bells catches my attention and my heart stops beating when I see him. Our eyes lock and the corner of his lip rises in a small smile. I am so fucked.

He takes strides toward me and signals with his hands for his guards to stay behind, near the exit. With each step he takes he gets closer to me and it feels like the connection between us strengthens when we are in the room together. The rest of the room blurs and he is the only thing that I can focus on. When he reaches the table, he stops, stands before the seat, and looks up at me.

"Is this seat taken, Lilac?" he asks me with a mischievous twinkle in his eyes.

The lump in my throat prevents my verbal response from coming out, so I nod instead. I watch him take a seat and scoot his chair closer to me so we can talk without needing to project our voices across the table and over the ambient sound. To stall and find my voice I take another drink of my coffee and then put my receipt in my book as a bookmark before putting the book back in my bag.

"You asked to see me and have a chance to explain. I am here and ready to listen," I tell him as I reinforce my spine and remember that he is married. Before he has an opportunity to speak, one of his guards appears at our table with a plate of pastries and a coffee for Aldo.

"Thank you, Enzo. Did you do what I asked?" he inquires with an even tone and quizzical expression. Enzo looks at him, smiling, and nods before taking a seat near the door to give us privacy. The baristas come out and go from table to table talking quietly to the patrons. Once they visit every table, they turn off the open sign and lock the door so it can only be opened from the inside. My jaw falls open in utter disbelief; this man just cleared out my favorite coffee shop so we could sit alone.

"Don't worry beautiful, the patrons were all compensated with coffee cards to take their drinks to-go. The staff and owner have been duly compensated for any losses they would suffer from shutting down early. I know you care about this place and I wouldn't want our meeting to affect your daily life negatively," he says to me and reaches out his hand offering for me to take it but not forcing me. Fear courses through my veins as indecision racks my system. I promised him a chance to explain but not a chance to touch me, so I gently decline by lacing my hands together in front of me. His face shows his disappointment for only a moment before he moves his hand and nods in acceptance.

"Let me start with the fact that I want to apologize for making you feel deceived. I only ask that you let me finish explaining before you leave. If you decide then that you never want to see me again, I will respect that." Aldo looks over my face, watching me take him in and all of his words as they sink into my being.

"I can do that but I may have questions, do you prefer that I ask them all at the end?" I inquire, as I grab the notepad and pen from my bag and flip to the ribbon marking my available page.

"I would prefer that the questions wait until the end and then I will answer them, but I need to know if you want me to glaze over the darker side of what I do. I will give you full transparency if you want it, but sometimes the truth is a lot to mentally handle. I am not a good man, Lilac. I am not a good man to the world but I promise that I can be a man deserving of you." His words spill out with sincerity and melt my heart and some of my resolve.

"I will take it all but if it becomes too much, can I have a safe-word? I am a nurse in the local hospital here and I know that there is a lot of violence in this city and that you play your part, but I might struggle to reconcile the man in front of me with the violence that you participate in," I ask, hoping for honesty but not sure that I am ready for the utter violence that the man in front of me can inflict.

"We will use the stoplight system. Green if you are comfortable, yellow if you want to slow down, and red if you want to stop. Please understand that your boundaries are very important, and I will not know them all as we start and I need you to communicate them to me. I promise that I won't push back. I might ask questions to understand, but you are in control. I might run a tight ship with my work but we do everything here with your informed consent," he answers earnestly without breaking eye contact with me.

"Okay, thank you. I'm ready," I say, taking another drink of my coffee and grabbing a cheese danish from the plate between us. The first bite passes my lips and the burst of sweet and savory causes me to moan. Fuck. That was not planned. The way that his fist clenches tells me that he isn't unaffected by my visceral reaction.

"Sorry," I whisper as the blush creeps up my neck, encompassing my face. My shame causes me to look down and avoid eye contact to prevent further embarrassment.

"Look at me," he asks me with a softer tone in his voice. I take a shaky breath and find my courage before looking up to meet his eyes.

"You do not have to apologize for the way your body reacts. You do not need to be ashamed of the beautiful noises that you make." He speaks softly before reaching over to provide comfort, stopping inches from my knee and looking at me waiting for my consent. I nod, allowing him to touch me for the first time since our kiss, and the reaction that sparks through my entire being is unmatched. My shoulders fall for the first time since I walked in and I am ready to hear whatever he has to tell me.

Chapter Five

"Honesty is the best policy, but the bloody truth might be my downfall."

Aldo

Finally seeing her relax with my touch brings a warmth to my heart that I never thought that I would be able to experience with my position in the family business. Patiently, I watch her breathe through her anxiety and take a sip of her coffee. I would happily wait all day for her to be ready for me to speak without a worry in the world. I have put all business on pause and cleared my calendar to ensure that she has enough time to be comfortable and get the answers that she deserves. Today isn't about me, aside from the information that I provide. Instead, today is about her and her comfort. I understand that my life and the deals that have been brokered are not easily understood but if she feels the same spark that I do between us she will give this a chance.

"Are you ready, beautiful? Did you want to finish your breakfast pastry first?" I ask to ensure her continued consent in all of this mess. She takes another sip of her coffee and it sounds nearly empty when she sets it back on the table. Before I can even utter the words, Enzo is at the counter, presumably asking the barista for another one. She settles into her chair before indicating that I should move forward with my story. With her pen in hand, she prepares to notate any questions she has.

"Fifteen years ago, the family business was far bloodier than it is today. The families had to beg, borrow, and plead for the weapons imported from outside of the country. In the first five years of my time as a made man, I saw countless of my friends and people that I grew up with die in front of my eyes. I knew at that moment that I would do whatever it took to secure a safer future for those who were left standing. I went to my father, the previous Don, and asked him what I could do to help save the lives of those who entrusted us. He spoke with the head of a powerful family in Italy whose daughter had just become of age and arranged our marriage. After the arrangement was made, he sat me down and explained that there was now a contract in place between our families that included a clause where I would marry their daughter and that we would at least have one child together to signify the unity that exists.

What I wasn't told was that my bride was in love with a woman in Italy and would not want to even try to be a true participant in the marriage. She came here so that her family would spare the person that she loves and agreed to be my spouse, but on paper only. We have not shared a bed throughout the entirety of our marriage and kissed only on the cheeks on our wedding day. After she settled here and found her footing, we used a clinic to impregnate her so that she would not betray her true love. My son's name is Leo, and as per our contract, his mother is primarily in charge of his care. I will introduce him to the family business and begin to prepare him to take over when he comes of age." I pause to let this sink in and and watch dutifully as she scrawls her question on the page. She looks up at me and takes another bite of her pastry as Enzo sets down her new coffee and walks to the other side of the room. Watching and waiting, I see her dip her chin indicating she is ready for more.

"There is no love between us and I know that Bianca resents me for keeping her from her love, but it was her father that forbade them from speaking again. With this arrangement, I knew that things would not be easy, and I have found my release with some of the local discreet call girls so that no one will get the wrong idea. I cannot leave my wife without it costing countless lives and jeopardizing the safety of everyone that I have sworn to protect. Everything changed for me the night that we met. Before you, I could live with the constant faceless women and having to pretend that our marriage was real. But then I saw you."

She takes a drink of her coffee before looking back up at me. For the first time since our kiss there is hope in her eyes and I will do anything and kill anyone to keep it there. She reviews the notes that she made and makes some adjustments based on the information that I provided.

"What is the plan? I understand the spark and the romance of this, and believe me I feel it too, but I need a plan. I work twelve-hour shifts at the local hospital and come from nothing. Our tax brackets don't even touch, so before I start something that could become serious, I need to know what your plan is," she says before finishing the danish that she has been snacking on throughout our meeting. I take a drink of my coffee and smile at her.

"My plan, you brilliant and beautiful woman, is to date you if you will allow me. I will easily fill my time while you are working and I respect that you have worked your whole life to get where you are. I am not here to rock your boat but to join you on it. If you want a step-by-step plan we can build one together to make sure that it fits in your life, but I want this and I am willing to ask for my chance on my knees for you," I promise her, knowing that I mean every word. She reaches out to place her hand on mine and my heart skips a beat. I do something that I have never done, I fall to my knees in front of her so she can understand the depths of my emotions for her. A pin drop could be heard in this cafe but I couldn't care less as long as she understands the lengths that I am willing to go for a chance.

"Aldo," she whispers with her free hand covering her mouth in shock at me on my knees for her. A moment passes in wonder and I think that maybe I have made it through to her when she moves her hand and reveals a smile below it. She scribbles something in her notebook before ripping out the page and handing it to me.

"It's my phone number, use it. We can date but I reserve the right to ask questions," she tells me before she stands up and I follow her from my knees to standing before the woman of my dreams. Before she moves she kisses me on the cheek, flustering me.

"I have a couple of errands to run today, but I would like to see you again when you can make time." She goes to leave and I quickly grab her wrist with light pressure.

"May I kiss you?" I ask with a level of uncertainty that I have never felt before.

"Yes." As soon as the word leaves her mouth I pull her into me and press our lips together. The passion unfolds as the kiss deepens and I groan. We come up for air with smiles on our faces before she walks out of the coffee shop. I stand there staring at where she left in utter disbelief.

"Don't worry boss. I have a discreet tail on her to make sure that she is safe." Enzo's voice breaks me out of my daze. I needed to hear that because this is the second time we could have been spotted together and it might place a target on her back.

"Good."

Chapter Six
"Bestie breakdowns and comfort snacks while I spill my soul."

Anna

Leaving the Cafe is one of the most difficult decisions I have ever made. I need to pick up groceries and prepare my food for the week or the next few days of long shifts will wear me down. Lucy agreed to meet me at home after her shift ends, and I know she is going to want a proper rundown. Today is my Sunday, and while I would love to spend the day with Aldo, I honestly did not think he would have any answers that would warrant us ever speaking again.

Walking down to the local grocery store I contemplate all of the information that Aldo told me. Even with everything that he covered today, I know that we have just scratched the surface of what secrets he has needed to keep close to his vest. His story is crazy, and for any other man I would consider it too much and too far-fetched, but, he is a mafia don who pours his money into financing the very hospital that I work at. His name isn't on any of the doors or buildings, but it was his family money that threw the fundraiser we met at. I was able to connect the dots between his name when his guard spoke it and the donor list for the party.

Shopping on autopilot, I gather everything that I think I could need for meals this week and head to the register. Placing my basket on the belt, I patiently wait my turn for the cashier to ring in my food, while the mother in front of me finishes her transaction.

"Ma'am, I apologize but it looks like the card declined." The cashier says as politely as possible so as not to embarrass her. The redness of shame finds its way to her face and her toddler squirms in the stroller while she digs in her bags and pulls out a few small bills but not enough to cover her food. Pulling out my card, I know that I will need to adjust my self-care budget for the month but I won't let a mother in my community struggle to feed her babies if I can help it.

"Let me get this for you," I say with a soft smile and a soft flutter in my heart. The cashier seems stunned and unaccustomed to kindness between strangers. She tries to hand me the little bit of cash that she has.

"No need. Please, just pay it forward where you can," I insist as I see the unshed tears fill her eyes. She nods and loads the groceries into her cart and heads for the exit. The young cashier rings in my groceries and I complete my transaction noting the new lightness in my chest knowing that today she will be able to feed her family regardless of her card and financial status. I see a man in dark clothes barely in my peripherals as I go to leave the store.

My heartbeat starts to increase at the potential danger and I reach into my bag to feel my concealed gun. I didn't think I would need it when I met with Aldo but I was more concerned with the after-effects of being seen with a mafia don than the don himself, especially when he got on his knees for me. Moving slowly, I slip my gun into the belt of my pants and place all the groceries on my left side, freeing my right to react as needed. I walk back to my car, checking every reflective surface to watch for the man as I near where I parked. Placing the bags in the trunk hastily, I unlock the driver's side door hating the exposure as I climb into the driver's seat and lock the doors.

The self-defense instructions from my years of classes start repeating in my brain.

Do not drive straight home.

Do not go down any alleyways.

Do not let them get in the car.

If you have to shoot, shoot to kill because it might be the only chance that you get.

My heart is beating fast in my chest but I force myself to take even breaths and keep my head on the task at hand. If I am being followed I am going to need all of the survival skills I have learned since college and Robert. I pull away from my parking spot and circle through the busy neighborhoods just south of my apartment, checking for any car that might be following me before I pull into the garage and park in my space. Keeping my head on a swivel and my right hand free, I pull out my groceries from the car and head inside. Once I enter the foyer, I set down my groceries and unsheath my gun before locking the door and carefully clearing every closet and hiding space in my apartment.

With the coast clear but the unease in my chest still present, I reholster the pistol and tuck it into my waistband to keep it nearby. I put away the cold food that I brought and proceed to prepare my lunches, listening for any sounds outside the door while I patiently wait for Lucy. Time passes quickly as I work through processing the veggies and prepackage all of my meals for this week. By the time I finish putting the lids on the containers, there is a soft rhythmic knock at my door that Lucy uses to indicate that she is on the other side of the door. I quickly saunter over to the door, unlock it, and open it only to be barrel-rolled by my beautiful best friend into a hug that sweeps me off my feet.

"Hey, Luce," I chuckle as she finally puts me down. Her responsive laughter is enough to lighten the mood. She gently pats my holstered firearm with a raised brow, waiting for me to fill her in.

"You, ma'am, have a lot to fill me in on, but don't worry I brought hot chocolate to make this easier," She tells me with a smile, pulling out the bag of her homemade hot chocolate mix that she covets the recipe for. I stand there with tears in my eyes and a full heart, knowing that no matter what I say next, Lucy will ride or die for me. While she will ask clarifying questions and advise me against things that are potentially harmful, at the end of the day no matter what decision I make she will respect it and be here to hold me if it ends badly.

While she stands there and makes our cocoa, I spill a recap of my entire day and she just listens. It all comes off my chest like a weight and I know in this moment that my platonic best friend is the best thing that has ever and will ever happen to me. Even if I end up old, grey, and alone romantically, I know that Lucy and I will always be together and hold space for one another. When I finally finish the recap of my day and stop talking, I just look at her waiting for the questions that I know are coming.

"Anna, I love you and I respect your decision but how can a relationship with him go anywhere if he has to stay married to his wife?" She asks me with softness in her eyes backed by fire.

"I didn't agree to forever but I did agree to go on dates and ask questions as we go. I don't expect him to have everything figured out without me and he seems to be willing to follow my lead on this. Luce, he was on his knees for me. You could have heard a pin drop with how quiet the room got," I respond, hoping that she understands my want to cautiously move forward and continue to get information.

"I love that, and maybe you could put that position to good use," she taunts me, causing me to be bright red at the thought of him on his knees bringing me pleasure over and over again until I physically can't stand anymore. I shake the dirty thoughts away as she laughs knowing exactly what she did to me.

"I love you. Are you staying here tonight or is it cocoa before you head home since I have work in the morning?" I ask, hoping that she will stay but also knowing that it might be safer for her if she isn't with me right now.

"I have time for cocoa and then I will let you get your beauty sleep. No one needs a crabby nurse tomorrow." She laughs, knowing that I am much nicer when I get sleep, especially for the start of my work week. When she finishes pouring the cocoa into two mismatched mugs before we sit down at the dining room table. We each take a mismatched chair next to each other before sipping the chocolate deliciousness in front of us. We have been friends long enough that I know when she has the need to say something so I reach over and put one of my hands on hers. Her mouth opens and closes a few times as she struggles to find the words.

"I am as worried about your heart in this as I am your safety. A man like him has more enemies than we can count. I know you can take care of yourself, but I promised that I would never leave you alone to fight your battles." She finally admits her fear to me with unshed tears in her eyes. I grasp her hand in mine and take a moment to cherish the amazing bond that we have built over the last five years.

"I promise that I will be honest with you the whole time and that we can continue to discuss everything as it progresses so you can help keep my expectations realistic and feet firmly on the ground."

"Good, because I love you and I might die, but I would take him out with me if it came to it."

Chapter Seven
"Is it stalking, or following around my queen?"

Aldo

I know that I need to give her the space that I promised her but my primal need to be near her is overwhelming my good senses. It only took one phone call to the hospital administrators to give me an office space to work out of the hospital with the ability to oversee the nurse's station from two floors above it. In an effort to respect her professional space, I have a view of her while she works on paperwork effortlessly as an elegant woman. She has worked so hard to get where she is in life, and yet, she does things like paying for a mother's food without batting an eye. The size of her heart is unlike anyone that I have ever met before. My whole life has been spent around spoiled and devious women who would not help someone in their family, let alone a stranger.

I spend hours of my day alternating between the makeshift desk and the landing where I can catch glimpses of her. The mountain of paperwork that would usually drain me seems easier to complete, which has never happened before. She is both fast and efficient at her job and I can't help but feel pride in my chest at my beautiful woman.

There is only an hour left of her day and Gio comes sprinting up the stairs, panic written on his face. Instantly I am in boss mode and have to focus on what needs to happen but by the time he reaches me, he is out of breath.

"What happened?" I ask, trying to understand

"I'm so sorry Boss. I was following Lucy from work to her car and I was less than ten seconds behind her. The quiet side road gave me minimal space to hide while she got in her car. Mere seconds passed as I got on my bike and headed toward the street where she was parked. There was a painting van that pulled quickly off the road and when I had sight of where she was parked, the driver's side door was open and she was nowhere in sight." He sputters out the last words and falls to his knees, waiting for my verdict.

This man that I have known most of my life is on his knees broken over his actions waiting for me to punish him for something that I know he would have died to prevent. I stand up and walk over to him. In the next moment, I place my hand on his shoulder, giving it a gentle squeeze to indicate that I need him to stand up. He lifts his head first and meets my eyes. Giving him as much reassurance as possible with my eyes I wait for him to stand up.

"I know you feel for the woman. There is no way you would have put her in danger or allowed her to exist in a dangerous situation without you. Stand up, we have some calls to make." I try my best to reassure him, knowing that the more I can calm his brain the higher clarity he will reach.

"The van said 'Ivan's Liquor' but that is all I got as it passed me," he says, his voice barely carrying to me.. I rub my face knowing that our next move may start a war but I can't think of one good reason to turn my back on this.

"That's one of the Russian-owned businesses in town," I utter but there is a pause as I let the information sink in to Gio. He needs the reassurance.

"Call our men, we are going to need every available hand. I will call my informant and see if I can get a location of where they would be holding your girl. Afterward, we will get a final plan together and I will summon my Lilac and tell her what happened." I give the instruction and then I dial the nurse's station.

"I need to speak with Anna, it's a family emergency. Tell her it's Aldo." I instruct the nurse who picks up the phone. I watch as she comes over to the station and picks up the receiver.

"This is Anna," she answers the phone, confused, but ready.

"Lilac, this is an emergency. I need you to come up to the third floor to office 322 right away. I promise that I would not ask this of you lightly, but grab your bag and let your supervisor know that you won't be back today and you will keep her apprised of the situation," I tell her, hoping to convey the seriousness of the situation.

"Give me five minutes," is the only response that I get before the line goes dead. I watch her sprint to her supervisor's office and then she disappears in the direction of her locker. As soon as she is back in sight and headed up the stairs I retreat to the office. This is a conversation that needs to be had in private where she can react however she deems fit instead of the person she typically has to be inside of these walls. Her soft knock on the door is all the time I have to prepare before she walks in face flushed and she stops, fear filling her eyes. I lean up and pull her into my arms.

"Lilac," is all I get out before her shoulders started shaking. Holding her closer to me and I feel my heart break knowing that I am going to have to tell her about Lucy.

"Tell me," she instructs through her sobs.

"The Russians have taken Lucy and I will have my men get her back..." is all I get out before this beautiful girl pulls out a gun. My jaw hits the floor as she grabs a couple of extra magazines from her bag and prepares for war.

"Baby, as hot as it is for you to be armed, I can handle this." In half a second she has the barrel of the gun pointed right at my dick as Gio enters the room. He lifts his gun and points it at her before he meets my eyes.

"Gio, I don't care if she fills me with more holes than Swiss cheese. If you ever point your gun at my woman, I will have your existence erased from history. Do I make myself clear?" I ask with no kindness in my voice and a hard edge to my tone that I have never used on him before. With trepidation, he lowers his gun but does not put it away.

"If you do not sheath your gun right now Gio, I will cut off your trigger finger and preserve it in a jar for my lady." At that moment she presses my bulge with the tip of the gun and kisses my cheek.

"I am going to get my best friend with or without your help. If you try to stop me I will shoot off your dick before I even have the chance to try it for myself." Her words cause my dick to get harder as they leave her mouth. This fucking incredible woman has no fear of me and it is the most refreshing experience that I have ever had in my life. She is everything that I need and more.

"Gio, when and where are we meeting the reinforcements?" I ask, unphased by the loaded gun aimed at my family jewels.

"All of our men are converging at dusk and meeting two blocks from the warehouse where we suspect they're holding her. It's their territory, and if we assemble too soon, they could move her or worse." Gio rattles off the information, his eyes bouncing between the two of us with uncertainty. She looks at her watch and we have enough time to change and drive over to the location.

"Lilac, I need you to give your keys to Gio. You and I will ride to the meeting point together and he will arrange for your car to be brought to your apartment," I say with a smile.

"You don't have the gate key to get it in after hours," She responds, lowering the gun and holstering it. I see Gio's shoulders relax at the sight.

"Babydoll, I own the building. There is no issue with any of my men putting your car away for you," I inform her and watch the crease in her brow as she processes the information.

"Since when?! I signed a lease renewal three months ago, and as far as I know, the company has not changed," She stutters, confusion and uncertainty filling her beautiful eyes.

"Technically, I took possession of the building this morning. I have the paperwork if you would like to see it." I reach back onto the desk and grab the envelope ready to hand it over to her so she will believe me. She just stands there opening and closing her mouth trying to find the words.

"Why?" She asks me pulling away for the first time since she walked into the room. As much as I want to force this, I let her pull away because even if she told me that she never wanted to see my face again, I would be in the shadows doing everything in my power to keep her safe.

"I started the process the day that we met. From the moment that we connected, I knew that I would do anything to keep you safe so I bought the building that you are living in so that I could increase the safety and security without disrupting your comfort," I answer her as honestly as I can. She searches my eyes for something before leaning into me and placing a soft kiss on my lips. The kiss kicks my primal need into overdrive and I dive deeper into the kiss, my hands finding purchase in her hair. She nips at my lip and I groan in response. A phone ringing disrupts us and we pull apart, breathing heavily.

Chapter Eight
"Hell hath no fury like a best friend on a mission."

Anna

As Gio answers the phone I feel embarrassment creep up my neck as the realization that I basically just climbed Aldo in this office with him still here hits me. I look down at my feet to hide my shame. Gio whispers into the phone and we catch our breaths from the impactful kiss the call interrupted. A strong hand finds my chin and brings it up to meet his eyes.

"Never be ashamed of the explosive chemistry that we have. I know that I'm not," he says to me with a taunting grin. He places a soft kiss on my cheek to reinforce the meaning behind his words as Gio wraps up the call. I reach into my bag and pull out my keys before handing them to Gio.

"I am not a damsel who sits in the car, so what's the plan?" I ask, hoping for something more concrete now that it is understood that I will be going to get Lucy. Both men's jaws fall open and they just stare at me. I stand there, cross my arms, and raise my eyebrow, waiting for a response.

"Love, I won't try to make you stay on the sidelines but I am begging you to stay by my side so that we can get both you and Lucy out of this situation in one piece. If you stay near me then we can jointly focus on getting your friend out of this with as little harm as possible. If you wander off, I will shift my focus to protecting you instead of finding the person that we came to get." He cups my cheeks and stares into my eyes, allowing me to see his sincerity and the fact that every action he has done since we met has been to respect my wishes to the best of his ability. He has given me choices that no one ever had before.

"When this is over, I need to sit down and tell you why I would gladly lose my life if it meant saving her, but for now, let's go save my best friend," I promise him and pull his hand toward the door. He is everything I could have asked for and more with his only flaw being his loveless marriage. We walk hand-in-hand to the parking structure and stop at his car. Gio opens the trunk and grabs something before heading over to us. Aldo takes the dark cloth items from Gio and it looks like a bulletproof vest. He opens the back door and sets one of the vests down in the seat before handing me one. I set my bag on the floorboards and examine the vest.

"Can you help? I have never put one of these on and I know you will feel better if you know that I am secured properly." As I finish my sentence, he laughs and it is a comforting sound that warms my soul. I pull my sweater over my head and throw it in the back of the car, leaving me in a camisole and yoga pants. The goal was comfort today after work, but luckily they will also work for the rescue without slowing me down. There isn't a thing in this world that I wouldn't burn down for Lucy, and God forgive the people who stand in my way.

Aldo smiles at me in my more relaxed state before he slides the vest over my head, positioning it on my body before securing the sides and brushing my hair out of my face. He grabs my sweater out of the car and hands it to me with a soft smile.

"What they don't know will surprise the shit out of them," he says with a smile as I pull on the sweater over the vest. We climb into the car and I grab the extra magazines from my bag and place them in my sweater pocket before I buckle into my seat. Gio takes the front seat to drive us to the location and we check our guns to ensure that they are loaded. It is a tenuous time traveling between the hospital and the meeting place, almost thirty minutes away, but Aldo holds my hand the entire drive, crazing the contact.

"I would pull you into my lap so I can keep you close but your safety will always be a much more prominent concern over my comfort," he tells me as we come to a stop in the alley with the rest of the cars. When the door opens, he steps out and holds his hand out to me to join him. I slide across the seats and step out as the men gather around us and I hop down from the seat. I shut the door behind me and look to Aldo, ready to hear him lead his people for the first time.

"Listen up, the target here is to get to Lucy. She is five foot five with brown hair and brown eyes. This is Anna and she will be by my side for this; do not let anything happen to her or you will meet the Angel of Pain," he instructs his people and I am in awe of the power that he commands every time he opens his mouth. This incredible and powerful man has been on his knees for me and while our connection is incredibly strong, we haven't even had sex yet. Finding the hair tie at my wrist, I pull back my hair in a braid to keep my field of vision clear. I run through my mental checklist; gun: Loaded, magazines: ready in my pocket, vest: secured, laces are double knotted so I don't trip over them. I don't think that there is anything else I could do to prepare.

Gio leads the team into position and Aldo and I file behind him as we make our way from the alley to the warehouse where they are keeping Lucy. The walk is made in silence with the team communicating in signals without spoken words. Aldo keeps his hand in mine, making sure that I move within the safety of the pack, and for the first time in my life, I felt like I belong somewhere. Lucy has always been family and I would rather die than give her up, but these men didn't even know my name until minutes ago and here they are protecting my life without a question or second thought.

We stop around the corner of the building and Gio goes ahead to secure entry to the warehouse door. Everyone but him freezes when it swings open from the inside. He moves so fast that it is hard to make out each individual movement in the dark, but he takes out the man's windpipe first before knocking him to the ground and using him as a prop for the door. He signals us all to come to him so we can enter the building as a unit. My heart is beating wildly but I put all of my feelings and emotions aside to focus on the task at hand.

As we enter the first door the strobe lights and the smell of urine take over my senses and I force my body to focus. We make it down the hallway to the first door that we open to find a stained bed and nothing else. The second door on the other wall opens to two armed men at a desk. They stand up and draw their weapons but before they have them out of their holsters bullets fire from one of our men and they hit the floor. Sadly our time moving stealthily is over with those gunshots. My shoulders tense but I do not raise my weapon for fear of hitting someone on our side from this angle.

We hear whimpering coming from down the hall and continue to move in that direction when I see a large man standing behind her with a knife to her throat. It's Lucy, and the rage in my chest goes wild. All of those years of training to perfect my aim come down to this.

"Put the knife down and you might survive this," Aldo booms from beside me as I raise my weapon. The ogre of a man has the audacity to smile like he has no control over what happens next. I steady my aim, breathe, and then fire. The bullet leaves the chamber of my gun, finds purchase in the center of his forehead, and blows the back of his head off. He falls to the floor as Gio and I rush for Lucy.

Chapter Nine
"This woman is akin to the air that I need to breathe"

Aldo

"Down!" I shout, hoping that they all hear me as I aim and fire three shots into the man, my heart rate increasing as the flash from his muzzle sends more panic into my heart. The man slumps to the floor but I turn away while my men deal with the fallout and I rush to find my girl crouched next to her friend clutching her arm and I see red. I blink and find myself next to her, grasping her arm to inspect the wound.

"It's a graze Aldo, I'll be fine. I have had worse." She attempts to comfort me, but now I'm mad that he died too quickly. I want to bring him back and force him to meet the Angel of Pain, but that isn't how life works. It takes an enormous amount of effort for me to ensure that my grasp on her is soft even with all of the anger coursing through my veins. While I may be a monster, I will never be her monster. Focusing on my breathing, I see that Gio has taken off his jacket and placed it over Lucy since she was almost naked and bruised when we walked in here. The delicate way that he zips her into his jacket and is careful not to add pressure to any of her wounds is heartwarming and genuine.

"I will go home with her, pack a bag, and keep her at my house until we get to the bottom of this and she is safe," Gio informs Anna with a reassuring smile. He places his hand on her shoulder before looking into her eyes.

"I promise I will do everything in my power including laying down my life for Lucy. Please let him take care of you and I will worry about her. We will check in after the doctor comes to my house to examine her and ensure she has what she needs to heal," He says looking directly into her eyes, unwavering in his admiration. She assesses him for a moment, weighing not only his words but also his body language before picking a response.

"That's fine with me if Lucy agrees, but understand this, Gio. My aim is spot on, and I protect those I love even against an army." My woman wows me yet again with her response, and I am ready to fall to my knees again for her. Her devotion to the people she cares for is unwavering and something to be admired. I nod at Gio, communicating that the only way to clean up this many bodies in another territory is fire.

"Baby, do you and Lucy want to burn this place to the ground as retribution?" I ask with a glimmer of excitement in my eye and the mischievous grin she responds with is indicative of her choice. My men start by dumping bottles of vodka all over the warehouse and ensuring that no one else here is left standing. The backdoor is open and one of the men might have escaped, but they will know that we wiped them out without any losses on our side. We walk out of the room together, my men flanking the women that we came here for, and stop at the exit. Everyone leaves us at the door and form a protective circle around the outer door, watching our backs.

"Okay, we are going to hand each of you a butane lighter. We will count down from three and then when we say 'drop', you drop them in the spill leading inside and allow the liquor to do the rest of the work. Are there any questions?" I go through the plan, making sure that both Lucy and Anna understand the instructions before we move forward. Both of us hand over a lighter to each of the girls.

"Light it up, Fighter" Gio whispers to Lucy and I do not miss the light in his eyes aimed towards her. Once his eyes connect with me and he nods, I know that we are ready. The girls maintain eye contact as they ignite the lighters.

"Three....two...one... drop." As the last word leaves my lips both women drop the lighters into the spill and the liquor ignites. We quickly leave through the door and shut it behind us, forcing the fire farther into the building. Quietly, we all walk back to the cars, watching for reinforcements or any additional problems. As we get to our vehicles we pause. Lucy hugs Anna and promises to contact her regularly and to see her as soon as she feels up for travel. With that, Anna and I get in the SUV that we arrived in but in the front seat instead of the back, and Gio uses the car next to us. Since our destinations are different, it is easier to travel separately instead of delaying the doctor seeing Lucy,

Our drive is quiet back to her place but we hold hands the entire time and I park in a guest spot near the door. As I put the car in park, our seatbelts unbuckle and we climb out of the car, the adrenaline starting to ebb. I walk quickly to her side, unwilling to be separated from her for even for a moment longer. We move quickly from the garage to the apartment, needing more skin-to-skin contact. She gets to her door and reaches into her bag only to frown.

"Fuck," she utters defeat evident in her voice. "I gave my keys to Gio which includes my apartment key. I refuse to stash one out here for safety reasons but I have no way into my apartment." Her voice starts to waver and I reach into my pocket and pull out my keys. I run my thumbs through the keys, finding the shiny new one that I had cut a few days ago, and slide it into the lock. She stands there too stunned to speak as the door opens for her.

I gesture for her to enter first and much to my chagrin she unholsters her gun and prepares to clear her apartment even though the door was locked and I could not be more proud of her. Unholstering

my gun and following her inside, I lock the door behind me. We clear
the space in under a minute before she sets her gun and holster on
the table and takes off her sweatshirt. I am by her side in a flash when
I hear her audibly hiss at the movement.

"Please let me take care of you?" I ask, and even though every
bone in my body wants to demand, I know that type of behavior will
get me nowhere with her. She stops moving and nods while
clenching her jaw. My hands find the edge of the material and gently
glide it the rest of the way off, careful to avoid her wounded shoulder.
Once the wound is uncovered, I am able to see that it is a bit deeper
than I would like but manageable at home.

"My medkit is in the closet in my bedroom, top shelf on the left
side," she answers my unspoken question without missing a beat. I
walk into the room and aside from the unmade bed, the room is tidier
than someone who lives alone. None of her furniture matches, but
none of that matters to me. I feel more at home in this apartment with
her than I ever have in the opulent family home that I inherited. I
walk over to the closet and slide open the left side, ready to grab the
kit and see the dress that she wore to the benefit. There is a small bag
exactly where she said it would be and I quickly head back to the
main room and find her on the couch.

"I figured that if this is going to hurt like a bitch, I might as well
be comfortable." She fills in the blanks for me and I love that she is an
open book for me even before I have to ask. It makes my heart sore. I
walk to the sink to wash my hands before digging into the kit since
clean hands are the first step in infection prevention. Coming back to
the couch, I reach in the bag and pull out all of the items that I could
need. Even with this being a compact kit, you can tell that she has
taken the time to properly stock it, and as much as I want to know
why, I think that is a question for a later time.

"I am sorry that this is going to hurt, Lilac, but I promise that I
will never purposely cause you pain unless it is medically necessary.
Even then, I will feel bad about it. Don't get me wrong, I am a bad
man, but I will never be a bad man to you," I declare before cleaning

the wound and causing her to hiss. I flinch at the sound of her pain but continue for her health. Once the wound is clean, I put in an antibacterial cream and wrap it. The whole time she just stares at me quizzically.

"I have never seen a non-medical professional who could clean and dress a wound so fast. Do you have to do this much?" she asks and her lack of hesitation brings a smile to my face.

"Not often anymore but before the deal my father made, I had to deal with a lot more gruesome wounds without a lot of help. I studied medicine in my free time as a way to save my friends and colleagues." I answer her truthfully, never wanting to hide anything from her.

She reaches into her bag and calls her boss to let them know that she won't be able to make it tomorrow and that her family emergency is going to keep her off of her shifts this week. Once the call is over, she looks at me and the vulnerability in her eyes pierces my heart.

"Will you join me to sleep? I am exhausted from today but I don't want to sleep alone," she asks, and I would never deny her this. I nod, grab the firearms, take her hand, and we head off to the bedroom. We change quickly, thanks to an extra set of clothes from the car, plug in our cellphones, and climb under her sheets. The moment she lays her head on my chest we both drift off for the most peaceful sleep I have ever experienced.

Epilogue
"Cinnamon rolls and movies are a great recovery."

Anna

The smell of bacon and cinnamon rolls wakes me from the best sleep that I have ever had to an empty bed and confusion fogging my brain. Forcing myself to climb out of the comfortable bed, I can still see Aldo's shoes by my bedroom door, which means he didn't leave. As I step through the bedroom door, I see him standing over the stove in my kitchen with a pan that sounds like where the bacon is cooking.

"Good morning beautiful," he greets me without turning around, causing a smile to cross my face. I walk up next to him and rest my head on his shoulder, unready to speak without some coffee. He kisses my forehead with a chuckle before popping open my microwave, exposing a coffee from Sly Fox Cafe and the tears brim my eyes. I can't believe he did this for me without asking. This man barely knows me and he got me breakfast and coffee without any prompting. No one in my life has ever done that but Lucy.

"I got a breakfast of cinnamon rolls and I am making bacon. I had one of my men get you the coffee while he picked up the food because I am not sure how you take it and I knew you would need something to start out your day." He fills me in before I can even ask. I wrap my arms around his waist and pull myself into him, enjoying all of the comforts that he brings with him this morning. At that moment his phone rings. It's Gio calling, and he rattles off questions about Lucy and what the outcome was of the warehouse while we were sleeping. I grab my coffee and take some big gulps to prepare for the depth of conversion I know will come after this call. Each drink brings me to more humanity as it enters my system. It is almost 9:00 AM according to the clock on my wall, which means I slept in from my normal schedule. The call ends and he turns toward me.

"The update is that Lucy is okay, but she has some bruising and damage from fighting back when they took her and when they tied her in that room. They didn't have time to sexually assault her but they stripped her of her clothes to make her feel powerless. I have no doubts that they would have if she had been with them longer, but we got there in time. She is going to stay with Gio until we can guarantee her safety at her own place. When I am not here I would like to post someone inside as backup so you are not alone. I understand that you might be uncomfortable with that but it is just until we understand why she was a target and increase the security here so that you can feel safer in your own home. Do you have any questions or need anything expanded?" he ends with the question without hesitation. I shake my head, unable to answer and just trying to process the information. While I understand that I may have questions later, my brain is barely functional at this moment. He dishes up breakfast and we sit at the table and eat in a comfortable silence. With the way that he looks at me, I cannot help but want to wrap myself in his lap so I can feel safe again.

"I had my guy drop off movies for us and we are going to spend all day relaxing on the couch together before I take you out for a real date that you deserve," he promises me as we make our way to the couches where he has pulled out the blankets and a couple of bags of snacks sit on the corner ready for us to enjoy. We make it partway through the first movie before I need his lips. My skin feels electric where we make contact. He leans into the kiss, passion escalating as our tongues dance and the rest of the room falls into the abyss. His warmth and touch consumes me and I reposition to straddle his lap.

"We can wait, baby, if you want to. I am happy to just be here with you," he reassures me without adding any pressure. His willingness to wait until I am ready makes the decision for me without concern. I pull my shirt over my head, baring my chest to him for the first time, lighting a new type of fire in his eyes. His hands explore my hips and work their way up to cupping my breasts. The soft moan that escapes me at his touch catches us both off guard as I press myself into his bulge. He tilts his head back and releases a groan.

In one swift movement, he grabs my hips and stands from the couch, carrying me on his hips toward my bedroom. I release a giggle at the sudden movement and the way it feels to be carried, most of my weight resting on his hips, rubbing as he takes steps. As we reach the bed he places me down and shucks his shirt, throwing it at the door before reaching for my pants. His fingers find their way below the hem of my pants and as he pulls them down, he places soft kisses on my exposed skin. Every kiss causes a surge of electricity to pulse through my body. As my pants find their way to the floor, he quickly removes his own, smirking down at my exposed skin. Heat floods my cheeks and in response, he climbs up the bed, kissing my skin lightly as he gets closer to my face. In one swift movement, his arms sweep under my ass and pull my knees over his shoulders before burying himself in my pussy.

"Oh, fuck," I moan at the sensation of his tongue exploring my body. The pleasure overwhelms me and forces my hips to buck uncontrollably before my orgasm crashes into me. It hits me with a force that feels fireworks being set off beneath my skin. With my eyes closed and breathing through the tremors, I feel him giggle against my inner thigh. His finger slides along the moisture gathered before he slides in a finger and rubs my clit with his thumb. The pressure builds as he slides his finger in and out of me before he adds a second finger.

Between the added finger and his thumb rubbing circles on my clit, my legs start to shake again as the cusp of another orgasm finds me. Bowing my back off of the bed and no longer in control of my body, the orgasm takes full control.

"This is just the start baby, I want to ravish you over and over again until your bones are jelly and you have screamed my name so loud that the rest of the building knows it," he promises me with soft kisses on my hips before making eye contact with me. As he brings himself higher on the bed, he leans over until his lips find mine. I can feel the tip of his cock against my entrance as excitement bubbles in my core.

"I'm ready," I whisper, still partially out of breath from my last orgasm. He searches my eyes before slowly pushing himself inside of me. With his dick fully seated in me, he begins to piston his hips driving my euphoria to new heights. In one swift movement, he pulls my legs up and places them over his shoulder, giving us a new position. The pressure from the changed position is enough to send me over the edge.

"I need you to cum again, Lilac. I can't cum until I feel the way that your pussy destroys me for anyone else as you come apart," he coaxes me and the words do exactly what he wants because I come apart at the seams from my orgasm, incoherently whispering fuck over and over again. His hips jerk as he thrusts into me again and spills his hot cum inside of me. As he pulls himself out of me and climbs out of bed he makes a promise.

"Baby, I will always choose you even in the darkest of times. My soul belongs to you."

About the Author

C.J. is born and bred in the desert of Nevada, where she currently resides with her husband. Having grown up in the Pacific Northwest, she has a soft spot for beautiful green mountainous areas and has an eternal love for the Oregon coast. When she isn't writing she can be found reading, listening to music, or working on her tattoo collection. She is an author of dark romance and loves connecting with her readers. Her love of dark humor and swoony characters heavily influences her work.

Connect with Me: https://linktr.ee/c.j.willis.author

tHERapy

By: Pandora Cress

About tHERapy

Mila Santos only leaves her home to attend therapy and participate in anonymous sex clubs. She's content keeping to herself and staying away from the abusive behaviours of men that she has all too much experience with. But when someone in her therapy group takes an interest in her, he's determined to show her that there is one man who won't hurt her. But he's happy to kill the others who have.

Beckett Holden is the quiet man who attends the SA Survivors support group every Wednesday. He doesn't talk much about his own past with his father, but he is an attentive listener. And that's how he learns about Mila, the beautiful woman who has lived through unimaginable trauma and sworn off men for good. Beck wants to show her that he's different. And if that means following her to a sex club and having anonymous experiences with her while tracking down her abusers, then so be it.

Content Note:

This work contains upsetting themes and situations involving mentions of childhood sexual abuse, childhood physical violence, hypersexuality, intentional harm to oneself both mentally and physically, murder, stalking and torture. While this list may seem off-putting without context, the story is essentially one of love, healing and justified revenge.

Relationship type: M/F

Prologue
Mila

I was eight years old when I was touched by a man for the first time.

I had been separated from my parents when they were deported and forced into a run-down home with dozens of other children. I learned quickly to try and make myself small, unnoticed. But it didn't matter how bad I looked or smelled. The men would find me and take what they wanted.

They called it a "Refugee Center," but it was anything but that.

I was eight years old the first time.

I was eight years old the sixth time.

I was eight years old the forty-second time.

And I was fourteen when I ran away because I had finally lost count.

Chapter One
Mila

"Mila," a voice calls out. "Mila Santos!"

I walk up to the counter at my local CVS and watch the tired-looking pharmacist scan my prescriptions. The circles under his eyes could rival my own, and that's saying something.

"Do you have a savings card you'd like to scan?" he asks, and I shake my head. I don't speak much in public if I can help it. I stare at his name tag: *Stefan.* I don't even know how to pronounce his name correctly, so I don't bother to try.

I look down again as he starts placing my items in a bag.

Xanax.

Birth control.

Paxil.

Ambien.

"Do you have any questions about your medications today?"

I shake my head again, and this time, I nervously brush my thick black hair behind my ears with both hands. I tap my card against the machine, and once 'APPROVED' shines on the screen, I snatch my bag and make my way out of the store before he can even finish his robotic, "Have a nice day."

I take a deep breath once the cold air hits my face.

And... this is why I'm a hacker. Not because of pharmacists, of course. But because my skills allow me to work from home. I keep to myself and prefer it that way.

It's safer.

At thirty-three, I should have a better handle on myself, but as the bag in my hand reminds me on the walk home, I don't.

I learned a long time ago that I can't rely on anyone but myself. When I was 14, I ran away from the center and ended up on the streets. I hustled, and I survived. I learned how to make money, and I learned how to hide it. I live modestly now, even though I've got a nice little nest egg saved up. It's a habit I picked up along the way. You never know when you'll need a quick exit, so always have the funds to get away if you need to. Which helped so much when I needed to leave my marriage.

I pull my thin leather jacket together in the front to shield myself from the chill of the morning as I grind my teeth when the memories come flooding back.

I thought I could trust him.

I thought he was *different*.

I thought I could let my guard down.

The first time he made me realize that our 3 year marriage was indeed *not* safe was when he broke the lamp in our living room by smashing it onto the ground at my feet. I seized up in fear, and when he calmed down and apologized, I believed him. And then, I told him about the men at the center and what they did to me. At first, he held me while I cried. Apologizing profusely. Made an effort not to lose his temper. But then, it changed. He started using it against me, bringing it up in arguments and accusing me of not trusting him because of my past.

It was only 6 months after the first incident when he broke my nose and dislocated my shoulder.

I fought back and managed to knock him out with the toaster I ripped out of the wall as I ran into the kitchen, my fingers slicing against the coils as I brought it down on him. I packed a bag of my most important things: clothing, checkbook, and birth certificate. The one thing that kept me from being deported like my parents. I made a report at the police station and filed for divorce. I asked for nothing but my freedom from him, and his lawyers were more than happy to grant the change.

I haven't seen him in 3 years, but I know he's miserable.

I check.

I know it's not healthy, but I do it because it makes me feel better.

I unlock the door to my apartment and throw my coat on a chair in the kitchen before putting my meds on the counter. The orange bottles look so jarring against the black-and-white tones of the room. But they are as necessary to my survival as the roof over my head, and I appreciate them more than I can put into words.

But I can't just live off the pills, obviously.

So, how do I manage my crippling anxiety, depression, CPTSD, and borderline agoraphobia?

Well, like any sane person, I frequent sex clubs. It's anonymous and safe. I don't have to get to know anyone; I don't have to open up or let my guard down. The clubs have security, so I know I'm protected. I can just go, fuck, and leave. I can use my body to try and forget what happened to me, to try and erase the feel of their hands on me. And to balance it out, I attend a Sexual Abuse Survivors support group each week. It's the only time I feel comfortable enough to open up to anyone or hold a conversation.

We're all survivors, so we understand each other. We share our stories, our struggles, and our triumphs. It's the only place I can be completely honest about my past without being judged or misunderstood. They get it when I say that sometimes I feel broken beyond repair, that I wish I could go back to save the little girl who endured so much and stop the young woman I was from getting married to yet another monster.

"You're safe now, Mila," Nancy, our group's main therapist, says to me as we hug at the end of each meeting. Dr. Wilson always tells me that, and I nod and tell her I know.

But the truth is, I *don't* feel safe.

I don't know if I ever will.

Chapter Two
Beckett

I can't believe it's been two years since I started coming here.

I spot Mila across the room, her eyes scanning the crowd as she picks her usual seat in the circle of chairs set up in the center of the room. She's a lone wolf, that one. Keeps to herself mostly, but I see her. How could I not?

We're both here at this Sexual Abuse Survivors support group, but our stories couldn't be more different. I moved to New York to escape my past, leaving my father and the memories behind. I've found a way to make a life for myself here.

Mila, though, she *runs*.

She's always ready to bolt since that is what her experiences have taught her to do. She runs from her demons and tries to outpace them. I respect that. We all deal with our trauma in our own ways, and I would never judge her.

I've never intruded on her space, but I have to admit I've wanted to.

I would be lying if I said there weren't several times my hand reached out towards her to lend a comforting touch before I clenched my fist and collected myself.

Maybe it's how she holds herself or the fire I see burning in her eyes despite how tired she appears. Whatever it is, I know better than to push. We're both damaged goods, after all. Sometimes, I wonder if she knows how beautiful she is. Not just physically, but the way she carries herself.

The way she survives.

"You okay, Beckett?" Dr. Wilson asks, snapping me back to the present.

I nod, feeling my face grow warm. I run a calloused hand through my short chestnut hair before responding, "Yeah, sorry. Just thinking."

The group starts, and we share our stories one by one. Mila speaks, and her voice is steady, but her hands are shaking. She tells of her marriage, of the man who was supposed to love her but instead used her past against her. He took advantage of her love, her body, and her mind.

My heart aches for her, but I don't show it. I know that's not what she wants.

Mila doesn't want pity.

She wants understanding. We all do.

I share my story next of my father and the control he tried to exert over my life. I don't actually tell the group that it's my father. I just say a "man I was close to" and no one pushes me to explain further. It's hard enough to talk about those times, anyway. When I didn't listen to his insane demands, I was punished with beatings and sexual assault so bad that I couldn't attend school for weeks at a time. My father didn't give a shit about me but *fuck*, if his reputation wasn't prioritized. The moment I turned 18, I was out of his home and in the city.

It's a story I've told before, but it still stings.

Mila listens, her dark eyes telling me without words that she cares. She gives me a slight nod when I finish, and I know she gets it. She understands the need to escape, to start over.

As the group wraps up, Mila catches me staring at her. Again.

Fuck. I gotta get a handle on myself.

She gives me a small smile, and I feel a connection form between us. It's not romantic—it's something more. It's a recognition of shared pain and trauma-based acceptance.

For now, that's enough.

That has to be enough.

Before, I would get tangled up in relationships, using them to distract myself. But since joining the group, I've stayed clear of romantic entanglements. I needed to work on myself, and that's what I've been doing. I know Mila is doing the same.

It's paid off, too; my career has taken off. I'm the highest-paid worker in my shop now and have a reputation for being the best. Being a steelworker in New York is rough, but I wouldn't trade the experience I gained for anything. Especially when they let me in at just 18 working the crane in order to survive on my own when I got here. I owe that company my life, because where would I have ended up without it?

But as much as I try to ignore it, something about Mila pulls at me. It's not just her looks although she is absolutely stunning with her dark skin and raven hair. Men would start wars over those full lips if we were from a different time.

Even as I try to tell myself not to speak with her, I find myself rushing out to do just that when the meeting is over.

I catch up to her as she's leaving the building and heading towards the subway. I spot her jeans and black jacket as her tall boots hurry her across the pavement.

"Mila, hold on a minute."

She turns, slightly frowning, and I wonder if I've made a mistake. I notice her entire frame is tense before she sees it's me. But then her expression softens, and she waits for me to catch my breath as I step before her.

"Hey," she says, her voice cautious.

"Hey," I reply, trying to sound casual. "I didn't mean to startle you."

"You didn't," she says defensively. "It's just that I wasn't expecting you to follow me out."

I let out a dark chuckle. "Following you is hardly what I was doing. I tried to catch you after the meeting, but you're quick for someone so short."

She rolls her eyes at my joke. "Not all of us can be giants like you."

I glance down at my body, pretending to notice it for the first time. I have on black jeans, a cream sweater, and a brown leather jacket. My father always wore black leather, and I'm careful not to keep it in my wardrobe. Mila has on black leather, but she's the only one who wears it that doesn't bother me. I hold my hand up to my chest and pretend to measure her height against mine, then look at her.

"I think I'm the perfect size for you."

I watch a pretty blush take over her face and smile at her in return.

Mila plays with the hem of her jacket and eyes me warily. "So, what did you want?"

I take a deep breath and rub my hand on the back of my neck to calm my nerves. "I'm curious if you'd like to grab something to eat tonight if you're not busy."

I don't know what expression I anticipate her to have, but sadness isn't one of them.

Mila's eyes close tightly before looking back up at me and I take note of how she looks at the scar along my jaw. "I'm sorry, Beckett. I'm not really ready for that yet." She pauses as she lets out a shaky breath. "I've got plans tonight, anyway."

I feel my face fall, but I try to hide it. "Oh, no problem. I understand. I really didn't mean to put you on the spot. Just thought it would be nice to talk about something else *with* someone else. Some other time, maybe."

"Yeah, some other time."

She backs away with a wave and then turns to continue down the street.

I stand there for a moment, watching her go. Part of me wants to call out to her to try again. But I respect her too much for that. I know she struggles with getting close to people, and I won't push.

Besides, I tell myself, *there's always next time.*

So, can someone explain to me why I actually *did* start to follow her?

I don't know what possessed me to jump in the subway car connected to hers, but I'm here now.

The ride is long, and I almost lose her a few times when she gets off the N train. I tail her from a distance as she walks through the station and up to the street.

Astoria. Huh. I guess it's safe as far as neighborhoods go around here. Definitely full of actors and struggling artists.

I follow her down the street, keeping to the crowds. She walks with purpose, her head down, hands in her pockets. Mila said she had plans tonight, which I never expected her to say. Part of me feels she might just be making it up so that I will leave her alone.

I mean, I just followed her home. Based on recent events, if her spidey senses were telling her I was a creep, I would have to agree.

As I close the distance between us, I bump into a group of college students complaining about their professor, and I spot her entering a beautiful old building. It's one of those pre-war apartments with high ceilings and intricate moldings.

Well, she definitely has some money.

I hang back, not wanting to be seen, and watch as she lets herself in. It's a spring night, so I grab a coffee and a pastry from the Greek bakery across the street. I'm unsure what to expect, but I'm determined to find out where she goes. She's mentioned a few times that she's a hermit, so where is she going?

Time ticks by, and I finish my coffee, but there's no sign of her.

Maybe she's not coming back out, and I contemplate leaving.

Definitely think I'm a creep.

But just as I'm about to give up, I see her emerge from the front doors. She looks different—her hair is up, and she's changed into a simple black dress with her jacket over her shoulders. It clings to her curves in all the right ways, and I feel my breath catch in my throat.

She walks as quickly as her red heels will let her, and I step behind her, keeping my distance. She heads down towards the old subway station, and my curiosity grows. There aren't many places down here—just a few old warehouses and...

That's when it clicks into place.

I know where she's going. There's a sex club down here, hidden away. I've heard about it from the guys at work but had never been. Mila mentioned it once, a while back but I didn't think too much of it at the time. She said it was a safe place to be herself without judgment. I assumed it was something she did once or twice.

My heart races as I realize what I've stumbled upon.

I stop following her, letting her disappear into the unmarked door under the single red light above it. I don't need to see any more.

Besides, I have a good idea of where this night is headed for her.

And if this is where she feels comfortable, I'm getting a membership.

Chapter Three
Mila

I step into the dimly lit club entrance, a familiar rush of anxiety coursing through me. I've been here dozens of times but it still stresses me out to check in. The bass from the music thumps softly in the background, but it fades as I approach the ornate gold metal security desk.

The bouncer, a massive figure with arms like tree trunks, nods as I approach. He checks my ID and scans me up and down. His eyes are impassive, like he's seen it all before, and nothing shocks him anymore.

"Same deal tonight?" he asks, his voice gruff but not unkind. I think his name is Ben or Bill, but I can't remember. There are a lot of bouncers here.

I nod. "Yeah, just checking in for the anonymous room."

He gestures toward the velvet rope behind him. "You're good to go. Just remember—no talking in there."

I walk past him, feeling that thrill tingle at the back of my neck and resist the urge to pull my hair down. This place had become a refuge of sorts—a fucked up opportunity to reclaim my body on my terms. In some weird way, I figure if I fuck enough people then I won't think of all the ones who took advantage of me as I grew up.

I make my way down the narrow hallway, walls adorned with flickering lights and heavy velvet curtains that hang like secrets on parted lips in the corners of this club.

As I reach the door to the anonymous encounter room, I hesitate for a moment. Plunging into darkness where anything could happen should terrify me, but I don't like to be seen. My body has been through too much, and I will not discuss where all my scars are from.

After discarding my clothing and putting my personal items in a small closet outside of the room, I turn the knob and step inside.

The air is thick with the heat from the thermostat and excitement, but it envelops me like a blanket rather than suffocating me. Pitch black takes over my senses; I can hardly see my hands before my face. I move deeper into the room, allowing myself to feel small and vulnerable.

It is *liberating*.

I often prefer this arrangement—the lack of sight meant no judgments, no expectations. Just bodies fumbling together in darkness; sometimes we fuck hard, other times with urgency. Sometimes, they became strangers who felt achingly familiar to my past.

In these moments, I allow myself to drift into darker fantasies. Sometimes, they took the form of faceless shadows—men or women whose bodies reminded me too much of those who had hurt me in the past. It twisted something inside me, an echo of pain wrapped in fleeting pleasure. But this is what I thought I needed to do to move on. Find a way to embrace what happened to me in some fucked up way.

But that's why I kept going back to the support group—to acknowledge that I wasn't okay, to remind myself that each Wednesday night didn't have to be an escape but a step toward confronting my truth... however dark it may be.

Then I feel it—a gentle touch on my arm, light but deliberate.

"Is this okay?" a voice murmurs close to my ear.

I nod even though they can't see me. My voice caught somewhere in my throat, the words lost in the thick air. I reach out tentatively and find their hands, fingers interlocking instinctively.

"No talking," I finally replied, slightly irritated.

I allow myself to lean into the man before me, feeling our bodies align like puzzle pieces seeking completion. A surge of something like freedom washes over me and drowns out my mind's thoughts. Adrenaline is my friend these days. And when it's not, that's what my meds are for.

But this was what I craved—intimacy stripped of expectations. At least, it's what I tell myself.

Because in the next moments, things change.

He forces himself inside me within minutes, and then he's spitting on my asshole before taking me there next.

It hurts.

It feels like I'm being ripped apart, and I cling to the cold vinyl cushions of the couch in front of me. This room only has this stupid couch and not a bed because that would be too intimate. No one wants that when they come to this room.

An extra hard thrust in my backside has tears streaming down my face, so I cling to Emily Dickinson as I dissociate and start to whisper to myself:

"Hope is the thing with feathers,
That perches in the soul..."

Chapter Four
Beckett

Three months. Ninety days. Two thousand, one hundred and sixty hours.

That's how long it took me to gather the courage to step into the darkness with her.

I'd followed Mila to the club every Wednesday night like clockwork, always keeping a respectful distance. I wanted our first encounter to be on my terms, possibly even let her know of my plans to join her in this world.

But tonight, something changed. The pull to be near and comfort her was too strong.

I joined the club weeks ago, so they had already done the necessary background checks on me. On the days when she wasn't there, I made myself comfortable with the building. Even though I had prepared for this mentally, I couldn't help the way my heart pounded, and my body warred with itself in terms of just simple breathing.

I waited until she disappeared into the anonymous encounter room from the opposing entrance. Without hesitation, I stripped my clothes off and put them in the locker in the adjoining room before placing my hand on the handle. I look back at the mirror that is leaning against the black-painted wall beside the locker and take in the burn marks on my upper arms and chest courtesy of my father. I only allow myself a minute to feel self-conscious because my physique is muscular and chiseled, even though my skin is marred with a broken childhood.

The lights in the room I'm in automatically shut off as I turn the handle into the anonymous encounter room and make my way inside.

I stand silently, my eyes adjusting to the pitch-black room. I can sense her presence, so I reach out and wait until I feel the wall beside me.

Her movements are hesitant at first, but soon, she's approaching me, and I let her. I let her come to me so she feels what I want her to feel—that she has control here, not me.

Because she does.

She reaches out, her touch gentle and searching. I stifle the urge to speak and tell her it's me.

When her hand finds my arm, she pauses, and for a moment, I think she might recognize me, which is ridiculous because I can't see an inch in front of me and know she can't either. But then, with a soft sigh, she continued, her touch tracing the contours of my body.

I allow her to explore me for several minutes. Once her fingers began to tremble, she led me over to another part of the room, and I felt her ass push against my hard cock. I gently try to turn her around to face me again, but she bends over and grabs onto something in front of her to push her backside into me again. This time, it's more forceful, as if to say, 'Let's get this over with.'

This is what I was afraid of. That she was using her body as a way to escape but not allowing herself the thing that she truly needed.

I pull her close, my arms wrapping around her protectively. I knew what she craved—the ache to be held and soothed. She reluctantly lets me hold her, and my heart breaks just a little as I feel her body relax into mine.

She whispers demands, urging me to be rough, to hurt her.

"You're supposed to fuck in here," she whispers as she gets impatient when I don't listen. "You're wasting time."

But I couldn't give her what she asked for. What she *thought* she wanted. Instead, I hold her tighter until I can feel her breasts and her heartbeat against my chest, my lips brushing her hair as I move my hands soothingly over her back.

I start kissing her. A deep, lingering kiss that has us both pressing our bodies into one another in hopes that it never ends. She tastes better than my thoughts conjured up these last months, and I love the noises she makes when I cup her jaw. When her tongue seeks mine out, I am more than happy to oblige and slant my mouth over hers over and over again. My fingers are trying to map her skin as we move together, and all I can think about is how soft she is. How perfect and warm. I run my fingers through her long hair after I find the hair tie keeping her hair up in a messy bun. She always had her hair up when she came here as if there was some sort of barrier between her and the things she was doing.

But I won't let her hide in here. Not with me.

I find the couch in front of her and gently sit her down as I kneel between her legs. Her breathing gets shallow, and I feel her tense up as my mouth sucks along the flesh of her throat while my hands lightly rub up and down along her arms. I can feel the goosebumps on her skin, and it's too warm here to be from anything other than what I'm doing to her.

Good.

Her hands grip my hair as I kiss down to her chest before taking a nipple into my mouth. She goes rigid, and I stop immediately, my mouth hovering over her breast.

A silent question hangs in the air.

Do you want me to stop?

Her surprised gasp is heart wrenching because even though I haven't spoken aloud, her reaction tells me she doesn't get this courtesy.

Her back arches off the furniture until her breast presses against my mouth, and I latch back on, lavishing it with the adoration it deserves.

When she's panting and trying to bring me back up by fisting my hair, I kiss down her body, instead inhaling her scent as I go. Her skin is like liquid velvet and supple, and the air smells of her arousal and a mix of butterscotch and roses. It is the most intoxicating thing that has ever entered my senses, and I'm drunk on it before I even reach her inner thighs.

She tenses again but doesn't try to push me away. Her grip hasn't left my hair, and she scratches my scalp with her nails as she lets out a long breath.

I take her thighs in my hands and gently widen them, pushing her knees up to her chest where I can have her wholly bared to me.

I wish that I could see her in this moment–see her stretched out for me and the way her cunt looks drenched in the light.

I must take too long with my thoughts because she starts to try and bring her legs back down. That simply won't do, so I immediately lean down to devour her.

"You don't have to do anything like that," comes out as a moan when my mouth meets her center, my tongue tracing a strip along her slick. "It's okay."

I growl, deep in my throat, as my lips wrap around her clit and suck. *Hard.*

I hope she knows that means that I need to do this.

When her hands grip my shoulders and pull me closer to her until I'm practically drowning in her juices, I take it as a yes.

Alternating between stealing air, sucking at her tender flesh, and licking her with quick flicks of my tongue is enough to send her over the edge in minutes. She's still trembling when I pick her up and position her on my lap while I take her place on the couch. I guide her entrance to meet my cock with my hands on her hips, but I don't pull her down. I simply drag her back and forth over the tip, coating myself in the aftermath of her orgasm.

She keeps making the sexiest noises, and it takes everything in me to not bury myself in her immediately. Luckily, she seems to feel the same way because her hands slam down on my chest for leverage as she lines herself up and sinks down.

If there was any doubt that I shouldn't have pursued this, it's gone forever as of this union.

It's the perfect fit, and when she starts moving on top of me, I can't remember any moment in my life being so exquisite.

She moves with confidence, chasing another precipice, and I allow my hands to roam over her curves. Eventually, she leans forward on top of me, breathing heavily against my ear as I feel her tighten around me. I cradle her face and kiss her tenderly, telling her without words that she's cared for and safe.

Our kiss deepens as her movements falter, and I know she's close because I barely hold on myself. My hands find her hips again, and I take over the rhythm, except I'm tilting her so her clit grinds against my pelvis as I thrust inside of her. It's just enough friction to have her nails scratching my chest and her moans breaking the silence throughout the room.

When I feel her walls spasm and she's coming on my cock until it's soaking the space where our bodies are joined, I allow myself to let go and join her.

The background checks make sure that we are tested and clean several times a month, and women must show proof of contraceptive use to participate. I get to spill myself in Mila, and it doesn't matter that we're in the darkness because the pleasure I feel would have blinded me regardless.

She collapses on my chest for a few minutes, and I gently stroke the skin of her back and leave kisses on the top of her head.

I wasn't surprised when the tears came, wet against my skin. I knew why—the weight of her pain was something I understood all too well. So I held her, sheltering her from the storm within her memories.

After that, she pulled away abruptly and stood up, her breathing ragged. The loss I felt when I slipped out of her was like a punch to the gut. I wanted to speak to her but remained silent because I didn't want to ruin the moment I had tried so hard to give her.

I love this woman. I want to heal her. And I'll wait as long as it takes for her to let me in. I'll be her light in the darkness, even if she doesn't know it yet.

Mila rushed to the door on her side. The light turned on and filled the room before me, but not enough to light the area where I stood. She paused at the threshold and experienced some sort of panic attack.

I recognized the signs almost immediately.

She scratched at her arms, digging her nails into her skin as if trying to erase the past encounters that haunted her. The club lights were too harsh, reminding her of those men who'd taken what they wanted without a second thought. I resist the urge to pull her back into the darkness with me.

Rage burned in my chest as I watched her--this beautiful, broken woman. I want to smash something, to put a stop to the pain I saw reflected in her eyes. I knew it was the past playing tricks on her, those bastards who'd left their mark, and her ex-husband—that son of a bitch who'd made her feel unworthy of love.

I made a vow then and there. I'll find those men, every last of them, and make them pay. They'd taken her innocence, her trust, and they'd pay with their lives. Especially that ex-husband of hers—he'd ruined her chance she had at a peaceful life, at happiness. He'd taken her trust and twisted it, even after she believed in him despite how she had been brought up and used. He took her for granted, and for that, he'd suffer.

Mila was strong; I already knew that. But seeing her like this, so raw and vulnerable, broke something inside me. I want to protect her, shield her from the world and its cruelties. I want to be her light in the darkness, to show her that not all men are like those who'd hurt her.

I am not the same.

But for now, I'll keep my distance, respecting the boundaries she'd unknowingly set between us. I'll bide my time, waiting for the right moment to show her that not all touches have to hurt, that not all memories have to be painful.

Because I love her, and in time, I know she'll let me in.

I will help her move on—one body bag at a time.

I just need access to her files first.

Chapter Five
Mila

I skipped the club next Wednesday, shaken by what had happened the week before. It wasn't like me to avoid it, but something about that man in the dark room had unnerved me. So, I locked myself in my apartment, burying myself in my work and trying to forget about the unknown man who'd held me with such tenderness.

That weekend, I received flowers—red roses, a whole bouquet, with a single white rose that stood out, dipped in blood. Tied around the stem, was my ex husband's wedding ring.

The card sent shivers down my soul, and my stomach twisted.

One by one, I will take them down.
And I will use their bodies to build you a sanctuary.

My breath caught in my throat as I realized someone knew of my past and cared enough to... what? Do me a fucked up favor?

I was scared, but a part of me also felt... protected. My ex was an evil man and I was surprised that I didn't feel bad about the fact he was gone. I felt... relief.

God, what was wrong with me? Too much, apparently.

Whoever this was seemed to want to exact vengeance on my behalf. But who?

I couldn't shake the feeling that the man from the club was somehow behind it. Had he been the one to send me the roses? If so, how had he found out where I lived? And why would he go to such lengths?

I wanted to bring it up in group therapy but stayed quiet. For a few weeks, I didn't do much besides pretend to listen and stare off into space as I contemplated what was going on in my life at the time. When I couldn't stay cooped up in my apartment any longer, I returned to the club the following week. I needed to work out the confusion and frustration that had been building up inside me before I drove myself insane. I went to the anonymous encounter room, my pulse quickening as I anticipated seeing him again.

And there he was, waiting in the darkness. I recognized his touch, the way he moved as if he knew every inch of my body and wanted to worship it with his hands. He took his time, caressing and exploring with his gentle and possessive touch.

It was him. The same man.

I had no idea who he was or why he was doing this, but I didn't care at that moment. All I knew was the comfort of his touch, the feeling of being cherished and avenged all at once. So I let him hold me, let him take away the pain, just for a little while.

And then I went back again the following week.

I felt him before I saw him, an electric charge in the air that crackled with familiarity. His presence filled the space, reassuring yet unsettling. I could barely make out his silhouette as he moved closer, but I could sense him.

"Thought you might not come back," he murmured, his voice low and inviting.

"I had my reasons." My voice came out steadier than I felt, laced with a mixture of defiance and curiosity. I didn't even care that we were breaking the 'No Talking' rule.

"Yeah? What kind of reasons?" He stepped closer still, his breath warm against my cheek.

"I don't know who you are," I reply, the words tumbling out before I can stop them. "Or why you sent those flowers."

"Flowers?" He chuckles softly. "Did they scare you?"

"Scare? No." The lie tasted bitter on my tongue.

He reaches for my hand and guides it to his chest. My fingers brush against something hard—a nipple piercing-- before my hand rests above his heart, which is pounding in time with mine. "What if I told you I'm coming here to help?"

"Help?" The word felt foreign, like a pebble lodged in my throat. "You think showing up here is helpful?"

He pauses, his silence heavy with intent, and his hand releases mine while I still keep my own pressed against his chest. "I think I'm treating you better than the rest of the men you've met here. You deserve better than what they did to you. And you have to stop seeking out pain in a way to try and erase your trauma. New trauma is not going to do anything but set you back."

I pull back slightly but don't drop my hand.

"What do you know about it?" I press, searching for answers hidden behind the veil of darkness around us.

"I've been watching." His words fell like stones between us, heavy and unyielding, and his arms encircled my frame and brought me flush against him.

"Watching?" My body stiffened, but not from fear–from awe.

"Yes," he continues, voice steady yet laced with emotion. "You don't need to be alone anymore."

I can't decide if that promise soothed or rattled me more. The heat from his body wrapped around mine, and our breaths mingling in the confined space didn't help my mental state either.

"What do you want from me?" The question escaped before I could stop myself.

"I want you to trust me. I know you have no reason to after what you've been through, and my promises are nothing compared to the hurt you have to go off of from the past. But I would rather slit my own throat than cause you an ounce of pain. And if you won't trust me–trust *that*."

It was true that I didn't know if I could trust him, but something in his words—how he said them—made me want to. It was foolish, of course. I barely knew this man, and yet... there was something about him that drew me in. Something that made me want to believe he could be different from all the others.

"Why should I?" My voice was stronger this time, belying the uncertainty swirling inside me.

"You don't have to. Not yet." His hands found my waist, his thumbs brushing the bare skin just above my pelvis. "But I'm going to prove it to you. That I'm not like the rest. That I can be trusted."

"How do you plan to do that?"

His lips curved into a shadowed smile I could barely make out, and I felt his gaze on me even though I couldn't see his eyes. "I'll start by telling you my name. It's Beckett. Beckett Holden."

Beckett.

Oh, god.

I know this man. And he's known me–for years.

It clicked simultaneously, and the air flew from my lungs as I struggled to catch my breath.

"Well, Beckett," I took a pause to catch my breath. "This is one way to get a girl's attention when she turns down a date from you."

He chuckles in answer and I can't believe I didn't register his voice this whole time. "I'm persistent when I want to be."

"So, what now?"

He pulls me closer, his breath warm against my ear as he whispers, "Now... I take care of you."

I let him hold me, letting his touch soothe the doubts and fears that still lingered. His hands were gentle yet firm, and I could feel the strength in them—a promise of protection. But it was more than that.

It was as if he understood the depth of my pain and was offering solace without asking for anything in return—something I had never had before.

"Why?" The word slipped out, raw and vulnerable. "Why would you do this for me?"

His thumb brushes my cheek, wiping away a tear I didn't realize had fallen.

"Because you need it," he whispers. "And because I want to."

I leaned into his touch, my body yearning for the comfort he offered, even if my mind wanted to push him away. "But—"

"Shh." His finger presses gently against my lips, silencing my protests. "Let me make you feel safe."

So, I do. I let him. I surrender to the darkness, to the comfort of a stranger, and for the first time in a long time, I let myself imagine that maybe—just maybe—I could be healed.

Beckett makes me finish with his mouth and his fingers before he enters me in the dark. It's not slow like the times before. It's fast and full of desire and hunger for each other. I love that he doesn't treat me as if I'm about to break and allows me to take charge with him. I think he likes it, too, because he's dripping down my thighs within minutes when I straddle him again on the couch.

We lay down together on the vinyl surface with my back pressed against his front before we speak again.

"Tell me something," he murmurs against my hair. "What do you want?"

My heart jumps at the question. It felt too raw—too vulnerable—to answer honestly. I craved safety, love, and maybe even redemption from the choices that had led me here.

"I want..." The words tangle on my tongue before they break free. "I want to feel normal."

His fingers trace patterns on my back as he contemplates my words. "You are normal," he replies softly. "Just because you've been through hell doesn't mean you're not deserving of happiness. Fuck, you're more deserving than most."

Happiness felt like a distant dream that slipped through my fingers every time I reached for it. But there was a part of me that wanted to believe Beckett.

"Do you really think so?" I ask.

"I know so." He shifted slightly, creating enough space for our bodies to comfortably fit on the couch as he turned me to face him.

I drew in a shaky breath, feeling exposed but strangely empowered by his promise. I couldn't see him still in the dark, but I could hear the smile in his voice.

"Let's just try being together. If I make your life harder in any way instead of better, then it just takes one word, and I'll be gone." He leaned closer, his forehead pressed against mine as if we were sharing secrets.

As his lips brushed against mine softly, time seemed to freeze around us—everything else faded away—and for the first time in ages, I allowed myself to believe it might be okay after all.

Chapter Six
Beckett

I had to force myself to breathe and keep my hands steady as I knocked on the weathered door. This was it—the moment I'd been planning for weeks. I felt a spark of fear as the door creaked open, revealing the frail old man who stood there, his eyes clouded with confusion.

It was him. My heart races as I recognize the weathered face from old records and grainy photos. The man who had stolen her innocence and left her traumatized and in shambles. I force myself to smile, feigning friendly confusion as I ask, "Mr. Roberts? I think I may have the wrong place."

"No, I'm Roberts. Who are you, lad?" His voice quavers and I see his knuckles whiten as he grips his cane.

"A friend," I lie, stepping past him into the apartment. I close the door behind me, the click of the lock sounding unnaturally loud in the silence. "You remember Mila, don't you?"

His eyes widen as he takes a step back, shaking his head. "No, I haven't seen her in years. Please, I don't know what you want."

I follow him into the house, my eyes adjusting to the dim light.

"You took something from her—something precious. And now I'm here to take something precious from you—your life." As realization dawns in his eyes, I watch him try to bolt, but his aging body betrays him.

I grab him by the collar of his flannel robe, my fingers tight around his fragile neck as I slam him against the wall. "You thought you would get away with it?" I hiss. "I guess you've made it this far without someone holding you accountable for your unspeakable acts. You and your friends were supposed to be protecting those children. They'd lost their families, and you took their innocence, too. You disgust me to the point that this next part will be so enjoyable for me."

For hours, I made him pay.

I reveled in his cries, his pleas for mercy only serving to fuel my anger further. I know there was a time when Mila cried out for a similar mercy, but she deserved one, and this piece of shit did not. I wanted to erase every trace of his touch from her memory, and for some reason, I had convinced myself that killing these men would do that. But as his lifeless body hung limply before me, I knew that no amount of vengeance could truly heal her wounds— or mine.

Yet still, I felt no remorse.

I stared at the body, feeling a strange sense of emptiness. This was the last one. The sixth man and head of the center during Mila's time there. I told myself it was for Mila, that I was avenging her, but was I really healing her or just feeding my own need for control over something I couldn't let go of for myself? For punishment?

No, I can't think like that.

These men deserved everything they got and more. They had taken away Mila's childhood, filling her life with pain and fear. And countless others. I would ensure they never hurt anyone else and would not go peacefully.

I turn to leave, but a movement in the corner of my eye catches my attention. A woman stands in the doorway, pushing the door open, her eyes wide with horror. She must have heard the commotion and come to investigate.

Thought that door was locked. Fuck.

"I have a key," she says and holds it up as if to shield herself.

"Please," I say, holding up my hands to show I meant no harm. "I'm not here to harm anyone else. I didn't want you to see this."

"What have you done?" Her voice shook as she took in the scene. She reminded me of Mila, only younger with the same dark skin and hair. She didn't have an accent like Mila; her English intonation was perfect, even in fear. "Oh God, I'll call the police."

"Wait!" I move towards her, and thankfully, I'm no longer covered in blood from my session with the old man. I had forgotten about the neighbors. "Please, just give me a moment to explain."

She backed away, her eyes darting towards the phone on the hall table. She was in a dirty nightgown, and when I looked closely, she had bruises on her legs and was barefoot. I knew I couldn't let her call the cops, not yet. I had to buy some time.

"I know it looks bad, but he deserved it. That man in there did something terrible to someone I care about. He wasn't a good man." I took a step closer, my voice softening. "Please, allow me to make things right before you involve the police. Or at least let me leave a message for Mila."

Her eyes searched mine, and she was scared. I couldn't blame her. My words must have sounded like madness, and I shouldn't have uttered Mila's name, but I panicked. But then, something shifted in her expression. I saw recognition, and her eyes widened as she looked at me.

"Mila," she whispered. "You did this for Mila."

I nodded, a surge of relief washing over me. "Do you know her?"

"I know what happened to her," the woman said, her eyes filled with a familiar pain. "I was there, too. Mila tried to make sure that us younger girls weren't visited as much at the center. She sacrificed herself so much to help us. No one blamed her when she finally ran away. I tried to take her place, but I couldn't get out."

I felt a punch to the gut as realization struck me. Another survivor. One who knew Mila and her story, one who shared in it. Her gaze flicked to the body on the floor, and I saw a mix of emotions play across her face—fear, disgust, and something that looked like relief. And then I realized why she had a key. Why she was a neighbor. She was still here to service this old fuck.

"*Please*," she said, her voice shaking. "You have to go. I'll...I'll clean this up and call the police. I can tell them I found him like this. Or just tell them I heard a strange noise from my apartment and they should check. But you need to leave now."

I hesitated, trying to figure out why this woman hadn't run away. I wanted to trust her but couldn't risk involving another person. Not yet. "I can't just leave you here with this. It's too dangerous."

"I know what I'm doing," she said, her voice steady despite the horror of the situation. "Go. I'll take care of it. This is one mess I'll happily clean up."

I couldn't force her to let me stay, so I relented.

"Thank you," I say, my voice gruff with emotion for the horrors she'd endured at the hands of this despicable human on the floor before us.

"Take the east exit out of the building; there are no cameras that way. And tell Mila...tell her Evie tried to make things right after she left."

"I read that the center was closed down shortly after she went on the run. No one was arrested or charged, though."

"No. I was able to convince the county that it wasn't safe and everyone was transferred to another center or adopted shortly after."

"But you stayed behind?" I ask, already knowing the answer.

Evie is looking down at the body on the floor--or what's left of it, and stomps her bare foot on his face, his chest, and then eventually brings herself to the ground where she begins using her fists. I don't stop her. She needs to let it out. When she's spent, she looks up at me with blood splotched on her face like crimson freckles and says, "It was the deal I made."

I nod, my heart heavy as I close the door behind me.

As I got in my car and drove, my mind raced, imagining the sirens, the flashing lights. But they never came. I checked the news over the next couple of days where I read about what happened as told by the media.

Carl Roberts, aged 76, was found brutally murdered during a home invasion where his valuables were taken along with a safety deposit box. Police believe the suspects to be a group of young men from the area but have no names.

There's no mention of Evie.

Today is Mila's birthday.

I sent her a small box-shaped gift topped with a blood-red bow to match its contents. I watched her open the gift through the window and look through the polaroids of the men I took out for her. She dropped them to the ground and let out a cry so devastating that I thought the glass I was staring at her through would shatter.

I'd been watching her for some time now. Not in a creepy way, but with a sense of protection. So, when she got that package, I was there to see her reaction. Her cry was one of relief and years of pent-up pain. All those men who had hurt her were finally gone. I could see the weight lifting from her shoulders as she realized those chapters of her life were now closed and she could move on. As she held the box, her entire body trembled.

I wanted to rush in and comfort her, but I knew this was a moment she needed to experience alone.

So, I waited, knowing that soon she would let me in.

Chapter Seven
Mila

I should've known he was serious, but I thought it was just for show. That once he'd taken care of my ex that he'd be satisfied. But no, he went after them all.

Every. Single. One.

I pride myself on my ability to track anyone down and hack into the most secure systems, yet here I was, blindsided by Beckett.

The gift left me stunned.

He'd been persistent in his pursuit after he told me who he was at the club, asking me out week after week following our support group meetings. I kept declining, telling him I had plans, which I did—my Wednesdays at the club were non-negotiable. He joined me on those Wednesdays in the dark but wanted to date me in the light.

It wasn't long before he wore me down with charm and unwavering determination.

"Please, Mila. Just give me one chance. I promise it'll be worth it," he'd said with a smile that melted my heart.

Date a murderer? Why not? As far as I was concerned, there were worse things than death.

So, now we're on our first official date. Besides doctor appointments and grocery runs, I hadn't been out anywhere besides the club and the support group meetings in years. I hoped my attire was sufficient for where he was taking me, choosing a velvet long-sleeved dark green dress that flared out at the knees and black pumps. Beckett was dressed in black button-downs and black slacks, looking sleek and elegant like a man of his stature.

We looked like we were ready for a nice night out at a restaurant or cabaret. Imagine my surprise when we went to the last place I suspected.

Beckett pulled into the familiar parking lot of the club and proceeded to tell me there was a very good reason. My heart was pounding as we walked inside, knowing that it would be different this time.

After we checked in with security, he took my hand and led me not to the anonymous room but to one lit by soft, warm lights. It was time to face each other, to bring our encounters into the light. This was a stark contrast to the dark anonymity I was used to. I hesitated, my eyes adjusting to the glow, taking in the familiar surroundings of the club but from an entirely new perspective.

Beckett sensed my nervousness and squeezed my hand gently. "You don't have to do anything you don't want to. I'm not rushing you, Mila. I just thought that this was the appropriate next step for us. But it's up to you. Take your time."

His words were like a salve to my wracked nerves. I took a shaky breath, still processing how much he knew about my private life. But instead of feeling exposed, I felt... *understood.*

I moved towards the center of the room, shedding my dress and undergarments as I went. With each item that fell to the floor, I felt a weight lift from my shoulders like I was shedding those terrible memories. Baring myself to Beckett in the soft light was liberating, with no shadows to hide in. It was time he saw the scars that marred my skin on the outside since he resonated with the ones within me so well.

When I was completely naked, I turned to face him, my heart in my throat. "Those photos... they were from you, weren't they?" I asked, finally confronting him about the Polaroids of the men I had received. "You sent them, didn't you, Beck? You made good on your word."

Beckett's eyes flicked to mine, then away, a muscle in his jaw working as he chose his words carefully. "Yes. I wanted to show you that I would protect you, Mila. That I could give you the closure you needed."

"But how were you able to find them? How did you know who they were?"

"Well, we can't all be hackers," he grinned and my eyes widened. "I was just determined."

I felt a rush of conflicting emotions—gratitude, surprise, and something warmer, more profound, that scared me. I took a breath to steady myself, my gaze holding his. "Why?"

His eyes met mine again, and he stepped closer. "Because you're worth it, Mila. You should have justice and peace. And if killing those bastards is what it took to ease your pain, then well...I was happy to do it." Beckett touched my cheek before adding, "Also, I met Evie."

I could feel the color drain from my face in an instant. "Evie?"

"Yes. Briefly. First, she's alright and will be fine moving forward with her life. Second, she was the one who got the center shut down after you left."

"She did?"

"Yes," Beckett says quietly. "And she wanted you to know she appreciated what you did for her and the others."

There's no reason to talk about what I did for them. What I had *done to me* for them. I'm just glad the center that housed so much abuse had disbanded. If it still stood today, I would go over with a gasoline can and light a match.

My voice was hoarse when I finally spoke. "Thank you."

His arms encircled me, and I breathed him in. I felt safe here, in this moment, with Beckett. His lips found mine. It was a kiss that spoke of new beginnings, healing, and a future I hadn't dared hope for until...now.

I poured all my longing and dreams of a family into that kiss, my hands tangling in his hair as I pulled him closer. He responded with equal passion, his hands roaming my body with a mixture of reverence and need.

He traced the scars on my body that I'd received in anger–both from others and from my own hands–with his fingertips and mouth. And when he undressed and I saw the lashings across his back, I did the same to him.

That night, in the soft glow of the room, we didn't just make love —we healed each other. It was a joining of two wounded souls, a union forged in the depths of our shared trauma.

When we finally parted, breathless and sated, I knew something had changed within me. Something that was needed for so long.

And I knew it was because of Beckett.

He held my hand across from a quaint table in a fancy restaurant later that same night, keeping me grounded in the sea of strangers around us.

"We'll take it slow, Mila. But you deserve to experience the good things in life, not just the bad. I am going to spoil the shit out of you until it becomes second nature."

I couldn't help but grin at the absurdity of his promise, but he just squeezed my hand tighter.

"I'm here for you now and I'm not going anywhere."

Chapter Eight
Beckett

The support group became our silent sanctuary, where we didn't need words to understand each other. Mila's presence there was a constant, her strength resonating through the room like a quiet hum because that was just how powerful she was. She still held herself tightly, but there was a softening around her edges and it filled me with such selfish pride that I played a small part of it.

We made our Wednesday nights at the club a mutual affair from that point forward. It was different now; there was no hiding in the darkness, no anonymity. It was just Mila and me learning the language of touch and trust. Each week, I watched her uncoil a little more, her breaths coming easier, and her body less like a taut string ready to snap.

It wasn't for several months that we started having sex outside of the safe haven the club became for Mila.

One evening, as we walked out into the cool night air, she surprised me by suggesting I spend the night at her house.

I agreed without hesitation, and we found that having actual beds and sheets to make love on only made it better.

Coffee dates before work became another part of our days. The little Greek place across the street served a strong coffee that could kickstart any morning. Sitting across from Mila, sipping the dark liquid as the world woke up, became a moment of peace I craved. She'd tease me about my work boots and how the knots were always lopsided or challenged my opinions on music, and I found myself looking forward to those debates more than I cared to admit.

Our relationship was evolving, becoming something neither of us had anticipated, but both desperately needed. With each shared experience, each moment spent together outside the confines of therapy or dimly lit rooms, Mila's confidence grew a bit more.

I knew we were far from okay or perfect; healing isn't linear or quick. But watching Mila smile as she waved goodbye from her doorstep after an evening out filled me with hope that maybe we were on our way to something like happiness. Real happiness.

It allowed me to open up more during our sessions as well.

"I was ten," I began, my voice steadier than expected. "I was already scared of him, of course. He'd beat me before, but this time... this time, he forced me to my knees." I had to pause, the memory a bitter taste in my mouth. "He shoved my head down hard. I couldn't breathe, couldn't scream. My only thought was to get it over with. I gagged and fought to keep my teeth from scraping him, but he was forceful and rough. I felt them dig in and draw blood. But I didn't mean it. Or maybe I did–I don't know–I can't remember. And then..."

I trailed off, running my fingers along the faint line that marked my jaw, a permanent reminder. "He pulled away so fast that my head snapped back. I heard the crack and felt the pain explode across my face." I took a shaky breath, the scar a phantom ache. "He broke a bottle on my jaw."

Nancy reached out to place her hand on my shaking knee. Her eyes were kind and encouraging, and she spoke softly. "Beckett, I don't believe we've ever heard you describe that particular incident before. Are you ready to talk about who did this?"

Ready felt like the wrong word, but I knew it was time. I glanced at Mila, seeking the strength reflected in her eyes. She offered me a small, supportive smile, and I turned back to the group, my voice steady.

"It was my father."

The words hung heavy like a fresh wound, raw and real. I had never said them out loud before, and at that moment, I felt exposed and vulnerable, but I also felt a strange sense of release.

The group murmured support, and I felt their collective embrace, a comfort I had come to rely on. The therapist nodded, her expression gentle. "It takes incredible courage to name your abuser, Beckett. Sharing this today is a significant step. Remember, you don't have to rush into further details. Take your time."

I offered a small smile of gratitude, knowing her words were genuine. This group, these people, understood the burden of secrets and the power of unburdening them.

I glanced at Mila again, grateful for her again to not only be in my life but to have her as a beacon of support in the room. We had shared so much already, and I knew we could only continue to heal.

I took a deep breath, my eyes locked on Mila's and told the whole story of my father that day.

Chapter Nine
Mila

I knew something was on Beckett's mind. We were curled up on my couch; our new Saturday routine of ordering takeout and binging a new show had reached the point where the food was gone, the show forgotten, and we were simply enjoying each other's company. But something was troubling him.

"Spit it out," I said, nudging him playfully. "You've been quiet all night."

He ran a hand through his hair, which I knew meant he was choosing his words carefully. "I was thinking... about your trip."

I stiffened before looking at him, my hand pausing on his chest. "What about it?"

"I know you want to do this on your own, and I support that. But..." He paused, his eyes searching mine. "I just want you to know I'm here if you need me. If at any point you feel like you can't handle it or you just want some company, I'll be on the next flight out."

I felt a rush of warmth at his words and tossed my hair over my shoulder as I adjusted myself in his arms. "Thank you," I said softly, leaning up to kiss him. "But I promise, I'm okay. I need to do this for myself. To prove that I can."

Beckett had nodded, his eyes never leaving mine. "I understand. And I'm proud of you for taking this step."

I smiled, tracing patterns on his chest. "I couldn't have done it without you. You know that, right? You've given me the strength to face my demons."

He pulled me closer, his voice intense. "And you've given me the courage to face mine. We're in this together, Mila."

I snuggled into his side, feeling safe and loved. "I know. And it's going to be fine. I promise."

The convention in California was a big step for me, both professionally and personally. It was a chance to immerse myself in my field, connect with colleagues, and prove to myself that I could navigate the world beyond my carefully constructed bubble.

And if I happened to drive by a specific address and leave a little surprise for someone, that was just an added bonus.

The convention was practically alive with excitement and bustling people. I weaved through the crowded hall, my senses on high alert. I'd attended events like this before, but this one felt different.

I was different.

I stopped by a booth displaying the latest in cybersecurity software and struck up a conversation with one of the developers. His eyes lit up as we discussed the nuances of encryption and data protection, our shared passion creating an instant connection. It felt good to talk shop with someone in front of me rather than through a screen.

As I moved from booth to booth, collecting business cards and making mental notes, my mind kept drifting back to Beckett. His support meant everything to me. He had his own demons, yet he was always there for me, grounding me when I felt like I might float away. He'd literally committed murder for me.

During a break between sessions, I found a quiet corner to check my phone. There, I saw a text from Beckett: **"Thinking of you. You got this."**

A small smile tugged at my lips as I replied with a quick thank you and a heart emoji.

In the afternoon, I attended a panel on emerging threats in cybersecurity. As they discussed the increasing sophistication of cyberattacks, I found myself scribbling notes furiously, ideas going off like rockets in my mind.

When the panel ended, I decided to take a short walk outside to clear my head. As I strolled through the nearby park, I couldn't help but think about the package waiting in my hotel room.

I had taken Beckett's father's watch during my so-called work trip —a symbolic act of reclaiming power over our shared trauma. It sat on the nightstand now, a reminder of what we'd both endured and how far we'd come.

The rest of the day flew by in a blur of presentations and networking. By the time evening rolled around, I was exhausted but wildly on edge at the same time. Back in my hotel room, I sat on the bed and stared at the watch for a long time. Beckett kept it all this time because he felt guilt and a plethora of other emotions regarding his dad. He took the watch because it was his father's favorite possession, and he wanted him to feel just a sliver of the pain he had been made to suffer.

It was time to get rid of it.

Beckett's text buzzed again: **"Miss you."**

I typed back quickly: **"Miss you too."**

And with that simple exchange, I knew we would be okay.

But I couldn't say the same for his father.

Chapter Ten
Beckett

I leaned against the wall, wiping the sweat from my brow as I surveyed the mess in Mila's living room. The Christmas tree stood tall against the row of windows, its branches still drooping from the packaging. I'd spent over an hour untangling lights and rummaging through boxes for ornaments from both of our apartments. I wanted it to be perfect for her return.

The faint sound of footsteps in the hallway drew my attention.

She was home.

I straightened up, stepping back to admire my handiwork—or lack thereof. The tree leaned slightly to one side, and half the lights flickered ominously. I chuckled under my breath; maybe it was a metaphor for us. Still standing but wobbling at times.

As she walked in, her eyes widened, taking in the scene.

"Beckett? What is this?" Her voice mixed surprise with amusement even though she looked from her travels, dressed in a plain white sweatsuit and sneakers. Her coat looked like it was eating her, a black puffy thing that came down almost to the floor.

Grinning, I took her coat from her. "Surprise! Figured we could use some holiday spirit."

She moved her bags to the side and stepped closer, inspecting the tree like a detective scrutinizing evidence.

"I thought you were supposed to make it look better than this." Her lips quirked into a smile that lit up the room more than any string of lights ever could.

"Hey now, I'm no interior designer," I shot back playfully. "But it's festive enough, right?"

Mila crossed her arms, leaning against the doorway with an air of mock judgment. "Festive? This looks like it survived a snowstorm."

"Yeah? Well, give me a chance." I stepped forward, reaching for an ornament—a simple glass bauble—and held it up like a prize. "See? We can fix this together."

She raised an eyebrow but took the ornament from me and carefully placed it on a lower branch. "Okay, Mr. Holiday Cheer. Let's see if you can salvage this."

I grabbed another ornament and joined her at the tree's base, our fingers brushing as we decorated together in comfortable silence.

"You know," she said after a moment, "you didn't have to stay here while I was gone and do all this."

I glanced at her sideways. "I wanted to be here—just in case."

"Just in case what?"

"Just in case you needed me when you got back."

Her expression softened as she looked down at the ornaments we had hung so far—each representing moments we'd shared or milestones we'd reached together since we met. We'd collected them the last few weeks while out on our dates.

I took a deep breath.

This was it—the moment I'd been dreading all day.

"There's something I need to tell you," I began, my eyes fixed on her reaction. "My father—he passed away while you were gone."

Mila's eyes widened, and her hands flew to her mouth in a dramatic display of surprise. "Oh my God, Beckett, I'm so sorry. When—?" her voice trailed off, her eyes searching mine.

I stepped forward and gently grasped her chin, my thumb

brushing across her soft skin. "I know it was you," I whispered, my gaze holding hers captive. "The watch. He was wearing the watch when they found him."

Her eyes flickered away from me, and she let out a strangled cough.

"I—I don't know what you're talking about." Her voice shook, and she took a step back, watching as my hand fell back to my side. I put my hands in the pockets of my jeans and waited until she looked at me again.

"Don't, Mila. Don't lie to me." I took a step forward, closing the distance between us again. "I keep an unhealthy tab on the where-abouts of my father. You're the only one who knows I stole that watch from him when I left. I saw the news article about his passing, and he was wearing that watch in the photo. The only part of him that wasn't covered in blood at the scene."

She swallowed, her eyes flicking downward briefly before meeting mine again. "I didn't— I mean, I—" she trailed off, her eyes filling with tears.

I held her gaze, the weight of my father's death heavy in the air between us.

"Mila, I'm not mad at you." I took a deep breath, trying to steady my racing heart. "I'm upset that you put yourself in danger going there."

Her brow furrowed, confusion mixing with pain. "I thought you'd understand. We both—"

"Understand what?" I interrupted, my voice rising slightly before I reined it in. "You think I want you to risk your safety just to prove a point? That you are every bit as capable of exacting revenge against that piece of shit? Don't you think I know that? You're a goddamn warrior to me. But you just started feeling comfortable being outside the apartment. Now you're off avenging me? That's not how this works."

She opened her mouth to argue but faltered, glancing away as if searching for the right words among the scattered ornaments on the floor. I softened my tone, trying to calm myself down because she was here. Standing in front of me. She's not hurt.

But Christ, she could have been.

"I know why you did it," I continued after a moment, keeping my voice steady. "And I appreciate it more than I could ever put into words. That man should have been wiped from the planet years ago. But I'm trying to keep you safe, baby. I know how sick that bastard is, and it would have killed me where I stood if I had read you died in that article instead of him."

Mila wrapped her arms around herself as if trying to hold in all that anguish we had both fought against for so long. The flickering Christmas lights cast shadows across her face, accentuating the pain etched into her features.

"I thought..." she whispered, tears pooling in her eyes. "I thought if I could just... get rid of your demon, we could both finally forget."

"Forget?" My voice dropped to a whisper. "There are things we will never be able to forget from our childhoods. But now we have each other and don't have to face it alone. We aren't alone anymore. You have to start getting that through your pretty stubborn head."

"I'm sorry," Mila whispered over and over as she walked into my outstretched arms, and I hugged her tight.

We hold each other for what feels like hours until time catches up with us.

"Stop saying you're sorry," I whisper harshly, kissing the top of her head. "I was just so worried. How did you even get close to him? The report didn't say much about how he died--just that he was the victim of a home invasion."

Mila buries her face into my chest before whispering, "I pretended my car broke down and needed help. He was more than happy to let me in the house, and once I was inside, I pepper sprayed him." She grabbed onto my thick wool sweater with her hands and I tightened my hold on her. "After I got him down on the ground, I kicked him in the head until he passed out. When he woke up, he was tied up on the floor in the kitchen, and I--I didn't, I don't know why I did it, but I just wanted him to suffer. I wanted him to pay for what he did to you."

"How did you do it, baby?" I ask again, rubbing a circle into her back with one hand. I reach over to grab one of her pill bottles from the counter behind me before passing her a Xanax. She's still prone to panic attacks, but at least her medication helps her when she starts to spiral. Luckily, she only packed what she needed for her trip and left the rest on the counter. She quickly swallows the small pill without water and continues clutching onto me as she tells me the rest.

"I told him I was there for you. I told him I loved you, and he needed to be gone so you could be free of him. I broke a bottle against his face and cut off his cock, and shoved it into his throat until he choked to death on it."

"You love me?" Beckett asks, gently cupping my face and tilting it upward so he can look into my eyes.

"That's what you heard from that?" I ask incredulously.

Beckett smiles. "The asshole died fittingly. Love how clever you are, you minx. You're a fucking beautiful savage and I am lucky to know you, let alone be with you. But I don't fucking care about my father right now. Do you mean it?"

"Yes."

"You love me?"

"Yes."

"You know I love you, too, right?"

"Yes."

"So, you'll marry me then?"

"Yes--Wait, what?" Mila asks suddenly, caught in her own trap. She tries to push herself back, but I hold her firm against me and kiss along her jawline.

"You already agreed. No takebacks. Besides, I can't keep carrying this around in my pocket. This is New York, and I will get mugged for it sooner or later." I'm trying to keep the energy in the room light as I get down on one knee and pull a small red box out of my pocket, but I'm shaking.

Can she tell I'm trembling?

This is the most vulnerable I have ever been, and it's totally not the right time, but I know this is my future. *She* is my future. I know she's the other piece of my shattered soul, and I don't even want to pick up the pieces. I'm just happy to lay with her amongst the shards.

"Beckett," she whispers as I slide the marquis-shaped diamond onto her finger. "Tell me this is real. Tell me I'm not just imagining you proposing to me because I'm so desperate to be happy that I'm making this up. *Tell me–*" A soft sob escapes her and cuts off her words as she sinks down to her knees in front of me until we're at eye level.

"It's real. We're real. And we're going to live a full, beautiful life. One with good therapists, great food, fantastic sex and love. God, I can't wait to spend my life showing you how much I love you."

Mila throws her arms around my shoulders and kisses me.

"I already know," she smiles against my lips.

And she does. I proved I would do anything for her. And I did.

And she showed me she would do the same.

There's no right way to heal, but there is a right way to love--

And we know how to do that.

About the Author

Pandora grew up in Atlantic City, NJ surrounded by pageant queens and saltwater. Growing up, she always had the need to create and loved writing, drawing and singing. She spent her middle school and high school years juggling cheerleading practices and musical auditions while managing to secure over a dozen scholarships and awards for her writing ability both locally and on a national level. She also won multiple singing and acting competitions during this time.

Always a flair for the dramatic, one could say.

During the last decade, Pandora has owned 2 successful Pole & Aerial Dancing studios, went back to school to become a mortician and funeral director, had 2 more children and remarried, won multiple pole dancing competitions and trained others to do the same, bartended, owned and operated a Beauty Pageant system during the pandemic and continued to write Fanfiction as she had throughout the years for her creative outlet.

After 20+ years of writing (and truly, her only constant), she decided it was time to pursue the career she wanted ever since she could remember. She released her first two books in October of 2024: Serpent Darling and Scaredy Cat with more to come in 2025.

Combining her love of horror, the macabre, an unhealthy obsession with quotes, dark romance and sarcasm, you get all the unhinged behavior in her stories.

Pandora resides in Pennsylvania with her supportive husband (truly, the ramblings he listens to when she has a new idea are unmatched) and 3 children where they spend their free time reading, browsing book stores and watching horror movies all year round.

You can learn more about Pandora by visiting her website at www.pandoracress.com

Toothtaker

By: Cait Alvarez

About Toothtaker

Vengeance. And teeth.

Those hadn't always been my goals, once upon a time I had been a simple creature with simple desires. But not anymore, now, the only thing that consumes my thoughts, my every waking hour, is finding the ones who hurt me and ensuring they feel every ounce of pain that I endured.

I am a toothtaker. And I will fulfill my purpose.

Content Note:

Mature content. For readers 18 & older.

Violence, torture, Gore, off-page SA, body horror, off-page captivity/confinement, mafia, sexual acts, description of rape.

Relationship type: MF

Chapter One

Edwige

The pain wasn't receding. I'd thought it would. That the gnawing, burning agony would fade as I slipped closer and closer to death. But it wasn't, it was just... there. Front and center and agonizing with every stuttering, gasping breath, as I tried to inhale past my shattered jaw and into my lungs, their delicate tissues shredded by the shards of my shattered ribs. No, the pain was not diminishing; the pain seemed to grow the longer I existed within its grasp, unable to move, barely able to breathe. Trapped against its razor sharp hold as my mind faded into the blackness of the afterlife. I couldn't think, couldn't focus. The sudden fear that perhaps the pain would travel with me, leap across the barrier between life and death, shot a bolt of fear through my ruined chest.

"Hush, be easy now." A low, feminine voice crooned.

I flinched in response, and the pull of what remained of my musculature against my ruined bones was positively agonizing. I released a weak, desperate wail, beyond terrified of the foreign presence coalescing above me.

That I was finally alone, allowed to die in what little peace that could be found amidst the roiling waves of agony, had been the only blessing offered since that feral nest of vampires had arrived at my front porch. When they'd surrounded my cottage and burned it to the ground, along with my herbiaries, my grimoires. All of it gone, and soon I would be too. I'd been relieved to finally be alone with my end, as painful as it was, because the end was in sight after days of agony at the hands of another.

"Broken little thing." The strange presence whispered, her voice even softer, as though she had regretted startling me, like she had regretted the pain she'd caused. *Was that even possible in this world?*

My remaining eye fluttered open, blurred gaze catching on sharp, angular features in a feminine, catlike face. The strange woman was the same deathly color as the underbelly of a dead fish, of the endless snows that blanketed the moors during the depths of winter. When the cold was so bitter and biting that even venturing outside felt fraught and perilous. When it seemed like the wolves of Maslenitsa were waiting in the shadows of the trees. Slavering behind the drifts that piled as high as my little cottage, their sharp teeth and jaws poised to snatch the breath from my throat and the beating heart from my chest. *She* was death; *she* was ice; *she* was darkness.

A glacial digit trailed its way over the bare flesh of my leg, awakening the forgotten ache of bruises and the sharper pain of the deep, torn bites that littered the flesh of my thighs. The pain stretched on for an endless agonizing moment, then abruptly ceased, replaced with... nothing. My eye shot down to where she touched me. Her fingers, blue and glittering in the dim light that filtered through the trees to where I lay, rested lightly on my flesh, the soft tissue frozen and stiff now, nearly as pale as her face.

It doesn't hurt.

The dawning understanding was a sweet comfort, a stark contrast to the bitter landscape of pain and fear I'd been dragged into. I wanted to tell her, but my shattered jaw couldn't form the words. She seemed to follow though, moving her hand up my other thigh, the icy balm of her fingers killing any sensation in its path.

"How cruel they were to you, my little witch." The woman murmured, one hand brushing my knotted, filthy hair back from my forehead. The other drew swirling patterns over my belly and breasts, leaving trails of ice in her wake, deadening the agony that had chewed at me, making every second an eternity of torment. "So much pain, so much cruelty. They painted it on your skin for me. I can read it like a tapestry. Your flesh, my love, it is a record of the horror."

I winced as she lifted my fingers. They were the first casualties in my kidnapper's attempts to stop me from fighting back. The goddess pressed her full, lavender lips to each of them, her touch fighting back the pain, forcing it to retreat. I could think for the first time in ages, enough to realize that even the balm of her touch couldn't keep my shredded lungs from killing me, from sending me into the darkness of death.

"Tell me, my poor creature, do you want peace?"

She turned my face towards hers, so gentle and careful with the shattered remains of my jaw. That tiny gesture brought tears to my eyes, the salty fluid burning in the shredded flesh of the one they had taken. She tutted her concern at the agony that stole over my face, burying her finger into the ruined socket up to the knuckle, making me squeal in shocked protest. For a moment, pain bloomed again, and I wanted to rail against it, to rail against her. But then, it was gone, so thoroughly replaced by nothingness that I wondered if I'd ever had a second eye to begin with. I pawed clumsily at the lovely creature that loomed over me, trying to touch her, to somehow show my gratitude.

"You are dying," she told me, her tone soft but words taking none of the brutality away from the statement. I gave a jerky nod, agreeing with her. I was dying. Her deathly pale face and wide eyes would be the last thing I saw.

"You don't have to go, lovely one, if you aren't ready yet. If you are bold enough to seek vengeance against those who have wronged you. Do you want to end them before they find another creature to torment? Do you want to use your wrath, your revenge, in service of something more?"

Vengeance... Did I want that?

I allowed myself to picture it, letting the knowledge of what she would make me sink into the threads of my consciousness. I would be a monster, a bloodthirsty, cruel creature, like the ones who'd tormented me if I denied myself the peace of death. I would be driven by need like them, satiated by blood like them. I would become a thing of rage. Would that be worth it? I was already so changed from who I'd been. Did I dare twist myself a little more? Would I break? Was the shattering worth it?

Yes. Yes. Yes. It would all be worth it to seek my vengeance. To give back the fear and torment those creatures had visited upon me.

I caught her gaze, grasping ineffectively at her silken slip, the wisp of fabric barely covering the emaciated form of the goddess.

"Teeth." I slurred, the words barely comprehensible coming from my swollen, bruised lips. Thinking about my broken jaw, and my cracked molars, only one thing was on my mind, "I want their teeth."

Hargrave

"Toothtaker!"

"Toothtaker!"

"Toothtaker!"

The word was echoing back and forth through the agitated crowd, all of them wearing their promenade finest, trying to catch a glimpse of the third gruesome murder of the week. The killing had been conducted with the same brazen viciousness on the grimy, gas-lit streets as the last two. Violence was commonplace here, but whoever conducted these latest killings had gone above and beyond, their cruelty documented down to the last salacious detail in every penny-rag and tabloid being printed.

I'd done my share of savagery, both as an orc and as the head of my criminal organization, but something about teeth and their removal had me shuddering along with the slowly panicking masses.

"Get out of the fucking way," my second-in-command, an unassuming wood-elf whose bite was far worse that her bark, demanded. Immer Venro's voice was as sharp as the crack of a whip and incredibly effective at creating a path through the milling crowd of frightened onlookers. I wasn't sure what they were so concerned about. It wasn't as though a toothtaker killed indiscriminately. They were made monsters, created by their tormentors and reborn with only one purpose in their vicious hearts.

Vengeance, and this toothtaker was getting theirs to the fullest extent.

The scene was gruesome, the hastily erected barricades stopping just before the initial splashes of drying blood. My eyes trailed over the splashes of gore. They caught for a moment on sprays of sliced flesh and viscera, cataloguing it as the mess grew worse, as the flayed flesh continued to multiply until the grime and slime covered cobbles of the street were entirely hidden by shredded remains.

Then there was the corpse.

Another vampire, based on his paper-white skin, though the mess of his mouth made it impossible to tell for sure. Every tooth had been removed, his tongue and gums pulped into nearly unrecognizable masses of red, the ribboned flesh marred by brilliant white shards of shattered bone. The mob was right for once. This was another killing by the toothtaker. Behind me, the sun continued to rise. It's rays brilliant enough to pierce the thick veil of fog that rolled in from the sea and blanketed the already damp city in a layer of salt and moisture that served only to make the sooty buildings dirtier and more depressing.

"Someone better do something before the corpse disintegrates," Immer muttered from her place beside me.

She was right. The rare sunlight shone down on us all, making the golden caps on my tusks gleam and wisps of ash rise from the dead vampire.

The sudden brilliance of gold was enough to catch the eyes of the milling constabulary, of whom there were many, each more useless than the last. I scoffed as they all froze. The silvery eyes of shifters, the black and orange gaze of other orcs, and the myriad of colors sported by humans all rising in unison to fall upon me. They took in the curled brim of my jet black Homberg hat, the razor sharp lines of my suit, and the sheen of my leather shoes an instant before pretending they hadn't noticed me at all. I scoffed as they continued their milling and muttering.

The body before us was decaying more rapidly, the plumes of ash scattering with the morning breeze. Soon there would be no evidence to examine, though anyone with half a brain wouldn't really need it. But it may make my life easier if all the evidence were to disappear into a plume of dust and smoke. I wanted to find the toothtaker before these bumbling buffoons got their hands on it.

I watched with interest as a bespectacled human, scuttling about so anxiously he could be mistaken for a goblin, approached the corpse with so much trepidation I had to wonder if this was his first crime scene. It certainly wouldn't be his last. Murder was rampant here. It usually just wasn't this messy. He would have to get used to being in the presence of corpses, especially in this line of work.

"Whatever the lad is up to, he better get to it soon. That body has about thirty more seconds of sunlight before its dust," my second grumbled.

I nodded my agreement. There was no point in pussyfooting about death. Accept it, hold your nose if you're squeamish, and do what needs to be done.

The trembling man pulled a vial full of candy-floss pink powder out of his worn coat, sprinkling it over the remains as thoroughly as he could while trembling like a kitten in a rainstorm. A brilliant gold light bloomed, followed by the scent of caramelized sugar and raspberries.

"That is-" I said with a laugh, "the most adorable spell I've ever seen." I looked more closely at the mage before us. He stood a little straighter now, using the confidence of success to unbend his anxious spine. The man was lithe, his smooth skin rich and dark, accented by a smattering of nearly black freckles over his button nose and cheeks. He ignored the uniformed creatures around him, tucked the nearly empty vial back into the recesses of his coat before stepping back into the sea of navy-clad officers.

"Ridiculous," Immer scoffed, turning away from the magical display, the now preserved crime scene and eyeing the increasingly fractious crowd. Only the most prestigious bloodsuckers who could afford the expensive charms needed to survive the daylight were present. Their thralls did most of the protesting on their creature's behalf, filling the morning air with despair and dudgeon in turn.

"Look him up, see if he'll be of any use to us," I replied, sweeping my gaze over the gory scene once more, still not catching sight of anything that could assist me in locating the toothtaker. I wanted a monster like that on my side, and I planned to find it before the milling, mewling vampires all around us did.

"Let's get out of here," I added with a jerk of my head towards the gaping maw of an adjacent alleyway. It would only get more and more difficult to stave off the rising panic of the citizenry.

I fought the urge to face them, to remind the gathered creatures they knew perfectly well this mess was their fault. But they knew that, provided they hadn't committed acts of barbarity against a witch and been stupid enough to leave her breathing, then they were safe from the wrath of their only predator.

There was just one way to make a toothtaker. They were created when a nest of vampires fed from a mage. At least, according to the lore, which I had to track down after the first brutally de-faced vampire had been found. But it was more than just a simple feeding, otherwise half the blood brothels in the red district would produce a toothtaker or two every night. No, these fiends were created when the vampires dragged out the process, when they kept their victim alive and tormented them, and fed them their own blood to ensure the wretched creature didn't expire too soon. Toothtakers were made from pain, from violation. They were reborn with only a few goals, vengeance, and teeth.

So far, the Toothtaker had taken her due from each of the corpses.

Chapter Two

Edwige

The bloodlust receded for a moment as the sun set into the glassy sea. It's fiery red a mirror to the crimson and rust that painted over my snow white hide, the color a perfect match to Maslenitsa, the goddess who'd found and transformed me. I enjoyed a brief, bright flash of sanity before I was engulfed by the roiling need for vengeance once again. The craving brought on as a familiar, rancid scent met my newly sensitive nose.

I hadn't always been so attuned to smells. Witches were like humans in form and most functions. I had been able to smell about as well as anyone else, which was to say not well at all. Now...now the world was a tapestry of not just color and sound, but smell, too. There are some odors that were impossible for the beast within me to resist.

I'd found one such scent last night.

I'd followed the bloodsucker emitting it through the twining, darkened alleys on the edge of the red district and into the emptier, dirty streets that branched out to the harbor docks. Those cobbled ways were abandoned every night as all the sailors and dock workers packed into taverns and bars, drinking away the aches they earned each day.

I imagined he had planned to snag one of them, making a quick unwilling meal out of a drunkard before going back to whatever hovel he inhabited in the perpetually dark, always smelling of sex and copper red district.

He'd fucked up, and I intended to show him just how much.

They were always so confident, these creatures. So stupidly sure of themselves, swaggering through the streets like they hadn't been in the nest that had torn up my home, my life, and my body. Like they weren't being stalked, as if their closest confidants hadn't been slowly picked off by me, left to burn in the sun with gaping, empty maws as testament to who'd killed them and why. Like they wouldn't fall to the silver gilding my teeth and claws.

I clacked the aforementioned gilded teeth together in anticipation. The sound was sharp as it echoed through the damp, salty air. The scent of low tide brewing with his personal smell, metallic and too-sweet, like the air around a plum tree once the fruit ripened and began to fall. The miasma was almost enough to turn my stomach.

The echoing clank of my teeth made him flinch. He looked over his wool clad shoulder. It was gratifying to see the flat cap that covered his dirty hair doing nothing to hide the widening of his eyes or the rising of his thick brows. The morphing of his expression as fear curled through the creature's chest and bloomed on his pale face.

Yes. Fear me. I am here for your pain, your blood, and your teeth.

I clicked my teeth again, harder, the sound so bright and pure. The sliver that coated them making the noise brighter and sharper. My claws echoed through the air as I stalked forward, the silver tips ring bright and fairy-like as I clambered through the gutter. I winced as my bare fingers and toes sunk into the unidentifiable muck that lined the gutters of the streets. It squished between them and coated my skin, skin that was still bloody from the last kill. Had it only been half a day ago? What had I done with the time? Time wasn't as linear as it had been before my near-death experience and transformation.

Now it keeled and yawed, like a ship on the rough seas, moving rapidly before stalling out, moments stretching for ages and hours condensing into a single breath.

"P-please," he whimpered. Fear was coalescing around him, filling the air with its bitter tang, wafting off his skin and trailing through the mist.

I pounced.

He was smaller than I remembered.

I knew a lot had changed about me when I took this curse of vengeance instead of accepting a clean death, but I hadn't gotten bigger. Perhaps it was that he cowered before me. Yes, that's what made him so much smaller, so much weaker. A pathetic little thing, just like the cowering worm he'd thought to turn me into. His vampire strength was useless now, his speed was gone, melted away in the face of the endless, rising fear that *I* inspired, that *I* was.

His first scream was music, the cry cut off as I rammed my razor sharp talons, the tips caked in muck and gore, through the base of his throat.

"I couldn't scream either," I whispered, gently pulling them back out, watching as the blood dripped onto the pristine white of his cheap shirt, the red blooming over it like the most decadent rose.

His sobs when I pried his mouth open were wretched and pitiful. When I peeled his jaw wider, tearing the flesh of his cheeks and giggling while I did it, I could feel the moment he remembered me. That he knew what he had done, and how he had created his own demise. I squealed along with him as my claws dug through the soft tissue of his gums, continuing to burrow into the bones of his face. Followed by the satisfying crunch when I ripped the first tooth free, one of the most precious ones, his dainty vampire fang. I held it up to the weak orange light of the gas lamp, admiring the brilliant pearly shine of it.

Oh, it was *perfect*.

His tears mixed with his blood, spooling off of his ruined face in long, thick strands of gore. The fluids, thick, warm and viscous as it pooled around where I knelt, mixing with the muck of the street, the piss and the shit, the grime polluting the already filthy cobblestones with gore.

"Tears, tears, tears," I sang, jabbing my silver claws into the ruins of his mouth, plucking out his teeth one by one.

I chittered, and he chomped. I rustled while he glommed, the sounds of my hands working over his flesh, an orchestra of the grotesque. His lips sucked, his tongue licked, the sloppy sounds they made a delightful counterpoint to the harsher crack of my inexorable claws and implacable greed. If only this silly little man would stop whining.

"Sticks and stones, and teeth and bones, and sticks and stones, and teeth and bones, and teeth and bones, and bones and teeth, and teeth, and teeth and-" I sang the nonsense words as I worked the teeth from their bony cavern homes, drowning out the weakening protests he was attempting to make.

"Have you had enough vengeance, little one?" The strange voice, calm and faintly amused, pulled me out of the bloody reverie I'd sunk into.

I whirled, baring claws littered with chips of bone and threads of flesh to the stranger who'd dared approach me, who encroached upon my kill and interrupted my meal. I hissed, ready to fight.

"Don't worry, toothtaker. I'm not here for your prize," he continued, holding pale green hands up in a placating gesture. I eyed his fingers. They were soft, especially compared to mine. His fingers would be weak and useless at any of the tasks my own excelled in. How would he strip the flesh from this corpse? My fingers were long and spidery, ending in sharp metallic points that I could sink into the flesh and bone of my victims to tear their teeth out by the root. His teeth were flat, useless, and soft.

The idea of plucking those bones from his face and pulverizing them turned my stomach, though. He wasn't one of the vampires I hungered for.

He had no fangs for my collection.

"Mine," I growled, crouching low over the moldering corpse, rooting through the shredded gums for the final two teeth, a pair of fat, squat molars.

Hargrave

"It's yours." I assured the toothtaker as she turned back to me once again, another pair of teeth in her hand. I stood very still, taking in her curtain of tangled, black hair, pale, gore-splattered skin, glittering teeth and claws. Her wide, reptilian eyes were like the black of an abandoned well, of a winter night, of the new moon. They ate the light as ruthlessly as she devoured her victims.

"He held me down..." she whispered, carefully weaving silver wire around the base of a fang. "He helped," she moaned, despair colored the words, and I froze.

"They hurt you?" I asked, careful to stay calm in the face of this awesomely violent being.

"Hurt me," she gasped, closing her bottomless eyes and clutching the remaining fang hard enough to draw blood. "In a sky so dark and so still, on a night with no moon, they came to kill."

"A kill, little demon?"

"A death, a kill, a maim, an ill will-" she was slipping away from me, heedless of anything around her as she created another fang pendant and threaded the two onto a necklace that, I realized with a shudder, was not ropes of pearls stacked around her slender throat, but a collection of teeth. A staggering number of ivory white teeth, vampire fangs interspersed with the more normal molars and incisors, all of them carefully strung along silvery, delicate chain.

"He helped?" I nodded to the vampire's corpse.

"He helped, he helped, he helped, he helped..." she was rocking back and forth, chanting the words.

Edwige

I had quite a collection now. The fangs, long and needle sharp, a perfect, brilliantly pure white, were my favorite. Even as the strange, massive orc spoke to me, I found it hard to focus. Not when I had all my new teeth.

They gleamed against the dainty, silver chain that hung from my neck. Each of my prizes were strung along it. They shone in the dim light. So, so perfect and precious and lovely. I stroked my finger along my newest set, the threads of flesh and speckles of gore still present, still marring the bright, smooth surface.

I held one up to examine it, spitting on the bone and rubbing it clean, the silver of my nails making the tiniest, musical little jangle as I touched my newest prize.

The teeth were getting heavy. I'd taken out five of the ones who'd wronged me, who'd hurt me so viciously, but there was still one more to end. The ropes of molars, incisors, and canines that were strung haphazardly hung around my neck like I was a sea queen with ropes upon ropes of moon-bright pearls.

I giggled, pressing the pads of my fingers together and peeling them apart, loving the tacky, sticky gooeyness of the semi-dry blood and spit coating them. Vampire blood decorated my neck and chest. It speckled my stomach and thighs, it painted my ankles and covered my feet like crimson silk slippers. I couldn't even feel the cold when I was coated in gore like this. It was the warmest coat, the balm against my soul, a friend that I could always rely on.

"Blood for blood," I whispered, pressing a kiss to the collected teeth that hung around my neck. They kissed me back, little bites of pain mixed with the heady thrill of revenge. I giggled and couldn't stop, the sound growing and growing until it filled my body and stole my breath, ripping at the sensitive membranes of my mouth and throat. I tasted my own blood now, and it just made me cackle harder.

Hargrave

She was beautiful, and terrible. She was perfect to behold.

I watched her as she crouched in the glow of the lone gas lamp, whispering nonsense words, swaying back and forth like a half-feral little goblin. Her pale skin decorated by the labors of her day, the blood nearly black, barely illuminated by what little light could penetrate the mist off the sea and smog from the ever-present miasma of smoke and soot that was pumped out by the factories and the boats that ferried their goods too and fro.

"Blood for blood," her hissed epithet came to an abrupt halt as the wind shifted and brought my scent to her. She raised her head slowly, stretching her curled spine, squatting beside her kill.

Perfect and uncivilized and, I realized as her too large dark eyes caught mine, *fucking mine.*

I stared in awe at her slight form, wraithlike almost to the point of emaciation, skin pale as moonlight, eyes wide and glaring, her vicious silver claws and moon-bright metallic teeth shining, burnished by the faint light. A ragged chemise was all that covered her, barely keeping the growling little thing modest. Her scent, like death, yes, but there were also roses, wet stone, and the burning of funerary resin.

I would cover her in silk, I mused as she shifted into a crouch, looking like the gargoyles that lurked over the stone buildings all around, their twisted face and forms failing to frighten away the bad luck they'd been tasked with banishing.

"Come here, toothtaker," I murmured.

Edwige

A single strand of his scent, a ribbon of something so intoxicating on the thick, salty night air, that it dragged me out of the wild mindset I'd sunk into. I needed more of it.

The scent belonged to me, the source of it was fucking mine. I owned it just as much as I owned my vengeance, as I owned my collection of teeth.

I turned my gaze from my newest acquisitions to the hulking figure that had waited so patiently at the top of the alley where I'd corned my panicked, gibbering prey. Vampires were all the same, proclaiming to be apex predators while they attacked the weak, the strays, torturing them in their nests. They always crumbled when confronted with a true predator. This one had crumbled so sweetly, especially when I bit my silver teeth into his spine, crushing it like the wild cats that hid, shy and aloof, in their snowy mountains.

I didn't think the orc watching me would fall as easily. I sniffed again, following the enticing aroma of winter, spice and pure masculinity to its source. *Him.*

"Mine," I growled, prowling forward, rolling to my feet with a little hop, heedless of the mud and blood I smeared over my bare limbs and ruined scrap of a chemise. I approached the male, making out a hint of green skin and a bulk so massive he could only be an orc. He didn't flinch as I came toe to toe with him and wrapped my iron claws around his thick throat. "You are mine," I growled, staring up into his dark eyes, orange fire blazing in the pupils, an amused smirk curling his darker green lips, highlighting where his tusks, gilded, just like my teeth, rose proudly.

"Yours," he assured me, wrapping a brawny arm around my slight, filthy form and lifting me off the ground, heedless of the threat in my silver teeth and of my claws tapping against the thin skin above his jugular. "All yours, little demon."

Hargrave

She purred in delight, those dark, strange eyes widening and softening like a contented cat..

"Yours," I assured her again. Feeling myself getting swept up in the possessiveness she was exuding, letting her will and her magic wrap around me as strongly as I wrapped my arms around her, heedless of the gore painting every inch of her slight form, the danger in her claws, or the icy hardness of her limbs.

She was mine; I was hers. It was settled.

A cry interrupted us.

The bellowed sound slowing our headlong fall.

She flinched, looking wildly over her shoulder, stiff, matted hair brushing my cheek as she sought the source of the noise.

Someone stood over her latest prize, a human, by the looks of them, swarthy and massive, with the thick mane of hair and beard. The onlooker yelled again, demanding help, crying out in horror at the sight of the mutilated corpse.

"Time to go, little demon," I growled, holding her tight enough that she hissed, her grasping claws digging into the flesh of my neck where she still gripped me, a master holding her hound. I ignored the pain, trusting, perhaps foolishly, that this creature would not truly harm me.

Hargrave

She was limp in my hold by the time I reached the wrought-iron gate of my townhouse. A now-stately edifice had been a baroque monstrosity when I purchased it. White marble had been weathered into black by the mist, rain and factory grime, its decorative work barely discernible even in the brightest of daylight. I'd had the entire hulking building modernized and now it gleamed, even in the late night darkness that had been compounded by mist and cloud.

I'd smoothed the corners and straightened the edges, turning the columns back to a more sedate Doric when they had been a very enthusiastic Corinthian, and toned down the more dramatic arches. The gargoyles had been banished to perches in the back garden, their snarling faces softened by the climbing roses, English ivy, and lavender. The gardener, a holdover from the estates' previous owner who did almost no gardening in his dotage, often gave me dire warnings that the creatures would awaken one day and clamber back to their original perches regardless of my decorative preferences.

I had conceded defeat to that bit of information and informed the arthritic old human that should the stone sculptures suddenly gain sentience, I would be happy to surrender whatever territory along my roof or gutter they deemed theirs.

"Just a little further," I murmured, pressing my lips to the tooth-taker's stinking, snarled hair, ignoring the stomach churning smell. She felt different in my arms, no longer a taught bowstring of half-mad fury and barely controlled violence.

"Where are we?" she replied, pliant in my hold her blinking eyes had returned to a more human shade, though they still sat too large in her gaunt, pale face.

"My home," I told her, snarling as my guards showed entirely too much curiosity as we passed through the barrier and into the safety of my home.

Chapter Three

Edwige

I'd been left to soak in a massive tub. The cast iron monstrosity was definitely custom made specifically with *him* in mind.

I wanted him to come back, as irrational as the thought was.

He had made me warm. It's been so long since I'd felt anything besides hunger churning in my gut and the icy cold of death aching in my bones. I wanted him to come back and help me be warm again, to remind me that I also had life within this pale, scarred flesh. I'd felt it rising in me as he'd carefully peeled the blood and sludge covered chemise off my body, the touch clinical and gentle despite how I'd thought we were going to devour each other a scant three quarters of an hour ago.

He'd shed his outer layers, wearing only trousers and a white shirt with the sleeves rolled up to show muscular sage green forearms. A smattering of thin scars over them, the delicate, lighter marks in stark contrast to the ragged edges of the bite marks that littered my flesh. I could feel him cataloguing each of my old injuries as he gently helped me into a smallish room at the corner of his opulent bathroom, the water streaming from a metal disc at the top warm and gentle as a spring rain.

"Magic," he'd said to my unspoken question, "a naiad owed me a favor, and instead of the usual drown-your-enemies payment plan, I chose this instead. There is a lot of bathing in my line of work," he'd added somewhat bashfully.

"It's wonderful," I sighed, keeping my eyes closed as the gentle downpour loosened the layers of dirt that clung to my skin until it felt like even my heart and soul had been gently scrubbed. He'd then set me to soak in this inane tub, with its clawed feet and curled lip. A luxury of luxuries, I could nearly swim laps in the damn thing.

A maid, who was an aging human woman with a carefully schooled look of neutrality on her face, added an oil that smelled faintly of something floral that I couldn't quite place, it floated over the surface of the water and clung to my clean skin.

I trailed my silvery claws through it, the marks of what I was never truly left, not that I wanted them to. I loved my teeth and claws. I loved the brilliant silver of their long, razor sharp points. I loved the designs that were etched into them, the miniscule twining vines of moonflower were so finely wrought and delicate they were barely discernible unless one was looking closely. Until now, the only eyes that had seen them were mine, and the terrified ones of my victims. I tapped them against the side of the tub, filling the still, humid air with the soft tinkling of fairy bells.

"I didn't expect them to sound like that."

His voice made me turn, and I gazed up and up at the orc, still in his suit pants and suspenders, the shirt marred with the gore I'd been painted in.

"No one does," I told him, a smirk twisting the corner of my pale purple lips. "I like it."

"I like it too, toothtaker," he replied. Coming forward, offering a him-sized towel, the length of fabric large enough to wrap around me like a throw blanket. Just seeing the orc sent a bubble of warm, delicious life burning in me, and I couldn't help but snuggle back against his broad form as he wrapped me up, and set about patting another cloth over my damp hair.

"It's Edwige," I said shyly, "not just toothtaker."

"And I'm Hargrave," he answered, smiling at my offering of a name.

"Why are you being so nice?" I asked the brusque question, tempered by how I leaned into his touch and practically purred with every pass of his hands over my hair.

"You're mine. My beloved, my treasure," he replied, carefully nonchalant, though I could feel the enormity of the statement behind his gently spoken words. "In orc tribes you would have been called a gift from the moon goddess."

"When I was a witch, I would worship the moon." I mused, allowing him to maneuver me onto a padded bench that sat before a mirror, looking at him in our reflection of the silver as he frowned down at his stained shirt, removing it and letting his suspenders fall around his muscular thighs. His bulk framed me as he began carefully combing through the tangled mass of my hair, scoffing when I suggested it might be easier to just hack it off and save us all some time.

It was nearly dry by the time he finished, running oil that he had said he used on his own mane of thick black hair through my thinner strands before quickly braiding it into a single neat rope that fell nearly to the center of my back. I was surprised when he laid me in his own bed, not so secretly pleased to continue being near him, to feel his warmth and his bulk, to smell the scent of earth, expensive cologne, and his maleness as he wrapped himself around me.

"How many are left, Edwige?" He whispered the question so softly against the shell of my ear.

"One more," I replied, running my ornate claws over his warm skin, bringing goosebumps up in their wake. "One more mouth." I growled the words, and I felt him pull me tighter against the broad expanse of his chest, as though he sought to shield me from the violence I contained.

"I'll help you find them," he growled. The promise making my heart and core throb in unison, "and I will revel in your vengeance."

Hargrave

"Word in the red district is there's only one left from that nest," my second-in-command, Immer, informed me, her breathless excitement making the sentence tumble from her lips.

"Who?" I growled, looking up from the wide window-seat I'd been lounging in, monitoring the toothtaker- no, Edwige's- progress through my carefully manicured green space. She was ravishing in just one of my shirts. I'd ordered clothing in her size to be procured, but I was already regretting it. She was much lovelier in my things, with her pale legs on display, feet bare, skin shining against the darker green backdrop of the plants.

"Gyrhorn Pavalur," she replied. "They call him 'The Duke' in the red district. He owns several blood brothels, all of them catering to vampires who've lived long enough to rise above the rabble."

"Let me call Edwige up for this," I said, ignoring the annoyed look on Immer's face. She could wait a few more minutes, this directly concerned my companion.

The woman in question was in the doorway a few moments later, her clawed fingers trailing over the white trim, leaving miniscule curling peels of paint in their wake.

Edwige

The territorial rage I felt seeing Hargrave in a room with another woman, even though she was across a desk from him and clearly here in some kind of professional capacity, surprised me. It awakened the toothtaker within me, and I felt myself baring my gilded teeth as I stalked towards Hargrave and positioned myself beside the oversized wood-and-leather desk chair, shining claws and teeth on full, threatening display.

The orc in question seemed to revel in the dramatics, leaning back and enjoying in my show of possessiveness. I rested a hand on his thick shoulder, uncaring that my gilded claws dug into his woolen jacket, leaving pinprick tears behind.

"Edwige," Hargrave purred, snaking an arm around my waist, pulling me closer. "Allow me to introduce my second-in-command, Immer Venro, formerly of clan Leaf-Fall."

The woman rolled her eyes, and the slight movement was just enough to reveal the pointed tips of her ears. An elf then, I mused, the predator in me cataloguing the information for later use. She seemed to take me in stride, a rare occurrence. My teeth and claws were usually enough to send anyone running, vampire or not. The whispered stories of creatures like me haunted all the magical species, even though we had been made to hunt only one of them. Her face returned to impassive politeness a moment later, her dark skin and delicate features facing towards me without a hint of irritation or fear. I thought I could grow to like her.

"Immer was just telling me some fascinating information about the nest of vampires that appear to have been targeted by these recent, brutal..." he squeezed me affectionately as he purred the adjective, "killings."

"There's only one left, which I'm sure Edwige is more than aware of," Immer said, raising a single, dark brow at our antics. I had been aware...though I had no plans to tell her that. The memory of my time under the attentions of the vampires was clouded by pain, fear and the odd, dizzying intoxication that being fed their blood had brought on. That had been what tied us together, what allowed me to recognize them by scent and aura, which had allowed me to trace and catalogue them.

"Gyrhorn Pavalur," Hargrave added, though the name meant nothing to me.

I looked down at him, questions wrinkling my brow.

"He owns several blood brothels, and rarely leaves the red district," He continued. The background information doing nothing but making my task more daunting than it had already been. I was astoundingly powerful as a toothtaker, but hunting a vampire within the borders of their territory would be incredibly stupid of me.

"Which means if you intend to finish your work, he will need to be drawn out of his hidey-hole and into the light," Immer finished, smirking at her little play on words.

Hargrave

"I suppose you know how to lever this asshole out of his den?" I drawled, running a soothing hand over the curve of Edwige's waist. I had felt her stiffen as we spoke. The information concerning her last target could hardly be categorized as good news.

"Gyrhorn is bored," Immer answered. "That's why he builds these nests, riles them up, then uses them to see how far he can push another living thing before they become-" her eyes darted to Edwige, and the pity in them was enough to make me cry. I wondered what horrors she had seen, that she understood the ones wrought about my moon-gift as well as she did. "But that boredom is going to work in our favor, toothtaker, because he is always seeking something, or rather someone," her eyes flicked to me at that, "new and interesting."

"And I'm new and interesting?" I asked, a brow raised.

"You're a mystery. Richer than the nobility, fingers in all kinds of unsavory pies, and a house in a fashionable district that no one has seen yet. I think he'll be more than a little *interested* in speaking with you, seeing the inside of your lair, and possibly even luring you into his after he'd made a few overtures. Or we can continue to let Edwige do her own work, waiting for him to get bored enough to seek his next bit of fun outside of the red district." Immer looked at her, a question in the twist of her lips.

Edwige was preternaturally still against me, and I could sense her desire to end the life of her final tormentor growing with each moment.

"How do you propose I lure this Gyrhorn into my home? Sending round a card might be suspicious when he goes missing immediately afterwards." I said, pinning Immer in place with a hard stare.

"I imagined you would host a ball. A rather large one," my second replied, as though she were informing me I was doing nothing more taxing than ordering lunch.

"A ball?" Edwige deadpanned, "like dresses, and dancing, and champagne?"

"Exactly like that," Immer replied easily. "Something opulent and decadent will be like catnip to Gyrhorn and the other hundreds of citizen we invite will create an even greater draw, and if he disappears into the night, it certainly cannot be pinned on Hargrave, who was hosting the entire time, and it won't be blamed on the phantom toothtaker either. Since he will simply vanish, along with his shiny teeth."

I opened my mouth to protest the entire ridiculous concept, but Immer was faster, holding up a slender, dark hand to forestall my words.

"She is a wanted woman, with a trail of corpses behind her. The constabulary is more interested in stopping her than in discovering how, or why, a toothtaker was created in the first place. If her next kill is somewhere on your property, no one will know there's another corpse missing its teeth."

"Won't it be suspicious if the last place he's seen is, well, here?" Edwige asked. "I don't want to land Hargrave in any hot water."

"Suspicions don't matter. They fall on him all the time," Immer replied with an easy shrug.

"One of the perks in my line of work, little demon." I told her with a chuckle. "Crime lords aren't ever not under suspicion... What's one more on the pile?"

"I'm sure the city's morbid curiosity about you will have every invitee frothing to accept." Immer added.

"Frothing..." Edwige deadpanned, her clawed hold on me relaxing just a little. I would do anything for her, I realized in that moment, anything she needed. Even if it was something as silly as a fancy party.

"Well, if it's going to make the citizenry froth, I suppose I must," I said with a small sigh. "Find someone to plan it. I don't know the faintest thing about what goes into planning a ball, I've never even hosted a party."

Immer smiled, the satisfied smirk of a cat that had gotten its cream, before standing up and marching out of the room to get started on whatever myriad of preparations needed to be initiated.

Edwige

The moment the door clicked shut I was climbing into his lap, my lips pressing firmly to his. The smooth glide of his tusks against my cheeks was achingly erotic as I asserted my claim on him, as I reminded this much-larger creature he was mine. I purred my approval as his mouth opened, darting my tongue in to taste Hargrave, to savor him. I couldn't believe he was so willing to help me, to put down all the time and effort it would take to lure the last piece of my vengeance out of his hiding place. To bring my enemy into his home for me.

"Thank you," I purred, pulling away to mutter the words before diving down to press kisses to the exposed flesh above his shirt collar.

"Anything for you," he replied, panting and breathless beneath me.

I grinned and nipped at his lower lip, enjoying the growing hardness that he thrust against my bare core. The shirt I'd stolen from him was riding up my legs, helped further by his warm hands travelling over my pale, cool flesh, grasping handfuls of my ass and kneading the flesh. "Perfect," He groaned, dragging me against the erection trapped within the confines of his dark pants. The single word, which yesterday felt so impossible, warmed me even more.

He thought I was perfect?

I sank to my knees, not wasting time with the fastenings on his trousers, instead using my claws to rend them from his legs. I gasped with delight as his erection, thick and tall, a deeper green than the rest of his flesh, the head just peeking out from his foreskin, with a single pearlescent bead of pre-cum decorating it, leapt free. I licked my lips in anticipation, turning my gaze from his perfect cock up to his handsome face and dark, glowing eyes.

Hargrave

She stared up at me, eyes wide, pupils blown out.

Edwige on her knees was so achingly lovely that I couldn't muster a single thought about my ruined trousers. She was the entirety of my focus. Every thought, every breath, every beat of my heart. It belonged to her. She looked so innocent like this, so sweet and docile on her knees. I knew in reality she was a savage, barbaric and untameable. That doing this small act of faith and trust was just for me. I revelled in it, revelled in her, her power, her strength, and her choice of me.

"Open your mouth," I growled.

She seemed surprised, hesitating for a moment before she obeyed. I knew this next move was stupid, supremely stupid. Her teeth and jaws had been crafted by the goddess of death and winter to rend flesh and shatter bone. Her teeth were coated in a metal that would poison many magical creatures. They'd been perfectly formed to destroy. I slid two fingers into her deadly mouth, fucking them slowly against her perfect, pink tongue, ignoring the danger of her sharp, hard teeth even as I admired how they sparkled.

Edwige

I don't think anything more erotic had ever happened to me before. I stayed perfectly still as he slid his soft, fragile limbs against my tongue, delving deep into my mouth, ignoring the scrape of my vicious, bloodthirsty teeth against the creamy, delicate flesh of his digits. I groaned, shutting my eyes to bask in the dual sensation of softness and trust. Slowly, so slowly, I closed my lips around them, sucking softly, reveling in the salty taste of his flesh.

It was delicious. His surrender. His skin. The taste of his trust was heavy, decadent and perfect. I slurped and sucked, teasing my tongue over the knuckles to show him how good it could feel against his cock. I adored him, the confidence he placed in me, letting me tease his fingers with my terrifying teeth. He was so close to them, and yet he showed not an ounce of fear.

I gagged a little as he thrust his fingers deeper, and the small sound brought a feral grin to his face. He did it again.

"Perfect," Hargrave groaned again, fisting his cock in his other hand. "Precious," he added, swirling his fingers over my tongue one more time before removing them and wiping them against my cheek. A gesture that had me panting for more.

My mouth watered as he continued thrusting into his own fist, and I leaned forward, just a little, to press a soft kiss to the head, tasting the salt of his pre-cum. I held so still as he fed me his cock, wanting him to feel safe, to know he could trust me to never use my vicious teeth against him. It was massive, filling my mouth completely and tasted of salty male. I sucked gently, still watching the orc that was towering over me as he began to claim his pleasure, fucking into my mouth with slow, steady strokes. I breathed through my nose and adjusted to his girth. I could feel my cunt weeping, feel its emptiness and need as he languidly fucked into my mouth. When I reached down to stroke myself, pushing the borrowed shirt out of the way, he grunted his approval, moving faster, going deeper into my throat.

"Touch yourself for me, little demon, get that pussy wet and ready for my tongue, and my cock," Hargrave moaned, his hips stuttering as though he could barely contain his pleasure. I cried out in protest when he pulled out of my mouth.

"You taste so good," I mewled, looking up at him from my place on his office floor. He pulled me to my feet, kissing the tip of each of my silver claws, sucking lightly on the last one, heedless of the razor sharp danger each one presented. The gesture, so sweet and giving, had me collapsing against his chest, overwhelmed with a tide of emotion I hadn't thought myself capable of any longer. Hargrave cradled me against his chest in an easy hold, wrapping a hand around my nape to pull me up for a deep, sensual kiss, sliding his other one down towards where I needed him most. Two fingers, thick and warm and so fucking perfect, slid between my greedy lips before burying themselves in my core, dragging a wild cry from my throat, one that he swallowed down with his greedy kisses.

"Mmph," I groaned as he curled them just so, brushing against that place inside of me that was built for the singular purpose of bringing me pleasure. "Hargrave!" I cried as he did it again and again, the gentle touch demanding my orgasm.

"First you'll come on my fingers, Edwige," he whispered against the shell of my ear before licking it. "Then you're going to come on my tongue," he continued, nipping the column of my throat. "Then when you finally come all over my thick cock, I'll think about pumping you full of my seed." I groaned as he thrust in time with his words, the pace as smooth and steady as how he'd fucked himself into my mouth.

"Yes, Hargrave, please!" I said between gasps and pants. I felt him smile against the column of my throat as he continued to press and curl those delicious digits inside of me. When he added his thumb, pressing it directly against my clit, I was lost. My orgasm crested through me, making me shake and sob as he kept fucking me through it. The self-satisfied smile he wore as I finally came down from my peak was so goddess blessed adorable that I just had to kiss him between gasping for breath.

Edwige

"You're so pretty when you come, little demon," he crooned, hefting me into his arms and sweeping out of the office. "I can't wait to watch you do it all over again in our bed."

"I don't know if I can," I sighed, using my claws to shed his shirt off, trailing them carefully through the hair decorating his broad chest, licking over one of his flat, deep green nipples and grinning as he shuddered. Then it was my turn to laugh as he kicked the door open with a booted foot, the rags of his trousers flapping as he prowled across the room before tossing me onto the freshly made bed.

I watched with my own satisfied smirk as he divested himself of his ruined clothes, revealing acres of thick muscles and dark skin.

"Perfect," I sighed, echoing his words back to him as he knelt on the bed and crawled towards me. A behemoth of a monster, the leader of a brutal criminal organization, with hands even more bloody than mine, was kneeling between my spread legs, gazing down at my cunt, looking like he couldn't wait to devour me.

The first lick was heaven. Hargrave, always so much warmer than me, was hot against my most intimate flesh. The pressure of his tongue, the heat. It was almost too much against my still sensitive clit.

"Hargrave!" I cried, digging my claws into the perfect bedding. He sucked at me gently, tongue delving just as deeply into my core as his fingers had. His hands clasped me in place as I bucked and writhed into his mouth, another orgasm approaching so quickly it seemed nearly impossible. I released a needy groan as he ate me out like a starving creature, his tusks pressing into my pale flesh, completely uncaring about the bite scars that were scattered liberally between my thighs. It was like every brush of his face and fingers worked to erase the damage and the memories associated with it.

"I'm going to-" I gasped, rending more holes in the bedding to keep from reaching down and slicing off his thick mane of hair, or even worse, cutting his perfect sage green skin.

"Come in my fucking mouth," Hargrave demanded before redoubling his efforts, and I was, for once, pleased to obey. Falling into my second orgasm in the span of less than a quarter of an hour, howling my pleasure as it rolled through me, until I was limp and languid in the nest of rags I'd accidentally created.

Hargrave

I couldn't help the smile that curled my lips as I crawled up the bed to where Edwige laid limp and spent amidst the ruins of my quilt.

"I'm going to worship that pretty pussy morning, noon, and night." I told her, pressing my lips to her slack ones in a filthy kiss, showing her what she tasted like and revelling in how she returned each press of my lips and tongue with her own. "I'm going to make you cum until you can't see straight and the neighbors know my name." She hummed a little approving laugh at that, carefully running her fingers through my hair until it came loose from the braid, flowing around us to mingle with her lighter curls. "But first, I'm going to make you cum all over my cock," I finished, rolling, so that she was poised above me, her gilded claws against my chest, her plump, kiss-swollen lips curled in a soft smile that set off her silvery teeth.

I leaned up just enough to catch one of her nipples, the tip just a little deeper purple than her lips, and sucked until she gasped before switching to the other one.

"Grind against my cock, little demon, get it soaked so I can fuck it into you," I demanded, my hands moving to her hips and grinding her against me, reveling the feel of her wet, silky cunt against my greedy, straining cock.

"I need you to fill me up," she groaned, wrapping one of those perfect, cool hands around my throat like she had the first night I'd found her, crazed from her kill and coated in gore. Fuck, I needed her. Keeping one hand on her hip, I used my other to guide my cock until it notched up against her entrance, and she tightened her grip on my throat, the demand in her eyes a clear command. I thrust into her, filling her perfect pussy all the way up and reveling in the shriek she released. I knew I was big, probably too big for her, but I was more than happy to obey my Edwige's demand, to be good and obedient just for her. When she held my throat in her deadly grip and clenched around my cock like that, I knew all I would ever want from now on was to be her perfect whore.

Moving my hand back to her hip, I tentatively thrust, pulling her forward so every movement of my hips would grind my pelvis into her pretty little clit.

"Perfect," she groaned again, head falling back, grip around my throat tightening.

"You are," I rasped against her tight hold, loving how she commanded me even as I filled her up. I moved her again, and she purred, starting to ride me in earnest, dragging the same needy sounds from me that I'd been so happy to pull from her lips. Soon we were bouncing together, filling the golden afternoon air with our lusty cries, our skin slapping together in wet, depraved cracks, and I knew I wouldn't be able to last much longer. She was so tight, so good, so *mine*.

I came with a roar, feeling lightning shoot down my spine, my balls tightening, and nothing had ever felt as good as filling her up with my cum. She was pressed against my chest, running her claws through my hair as I relaxed into post-orgasmic bliss, adoring how her slight form felt perfect sprawled across me.

Chapter Four

Edwige

We were so busy fucking that as the night of the ball loomed only a few hours from now, neither had any idea how it had come to fruition. But I was more than happy to see it arrive. The thirst for Gyrhorn's teeth had been growing, a need for vengeance clawing and scraping inside my chest had left me hollow, and raw, and fucking hungry. Hargrave had kept it at bay, sitting with me as I lost myself to the madness. Watching me as I crouched, counting my teeth and murmuring gibberish. Letting me fuck him and myself into oblivion when that was the only way to expel the need to hunt and maim.

"You look ravishing Edwige, darling."

I turned in place, being far more careful than I usually was. My wardrobe had been steadily increasing over these last few weeks, though it was no secret I preferred Hargrave's shirts whenever we were simply relaxing at home. Fittings for a ballgown had been added into my routines, the seamstress and her assistants, a family of house brownies, had been paid an exorbitant amount to come to his hulking townhome, rather than have me wandering the streets with my tell-tale teeth and claws.

I secretly enjoyed the sweetness of the creatures. A trio of sisters, each smaller than the last, with bright smiles and warm, brown eyes. They'd created a masterpiece. The silk tinted a delicate heliotrope, with a deeply scooped neck and sleeves of the finest chiffon that fell just to my elbows. My pale skin glowed against it, and the deathly purple tinge to my lips was enhanced. The carefully draped skirt fell down the length of my legs, coming to the floor in a delicate little train that followed where I walked but could be collected and held by a single gold ring should I need to dance, or, more likely, need to ambush and chase down my last kill.

That thought had me grimacing, because this was the most beautiful thing I'd ever seen or owned, and I was absolutely going to ruin it tonight.

Hargrave caught the change in expression and rushed towards me, gathering my face in his wide, warm hands and lifting my gaze to his.

"What's wrong?" He demanded gently, "do you not like it?"

"I love it!" I protested, running my hands over his suit, admiring the heavy dark fabric that had been expertly cut to highlight his broad shoulders, the little tails on the back of it mimicking my train in a way I found adorable. "I'm just sad that it will be ruined by the end of the night."

"Oh, love," he chuckled, pulling me into his embrace and pressing a kiss to the top of my head, uncaring about all the work Immer and her army of housemaids had done to turn my wild curls into an updo that rested almost like a crown on the top of my head. Each hair had been tamed and woven into perfection, decorated with jeweled pins that winked purple and brilliantly glittered when the light hit them just so. "I'll buy you a thousand more dresses. You can ruin one every night if you want."

"I do not want to ruin dresses every night," I groused, pressing my face into his sternum and inhaling a calming lungful of his scent. "I would like to ruin fewer things, if that's an option."

"You have not ruined a single thing, Edwige. Not even one time," he growled, holding me tighter at the words. "You've only made them better."

Hargrave

This is going to be my first and last ball, I groused internally after yet another polite greeting to a trio of simpering idiots that I had never heard of, and certainly had no desire to interact with again. I worked to school the annoyed expression on my face. A pace behind me, in a modest dress that did not suit her at all, Immer was whispering names and titles into my ear as people approached to greet their host before fucking off to the buffet or the half-populated dance floor.

I had to hand it to the elf; she had outdone herself.

Flowers were everywhere, perfuming the air, festooning every rail, brightening even the darkest of corners, dripping over the edges of the tables and around the backs of the chairs. A sea of delicate white tapers burned among the burgeoning greenery, softening the harsh, orange light from the recently installed gas lamps. Life size marble statues, depictions of the maenads as they danced madly for their god of wine and chaos, were arranged around the perimeter in poses that seemed to change between sexual and violent. Each one more arresting than the last, and wreathed in so many flowers it seemed as though we were giving them offerings, and that this ball was actually a religious ceremony.

Everything that could have been gilded was, and it glimmered luxuriously. Beyond the second set of doors, thrown wide open the gardens waited, lit with torches the gargoyles cleaned to the brilliant marble white of the statues, with flowers added into every plant not currently in bloom, so it appeared a second spring had taken hold within the boundaries of my high walls.

I glimpsed Edwige as I surveyed the expanse of my rarely used ballroom. She was radiant in purple; the color highlighting her deathly pale skin and the enchanting shade of her lips, and her nipples, though none of the attendees knew that particular fact.

The flickering candles made her wide eyes shine as silvery as her teeth and claws.

Then she froze, going exceptionally still in the same manner as a great cat about to pounce. I turned my gaze to the entrance, already knowing what I would find when I looked there. A lithe, blonde male stood proudly in the center of my thrown open doors, the candle and gaslit lamps bathing him in an ethereal glow. The vampire must have fed recently, and well too. His skin was dewy, and a blush tinged his cheeks. His scarlet lips were twisted in a smile of genuine awe, his pale grey eyes, rimmed in red, seemed to take in every detail with the wonder of a child.

For a moment, I could understand and empathize with his expression. Immer had created something truly beautiful. The ball, a term that seemed so trite, was spectacular, every aspect of it lush and spellbinding. I searched through my vocabulary, trying to find the right word to describe it even as the vampire approached me. That she had done it for Edwige, a woman she'd barely known, a woman who could be a genuine threat to her, to me, to our entire organization, was astounding.

"There he is," Immer whispered into my ear before stepping away, and I watched her approach Edwige from the corner of my eye before turning my focus back to the second most dangerous predator in the room.

"Mr. Rutledge." the vampire said, his voice somewhat breathy, "Please allow me to introduce myself."

"No introduction needed, Mr. Pavalur," I replied warmly, taking his proffered hand and shaking it heartily, fighting the urge to crush it between my larger ones. "I am thrilled you could attend this evening. I know the invitations were rather last minute, but once I had the idea, I simply couldn't wait a moment longer than necessary."

"Strange, you seem like one of the more patient... business

owners I've ever heard of," Gyrhorn replied, returning my warm greeting with a look of suspicion.

"I am patient with my work, and meticulous to a fault if you ask my staff, but waiting for my pleasure is not something I'm not in the habit of doing," I replied breezily.

"It seems you don't skimp on it, either," he answered, leaning towards me as though we were co-conspirators. When I didn't back away, he seemed gratified, smiling winsomely at me as he threaded an arm through mine, like we were a couple about to perform our afternoon promenade. I allowed the liberty, feeling a thrill at the idea that Edwige would see, would become jealous, and take it out on me later.

"I do not," I assured him, gesturing to the overstated grandeur that surrounded us, taking the opportunity to lead him deeper into the crowd, closer to where Edwige watched and waited for me to deliver her revenge at her perfect feet.

Edwige

I was vibrating with need. His scent was all I could breathe. It wove through the air to strangle me, to awaken the barely contained violence that lurked beneath my skin. Glee, anger, and vengeance all roiled under my skin, warming me and filling me to the brim. He was here, the final set of teeth I needed. My vengeance would be complete, their debt of pain fulfilled. Even as I moved to stalk him, slinking through the shadows, I could already see the long, twisting rope of teeth that waited upstairs, so close to being finished. It needed me to complete my work, to take the teeth of the vampires who had done me wrong.

"Edwige." I twisted, baring my silvery claws as Immer approached me, her understated gown's train brushing over mine, her hand wrapping around my bicep to halt me.

"Mine," I growled.

"Yours, he is yours toothtaker," She agreed, gently urging me deeper into the shadows. "Come to the garden with me, and you can hunt, you darling, vicious thing. Your vengeance is waiting."

I was done waiting.

The garden was swathed in the deepest shadows, the pinpricks of brilliant light from the added torches searing my eyes, and I hissed, drawing further into the shelter of the branches, uncaring of the roses. I could smell sex emanating from a few nooks and crannies, and the scent irritated me. It diluted my prey. It interrupted the hunt.

Immer had led me to a massive stone gargoyle. It sported a bull's head, and massive bat wings. Its hands were wrapped around a pomegranate in offering, the cloven hooves buried deep in the damp, stony soil. I wriggled as she worked to divest me of the lovely gown, trying to hold on to my sanity as she rushed through the process, popping off several buttons. As the dress fell, I let my veneer of propriety fall with it, sinking into the feral rage of the toothtaker, becoming her, savoring her need for vengeance.

My claws tinkled against the stone of the gargoyle she'd secreted us behind, my teeth clattering and chattering with glee. I could smell him, I could taste him. I would have my vengeance. I would sate my rage. I would wear his fucking teeth as a goddess cursed trophy while his corpse disintegrated into ash beneath the pink Gallica roses my lover's gardener was so fucking fond of.

Hargrave's voice reached me, the deep, rich timbre of it sending a shiver through my spine, making the beds of my claws tingle and my gilded teeth chatter in a flurry of chimes. I crouched lower, crawling forward, skittering around pools of golden light, hunting my last tormentor and certain of his demise.

Hargrave

The faintest flurry of silvery bells reached me, and I had to suppress a feral grin at the sweet, delicate noise.

"What was that?" my companion asked, the vampire turning to look into the night, his preternatural gaze spotting far more than mine could. I trusted Edwige, trusted her abilities and instincts. She would hide herself in the shadows until the perfect moment to take her prey. That she had allowed me to take part in her vengeance was a gift I would never take for granted.

"I have been informed by the staff that the gargoyles come alive under the moonlight." I told him, gesturing to the waxing orb floating high above us in the rare, clear night.

"Gargoyles, truly?"

"You are a vampire, and I am an orc. There are whispers of a toothtaker roaming the streets, and yet you don't think that the gargoyles can awaken under the moon and cavort through my roses? Especially on a night of such... revelry?" I asked, chuckling a little at the annoyed little twist of Gyrhorn's too red lips. That sent the man whirling away from me, the wonder and delight completely abandoning his features, cold fury sharpening them into what I was certain was his true face.

"What do you know of the toothtaker?" He hissed, sinking into a crouch as though he planned on attacking me.

"I know every scar," I whispered, taking a step back, then another, as though his posturing was intimidating, my eyes on Edwige. She was beautiful in her nudity, snow white skin shining in the moonlight, brilliant silver teeth bared and claws extended. "I know every wound... I know her name," I growled.

Edwige

I leapt, landing on his exposed back like a jungle cat, silent and deadly.

He didn't even have time to scream as I tangled one of my hands in his greasy blonde hair, the scent of expensive oil turning bitter with the sudden fear he emanated. I wrapped the other around his throat, revelling in the sensation of my claws as they sunk into the cartilage and flesh before burying themselves between the hardness of his delicate vertebrae. He released a wail, the sound bright and pained before it stuttered in a gurgle, and then silence when I stole his ability to speak, to breathe.

So perfect, this final vengeance. The night above me, its moon silvering my prey and my flesh and the hothouse flowers around us. None of it soiled by a single cry from the creature I fully intended to destroy.

"I couldn't scream, either," I said, giggling into his pale white ear. "I could cry, though. Are you crying?" I jerked his head back by his platinum hair, looking at his frozen face. "There they are. Sweet, sweet tears just for me. A gift for me, a curse for you," I crooned. I groaned as I dug into a juicy vein, feeling the viscous, red fluid gush into my palms, pooling in them before sliding out of my grip and down his ruined throat.

My feet were planted on either side of his sloping shoulders and I squatted atop of him. "I care a great deal," I whispered into his dirty, hairy ear as I tore his head from his neck.

The wet crackling *pop-pop-pop* sound of ripping his head from his shoulders was a new and thrilling sensation. The hot spray of blood across my skin, however, was not. It was red, and wet, and stank enough that my own gorge rose in my throat.

"Blood and bones, and teeth and groans," I muttered, dropping the still-blinking head to the earth and shaking myself like a wet dog. Blood droplets fell off of me, but mostly it just spread the viscous fluid over my skin. The head stared at me, its eyes going dull as I watched.

"Take your due, little demon," Hargrave urged, the soft words drawing me out of the reverie I'd slipped into, entranced by the way the blood seeped out of the ragged stump and oozed through the network of pea gravel. He would need to replace the path, or at the very least rinse it thoroughly. I reached out, my claws shining black, the miniscule designs on them obscured by the gore. I crouched once again, peering into the dead, dull eyes of my lifeless tormentor, before reaching out with my deadly claws and sinking them into the brittle bones of his mouth, the visceral crunch drawing a moan of satisfaction from me. His teeth fell to the ground, the faint pinging of bone and stone so barbaric when compared to the lovely, clear bells of my claws. Scorn filled me. He was all bluster and no substance, even in death. I twisted my fingers, dislodging the deeper molars and fishing them out, piling my cache of bones in the thin fabric of my chemise where it stretched into a basket between my thighs.

Soon I had them all, 32 perfect teeth rattling in my grasp, shining in the moonlight, ready for my collection.

"It's done," I whispered, holding one of the fangs up to the light, carefully pressed between my claws.

"It is indeed, my perfect creation," I flinched at the voice, turning to face the woman I had not seen since that fateful night, when I had chosen fury over peace, when I'd needed to sate my rage more than I needed to allow myself to finally rest. A choice that I could never regret, not with a palm full of teeth and a hulking orc at my side.

"Maslenitsa," I whispered, dread pooling in my gut, replacing the half-mad glee that had been there.

"Smart little witch," she crooned, reaching out to me with her pale blue fingers crooked. I took a step back, recalling the last time she'd ran the icy pads over my flesh, how she'd frozen my skin solid, killing it along with the pain. The movement didn't seem to surprise her. She even smiled, as though I were one of her more clever pupils. "You will be a lovely addition to my court."

"What do you mean?" Hargrave was beside me, going toe-to-toe with the terrifying deity.

"She has completed her vengeance," the goddess said, turning her brilliant sapphire eyes on my lover. "Unless she has more deaths to offer me, she must accept her demise and enter court, as an honored member, of course. Edwige will want for nothing at my side, orc."

"If it's death you need..." Hargrave said, a vicious smirk cursing his lips, "then I think I can keep Edwige busy. If that's what you want, my love?" He asked, turning to me, "I don't mean to speak for you," He added, looking so contrite that I almost laughed.

"Are you asking me to be your... assassin?" I replied, looking up into his dark eyes, the fiery light in their very depths seeming to burn brighter the longer I held his gaze.

"I am asking for so much more than that, little demon, but if having you maim and kill my enemies will keep you by my side, then yes, I hope you can be my assassin."

"I think I prefer wife," I told him, wrapping my free hand, dirty as it was, in his warm one, "but I will kill whoever you want me to."

The fading snickers of the terrifying goddess punctuated our kiss.

About the Author

Cait is an author, acupuncturist, and army veteran currently living in the hill country of central Texas. When she isn't working she enjoys creating lush, decadent, and dark worlds where the heroines are unapologetically themselves and their heroes are here for it. Her stories are laced with myth, magic, and just enough horror to keep you on the edge of your seat.

If you enjoyed this story check out her dark, paranormal romance The Witch Bottle here: https://tinyurl.com/The-Witch-Bottle

Acknowledgments

First, thank you, dear reader, for picking up this anthology and for your solidarity as we express our RAGE at the never-ending restrictions on reproductive rights, including abortion. All proceeds from RAGE will be donated to the Chicago Abortion Fund, and we encourage you to donate to the abortion fund of your choice to help folks from places with abortion restrictions to receive vital reproductive healthcare.

Thank you to all the authors and artists who contributed creative works to this anthology.

Thanks to Danielle Romero, who generously donated covers for both the ebook and all of the paperback editions.

Thank you to Kelly, Jasmine, and Raeleen, whose behind-the-scenes support made this anthology possible.

An enormous thank you to the editors who either offered up their services for free or at a discounted cost to anthology participants: Raeleen Nelson with Book Witch Editing, Alexa Thomas with the Fiction Fix, A.N. Stauber, MP Starkweather, Ashley Oliver, Raven Heidrich, Kyla Lee, Rosie Sloane of All the Proof, Bookish Services by Kay, Fae Darling, Scarlett of Scarlett Pen Edits, Alexandra of Sinful, Nooks Editing, and Nikki Grant.

Our deepest appreciation to all the influencers and readers who volunteered their time and their platforms to get the word out about this important fundraiser.

And finally, once again, thank you for putting your foot down and saying, "ENOUGH." We are so grateful to each and every one of you for joining us in this fight. It's going to take all of us.

It's not over. We've barely begun.

Yours in solidarity,
    Poppy, MT, and Jo

Made in United States
Troutdale, OR
04/14/2025